The Eye of ETERNITY

By Maggie Furey

The Artefacts of Power

AURIAN
HARP OF WINDS
THE SWORD OF FLAME
DHIAMMARA

The Shadowleague

THE HEART OF MYRIAL
SPIRIT OF THE STONE
THE EYE OF ETERNITY

THE EYE OF ETERNITY

Book Three of The Shadowleague

MAGGIE FUREY

orbit

www.orbitbooks.co.uk

An *Orbit* Book

First published in Great Britain by Orbit 2002

Copyright © Maggie Furey 2002

The moral right of the author has been asserted.

A CIP catalogue record for this book is available from
the British Library.

ISBN 1 84149 114 4 (Hardback)
ISBN 1 84149 115 2 (C format)

Typeset by Palimpsest Book Production Limited,
Polmont, Stirlingshire
Printed and bound in Great Britain by
Clays Ltd, St Ives plc

Orbit
An imprint of
Time Warner Books UK
Brettenham House
Lancaster Place
London WC2E 7EN

The new girls, Freda and Sparkle.
Welcome to the family.

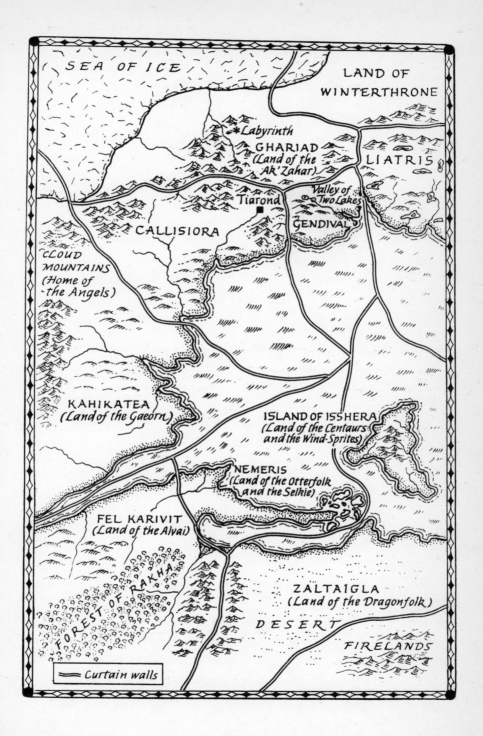

ONE

TO THE RESCUE

Everything looked the same as usual. The scattered buildings of the Loremaster community were unchanged, their lichened grey stone blending with their surroundings as though they were a natural part of the landscape. Though the usual bank of low cloud hung over the Upper Lake, the waters of the Lower Lake glittered in the pale, cool sunlight of an early autumn morning. The great oak forest that cloaked the steep southern slopes of the valley was resplendent in bronze and gold, and fallen leaves lay like hoarded treasure across the paths and down to the shores of the lakes.

It could have been any normal day in Gendival – had it not been for the strange absence of inhabitants. At this hour, both in the Shadowleague settlement and the village beyond, people were usually going about their business, sparing time from their errands to stop awhile and engage in talk. Today, however, was not a normal day. Cergorn, the Archimandrite, was grievously wounded and barely clinging to his life. Amaurn the renegade had returned, and had proved to have a number of covert supporters in Gendival. There had been a titanic battle between two Senior Loremasters: the fearsome Maskulu, with his long, low-slung body and many legs, and the mantis-like Skreeva – the former a supporter of the renegade Amaurn, and the latter a Dragonfolk spy.

In the aftermath of these events, an uneasy, unnatural quiet had fallen. The villagers were at home with their families, aware that the future of the Shadowleague hung in the balance, and keeping out of the way while its members settled the differences that had split their ranks. The Senior Loremasters – those few who remained in Gendival – were convening at the lakeside. It would be up to them to make sense of the shocking events of the last few hours, and pull the Shadowleague back into a cohesive, functioning team.

It was one meeting that Veldan would be glad to miss. She considered herself and Kaz extremely fortunate to be heading, with Elion, out of the settlement at this time. With luck they would be far away before anyone got round to considering the part they had played in Amaurn's sudden bid for power and hopefully, by the time they returned, all the fighting would be over, and the important decisions made. On Amaurn's instructions, they would travel downriver to the coast to find their lost companions Toulac and Zavahl, who had been kidnapped by agents of the Dragonfolk. Zavahl carried in his mind the spirit of their Seer, guardian of the tribal memories, and the Dragons wanted him back. The Shadowleague, however, were desperately in need of the information he carried, and Amaurn wasn't prepared to let him go.

Veldan, Kazairl, and Elion parted from Amaurn on the lake shore. 'Are you sure you don't want us to stay, and explain to the Afanc about Zavahl and the Dragon?' Veldan asked in mindspeech. The lake monster Afanc was the only other Senior Loremaster in Gendival at that time. Given his close friendship to Cergorn, she had a feeling that he would object in the strongest possible terms to the centaur being replaced by this interloper from the past, and he would be a good deal less easy to persuade than the other Loremasters. Though Amaurn had managed to snatch the reins of power from Cergorn, whether he could hold onto them remained to be seen.

Amaurn shook his head. 'I'll manage the Afanc Bastiar – and any other objectors.' His face was set and bleak, as though he had pulled the mantle of Lord Blade around his shoulders once again. Veldan shivered. It was as though the moment of closeness that they had shared in the aftermath of the titanic battle in the clearing had never existed. 'You and your friends get out of here,' he continued, 'before you become embroiled any further in this mess. I'll have Bailen send messages downriver to arrange ahead for your transport. Just get Zavahl back. Everything depends on that. If we can show Bastiar that we were right, and Cergorn was wrong, then even *he* cannot deny my claim to take over the leadership.'

He turned away, and looked out across the waters of the lake. Veldan and Elion exchanged a glance, she raising her eyebrows and he replying with a shrug. Clearly, they had been dismissed. The firedrake snorted loudly – there was no need to ask what *he* thought of Amaurn's attitude. 'It's a good thing for him that the Wind-Sprite isn't here,' Kaz muttered. 'He may be able to get round the Afanc, but Shree wouldn't allow him to take over from her partner.'

The three Loremasters set off back up the wooded slope towards their own hillside dwellings. At Veldan's side, the firedrake rumbled softly in his throat. Clearly, there was a lot he didn't like about this business – which was no surprise, as she found herself harbouring the same doubts. How had it happened so quickly, the transformation from Blade the foe to Amaurn the ally? It felt as though she and Kaz had been swept away in a torrent of circumstances, and had been too busy fighting the conflicting currents and trying to keep their heads above water to know, or care, where they would be washed ashore. She couldn't understand how they had ended up supporting Blade, yet somehow it had happened, and now they would have to live with the consequences. Waiting until Elion had left them at the fork of the path, heading for his own home, she mentioned her misgivings to the firedrake.

He tilted his head in a draconic shrug. 'Me too. Well, we won't be the only ones.'

Veldan glanced back over her shoulder, towards the settlement. 'True. I don't think Blade, or Amaurn, or whatever he wants to call himself, is home and dry yet. Now that all the excitement has died down, there are a lot of doubts flying around.'

'Doubts?' The firedrake snorted. 'You mean they're scared out of their tiny wits.' He stopped for a moment, turning his great, glowing eyes on his partner's face. 'What do *you* think, Boss? Honestly?'

Veldan shook her head. 'I don't know. I can scarcely believe I could support a man who has been capable of such ruthlessness, and who so recently threatened our own lives. But I do. I don't trust him entirely, but I think Gendival needs new blood and new vision right now. What worries me, though, is that he seems so familiar, somehow. Even though I never met him before, I feel as if he's always been there, somewhere in the back of my mind, just waiting to emerge. Does that make any sense to you at all?'

'Make any sense? Are you crazy? Of course it doesn't!' snorted the firedrake.

'You're probably right,' Veldan sighed. 'All my life I've had the tale of Amaurn the renegade held up before me as an example and a warning. In a sense, I grew up with Amaurn, and that's probably why he seems so familiar now.'

'It's as good an explanation as any,' the firedrake agreed. 'And you're tired, Boss: no wonder you're not thinking straight. There's enough to worry about in this Amaurn business as it is, without clouding the issue with fancies.' He turned his head to look at her. 'Just think about it. Firstly, the world's in a state of crisis, and we need to take some kind of positive action. Secondly, Cergorn failed us, and wouldn't listen when we tried to tell him that the Dragon Seer was trapped inside Zavahl. Thirdly, it turns out that Amaurn was a friend of your mother's, so it's natural that you'd want to trust him. Fourthly, he offered to help us save Toulac and Aethon, not to mention that Hierarch, when Cergorn wouldn't. We have enough reasons to make us change sides, without worrying about mysterious feelings.'

'I suppose you're right. Anyway, in the end, it won't make much difference what we think. We'd better leave the problem of Amaurn to the Senior Loremasters right now, and attend to our own affairs.'

Veldan's mind leapt ahead to their journey in search of Toulac and Zavahl. By this time, Bailen would be sending messages down the river, and a boat would be waiting for them at the nearest settlement of the Navigators. These river traders were an essential part of life in Gendival. The realm consisted mainly of mountains and lakes, and the land was so wild and broken that the easiest way to get from place to place was by river. The Navigators were nomads of the waterways; they built locks, they dredged the shallows and, in truly inaccessible places, they constructed portage ways and transferred their goods to smaller boats that could be hauled on rollers by sturdy horses. All up and down the rivers they carried news and goods, and sometimes passengers. Their great sailing barges even went to sea, trading along the coastlines as far as the Curtain Walls would permit, and like all the natives of the Gendival realm, the Navigators worked to aid and support the Shadowleague whenever necessary.

'It'll make a nice change,' Kaz remarked, 'to float down the river at our ease, and let somebody else do the work. My poor old legs have been practically worn down to stumps, these last months.'

'Make the most of it,' Veldan warned him. 'With the Curtain Walls still failing, our work is far from done, and somehow I get the feeling that Amaurn will have plans for us when we get back.'

'If he's still in charge when we get back,' the firedrake snorted. 'He hasn't convinced Bastiar yet.'

There was a harsh edge to Veldan's laughter. 'Want to bet on it? Let's not forget that Amaurn is still the ruthless Lord Blade, and a man doesn't change overnight. If it comes to a contest, I'll back him against the Afanc any time.'

When Kaz and Veldan reached their home, they found the indefatigable Ailie already there. While they had been down by the lakeside, the innkeeper had clearly been busy. She was in the middle of making breakfast, and the glorious smell of frying bacon filled Veldan's kitchen. The innkeeper looked up as they entered. 'Just in time,' she said cheerfully. 'But where's Elion got to?'

'Gone back to his own house to change, and get a few things together.' Veldan had to swallow hard before she could get the words out. It had been a long, eventful time since last night's supper, and her mouth was watering at the smell of the food.

The firedrake was stretching his neck out as far as it would go to sniff at the bacon in the pan, oblivious to the spits of hot fat that stung his nose. 'What about me?' he demanded. 'Veldan, ask her if she brought anything for me.'

'Shut up, Kaz.' Veldan cast a despairing look at the frying-pan. 'Ailie, this is tremendously good of you, but we have to leave as soon as possible. The Navigators will have a boat going downriver this morning, but they won't delay too long, because of catching the right tides at the estuary. We just haven't got time for breakfast.'

'That's all right,' Ailie said tranquilly. She began to fish crisp, brown rashers out of the pan, slipping them between halves of round, flat loaves, split lengthways. 'We can take these with us, and eat them on the way.'

'We?' Veldan's eyebrows shot up almost to her hairline. For the first time, she noticed several bags and bundles which had been stacked neatly in the corner. 'And just what are those?'

'Oh, that stuff isn't for me,' Ailie told her. 'Well most of it isn't. I brought Toulac's coat with me – that disreputable sheepskin object she's so attached to – and one of my dad's old coats for Zavahl, and a change of warm, dry clothes for the pair of them. Then I thought we should take some food, and blankets, and—'

'Now just hold on there, Ailie. I really appreciate all your help, but I can't possibly take you.'

'Why ever not?' Ailie interrupted. 'If this had been one of your normal missions, I would agree with you. I'm no Loremaster, and I don't want to be. But this time you're only going to pick up Zavahl and Toulac. We'll be travelling by boat most of the way, and we aren't even going outside the Gendival Curtain Walls.'

'But Cergorn doesn't let villagers—'

'Oh, stuff Cergorn,' Kaz interrupted with a snort. 'He's not in charge any more. For goodness' sake, Veldan, the woman has *food*! Bring her along. And you forgot to ask her if she had any breakfast for me.'

With a laugh, Veldan surrendered. 'All right,' she said aloud, to Ailie as well as the firedrake. 'It'll be a joy and a revelation to have someone with us who can cook, for a change.'

The innkeeper grinned. 'I knew you'd see sense.'

Leaving Ailie to finish packing up the food, Veldan went to throw together a few things of her own. Although a quick wash and a change of clothes made her feel better, she couldn't keep her thoughts from dwelling wistfully on a steaming hot bath followed by her soft, warm bed. Stifling a yawn, she splashed cold water on her face. 'You can sleep on the boat,' she told herself. 'Once we get going, there'll be plenty of time.'

At that moment, she heard the sound of voices. 'Slime-bag's here,' Kaz informed her, but she noticed that the usual venom had vanished from the epithet. Wisely, Veldan said nothing, but hurried back to the kitchen, where Ailie was using Elion as a packhorse, and loading him up with her collection of bundles.

'What did you bring?' Elion was grumbling. 'The entire contents of the inn?' Turning away from the innkeeper, he glanced across at Veldan, and she saw the faint line of a frown between his brows. 'Is this wise?' he asked her in the silent mind-to-mind communication of the Loremasters.

She answered in mindspeech with an almost imperceptible shrug. 'What harm will it do? As Ailie was quick to point out, this isn't like one of our normal missions.' She grinned slyly. 'And since she gets along so well with Zavahl, it should be greatly to our benefit to have her along.'

'I hadn't thought of that, but you're right.' Aloud, for Ailie's benefit, he added: 'Let's go then, before I collapse under the weight of all this baggage.'

They walked down through the trees to the bottom of the hill, and turned right to follow the river as it flowed out of the valley, which began to widen as the settlement was left behind. Stubbled harvest fields and green meadows had replaced the shining lakes. Further down the valley, cows and sheep were browsing peacefully in the cool autumn sunlight, but first, not far from the outskirts of the village, there was a cluster of neatly kept stables and barns, and horses grazed in the surrounding fields. Elegant heads were raised as the Loremasters and Ailie approached. Unlike the beasts in the realms outside, the horses of the Shadowleague were far too accustomed to the presence of the firedrake to be afraid. They all seemed to sense that he was not permitted to eat them, but Kaz always seemed to fascinate them, none the less.

The proximity of so much food, however, was driving the firedrake wild with hunger, so he elected to wait outside while the others went on into the stable block. As Veldan and her companions walked into the neatly swept yard, they were met by a square-set, stocky man with bristly, greying dark hair and a pugnacious jaw. He emerged from the stables with a hayfork in his hand, and when he saw Elion, his face fell, and his knuckles tightened around the shaft of the fork. 'Not *you* again! How dare you show your face back here?'

The Loremaster edged backwards, trying to put Veldan and Ailie between himself and the stableman, but the two women were having no part of it, and drifted away to the side, leaving Elion to his cruel fate. 'Er . . . look, Harral,' he muttered. 'I'm really sorry about the chestnut . . .'

Harral's black, bushy brows were singularly effective for scowling. 'Sorry?' he barked. 'You're *sorry?* Is that all you've got to say for yourself? Against my better judgement, on Cergorn's orders, I let you have the best mare in the place, the darling of my heart, the apple of my eye. And you, you incompetent buffoon, YOU GO AND LOSE HER!' His face had turned brick-red and veins were standing out on his neck and forehead.

'But I brought you a replacement,' Elion protested weakly.

'You call that a horse? That ill-favoured, iron-mouthed offspring of a donkey and a cow?' Harral brandished his pitchfork menacingly, forcing Elion to step back from the flashing tines. 'I had plans for that mare, you moron. She was going to be the foundation for an entire line. I should never have given her to you. I should have known better. If the Archimandrite hadn't . . .' He broke off at the mention of Cergorn's name, and changed tack abruptly. 'Do any of you know how he is?'

Veldan shook her head. 'The healers are working desperately to save his life. That's all we've heard so far. We'll just have to hope they succeed.' She was surprised at the strength of her feelings. Despite the recent conflict between them, Cergorn and his lifemate had always been a strong, sure presence in her life. Though they had not been on the best of terms lately, and though she no longer felt that he was the best choice for the role of Archimandrite, she owed him far too much to wish him any harm.

Harral muttered an oath and spat on the ground. 'That thrice-cursed renegade Amaurn! Why couldn't he have stayed away? If only we'd managed to kill the slippery bastard the first time around.'

Veldan, her curiosity piqued, was longing to ask him more about the events that had taken place back then, but time was pressing. The Navigators wouldn't wait for passengers. Down near the mouth of the river, the estuary waters were strongly tidal, and if they arrived at the wrong time, their progress could be held back for hours.

Harral also knew better than to delay the rivermen. 'Well, I'd best let you get away,' he said. He beckoned impatiently to the lad who was leading out their mounts. 'Hurry it up, Sem! These folk haven't got all day.'

They were taking four horses, because they would need mounts for Toulac and Zavahl, if all went well. Ailie had her own plump dappled mare called Daisy. Her bundles were loaded and secured on to one of the spare beasts, which would be led, and Veldan elected to ride the other on the outward journey. Though she was usually carried by Kaz, she still enjoyed the occasional ride on horseback. As she mounted, she heard the firedrake's snort of disgust. 'How thoughtful of you to bring breakfast along,' he sneered.

'You were the one complaining that your poor legs needed a rest,' Veldan retorted.

Elion was given the ex-Godsword horse that he had ridden from Tiarond. Harral eyed the brown, nondescript creature critically as it was led out into the yard. 'The poor thing could do with feeding up, but you won't be riding it too far this time. Anyway, it'll have to do. I'm not risking any more of *my* precious animals with you, Elion. You have no sense of responsibility towards them. Since you brought this bag of bones here, it belongs to you as far as I'm concerned, so I suggest you look after it better than the others I've allotted you.'

Elion shrugged. 'Fair enough,' he said. 'At least this horse is quiet. *He* doesn't buck, roll, bite and kick – unlike the beasts you give me.' Patting the ugly beast on the nose, he scrambled clumsily onto its back.

Kaz, who had seen the exchange through Veldan's eyes, snickered. 'Just wait until that walking hat-rack is fed and rested. I wonder if he'll find it such an easy ride then?'

'I don't know.' Veldan grinned. 'It'll be fun finding out, though.'

Down on the coast, the former Hierarch of Callisiora had a few things of his own to find out. He had never been in this position before: lost in the wilds with no food, no shelter, and not even a coat or a cloak to his back. During these last few days, he had discovered just how little he knew about himself, about the people around him, and about the world outside his city, which had turned out to be so much more varied and intimidating than he could ever have dreamed.

At least, thank Myrial, he was not alone. Toulac was proving to be an unexpected comfort. When he had first encountered the former mercenary, Zavahl had dismissed her as a foul-mouthed, ignorant old harridan with a primitive love of violence. Now, in the face of her calm, businesslike demeanour, he was revising those opinions rapidly. She had informed him that in her wandering days, she had learned to live off the land. In their current predicament, her knowledge and skills could keep them alive until help arrived.

At least, according the veteran, they had ended up in a good place. 'Look around,' she said, with a sweeping gesture. Zavahl looked, but all he could see was a long stretch of wild, inhospitable coastline. This was a *good* place? Had the woman lost her mind? Great reefs of razor-edged rock thrust out into the ocean and vanished in the churning surf. The sloping shore was strewn with a jumble of stones: on the lower beach sea-smoothed pebbles rolled and made walking difficult, but nearer the cliffs, the rocks at the foot of the escarpment were gigantic boulders, some as big as a house, which had been broken off by the inexorable power of the sea.

The former Hierarch was overawed by the bleakness of his surroundings. The sky was grey with a high covering of racing clouds, the sea had a steely aspect that made him shiver, and nothing grew on the stark stone of the cliffs. It was as though all colour and warmth had been leached from the world. A cold, cutting wind, damp with salt spray, snivelled and whined between the stones, and cries of seabirds added a plaintive counterpoint to the rumble and sigh of the churning surf.

Zavahl shivered. He yearned with all his heart to go home – but not to Tiarond. To his astonishment, he realised that the home he longed for was not the bleak mountain city he had ruled, but the bright, cosy room in Ailie's village inn.

His wistful thoughts of the innkeeper were punctured by a sharp dig in the ribs from Toulac. 'I said look around, not stand there wool-gathering.'

'Why?' Zavahl grumbled. 'There's nothing in this place worth seeing.'

Toulac grinned. 'There is if you know what to look for. It may be cold and wild and intimidating now, but it'll seem smaller when we've built a shelter, and safer when we have a fire.' She clapped him on the shoulder. 'Why, by the time you've put some hot food into your belly, you'll be feeling right at home.'

Zavahl couldn't help but resent the fact that though she was only clad, like him, in breeches and shirt, she didn't seem to be shivering. She was almost twice his age – how in Myrial's name could she do it? He glared at her. 'And just where is this hot food going to come from?'

'The seashore is one of the best places for foraging I know. There are all sorts of edibles, right here for the finding. Don't worry, you'll soon learn the tricks, and by the end of today, you'll know a fair amount about surviving in the wild. Right now, though, leave the business of the food to me. I know what I'm looking for. You collect any other useful stuff you can find. Now, sonny, we'd better shift ourselves. Freezing our backsides off on a cold beach isn't going to get us anywhere. Don't forget we'll need driftwood for a fire – as much as you can carry. Keep a lookout for any longer or thicker pieces that we might use to make some kind of shelter.'

'But couldn't we just shelter in a cave?' Zavahl asked.

Toulac rolled her eyes up to the heavens. 'Can you *see* any caves?'

'Well, no, but . . .'

'Unfortunately, in real life, you rarely get caves just for the asking. And even if you do, they're usually damp, cramped, prone to rock-falls, difficult to get into, or they already have a resident bear. All the same, if you *did* happen to find one we could use, a cave would be an enormous help to us. And while you're looking at the cliffs, keep an eye open for fresh water. There may be a spring, or a trickle draining down from that swampy area above.'

Zavahl nodded. 'Anything else?'

'You can bet your life on it.' Toulac's eyes twinkled. 'The shore-line can be a real treasure trove. Stuff gets washed off boats in rough weather. People throw their garbage into rivers or harbours – it's a foul habit, but they do it anyway – and all sorts of things end up here. And with all these rocks and reefs, it looks like a wrecking coast to me. If ships tend to get smashed up in this area we could find all sorts of useful items. Keep a lookout for any bits and pieces that might come in handy: bits of rope, discarded fishing nets, anything that could be used as a container for cooking or carrying water. The possibilities are endless. Just use your imagination and your ingenuity. You'll be amazed at what you can find, and I'd be willing to wager that one you get started, you'll find that beachcombing is a damn sight more fun than being Hierarch.'

'The way things have been lately, having my fingernails pulled out with red-hot pincers would be a damn sight more fun than being Hierarch,' Zavahl said sourly, not wanting to be reminded of his failures, and the mess he had left behind him.

'Think how lucky you are, then, to be the first person in the history of Tiarond to escape from the job with your life,' Toulac told him briskly. 'Now, you go that way and I'll go this. Bring anything you find back here – you're sure you can recognise the place when you come back?'

'With that big bit broken off the clifftop and a pile of soil at the bottom, where you nearly went over – yes, I *think* I can find it again.'

Toulac looked at him with narrowed eyes. 'You ought to be careful, sonny. The next thing you know, people will accuse you of developing a sense of humour, and *then* where will you be?'

Before Zavahl could think of a retort, she was all business again. 'We'll meet back here about noon, and see what we've managed to find between us.'

'What about them?' Zavahl gestured towards the group of large, otter-like creatures: some fishing beyond the surf, their compact round heads occasionally appearing above the waves, while others turned over rocks among the tide pools with deft little black paws that seemed, in structure, very much like human hands. 'You say they are intelligent, but can you be certain they can be trusted?' He was still finding it difficult to believe Toulac's claim that she could communicate from mind to mind with such creatures. Had it not been for the fact that he had been doing very much the same thing with Aethon, the Dragon for whose mind and spirit he was an unwilling host, he would have been certain that she was lying, or that age was befuddling her thoughts.

'What, the Dobarchu?' Toulac's expression softened as she regarded the brown-furred creatures. 'Well, they're certainly friendly enough, and I've a feeling in my bones that they can be trusted. They offered to share their catch with us, and later, when we have time, I'm going to have a long talk with them.' She turned back to Zavahl. 'So let's see about getting ourselves settled, shall we? We have a lot to do.'

As he turned to go, she added, 'Just one more thing. Unless you find a cave, or traces of fresh water, stay away from the foot of the cliff. We already know to our cost that the rock in these parts will crumble very easily.' She gestured at the boulders and piles of smaller rubble at the bottom of the escarpment. 'Having survived being captured by those horrible great monstrosities, you don't want to end up being buried under a pile of stone.'

'I'm not *that* stupid,' Zavahl protested.

'I wouldn't count on it.' With that, Toulac turned away and went stumping off along the beach, her eyes fixed on the ground.

Being on his own changed everything. Zavahl, born and bred in a city, was unnerved for a time by the lonely, empty expanse of sea and beach and sky. He longed to find an excuse to run back to Toulac, whose sturdy, capable presence he was coming to appreciate more and more. Only one thing stopped him. To his surprise, he was aware of a new-found sense of pride, far different from the Callisioran Hierarch's haughty superiority. That sort of arrogance had come from privilege and wealth: the luxurious trappings of his rank, the servants to wait upon his every need, and the powerful backing of the feared Godsword soldiers. This tentative new confidence, however, came from within – and now that he was utterly destitute, with nothing in the world but the clothes on his back, each fear he conquered, each new skill that he could learn, would contribute to his growing sense of self-respect. How ironic. Only when he had been stripped of everything that mattered in his life did he begin to feel that he might be worth something at last.

Zavahl squared his shoulders and set off along the beach, heading away from the foraging Dobarchu. He had not really become used to the intelligent non-humans of this mysterious land to which Veldan and Toulac had brought him, and they still made him a little uneasy – though after the women's alarming firedrake companion, it would take a lot more than these new creatures to actually scare him.

He soon discovered that if he concentrated on the ground around his feet, his surroundings became less intimidating. After his first discovery – an old sack that was still perfectly serviceable, once the sand had been shaken out of it – he began to get into the spirit of the hunt and, before very long, found out that that Toulac had been right. Beachcombing *was* a damn sight more fun than being Hierarch.

Two

A Question of Conscience

As the long night drew to its close, it was Aliana's turn to watch. Dawn always came late to the Sacred Precincts in their shadowed canyon, but for some time now the light that filtered through the cellar's high ventilation gratings had been growing brighter. Though she and her companion were by no means safe yet, Aliana felt her weariness lift a little as relief flooded through her.

I did it again. I lived to see another morning!

For the small band of survivors, all that remained of the Holy City of Tiarond, every dawn was another hard-won victory, but yesterday she and Galveron had scored their own personal triumph by recovering the Hierarch's ring from their foes, and were halfway, at least, to bearing it back to Gilarra in triumph. During the hours of darkness they had taken shelter in this cellar beneath the abandoned brewhouse, while the dreadful winged creatures had roamed at large in the Sacred Precincts. Soon it would be safe to venture out again, and make their way back to the Temple.

To celebrate, Aliana threw the last of their carefully hoarded fuel on the fire. As the flames flared up into fitful golden light she looked down at Galveron, who slept beside her. Even in sleep, his face was haggard with exhaustion, and the jagged wounds across his cheek and forehead, souvenirs of an earlier encounter with the monstrous Ak'Zahar, stood out livid on his skin. Aliana frowned. Only with the greatest difficulty had she persuaded him to let her take her share of watches. The new Godsword Commander took his responsibilities very seriously. Almost *too* seriously: to the point where his friends – among whom she numbered the Healer Kaita, the Smithmaster Agella and, of course, herself – were going to have to ensure that he didn't kill himself in his zeal.

One person Aliana did *not* number among Galveron's friends was Gilarra, the recently made Hierarch. What she had seen of the woman so far had failed to impress her in the slightest. To the thief's mind, Gilarra was too self-involved to be much use to the bereft and terrified survivors of Tiarond. Why, if she didn't have Galveron to prop her up, there probably wouldn't *be* any survivors by now.

And then she risks the poor man by sending him off with me on this mad expedition to find some stupid ring!

Though Aliana understood the significance of the ring well enough – it was the symbol of Myrial's divine power, which must be passed from one Hierarch to the next – this hardly seemed to be the time to be bothering about such trifling details. After all, Gilarra had been Suffragan. Of *course* she was the new Hierarch! In the current situation, who was going to argue the point? So what did she need the stupid ring for?

The thief stared into the fire, absently chewing at a grubby thumbnail.

There's got to be more to this than meets the eye. Galveron has more sense than to drag us both out here for a mere symbol. The ring must have a more practical function that we ordinary people know nothing about.

So is it only the designated Hierarch that can make the ring do whatever it does? Or does whoever holds the ring possess the Hierarch's power?

And if that's true, then the Hierarch doesn't need to be Gilarra at all . . .

Aliana held her breath, overawed for a moment by the enormity of such a thought. Could it be true? But surely that would make the whole religion of Myrial nothing but a mockery!

So what? A fat lot of good Myrial ever did me, or my parents, or Alestan – or for that matter, anyone else in Tiarond. And I don't think much of the new Hierarch, either. Why, Galveron could do a better job than that!

Suddenly, her mind was racing. Why not? Why not indeed? Galveron was a far better leader in every respect. He was a soldier, and therefore had a better grasp of fighting and tactics. He was organised, and had an unerring instinct for the matters which were important. He was a true leader, who was genuinely interested in his people. He could inspire confidence and hope in even the most desperate refugee. The more Aliana thought about it, the more certain she became that the new leader of the Godswords was the only man who could get the remnants of the Tiarondians through the crisis that had beset them.

There was only one problem.

Galveron was also honest, straightforward in all his dealings, and loyal to a fault. As Godsword Commander, he took his position of trust very seriously, and there was no way he would betray the Hierarch. The thief sighed in exasperation. If only the wretched man wasn't so decent and noble! In her opinion, his treachery would do Tiarond far more good at present.

I wonder if I could ask him about the ring's significance – in a round-about way, of course. The idiot could be wasting a tremendous opportunity!

Bringing up the subject, however, would be the worst thing she could do. It hadn't taken her long to work out that, no matter how subtly she thought she was acting, Galveron could see right through her. He would be horrified to learn what schemes she was hatching behind his back, and would watch her like a hawk thereafter.

But I won't be beaten that easily. When we get back to the Temple, I'll ask Kaita about the Hierarch's ring. She's bound to know.

As Aliana looked down once more at her sleeping companion, Galveron began to stir. He rolled over, rubbing his eyes, and sat up quickly. 'It's daylight! Why didn't you wake me?'

She shrugged. 'What's the rush? It's only just turned light. There was no reason why you shouldn't have your sleep out.'

It was as if she hadn't spoken. Galveron stood up and started gathering their paltry belongings together. 'The Hierarch will be worried. We'd better get back.'

Damn the Hierarch! She can jump off a precipice, as far as I'm concerned.

But she knew better than to speak the words out loud. With a sigh, she got to her feet. There were advantages to returning to the Temple with all speed. For one thing, she'd get a chance to ask Kaita about the ring, and for another . . . breakfast! Surely the heroes who had done Gilarra such a tremendous favour would be allowed a few extra rations. After all the adventures of the previous day, and a night spent without any food, Aliana was just about hungry enough to eat her shoes.

Wary as hunted animals, the thief and the warrior crept out of the brewhouse door. Even though it was unlikely that the winged predators would be active in the daylight, the clouds were low and the day was gloomy, so the threat was always there. Both Aliana and Galveron had, at various times, narrowly escaped with their lives from the deadly creatures, and they were taking no chances now.

The Precincts were shrouded in thick, clinging mist which drifted, swirling, with every movement of the sluggish breeze. Grey tendrils of vapour brushed, cold and clammy, against their hands and faces, catching in their throats and silvering Aliana's tawny curls with a sheen of fine droplets.

'It's not all bad,' Galveron whispered. 'We certainly couldn't ask for better cover.'

'True. We'll just freeze our backsides off instead.' The thief shivered, and tried to pull her Godsword cloak more tightly around her shoulders. The day was raw and damp, and there was a chill in the air which made her suspect that snow might be due again before nightfall. Suddenly the Temple, noisy, overcrowded and smelly, seemed like home – and she couldn't wait to get back there.

As they made their way through the lower area of the Sacred Precincts, the artisans' village was eerily deserted. The Godsword stables, kennels and mews were silent, the last of their occupants having gone to fill the bellies of the winged invaders. Smithmaster Agella's forge was grey and cold, its fire extinguished long ago, and the ovens in the bakery were the same. Other workshops – potter, tanner, weaver, silversmith, and all the others – were empty of life, with materials, tools and half-finished work spoiled and scattered. From the laundry there no longer came the raucous, cheerful sound of the washerwomen's gossip and laughter.

Among the clusters of neat little houses, the mist drifted, revealing and concealing abandoned dwellings as it moved. To Aliana, it seemed to hide a multitude of ghosts. Dim shapes seemed to move in the shadows behind the shattered windows. A loud crash caused her to gasp and whirl, her heart pounding, but it was only a loose tile sliding from a roof. Here and there, a shutter caught the breeze, creaking gently back and forth on its hinges, and in every pile of rubble, rats rustled and scratched, surviving as always, in the midst of death and ruin.

Then suddenly Aliana heard a something that was not a rat – a sound so unexpected that she thought she must be imagining things. She clutched at Galveron's arm. 'Did you hear that?'

He nodded, peering round in an attempt to locate the origin of the sound. Then it came again, briefly, choked off suddenly as though it had been muffled by a hand. But this time there was no more doubt. Unmistakably, it was the whimper of a baby.

'Holy Myrial!' Aliana muttered. 'How in the name of wonder could a child as young as that survive on its own for so long?'

'Maybe it isn't alone,' Galveron said. 'Anyway, we have to find it, though I don't much like the idea of lingering out here.'

'Me neither. If the day gets any more gloomy, we'll have those damned creatures on the hunt again.'

'We shouldn't take that risk – especially when we're carrying the Hierarch's ring.' Galveron paused in thought. 'I have an idea.' He dug in his pocket, and handed her the ring, wrapped carefully in a piece of rag that they had found in the brewhouse. 'Here. You take this and go back now. Then at least the ring will be safe, and Gilarra will know we're all right.'

Aliana crammed the ring into her pocket with some force, her mouth tightened to a thin line. 'Absolutely not – and don't waste time arguing. We should stick together, and you may need my help. I'm not going back without you.'

Galveron scowled at her – but she knew that he knew he couldn't *make* her go back. 'All right,' he said coldly. 'Since you've decided to be stupid and irresponsible, so be it.' He turned away from her as if in disgust, and headed towards the nearest building.

Aliana's cheeks burned at the rebuke, but she said nothing. This was not the time – but she'd be sure to pay him out later. Much more important was the fact that he seemed to have forgotten that he'd given her the Hierarch's ring – and she didn't want to do anything to remind him. She might not understand what, exactly, the ring did – but she knew that while she held it, she possessed a great deal of power over Galveron and Gilarra.

There's no going back now. Tiarond is finished, and even if I had the chance to return right now, what would be the point? So feeling home-sick is a waste of time – and so are regrets.

Seriema leaned on the sill of the deep window embrasure, and looked out across the moors and the tarn below. The world seemed so wide here in the territory of the Reivers, with no buildings to block the horizon. In the distance, she could see the mountain on which she had lived her entire life. Somewhere up there was Tiarond, and her opulent home: a far cry from this draughty tower chamber walled in dank, chill stone which, unfortunately, was her sleeping quarters for the foreseeable future. After a supper which had been far from a feast, as Tormon's news had persuaded Arcan, the clan chieftain, to conserve supplies, she had spent the night here, along with Rochalla and four unwed Reiver girls. Though none of them had been happy about the arrangement, there had been no alternative. Now that danger threatened, the clan was being brought into the shelter of the fortress, and accommodations were in short supply. The young women had slept on the floor of their cramped quarters, on thin pallets stuffed with bracken, and considered themselves lucky to be only six. In other parts of the building, folk were sleeping as many as twelve or fourteen to a room this size.

Well, at least she had a bed. She told herself that she should be grateful. And clothes, too. To replace the torn and mudstained Godsword clothing she had taken from the Tiarond guardhouse, the Reiver women had supplied her with a dress of thick woven wool, in mingled shades of heather and twilight. The soft colours were beautiful but more to the point, the gown was warm and hard-wearing, and Seriema was grateful for the generosity of her hosts.

Tormon's little band of wanderers had breakfasted that morning with the chieftain, his lifemate and his sons. The meal had consisted of broth, cold mutton, oatcakes, and creamy ewe's milk cheese, washed down with ale – a change, to say the very least, from her usual fare, though she supposed she would get used to it eventually. Maybe. In about a hundred years. Afterwards, Arcan had closeted himself with his sons and his warriors to discuss, once again, the threat that would face them when the winged invaders from Tiarond should venture further afield.

Seriema had found herself at a loose end after breakfast. Presvel and Rochalla had gone off somewhere together – but not alone. To the conspicuous annoyance of Seriema's former assistant, Rochalla had offered to mind little Annas while Tormon was busy. The trader himself, accompanied by his shadow Scall, had headed down to the ground floor of the fortress, where the livestock was kept, to see to their precious horses. Tormon had invited her to accompany them, but Seriema had made the excuse (mostly untrue) of fatigue after yesterday's long ride. Apart from stiffness and complaining muscles she felt fine, but that wasn't the point. Now she'd had time to get used to the idea, she could see the sense of looking after her horse when they were on the road, but she was damned if she was going to turn herself into an unpaid groom in this place, where there were so many big, strong men around, who apparently had nothing better to do with their time than bragging, gambling, and sharpening their swords.

She had wandered round the fortress for a while, learning to find her way about, and watching Arcan's folk busying themselves with their various tasks. The dour Reivers, however, did not seem to welcome her presence, for the place was in a ferment with the preparations for a siege, so eventually she had come up here to be out of the way. Feeling lonely and a little unsure, she had just been giving herself a good talking-to. She didn't miss the city – not she. It would do her good to be away from the weight of her responsibilities, the endless documents on her desk, the crowded streets and the tedious daily routine. And Lord Blade. At the memory of the Godsword Commander, her fingers clenched on the stone of the windowsill. The further she was from *him*, the better.

That's all very well, but what's the alternative? What place would there be for me here? I had an empire, and now it's gone . . . But damn it, I won't let that beat me. Somehow, I'll think of a way to start again.

Suddenly, she felt unbearably constricted in the little chamber. It was well enough for sleeping in, but in daytime the turf fires were allowed to go out, and the cold, dismal place smelled stale because so many sleepers had occupied it through the night. Acting on impulse, she grabbed the thick Godsword cloak that she now wore as a matter of course, and left the room, continuing on up the narrow staircase, instead of descending into the body of the fortress itself. In a moment, she had opened the narrow door that led out onto the roof, and was leaning perilously over the crenellated wall, the icy wind blowing her hair out of its fastenings to fly and tangle in the wind.

She had better make the most of this, she told herself. By the look of the sky, there would be rain again soon. The far horizon was stacked with an inky mass of cloud that was approaching swiftly on the wind. From the fortress's vantage point, high on the hill, Seriema looked out over the valley in which the Reivers made their home. Everything seemed so primitive here! Tormon had explained to her that, despite the harsh climate, the clan had limited use for dwellings. For the most part, they inhabited the wild landscape itself, camping in the open in temporary shelters or sturdy hide tents, either roaming the moors with their livestock, hunting game, or fighting with other clans. In the valley bottom, huddled in the lee of the high, steep slopes, was their one little settlement with its straggle of rough-and-ready houses: low stone dwellings half-sunk into the ground, and roofed with sods. They looked like dens of some wild animal, not homes for people, and were mainly used by those with small children, the sick, and the elderly members of the clan.

Today the hills were bare of sheep and the Reivers' wild, white cattle. They had been rounded up and penned in the yard of the keep. If the winged fiends came, many of the beasts would be slaughtered, and the meat smoked or salted to feed the people taking shelter in the stronghold. People went to and fro below her, transferring provisions, clothing, bedding, and any small treasures to the safety of the keep. Some were grubbing up any root crops that could be lifted now, while others brought in supplies of peat for the fires, and bracken to bed down both animals and humans alike. There was an air of grim purpose about the Reivers this morning. Even small children trotted to and fro on errands with an air of self-importance: fetching and carrying, scavenging round the shores of the tarn for odd bits of firewood, hunting around the settlement for eggs, and rounding up the chickens and pigs to be transferred into the keep. Dogs, overexcited by all the activity, yapped and darted around people's feet, chasing the livestock and hindering more than they helped.

If only Tiarond had had some warning like this. How many lives could have been saved?

Turning away from the settlement, Seriema walked across to the other side of the roof. Leaning on the parapet, she looked across the wild moors to the far horizon, where the iridescent barrier of the curtain walls stretched from earth to sky. It was many years since she had seen them – not since her father had brought her, as a girl. Below the keening of the wind, she thought she could just make out the faint crackle and roar of the energy barrier. What must it be like to live so close to such a phenomenon? She wondered what, if anything, lay on the other side. Was that where the winged invaders had come from? Beyond the mysterious boundaries which enclosed Callisiora?

I wish I knew. Maybe if we could find out where they came from, we might discover a way to fight them.

Lost in thought as she scanned the wild horizon, she suddenly heard her name being called. Turning, she came face to face with Cetain, the chieftain's second son. 'So this is where you're hiding,' he said with a smile. 'I've been all over the fortress trying to find you.'

'Why?' Seriema asked in surprise. She hardly knew this man. True, she had spoken to him the previous day when he had escorted the wanderers to his father's fortress, and they had exchanged a tentative smile or two at supper the previous evening, though they had not been seated near one another. That had been enough for her to decide that she liked him. He must have been close to herself in age, and though she wouldn't have called him handsome, he looked very striking, with his twinkling green eyes and his long, dark red hair, braided this morning and tied back from his face with a silver clasp.

'You've no nonsense about you, have you, lass?' He smiled. 'Short and to the point, the way a warrior speaks. Just what I would have expected from the merchant queen of Tiarond. And what if I said I just wanted to pass the time, and to see how you were settling in with us?'

'I would say that tripe coated in honey is still tripe. You have too much to do today to stand around and gossip, and you wouldn't have been searching the place for me if it was only company you lacked.' Seriema answered his smile with one of her own. 'So come on – out with it. What do you want?'

Cetain's smile vanished. Instead of answering her question, he came to lean on the wall beside her, and looked out towards the horizon, and the fast-approaching clouds. 'I should have known I would find you up here,' he said softly. 'This has always been my favourite place for thinking things through. And from what Tormon has been saying, you must have a very great deal to think about. These last few days can scarcely have been easy.'

Somehow, Seriema was unable to dissemble with this grave young man. 'You're right. So many terrible things have happened, and all so fast, that I hardly have them settled in my mind, as yet. I just keep telling myself I'm one of the lucky ones to have survived at all.'

'You're very brave. I'm not sure that many of my warriors would have been so steadfast, under the same circumstances.' Cetain looked down at his hands, clasped before him on the top of the cold stone wall, and sighed. 'In a way, that makes it harder for me to ask of you what I must.'

Seriema frowned. 'What do you want to ask me? I'm grateful that you've sheltered us here, and I'm willing to help in any way I can. As long as it isn't cooking or sewing,' she added hastily.

Cetain laughed. 'The minute I set eyes on you, proudly wearing your soldier's cloak, still unbowed after your arduous journey, and handling that great black horse as easily as if it were a gentle old pony, I knew I had a warrior-maid on my hands.'

But Seriema wasn't about to be flattered. 'And?' she said pointedly.

'And . . . Look, please don't feel that anyone is forcing you to do this. I know it's a lot to expect after what you've just been through.'

Her patience gave out. 'Do WHAT?' she shouted.

'Come with me to persuade the other chieftains of our danger.'

Seriema's jaw dropped open. 'You – you want *me* to ride with the Reivers? But I scarcely know one end of a sword from the other. What use would I possibly be?'

'It's like this, you see.' Cetain turned to face her. 'If my men and I go to the other chieftains with this tale of winged invaders, why should they believe me? They're bound to think it's some kind of trick on the part of my father. It would not be the first time in our history that the leaders of all the clans have been lured together under a flag of truce, and murdered. But if we take a witness from the city – someone who saw these terrible killings happen with her own eyes – well, we'd stand a better chance of succeeding. So my father thinks, and I agree, though I'm far from happy to be taking you into danger . . .'

'Why me?' Seriema interrupted. 'Why me, and not one of the others?'

'Well, for a start, you'd be better-looking company than Tormon . . .'

'Be serious!'

'That you're better looking than Tormon? What makes you think I'd *not* be serious about a thing like that?'

She glared at him, and he held up his hands in surrender. 'All right, all right. I'll tell you. Stop glaring at me like an eagle about to pounce on a sheep. I should have known better than to rely on my poor indifferent charms to talk you around.'

'If you would just tell me why you want me to go, you might not have to talk me around at all.'

He nodded. 'One reason is that you *are* a woman. We go to parley this time, and the less warlike we look, the better. And though we do have a number of female warriors, with all due respect, you don't look like one of them – yet. Another reason is that you are who you are. All the Reivers have heard of the Lady Seriema, the foremost merchant in Callisiora – mostly because your caravans are such prized targets for us. But better still, some of our folk have seen you in the city, for we do visit – unobtrusively, of course – from time to time, to do a little trading, and gather information.'

'And because the Reivers are not normally my friends,' Seriema said wryly, 'I would have to be riding with you for a damn good reason.'

'Exactly.' He searched her face with his eyes. 'So will you come? It may be dangerous – I won't lie to you about that. If any of the chieftains decide not to honour our flag of truce, then we'll end up fighting for our lives. But, on the other hand, if the clans can be persuaded to co-operate for once, many innocent people might be saved.'

An image of the foul winged monstrosity, with its bloodstained talons and fangs, bursting into her room, flashed into Seriema's mind. She thought of the women and children she had just been watching, as they went about their tasks in the village. 'Of course I'll come,' she said.

'I knew you wouldn't fail us!' Was it her imagination, or did Cetain look on her with new respect? 'I'll find a good horse for you – that great black beast of yours will need a good rest after all its exertions yesterday, and besides, I'd not be willing to take a beast of such quality and breeding into the lands of our enemies.' He grinned. 'Best not to put temptation in their way, eh?'

Seriema did not smile back. Speaking of horses reminded her of Tormon – and she knew that the trader wasn't going to like this expedition of hers one little bit.

Well, tough. I don't have to ask Tormon's permission for anything. I carved out my own life in the city, and I'll damn well do the same out here.

It was amazing how the prospect of having something useful and practical to do had boosted her spirits and her confidence. She owed Cetain her thanks for letting her, an outsider, be part of the Reivers' world.

He held out his hand. She took it willingly, and together they went down into the keep.

Three

The New Hierarch

Galveron held up a hand for silence and crept towards the house, trying to move as silently as possible over the broken glass and other debris underfoot. Though the windows had been shattered, the door was still intact. He pushed at it, then put his shoulder to it, but it would not move. 'The accursed thing's locked,' he said softly. 'I don't want to break it down, in case the noise attracts those vile creatures, but I can't seem to budge it at all.'

'I can see that.' Aliana pushed past him. 'Here – let me.' Before he had a chance to protest, she picked up a stone and knocked the last shards of broken glass out of the window frame. Then she hoisted herself up, and with a twist and a wriggle, was inside.

'Come back, you idiot!' Galveron hissed. She pretended not to hear him. After a moment, however, she heard him climbing through the window behind her, and making a lot more noise about it than she had done. Grabbing her arm, he spun her round to face him. 'What in perdition do you think you're playing at?' he demanded.

Aliana twisted out of his grasp. 'If there's a child in here, we've got to find it.'

'I know. But don't go off without warning like that. Out here, we ought to stick together.'

Aliana knew that he was right – this time – but she was damned if she was going to admit it. 'Try keeping up, then,' she snapped. In a chilly silence, they commenced their search of the house.

29

Apart from the rain and dirt that had blown in through the shattered casements, the interior of the building seemed undisturbed. Aliana suspected that the winged fiends had gone through the village smashing the windows of the houses so that they could look and listen for any people that might be concealed within. So far, however, there had been enough food in the Temple courtyard to distract them from a more thorough search.

The little house was cosy and well-kept. It had the feel of a happy home about it, the sort that Aliana had always longed for while she was living with her brother in the rough-and-ready squalor of the Warrens. She felt a pang of deep regret for the loss of the family who had dwelt here. Signs of the loving attention they had lavished on the place were everywhere. There was intricate carving on the furniture and the wooden overmantel. Rich tapestries hung on the walls. The handmade rugs on the floors and the bright, embroidered cushions on the chairs had all been crafted with great skill. 'It looks as though both of them were Temple artisans,' Galveron whispered. 'He was a carver, and she probably embroidered the great tapestries and the vestments of the priests.'

Aliana snorted. 'What makes you so sure it was that way around?'

The lower floor of the house was deserted, as were the bedrooms upstairs. The kitchen was filled with a sharp reek of burning, which came from a neglected stew pot, that hung over the ashes of the fire. The contents had burned dry, and congealed into a blackened lump in the bottom. Presumably this would have been their supper on the night of the Sacrifice, simmering over the fire to be ready for the little family when they returned. Aliana bit her lip, hard. This place was so sad! Somehow, it underlined the sheer extent of the human tragedy that had beset Tiarond, far more powerfully than the decaying pile of dead meat in the courtyard ever could.

She shivered. Suddenly her irritation with Galveron, and his with her, seemed stupid and petty. She caught his eye, and knew that he was thinking exactly the same thing. Somehow, apologies passed between them without a word being said, and they were back in accord once more. 'Let's get out of here, Galveron,' Aliana whispered. 'It's time we were heading back. We've searched the house from top to bottom, and there's no baby. We must have been mistaken.'

The Godsword Commander frowned. 'But I'm sure that's what I heard.'

'Me too.' Aliana shrugged. 'But there's nothing here. It must have been a cat or something, and Gilarra wouldn't let us take an animal back to eat her precious rations.'

Galveron sighed. 'Can't you be a little more charitable towards her? Please? Remember that Gilarra has a difficult job to do. Just think how *you* would manage, in her place. Anyway, I think a cat would be a good idea, if we can find one. Quartermaster Flint has been complaining about vermin in the storage caves.' He paused, his brows knotted in thought. 'But I'm sure that wasn't a cat I heard.'

He raised his voice a little. 'Ho! Is anybody here?'

There was a moment's silence then, from under their feet, came a weak little cry. 'Myrial save us!' Galveron punched his fist into the palm of his other hand. 'There's a cellar.'

After a brief but frenzied search, they discovered that a rug in front of the kitchen range had been hiding the trapdoor. Aliana found a little oil lamp in the kitchen and Galveron lit it, then they scrambled through the opening and down some rickety stairs which were little more than a ladder with delusions of grandeur. At the bottom, Galveron held up the lamp to illuminate the room.

The cellar was very small, and stank of blood and human waste. The wall to their left was lined with shelves to accommodate the family's food supplies, though much of the space was now empty. On their right was a long table, its surface gouged and scarred, but spotlessly clean. The carver's tools were there, in a lavishly decorated wooden chest, and the space between the table and the steps housed a lathe. But Aliana and Galveron were not looking at the little underground room. Their attention was fixed in the far corner, where a pile of boxes, casks, and one or two broken bits of furniture were stacked. From behind this pile of discarded odds and ends came a weak and pitiful cry. 'Help me, please.'

They darted forward, and Aliana held the lamp while Galveron pulled some of the boxes away. In the corner, shrinking away from the light, was a grey-faced, tangle-haired woman in a nest of blood-stained blankets. By her side, wrapped up in what looked like an old flour sack, was a tiny infant.

Aliana was frozen with horror and pity. For a moment she felt utterly powerless to help this poor, wretched creature. Not so Galveron. Snatching the lamp from his companion, he knelt down beside the woman.

'Are you real?' she whispered.

'We're real.' He gave her a reassuring smile. 'What's your name?'

She licked her dry lips. 'Cerella.'

'I'm Galveron and this is Aliana.' He looked round at the thief. 'Will you get some fresh water, please?'

'Of course.' Aliana couldn't wait to get out of there. Something about this pitiful woman tore at her heart. She rummaged in the kitchen, collecting together a pitcher of water, a cup, and a towel. Juggling her burdens, she slithered down the ladder with difficulty, and returned to the dark and fetid corner just in time to hear Cerella telling the Godsword Commander what had happened.

'And as I was so near my time, Essel – that's my lifemate – wouldn't let me go to the Sacrifice, even though I was supposed to. He said that the Hierarch wouldn't miss me, and if Myrial was any sort of God, He wouldn't mind a woman so near her time staying out of the crowds . . . But I think Myrial did mind.' Her face twisted with grief. 'I should have gone, but I didn't, and now these dreadful things have happened. I thought everyone was dead. Everyone but me.' Tears began to course down her sunken cheeks.

Galveron gripped her hand. 'Not everyone,' he said. 'A good number of people survived, and we all found shelter in the Temple. We'll take you there.'

But Cerella turned her face to the wall. 'Too late,' she whispered. 'I heard screams. I looked out of the window and saw those vile creatures flying overhead. Then the baby started to come, and I hid down here. It was the only thing I could think of. I tried to pull the rug back as best I could from inside, so that the trapdoor would be hidden.'

Aliana felt tears prickling behind her eyes. *She had her baby all alone here in the dark, knowing that her man must almost certainly be dead, and with those fiends rampaging outside.*

Galveron's face was oddly immobile, and she admired his ability to keep his feelings from the woman. 'And afterwards?' he asked softly.

Cerella shook her head. 'I had such a bad time,' she whispered. 'Somehow the baby survived, but something's wrong inside me. Every time I move, I start to bleed again.' She took a sip of water from the cup that Galveron held out to her. 'I'm finished, I think, but my poor little girl still clings to life. Please, if you can only take her . . .'

'We'll take both of you,' said Galveron in a voice that brooked no argument. 'I'm going to carry you, so that you won't strain yourself, and Aliana will take the baby. All you have to do is make it as far as the Temple. We have a very skilful healer there. She'll take good care of you.'

'But the bleeding . . .' Cerella protested.

Aliana knelt down and took both the woman's hands in her own. 'Listen, Cerella. If you stay here, you'll die for sure. It's a terrible risk, I know, but surely it's worth a try.'

What's the point of this? She's going to die anyway.

Not for nothing had the thief spent so much of her life in the Warrens, where death was an everyday occurrence. She could recognise the signs. Cerella's waxen appearance, the cold, clammy feel of her skin, and the laboured rasp of her breathing: they all signified that her life was fading. Once again, Aliana felt her throat tighten, thinking of what this poor woman had suffered in the last few days. Somehow, through a tremendous act of will, she had managed to keep herself and her newborn child alive until help came. The effort had taken every ounce of strength she possessed, but now that she knew her baby would be safe, her overtaxed body was ready to admit defeat.

The poor thing doesn't have much longer. Why put her through the rough handling it'll take to get her out of here? We could stay with her, surely, until she slips away?

Then all at once she felt ashamed. Who was she to say that Cerella would never make it back? Given the tremendous effort she had made to live, surely she might just hold on for a little while longer, until she reached help? Besides, Galveron wasn't about to *let* her give in. A single glance at his face as he knelt by the woman's side told Aliana all she needed to know. He was a Godsword. He was pledged to protect the people of Tiarond, but an uncountable number of citizens had died. And Kaita had told her about the death of his old friend, Sergeant Ewald, when the winged fiends had invaded the Temple.

He couldn't save all those others, so he's determined to rescue this one. And he doesn't seem to realise that he's setting himself up for more heartache. Oh, Galveron! Don't do this to yourself.

As though he had sensed her eyes on him, Galveron turned to her. 'Stay with Cerella,' he told her. 'I'm going upstairs to find some blankets.' He climbed out of the cellar, leaving the two women face to face.

'He's a good man,' Cerella said softly.

Aliana nodded. 'The best.'

'He'll break his heart trying to put this city right. Don't let him.'

'I can't stop him. It's just the way he is.'

'Are you his girl?'

The thief smiled. 'No. He's the Godsword Commander, and I'm – at least I was – a thief. Under the circumstances, we haven't got much in common.'

'He's Godsword Commander? So Lord Blade was killed?'

'I suppose so.'

'It's time we had a good man in charge. And Zavahl? Did they sacrifice him after all?' Suddenly, there was a new urgency in the woman's voice.

'To tell you the truth, Cerella, I wasn't there either.' Aliana squeezed her hand. 'As far as I can discover, neither were quite a

few other people. So you see, it's pointless to go on blaming yourself for this catastrophe just because *you* stayed at home. But to get
back to Zavahl, he isn't among the folk in the Temple, and Gilarra
is the new Hierarch, so I expect we can assume that he's dead.' She
frowned. 'Why do you ask?'

Cerella's eyes were wide and dark. 'My baby,' she whispered. 'I
was in labour when a Hierarch died. Unless another child was born
last night, my little one should be his successor.'

The thief felt her jaw drop. 'Myrial's name! I never thought of
that.'

'I've had a lot of time to think, down here alone. So you see, it's
just as well I'm dying. Had I survived, how could I ever have given
her up?' She sighed. 'After all that's happened in the last few days,
there's probably not much of a future in being Hierarch of Callisiora.
But at least she'll be looked after, and that's all that any of us can
ask.'

Aliana squeezed Cerella's hands. 'And you'll be looked after too.
You've come this far. Don't give up now, when you're almost safe.'

Cerella's eyelids drooped. 'Her name is Ruhanna,' she whispered.
At that moment Galveron came sliding down the steps, his arms
full of blankets. Aliana had never been so glad to see anybody in
her life. She ran to meet him. 'You'd better hurry,' she whispered.
'She has no strength left, and she's ready to give up.'

Galveron knelt down beside the half-conscious woman. Reaching
across her, he picked up the baby and handed it to Aliana, who took
it very gingerly. The little face, topped with a thatch of dark hair,
was pale and sunken. She was still breathing, but did not awake,
even when the thief wrapped her, very clumsily, in another blanket.
Aliana frowned. She didn't don't know much about babies, but
surely such stillness couldn't be a good sign.

Galveron, in the meantime, had wrapped the child's mother in
blankets, and gathered her into his arms. 'Are you ready?' he asked.
'Then let's go.'

The worst part was getting the woman up the steep cellar steps
and through the narrow trapdoor. Aliana went first with the child,

and Galveron followed with Cerella, pushing her up through the hole while the thief pulled and steadied her from above. By the time they had got her out, she was unconscious, and by the time they left the house, blood was already beginning to soak through the blankets.

They hurried through the village, Galveron carrying Cerella, and Aliana clutching Ruhanna, the baby girl. She was glad to reach the towering golden gates which were the entrance to the wide plaza in front of the Temple, and put the artisans' settlement behind her. Even the grisly mounds of the decomposing dead were preferable to the eerie shells that had once been happy homes. At least here she and Galveron were out in the open, where nothing could creep up on them.

At least, I hope not. The thought of some enemy lying hidden, just as she had done, amid these rotting, stinking corpses, sent a shudder through her.

Galveron nudged her, giving her a welcome respite from such thoughts. 'Come on,' he whispered. 'Hurry. Bleeding like this, I don't think Cerella will last much longer. The sooner we're all safely back in the Temple, the better.'

One by one they slipped through the gates and began to pick their way around the edges of the plaza. Mist and cloud might conceal their progress, but they were still too wise and wily to attempt to cross open ground without any cover. Besides, the centre of the square was choked by the dead. Even at the edges, where bodies were thinner on the ground, they were forced to clamber over ghastly human remains, burdened by the mother and child they had rescued. Aliana had wrapped her scarf across her nose and mouth, but it did nothing to block out the thick stench of decay. She had pulled on her gloves so that she wouldn't have to touch the cold, decaying flesh, but still her throat contracted with nausea at the sight of viscera torn loose from gaping bodies, faces that had been half-eaten away by rats and crows, torn limbs, and bloodied eye sockets staring emptily at the sky. Time after time, her feet slipped in putrid slime, and she only just managed to save herself from pitching headfirst into the pile of decomposing flesh.

How did we ever manage to do this the first time?

Aliana remembered when she and the other Grey Ghosts had first climbed into the Sacred Precincts, looking for shelter in the Temple. Pursued by the winged predators, running in terror for their very lives, they'd had little chance to consider the scenes of carnage around them. With a shudder, Aliana thought of the children Tag and Erla, the youngest surviving members of the Grey Ghosts.

I hope they don't remember much about this.

Getting across the square had been easier the next time too, when Aliana had made her lonely journey in the dead of night from the Citadel to the Temple. The snow and darkness had hidden many of the horrors that she was seeing now, and the bitter cold of that freezing night had diminished the awful stench. Then there had been yesterday, when she and Galveron had passed this way on the outward leg of their search for the missing ring. How many more times would she have to endure this dreadful journey? Each time the horror, rather than diminishing, seemed to grow worse. Some sights were so appalling that it was impossible to become accustomed to them. She clutched the baby closer to her, and tried to move a little faster.

She reached the Temple door ahead of Galveron, with his heavier, more awkward burden. Clasping the child to her with one arm, she gave the coded knock on the Temple door. It was opened by Smithmaster Agella, and Flint, the one-armed Quartermaster. 'Thank goodness you're safe.' Agella put an arm round the shoulder of the weary girl, and pulled her into the safe haven. 'The Hierarch has been out of her mind with worry.' Then she caught sight of the baby. 'Holy Myrial! Where in the name of wonder did you find *that?*'

'We have its mother, too,' Aliana said. 'Galveron is bringing her. Quickly, send someone to warn Kaita. We think the woman's dying.'

Agella beckoned to a child who was lurking nearby. 'You, lad! Go and tell the Healer we're bringing her a very sick woman. Run!'

At that moment, Galveron came staggering into the Temple, helped by a steadying hand from Flint. Without pausing, he carried straight on to Kaita's makeshift infirmary in the old Guardroom, Aliana following with the baby. The Healer was helping a Godsword soldier, whose arm was swathed in bandages from shoulder to wrist, out of bed. 'I'm sorry to throw you out, Lomin,' she was saying, 'but you're on the mend now, and we have an emergency on our hands.'

The soldier grinned at her. 'Don't you worry, Healer Kaita. I got no complaints. You've looked after me like I was the Hierarch himself.'

'What – burned him at the stake?' someone muttered, as she passed Aliana with a can of hot water. The thief hid a grin.

Kaita, in the meantime, had taken charge of Cerella. 'Put her on the bed,' she ordered Galveron, 'and let's have a look at her.'

As they unwrapped the woman from her blankets, Aliana was horrified to see that they were soaked with blood.

Dear Myrial! I'm amazed she's still alive. And what about this poor child?

Desperately she looked around for one of Kaita's helpers. Frana, a plump, motherly woman who had been a midwife in the city, was straightening beds at the other end of the room. Dutiful as always, she continued with her allotted task, but Aliana could see by the way she kept darting glances at the new patient that she was longing to assist. She ran over to the midwife, proffering the baby. 'Frana, will you help me? I have that poor woman's child here. It's in a bad way too, I think.'

'Gracious!' With expert hands, Frana undid the thief's clumsy wrappings. The pallid, scrawny babe lay limply in her arms. 'Why, she's nothing but skin and bones,' she said indignantly, glaring at Aliana as though it was *her* fault. She gently pinched the skin on the child's arm, and frowned. 'The first thing we need to do is get some liquids into her. Poor little scrap . . .' She was addressing the baby now. 'You haven't had much of a start in life. Never mind, we'll soon put that right. Auntie Frana will take care of you . . .'

Clearly, Aliana was no longer needed. 'Her name is Ruhanna,' she told the midwife, and fled – but not far. She continued to hang around the sickroom, feeling useless, but unable to leave until she knew whether the woman she had found would live or die. As she waited, she found that her eyes were drawn to one of Kaita's helpers, who was boiling surgical instruments in a large pot on the fire. It was the same woman who had made the jest about the soldier being burned at the stake like the Hierarch. She turned, and beckoned surreptitiously to Aliana, and with a sudden shock of recognition, the thief realised that it was Gelina, looking completely different – and much older – with her abundant hair tied out of the way in a kerchief, and her colourful, swirling gypsy skirts covered by a clean white apron. Aliana hurried over to her. 'Gelina! What are you doing here? I thought you would be keeping an eye on Packrat for me, and taking care of Tag and Erla.'

The woman glanced furtively over her shoulder. 'Quick,' she said. 'In here before they see us.' She tugged Aliana through the back of the sickroom and into the passage that led to the store caves further up the mountain. 'It's the Hierarch,' she said softly. 'She split us all up, and put us to work.'

'*What?*'

'Shhh. Somebody will hear you. Once you and Galveron were out of the way, she came over with some Godswords, and said that the best way to keep us out of mischief was to make us do an honest day's work for once in our lives, and if we were kept apart we would be less likely to make trouble.'

'Of all the bloody nerve!' Aliana exploded, keeping her voice down with difficulty. 'How dare she!'

'I know.' Gelina nodded mournfully. 'The bitch sent me here to Kaita, sent Packrat down to clean the privies, and put Tag and Erla with the rest of the orphaned kids that Felyss is looking after.'

'But what about Alestan? Surely he objected?'

Gelina glanced over her shoulder again to make sure that they were unobserved, but everyone's attention was fixed on the ailing woman. 'Oh, he objected all right,' she said bitterly. 'And that was when they arrested him.'

'I don't believe this! Why, that treacherous, two-faced bitch . . .'

The thief's tirade ended abruptly as Gelina clamped a hand across her mouth. 'Hush, Aliana, for goodness' sake! Don't you see, she'll be trying to provoke you? She's already got Alestan out of the way. He was accused of stealing bread, but I saw one of the Godswords slip it into his pocket myself. Now that she has him locked up, she has a hold over you right there, and Galveron is unlikely to defend him because of all the acrimony between the two of them. As things stand right now, she can't very well arrest *you* because she owes you, and Galveron wouldn't stand for it, so she's trying to goad you into some sort of confrontation. All she's looking for is an excuse to get you out of the way, and she'll pick the rest of us off one by one, probably with more trumped-up charges of theft.'

'Where is he?' Aliana demanded. 'Where did she put my brother?'

'He's locked up in one of the little rooms beneath the Temple,' Gelina told her. 'You can't get near him, Aliana – I already tried. That corridor is thick with guards.'

'I can see what she's up to, I think,' Aliana said with a frown. 'Now that we know her secret she thinks we're a danger to her. She doesn't have to worry about us blackmailing her if she has the ring back, but if we told people she had been careless enough to lose it in the first place, it would still undermine confidence in her to a certain extent.'

Gelina nodded. 'People are already wondering why you and Galveron went outside, and where you went. Any rumours that the ring had been lost would cast a certain amount of doubt on whether or not she had the real one now.'

Aliana's mouth tightened. 'Well, she doesn't have it – not yet. And if she thinks she can do this to my friends, she's made a big mistake.'

'What do you plan to do?'

'Don't worry. I have an idea.' Aliana hugged her friend. 'Take care of yourself, Gelina, and look after the others – whatever Gilarra says. You may not see me for a while.' She hurried away, before Gelina could ask any more questions.

As she left the room, the Hierarch's ring seemed to be burning a hole in her pocket. She had plans to make – and she would have to make them quickly, before Gilarra had time to ask about her prize. Aliana glanced back at Galveron, who was still lingering near the sick women, despite Kaita's attempts to chase him away, as though he felt that he could somehow use his own strength to hold her to this world.

Damn Gilarra. That good man ought to be our leader – and if she doesn't have the ring, perhaps he can take her place.

FOUR

BEACHCOMBERS

Toulac set off down the beach in the opposite direction to Zavahl, and as the distance between them widened, she felt herself beginning to relax. Though it wasn't his fault that he knew so little of the world beyond the walls of Tiarond's Temple, he couldn't help but be a burden. Still, he was company out here on this wild shore, and he was doing his best. Her mind went back to the terrified, hysterical wreck of a man that she and Veldan had rescued from the sacrificial pyre, and how far he had come since then.

That's what happens when you cage a man within walls of stone, and wait on him hand and foot for the whole of his life. After such a cosseted existence, how could we expect him to cope with the tough and dangerous world out here? All things considered, the poor bugger isn't doing too badly. I suppose we have that bonny lass from the inn to thank for the improvement. It's amazing how love – or lust – can wake up a man's ideas.

She chuckled as she walked along, but soon her thoughts began to stray to a less happy subject. By Myrial, but she missed Mazal! It had broken her heart to leave the big, grey warhorse behind, but what choice had there been? She and Veldan had been fleeing for their lives from Lord Blade and his Godswords, and there had certainly been no time to go back and rescue a horse. But she had owned him since the day the lanky colt had left his mother, and he had felt the touch of no one's hand save hers. He'd been more than a useful animal. While they had still been warriors, he had saved her life more times than enough. He was a true companion. He was all the family she had.

I wonder where he is now? Is he still alive?

Toulac doubted it. The mountain had been swarming with Godsword soldiers. If they couldn't tame the horse – and he had been trained so that no one could ride him except Toulac – then they might very well slaughter and eat him instead. There was plenty of meat on a horse, and given the current shortage of food in Callisiora, it would be more than welcome.

I left him tethered in the barn. A sitting target. All they'd have to do is put a crossbow bolt between his eyes. And even if, by some miracle, they don't find him, he'll suffer a slow and horrible death from starvation.

Tears burned behind her eyes, and overflowed. She wiped them away roughly with the back of her hand.

Stop that, you daft old baggage. After all these years, now is not the time to start turning all sentimental on me!

It was true enough. A warrior couldn't afford to go to pieces every time a comrade fell. You learned that early, or you didn't survive for long.

All the same, if someone was to bring him back to me right now, I swear I'd give them anything they asked.

Toulac was annoyed with herself. That sort of sentimental, woolly-headed wishful thinking was a complete waste of time. Firmly, she pulled herself together. Things could be a lot worse, and well she knew it. Not only had they ended up in this scavenger's paradise, but she also had her sword, which she had buckled on in Zavahl's room just before the kidnappers struck.

And a good thing I did, too, or I would never have managed to kill that creature who captured me.

Though the area appeared to be deserted, the sword was a great comfort to her, none the less. Out of habit, she checked the blade, tutting at the slight notch where the creature's chitinous head had been severed. If only she'd had time to grab her coat, she would have had her oilstone with her, not to mention being a damn sight warmer. Well, the best way to cure that was to get busy, and to keep moving. With a shrug, she turned her attention to the job in hand.

Even while she was thinking, Toulac had been scanning the beach.

Spotting a dull gleam in the shingle, she darted forward and, squatting beside her find, began to dig, scooping the damp, gritty sand away with her bare hands. To her delight the object turned out to be a sturdy metal box, about as long as her forearm. It was patched with rust, but otherwise intact. It was heavy but, she suspected, the weight probably came from the water she could hear sloshing around inside it. But was seawater all that it contained?

'Well now,' muttered Toulac. 'Let's have a look at you, shall we?' She carried the box further up the beach, and then went in search of a rock of the right size and weight. Having found what she was looking for, she knelt down in the dry sand beside the box, which was fastened by a hasp and pin, rusted into a solid red lump. After some time spent grunting, swearing, and hammering with her rock, she succeeded in smashing off the clasp. Throwing her rock aside, and barely able to restrain her curiosity, she prised open the lid.

The veteran swore as a couple of pints of seawater poured into her lap. She tipped out the remainder of the water and a sludge of wet sand. In the bottom of the box was a sheaf of saturated pages, which fell apart when she tried to lift it out. When she examined the fragments, she discovered that the ink had run out of all recognition, and all that remained was a smudged blue mess. Toulac's heart sank with disappointment. 'Bugger!' she muttered. 'I wonder what it was. Love letters, maybe? A treasure map? Now I'll never find out.'

Beneath the papers lay a small, leather drawstring bag, and she felt her excitement rise again. The leather was soaked and stiff and the string had swollen so that the knots were very tight. Toulac picked at them for a moment or two with her blunt, short nails, before her impatience got the better of her. Removing her right boot, she felt around inside the leg until she found the small, flat pocket, sewn into the leather. Out of it she pulled what had to be her most precious possession at this time: a small, but very sharp knife in its own little sheath. She had carried it around in its hiding place for so long that she had almost forgotten it was there. After putting her boot back on, she attacked the bag again, slicing through the strings and pouring the contents into her hand.

'Plague on it!' The bag, of which she had held such high hopes, contained nothing but some poor sailor's worldly treasures: a few tarnished coins of no particular value, and a handful of poor quality pearls wrapped in an old handkerchief. Toulac shrugged, returned the paltry items to the bag, and dropped it in the sand. Oh well. At least the metal box would come in extremely useful for cooking, and a hot meal, right now, would be more welcome than a whole chest full of treasure. She wondered how long her find had been in the sea. If there had been a fairly recent shipwreck nearby, then the beach could be littered with all sorts of useful items. Tucking the box under her arm, she set off again along the beach, to see what she could find. After a while, she had accumulated several useful items and, thankfully, managed to take her mind off Mazal.

Zavahl, tired from walking and stooping and carrying his booty back to the meeting place, was ready to sit down and rest when he returned. Toulac, however, seemed tireless. She arrived shortly after he did, laden down with an assortment of items, and made him spread out his own finds for inspection, alongside her own. 'There you are,' she said. 'I told you this place would be a treasure-trove.'

Still dubious, he looked down at the motley pile of flotsam. Between them, he and Toulac had amassed a length of sturdy chain which was probably from the anchor of a small boat, a tin box, various lengths and thicknesses of rope, a sizeable piece of fishing net – about which, for some reason, the veteran seemed inordinately pleased – a long spar, broken at one end and with a ragged strip of canvas still attached, assorted driftwood, Zavahl's sack, and his proudest find, the bottom part of a broken earthenware jug which, though it was cracked, seemed fairly watertight. He poked the haphazard pile with his foot. 'Myrial only knows what you could possibly make from this lot.'

The veteran chuckled. 'Luckily, Myrial isn't the only one.' After allowing herself a brief respite to gloat over their discoveries, off she went again, poking around among the rocks that littered the upper part of the beach. After a while, she selected her location: a cluster of boulders close enough to the foot of the cliff for shelter, but far enough away to be safe from any falling rocks. Clambering between the massive stones, she found a sheltered space in their midst that would accommodate a fire and two people. With the help of the taller Zavahl, she jammed the spar high up between two of the boulders to make a ridge pole, and draped the length of netting over the top. 'Now,' she said, 'we need some greenery from up above to thread through the holes in the net.'

The only vegetation in the area was at the top of the cliff. After he'd had so much trouble getting down, Zavahl was not keen to tackle the crumbling rock face again but, in deference to his companion's age, he felt that he ought to volunteer. Toulac laughed. 'Thanks for the offer, but I'll go. I'm used to scrambling up cliffs and the like, but I'll wager that in your whole life you've climbed nothing more than stairs.'

Zavahl felt himself going hot all over with chagrin. 'I'm not *completely* useless, you know!'

The veteran patted his arm. 'It's not your fault, sonny. You can't help the kind of life you've led. But climbing cliffs takes practice. If we get the chance I'd be more than glad to teach you, but this kind of crumbling rock isn't a good place to start. I don't want to have to scrape you up from those rocks at the bottom!'

Despite his wounded pride, Zavahl had to admit that he was relieved – and even more so when he saw that even Toulac, with all her experience, was finding the cliff far from easy. Hardly daring to breathe, he watched her slow, painstaking progress up the escarpment, as she tested every hold and crevice in the friable rock before trusting her weight to it. Even so, she twice lost her footing as the surface crumbled away, leaving her hanging precariously as her feet groped for another secure position, dislodging a barrage of stones in the process.

Myrial, save her! Zavahl had to dive out of the way as a chunk of rock clouted his shoulder, narrowly missing his head. Only when the veteran had found a new foothold and started moving again, did he dare to breathe.

'Are you all right?' he yelled.

'Shut up – I'm concentrating.' Toulac spoke through gritted teeth, and climbed grimly on. The former Hierarch shook his head. *She's old enough to be my grandmother! How can she do this?*

But Toulac could, and did. Before much longer, she had reached the top of the cliff, and with one last scramble and another shower of stones, she vanished over the edge and out of sight. A voice, very breathless, came floating down. 'I'm fine. Just give me a moment or two to collect myself.'

A moment or two? Zavahl had only been watching, and he was wringing with sweat, trembling and exhausted from the tension. He waited, shivering, in the raw wind, steeling himself for a long delay while Toulac recovered. But long before he expected to hear from his companion, the voice came again. 'Mind your head!'

A moment later a large bundle of russet bracken was dropped over the brink of the escarpment. When Zavahl picked it up, he saw that it had been secured by an unravelled strand of the rope he had found earlier. Several more bundles followed: a mixture of bracken, reeds from the marshy ground, and long, flexible twigs from a leafy shrub.

After a time, Toulac's head appeared again over the edge of the cliff. 'Look out – I'm coming down.'

And once again Zavahl had to watch, with his heart in his mouth, while she made a descent that looked, from his point of view, to be even more perilous than her initial climb. Finally she reached the bottom, dropped the last few feet, and dusted the knees of the breeches that Ailie had lent her back at the inn. 'Good, hard-wearing cloth, this,' she said approvingly. She turned to Zavahl and grinned.

'What are you standing there for? Come on, pick up a bundle or two. We've got a shelter to build.'

Building a shelter sounded like a lot of work to Zavahl. He'd had no sleep the previous night, no breakfast today (or any other meals, for that matter), and had been forced into a lengthy trek along the beach and back, hauling a load of heavy junk. He was weary and stiff and cold, his head was throbbing and his stomach ached with hunger. Completely unaccustomed to any form of physical labour, he had just about reached the end of his endurance – or so he thought. 'Are you sure we really need a shelter?' he wheedled. 'I thought you said that Veldan and the others were coming for us.'

'They are – eventually,' Toulac replied. 'But if you think how long we were in the air last night with those awful critters, and how quickly they seemed to be moving, you can work out for yourself that we must be a good long distance from the settlement. Goodness knows how long it'll take them to find us – so in the meantime, we need a shelter.' She looked at him and scowled. 'Besides, making me climb all the way up that bloody cliff for nothing would be a *very* unwise move on your part. Now let's get moving, sonny. We don't have for ever.'

Toulac was more correct than she knew. From the top of the cliff, hostile eyes looked down on the two lost beachcombers, and voices spoke in low and furtive tones.

'Phew! That was close! I felt sure the old baggage would see us when she was poking around up here.'

'So what if she had? A knife in the belly would soon solve that little problem. In fact, I still don't know why you didn't let me kill her while she was up here. They would have been much easier to deal with one by one.'

'Have you gone soft or something, Pelorm? If the four of us can't manage an old granny and a clueless whiner, we should give up this business for good.'

'Anyway, you fool, Tuld was right to wait. It paid off, didn't it?

Now we know they have friends coming to find them, which is good news for us. Word's getting round, and ships don't come close to this bit of coastline any more. Pickings have been getting mighty slim. But the terrain's too rough around here to get far by horse or on foot. The only way these folk will be able to search for their lost mates is by boat – and that's where we come in. We'll make our signal in the usual place, just like we always do and—'

'What about the pair on the beach? It'll be a bit suspicious if there are *two* signals.'

'Oh, don't be stupid, Shafol. You heard the old one say that it'll take their friends a good while to find them. We'll have something to eat now, and a bit of a rest, and wait until it's dark. Then we'll slip down and stick a knife in them – and when their friends come, we'll be waiting.'

Congratulating themselves on the cleverness of their plan, the wreckers crept away into the bushes.

Despite all the problems that were accumulating back in Gendival, and the fuzziness in her head from a night's missed sleep, Veldan was beginning to enjoy the day as she rode the spare horse along the river path. She and her companions were heading for the nearest jetty owned by the Navigators, where they would pick up the boat that would take them down to the coast. It should be a pleasant journey on a day as lovely as this. The fragrant autumn air had an invigorating bite, and the sunlight sparkled and danced through a dappling of bronze oak leaves that still clung to the boughs over-head. The path was soft with a deep bed of leaf litter that muffled the horses' hoofbeats and left the birds and the rippling song of the river as the only sounds.

This was a chance to rest a little: an island of calm in the surging currents of change which had beset Gendival. But though she was enjoying the ride, Toulac and Zavahl were very much on the Loremaster's mind. She wanted to send a mental call out to the veteran, though she wasn't sure of Toulac's ability to answer her.

Had the last time been a chance occurrence, brought on by desperation? Or were her friend's abilities beginning to strengthen and grow, as she was exposed to an increasing amount of telepathic communication?

Kaz interrupted her thoughts. 'Boss, you're getting tempted again.'

Veldan felt a prickle of annoyance. 'All right, I'm tempted. So what?'

'You know what. If, for some reason, Toulac isn't able to answer you, you won't know whether it's because she can't manage to broadcast another message so far, or whether she's in trouble. And then you'll worry. All the way down the river, you'll be fretting. And you'll take it out on me.'

'If that's all you're bothered about, I'll take it out on Elion instead.'

'A plague on Elion,' the firedrake snorted. 'I'm your partner. If you're worried about anything, you talk to *me*. But this time there's no need. Just be patient, Boss, and restrain yourself. Toulac can look after herself. She'll be fine.'

'I suppose.' Veldan sighed. However, since she was riding on horseback and not on Kazairl, at least she had some means to distract herself. She turned to the innkeeper, who rode beside her. 'Hey, Ailie. Want to race?' Urging her horse into a gallop, she took off at speed along the path, leaving her worries behind for just a little while.

The Navigator jetty was on a pleasant, tree-lined stretch of the river, where the stream flowed steady and deep. Small clearings had been cut in the woods nearby, where clusters of low wooden sheds held cargo, and occasionally people, when the boatmen or their passengers wished to spend a night on land. The largest of the buildings had been given over to a trading post, where folk from the Gendival settlement came to bargain for luxuries from downriver and, in the case of the villagers, to sell goods and implements of their own skilled crafting. The Loremasters also had curios to trade: unusual bits and pieces that they had picked up on their travels in the other realms.

The place was run by Skeryn who, in all his thirty-two years, had never taken to life afloat, though he was a Navigator born and bred. He was a clever man with a great thirst for knowledge, but he had neither aptitude nor love for the hard manual work of a boatman. So instead he stayed at the trading post with his books and scrolls, and cared for the two youngsters of his widowed sister Meglyn. She, by contrast to her scholarly sibling, was a proper water-gypsy who could handle any sort of boat with consummate skill. She now owned three boats: two of the shallow-hulled sailing wherries – sixty feet long, built of oak from the Gendival forests, and especially designed for carrying cargoes in river waters – and a seagoing barge which carried cargoes back and forth along the coast. This latter had belonged to her lifemate's father, Ruthar, who had now retired from the sea and lived with Skeryn and the children at the trading post, where he managed the store itself, exchanged gossip, and did a roaring trade with the strong, dark ale he brewed in his own little shed around the back.

When the Loremasters rode up, the wherry was unloading cargo at the wharf. Meglyn, tall and lanky with her dark hair cropped short for convenience and safety on the boat, stood on deck supervising the hoists while Chalas, her brawny crewman, shifted crates and bales. When she saw them, she gave them a cheery wave. 'Nice and early, I see,' she called. 'Don't get too settled. We'll soon be done here, and then we'll want you all aboard as quickly as possible.'

Elion grinned. 'At least that spares us from having to drink Ruthar's deadly black brew.'

'If you're not man enough for my beer, Loremaster, there's plenty of water in the river.' Ruthar had come out of the trading post to welcome them. Though rheumatism had stiffened the old man's gait, he still managed to carry himself with a jaunty air. He had a round, cheerful face, a head of fine, silver-white hair, and twinkling eyes. His skin was surprisingly unwrinkled, considering its years of exposure to the salt winds of the sea and, all in all, he looked much too young to have been in the world for more than eighty years. Veldan was very fond of him: Ruthar was sociable, kind, and full of fun, and she had never heard him complain, or speak ill of folk behind their backs. He was lively company for his grandchildren, and enjoyed food, drink, good company, and keeping busy. He virtually managed the trading post for the studious Skeryn, who was more than happy to do his share of the physical work and keep the accounts, while Ruthar bustled around, taking inventories, arranging goods and, best of all, yarning with the boatmen and the folk who came down from Gendival to trade.

He greeted Ailie with delight, for she was a frequent visitor to the trading post when purchasing her supplies for the inn. 'Well, lass, but it's good to see your pretty face again.'

Unconsciously, Veldan's hand went to the jagged scar that ran down the side of her face, but no one noticed save her partner Kaz.

As Ruthar welcomed them all, the human Loremasters dismounted, somewhat stiffly in Veldan's case. Kaz was a lot more comfortable to ride. In the background of her thoughts, she could feel his smirk. It spoke volumes. 'Oh, shut up,' Veldan growled.

'Me? I never said a word.' The firedrake was all injured innocence.

'You didn't have to.'

'Maybe you'll believe me now, when I tell you that those creatures are for eating, not riding,' said Kaz. 'And on the subject of eating . . .'

'There's no time now,' Veldan told him firmly, 'but I'll see if I can get something from Skeryn to eat on the boat.' With that, she followed Elion and Ailie into the store.

The trading post was a fascinating place. So that the merchandise could be seen clearly, the interior was well-lit by many oil lamps that hung from the low beams above, and a small stove in one corner provided a welcome warmth on this cool autumn day. There were goods stacked everywhere: in barrels, in bales, piled up in the corners and crowded onto shelves. Flour and fleeces, lamp oil and twine, pottery and knives, honey and herbs for medicines and teas – all of these things and more found their way, sooner or later, up the river in the big, shallow-draughted wherries of the Navigators. The air smelt of leather and fruit, spices and soap, tarred rope and smoked fish, all blended with a whiff of woodsmoke from the stove.

Veldan, Elion and Ailie all glanced at one another and smiled. As children growing up in Gendival, it had been their greatest treat to be allowed to come down here with the adults and rummage (while the adults' eyes were elsewhere) through all these treasures from distant places. Even better for adventure had been the jetty and the wherries themselves, and if some eagle-eyed adult should spot the youngsters and chase them ashore, there had always been the swing: simply a piece sawn off a plank of wood, with a hole pierced through the middle and a thick rope passed through and knotted on the other side. The other end of the rope was tied to the thick bough of a tree on the bank, and you swung right out across the river, spinning round and round . . .

'. . . And the day wasn't complete until at least one of us had fallen in, and had to be fished out and dried, and sent home in borrowed clothes.' Only when Elion finished her thought aloud, did Veldan realise how strong and clear the memory had been. Sometimes the past was a much more comfortable place to be than the present.

Skeryn was sitting by the stove. He was lanky and dark-haired like his sister, but his hair was longer, and tended to curl, where hers was straight. His feet were up, his chair was tilted back and, as usual, his nose was buried in a book. As the Loremasters entered, he looked up and blinked, gathering his thoughts from far away. 'Veldan! Elion! It's ages since you've been here! And it's always good to see Ailie.'

He got up and came to greet them, arms outstretched, and enfolded Veldan in an enormous hug. It was only then, when she felt the stiffness going out of her spine, that she realised she had been waiting for him to flinch away from her scar. But, bless him, apart from catching it with a single, piercing glance, he had taken no notice whatsoever of her disfigured face. It came as a great relief to Veldan. Caught up in the tide of events in Gendival, she'd had little time to think about scars, and besides, she had been around and about the settlement while the injury to her face was healing, and they were familiar with the way she looked now. But Skeryn was an old friend, and it was the first time she had seen him since she'd been hurt.

Suddenly, the Loremaster remembered something that Toulac had told her a long time ago, back when they first met:

'That scar is not a pretty sight, but it's not near as bad as you think, and it'll be better still when it silvers out. No one but a complete imbecile would turn away from you in revulsion – and I can't see you scaring people into fits.'

'I don't want them to pity me . . .'

'What? Pity you? My dear child, take a look at yourself. You've a brain in your head, you're a warrior, and you have the air of a woman who knows how to take care of herself . . . And whatever you may think, your face is lovely. Granted, it may not be as flawless as it once was but believe me, the plain old rest of us would gladly trade a scar like that to be as beautiful as you. Really and truly. So you see, Veldan, folk will sympathise with your injury – and that's fair enough – but no one is going to pity you longer than two minutes together.'

Maybe the veteran had been right after all.

'I bet you're glad now that she threw that stupid mask on the fire,' Kaz commented, smugly, from his position outside. 'And I'm sure you remember what *I* always used to tell you . . .'

'Yes, I know,' Veldan interrupted. 'You and Toulac are too damn clever for your own good.'

'But not too clever for *yours*, sweetie.' As usual, the firedrake had the last word.

Veldan barely had time to negotiate a haunch of venison for Kaz before Meglyn was in the doorway, hurrying them away. 'Come on, you folk. The cargo has been unloaded, and we're ready for you now. Never mind settling your stupid horses. Ruthar will see to them until you get back.' The Navigator had little time for any mode of transport which couldn't go on the water. 'Come on. Stir yourselves quick, or we'll be missing the tide.'

'You'd better do as she says,' said Ruthar. 'The last fellow who made her miss the tide left a few possessions behind on the boat. His liver, his kidneys, his—'

'All right, all right.' Elion stood up hastily. There was a scrape of chairs as the two women followed suit.

'Come back soon for a proper visit,' Skeryn said quietly to Veldan. 'We don't see enough of you these days. Maybe the new Archimandrite won't keep you gallivanting around the world so much.'

The Loremaster blinked in surprise, then remembered that Blade had sent messages down the river to arrange transport on Meglyn's boat. 'Do you know anything about Amaurn?' she asked softly.

Skeryn shrugged. 'Not me. I'm too young. Ruthar remembers him, though.'

'Are you on his side?' There weren't many people she would dare to ask so openly.

'We Navigators aren't on anybody's side.' He grinned. 'Only the riverside.'

'Veldan! Get yourself out here *now*!' Meglyn roared – and when she used that tone of voice, it was wise to hurry. Veldan fled.

The wherry was waiting for her, with the mast up and sail ready for hoisting. Clearly the captain was in a hurry to be off. When everyone, including the firedrake, was safely aboard, Chalas cast off and was hoisting the sail up the tall mast while Meglyn, at the tiller, steered the craft out into the current. Ailie immediately found a sheltered corner on deck and dragooned Elion into helping her get out the food. Veldan, leaning on the rail, waved goodbye to Skeryn as the trading post dwindled behind, but her mind was already leaping ahead to the journey's end, when she would find Zavahl and Toulac, and bring them safely home.

fIve

eye on the world

Firefly, Scall's chestnut mare, was coming into season. This morning, the signs were clear – as was the interest of Rutska, not to mention several of the thick-coated, long-maned little stallions belonging to the Reivers.

Oh, no, Firefly. You would have to do this now!

Anxiously, Scall went around checking the tethers of the stallions, but like the Sefrian, they were all restrained with lengths of light chain, to stop them biting through in just such a situation as this. It wasn't an absolute guarantee that one of them would somehow get loose and molest his precious mare, but under the crowded circumstances, with so many beasts stabled so close together, it was the best that could be done.

Firefly had been groomed so hard that she gleamed like a copper coin. In fact, he had brushed her for so long that she'd had more than enough of him for one day. When finally she turned her head and nipped him, none too gently, he decided that, reluctant though he was to leave her for the company of his strange, rough hosts, perhaps he ought to take the hint and give her some peace. Nevertheless, he kept finding ways to put off the evil moment. Maybe he should check her hooves once more . . .

Just when he had made his mind up that he would really have to go, there came the sound of angry voices, from the place where Tormon's sturdy Sefrians were tethered.

'Are you insane? You're *not* going off with those Reivers!' It was Tormon's voice, harsh with anger.

'Who in blazes do you think you're ordering around?' The other voice belonged to Lady Seriema. 'This is important,' she said. 'I'm not going off on some pleasure jaunt, you know. Cetain asked me to go with him and meet the other clan chieftains because he thinks that the testimony of someone who actually witnessed the attack on Tiarond will help convince them to join us.'

Scall's eyes opened wide. She was thinking of going off with the Reivers?

Better you than me, Lady. You must have lost your mind.

Clearly Tormon was not impressed, either. 'If you ever *get* as far as talking to them,' he snapped. 'Don't be fooled by your welcome in this clan, Seriema. These are not civilised people but ruthless barbarians. Their life is hard, and they survive through banditry and murder. If clan chief Arcan didn't owe me a favour or two, your fate would have been rape, and either servitude or death, depending on whether they could spare enough food for you.'

Scall heard Seriema gasp. Tormon must have been desperate indeed to bring up such a painful subject. In Scall's opinion, she had kept going with exceptional courage since she'd been attacked by a brutal madman, but it had all happened so recently that she still had yellowing bruises on her face, and a constant shadow behind her eyes, mute testimony to the memories of pain and fear that must still haunt her. Surely her resolve would waver now?

From his place of concealment, he heard her take a deep steadying breath. 'I'm not afraid,' she said firmly. 'We'll have a company of picked warriors with us, and we'll be travelling under a flag of truce. Cetain won't let me come to any harm.'

Tormon clapped a hand across his eyes. 'Give me strength!' he muttered. 'It's touch and go whether he can manage to keep himself from coming to harm. What does the young idiot think he's playing at? I'll go and have a word with him right now.'

'You will mind your own business.' The words carried the bite of a whiplash, spoken in the tones of one who'd been born to command. Scall was extremely glad she'd never spoken to *him* like that. 'This has nothing whatsoever to do with you,' Seriema went on. 'I have conferred at length with Cetain, we have reached a decision, and I am informing you out of courtesy, not asking your permission.'

'Well, you needn't think you're going on *my* horse.' This sounded so much like capitulation that Scall blinked in surprise. Someone get the better of Tormon? He had developed such a healthy respect for the trader in the last few days that he had never considered the possibility that anyone might defy him.

'Cetain will be lending me a horse,' said Seriema, with great dignity. 'We already discussed that, too.'

'In that case, there's nothing left for me to do but wish you luck,' Tormon replied stiffly. 'Frankly, my Lady, you're going to need it. But let me tell you one thing. When you were attacked in Tiarond, you were fortunate that I happened to be there to help you out. If you get into trouble this time, you're on your own. I have my daughter to consider, and I've no intention of making her an orphan just because some silly woman deliberately walked into danger.'

There was a hiss of indrawn breath. 'Silly, is it? Well what you consider folly, *some* folk would call courage. I'm sure Cetain and I can manage very well without your assistance – and risk or no risk, at least we're trying to do something positive, instead of skulking behind stone walls like a coward.'

Scall heard Seriema's footsteps receding, across the floor and then up the stone steps that led into the main part of the fortress. He held his breath. He didn't want Tormon to discover him now. There was a long moment of silence, then the trader began to curse, his voice low and baleful, not giving vent to his anger around the horses, but letting it out in a soft, steady stream of invective, without once repeating himself. Scall's eyes grew wider and wider. He had never imagined that Tormon would know such words! He didn't know half of them himself.

Finally, the trader ran out of curses, and stalked out of the stable without a backward look. With a sigh of relief, Scall emerged from his hiding place. What could he do now? Clearly, it would be best to keep out of the way for the next few hours. Suddenly the answer came to him. He would go and fetch the mysterious artefacts he had found beneath the city of Tiarond, and take them to show the Summoners, as Tormon had suggested. Right now, the eldritch figures in their sinister skull masks seemed a far less alarming prospect than Tormon in his current mood.

No one took any notice of Scall, as he went to upstairs through the draughty stone corridors to fetch the strange, nameless items from his pack. The Reivers were all too busy settling into the stronghold and preparing for a siege to take any notice of one stray lad. Nevertheless, Scall bustled along with a calculated air of purpose that he had learned as an apprentice. If you looked as though you were on an errand, people left you alone. If you skulked, or wandered, or wool-gathered, they inevitably found you a host of tasks, usually unpleasant, inevitably inconvenient, and all to be accomplished before supper.

Scall shared his quarters with Presvel, and a number of Arcan's young, unwed warriors, while Tormon and Annas had been allotted their own tiny closet of a room elsewhere. When he reached the sleeping chamber, he opened the door just a crack, and peeped cautiously round the edge. He didn't want to risk meeting Presvel, who seemed to be behaving more and more strangely, skulking and muttering, and who had made it quite clear that Scall had better stay out of his way.

Luckily, the room was empty and, with a sigh of relief, he slipped inside. His peculiar finds were stuffed into the bottom of his pack. Myrial only knew why he had dragged them so far. As far as Scall knew, they had no practical use whatsoever. But they reminded him of his adventure beneath the city which, now that it was safely over, he looked back on with pride. The objects were rare and fascinating, he had found them by himself, and he had so few possessions to call his own that he wasn't prepared to let any of them go.

To keep his finds safe, he had wrapped them in his ragged old shirt, which he had given up wearing when he'd replaced it with a warmer soldier's garment from the guardhouse on the outskirts of Tiarond. Squatting on the floor, he took the untidy bundle out of his pack, unwrapped it, and looked at the items again: what appeared to be a thin, round, silver mirror, and a small silver sphere about the size of a walnut. But, as he had accidentally discovered, there was a great deal more to them than there seemed to be at first sight.

Tormon was right. These things are beyond me. Let the Summoners decide what to do with them.

Unfortunately, there proved to be two small problems. It took him some time to screw up his courage to go looking for the Summoners. They gave him the creeps with those black robes, and the chilling death-masks that hid their faces. Then, when he finally did go, they were nowhere to be found. He hunted high and low, all over the stronghold – except for the clan-chief's chambers, and he wasn't about to go in *there* without Tormon's protection. However, the warrior on guard at Arcan's door was a young man who seemed disposed to be friendly. 'You'll be one of the wanderers from the city,' he said, looking Scall up and down with piercing blue eyes.

Scall nodded. 'That's right,' he said warily. 'I'm Scall.'

The young guard, his long braided hair red-gold, like so many of these Reivers, held out a broad, callused hand. 'I'm Riol.' He leaned close to Scall. 'Tell me, is it true what they're saying about monstrous brutes with wings? Did they really massacre all the Tiarondians?'

'Well, if they didn't kill them all, they certainly had a damn good try.' Scall strove to keep his voice steady and offhand.

The guileless blue eyes grew wider. 'And did you *see* them?'

Scall remembered the sinister winged shape dropping, with outspread wings, from the roof of Lady Seriema's mansion. He remembered the hideous fiend exploding through the window in a shower of glass, its red eyes burning with a murderous light in its gaunt, grey face, its lipless mouth gaping to display the bloodstained fangs, with shreds of nameless flesh caught between them. He remembered the foul stench of it, as it closed upon its prey with unnatural and terrifying speed. A shudder ran through him, and clammy sweat iced on his brow. 'Oh yes,' he whispered. 'I've seen them – and I pray that you never will.'

But Riol seemed unconcerned, and Scall realised that he had

barely been listening. His thoughts were elsewhere. 'Ach,' he said softly, 'can you not imagine it? All that booty – just lying there for the taking. A whole city full of loot . . .'

Scall felt anger explode within him. 'Are you insane?' he yelled. 'You have absolutely no idea what you're dealing with. Those creatures massacred the entire city!'

Riol shrugged. 'Ach, city folk. They're all soft. Put those creatures up against proper warriors, now, and we'd soon see them off. And then Tiarond would be ours, our stronghold, with all its wealth and its mines. Arcan's clan could rule all Callisiora . . .'

Scall stared at him in horror. Was that what these Reivers were saying amongst themselves? Was that what they were all thinking? Well, if the idiots were hatching some crazy plan to march on Tiarond, it was none of his concern.

But one thing's for sure. There's no way I'll be going with them.

Still, Riol seemed a cordial young man, and Scall had enjoyed talking to someone nearer his own age – even if he did keep his brains in his backside. It would be nice to have a friend among these warriors. He decided not to argue the point any further – yet. Maybe if Riol got to know him better, he would be more amenable to listening to sense. In the meantime, he remembered, he was on an errand of his own. 'Riol?'

'Eh?' Clearly the guard had been lost in a daydream – probably already looting Tiarond, Scall thought disgustedly. The notion of this fresh-faced, friendly young man marching cheerfully off to certain death filled him with profound sadness.

But if that's really what the clan chief is planning, surely Tormon will be able to talk him out of it? Supposing Arcan confides in Tormon, that is.

'Riol?' he tried again. 'Could you tell me where I can find the Summoners?'

'*What?*' That got the Reiver's attention. 'What in the name of perdition do you want with *them?*'

'I just need to talk to them about something. Are they in there with Arcan?'

'Arcan isn't here. He's downstairs seeing off Cetain and his warriors. They're leaving now to warn the other clans.' He spat on the ground. 'I wouldn't warn the bastards. Let them shift for themselves, I say!'

Dear Myrial! If this is the attitude of the average Reiver, we'll never get though this crisis in one piece!

'Er . . . The Summoners?' he reminded his companion.

Riol shook his head. 'I don't know what you want with those accursed spooks,' he said. 'They're not natural, with their death's-head faces and all their weird powers. I'm not looking forward to sharing the citadel with them, that's for sure. If it were up to me, I'd take my sword and I'd . . .'

'You mean they don't live here normally?'

'Nah,' Riol replied scornfully. 'We don't want them living among decent folk. They have a tower of their own, down by the lake.'

'Would they be there now, do you think?'

'I expect so.' The guard shrugged. 'They'll be packing their stuff to come up here, just like everybody else. But you don't want to go there, Scall. It's a bad place, by all accounts. It's said that they eat . . .'

'Yes, yes,' Scall said hastily. 'Well, it's been nice talking to you, Riol. Maybe I'll see you later.' With that, he fled.

When he left the fortress, he found that the clouds which had darkened the horizon in the early morning had spread right across the sky, shrouding the landscape in gloom. The rain was being driven across the moors by a cold, raw wind, and the Reivers were rushing to complete their tasks, pulling up the hoods of their cloaks against the weather, and cursing as they splashed across the muddy ground. Scall hesitated in the entrance to the stronghold, standing to one side to keep out of the way of Arcan's folk as they went dashing in and out. It would have been easy to use the foul weather as an excuse to put off his visit to the Summoners, but he knew that if he didn't go now, he might never pluck up the courage again.

Though he didn't set much store by Riol's superstitious mutterings, Scall found his heart beating faster as he approached the solitary tower on the edge of the sombre tarn. Who would want to live in such a godforsaken spot, unless they had evil deeds to hide? The place was very isolated. Anyone calling for help here would never stand a chance of being heard. To speak to the Summoners in the fortress, where there were folk around to help if things got too alarming, was one thing, but to approach them here, alone, on their own sinister territory, was almost too much for Scall's faltering courage. All at once, he began to wonder if showing his strange new possessions to them had been a good idea after all. As he neared the tower he found his footsteps getting slower and slower until he stopped altogether, within the shadow of its walls. He could go no further.

He lingered before the door, rain dripping from the hood of his cloak, clutching the untidy bundle that protected and concealed his finds, and trying to pluck up sufficient courage to lift his fist and knock. He might have stayed there all day, had it not been for a sudden commotion from within. There was a long, low moaning sound, followed by a female voice, shrieking curses. 'Get out, you damned infernal monster! Out, out, you damnable brute!'

Scall's blood turned to ice in his veins. Had the Summoners called up some hideous demon? What was it doing to the woman inside the tower? He knew he should go to her aid, but he was frozen to the spot in horror. Suddenly the door slammed open, and a huge, inhuman, white countenance, horned and hairy, came looming out of the shadows. Scall let out a shriek. Cloven hooves clattered across the doorstep, then the monster barged past him, snorting hot breath in his face, and knocking him to the ground, where he floundered, winded, in the slippery mud.

'Blasted cow!' yelled the female voice from the tower. 'Good riddance! The next time I find you in my storerooms, it'll be beef-steaks for supper!'

A cow. Oh, dear Myrial, what an idiot I am. Terrified out of my wits by an ordinary cow.

Scall, cringing in embarrassment, was about to scramble to his feet, when the owner of the voice appeared in the doorway, brandishing a broom. Slowly, she lowered the weapon and stared at him in astonishment. She was a pretty young woman, whose bodice seemed to be cut a great deal lower than was customary in Tiarond. Scall felt his face turn crimson. Suddenly, to his utter mortification, he couldn't seem to put his eyes anywhere else. Apparently unaware of his discomfiture – maybe she was used to having this effect on men, Scall thought – she reached down and helped him up. Hands on her hips, she regarded him quizzically as he juggled with his unravelling bundle, trying to hold on to it and dust the mud off his pants at the same time. 'And who the blazes may *you* be?' she demanded.

'I'm – I'm Scall.' With an effort, he kept his eyes glued to her face. Were it not for the distractions lower down, it would have been well worth looking at. He tried to pitch his voice down to a more manly tone. 'We – me and my companions, that is – are guests of clanchieftain Arcan. We came from Tiarond yesterday. I want to talk to the Summoners.'

Her eyebrows rose. 'You *want* to talk to them? Now that's a first! Come on up, then. Follow me.' She turned and walked into the tower, hips swaying, and as she mounted the steps in front of him, Scall discovered that the view from the rear was nearly as good as the visions of delight at the front.

Though it was of smaller size, and a different shape, the tower was constructed on a similar plan to Arcan's fortress. On the ground floor were animal quarters and on the next the storerooms, with a staircase leading up in a tight spiral to the living quarters on the floors above. As the woman led him up the tower steps, she kept up a continuous flow of talk. 'That dratted cow! I'm sorry she knocked you down. The problem is, the Summoners dote on her. Between them they've got her so spoilt with titbits and treats that she won't go out on the moor with the others, but hangs around the tower all day, making a nuisance of herself. When she was a calf, Dark thought it would be amusing to teach her to climb the stairs, and it's a nightmare to get her down again. She's played havoc in my storerooms this morning, today of all days, when I don't have time to turn round.

She's a cow, I keep telling them, not a pet, but they . . .' She paused in mid-sentence to yell up the stairs. 'Summoner Grim! Summoner Dark! You have a visitor.'

Scall wondered why she had called out like that, instead of announcing him when they arrived. It seemed very rude. Then all at once he realised that she had been warning the Summoners, so that they would have time to put on their sinister masks – and in that moment, the eldritch figures, who had scared him so badly the previous day, turned into human beings.

Why, of course they can't wear those masks all the time. It would be dreadfully uncomfortable. It's funny – I never thought of them having a home life, and doting on a pet cow, of all things.

At the top of the stairs was a sturdy door. The woman gave a perfunctory knock, and went straight in. Scall followed her into the room – and stopped short, blinking in astonishment. The chamber was warm, cheerful and cosy; a startling contrast to the stark exterior of the tower. He stared at the thick, colourful wall hangings, the sheepskins that padded the two deep chairs by the roaring fire, the well-polished glow of the wooden shelves and storage chest, and the homely clutter of books and teacups on the table.

Well, who would have thought it?

A black-cloaked figure was kneeling by the lowest shelves in a corner, sorting books and packing them into a wooden box. He straightened, turned, and looked at his visitor, who could see the glitter of his eyes behind that smooth, anonymous mask of palest bone.

Dark looked from Izobia to the newcomer, and wondered why he had come. Visitors to the tower were few and far between.

Surely this is the youth who arrived yesterday with trader Tormon. What in the world is he doing here?

To his astonishment, the lad didn't look particularly scared. Accustomed as he was to constant fear and distrust from the folk around him – a sense of awe deliberately fostered by the Summoners for their own protection – he found such courage refreshing, if a little disconcerting. He smiled behind his mask. 'You're Scall, aren't you?'

'He said he wanted to speak to you about something.' Clearly, Izobia had realised that no one was paying her any attention.

Dark sighed. 'Thank you, Izobia. Don't let me detain you. I'm sure you have a great deal to do today.'

'As a matter of fact I do. Cleaning up the mess your accursed cow has made in my storeroom – again. Just when we're so busy, and all. You think more of that animal than you do of me. I don't know why you don't just give her my room and turn me out on the moor with the cattle.' With that, she turned on her heel and left.

'Izobia sulks better than anyone I've met,' Dark said. 'I won't hear the last of this for weeks. Come and sit by the fire, Scall, and tell me what I can do for you.' As they went to the fire, the Summoner reflected that he was doing little to encourage a sense of dread in his visitor. He was glad that his mentor was upstairs packing. Grim was always reprimanding him for being too approachable but, while he understood the need to foster a sense of awe in ordinary folk, it just wasn't in his nature to scare them in that way.

When they were settled, he listened with growing amazement as the lad began to tell of the marvels that lay beneath the city of Tiarond.

How I would love to see that extraordinary cavern for myself! It's incredible that such a place has been there for centuries, secret and undiscovered, its existence unknown even to the Summoners. What wonders must be within!

Dark leaned forward as Scall unwrapped his muddy bundle to reveal two strange items: a small silver sphere about the size of a walnut, and a flat, circular object about a foot across, which appeared to be a silver mirror with a narrow band of gold around the edge. Glancing at the lad for permission, he picked it up carefully and, as he took it in his hand, its surface darkened to black. Strange lines of bright green light appeared, forming patterns that materialised at the bottom and moved slowly up the face of the object, to vanish at the top. Dark looked closely at the lines of moving symbols, which were grouped in clusters of varying length.

This is writing – it must be! Just wait till Grim sees this!

'Er . . . Sir?' Only when Scall interrupted did the Summoner realise how long he had been gazing at the indecipherable writing. He looked up, blinking, to see that the lad was holding out the other item, the one that looked like a silver nutshell, still nested in its wrappings, as though he didn't want it to touch his skin. 'I think you should look at this, too,' he said. 'It's even more amazing than the other. It starts working when you pick it up, just like the mirror-thing does.'

Dark picked up the artefact, cupping it in his palm, as Scall advised. The hiss of his indrawn breath was loud in the quiet room as an image began to revolve in the air above his outstretched hand: a sphere, as solid-looking as a child's ball, coloured in patchwork shapes of green, blue, brown and gold, and covered in a curious network of shining, blue-white lines. He reached out cautiously with his other hand to touch the orb – and his fingers passed straight through. Solid though it seemed, in reality it was as insubstantial as the air he breathed.

The Summoner's hand was shaking so hard with excitement, that the little silver object, the source of this miraculous manifestation, threatened to spill from his palm. He snatched at it in alarm, and when he opened his fingers again, the image had changed. A new vision had appeared, hovering in the air where the sphere had hung before. This time he seemed to be looking down on a vista of wild moorland, in the midst of which he could see, quite clearly, the mere in which he had so very nearly ended his life, and the tower in which he now sat. On the hill above was the blocky shape of Arcan's fortress, and in the valley bottom he could see the hummocky shapes of the Reivers' turf-roofed dwellings, with people, tiny as ants, passing to and fro.

Shock ran through Dark as though, once again, he had plunged into the icy mere. As if to hide the image, he closed his fist around the artefact. Once more, the image vanished, but the insatiable curiosity of a Summoner won out. He opened his hand again, and a vision sprang into the air of the river-girt city of Tiarond on its mountain eyrie, and the great waterfall streaming over the plateau's edge. In this way he viewed a series of landscapes: a vista of silvery lakes and rivers; white, snow-clad mountains, vast beyond all his imaginings; a cluster of islands in a lapis-blue ocean; a dense green forest which stretched away to the horizon; a settlement of strangely wrought buildings on the edge of a lake.

Dark, his heart beating fast with excitement, wondered where these places could be. The visions of Tiarond and the moorland home of the Reivers had been accurate and – judging from the people running back and forth from Arcan's citadel, and the flooded, muddy plateau of Tiarond – they were scenes of events and conditions in the present time. There was no reason, therefore, to believe that the other places that Scall's strange device had shown him were any less real. But he had done some travelling with Grim who, in his time, had walked every inch of the realm, documenting his discoveries with journals and clever little sketches. Consequently, Dark knew perfectly well that most of the places depicted by the strange artefact were not in Callisiora at all. Which only left one possibility . . .

There must be other realms, beyond the Curtain Walls! I always suspected as much! What's more, I have a feeling Grim already knows that, from the way he always takes such pains to avoid the subject of the Walls. He's full of secrets, that's for sure, and it's high time he started to share them with me. Why, if only we could find some sort of artefact that would permit us to pass through the barrier, the possibilities would be staggering . . .

Once more, he turned his attention to the little silver sphere in his hand. Who had crafted such an incredible device? How had it come to lie beneath the city of Tiarond, and what else might Scall's cavern contain? If this artefact really showed the present, then, if they could learn how to control it, it could be used to watch over Cetain's journey, in case there should be treachery from the other tribes. It could also warn the Reivers if the winged predators, or any other dangers, approached.

Dark looked up at his visitor. 'Scall, do you think there was any more stuff like this in the cavern that you found?'

'There might have been,' the lad said carefully. 'I didn't see anything else lying around that was small enough to take away, but the place was so big that I only explored a bit of it. Sir . . .' He bit his lip. 'You aren't thinking of going there, are you?'

Dark felt sorry for him. Clearly, Scall was afraid that he might be asked to go back there to the cavern as a guide. 'It's all right,' he said gently. 'We may go back to explore, but I'm sure we can find the place, if you can describe to us exactly how you got in. I don't blame you for not wanting to return, Scall. You've done your share for the present, and you deserve to rest in safety – for as long as any of us can. We already owe you a debt of gratitude for bringing your precious finds to us.' He leapt to his feet, his voice ringing with excitement. 'Grim must hear of this at once. If we can work out a way to use these items properly, you've put a weapon of tremendous power into our hands.'

Leaving his visitor by the fire, Dark sped up the tower steps to his mentor's workroom on the topmost floor.

Six

The Girl Who Wasn't There

Gilarra only realised how much time had passed when Healer Kaita finally straightened up from Cerella's bedside. 'Well, we've stopped the bleeding at least. It's up to her, now,' she said, and wiped her brow with a bloodstained hand, leaving a russet smudge behind.

Galveron had been hovering anxiously on the edge of the little knot of activity around the sick woman's bed and assisting where he could, by fetching and carrying for the Healer. Now he stepped forward with a smile. 'Well done, Kaita. No one else could have pulled her through. She owes you her life.'

'She will if she survives,' Gilarra said sharply. 'And what of the child? After all, the babe is the important one. It is she who will become the next Hierarch.'

They turned to look at her, accusation in both faces. Galveron's smile had vanished, and Kaita's eyes were hard. Gilarra felt a stab of annoyance. 'It's no use looking at me like that! Why can't you people realise that as Hierarch, I have to take thought for these matters?'

Kaita took a deep breath. 'Let's go and see how the little one is getting along,' she said.

As they crossed the room, Galveron took Gilarra's arm, drawing her aside. 'Your rule of this place would be far more effective, Lady, if you would learn to give praise when it's due.' The words were little short of an open rebuke. 'We all owe a very great debt to Healer Kaita. She has laboured tirelessly on our behalf ever since we took

70

refuge here. Even though her greatest friend and companion was the first victim of the winged fiends, and she is still grieving deeply, she has put her own considerations aside to help the people of Tiarond. But for her, our death toll would have been far greater. And what of her helpers? An occasional word of gratitude from you would be a great encouragement to them.'

First it was Galveron sticking up for that grubby little thief, and now he's supporting the Healer! Am I the only one around here that he doesn't defend?

Gilarra felt the flush of anger burning her face. 'Those folk must do their duty, as I do mine,' she snapped. 'I have no time to run after them, fawning and flattering.'

'Lady, listen . . .' Galveron began, but was interrupted by the approach of Kaita. 'The child is gaining ground,' she said. 'Frana the midwife found a wet-nurse: the woman who gave birth shortly after we took refuge here.'

Gilarra raised her eyebrows. 'Ironic, is it not? The future Hierarch and the future Suffragan both suckling at the same breast. It's to be hoped that the mother does not come to realise that one day this new babe will take precedence over her own. Loath though I am to deceive her, I think it would be as well not to mention that her foster-child was born before her own.'

Kaita shook her head. 'You know, Lady, there are other things in life besides being Hierarch. You might do well to think of that now and again.' She turned away and went back to the bedside of the sick woman, but her words, annoying though they were, had reminded Gilarra of Galveron's errand. She clutched at his arm. 'Galveron! The ring! Did you find it?'

He nodded. 'Let's go somewhere more private,' he said softly.

Gilarra was bone-weary. She felt guilty, because she had so little time to spare for Bevron and Aukil, and she knew that they were missing her. She was apprehensive, too, because she knew that Galveron would be far from impressed with the way she had dealt with those scheming thieves. She hadn't slept all night, or eaten all day, for worrying about the absent Commander and the missing ring, and her Hierarch's robes, which she had continued to wear as a badge of her authority, were now wrinkled, stained, and spattered with Cerella's blood. She was uncomfortably aware that they didn't smell too good, either.

By Myrial, what I wouldn't give for a bath and a change of clothes! Nevertheless, her heart was singing.

The ring! The ring is safe! Now at last I can truly be Hierarch!

What did robes matter, when soon she would possess the highest symbol of authority in all Callisiora?

Galveron picked up a lamp and led the way out through the back of Kaita's sickroom, and up into the passageway that led into the mountain, connecting with the storage caverns above. When they reached the place where they had spoken the previous day, he set the lamp down on the shelf of rock. 'Aliana was right,' he said. 'The ring was exactly where she had hoped it would be. She was very brave . . .'

But Gilarra didn't want to hear about Aliana. 'Quick!' she said. 'Where is it? Give it to me!'

A shadow crossed Galveron's face. 'As you wish.' He spoke so coldly that Gilarra, preoccupied as she was, realised how ungracious she sounded. 'Oh, Galveron, I'm sorry. I am grateful to you, truly. It's just that I've been so anxious about the ring. It's important to all of us, not just to me.'

The Commander's expression softened a little. 'I understand – or at least, I'm trying to,' he told her. 'But please, Gilarra, don't let your own concerns blind you to the feelings and the needs of others.' He began to dig around in his pockets. 'Maybe when you have the ring, you'll be able to . . .' His voice tailed away, and his expression changed. Before Gilarra's eyes, he went, in an instant, from doubt to anxiety to a panic that was contagious. She watched, cold with fear, as feverishly he began to rummage through each pocket in turn, pulling out the contents and throwing them on to the ledge of rock. A few coins, a tinderbox, a small whetstone, a large iron key: there was nothing more. The look he turned on her was one of utter horror. 'I had it. I swear I did! It was right here in my pocket, wrapped in . . .' Suddenly his face cleared, and he clapped a hand to his forehead. 'Of course! How stupid of me. I gave the ring to Aliana, in the Precincts. I wanted her to bring it back here to you, while I hunted for the child we'd heard, but she wouldn't . . .'

'Why am I not surprised?' Gilarra muttered sourly, but he didn't hear her.

'What with one thing and another, I clean forgot to get it back,' he was saying. 'I'm sorry, Gilarra. I must have given you a dreadful shock, just then.'

'You don't know the half of it,' she murmured. 'Come on,' she said, even more anxious than before to have the ring safely in her hands. 'Quickly! Let's go and find that wretched girl, before—'

'Before what?' Galveron was looking at her oddly, making her feel increasingly uncomfortable.

Oh damn! He'll have to learn the truth sooner or later. Who's the ruler here, anyway?

The Hierarch took a deep breath. 'Before she finds out that I imprisoned her brother.'

Galveron looked dumbfounded, then angry – whether at Alestan, or at herself, Gilarra was uncertain. 'You imprisoned him? In the name of Myrial, why?'

'He was caught with stolen food on him.' Squirming under that frank, blue gaze, she prayed that he would not detect the lie behind her words. 'He denied it, of course,' she went on quickly, 'but the evidence was right there.'

'And what of the others?' The Commander's voice was ominously quiet.

'I separated them and set them to work.' Gilarra was aware that she was gabbling now, and made herself take a deep breath. 'It seemed to be the best way to try to keep them out of trouble.'

'Poor Aliana.' Galveron was already moving. 'She deserves to hear this from your lips, not have it passed on to her by some Temple gossip. Maybe it really *was* a mistake,' he added hopefully. 'I'll look into it immediately, Lady – just as soon as we've restored your ring to you.'

When they returned to the sickroom, there was no sign of the thief, so Galveron asked the Healer if she had seen her. 'She was here at first,' Kaita said, 'but I don't recall seeing her for a long while. I expect she went to find some breakfast, Galveron, and I'm sure I needn't point out that you could do with some yourself.'

'As soon as we find Aliana, I'll eat, I promise,' he said.

Gilarra, sick with worry now, glared at Galveron. Damn him, how could he stand there exchanging pleasantries with the healer as if it were just a normal day? She led the way across the crowded Temple floor, almost stepping on the people in their little encampments in her hurry to find the thief. A quick glance in the direction of the doors told her that the girl was not with her friends in their exposed little enclave. Vexed and anxious, she turned back to Galveron, who was following more slowly. 'Where in perdition can she be?'

'She'll already be down in the caverns, I expect, trying to speak to her brother,' he said, with the slightest note of irritation in his voice. 'Why are you worrying yourself unnecessarily? You know she can't be far away. She's not exactly going to leave the Temple, is she?'

He led her through the doorway at the back of the Basilica, past the rubble-choked stairway that even now was constantly guarded, and Gilarra ground her teeth with impatience as he paused to have a quick word with the two young Godsword soldiers on duty.

Come on, Galveron, for goodness sake! Just let me get my ring, and then I don't care if you want to stand around and gossip with everyone in the Temple.

Unable to wait for him any longer, she set off down the other stairs, which gave access to the network of caverns beneath the building. Down here there was an air of purposeful bustle. Folk were working at cooking and laundering, mending what little gear the community possessed, and adapting the materials in the Temple to other uses. Despite her anxiety, she noticed that the atmosphere was perceptively lighter and more cheerful that that of the Temple itself, and Gilarra reflected that these people were far better off for being occupied with useful tasks that would benefit the whole community, instead of sitting round brooding on everything they had lost.

'You know,' she said to Galveron, as he caught her up, 'since we seem to be stuck here for the time being, we should try to think of useful tasks to occupy our people.'

He nodded. 'You're right. Maybe I could get some of my men to set up a weapons school, then anyone who wishes can be trained to fight.'

You can train them as much as you want, but they still won't be able to rid us of the winged fiends.

This was Gilarra's constant worry. No matter how hard she tried, she couldn't see any way forward. Eventually the food would run out, then her people would have the choice of leaving the Temple and being hunted down one by one in the streets of Tiarond, or staying here to starve, like rats in a trap.

For now, however, she had other pressing concerns, as she and Galveron began their systematic search of the caverns and vaults beneath the Temple. Aliana was not in the bathing caves, where both people and laundry were washed in the stream that ran through in a series of little falls and pools. Nor was she in the vast cavern which contained the lake that was the reservoir of drinking water for the city, and now for the refugees. From there they took the side tunnel that went to the Temple vaults, which boasted fire-places for the comfort of the artisans and archivists who normally laboured there. These rooms had now been taken over by Telimon and his team of cooks, and their precious contents – the old books and scrolls; the priceless documents dating back hundreds of years; the tools of the artisan; the gilding, the jewels, the paint, the precious carved woods and cunningly wrought silver and gold, the velvets, satins and silks – had been carefully moved elsewhere. Teams of tailors and seamstresses were hard at work in chambers of their own, turning the precious old tapestries into blankets, and the rich materials of curtains, altar cloths, and embroidered priestly vest-ments into clothing for the refugees.

In Telimon's domain, the workbenches of the artisans had been scrubbed, and were now being used for the preparation of food on a tremendous scale, but there was no sign of Aliana anywhere. When asked, the head cook said he'd seen her some time ago. 'Yes, she had some porridge, and she managed to wheedle some bacon out of me, too.' He frowned. 'I was busy at the time, and I didn't notice what else had been taken, or I would have reported it to you sooner.'

'Taken?' Galveron said sharply. 'What do you mean?'

Warned by the edge in the Commander's voice, Telimon hesitated. Since the death of his twin he had aged perceptibly, Gilarra thought. The plumpness was melting away from his frame, and his clipped blond curls had lost their lustre. His skin was grey, his shoulders sagged, and the merry twinkle had gone from his eyes. 'I was just checking my supplies when you came in,' he said. 'I know for certain the wretched girl took cheese, a couple of the griddlecakes we've been baking to make do as bread, some pasties, and a small bag of nuts. I'm not sure yet, whether anything else is missing. Galveron,' he added testily, 'we simply cannot permit such pilferage. It endangers the lives of us all.'

'I'll send you down a couple of guards,' the Commander said absently. It was clear to Gilarra that the news had hit him hard. His face had turned absolutely white, with the jagged, half-healed scars standing out livid against his skin. He was now in a cleft stick of his own making. The Hierarch knew that he had grown fond of Aliana, yet he himself had made the rule that anyone caught stealing in the Temple would be ejected without appeal.

Gilarra, however, was too busy with her own concerns to worry about Galveron's distress. If Aliana had taken food, then she intended not to be found – at least not for some considerable length of time. As she considered the alarming implications of the thief's disappearance, with the precious ring, she felt rage sweep over her.

Curse her! This is some kind of attack on me, I know it. She's taking her revenge because I arrested her brother. No matter what Galveron said, I should never have trusted that filthy, light-fingered, backstabbing little bitch from the Warrens! When I get my hands on her, Galveron won't need to throw her out. I'll throttle her myself! But why did she do it? What is her plan?

And more to the point, where in Myrial's name can she be?

By this time, Galveron seemed to have pulled himself together. 'Come on,' he said grimly. 'Let's go and talk to Alestan. He might have some idea of where she could be hiding out.'

Alestan was sitting in one of the vaults, that had been hastily converted into a cell. He was trying to push his fingers under the tightly wrapped splints and scratch his fiercely itching skin when some instinct for danger, developed over years of dodging and hiding, made him look up. He could hear voices on the other side of the door, and though his anger flared as he heard Gilarra, his heart leapt at the sound of Galveron's voice. News of Aliana at last! He had been frantic with anxiety because she had been gone so long. The door opened, and the two of them entered. Alestan took one look at their faces – the thunderous expression of Gilarra and the Commander's frowning concern – and knew there was even more trouble in store, as if he wasn't in enough already. He leapt to his feet. 'Aliana? Is she all right?' he asked.

'Don't worry,' Galveron told him. 'She got back safely.'

Alestan knew at once that he was hedging. 'Then where is she?' he demanded. 'What have you done with her, you bastard? Tell me or I'll—'

'You're in no position to be making threats and demands,' Gilarra said. 'You and your little gang of Warrens scum are in more than enough trouble. If you want to continue to shelter in this Temple with the *civilised* people, I suggest you cooperate with us and tell us where your sister might be hiding.'

'Aliana? Hiding?' For a moment he thought he hadn't heard her right. 'Why in the name of perdition would she be hiding?'

'Because she's a thieving little bitch,' snapped the Hierarch.

Alestan's heart sank. Poor refuge though this was proving to be, how had Aliana managed to make the most powerful person in it so angry? He looked uneasily from Gilarra to Galveron, and fought to keep his alarm from showing on his face. 'Why? What's she supposed to have done?'

The Hierarch's eyes narrowed, and she went to the door and looked out quickly, to make sure that no one else was listening. 'You know the item she and Galveron went to fetch?' she said quietly. 'Well, she seems to have stolen it, and disappeared. You know our laws concerning stealing.'

'She's stolen the *ring?*' Alestan said.

'Shut up, you idiot!' Gilarra hissed. 'Do you want everybody in the place to hear?'

Alestan ignored her, and turned to the Godsword Commander. 'I don't believe this! Look here, Galveron, there must be some mistake. You must have missed her, down in the cavern. She was probably bathing, or something.'

Galveron shook his head. 'No,' he said dully. 'We looked everywhere. There was no sign of her. And there's something else you should know, Alestan. Telimon says that she stole food from the kitchens, so wherever she's hiding, she plans to be staying there for a while. I'm sorry.'

Alestan felt himself turn cold all over. 'Did Telimon actually *see* her stealing this stuff?'

'No, but . . .'

'Well, there you are then. You have no proof whatsoever. Why, it could have been anyone who took the food. There are people in and out of those kitchens every minute of the day. I know that from bitter experience. It was easy enough for someone to falsely incriminate *me*, and get me out of the way.'

'No one else but your accursed sister stole my ring,' Gilarra spat. 'And I don't believe for a single moment that you aren't in on her plan, whatever it may be. Well, you've just signed your own death warrants. You, her, and the rest of your pack of vermin are finished here.'

Alestan was stunned and appalled by this sudden turn of events, but he kept his head. His sister and all the Grey Ghosts were depending on him now. He wasn't going down without a fight. 'I don't think so.' He faced up to Gilarra. 'Even before you arrested me, I suspected that we'd have trouble from you sooner or later. That's why I left instructions with the others. If you threaten our lives, we tell everyone your little secret. There's no way you could kill us all fast enough to stop one of us shouting out to the entire Temple that you've lost the Hierarch's ring.' He glared at her. 'Care to give it a try, Lady? If you're sick of being in charge here, we can soon arrange it so you aren't.'

As Gilarra's face turned red with anger, Galveron stepped in. 'I suggest we all take a deep breath, and start again on better terms,' he said. 'First of all, we could all be panicking needlessly. This could still all be a mistake. After the last few days, Aliana must have been exhausted. What if she's just fallen asleep in a corner, somewhere out of sight?'

Alestan gave him a grateful look. 'You're right. I hadn't even considered that possibility. And we know that no one has gone in or out of the doors, so she must still be in the Temple somewhere. If you let me out of here' – he gave Gilarra a dirty look – 'I'll help you look for her, and so will the others. When it comes to finding things, the Grey Ghosts are second to none. Then the Hierarch will get her ring back, and we'll hear no more about this little misunderstanding.' He looked coldly at Gilarra. 'Will we?'

Galveron looked at him narrowly. 'You said that you were falsely accused. Do you swear you never took that bread?'

Alestan returned his look with one just as direct. 'I swear it on my sister's life,' he said quietly.

'Then that's good enough for me. We can look into the circumstances of *your* arrest when we have more time but for now, let's get the search under way for Aliana, and—'

'Commander Galveron! I never gave you permission to release this criminal!'

Both men looked round at Gilarra's interruption, and Alestan was glad to see the look of anger that flashed across the Godsword

Commander's face. He didn't like Galveron any better than he had ever done, but at least he looked like being a useful ally in this unholy mess, and for Aliana's sake, her twin was willing to set aside his enmity – at least for now.

When Galveron spoke, there was no trace of his anger in his voice. 'Lady,' he said quietly, 'as Godsword Commander, criminal matters such as these are my concern, and you must let me deal with them as I see fit. You do *want* your ring back?'

'Of course I do,' Gilarra said icily. 'But I object to being held to ransom by a bunch of common criminals. Don't you see that this is all a trick? They must have planned it beforehand.' She turned to Alestan. 'Was that your plan? She hides, and you use her absence to blackmail me – then suddenly you find her, and earn gratitude and rewards. Is that the way it was meant to work?'

Alestan bit down on his anger. 'I love my sister,' he said. 'She risked her life for you yesterday, and I couldn't stop her, but there's no way I would let her put herself – and the rest of us – at risk like this. It would be a stupid idea, and too chancy by half. If she really *has* stolen your accursed ring, I expect she heard that I had been arrested, and she simply wants to put pressure on you to release me. Now, I'm very worried about Aliana, so I'm going to get busy searching for her. I suggest you do the same, instead of wasting everyone's time with these wild accusations.'

Galveron intervened before Gilarra could speak. 'I think that's a very good idea, Alestan. If you and your companions will search the Temple and the caverns again, I'll go up the other way, into the storage caves. We haven't looked there yet. Lady Gilarra, I suggest you rejoin your family for the present, and get some rest. Try to act as if everything is normal – or as normal as it can be, under the present circumstances. If people see the Hierarch turning the Temple upside down, they're bound to suspect that something is wrong. Alestan, will you gather your friends together and start to search? If you find her, or when you've looked everywhere you can think of, meet me in the corridor behind Healer Kaita's sickroom. It's best we keep this business as private as possible.' He lifted his hand in salute to the thief. 'Good luck to you.' Taking a mutinous-looking Gilarra by the arm, he led her away.

Alestan gathered the other Ghosts together where Galveron had told him they should meet. When he explained to them what had happened, they simply stood for a moment, trying to come to terms with their companion's disappearance. 'I just don't believe she would go off like this,' Gelina said at last. 'Unless you're right, Alestan, and she wanted to get the Hierarch to release you. But if that's the case, what does she plan to do next? Why would she just disappear without a word and leave us in this mess? There's no sense in it.'

'What if she was attacked, though?' Alestan's mind was racing now. 'We Warrensfolk aren't exactly popular around here. I've heard the whispering behind our backs. Why should a bunch of thieving scum be allowed to eat up good rations, they're saying. Galveron promised no one would know where we came from, but word has leaked out somehow.'

Tag shook his head. 'Aliana can look after herself in a fight.'

'But what if there was a bunch of them?' said little Erla. 'What if they jumped on her out of the shadows?'

'Well, we won't find out by standing here,' said Alestan. 'And another thing – where has that wretch Packrat gone? When he's missing there's always trouble brewing somewhere. Look for them both, but it's most important that we find Aliana – and that accursed ring.'

It was some time later when Galveron came wearily back to the meeting-place. He had just escaped from a very unpleasant inter-view with the Hierarch, who still had strong objections to his release of Alestan, and had not been happy when he'd been forced to confess that he'd found no sign of Aliana. He only hoped and prayed that Alestan and the rest of the girl's adopted family had done better. He had seen Gelina and the two youngsters across from the far side of the Temple, and knew they would be with him in a few moments.

He had also seen that Aliana was not with them. Feeling tired and discouraged, he slumped down on the bench-like shelf of rock to wait for them.

I only hope that Alestan has done better.

Galveron felt sick with disappointment over the way Aliana had acted. He had trusted her. Had his judgement really been so flawed? He still couldn't believe that she would betray him, and her other companions, so thoughtlessly. So far as he knew, it just wasn't like her at all. He thought of her courage in bringing the blasting powder across from the Citadel, and her further bravery the previous day, when she had helped him climb up onto the canyon rim. He could never have managed it without her. She was direct and forthright – *surely* he would have known if she had been deceiving him? So what had gone wrong? Was it only the arrest of her brother that had prompted this insanity, or had something else happened in the short space of time between their return to the Temple, and the discovery that she had vanished into thin air?

Most perplexing of all, however, was the realisation that he missed her.

Aliana, please come back. It's not too late. Whatever you've done, we'll make it right somehow.

At that moment, and not before time, Alestan returned, red-eyed and looking ten years older than he had seemed before. 'I can't find her,' he said hoarsely. 'I'm beginning to wonder whether my earlier suspicions weren't right, about her being attacked somewhere down in the caverns by dutiful Warrens-hating citizens. There are plenty of crevices down there where they could hide a body.'

Galveron's blood ran cold at the thought. 'Why didn't you tell me things were that bad?' he demanded.

'I didn't think they were,' Alestan admitted. 'There has been some bad feeling against us, but not more than we could handle – or so I thought. But apart from this business of my arrest, I simply couldn't think of any other explanation for my sister's disappearance. She—'

'She can't be anywhere in the Temple,' said a voice behind him.

'We've looked everywhere.' Gelina had returned, with the young-sters in tow. She hesitated, and looked from Alestan to Galveron. 'Packrat is still missing, too. Could they be together?'

'Packrat?' snapped Galveron. 'Since when has *he* been missing?'

Alestan sighed. 'Since before we spoke to you first,' he admitted heavily. He knew that Gelina had been right – things had come to such a pass that they had no option but to be completely honest with the Godsword – but Galveron finding out about Packrat now, when they had failed to mention his absence earlier, certainly made things more difficult.

'Why didn't you mention this sooner? You'd better tell me what's going on here, Alestan, or—'

'Sir, sir, sir!' The voice came from Tag, who had been gently tugging at his sleeve for some time, and was now swinging on his arm like a monkey. Galveron prised loose the clutching hands, and Alestan admired his control as he swallowed his anger to speak patiently to the child. 'What is it, Tag? Do you have something to tell us?'

'Yes,' Tag piped up. 'There's one place we haven't looked.'

'Where?' Both Alestan and Galveron spoke at once, and the child took a hasty step back. 'That place I wanted to explore before, but the guards wouldn't let me go in.'

Galveron grabbed him by the shoulder. 'Show me where you mean.'

Tag led them out to the sickroom doorway, and pointed across the Temple floor at the silver filigree screen that hid the way into Myrial's most hallowed sanctum. 'Down there,' he said.

SEVEN

Ray of Hope

In the clean, neat room in the Shadowleague infirmary, it was difficult to believe that a battle was taking place for the survival of the former Archimandrite. Syvilda had never left her lifemate's bedside, except on those odd occasions when the healers had chased her out so that they could work. It seemed to her that her presence in the room was vital; that he needed her strength and her will to help him hold fast to the world. Nevertheless, she could hardly bear to look at Cergorn. The Centaur lay so white and still, with no outward sign of his desperate battle to cling to life. He looked so frail and diminished that it was impossible to imagine that only yesterday he had been the leader of the Shadowleague: vigorous, powerful and strong. His broken foreleg – just as bad an injury for a Centaur as it would be for an ordinary horse – was braced and held immobile in a casing of some shiny material that Syvilda did not recognise. The appalling injuries inflicted by the dying Skreeva, which had caused the healers so much labour and anxiety, had been cleaned, stitched, swathed in bandages, and now were hidden beneath a clean white sheet. Strange devices, a testament to the skills and knowledge of a long-gone civilisation, sprouted from his body like the tendrils of some parasitic plant.

Three great crystals, each larger than a human head, were suspended above the bed. They hummed and glowed, each one a different colour. One gave a swirling green light that bathed Cergorn's body in a deep glow that lapped slowly around him, rippling and shimmering, making him look as though he had been immersed in viscous liquid. Another gave off a scintillating golden effulgence that rained down onto the bed like glittering sparks. When Syvilda put her hand under it, she could feel her skin tingle, and a vibrant energy coursed through her veins. The third crystal, the largest, bathed the centaur in an intense beam of blue-violet light. According to Quave, one of the healers, the green glow would help prevent infection, the fall of sparkling gold would help give Cergorn the energy to fight the dreadful shocks his body had suffered, and the deep blue radiance would help speed healing.

'How do they work?' Syvilda had asked.

Quave shrugged. 'Who knows? We've never been able to find out. We only know they *do* work, and we thank providence that we're lucky enough to have them.'

Syvilda did thank providence – not only for the alien devices, but for the healers who, without a doubt, had saved the life of her mate. Quave, the human: a grey-haired, tireless crusader against ignorance, disease and death. The petite, black-furred Myssil of the Dovruja, lithe and tirelessly active, with a ferocious intelligence burning behind her dark eyes. The eldritch Shimir of the Takuru, a race of shapeshifters from the Forest of Rakha, in the south.

Shimir was present now, keeping watch over the unconscious Cergorn. So as not to distract his preoccupied lifemate, she had taken the form of another Centaur, a mature female whose black hair, streaked with white, matched the attractive piebald markings on her equine body. Syvilda appreciated her tact and consideration – but it was as a physician that the Takur's odd skills really came to the fore. She could make her limbs incredibly sensitive to changes in temperature, moisture and elasticity of the skin. She could adapt them for intricate and delicate surgery, no matter how complex. She could alter her vision to view, in minute detail, the composition of cells and blood, or change it to see right into a body, viewing the shadowy shapes of organs and bones for evidence of damage or disease.

It was easy to forget about the Takuru, Syvilda mused. Though a handful did dwell in Gendival, they tended to keep to themselves and, because they were able to alter their forms to resemble just about anything, they were rarely seen – unless they wanted to be. This should make them perfect agents for the Shadowleague, but the other Loremasters tended to dislike the shadowy creatures with their odd, amorphous shapes which seemed to melt from one form into another. Though their reputation was largely undeserved, there was little trust for a being who could be in a room, unknown and unseen, looking like part of the furnishings, but spying on all that took place. Cergorn, who had foreseen their uses and appreciated their skills, had always insisted that they be represented in the Shadowleague, but the Takuru were pariahs, nevertheless. They dwelt on the outskirts of the community, far up in the bleak, stony valley of the Upper Lake. Their company was not welcomed by the other Loremasters, nor was their assistance sought – unless there was no alternative.

'Because of all the information available to us, it's easy for us to trick ourselves into feeling that we're better, wiser, more clever than the rest of the world. But in reality, the Shadowleague is just as riddled with prejudice and its own injustices.' The mental voice came from Shimir, who had come to check on Cergorn, and had plainly caught the drift of Syvilda's thoughts.

The Centaur looked at her unconscious lifemate, and shook her head sadly. 'The difference is that when we make mistakes, they have far greater repercussions.'

It was true that, because of his isolationist policies and his diffi-culties in handling the current crisis, Cergorn had left himself open to this coup by Amaurn and his supporters. Much as she loved him, Syvilda was honest enough to admit that to herself. But she wasn't going to admit it to Shimir, though she knew that the Takur – and indeed all her kind in Gendival – were utterly loyal to Cergorn.

'Nevertheless,' she told the physician, 'I am not about to sit idly by and see the Shadowleague taken over by a renegade outsider whose ideas were at least subversive and at most, downright dangerous. Repercussions or no, he must be removed, and quickly – even if . . .'

'Even if Cergorn's injuries mean that he can no longer be Archimandrite?' Shimir voiced the thought that Syvilda had been unable to face. 'The Takuru owe him our allegiance – after all, were it not for you and Cergorn, we would not be permitted here in Gendival at all – but the Shadowleague must have a leader, especially in these dark times.'

'If Cergorn is unable to lead, we must choose someone else,' said Syvilda firmly.

And why not me?

'Someone from among our own,' she continued aloud, 'who deplores the ideas of this unscrupulous upstart Amaurn. Even when he lived among us before, he never really belonged. While he remains in control, there will be no hope of returning the Shadowleague to its true goals and precepts.'

'And the longer he remains in control, the more powerful he becomes,' said the shapeshifter thoughtfully. She gave Syvilda a sly, veiled look. 'Already he is too strong to be deposed by legitimate means . . .'

For a long moment, the thought hung in the air between them.

Amaurn must die.

It would have been a shocking thought to yesterday's Syvilda, yet the one who sat there today, watching her love of so many years fight for his life, found that she could view the notion as calmly and dispassionately as she would consider squashing a fly.

Or spider, more like.

Carefully, the two conspirators considered the idea between them, examining it from every angle.

'Clearly, assassination is the only option,' Syvilda said. 'An overt challenge isn't possible at this time. Furthermore, the assassin must be able to get close to the new Archimandrite without arousing suspicion.'

Shimir nodded agreement. 'He or she must be swift, skilled, and deadly. If Amaurn is put on his guard by a bungled attempt, there will never be another chance.'

'It must be soon, before the renegade has a chance to put his insane plans into action. Once the knowledge of the Ancients is let loose in the world, things will be changed for ever, and there will be no going back.' Syvilda frowned, her fingers idly stroking the fine wool of Cergorn's blanket while her thoughts were focussed elsewhere. 'And there's one thing more. Our assassin must be utterly trustworthy. When Amaurn took over, I was stunned and appalled by the number of his supporters who'd been lying low in Gendival all those years, unsuspected and undiscovered. Whoever is chosen to rid us of Amaurn must, without a shadow of doubt, give all their loyalty to Cergorn, and to me.'

Again, came the oblique and furtive glance from Shimir. 'In that case, you only have one choice.'

'I agree,' Syvilda said softly. 'Which of your people are here in Gendival at the moment?'

Shimir hesitated. 'Syvilda, if we do this thing, you must give your word that you will protect us, afterwards. The position of the Takuru is precarious enough within the Shadowleague. If it should come to light that one of my people carried out an assassination here in Gendival – and killed an Archimandrite, no matter how dubiously he came by his position – there will be great pressure to have us cast out. Or worse.'

'I promise,' Syvilda said quickly. 'Furthermore, Shimir, I give you my word that, once Cergorn, or his true successor, returns to power, the Takuru will no longer be treated as outcasts, but will be given the best of everything that Gendival can provide.'

'Very well.' Head tilted on one side, the shapeshifter considered for a moment. 'I think that Vifang would best fit your needs.'

'Could you send a message, quickly, without anyone knowing?'

'Of course.' Shimir looked at the pale, unconscious figure of Cergorn. 'As you know, for many years now, Vifang has been the Archimandrite's most secret spy and assassin, and will be able to come to you without being seen. What you ask does not present a problem.'

Syvilda's eyes narrowed. 'I never knew anything about a secret assassin, and Cergorn always told me everything.'

The Takur chuckled. '*Everything*, Lady? I think not. In my experience, we all harbour a secret or two within ourselves. If you look carefully, I'm sure you can find your own.'

Syvilda recovered well. 'My secrets are none of your concern, Shimir – apart from the chiefest one, which at present, involves you and your people. Know this, however. As this assassin was loyal to my lifemate, I would now have him loyal to me.'

The shapeshifter smiled. 'You need not worry. I am certain that you can consider Vifang's loyalty to be yours. Now – what, exactly did you want our assassin to do?'

'Haunt Amaurn.' Even though she was using mindspeech, Syvilda spoke in a low hiss. 'He must be followed, and his every footstep shadowed. Then when he finally drops his guard and is alone, without his traitorous friends to protect him, he must die – and the more painfully, the better.'

'Lady, it shall be done.'

Though Amaurn had spent the whole of his exile with one goal in mind – to return to Gendival – it was unsettling to be back after all these years. So little had changed under Cergorn's rule that he might have been transported into his own past, and there were memories, both good and bad, but always deeply haunting, around every corner. The same ambivalence was evident in the welcome he had received from the Loremaster community. A good number viewed him with suspicion at best, and hatred at worst while, on the other hand, there were many who welcomed him back with delight. He was pleased and touched by the number of folk who had supported him in secret, though he was cynical enough to realise that some people would always espouse the winning cause. No doubt, had Cergorn been the victor, these same so-called supporters would have been baying for his blood by now.

For the time being, Amaurn had set up his headquarters in the spacious Meeting House, near the Tower of Tidings, for he felt that, with Cergorn barely clinging to life, this was not the time to be claiming the Archimandrite's traditional residence for himself. Besides, those quarters had been adapted for use by Centaurs, and would not be comfortable for a human without a number of changes. On reflection, since he planned to make so many changes in the Shadowleague, it might be appropriate to relocate the Archimandrite's home – when he had time to find a suitable dwelling, or have one built.

In the meantime, there was always the Meeting House, and while no one could call the vast chamber cosy, at least it was big enough to accommodate most shapes and sizes of Loremaster – not to mention the menacing bulk of Maskulu, who was a perfect deterrent to any would-be enemies, declared or covert, of the new Archimandrite. After his lengthy and far from cordial meeting with the Afanc which had concluded in a reluctant truce, at best, Amaurn had had his fill of opposition for one day.

In one corner of the room a chair had been placed, with worktables set around it. In the course of the morning, these had disappeared beneath piles of maps, despatches and reports from eyewitnesses, not to mention many papers covered with his writing – though he would be lucky indeed if he could ever decipher what he had scrawled there. His writing hand was out of action and he had been forced to get by as best he could with the other, for his arm was bandaged from fingertip to elbow and bound up in a sling as result of an injury he had received when Cergorn had kicked his sword out of his grasp. A similar bandage was wrapped tightly around his ribs, and the painful catch with every breath served as a constant reminder that the centaur's hooves were formidable weapons indeed. When those injuries were added to the after-effects of the battering he had received when he'd fallen down the cliff, there was very little left of him that didn't hurt, in one way or another. Today, however, the Archimandrite had no time to worry about pain as he strove to put together a complete and coherent picture of the widespread disasters that had befallen all the realms since the Curtain Walls had begun to falter.

Wherever possible, Amaurn had been interviewing Loremasters

and refugees from the areas which had been hit. Their experiences made for harrowing listening. Many realms had suffered natural catastrophes. Drought, flooding, landslides and violent storms were causing hardship and havoc, and he realised that Callisiora, with its eternal rain, had not come off worst, by any means. Only Gendival, which could have the power of its Curtain Walls illicitly boosted by the technology of the Ancients, had escaped – so far. One look at the state of the energy barrier on the Callisioran border had convinced him that even the Shadowleague was living on borrowed time.

Other lands, such as the peninsula of Nemeris and its archipelago beyond, had been ravaged by war, as beings from other ocean realms tried to annexe the warm coastal waters with their bays and reefs which provided both dwellings and bountiful food. Amaurn had spoken at length with Kyrre, Loremaster for the Dobarchu, who had first brought word of the atrocities which were taking place in her land. She still had not recovered from her dreadful experiences and from the wounds she had suffered. She had told him how an undersea volcano had erupted, causing great loss of life and the invasion, in the subsequent chaos, by Merfolk and sharks. When she had left, her folk were had been reduced to a mere handful, besieged in a sea-loch and fighting for their lives. Nothing had been heard from them since she had arrived in Gendival, and she feared the worst.

When Kyrre, who still tired easily, had left him to return to the healers, Amaurn found himself unable to concentrate. Surrounding him was all the evidence of the dreadful thing he had done when he had interfered with the Curtain Walls.

How could I have known I would unleash such horrors? I never intended that!

But the voice of his conscience, which had lain dormant for so long, seemed to have reawakened here in the wholesome air of Gendival.

You knew, none better, that the risks existed. You just didn't want to consider the possibility. It would have interfered with your plans.

Only the iron discipline, learned the hard way in his years as Lord Blade, kept Amaurn seated at his worktable, outwardly calm and focussed as he correlated more and more information that would, if the other Loremasters ever discovered his tampering, condemn him utterly. In a settlement where the population consisted entirely of telepaths, how long could he keep his guilty secret? And what would they do to him if they ever found out the truth? The former Archimandrite still lived, and he had allies. The supporters of the newcomer would vanish like the snows in spring if they found out that, as Godsword Commander in Callisiora, he had exchanged the Hierarch's ring for a false stone. The collapse of the Curtain Walls had dated from that time, and there was no doubt whatsoever about the connection between the two events.

This is a nightmare! Somehow, I must put right my mistakes before they can be discovered – yet how can I, when that stupid idiot Gilarra lost the genuine Hierarch's ring, and that filthy, thieving Ak'Zahar snatched it up, right from under my nose? I can't see any way of getting it back now, and without it I have no idea how to repair the damage to the Curtain Walls.

Nevertheless, this whole disaster is my responsibility. I need to devise a plan, and quickly, to get us through these difficult times. And whatever scheme I come up with, it had better be a damn good one. Maybe it's just as well I sent Veldan to fetch Zavahl – because what we need right now is a miracle. I don't hold out much hope that his precious Myrial will do the trick but the dragon, hopefully, will be of far more use.

In the meantime, there were some practical things that could be done and Amaurn began to jot down some notes. Though nothing could be done about the climatic problems, surely the issues of the invaders across the Curtain Walls could be addressed. First of all, he must ask Vaure to assemble the few resident Loremasters who could fly. The barriers around Gendival must be patrolled, to make sure that the Ak'Zahar could not get through. He would need a roster of all agents currently in service, both here in Gendival and in the field. Teams of Listeners must work around the clock to try to locate, by telepathy, those Shadowleague members who had not been heard from in some time. Maybe some of the retired Loremasters could come back to work in Gendival and free their fitter colleagues to go out into the field, and the most advanced Loremasters-in-training could be pressed into active service immediately, perhaps with a more experienced partner.

A council of artisans and academics must be formed to come up with examples of the forbidden knowledge of the Ancients which could be used to help sick and starving people – though if recent events had taught Amaurn one thing, it was caution in tampering with the balance of the world. Any information or devices must remain in the hands of Loremasters only for the present, and should only be used so long as the current crisis lasted. Afterwards – if there was an afterwards – there would be time to study in detail their potential impacts on the realms, and decisions could be taken at leisure on what information could be safely released, and where.

Maybe the Navigators could assist in getting food and medical supplies to stricken regions – though both of these essentials would be difficult to come by in sufficient quantities . . .

'Amaurn? Amaurn? Are you there? Can you hear me?' The faint mental voice that interrupted the Archimandrite's deliberations had not come through the Listeners, which meant that one of his secret supporters somewhere had either not yet received the news of his return, or had something to tell him that should not become common knowledge. At once, Amaurn felt the prick of the old Magefolk curiosity.

They robbed us of our magic, but they couldn't take away the basic characteristics of our people.

'I'm listening,' he answered. 'Who is this?'

'It's me, Grim. Amaurn, I have some staggering news for you . . .'

'And I have some staggering news for you, old friend. You are speaking to the new Archimandrite of the Shadowleague.'

A surge of delight came from the old Summoner. 'Well done! You didn't waste any time, I see. Did you have any difficulties?'

'Actually, it was much easier than I had expected.' Even as the casual reply formed in his mind, Amaurn had flashes of memory: Cergorn charging at him wielding a massive broadsword; an explosion of pain as the centaur's hoof connected with his hand; Skreeva's head being crushed in Maskulu's jaws; the clearing awash with blood; Syvilda's open loathing and utter contempt; Veldan's eyes, hostile and wary, in her mother's face.

Grim, far away, snorted. 'May providence grant that *my* life never gets that easy. But now you must listen, Amaurn. What I have to tell you will be of even greater importance, now that you are Archimandrite.'

Quickly, Amaurn told Maskulu not to let anyone else into the Meeting House for a few moments. He knew it was an effort for Grim to send so far, without the aid of any Listeners, and he wanted to make sure that they were not interrupted. The Summoner's excitement was contagious. He settled back in his chair and heard, with growing astonishment, the tale of the gangling boy who had come from Tiarond, and the wonders he had found beneath the city.

By the time Grim had finished, Amaurn was on his feet, and pacing back and forth across the room, unable to sit still in his excitement. This could be the answer! Maybe it was possible to get through the tunnels and reach some kind of interface that controlled the Curtain Walls, removing the need for the Hierarch's ring completely. He didn't have a clue how to go about this – but he could recognise a hope when he saw one, and had the sense to seize it with both hands. Could the strange objects that the boy had found be of any help?

'Grim, this is wonderful news. Can you come at once? Those artefacts must be in the hands of our experts as soon as possible. They may prove crucial in our search for what ails our world. And can you bring the boy, too? I want to question him myself.'

He felt the Summoner hesitate. 'Amaurn, is that really necessary? The poor lad has been through a very great deal in the last few days, and he only reached this sanctuary yesterday. Surely he deserves to spend a little time in peace and safety? Besides, he's terrified that we'll ask him to go back to the city.'

The Archimandrite shrugged. 'Too bad. Lately we've all had to do things we'd rather not have done. Why should he be the exception? But I shouldn't think he'd need to return to Tiarond. We'll send a search party back there, of course, but a callow lad would be more of a hindrance than a help. No, I simply want to probe his mind, to learn the details of this cavern and its whereabouts, so that I can come up with some kind of plan.'

'And what will happen to poor Scall after that?' There was a note of concern in Grim's mental tones.

'Don't worry about it. We'll think of something.'

There was a wary pause. 'Are you speaking as Amaurn now? Or as Lord Blade?'

Amaurn was angered by the implication. 'I'm speaking as the Archimandrite of the Shadowleague,' he said coldly. 'I am deeply grateful to you for your help, Grim, but I need this one thing more. Bring the boy to me – and hurry. I'll see that he's taken care of, you have my word on it.'

'Very well,' the Summoner said sternly. 'If your recent experiences haven't taught you the difference between right and wrong, then we're all in trouble – but you are in the worst danger yourself.' With that, he was gone.

'Damn!' Papers flew as Amaurn's fist crashed down on the table. It had suddenly come home to him that Lord Blade would be harder to shake off than he had thought.

EIGHT

THE BREAKING STORM

As Seriema looked across the high, wild lands of the Reivers, she felt as though she had come to the top of the world. Riding with Cetain, the chieftain's son, at the head of two dozen picked warriors, was the best thing that had ever happened to her.

Today, as she had ridden out of the gateway of Arcan's fortress, she had felt as though she'd changed overnight from a terrified fugitive to a triumphant queen. The busy folk in the settlement had paused in their tasks to watch the chieftain's son ride by, the children dropping their burdens in the mud to wave at the bright-eyed warriors. As the column of riders left the fortress and rode along the top of the ridge, the two Summoners in their sombre robes, their black cloaks flying in the wind and their white skull masks gleaming in the sombre light of the approaching storm, emerged from their tower by the mere and called out a blessing.

Now, riding fast, they were far out across the moors, and Arcan's fortress had vanished somewhere behind them, blending into the background of heath and fell. Seriema's shaggy, wiry little horse, so very different from Tormon's massive Sefrian, felt quick and responsive beneath her, and she wished that she was simply going out to race with Cetain, instead of accompanying him on this desperate, dangerous errand to rally the other clans. She looked across at the tall warrior, a magnificent sight with his long, dark red hair escaping from its single braid and streaming out behind him. He looked across at her and smiled. 'You ride well, for a city lass.'

'It was always something I enjoyed, and my father encouraged me,' Seriema replied. She smiled wryly. 'It was the age-old story, I'm afraid. What he really wanted was a boy.' Normally, when she spoke of her father, she found her inner self at war between her great love for him, and her resentment that, no matter what she had achieved, no matter how hard she had tried, it had never been enough. Today, however, much to her surprise, much of the secret bitterness that festered within her seemed to have been blown away in this clean moorland air.

Cetain was looking across at her with sympathy on his face. 'And so you had to do everything ten times better than a boy, to compensate – both in his eyes and in yours.'

Seriema gasped. 'How did you know that? Apart from Presvel, you're the only person I've ever met who understood.'

'You'd be surprised how well I understand,' Certain said softly. 'I had a sister, the next youngest of our family to me, and the only girl among eight brothers. Her name was Amellin. Being the only girl, she too felt she had to prove herself in our father's eyes; to ride better, to hunt better and to fight better than all the menfolk of our family put together.' He shook his head. 'To take more risks. Time and again I warned her to be more careful, but she would just shake her hair back across her shoulders and laugh at me. Until the day we made a raid on the Wolf clan's cattle that went very wrong.' He swallowed hard. 'They were waiting for us. To give us time to escape, my sister charged their chieftain himself, and fought him hand to hand. When I saw her fall, part of my heart went with her, to be trampled beneath the horses of our foemen.' Cetain's face was an expressionless mask, his eyes far away. 'Amellin saved our lives that day – competing.' He spat on the ground.

'I'm sorry,' Seriema said softly. 'She must be a great loss to you.'

'To me, aye – but not to our father. Not so long as he has his sons.' There was a bitter edge to his voice. 'Amellin died two years ago, and from that day to this, I've never heard him mention her name.'

His tone of voice invited no reply, and wisely, Seriema did not pursue the subject. She could sense that Cetain had come near to weeping, and that would be unthinkable in front of his warriors – and her. They rode on in silence for a time. Her tough little horse, wise to the ways of this terrain, had worked off its first high spirits and had settled into a steady, energy-conserving lope which gave her plenty of opportunity to turn her attention to her surroundings.

The wind was gusting now and strengthening to a gale, and in it she could feel the approach of the threatening storm. The bank of indigo cloud which she had seen at a distance from the tower of the stronghold was almost overhead and coming up fast, and she could feel the first cold spits of sleet against her face. She didn't have to be as weather-wise as a Reiver to tell that this was going to be a bad one. Surreptitiously she looked around, searching for a place to shelter, but there was nothing in sight in any direction but the bleak, bare fells.

Oh, Great Myrial! It looks as though we're just going to ride right through it.

Seriema shivered. So much for the joys of this wild life. She should have had the sense to see that there would be another side to it. For an instant she thought, with longing, of her cosy study in her solid mansion, with the fire roaring up the chimney, and Marutha – poor Marutha – bringing her a cup of hot, fragrant tea.

Never again. No matter what happens in the long run, whether we win out against those monsters or we don't, nothing will ever be the same. The old days are gone for ever.

Quickly, Seriema strangled such thoughts. Gone they might be, but that wouldn't stop her making the best of these new days. And if she had to ride through that black tempest up ahead, so what? Cetain seemed to think that she was tough enough to ride with the Reivers, and not for anything would she let him down.

As though he had sensed her thinking about him, Cetain sat up in his saddle and straightened his shoulders, as though flinging his sadness to the winds. 'My apologies, Lady. This is not a day to be dwelling on old sorrows. We should be thinking of what lies ahead of us, not what's in the past.'

Seriema took up his words gladly, pitching her voice to be heard over the relentless, keening wind. 'What does lie ahead? Are the other clans much as our own?'

'Ours?' He looked at her with a lifted eyebrow, and Seriema felt herself colouring. 'Well, you know what I mean,' she said. 'Right now, Arcan's stronghold is the only home I have.'

'You're a forgiving lass indeed, to adopt the Reivers as your own, when we've been responsible for so many of your losses over the years. Aye, and brave too – or foolish – for we're disputatious folk, always ready for a fight and not the easiest to get along with, so I'm told.' But Cetain had been pleased by her words. She could see it in his eyes, and in his smile.

'Tell me about the clans,' she said.

'Forewarned is forearmed?'

She laughed. 'Something like that. I want to know what I'm letting myself in for, if I'm going to tangle with such difficult folk. You mentioned the Wolf clan before; do all the clans have animal names, or is Wolf the name of that particular chieftain?'

'No, we all have animal names, and a totem animal or bird who carries the spirit of the clan, though you'd have to ask the Summoners if you want to know why.'

'Well, that forestalls my next question,' Seriema said. She thought for a moment. 'Maybe it's because the Reivers lead such violent, blood-steeped lives. The actual chieftains themselves must change fairly often, so the totem animal names give the clans a sense of continuity, and identity.'

Cetain's eyes widened. 'All these years, and I never though of that! Sometimes it takes an outsider to see the things that are under our very noses – not that I really look on you as an outsider, which is odd in itself, for we're not accepting of strangers, as a rule. If you weren't born to the clan, you don't count.'

Seriema grinned at him. 'What is the name of your – of *our* clan, then?'

'Arcan's folk are the Eagle clan. There are seven clans in all: Eagle, Bear, Horse, Bull, Raven, Wildcat, and Wolf.'

'And we have to convince them all?'

'Aye – if they'll let us,' Cetain replied dourly. 'With the Bull and the Wolf clans, we'll be lucky to get anywhere near them without picking arrows and spears out of our teeth. Under the present chieftains, they are no friends to the Eagle clan.' He frowned. 'You have to understand that the balance of power among the Reivers is always shifting. Sometimes, if one clan is seen to be getting too powerful, then two or more of the others might band together in a loose alliance. There's little love and less trust between them however, and once the common enemy is dealt with, they might just as well turn on one another.'

Seriema thought long and hard before she actually dared speak the next thought that came into her mind. 'I know that the way the clans run their lives is absolutely none of my business,' she said cautiously. 'In fact it's a lot better for the merchants that they act the way they do, but . . . Well, don't you think it's awfully wasteful?'

Cetain's face lit up. 'Ach, you don't know what a relief it is to hear that from someone else, for a change! I can't count the times I tried to tell my father, or my brothers, that our lives were hard enough already in this wild, bare place, without making them harder by fighting one another. But they wouldn't see it. I was called coward, and worse, and my father broke my head a time or two for the speaking of such heresy.' Abruptly, his expression darkened. 'Then finally I stopped thinking that way. After seeing Amellin die, I could never make peace with the Wolf clan. I'm afraid it's the same for all of us. There are too many old grudges; too much buried hatred. We kill them, they kill us in revenge – and so it goes on, never stopping, throughout all the clans, until the end of time.'

Seriema took a deep breath, feeling her usual fighting response to a challenge rise up within her. 'It'll have to stop, though – and right now. Otherwise everyone will die when the winged fiends come.'

Something in her voice made Cetain turn to look at her. 'Are they really so dreadful as all that?'

'Yes,' Seriema said. 'More dreadful than you could possibly

imagine. And it'll be our job to convince the other clans of that.'

'And if we fail?'

'Then that will be the end of the Reivers. So we'd better not fail, Cetain, for all our sakes.'

There was no chance to say anything more. While they had been talking, the sky had darkened overhead and now the storm began in earnest. Curtains of sleety rain came driving across the exposed fells, obscuring the view ahead and hitting the riders full in the face. Cetain, riding beside her, turned into a veiled, blurred shadow, and she could no longer hear the other warriors following for the noise of the wind. The horses slowed from their brisk canter to a stoical plod, their heads down and their strong little legs working hard to thrust their bodies forward against the wind.

'We must try to keep going if we can,' Cetain shouted. 'We have no time to waste. If your fiends are truly coming, then the sooner we get back to the safety of our stronghold, the better.'

Seriema nodded, though it wasn't what she'd been wanting to hear. Though the thick, oiled wool of the Godsword cloaks repelled a certain amount of water, they were no match for this downpour, and soon her sodden cloak was dragging heavily at her shoulders. The wind kept blowing her hood back, so she either had to keep a hand free to clutch it around her face, or just give up on it altogether. As soon as she felt the water soaking through the fabric, she took the second option.

Within moments, the temperature had plummeted still further. Seriema's head, jaw and ears were aching with the cold, and though her hands still clutched her slippery reins, she had ceased to feel them.

To perdition with the wild, free life! Right now I would give it all up for a nice big fire, a hot bath, and the biggest glass of brandy in the world.

Cetain shouldered his horse in close to hers. 'Are you all right, lass?'

When Seriema tried to answer, her mouth filled with rain. She spat it out, wiped the water from her streaming eyes, and tried again. 'Never better,' she shouted.

Above the howling wind, she heard him laugh. 'You're an accomplished liar, too.'

'What do you expect? I'm a merchant, remember?'

'You don't look much like a merchant any more. You look as though you belonged right here on the moors, in the wind and the storm.'

And I feel like a drowned rat – but I'm certainly not going to spoil his illusion by telling him I'm freezing, or asking about shelter.

Seriema clawed a tangle of soaking hair out of her eyes and freely damned the wind and the storm. But it was no use trying to pretend to herself that she wasn't delighted, and the new warm glow inside her proved a perfect antidote to the freezing wind.

Grim was in his workroom, wrestling with his conscience. Following his conversation with Amaurn, the fates of not one but two young men lay in his hands. He felt dreadfully guilty about having to uproot poor Scall again, and tear him from his friends, just when the lad could reasonably expect himself to be safe – at least, as safe as anyone could be in these days. But guilt or no, he knew that in the end he could not defy Amaurn. Not when there was so much at stake. He was determined, however, to make sure that the Shadowleague took good care of Scall.

Surely we can wipe out his memories of Gendival, and return him to his friends when we're done. After he found those devices for us, we owe him that much. I'm going to do everything in my power to persuade Amaurn to deal kindly with the boy.

The other young man was an even greater problem. Grim had intended to plead Dark's case to the Archimandrite, and bring him into the Shadowleague as a new Loremaster, as he deserved. Because of Scall, however, their conversation had ended badly and, once he'd angered the new leader of the Shadowleague, there had been no chance to put forward his request.

So what do I do now? Take Dark with me anyway and risk him being rejected by Amaurn? Or leave him behind, to cope as best he can with the attacks of the winged demons and to bear the brunt of Arcan's wrath when the chieftain finds out that his Summoner has deserted him?

A persistent chattering and squeaking from the cage in the corner pulled Grim's attention away from his musings. His imps, bored with being shut in when they wanted to be loose in the room wreaking their usual havoc, were determined to attract his attention. Gar, of course, was still in Gendival with Maskulu, and Grim, anticipating his own journey home, had asked the Senior Loremaster to keep the little creature there for the present. The others, however, were making more than enough noise to compensate for the absence of one of their group. Bad-tempered Iss was squabbling with mischievous Bir, and the two females were behaving no better. Lively Vai was throwing her bedding and playthings out of the cage onto the floor, and affectionate Ell was rattling the bars; trying to reach Grim and shrieking for attention at the top of her piercing voice.

Well, at least the imps would present no problems. Now that he was leaving, he didn't have to think of a way to transport the little creatures up to the stronghold, and keep them safe and secret once he got there. He would simply send them all to Maskulu (he tried not to picture the Loremaster's horrified response when the imps all descended on him) and he would collect them when . . .

At that moment, the door came crashing open. He turned quickly, with a flash of anger, and saw his assistant in the doorway. 'How dare you come bursting in here. Get out at once!'

Dark was standing with his mouth open, staring into the big cage that filled the far corner from floor to ceiling. 'What in the name of wonder are *those?*' he demanded, as the small black imps chittered and fluttered, clearly excited by the unexpected visitor.

'None of your business,' Grim replied testily, 'though no doubt you'll be pestering the life out of me for evermore until you find out. Why do you think I forbade you and Izobia to come in here?' He frowned at his assistant. 'Would you kindly explain why you chose to defy me?'

'Because you're up to something,' Dark said frankly. 'You

wouldn't even discuss those objects of Scall's with me – and you always want to talk about anything new, even if it's just to increase my experience. You didn't take much time to examine them, either. You simply grabbed them and shot up here as though the fiends were after you, leaving me floundering, trying to think up some kind of explanation to give the poor lad. You've been closeted in your workroom ever since, and I want to know what's going on. I meant to knock and wait, as usual, but then I thought "Why should I?" I'm a fully-fledged Summoner now that I've conducted my first Passing . . .' For a moment he faltered, and Grim knew he was thinking of the sick child whose suffering he had ended. Then he rallied once more. 'And I don't see why I should be kept waiting on your doorstep like a mendicant or a child.'

He was working himself up into a fine old temper, and Grim, more than a little taken aback by the outburst, smiled to himself.

Finally, Dark has grown into a true Summoner, and it's time I started to treat him as one. How could I even have thought of leaving him behind? He has the makings of a superb Loremaster. Besides, whether he's annoyed with me or not, Amaurn is no fool. With the Shadowleague so short of agents at present, he should jump at every opportunity to recruit new blood.

'You're absolutely right,' he told his assistant, 'and I apologise. Ever since you came to me, I have been forced to keep secrets from you, but it's time to put that right.' He almost began to tell Dark about the Shadowleague, then realised that at present, there would be no time to explain it properly. Quickly, he thought again. 'Dark, my boy, what would you think about leaving the lands of the Reivers? There's no time to explain now, but I can tell you every-thing you need to know when we're on our way. Would you like to go travelling with me?'

'Travelling? Where?'

Grim never took his eyes from his assistant's face. 'Beyond the Curtain Walls,' he said quietly.

Dark's jaw dropped. 'Beyond . . .' His voice was shaky. He took a deep breath, visibly getting himself under control. 'I knew it. I always *knew* there had to be something beyond that barrier! And those dreadful creatures that slaughtered the Tiarondians, they had to come from somewhere . . .'

Grim's mouth twisted in a wry smile.

Since the barriers began to fail, more and more ordinary folk in all the realms have been thinking about them and realising that there must be something beyond. Amaurn was right, Cergorn. No matter how hard you tried, you couldn't have kept the nature of our world a secret for much longer.

'When do we leave?' Dark was too excited to be patient with Grim's musings, but his words brought the Summoner back to life's practicalities with a vengeance. It was all very well to talk about leaving, as though it was no more difficult than a stroll down to the lake and back, but given the current crisis, Arcan wasn't about to let his Summoners go wandering off, for any reason whatsoever. Their escape – for escape it must be – would have to be conducted with great stealth, at a time when the Reivers were very much on their guard. In addition, they would be dragging a scared, reluctant boy with them, and if they should be caught fleeing, Scall would share their fate.

Not that Arcan would harm us. He needs us too much, though he would be very angry, and with good reason. We'd be imprisoned, and no worse, I expect. No, the chief risk is being mistaken in the darkness for a raiding party from another clan. There are always patrols of mounted warriors guarding the settlement and the cattle, and it's more than likely that they would cut us down before there was time for explanations.

Clearly, Dark had also been considering Arcan's reaction. His look of bright-eyed excitement had given way to a frown. 'Grim, I want to go travelling with you more than I've ever wanted anything in my life, but . . . Do you really think it's right for us to leave Arcan and the clan just now, when they might be facing such danger? Surely they'll need our knowledge more than ever before.'

Dark, I'm so proud of you. Had I searched the world over, I couldn't have chosen a better apprentice.

'You're right of course,' Grim said aloud. 'It's treacherous and irresponsible and downright wrong of us to be deserting the clan at this time. But I'm afraid it can't be helped, lad. I have another life from the one you know, and other, greater loyalties. If I can get Scall's artefacts to *my* masters, there's a good chance that they might help us solve not only the threat of the winged fiends, but also the problem of this constant rain that cripples our land. And Callisiora isn't alone, Dark. There are many other realms beyond our own that are suffering great hardship and catastrophe. My true people must take the whole world into account, not the fate of one small tribe in one small land. It doesn't sit easily with me either, but I know that we can help Arcan's folk far more effectively, in the long run, if we go.'

Dark look at his mentor for a long moment, before he spoke. 'I don't know how far you plan to go, but we'll have to travel light, Grim. The only way we'll get out of here is to sneak away in the night – and even then we'll be lucky if we're not seen by one of Arcan's guard patrols.'

Grim nodded. 'This would have to happen today, when the danger of invasion is making everyone so watchful.'

Dark grinned. 'I know. It'll be like trying to get downstairs past Izobia's room, without her popping her head out to find out what's going on . . .' His eyes widened. 'Guardians preserve us! What are we going to do about Izobia and little Lannol? Since Arcan cast her out, she has no one but us to take care of her.'

'You're right again,' Grim said. 'We have a responsibility to the poor girl, and we must make sure that Arcan will give her care and shelter in our absence. He has a right to be angry with the two of us, but I won't have him cast out that girl and her child a second time.' He sat back down at his workbench, gazing out through the window with narrowed eyes while he thought. 'Also, there's something I haven't told you yet, Dark. Another complication, I'm afraid. When we go, we have to take Scall with us.'

'*What?* Grim, that really isn't fair on the poor lad.'

'I know.' The Summoner sighed heavily. 'I don't like it any better than you, but I don't have any choice. Those are my orders. My master wants to question him about the cavern he found.'

Dark sighed. 'I just don't see how we can do this. We've got to make sure Izobia is safe, kidnap Scall from the stronghold, and avoid Arcan's warrior patrols – hoping against hope, of course, that the winged fiends don't decide to arrive when we're out on the open moor. How in blazes are we going to manage all that?'

The Summoner shook his head. 'I don't know, but we have very little time to come up with a plan. Arcan wants everyone inside the fortress by sundown, and he's planning to lock and bar the doors until morning.' He shepherded his assistant out of the workroom and locked the door, before he set off down the twisting staircase. With one last, regretful look behind him, Dark followed, but when they reached the bottom of the stairs, he detained his mentor with a hand on his arm. 'Grim? What were those creatures? I've never seen anything like them.'

Grim smiled at him. 'As with everything else, I'll explain on the way.'

But one thing's for sure, my boy. You'll see creatures a good deal stranger than that, if I can get you through the Curtain Walls to safety.

Nine

Sunset

The wherry got down to the estuary just in time to catch the last of the ebb, which was just as well. According to Meglyn, the wind usually dropped around sunset, but the last of the receding tide would carry them down to the settlement that perched on the coast at the south side of the river's mouth. Elion, standing on deck with Veldan and the firedrake, drank in the beauty of the scene. The estuary faced south-east, so that the light of the setting sun was almost directly behind the ship. The hills were silhouetted against a blazing sky, and the ocean looked like molten gold. Ahead, on the ocean's far horizon, the cloudless sky shaded down to sapphire and amethyst as evening crept towards the land.

Beyond the mouth of the estuary, islands seemed to float on the evening sea, the dark stone of their pinnacles and crags still catching the light of the setting sun. It was a sight to lift the heart, but for Elion, it was tinged with sorrow. Melnyth had loved the coast, with its little ports and secluded fishing villages. She had been quite an accomplished sailor herself, good at reading wind and wave, and at home with the sea in all its changing moods. She had loved the rough dockside taverns, and the raucous company of the fishermen and fishwives, the stevedores and strumpets, the wayfarers and traders and the itinerant fish gutters who worked their way from port to port, as the fish shoals passed in their due seasons. She was never happier than when she was yarning with the old sailors exchanging travellers' tales until the break of dawn, and once again, in his mind's eye, Elion saw her rapt face as she listened, her generous mouth curved in a smile, her copper hair gleaming in the firelight.

Go away, damn you! Stop haunting me!

The thought took the Loremaster by surprise. Before, he had always embraced the painful memories, no matter how much they hurt him.

'Are you sure that Melnyth is haunting you, and not the other way around?' said a soft voice. It was Veldan, using mindspeech. 'Maybe you're ready to let her rest in peace at last.'

Elion shook his head. 'I can't let her go, Veldan. So long as I keep her alive in my heart, it's as though she's still in the world, somewhere round the next corner, just out of sight.' Tears blurred the sunset sea into a haze of gold. 'If I let her rest in peace, as you say, I'll finally have to admit to myself that I'll never see her again – and I don't think I could bear that.' Yet, even as he spoke, it came to him with more than a little guilt that, during the last few days of crisis, he'd had little time to think of his former partner and, if he was being completely honest with himself, the respite from his constant grief had not been unwelcome.

The estuary ended in a pair of headlands that jutted out into the sea. Near the end of the southern promontory there was a deep cove, ringed by a cluster of low houses built from pale grey stone. The ship listed to one side as Meglyn put the tiller hard over, and the boom creaked as it swung sluggishly across. 'We got here not a moment too soon,' she muttered. 'There's practically no wind to speak of.'

On the last breath of the dying breeze, they coasted into the harbour, passing the lofty cresset of the navigation beacon at the end of the wharf. Two fishermen, an old man and a young boy, were seated on the edge of the dock, dangling their lines in the water. They waved as the wherry glided past, their jaws hanging open at the sight of the firedrake, who was crouched in the bows. Coming skilfully alongside the stone wharf, Meglyn moored the wherry beside a long, dark sailing barge, and greeted its skipper with a hail. 'Hey, Arnond! I've brought you your passengers.'

A broad-shouldered, bullnecked young man with cropped dark hair emerged from one of the barge's open hatches, grinning broadly. 'Hey, Meglyn! You made good time.'

'Just caught the last of the tide.' Meglyn leapt ashore to help Chalas make the wherry fast, and the crop-haired young giant clambered off the barge and caught her up in a hug. 'Ouf! Put me down,' she gasped. 'You'd better not let Rowen catch you embracing other women. How is she?'

Arnond's grin grew even wider, as his arms described a great circle in the air in front of him. 'Blooming. She'll be up in a minute, but she's so big now, it takes her a while to climb through the hatch.'

'It can't be very long now.'

'It isn't. Today's little jaunt down the coast is the last trip we're going to make, then we're staying here in Neymis, until the baby comes. After that, we'll get back to normal as soon as possible. It's going to be interesting to sail with a little one aboard.'

Meglyn laughed. 'It might just be more interesting than you think.'

Arnond shrugged. 'It'll be all right. Why, I grew up on a boat myself, and so did Rowen. The main thing is that we're all together.'

At that moment, a tall young woman clambered clumsily up through the hatch of the barge, and Arnond leapt back aboard to help her ashore. Rowen had a lovely, delicate face, and long hair that was dark in shadow, but glowed deep red where it picked up the light. Meglyn embraced her. 'Arnond was right, love. You do look blooming.'

Rowen laughed. 'Well, it's nice to be decorative at least, because apart from the cooking, I'm not much good on board right now. My days of hauling on ropes and shifting cargo are finished for a little while.'

'Well, that doesn't matter when we've got Sidras to help out with the heavy stuff,' Arnond said. 'When we can prise him out of the tavern, that is.'

Meglyn raised her eyes to the heavens. 'That old reprobate never changes, does he? While we're waiting for him, let me introduce you to your passengers.'

Elion, Veldan, and Ailie, not wishing to intrude, had been waiting by the wherry's rail. Now Meglyn beckoned them ashore, and introduced them. With some difficulty, Kaz followed them, making the boat list ominously beneath his weight. 'And that,' Meglyn finished, indicating the firedrake, 'is Kazairl.'

'He's enough to scare Rowen right into labour, isn't he?' said Elion.

Rowen laughed. 'I don't scare that easy. I think he's beautiful.' She reached up and patted Kaz on the nose. For a moment, he looked astonished, then he gave a pleased rumble, almost a purring sound, deep in his throat. 'Clearly a woman of great intelligence and discernment,' he said, with a poisonous look at Elion. 'Which is more than I can say for some people.'

The Loremasters and Ailie said their farewells to Meglyn, who had agreed to remain with the wherry in Neymis until their return, and moved their belongings to the other ship. Chalas was about to go to the tavern to fetch Arnond's crewman, Sidras, when Meglyn stopped him. 'Wait! There's no need to pull Sidras away from his rum for a little run like this with no cargo. Why don't I take his place, and be your crewman, instead of kicking my heels in port? I love the river, but being out at sea would make a lovely change.'

Arnond looked doubtful, but Rowen was more frank. 'As long as no one's in any doubt that Arnond is the captain,' she said. 'In a boat, you can only have one person giving the orders.'

Elion looked at her in astonishment, wondering how she dared talk like that to the owner of the barge. Meglyn, however, just laughed. 'I asked for that! And you're quite right, Rowen. Just yell at me if I start getting out of line.'

Arnond put an arm around his pregnant lifemate's shoulders, pride shining in every line of his face. 'Yell at you? If you start getting out of line on our ship, Rowen will probably keelhaul you.'

'Well, if I can't give any orders how about a polite suggestion?' Meglyn glanced up at the darkening sky. 'I thought I felt a breath of wind just then. Why don't we get ready to leave?'

Within half an hour, the barge moved slowly out of the harbour, making for the open sea. Veldan, standing in the bows, looked considerably relieved. She turned to Elion with a smile. 'It's good to be on our way again. I've never had an easy moment all day, wondering if the Dragons would make another attempt to kidnap Toulac and Zavahl. The sooner we can pick them up, the better I'll be pleased.'

It was getting on for evening by the time the shelter on the beach was finished.

'Well,' said Toulac, dusting her hands on her long-suffering breeches. 'That should get us through the night. I reckon we've done a good job, there.'

Zavahl looked at the lopsided creation with pride. It had taken a long time to weave the twigs, reeds and bracken through the holes in the net, but this was the first thing he had ever built with his own two hands, and he had a collection of scratches, scrapes and blisters to prove it. His filthy, reddened palms felt hot and sore, but he didn't mind a bit. His sense of achievement gave the shelter a beauty which, to a less prejudiced eye, it certainly did not possess, and he couldn't wait till evening came so that he could try it out.

But Toulac the slave driver clearly had no intention of letting him stand around in self-congratulation. Before he knew what was happening she had thrust both the broken jug and the tin box she had found, now minus its lid, into his hands. 'Fetch us some water, will you? I found a trickle running down the cliff about a couple of hundred yards or so along the beach. In the meantime, I'll get a fire started.' Rummaging in the breast pocket of her shirt, she produced a flint. 'Always keep one of these on you – or several, if you can manage it. Just in case. Never go anywhere without a flint. It's a habit that'll stand you in good stead for the rest of your life.'

Zavahl trudged off along the beach. Though he kept a close watch on the cliff face so that he could spot Toulac's water, in reality he was deep in thought. *I'm actually learning to survive out here. Who would ever have imagined that?*

He soon found what he was looking for, lodged the box beneath the dripping trickle, and waited, with scant patience, for it to fill. When it did, he was dismayed that it held so little. Why at this rate, he was going to be trudging back and forth all night! Sighing, he set the jug in its place, and stamped around impatiently, shivering in the cold wind, until it too was full.

When he returned to the shelter, the sun was going down, bathing the beach in gold and copper light. There was a small but cheerful fire blazing in their little den between the rocks. Crabs were baking in their shells on the flat lid prised from the metal box, hissing and crackling in the heat of the fire. The savoury aroma made his mouth water. Toulac was down by the ocean, sitting on a rock by the water's edge while several of the Dobarchu bobbed in the water around her feet. Zavahl wondered what they were telling her – then marvelled that he should be so accepting of the fact that the furry little creatures were communicating at all. He put down the water carefully – for now that he had to carry every drop, it had suddenly become very precious – and went to join her. A silvery pile of fish lay on the rock beside her, and she was gutting them, swiftly and expertly, with a little knife.

'Where did you get that from?' Zavahl asked in astonishment.

Toulac stopped cleaning the fish, and looked up at him. 'I had it hidden in my boot.'

'Well, why didn't you use it when we were building the shelter, then? I nearly took the skin off my hands, breaking twigs.'

'Because we need to keep it sharp for tasks like gutting this fish,' Toulac replied. 'It's only a little knife. It's our only utensil and our only tool. We can't risk blunting it, or snapping the blade by hacking away at a bunch of branches that we can break just as easily with our hands. It's the same with the sword. You never know when we might need it.'

Zavahl sat down on the rock and sighed. 'I suppose.' These practical details seemed so obvious when Toulac explained them. 'I feel so stupid out here.'

The veteran looked at him in surprise. 'I never thought I'd hear *that* from the Hierarch of Callisiora.'

'I'm not the Hierarch of Callisiora any more.' Zavahl didn't look at her, but kept on staring straight in front of him. 'I don't know what I am.'

'Well, think of all the fun you're going to have finding out,' said Toulac. 'Especially the parts that involve Ailie.' She winked at him, and Zavahl felt the heat rising into his face. 'Listen,' she went on, 'there's nothing wrong with you, as long as you don't fall into self-pity. Of course you don't know anything about this outdoors stuff, but you've had an appallingly sheltered life, and you haven't exactly had long to learn. You're as able as the next man, Zavahl. It's all a matter of experience, and there's only one way to get that. But you'll be fine, you'll see. And the next time something like this happens, you'll have a knife in your own boot.' She grinned at him. 'I'll show you where to get one made.'

They left the water's edge and went back up the beach to the shelter, their footsteps crunching in the damp shingle. Toulac had laid flat stones at the edge of the fire, and now she wrapped the fish in broad leaves that she'd brought from the top of the cliff and laid them on the hot stones to bake. While they waited for them to cook, she passed on the information she'd gained from the Dobarchu, while she'd been down on the rocks gutting the fish they had brought her.

'Their country was invaded,' she said, 'by some other creatures – I couldn't quite get the straight of it. I think they came from outside their Curtain Walls, like those winged monsters Elion told us about, that attacked Tiarond. Poor things, there's only a handful of them left; in fact they think that this small group might be the only survivors. There's a Loremaster with them, Mrainil, who decided that rules or no rules, he would have to bring his folk to Gendival. Otherwise, the Dobarchu would be wiped out completely. He seemed quite relieved that Cergorn wasn't in charge any more. He's hoping that whoever takes over has more lenient views.' She shrugged. 'As are we all, or you and I will be finding ourselves without a home, too.'

'Did Veldan sound concerned about that when you spoke to her?' Zavahl asked.

Toulac smiled broadly. 'That's a very good question. No, she didn't say who was in charge now, but she didn't sound worried at all.'

'Good.' Zavahl wriggled his buttocks into a more comfortable position on the rounded rock on which he sat, and stretched his hands out towards the crackling fire. 'You know, you were right when you said a fire and a shelter would make all the difference. This is almost pleasant. Will those fish be ready soon?'

Toulac poked at the steaming fish with the point of her knife. 'They're ready now – and so am I.'

Zavahl agreed. He had never been so hungry in his life.

Taking turns to use the knife and a clam-shell scoop, they ate the fish directly from the hot stones, and cracked the shells of the crabs to get at the chewy white meat. After they had finished, Toulac built up the fire, and they huddled close over the smoky flames as the wind grew colder. The night deepened, and the stars came out in the sky above.

Though the Dragon Aethon no longer had a corporeal form of his own, he still found himself attracted by the warmth and glow of the fire. Though it was only a pale echo of his own land's blazing sunlight, it stirred memories of home: of the glittering crystal city of Altheva; of long-missed friends and companions; of stretching out his magnificent golden wings to drink his fill of radiant, life-giving sun . . .

Never again. Never again. His great, lithe, golden form was a pile of decaying meat now, the shimmering wings were battered and broken by the landslide that had destroyed his body and, had it not been for the timely arrival of Zavahl, would have snuffed out his existence like a candle. Now, the only surviving parts of Aethon the Seer were his mind and spirit, and the precious memories of his people, which clung to a precarious and awkward existence as a guest within the mind of this vulnerable human. It wasn't much of an existence, but it was all he had, and all he could ever expect.

Sorrow gripped the Dragon, and a loneliness so profound that he wanted to howl his pain to the skies.

This is all that's left to me. All that there can ever be. I can never go home again.

His capture by the Dierkan drones had forced Aethon to face up to some painful truths. He had been aware the Skreeva of the Alvai was an agent of the Dragonfolk in Gendival. Unfortunately, the decision had not been his to make, but he had always deplored his people's use of a spy in a relationship which was meant to be founded on trust and cooperation. As soon as he had seen the wicked, predatory forms of the Dierkan, he'd known that his people had somehow discovered his whereabouts, and had found a way to bring him home. For an instant his heart had leapt. Then, all at once, it had struck him with stunning force just what such a summons meant. Once the dragons found a way to retrieve the memories of his race, and pass them on to his successor, then what remained of Aethon would be expendable – and so would his host, Zavahl.

But I don't want to die!

Zavahl, nodding in front of the fire, leapt up as the Dragon's anguished words resounded through his mind. Throughout that day, his thoughts had been for his own immediate survival, and he had almost forgotten the bizarre passenger who shared his body.

Toulac was also on her feet, her sword out of its scabbard. 'What? What happened?'

Taking a deep breath, Zavahl sat down again. 'I'm sorry. False alarm.' Until he found out what had caused Aethon to cry out like that, he preferred to keep his own counsel.

The veteran remained on her feet, peering fiercely into the gloom that ringed the fire. 'False *alarm?* What in perdition do you think you're playing at?'

'I'm sorry,' Zavahl repeated. 'I must have dozed off for a moment. I thought I heard a voice.'

Toulac sat down again with a long-suffering sigh. 'There wasn't any voice,' she said testily, 'but just in case, I'll get out of this firelight for a while and keep an eye open for any intruders. Besides, it's probably too early to be looking out for the ship yet, but you never know.'

She slipped away into the shadows, leaving Zavahl alone and feeling guilty.

But I'm not alone, am I?

There had been no word from the Dragon since they had been kidnapped. It was almost as though Zavahl's uninvited guest was deliberately lying low. But why? Closing his eyes, he turned his thoughts inward. 'Aethon? Are you there? What's wrong?'

'It seems I owe you an apology. Inadvertently, I have brought great trouble to your life.' When the Dragon spoke he sounded uncertain and subdued: not at all like the confident and knowledgeable creature who had first accosted a terrified former Hierarch. Zavahl frowned. Why, it almost seemed as though their positions had been reversed!

'When I hurled myself into your mind, I was desperate,' Aethon continued. 'I was dying; almost at the end. There was no time to consider the consequences. But I carry knowledge locked within me that is vital to the future of the Dragonfolk, and the events of last night prove that that they will stop at nothing to recover it.'

A chill went through Zavahl. Toulac had told him that, according to Veldan, the Dragonfolk were behind their abduction, but she didn't know any more than that. And since his capture, the demands of survival had preoccupied him so deeply that he'd had no time to consider motives and consequences. 'So they want you,' he said slowly, 'and in order to get you, they would have to capture me. And then what?'

'Unfortunately, my racial memories are not conscious, so I cannot pass them on verbally – indeed, you would die of old age before I would have time to put more than a fraction of them into words. So they would have to be retrieved by some other means, and passed directly into the mind of the new Seer. It is very likely that their recovery would either eradicate me altogether or, at the very least, ravage my mind beyond all recognition,' Aethon said heavily. 'And the human brain was not designed to stand up to the methods they would be forced to use. It is more than likely that you, or at least all vestiges of your personality, would perish too.'

'But that's monstrous!' Zavahl gasped.

'Not to them,' said Aethon. 'You see, to them I'm dead already. The way they see it, I only took up residence in your body to preserve the memories. They weren't really considering that my very essence would also make the crossing, but it did. Everything that makes up Aethon the Seer is here within you, Zavahl – and I don't want to die yet.'

'Well, nor do I,' said Zavahl. 'Not that your wretched relatives seem to be remotely concerned about *that*.' What a mess! While Aethon remained in his mind he would continue to be a hunted man, yet the price of getting rid of his uninvited passenger was his own sanity, and probably his life.

TEN

ILLUSIONS

She didn't want him. How could she not want him, after all he'd done for her? But the evidence was right there, before Presvel's eyes. From his shadowy corner of the stronghold's great hall, he watched Rochalla, the firelight haloing her hair in bright gold, as she sat to the side of one great fireplace listening to a storyteller. Little Annas snuggled sleepily on her lap, her thumb in her mouth, absorbed in the tale of heroes and hidden treasure, and beside them – much too close – sat Scall. Had it not been for the obvious youth of the lad and lass, the trio might easily have been a family. They looked so comfortable together. As if they *belonged*. Presvel gritted his teeth.

It's not fair. She should be mine. I've loved her ever since the first time I saw her. Had I not brought her, she wouldn't even be here, she'd be demon-bait in Tiarond.

It had not been a good day for Presvel. He'd felt out of place among these rough, hulking warriors; despised and dismissed. The busy Reiver folk, preparing their stronghold for a siege, had made it abundantly clear that he was getting in their way. Tormon, having quarrelled with Seriema, was ill-tempered and taciturn, and Seriema herself had left the safety of the fortress without a word to him, taking ridiculous risks with her own life.

I used to be important to her. She used to depend on me for so many little things, and now she has no time for me – but no wonder she turned to someone else. I've had no time for her. I've been wasting it on that ungrateful little slut by the fire.

Presvel buried his face in his hands. In his heart of hearts, he knew he was being irrational and unfair. When he had first brought Rochalla into Seriema's household, he had told himself that he could no longer expect her to be his whore, and had steeled himself for rejection and failure. He had warned himself to expect heartbreak, and had thought he had the courage to watch her take wing without him – but the reality had proved far worse than he had bargained for.

All that day, he had wanted to be alone with her, but it had seemed that she was deliberately avoiding him, and she had kept Annas with her all the time, as if to prevent him from speaking to her privately. Then tonight, after they had eaten, she had joined Scall by the fire. At first, Presvel had thought that this was simply another ploy to keep him at arm's length, but now, as he watched her whispering and laughing with that callow youth, a dark, ugly stain of jealousy spread throughout his heart.

How dare he?

How dare they?

As he looked on, the boy put a tentative arm around the girl's shoulders. Presvel saw her stiffen, and glance round at the unfamiliar touch. Surely now she would send the temeritous upstart packing? But after a few moments, he realised that she was actually permitting the little bastard to maul her.

Presvel couldn't bear to look any longer. Rising hastily, he hurried out of the room, tripping over outstretched legs and stepping on toes as he went. Once outside, he leaned against the cold stone wall, breathing hard and fast.

That does it. I won't let this happen. I'm going to deal with that little wretch, if it's the last thing I do.

He was still carrying the long sharp knife – he bore it all the time now. And there was one place he could be guaranteed to get the boy alone. Whatever else happened, the little rat was certain to visit the stables this evening, to check on that precious horse of his. Assuring himself that he only meant to scare Scall off, Presvel headed downstairs to the stables, fingering the hilt of his knife.

*　　*　　*

Dark bounced up and down on the well-stuffed mattress, and ran an appreciative hand over the luxuriant bearskins that covered the bed. 'This is the life,' he said. 'I wish we didn't have to leave so soon.' He hesitated. 'You know, I still feel guilty about deserting Arcan when he's treating us so well.'

Grim turned away from the window, where he had spent the last ten minutes scowling out into the darkness. 'Oh, grow up, Dark. Do you think that Arcan put us in the chambers next to his own out of the kindness of his heart?' he barked. 'He treats us with such deference because he's nothing more than a superstitious primitive, and he's afraid to do anything else.'

And you're feeling as guilty as I am, Grim. That's why you're so peevish.

Dark kept his thoughts to himself. When his master was in this mood, silence was definitely the best policy. While Grim brooded at the window, he checked the packs again. They were taking very little with them: some food, a blanket each and one for Scall, a spare cloak, warm jerkin, and gloves for the boy, plus a rope to tie him in case he should get difficult, one or two precious oddments that were small and light. With a wrench, Dark thought of all the precious books and scrolls they were being forced to leave behind them in the Summoners' tower; all the clothing and the personal items that could never be replaced.

I wonder if we'll ever come back?

Like the man said, grow up, Dark.

I'm scared.

The younger Summoner hoped the results of this venture would be worth the risks – but he had to admit that the prospects were exciting, as well as frightening. While they settled into this chamber, waiting for dusk to fall, Grim had told his astonished assistant a little about the Shadowleague, and Gendival; the reality beyond the Curtain Walls and the peril the world now faced. Dark was still trying to take it all in. He was beset with a sense of unreality. He was finding it impossible to imagine that soon he and Grim would be escaping in the night, and heading for a place of strange powers and outlandish creatures.

And I'm going to be a part of it! No more skulking in a mask, a freak who is feared and hated. Finally, I'll be able to develop my mind properly, and use my abilities to do some good.

At last, Grim turned away from his contemplation of the night. 'It's time to go,' he said. 'I'll meet you down in the stable, as we planned.' Putting on his skull mask and picking up both packs, he left the room. With the door opened a mere chink, Dark peered through the crack and watched him go down the passageway. Around him there was a shimmer in the air – a faint distortion that only the trained eye of Summoner could see. When Grim passed the sentries at Arcan's door, they did not move, or blink, or show any sign that they had seen him at all. Cloaked in illusion, Grim faded past them, unseen.

I wish I could do that.

Though Dark understood the basic techniques of glamourie, he did not, as yet, have the skill to sustain an illusion for long. Fortunately, it would not be necessary tonight. He returned to the fire, soaking up all the heat he could get, while he could still get it. It would take a little time for Grim to get into position. While he waited, Dark ran through the previous hours in his mind, trying to think of anything they might have missed. Grim's little creatures (when *would* he explain them to his apprentice?) had been sent on ahead to wherever the Summoners were going. Their livestock had all been brought up to the fortress and, though Arcan would not allow Izobia and little Lannol to lodge in the luxurious guest chambers near his own, she had been settled in the crowded but lively rooms that housed the clan's widows and orphans. To Dark's relief, Damaeva, the chieftain's lifemate, had taken the girl under her generous wing to make sure that she was not bullied or ostracised by the others. No matter how angry Arcan might be when he discovered that his Summoners had fled, kind-hearted Damaeva would not let him take his wrath out on Izobia – and despite all his brag and bluster, the Chieftain knew better than to cross his diminutive partner who, when roused, could prove to be a formidable adversary indeed.

So that was it. Everything had been settled, and it was time to go. Dark straightened up from the fire and, with a last regretful look at the cosy room, he went to the door. Following a habit as ingrained as breathing, he paused there to don his skull mask, and as he did so, he noticed that the stitching round the buckle had become frayed, and the fastening was hanging by a thread. For a couple of days now, he had been meaning to repair it, but the news of the invaders and the chaos of packing up and moving to the stronghold had meant that he'd just never had the time. Oh, well. There would be no chance to do anything with it now, and it had held out so far. It only had to last a little while longer and then, he hoped, it wouldn't ever be needed again. The Shadowleague, according to his mentor, had no need of such artificial props. With a lot more care than usual, he fastened the mask into place, and left the room.

Unlike Grim, the Summoner had no need for stealth. He stepped out boldly into the stone-flagged passageway, acknowledging the respectful salutes of the sentries as he passed the door to Arcan's chambers.

It's a good thing this mask hides my face. At least I don't have to worry about looking nervous.

Earlier, when Scall had visited the Summoners, Dark had asked the boy whereabouts in the stronghold he was sleeping. He made his way there now, moving quickly through shadowy, draughty corridors that were almost deserted. At this time of night, most folk gathered together in the great hall of the stronghold, firstly to eat, and afterwards to while away the long, dark evening with flirting, gossip, gambling, and song. With so much going on elsewhere, there was only a slender hope that Dark would find Scall in his cramped, cold room he shared with several others, but since it was on his way, he poked his nose in for a quick look. No such luck. The room, strewn with the clutter of eight untidy young men, was empty.

Pity. Had I found him here, it would have made life so much easier.

Shrugging, he made his way down to the great hall and stood in the doorway, scanning the crowded chamber. The place looked cosy and welcoming, with its two great fireplaces throwing out both warmth and a welcome blaze of light, to supplement the great tallow candles which burned in sconces round the walls. Someone was playing a harp in a corner. By one of the fireplaces, a group of warriors were blocking most of the heat, playing dice on the hearth-stones. By the other, a storyteller had gathered a rapt group around him, and Dark saw Scall, sitting with the small child and the pretty young girl with whom he had arrived.

Drat! Now what? Under the circumstances, whatever I suggest won't be enough to tempt him away from that charming creature.

He lingered for a time in the doorway, unsure of the best way to proceed, but luck was with him. The storyteller ended his tale, and Scall's friend bent down to whisper something to the drowsy child in her lap. Motioning for Scall to stay where he was, she set the little one down carefully and stood up, then, taking the child by the hand, she led her out. When she passed him, Dark heard her say, 'I know you want to hear another one Annas, but it's past your bedtime. Come on, let's find your dad and say goodnight. You can hear another story tomorrow.'

As soon as she was gone, Dark entered the great hall, knowing better than to try to slip in unobtrusively. The gleaming, death's head mask was enough to cause a stir wherever he went.

Honestly! You'd think the idiots would be used to seeing it by now!

Scall's eyes widened with surprise to see him, at least they held nothing more than a healthy respect. It made a nice change from the usual fear. Dark beckoned the lad away from the fire and led him out of the room.

'Good evening, Sir.' Scall sounded a little puzzled. 'Did you settle in all right? Did you find out anything more about those objects I discovered?'

'We didn't have time.' The lie came with difficulty to the Summoner's lips. 'My mentor is looking at them now, so I came out to let him have some peace and quiet. I remembered you mentioning your lovely horse, so I thought that, if you aren't busy, now might be a good time for you to show her to me.'

The young lad's face lit up. 'Of course, Sir. I would love to.'

'You don't need to keep calling me Sir, Scall. Dark is fine.'

'Yes Sir . . . Dark.' Chattering enthusiastically about his mare, Scall led the way downstairs, using the cramped little back staircase, which was nearest. Dark followed, gnawed by guilt.

The back staircase down to the beast quarters was a tight, narrow spiral of hewn stone, lit by sconces set at intervals in the curving wall. It was cold and dank, with a whistling draught, and there was barely enough space for two people to walk side by side. The Summoner let Scall go ahead of him, so that if they met anyone ascending, there would be room for them to pass.

And at least I don't have to look that poor lad in the eye.

Halfway down the stairs, it happened. Dark felt the skull mask slip as the broken buckle finally gave way. 'Damn.' He grabbed at the falling mask, catching it just before it hit the hard stone steps and shattered the delicate bone. Had the staircase been straight, he would have overbalanced and fallen to the bottom, but as he lurched forward, he managed to catch himself against the curving wall.

'Dark, are you all right?' Scall reappeared from below, and Dark heard him gasp as he saw the maskless Summoner.

Well, what does it matter if he sees my face? He'll be seeing enough of it when we take him out of here to Gendival. All the same, I had better keep the mask on for a little longer. It wouldn't be too likely that we'd meet anyone else in the beast quarters at this hour, but it would just be our luck, and a maskless Summoner would create just too much interest.

Dark shrugged. 'I'm fine,' he said. 'This wretched thing broke, that's all.' He held up the mask with the dangling buckle. 'Why don't you go on ahead, and I'll be with you as soon as I've fixed it.'

'All right.' With one last, curious look at the Summoner's uncovered face, Scall turned and went on down the stairs.

Following the lad as far as the next sconce, Dark paused underneath it, and fiddled with the broken fastening of his mask. It proved a lot more awkward than he'd expected, and he muttered and cursed, glad that he would soon be rid of the accursed thing for good. Finally he was saved by a length of twine he found in his pocket, left over from tying up the boxes of books he'd packed that afternoon. With its help, he managed to fasten the mask precariously to his face, and hoped that it would last long enough to see him through.

Soon it won't matter any more. But in the meantime, I hope I don't run into anyone. A Summoner can hardly inspire awe and terror if his mask is held on with a bit of string.

Dark hurried on his way, aware that his mentor would be wondering what had become of him. Coming out into the warm darkness of the beast quarters, Dark took one of the carefully shielded candle lanterns from the shelf at the bottom of the stairs, and lit it at the final sconce. Arcan's prohibition of candles and torches down here would stand the Summoners in good stead. Cloaked in illusion and hidden in the shadows, Grim would have had no difficulty concealing himself.

In the enclosed space, the moist air was thick with the smells of manure, and hay, and horse. Trying not to breathe too deeply, Dark picked his way fastidiously through the ranks of tethered horses, holding his lantern aloft and trying to keep the worst of the muck off his boots. As he passed along the rows, curious heads, their ears pricked, turned to watch him, and the lamplight glowed eerily in one pair of eyes after another. Spotting the faint glow of a lantern in the far corner, the Summoner headed towards it. He was only halfway there when the commotion broke out.

It seemed to Presvel that he had been hiding for ages down here in the beast quarters, waiting for that wretch of a boy to turn up. However, the heat of so many animals made the place comfortable at least, if not fragrant, and the long wait had given him plenty of time to dwell on ways to terrify the life out of Scall, so that the little rat would be too scared to go tattling to Tormon, but would stay away from Rochalla in future. Without her new suitor in the picture, surely she would come to her senses, and choose the right man. In the darkness, he fingered his knife. When Scall saw this, he would know that he was dealing with someone who meant business.

Though the beast quarters were short of good places to hide, there were large wooden barrels placed at intervals throughout the big chamber, to make it easier to water the horses and other livestock. Hidden by the darkness, Presvel crouched behind the cask that stood nearest to the chestnut mare, waiting, waiting. Once he thought he heard the sound of soft footsteps, and someone moving about at the far end of the vast room, but there was no glow of lamplight from beyond the barrel, and no greeting for the little mare who was tethered nearby. Since Scall had talked to the blasted creature most of the way from Tiarond, it hardly seemed likely that he would tend it in silence now.

As time passed, Presvel began to doubt. Maybe the boy wasn't coming after all. Maybe – Myrial curse his name! – he was with Rochalla, instead, pawing her and slobbering over her, and much too preoccupied to think about horses. Presvel, tasting black bile at the thought, leapt to his feet, but as he did so, he caught sight of a glimmer of lantern light, working its way towards him. Quickly he ducked back down behind his barrel. Could this be Scall? Surely it must be! Sure enough, there was the little idiot, calling out to the horse as if it were a person who could understand. Presvel waited until the boy had hung his lantern carefully on the iron hook which had been set for it above the manger. He didn't want to risk it being dropped or kicked over in a scuffle. Being burned alive was definitely not part of his plans.

Wait, wait. There's plenty of time. Don't rush in and scare the horse – there's no point in being kicked to death. He's sure to give the stupid animal some water, and that's the time to strike.

It couldn't have worked out better. Whistling, Scall approached the barrel, swinging a bucket by its handle – and Presvel struck. Leaping out from his hiding place, he took the boy completely by surprise, knocking him to the ground and holding him down with a knee in his back. While he had been hiding, he'd found a dirty rag lying on top of the barrel, and now he wadded this into Scall's mouth, making him choke and splutter. The next moment his knife was at his captive's throat. 'Now,' he hissed. 'I'm going to tell you exactly what will happen to you if you don't leave Rochalla alone.'

Before he could continue, a voice came from behind him. 'What do you think you're doing? Let that boy go!' A figure loomed out of the shadows, cloaked in darkness, its face a grinning skull. Arcan's Summoner had found him! Panicked, he leapt to his feet and turned to run, all in one movement, forgetting the knife clenched in his hand. Tangling his feet in Scall's recumbent form, he tripped and fell headlong, colliding with the masked figure. There was a grunt of pain, he felt the knife wrench in his fist, and a gush of warm wetness across his hand. Then the black-robed figure crumpled, and lay still.

'No!' Presvel shrieked. Throwing down the knife, he bolted towards the main stairs, and as he ran, he heard Scall's voice yelling 'Dark! Dark!'

The Summoner ran up in time to see a figure rush off into the shadows, but he paid it little heed. All his attention was riveted on the crumpled form that lay, unmoving, at his feet and, unable to speak for the terror that assailed him, he sank to his knees beside it. Scall was already bending over it, muttering, 'Oh no, oh no, oh no, please, no . . .' Together they rolled the still body gently onto its back, and Scall stifled a sob. 'Oh, Dark, I'm sorry . . .'

'It wasn't your fault.' With shaking hands, the Summoner removed the mask from his companion's waxen face, and felt for a pulse beneath the jaw. 'Grim? Grim? Can you hear me?' He tore away his own mask, his face wet with tears.

Scall gasped. 'I thought it was you!'

Dark wasn't listening. 'Hush,' he said urgently, putting his face down close to the old man's lips.

'Listen, my boy.' Grim's voice was reedy and faint. 'You must go on as we planned. Take Scall and the artefacts to Amaurn in Gendival. Tell him it's my dying wish that you become a Loremaster . . .'

'No!' Dark was shaking with anguish. He couldn't imagine a world without his mentor.

'There's no time for that!' Suddenly, Grim's voice was an echo of its old waspish self. 'Listen carefully, Dark. I must tell you how to pass the Curtain Walls.' He pulled Dark's head down, whispering urgent instructions in his ear then, exhausted by the effort, he fell back, his head lolling limply against the younger Summoner's arm. 'Tell Amaurn good luck.' The words were fainter now. 'And Dark . . . You were the son I never had. I'm proud of you, my boy.'

'Farewell, Grim. Thank you for everything.' Dark bowed his head, weeping – and then felt a gnarled old hand clutch his arm. Grim's eyes had opened once more. '*Will* you stop that? You're running out of time.' His face creased in a twisted smile. 'You can do this. I have every confidence in you.' Then suddenly his body was limp and heavy, and Dark felt his spirit pass away. Blinded with tears, he laid his mentor gently down, and straightened the bloodstained black robes. There was no time to mourn, however. Grim had given him his last instructions, and they must be obeyed. For an instant, Dark felt himself quailing from the responsibility.

How can I do this alone? How can I dodge Arcan's patrols, get through the Curtain Walls, and find this Gendival place without Grim to help me? He's always been there, a solid rock in my life, but I never realised how much I truly needed him until now, when it's too late.

But he had faith in me. Every confidence, he said. Grim, I promise I won't let you down.

Scall was sitting back on his heels, his eyes dark and wide. Dark saw that he was shaking all over. 'I thought it was you,' he whispered.

Dark wanted to ask him who had done this dreadful thing, but Grim had been right – there was no time to delay, and no time to be subtle, either. Holding Scall's eyes with his own, he reached out and touched the boy's forehead, sinking into his mind, much as he had done with the child whose Passing he had accomplished. This time, however, it was not physical control he was seeking, but control of the will. It was a cruel and frightening thing to do to Scall, and he was sorry it must be so, but it could not be helped. The skirmish was brief and ugly. Scall fought back, clumsily, but with a ferocity born of desperation. What chance did he have, though, against a man with the training, abilities, and intellect of a Summoner? Dark wrestled the boy's will into a corner of his mind and penned it there, while he himself took control.

After a moment Scall's eyes lost their animation, though they still held the shadow of that dreadful look of fear. Dark leaned back against the water barrel and took a long, shaky breath. 'I'm sorry about this, Scall,' he said. 'Get your horse ready quickly. We have to go.'

Dark found his own horse, a dark, dappled grey, beside Grim's white beast. Both were tacked up and ready to go, with the Summoners' packs and Scall's bulky bundle fastened behind the saddles. Quickly he mounted then, on an impulse, he leaned over and untied Grim's mount. Forced to go on alone, and desperately unsure of himself, he needed to take with him something belonging to his mentor.

He returned to Scall, and found him already mounted on the restive chestnut mare. 'Follow me, and keep quiet,' he ordered, re-inforcing the command with all the power of his will. He would have liked to promise the boy that he would be safely returned to his friends, but Grim had not had time to confide the Shadow-league's plans for him.

I don't even know what their plans will be for me! It's all very well for Grim to blithely talk about them making me one of their own, but what if they don't want to?

With Dark leading the spare horse, they moved out, threading their way between the ranks of tethered animals. As he passed, the Summoner couldn't bear not to take one last look at Grim's body. It tore the heart out of him – but it also filled him with a cold resolve.

I won't fail you, Grim – and I'll hold your memory in my heart for as long as I live.

Though Arcan saw no point in wasting men to guard the inside of his beast quarters, outside was a different matter. The strong-hold's inner courtyard was well-guarded, as was the outer gate. Dark remembered Grim walking out of their room in front of

Arcan's guards, cloaked in the illusion that no one was there. He knew that he lacked the skill of his mentor at glamourie, yet now he was not only going to have to shield himself for the length of time it would take to get across the courtyard and out of the main gate, but accomplish this miracle for two people and three horses – and, on top of all that, to retain his control of Scall.

Grim, wherever you are now, I hope you're watching over me.

Dark extinguished the lantern, and opened the door of the beast quarters a cautious crack. As he peered through, an icy wind blasted into his face, almost taking the skin off – or so it felt – and threatening to pull the door out of his hand. The wind was getting wilder all the time, and the sleet had turned to hail, yet the wild weather was a lot more providential than it might first appear. Though the storm would make travelling a nightmare, at least it would mask any noise he might make during his escape. Biting his lip in concentration, the Summoner prepared his cloak of glamourie, surrounding himself, Scall and the horses with a shimmering nimbus that would seem, from the outside, to be nothing but shadows and swirling, wind-driven hail. At least, he hoped it would. Pushing the door open, he sent Scall through ahead of him, and followed with his own horse and the spare.

The strain of maintaining the illusion was tremendous. His head and clenched jaws ached from all the concentration, and he was trembling from the strain. It was as though the shield was draining the energy from his body, in order to feed itself. Dark knew he couldn't keep it up for very long. Instead of creeping cautiously around the sides of the courtyard, as he had originally intended, he struck out boldly across the centre, keeping Scall on his right-hand side and Grim's white horse on his left. The closer they could stay together, the easier it would be for him, as it would make for less of an area to shield. As he had hoped, the guards were all huddling under shelter, and he was able to cross the courtyard unmolested. *Unfortunately*, they had decided to shelter from the weather beneath the deep arch of the entrance gate, and were blocking his way out.

Damn! Now what?

Then suddenly, he remembered what Grim had taught him. *'Sometimes, you scarcely need to cloak yourself at all. If you can manage to divert people's attention elsewhere, it's amazing what they won't see.'*

Thinking with feverish speed, Dark pulled Scall and the horses close to the courtyard wall on the right-hand side of the archway then, concentrating until his brain felt as though it would burst from the strain, he directed energy from his mind into a wooden cart which had been left near the door of the beast quarters, altering its underlying structure, to heat the wood from within. It wasn't easy. The wood was wet and cold, and Dark could spare only a fraction of his attention from maintaining his shield and restraining Scall. Doubt began to gnaw at him. Would he be able to create his diversion before he lost control of the lot?

Without warning, the cart burst into flames – a beacon that burned brightly despite the wind and hail. Shouts and curses sounded from the archway, and the guards came pouring out, pelting across the yard to put out the roaring blaze. Dark reacted instantly, pushing Scall ahead of him through the arch, and dragging Grim's horse along behind. He had minutes, at most, to get out of there, before they put out the fire and returned. The bar of the gate was heavy; normally it took two men to lift it. The Summoner cursed and struggled and, bolstered by the fear that jolted like cold fire through his body, somehow he found the strength. The bar grated loose from its socket, and with a relief that was almost bliss, he dropped it with a clatter that was magnified by the echoing archway and could be heard quite clearly above the wailing of the storm. There were shouts from the courtyard behind him and the sound of running feet – and then Dark realised that he had lost control of his shield.

'Go!' He gave Scall's horse a whack in the rump and the little chestnut bolted off into the night with the Summoner following, his stockier horses labouring to keep up with the fleet-footed mare.

It'll take them a while to get mounted, and hopefully they'll never find us in this dreadful storm.

In spite of his exhaustion, jagged nerves, and the sorrow that beset him, Dark laughed aloud. He had done the impossible! He had escaped from Arcan's fortress, right under the noses of the guards! Then, to his dismay, he realised that he had only accomplished the first step on a long, hard road. The laughter died on his lips as he considered his prospects of success. He had to keep Scall under control, dodge the patrols, and survive this beast of a storm. *Then,* if he accomplished all that, he had to find his way to the Curtain Walls and the valley Grim had described to him and manage, somehow, to pass through the energy barrier. After that, it would simply be a case of finding his way through an unknown landscape to a place he'd never seen – and once he'd got there, persuading a bunch of total strangers to take him in.

Grim had every confidence in me – I only hope he was right.

Eleven

Esmeralda and the Magic Sheep

For most of the day, Tormon had been keeping to himself. Not because of his argument with Seriema – though that had not put him in the best of moods – but because, now that the searching and fighting and running had all come to an end, he was being forced to confront the death of his lifemate Kanella, and the unbearable notion of spending the rest of his life without her. If he survived the current peril – and survive it he must, for Annas's sake – the long years would stretch out ahead of him, bleak and lonely. How would he ever get through them? How could he manage to bring up a small daughter on his own? The frantic preparations of the rest of the fortress meant nothing to him. Disconsolate and sick at heart, he had kept to his chamber and mourned.

The sound of approaching footsteps in the passage outside, and the birdlike sound of his daughter's prattle, roused him at last from his dismal reverie. Wiping a hand across his wet eyes, he rose from the fireside just as Annas and Rochalla entered, hand in hand. 'Dad!' Letting go of Rochalla's hand, she flung herself on him. 'Where have you been all day? I missed you! Rochalla and me have been busy. We went for a walk, right up on the roof, but it was too cold up there, so we came down and helped the other children stack up the blocks of earth for the fires. Isn't it a funny idea, putting earth on the fire, instead of coal or wood? And we went to visit Rutska and Avrio, and I saved my breakfast apple for Esmeralda, and patted a sheep, and . . .'

'Whoa!' Tormon hugged his little girl. 'Slow down.' Over the top of her head, he looked at Rochalla with gratitude. While he had been feeling sorry for himself, she had been doing his job for him, entertaining Annas and making sure that the child had no time to feel as miserable as he himself had been.

Rochalla perched herself on a low wooden stool, close to the fire. 'If Arcan doesn't need you for anything tomorrow, you should come with us,' she said. Her voice and manner betrayed her concern and Tormon clearly heard the additional words that she didn't speak aloud: *It's not good for you to brood alone for too long.* He blessed her for not saying them.

'Oh, yes, Dad, please do!' Annas took up the idea with alacrity. 'We've been listening to the storyteller tonight, and he's really good, you would have liked him, but we can hear him tomorrow, and play with Scall, and I'll show you my sheep – it has a black face – and . . .'

'You know,' laughed Rochalla, 'I sometimes think you must breathe through your ears.'

With a giggle, Annas clapped both hands over her ears. 'No I don't. That's silly!'

'Well, when you talk so much, I don't know when you have time to take a breath.' Rochalla smiled at the little girl.

'Maybe she has gills like a fish,' proposed Tormon.

'I do *not*!' his daughter protested.

'Well, however you breathe, it's time you were getting into bed,' Tormon said.

Since there were a large number of children running round the settlement and stronghold, it had been easy to obtain some hand-me-down clothing and nightdresses for Annas. As soon as she was in bed, she asked the inevitable question. 'Dad, will you tell me a story?'

'All right. Which story would you like?'

'Tell me some more about Esmeralda and the magic sheep.'

'*What?*'

'Rochalla told me a story about them today,' Annas said happily. 'The sheep I patted was a magic sheep, and it went off with

Esmeralda to find some treasure, and bring it back for you and me.'

Tormon looked helplessly at Rochalla.

'I'll tell you what,' the blonde girl said quickly, 'you pick another story for tonight, and I'll tell you more about Esmeralda and her friend tomorrow.'

'You promise?'

'I promise.'

'Oh, all right then. Can I have the one about the Cat and the Moon instead, Dad?'

Again, Tormon felt the knife-twist of grief in his heart. Kanella had made up the story of the Cat and the Moon for Annas some time ago, and it had been her favourite ever since. He had a sudden picture in his mind, bright and vivid as a jewel, of the cosy interior of the brightly painted wagon which, until a few days ago, had been a happy family home. Annas was in the recessed bunk, her big eyes peeping over the edge of the blue and white woollen blanket, while Kanella sat beside her on a pile of sheepskins, her face rapt and smiling in the lamplight as she spun her tale.

Rochalla leaned down to kiss Annas goodnight, and the vision shattered like crystal, leaving only the gaping void of a loss so deep that for a moment, it robbed him of breath. As she passed Tormon to go out, she put a sympathetic hand on his shoulder. 'If you get on with your story,' she said, 'I'll go down and get some food for you. I'll wager you haven't eaten all day.' Then she was gone, calling out a last goodnight to Annas as she closed the door.

The little girl smiled sleepily. 'I like Rochalla,' she said. 'But Dad . . . When is Mama coming back?'

Tormon froze. He kept forgetting how different the world looked from the viewpoint of a five-year-old. It was impossible for someone who had lived such a short time to truly comprehend that death was both immutable and irrevocable. And what could he tell her? How could he explain? He took hold of her hand. 'Annas,' he said softly, 'you've got to accept that you won't be seeing your Mama for a long, long time – not until you're an old, old lady, and you can follow where she's gone.'

I can't tell her she'll never see her mother again, but maybe this way will soften the blow just a little. And after all, I hope with all my heart it's true. If we do continue after we die, then one day we will see Kanella once more.

The child's lip trembled. 'But I miss her. I don't want to wait a long, long time.'

With tears in his own eyes, Tormon enfolded her in a hug. 'Nor do I, love. Nor do I. But we don't have any choice.'

All the way through her favourite story, Annas was very subdued, and the trader was relieved when she fell asleep before the tale was done. Bless Rochalla for keeping her so busy all day! Even as he thought of the slender, fair-haired girl, the door flew open, and she came rushing through, grabbing frantically at his arm. 'Tormon,' she cried. 'You've got to come!'

'Sssh.' Gesturing at the sleeping Annas, he pulled her out of the room and closed the door behind him. 'Now, lass – what's wrong?'

Rochalla had obviously run all the way upstairs, and she could only breathe in gasps. 'Somebody killed Arcan's Summoner . . . They found his body in the beast quarters . . . And Scall is missing – his horse is gone . . .'

Horror gripped Tormon like a choking hand around his throat. 'Look after Annas,' he ordered. 'Don't leave her.' With that he was gone, charging headlong down the stairs. What in the name of perdition had become of Scall? In the last few days, he had grown as dear to Tormon as his own son. He had to find him quickly. Whatever had happened to the boy, it was certain to be bad, bad trouble.

Cetain had told Seriema that she looked as though she belonged out on the moors in the wind and storm, but it didn't take her long to decide that the man must be an idiot. *No one* should have to belong out here, in such filthy weather! At nightfall, the sleet turned to hail, and the warm glow of belonging with which Cetain's daft words had originally filled her were no protection whatsoever against falling chunks of ice. And it had been so sudden, without any gradual change: suddenly, or so it seemed to Seriema, the cold, wet flakes had turned into hard icy pellets which came hissing through the air and smashed against her unprotected skin with stinging force. Quickly she pulled up her sodden hood again, feeling it cold and clammy on her wet hair, and tucked her head down to protect her face.

The wind was wailing on a new pitch now; it sounded just like the ghastly cries of the winged fiends as they hunted. Seriema felt a chill run through her that had nothing to do with the weather. It couldn't be, could it? Surely they wouldn't have spread out here from Tiarond quite so fast. Would they? But what was to stop them? They could move very fast when they wanted to, and there was precious little prey to delay them between the city and the moors.

With an effort, Seriema took herself firmly in hand.

Will you stop this childishness! It's just the wind, and your own imagination. Right now you have enough problems, without inventing non-existent terrors in the night.

As the clouds came down even lower, the darkness deepened further, until soon the night was black as the inside of a glove. Until now, Seriema had been able to discern her pale, cold hands as they gripped the reins and, to her right, the moving, shadowy shape that was Cetain's horse. As long as she could see that, there had been no chance she that she would get lost, but now, to her utter horror, she realised that she was riding blind. Panic gripped her. Frantically, she shouted for Cetain, yelling at the top of her voice to be heard above the storm. In less than a moment, he was at her side. 'Seriema! Are you all right?'

'I can't see!' She couldn't keep the tremor out of her voice.

'Ach,' the Reiver said ruefully, 'I was forgetting you'd got town-bred eyes. We've been running around on these moors in the dark all our lives, and we've learned to find our way around, even on the blackest night.' Unhooking a coil of rope from the pommel of his saddle, he measured off about a yard, and fastened the end to her bridle. Even Seriema could see the pale glimmer of his smile in the dark. 'There. That should stop you running away from me.'

For an instant, Seriema's pride reared up. The humiliation, to be led about on a tether like a child!

Don't be stupid. Would you rather be lost in this shelterless place on a night like this?

When she looked at things that way, the piece of rope suddenly became the most comforting thing in the whole world.

Now that she didn't even have to worry about where she was going, Seriema let herself sink into a miserable daze as she rode along, feeling grateful for the deep hood that hid her expression from Cetain, and saved her from having to put on a valiant face. The shrieking wind seemed to be growing louder, with a discordant, keening note that set her teeth on edge. The hail seemed to be hitting her shoulders with increasing force; hard enough, she realised, to leave small bruises. She gritted her teeth, and endured.

After all I've been through these last few days, I can surely put up with a bit of weather.

After a time, she felt a tapping on her shoulder, gentle at first, then harder. She lifted the dripping brim of her hood to hear better, and looked in what she assumed was the direction of Cetain. 'If these hailstones get much bigger, someone will be hurt,' he shouted. 'We must take shelter.'

'Where?' Seriema yelled.

'If we haven't lost ourselves in the storm, there's an old, half-ruined tower not far from here. We can shelter in the cellars underneath.' She felt him tug on the rope that bound them together, then they were off again.

A whole cellar! A wonderful, cosy cellar with walls, and a roof. I hope it's not too far away.

In the meantime, she pulled her hood back over her face, and retreated into her own little world.

Warm sunshine, hot baths, tea and toast beside a blazing fire . . . Seriema was deep in a daydream of these happy things when the dreadful scream of a dying man tore through the darkness. Terror went through her like a spear of ice. She knew at once that this was no Reiver ambush, and that her earlier fears had not been due to an overactive imagination. It was them. Dear Myrial, it was *them*.

She heard Cetain curse, and turn back as if to fight. 'No!' she yelled. Taking a twist of her lead rope around her hand, she pulled back with all her strength. Cetain was fighting her, pulling so hard on the rope that it crushed her hand. 'Let go!'

'Run, you fool!' Seriema shrieked. 'Tell your men to run. You can't fight these fiends. Get to the tower – it's our only chance.'

For a split second Cetain hesitated, and another shriek ripped through the night as a warrior was struck down. The Reivers were milling about in confusion, unused to this deadly attack from the air and unable to see their enemy clearly in the dark and storm. 'Come on,' Seriema roared. 'To the tower!'

She made as if to ride off, but Cetain hauled her back. 'It's this way,' he yelled, and pulled her after him in a different direction. 'Follow me, Reivers! Retreat!'

It was a desperate race against foes who were stronger, faster, and more deadly. Once Seriema was almost knocked from her horse by a blow from a great, black, leathery wing. Twice there were further shrieks as the predators plucked a warrior from his saddle, but each time someone was lost, Seriema knew that a number of the creatures would break off the attack to feed.

Thank Myrial it wasn't me.

It was impossible to keep the shameful thought from her mind.

The fleeing humans were aided by the storm, which tended to confuse the aim of the airborne creatures, and buffet them off course. Also, the horses were so terrified of this strange and fearsome threat that they discovered an incredible new turn of speed. Seriema's heart was in her mouth as they hurtled across the rough moorland, terrified that her mount would catch its foot in a hummock or rabbit hole and fall, taking them both to their deaths, but the little horses were surefooted and familiar with this terrain and, so far, every one of them was managing to keep on their feet. All the time, a litany of terror was pounding through Seriema's head.

Not again, not again – oh, sweet Myrial, not again . . .

It had been so hard to escape the terrors of Tiarond, and the journey to the Reiver stronghold had been arduous, but once she had arrived there, she had felt safe for the first time since the night of the Great Sacrifice. It was too cruel that her respite had been so brief, and now that those hideous creatures were loose in the world, nowhere in Callisiora would be safe again.

Without warning, Seriema's horse plunged to such an abrupt halt that she almost went straight over its head. Above the screaming of the wind, she heard Cetain's shout. 'Here it is! Duck, Seriema!' Then they were moving again, the horses jostling and barging into a narrow opening in their haste to get away from the horrifying creatures that pursued them. Seriema, bent double with her face pressed into the soaking mane of her mount, banged her knee hard on something that could only have been the edge of a doorway, and then there was a loud clatter of hooves on stone, echoing hollowly in a confined space. Other warriors, crowding from behind, were pushing her forward and, groping for the trailing rope, she realised that she had lost Cetain in the crush. The only sensible thing to do was to keep low to avoid banging her head on the ceiling, and stay on her horse, to avoid being trampled underfoot.

Someone lit a torch, revealing a confused melee of horses with laid-back ears, tossing manes and rolling, white-rimmed eyes. Some of the riders were sporting tattered cloaks, and several of them had torn backs and shoulders, with blood glinting in the smoky light. Behind Seriema, a long ramp led up to a heavy wooden door in a deep, arched doorway, and she could see Cetain and a handful of others, off their horses, and trying to bar and wedge this only defence between the Reivers and the fiends outside.

A hand touched her arm, making her jump violently. 'Through here, lass. Let's clear ourselves a bit of space.' A grizzled, scar-faced Reiver was gesturing towards another arch behind him, and Seriema realised that this must only be a sort of anteroom to the cellar proper. One by one, the shaken warriors were dismounting and leading their horses through, and she was just about to do the same, when she heard Cetain calling her name from the top of the ramp.

'Seriema – will you come up here?'

She could hear the fiends quite clearly, scratching and battering on the other side of the door, and there was no way she wanted to get any closer, but now that she had started with this business of appearing brave and tough, there was no going back. Handing her reins to the veteran, she slid to the ground, and set off up the ramp. Cetain, when she reached him, was pale and wild-eyed, but when he spoke his voice was calm. 'It's them, isn't it?'

Seriema nodded. 'I'm sorry. I never thought they'd get here so soon.'

Cetain took hold of her cold hands. 'Don't fret, Seriema. If it hadn't been for you and your friends, we would have had no chance to prepare. Now, at least, we have food and fuel stored, the beasts under cover, and Arcan's folk all safe up in the fortress. Is there anything you can tell me about these fell creatures, that might help us tonight?'

'You're welcome to what little I know, but the reason we got out of Tiarond in one piece is that we didn't wait around to find out more about them. They're fast, ferocious, and deadly, and once they have their sights fixed on their prey, they don't give up easily. They're very strong and tough – one burst right in through a window pane in my house, without sustaining much damage. They have sharp and powerful claws, so we'd better hope that's a damn sturdy door.'

'Don't worry, lass, it's good, thick, solid timber. These towers were all built for defence. A door that an enemy could get through with a couple of axe blows wouldn't be much use out here.'

'Let's hope you're right,' Seriema said. 'Because they don't show any signs of going anywhere, and daybreak is a long way off. Tormon thinks they must hunt by night, but we don't know for sure. Hopefully, we should be able to ride out of here in the morning, but . . .'

'Someone will have to go out there first, and test whether it's safe,' Cetain finished for her. He swore bitterly, while behind him, the creatures screeched and battered the door in a renewed onslaught. 'Well, so much for warning the other clans. There's going to be a bloodbath – and while there are a lot of folk whose loss I won't regret, this disaster will weaken the Reivers to the point where the Hierarch and the accursed merchants will just be able to pick us off one by one.'

'If there *is* a Hierarch,' Seriema said. 'You're forgetting what happened to Tiarond. And as far as I know, I'm the last of the accursed merchants, and I'm hardly in a position to pick anybody off.'

Cetain rubbed a weary hand across his face. 'You know, until tonight, I don't think I ever understood the true horror of this invasion – nor the scale. How can such creatures be defeated?'

'I don't know.' After the long ride in the biting cold, Seriema found that her legs were shaking with fatigue. Something in her sagging posture must have conveyed her exhaustion to Cetain. 'Come on,' he said. 'You've done wonders for your first day's riding as a Reiver, but you've had enough now. Give me a moment to organise some guards for this door, and then we'll rest, and get something to eat.'

The inner chamber, a large, echoing room with a crudely carved vaulted ceiling, appeared to have been hollowed out from the rocky bones of the moor. One wall boasted a generous fireplace, in which someone had already kindled a fire. 'What on earth is a fireplace doing down here?' Seriema asked in surprise.

'This tower was built for defence, remember?' Cetain replied. 'We are far from the first folk who've sheltered down here, with the enemy hammering at our door.'

The horses had been taken back out and tethered in the anteroom with some hay and a small ration of grain. 'We keep a few supplies here in winter – firewood, fodder, that sort of thing,' Cetain explained. 'There are several of these towers scattered about on the moors, which don't belong to any one clan, but are there to shelter anyone who needs them. When the snows come, they always save lives. That's why all the clans respect their neutrality. Any one chieftain foolish enough to try to claim one would have all the other clans down on top of him faster than he could blink. Of course,' he added wryly, 'if it comes down to a raid or a fight, whoever can claim a tower first will often have a great advantage.'

'I can't tell you how glad I am that we've claimed this one,' Seriema said.

The warriors were settling in for the night, and this crisis had not found them unprepared. Whenever the Reivers rode out, each horse carried a blanket wrapped in a thin, oiled hide to keep it dry, a water bag, and a small pack of rations, and clearly they had done this many times before, for everyone was getting on, quietly and efficiently, with some allotted task. Along one of the side walls, some of them were spreading blankets. Others were close to the fire, laying out food, and a third group was in a corner, where the wounded were being tended. The scene was cosy in the firelight – almost domestic, had it not been for the fiends that were ravening outside.

Cetain found the chilled, wet Seriema a place beside the fire, and the men moved aside to make room for her. As she stretched out her hands towards the flames, steam began to rise gently from her clothing. Though it was impossible to disrobe in front of all these men and, in any case, she had nothing to change into, she began to hope that eventually she would dry out. One of the warriors handed her some food, and she took it gratefully. Oatcake and cheese had never tasted so good, even if what she really wanted most in the world at that moment was a nice, hot cup of tea.

Food and heat were making her drowsy, and soon she found herself beginning to nod. She turned to Cetain, who was talking quietly with his men. 'Where will I be sleeping?' There was a coarse laugh from one or two warriors, and for an instant, she felt a flicker of fear. The memory of her attacker flashed through her mind: the pain, the helplessness, the humiliation and terror, and for a moment she was assailed by doubt.

Was Tormon right? Was it a dreadful mistake to come out here with these wild barbarians?

Then Cetain looked around his men with a steely glare, and in the sudden silence that followed, she discovered her courage once more.

Remember who you are, Seriema. If you let yourself be cowed by this bunch of lecherous, foul-minded louts, you'll have lost any hope of gaining their respect.

Taking her cue from the chieftain's son, she lifted her chin and favoured the culprits with her most imperious look – the one that could intimidate even the Hierarch Zavahl. Now it was the turn of the men to drop their eyes and look away. She did not sustain it for any length of time – just long enough to make her point. She had enough sense to realise that she was only getting away with it because she had Cetain's protection.

He showed her to a quiet corner, not too far away from the fire, and handed her two blankets. 'Here you are, lass. You take mine, too. I'll be keeping watch up by the door, with my men.' He smiled at her. 'You won't have any more nonsense from the lads, I'll see to that. Don't worry – when I asked you to come out here I promised I'd take care of you, and I will.'

Seriema sighed. She was too old for fairy stories at bedtime. 'Look, Cetain – I appreciate your intervention with the warriors, but when it comes to those winged fiends, let's not fool ourselves. If they manage to get in here, you won't be able to save me, yourself, or any of your men.'

The warrior frowned. 'That may well be true. After all, you know these creatures far better than I do. But though it's best to be realistic, so we don't get any nasty surprises, hope is just as important if any of us are to get through these dreadful times.'

Seriema thought about that for a moment. After all, without hope she would never have escaped Tiarond. Without hope, they all might just as well roll over and die right now. She took a deep breath and straightened her spine. 'Cetain,' she said, 'you're absolutely right.'

Twelve

Fugitives

Packrat wasn't averse to stealing, or sneaking around in the dark, and normally he didn't have a problem with going where he was not allowed to go. This latest escapade, however, was quickly getting out of hand.

That Aliana! All those times she's been down on me for being where I shouldn't be, and taking things I shouldn't take – and now she goes and does a damn fool thing like this!

But she had welcomed him into the Grey Ghosts, and in all his time with them, she had never once let him down. Even though she seemed determined to give him the slip, he wasn't about to abandon her now, no matter how much trouble she was in.

He had seen her come back into the Basilica, for the simple reason that, Hierarch or no Hierarch, he had no intention of spending his days cleaning the privies, and had quietly faded out of there the first opportunity he got. He'd been lurking in the Temple itself, staying inconspicuous among the other crowds of refugees, when Aliana had gone into Kaita's sickroom with Galveron and the woman they had brought in. Packrat had stayed where he was, rather than intrude where he wasn't welcome. The last time he had tried to go in there, one of the healer's helpers had chased him out with a broom, calling him unhygienic – whatever that meant. Though he had not been especially aware that he was keeping one eye on the door, he had noticed when Aliana came out, and had immediately been aware that something wasn't right. Instead of coming over to look for her companions, she had slunk along the far wall of the Temple, and disappeared through the doorway that led down to the basement areas. Had it not been for her sneaky behaviour, he would simply have thought she was going to scrounge something to eat, but there was more to it than that, he was certain. Afire with curiosity, and not a little concerned, he had followed her downstairs.

When he saw Aliana talking to Telimon, he'd thought he had been wrong about her suspicious behaviour – until he saw her steal the extra food. He was dismayed and angry to see her pocketing the Temple rations, not because he had any moral objections to a bit of pilfering here and there, but because of the insane risks she was courting. How dared she put herself in danger like that, not to mention her unsuspecting friends! For the first time, he understood how she felt when *he* did this sort of thing – and it wasn't a very comfortable sensation.

Well, the damage had been done. The food had been stolen, and there was nothing he could do about it. But Packrat knew that Aliana wouldn't do such a stupid thing without a damn good reason, and when you added this latest exploit to her earlier sneaking around and avoiding her friends, it became more and more clear that she was definitely up to no good.

The leader of the Ghosts had been chatting to Telimon, the picture of innocence, while her pockets bulged with stolen food. Now she was taking her leave, so Packrat, almost absent-mindedly, swiped some cold sausage, some cheese, and a couple of griddle cakes. Wherever Aliana was going, he planned to tag along, and if she needed supplies, then so would he. He faded out of the room as unobtrusively as he had faded in, and looked around to see where she had gone.

When Aliana went back upstairs, Packrat was astonished. What was she playing at now? There was nowhere to hide up there! Surely the caverns down here offered a better choice of places? When he came back out into the Temple itself he thought, for a moment, that he had lost her in the huge, crowded chamber, with all its activity and noise. Then suddenly he spotted her again, slinking along the side of the mysterious – and valuable – silver filigree screen, that the Hierarch didn't want anyone going near. There was a guard at the entrance, but he didn't seem to be taking the job too seriously. He looked sleepy, inattentive, and bored out of his mind, and Packrat was pretty sure it would be possible to sneak up on Aliana without attracting any unwanted attention. Perhaps he could catch her up, and stop her before this craziness went any further? For a moment he was torn between the urge to protect her from her own idiocy, curiosity about what she was up to, and fear that he might get them both caught, with stolen food in their pockets, if he interfered.

While he was wrestling with his indecision, two small children broke out of a nearby refugee encampment and came chasing towards the heavy-eyed guard. The one in the lead tripped over the broken corner of a flagstone and tumbled down, wailing loudly. The guard ran forward to pick it up, at the same time as the child's young and pretty mother came darting across to rescue her offspring. Packrat, suddenly realising that he had taken his eyes off Aliana, looked back quickly – but she had vanished. Clearly, while everyone had been distracted, she had slipped behind the screen.

Well, two could play at that game. The guard was still helping the mother comfort the sobbing little boy – while getting in a bit of flirting, at the same time – so Packrat, after waiting a few minutes until the man was completely distracted, moved across to the screen, and ducked behind it. There was nothing in front of him but a narrow doorway, with nothing to be seen beyond that but utter blackness. Well, that was all right. He had been in plenty of unlit places in his time, and he'd never had any problems. Quickly, before the guard came back, he plunged into the darkness.

A hissing noise and a loud click from behind him made him spin round with an oath unspoken on his lips. The light from the doorway had vanished abruptly, as if to cut him off from the world he had known. He took a couple of hesitant steps forward, and his fingers encountered what felt like a smooth, featureless wall. The doorway had vanished completely, and though Grey Ghosts weren't scared of the dark – they wouldn't have survived very long in their business if they were – he was unnerved by the feeling of being shut in, and annoyed that he had been trapped when he was in a hurry to find Aliana.

Well, bugger this for a game of soldiers!

Packrat didn't know about the constraints under which the Hierarch must enter this sinister portal, and had he known, he wouldn't have cared. He groped in his pocket and found tinder, striker, flint and candle – standard equipment in his line of work – and made a light. To his surprise, the flaring flame reflected softly in walls made from a smooth, dark metal with a bluish tint. He was just about to examine it more closely when all at once, his stomach gave a lurch, and he felt as though he were falling, though the floor remained beneath his feet. He overbalanced, and dropped the candle, which immediately went out. Blackness, dyed with little afterimages of the candle flame in purple and green, surrounded him once more. Sticking out a cautious hand, he encountered the wall, and felt the heat of friction like a rope burn on his skin as the surface whipped upwards. He stayed where he was, flat on the floor, his heart racing, until a slight jolt told him that he had stopped moving.

'Myrial's teeth and bloody toenails!' Having tested the wall with a cautious hand to make sure that it was still now, Packrat began to crawl about on hands and knees, searching for the candle, which must have rolled away when he'd dropped it. That was the point at which he decided that this entire escapade was getting out of hand, and when he found that wretched Aliana, he would have words with her, and no mistake. He tried calling her name, but only dared do it softly, because he had no idea what else might be down here. There was no answer, which was about what he'd expected.

There was another click, and a hiss of moving air. Packrat still couldn't see, but he was willing to bet that the door had opened again. He had become totally disorientated in the darkness however, and since there was not even a glimmer of light beyond it to guide him, he had no idea where the exit lay.

They certainly don't want people to see what it looks like down here. I wonder what they've got to hide?

A moment later his searching fingers found the smooth, waxen surface of the candle, and he sighed with relief. He'd had about enough of the dark by now. His other senses were stretched to breaking point to compensate for his lack of vision and, frankly, so were his nerves. Things were decidedly weird down here, and if there were any threats around, he preferred to see them first. He lit the candle again with a slightly shaky hand, and got to his feet, spilling hot wax over his fingers.

He got out of the little, moving room very quickly, just in case it decided to do it again, but it was just as well for him that he didn't keep on going. An instant later, he found that he had run out of floor, and was teetering on the edge of a yawning black pit. With a lurid oath, Packrat sprang backwards. 'What sort of bloody stupid place *is* this?' he growled.

He was standing on a small, square platform, about three steps across in any direction, that extended out over the abyss. It seemed to be made from the same, smooth, dully gleaming blue-black metal of the moving room itself. A narrow metal bridge – a criminally ridiculous design about two feet wide, without a railing or hand-holds of any kind – sprang out across the chasm to another small platform, which seemed, most unnervingly, to be hanging in space without any visible means of support. Above it, again, seemingly suspended in the air, was a massive shape like a circle or hoop, balanced on its edge.

There was no sign whatsoever of Aliana. Packrat was reluctant to call out to her again. After all, who knew what might be lurking down here? Instead he made a careful inspection of the platform on which he stood but, as he had suspected, there was no way off it except back the way he had come, via the moving room, or across the chasm on the flimsy-looking bridge.

Typical!

The light from the candle didn't reach very far down into the dark well of the pit, and there was certainly no sign of the bottom. With a shrug, Packrat walked quickly and competently across the bridge. Second-storey work had never been his favourite form of theft, but he had done enough of it, especially in these hard times, to have developed excellent balance – at least when the floor stayed put. Once he'd reached the other side, he made a quick examination of the slender plinth that stood there, but as far as he could tell, it was neither use nor ornament.

So where in blazes is that blasted Aliana?

Once again, Packrat began to make a minute examination of the structure on which he stood. The rounded plinth rose seamlessly from the floor, as though they had somehow been crafted in a single piece. Beyond that, there was simply the edge of the platform. Above, and some unguessable distance further on, the great circle hung in midair. Below, there was more black nothingness.

Damn it, there must be a way off this thing! She can't have flown away!

He kicked the plinth, stubbed his toe, and swore inventively, and at some length. Then, gritting his teeth, he got down on his hands and knees, and began to feel along the periphery of the square, inch by inch. The only way off this thing was down. There must be some kind of steps or ladder hidden somewhere. Sure enough, he found it on the third side; a slender rope ladder fastened out of sight, beneath the platform's edge. Aliana must have worked things out a great deal quicker than he had done. He'd waited until he'd been certain that the guard up in the Temple had been fully preoccupied before making his move, and that had delayed him a little, but he hadn't been all *that* far behind his fellow thief.

Packrat stuck his candle on the brink of the platform in a little puddle of its own wax, and lowered one leg over the side, feeling around with his foot for the ladder. Getting onto it was one of the least pleasant experiences of his life. The smooth metal floor meant there was nowhere to grip, and he had to scrabble on the edge, with his body hanging out over the unguessable drop, while he got his feet into position then – even worse – had to let go with one hand, then the other, while he made a grab for the nearest rung. By the time he was clinging to the ladder, swinging out over empty space, he was sweating and shaking, and his bowels felt as if they were in knots.

When I get my hands on that girl, I'm going to throttle her!

Getting off the platform and onto the ladder was the worst part of the operation, however. Once he had managed that tricky manoeuvre, the descent itself should present no real problems. Holding on with one hand, Packrat reached up with the other for his candle, blew it out, and stuffed it back in his pocket. Then, taking a deep breath, he started to make his way down.

It was a long descent, made in pitch darkness, on a flimsy, swinging ladder, with nothing to distract him from worrying about Aliana's fate, and his own. After some time, aware of weariness and the aches in the muscles of his shoulders, back, and limbs, he stopped to rest, using one of the rungs as a seat, and hooking his arms over another, to keep himself balanced. He had better pace himself, he decided. He didn't want to succumb to exhaustion or cramps and fall off – not when he had no idea how far it was to the bottom. When he had recovered a little, he continued, but he had to rest twice more before the ladder finally came to an end. He could hardly believe it when his feet touched a solid, level surface. It had seemed that he'd been condemned to climb down for all eternity.

With a sigh of relief, Packrat let go of the ladder, feeling oddly shaky about the knees, and started to rummage in his capacious pocket, looking for the candle and his flint. Suddenly something hit him hard, knocking all the breath out of him and hurling him to the ground. Before he could recover himself, he felt his arms pinioned, and a cold edge of steel biting into his throat, then suddenly, a voice came out of the darkness. 'Packrat? Is that you?'

Relief flooded through him. 'Let go of me, you stupid cow,' he snapped back. 'Haven't you caused enough bloody trouble for one day?'

The pressure on his arms relaxed, the knife vanished, and then he heard the rapid succession of scrapes and clicks as she tried to strike a spark. After a moment or two, a candle flared into life, and in the orb of pale light cast by its flame, he saw Aliana's face, frowning, smudged and pale. 'What the blazes do you think you're doing?' she demanded crossly.

For a moment they glared at one another in the flickering light. Packrat was the first to speak. 'Why did you run away?'

'Why did you follow me?' Aliana countered.

'I saw you sneaking around, up there in the Temple.' Packrat couldn't keep an accusing edge out of his voice. 'I followed you and saw you steal that food from Telimon. I want to know what the bloody blazes you think you're doing, mucking around like that.' With each word he spoke, he was becoming more angry. 'You know what your friend Galveron said. If one if us is caught pinching stuff, we'll all be thrown out of the Temple.' By this time, Packrat was actually shaking her shoulders. 'Are you trying to get us all killed, you gormless bitch?'

Aliana knocked his hands away, and started to laugh, though there was more hysteria than humour in her mirth. 'Stole food? You think that's bad? Packrat, you have no idea how serious this is. I've gone and done the most dreadful thing. I've stolen far more than a few meagre provisions. I took the Hierarch's ring, too.'

'You did WHAT?'

She winced. 'Don't shout at me, Packrat.'

'Don't *shout* at you? HAVE YOU LOST YOUR MIND?'

'Well, what did you expect?' Aliana flared. 'That cow arrested Alestan and split up all the Ghosts. Galveron hadn't been out of the place two minutes, and she was breaking his promises into a million pieces. I've had enough of her, Packrat. She's no more fit to be in charge than – than you are!'

'Thanks,' said Packrat drily, but his friend was still in full flow.

'I'm going to make her sorry. Without the ring she can't be Hierarch, and I'm going to hide it somewhere down here, where no one will ever find it.'

'And then what?' Packrat asked her.

'I'm going to make her release Alestan, and then . . .' Her face fell. 'I, er, haven't exactly worked the next bit out, yet. But I will,' she added defiantly.

Packrat sighed. One way or another, Aliana usually managed to get away with these impulsive acts of hers, but this time, she might have pushed her luck too far. She had been tired and angry, and she hadn't been thinking clearly. What if the Hierarch threatened to kill Alestan if the ring was not returned? It seemed the obvious action to take. With a shudder Packrat realised just how much trouble they could be in. For the time being, protectiveness took over from his outrage, though anger at this thoughtless act of hers still lurked in the background, waiting its turn. 'Come on.' He took her arm. 'We can't stay here. It won't take Galveron long to work out where we've gone.'

Aliana took a deep breath, and nodded. 'I had a bit of time to look around, before I heard you coming down. We're on another platform, a bit like the one up there—'

'Oh, bollocks! Not *more* ladders!'

'No. It's all right. There's another bridge – a much more sensible design than the first one. I didn't have time to find out where it went.'

'Then let's find out now. Which way?'

'Over here.'

'Good. We'll go on until we find some safe place to hide out – then somehow we have to find a way out of this mess.'

In the stronghold of the Reivers, it was the clan chieftain who was demanding explanations. As Tormon ran down the staircase into the beast quarters, he could see, from his high vantage point, a collection of men and women clustered around the lifeless form of the old Summoner. Arcan was kneeling over the body, his face livid with rage. He got to his feet as the trader shouldered his way through to the front of the group. 'Ah, Tormon. Your arrival is timely; I was about to send for you. As you can see, a great evil has been committed here. Our Summoner, Grim, has been murdered. It would appear that his assistant is missing, and so is the boy you brought with you from Tiarond. Can you shed any light on this mystery?'

Until that moment, Tormon had been praying Rochalla had made a mistake: that Scall wasn't really missing but had merely, in the manner of adolescents everywhere, gone off for his own reasons to be alone in some quiet place. 'I'm very sorry for your loss, my Chief,' he said. 'Summoner Grim will be sorely missed. But are you absolutely sure that Scall is gone? He's not the sort of lad to be involved in such a dreadful business, I'd swear it.'

Arcan frowned, and the onlookers suddenly discovered pressing business elsewhere. In that moment, Tormon was all too aware of the fragility of his own welcome here. 'I have parties searching the entire fortress,' the chieftain said brusquely. 'They have already looked in the obvious places, and there has been no sign of either of the missing young men.' He sighed. 'For what it's worth, I am already certain that we won't find them. I don't know how deeply your boy is involved in this dreadful business, trader Tormon. It may be that he was witness to a quarrel between the two Summoners, and saw Dark kill Grim. Maybe Dark took him away as some sort of hostage – but that begs the question of why, having murdered his master, the rogue Summoner didn't just kill your lad too. And Dark and Grim have been together for a long time, now. As far as I could ever tell, with such strange beings, they seemed almost as close as father and son.'

'Sons have killed fathers before now,' Tormon pointed out.

Arcan nodded brusquely. 'True enough. But something about this whole business doesn't sit right with me. Maybe it was Scall who killed Grim, and Dark went after him. But then how did Scall manage to leave the stronghold without my guards seeing him?'

'How would either of them have managed to get out?' Tormon asked.

'Apparently someone set a cart on fire in the courtyard, and while my men were all distracted'– Arcan's scowl boded ill for his in-attentive sentries – 'the culprit simply opened the gate and left.'

'With a horse? And they didn't notice him until the gate was opened?' Tormon asked.

The chieftain sighed. 'I see where you're going. Actually, it was three horses: Dark's mount, Grim's animal, and that pretty chestnut belonging to your lad. And you have a point. My men aren't totally useless – though sometimes it may seem that way. Only a Summoner would be able to spirit three such large and noisy creatures out from under their noses.'

'Then one way or another, Scall couldn't have left this place on his own,' Tormon pointed out triumphantly.

'But that doesn't necessarily mean he's innocent,' Arcan said. 'Another explanation I can think of, is that Dark and Scall plotted together to kill the old man. Witnesses certainly saw Scall going into the tower of the Summoners earlier today.'

'That's ridiculous!' Tormon protested. 'Scall's a good lad. There's not an ounce of harm in him.'

'Then how do you account for this?' Arcan held our a bloody blade wrapped in a cloth. 'This was the weapon that killed Grim. It is not a Reiver knife. It must have belonged to one of your party. No matter what happened to the boy, this puts all of you under suspicion.'

With a shiver, Tormon recognised the blade. It was a Godsword knife, with a long, keen blade. They had all armed themselves from the weapon store in the guardhouse before descending the cliff. This knife could have belonged to any of them.

Just then one of the chieftain's warriors came pelting down the stairs. 'We've searched the whole tower, my Chief, right up to the roof,' he panted. 'No one can be hiding there, and Lewic asked me to tell you that the kitchen and the storeroom are also clear.'

Thanking the man, Arcan turned back to the trader. 'We've run out of places to look, Tormon. We already knew that Dark must have fled. Now we're certain that your lad has also gone missing.'

A chill went through Tormon. 'What if Dark killed him too, and hid the body?'

Arcan shrugged. 'Where? And if he didn't bother to conceal his master's corpse, why would he waste time hiding a dead youth? No, Tormon. That doesn't make sense, and you know it.'

'Your words give me hope, at least,' the trader said. 'So long as the lad's alive, he can be found, then maybe we'll get to the bottom of this dreadful business. Will you send out a search party tonight, my Chief?'

'Have you taken a look outside lately? There's no point in sending my men out into a foul storm like that. They couldn't even find their own backsides on such a wild, black, night. We'll wait until first light. Once we can see what we're doing, I have trackers who'll hunt the culprits down in no time. In the meantime, I must see that my Summoner is taken to the great hall, where he may rest in state. You have brought black days upon us, trader Tormon. If half of what you say about the fate of Tiarond is true, we couldn't have lost Grim at a worse time.' He turned away, to supervise the warriors who were lifting the Summoner's body on to a bier, and said no more.

Tormon knew that he had been dismissed, but he lingered in the beast quarters, waiting until Arcan and his warriors had departed with their sad burden. The empty space where Scall's mare had stood seemed to mock him. He knew it wasn't his fault that the lad had met with some sort of mishap – after all, he couldn't lock Scall and Annas away from the world, just to keep them safe, and he couldn't be watching them every minute of the day. But somewhere along the line, Scall had become part of his family, and the thought of losing another loved one, so close to Kanella's death, was not to be borne.

Tormon was in a quandary. He knew he should ignore Arcan's advice, saddle up Rutska immediately, and head out onto the moor in search of the missing boy, but he was also aware that the chieftain had been right. On a night like this, how could he even discover the direction in which they had gone? And how could he leave

Annas again? So soon after her mother's death, she needed him to be there for her, and his first responsibility must be to her. He had no right to put himself at risk by riding out alone on such a cold, tempestuous night.

But that poor boy . . .

Shaking his head, Tormon turned away, and headed reluctantly back upstairs, his heart as heavy as his footsteps. He wasn't looking forward to telling Rochalla what had happened. He knew she'd be upset. Nevertheless, her presence would be a comfort to him right now. She seemed to be just as much a part of this strange new family he was collecting together as Scall had become. How different she was from Seriema, who, as today's quarrel had proved, would go her own way, no matter what . . .

Halfway up the stairs, Tormon stopped in his tracks.

What about Presvel? He didn't go off with Seriema today. And he was conspicuous by his absence when the word went out that the Summoner had been killed.

Frowning, the trader went on his way, vowing to keep an eye on Seriema's assistant. Since they had left Tiarond, the city man had been coping less and less well with the tough world outside, and for a while now, his behaviour had been giving Tormon cause for concern.

If I can do it without alarming her too much, I'll warn Rochalla to stay away from him, too. There's something about him I just don't trust any more. He's a desperate man right now. He feels that his life is out of his control, and such folk are always dangerous. But if he had anything to do with what's happened to Scall, I'll wring his neck with my own bare hands.

Dark knew that if Arcan caught him, he would never be able to explain his actions. His mentor had laid this journey on him with his last, dying breath, but there had been no witnesses to that save Scall, and since he had kidnapped the lad, he couldn't realistically expect any help to come from that quarter. When someone found

Grim's body, it would look as though *he* had been the murderer, and had fled to escape the consequences of his crime. It was no use wondering if he had done the right thing. There was no chance now for second thoughts. The young Summoner was grieving, sick at heart, and scared, but now he was also homeless, a fugitive, and an outcast from his clan.

Not to mention soaked and freezing – but that's the least of my problems. I had better concentrate on where I'm going, or I'll be lost, too.

Not only that, but he also had to concentrate on keeping Scall under control. He could feel the boy's resentment burning like a smoky flame, and feel his frantic struggles to reassert himself. If Dark should lose him now, he would have failed in the task with which Grim had entrusted him, and everything would have been in vain.

Like all Reivers, Dark had excellent night vision, but he could see next to nothing in the icy black turmoil of the storm. Though he was aiming for the Curtain Walls, and it was possible to see them from the high tower of Arcan's fortress, at ground level they were over the hilly horizon, their glimmer obscured by driving hail. The only way he could gauge his direction was by the wind. He kept it on his left shoulder, crossed his fingers, and prayed that it wouldn't veer. It might as well be of *some* use, he thought grimly, because it was certainly making life difficult when it came to managing the horses. None of them was happy about exchanging a nice, warm stable for this freezing nightmare, none of them liked being pelted with stinging hail, and all three of them were badly spooked by the gusting wind that howled and shrieked like a host of restless demons.

Scall's little chestnut was finding it particularly difficult to cope with the vile conditions. Her ears were back, her tail was tucked in, and he could feel her shivering all the way through the leading rope. Dark cursed himself for bringing her: he would have been far better off to have chosen one of the robust Reiver horses, who were used to all sorts of black nights and wild weather. His reasoning had been that if he must tear Scall away from safety and friends, at least the lad would have the comfort of his beloved horse, but . . .

If the animal dies, he'll be utterly heartbroken. He'll never forgive me – and who could blame him?

Dark could no longer fight against the tide of despair that rose to engulf him.

Oh Grim, Grim! How I wish you were here. This seemed like such a simple plan when you first worked it out. How could everything have gone so wrong?

For some time now the going had been a steep uphill climb, and as the horses crested the ridge, the strengthening wind in this exposed location nearly knocked the Summoner out of his saddle. Once more, the two animals that he was leading tried to turn and bolt back towards the Reiver stronghold, and his own mount seemed to have the same idea. He spent a frantic few moments wrestling with the recalcitrant creatures, who seemed bent on pulling his arms out of their sockets. It took all the power of his Summoner's trained will to get them going again in the direction he wanted, not to mention keeping Scall safely in the saddle in all this confusion, but finally he managed it, and as the horses picked their way down the steep slope on the other side of the ridge, and were shielded once more from the very worst of the weather, they seemed to become resigned to their lot, and stopped giving him so much trouble.

As he rode, Dark wondered whether anyone had found Grim's body yet, and if the hunt had gone out for him already. As soon as they discovered the missing horses, they would know he had left the stronghold. Would they think it was worth searching for him on such a black and stormy night? He suspected not. Probably they would wait until the morning, and try to pick up his trail in daylight. It made much more sense than blundering about on the moors in the darkness. Some of the Reivers were excellent trackers, and with the ground being so wet they should have very little difficulty in following him after daybreak.

I hope they decide to wait. That way, I should beat them to the Curtain Walls, and as long as Grim was right, and I can manage to get through, I'll be safe from my own people, at least. Then all I'll have to worry about is the strangers on the other side.

Reaching across, he pulled up Scall's hood, which had been blown or jolted back while the horses were plunging around. At least, under the circumstances, he could try to make his captive comfortable, if nothing else. He was glad that he could see so little in this dim light. If he'd had to witness the misery and confusion that he knew must be written on the lad's face, and the hurt and hatred – not unjustified – that must surely be in his eyes, he wondered if he would have the resolution to carry on with this.

It would be different if I really knew what was going on. If only Grim had introduced me to his mysterious friends before now, or even told me about them, then I might have a better idea of what they intended to do with Scall, and why the artefacts he found are so important to them.

The Summoner rode on, worrying, even though he knew there was no point. He was committed now, and what would be would be. After a while, he realised that he had lost all track of time while he'd been preoccupied, and decided that he had better start paying more attention. Pushing his hood back a little, he looked around, and was horrified to see that over his left shoulder, the driving hail was glowing with a dim and eldritch light. Driving his fist into his knee, Dark swore. That pale glimmer could only be the Curtain Walls. The blasted wind must have veered while his thoughts were elsewhere, and now, instead of heading towards the barrier, he was actually heading away from it at an oblique angle.

Annoyed with himself and feeling a little foolish, he corrected his course, and found that now the wind was driving right into his face. Surprisingly, his improvised repair of the skull mask was still holding, and at least it provided some protection from the weather. He had something to head for, now that he could see the glimmer of the barrier, and Grim had told him that the weather conditions on the other side would probably be completely different.

Dark hoped so. Right now, he'd do just about anything to get out of this unrelenting storm. The hail and freezing temperatures were bad enough, but the wind was definitely beginning to make him uneasy. The gale's discordant screeching sounded like some foul, hideous creature from beyond a man's most grisly nightmares. He told himself not to let his imagination run away with him, but to no effect. There was something in this weather that wasn't natural, and that extra awareness that came with a Summoner's training kept warning him that he was in increasing danger. Once more, he looked uneasily over his shoulder. The sooner he got through the Curtain Walls, the safer he would feel.

Thirteen

A Light on the Horizon

As the night drew on, Toulac sent Zavahl into the shelter to get some rest. 'One of us has to stay awake,' she said, 'to keep the fire going and keep a lookout for Veldan's ship. They might see the glow from our fire, but it's pretty well hidden down amongst the boulders, so we can't very well count on that.' As she spoke, she was sorting some long, straightish bits of driftwood from their fuel pile. 'These should do as torches, for signalling, if we see a light out at sea. Mrainil of the Dobarchu says there are some tricky reefs out in the bay, but he'll be able to guide a small boat to shore, to pick us up.'

Having put her torches carefully aside, she built up the fire with rapid skill. 'There. That should keep it going for a while. You take yourself into the shelter, sonny, and get some sleep. I'll wake you later, when it's your turn to watch.' She looked up at the clear, starry sky, and shivered. 'Our main problem will be the cold. Without coats or cloaks on a night like this, the person on watch will have to keep nipping back to the fire.' She shrugged. 'Oh, well. We'll manage. See you later.' With that she was gone, into the darkness beyond the firelight.

Zavahl, still wondering when he was going to get a word in edgeways, sat on for a few moments, but the scares and sleeplessness of the night before, coupled with all the exertions of his day, had left him exhausted. He took a sip of water from their dwindling supply in the broken jug, and crawled into the shelter. Ever since the structure had been completed he had been looking forward to this part, but soon he found that camping on the beach was not as romantic as it had seemed. With nothing to put between himself and the shingle, it was impossible to get comfortable. The pebbles beneath his shoulders and hipbones seemed particularly sharp and lumpy, but each time he thought he had removed the worst of them, others arrived to take their place. The other problem was the cold. Though the shelter caught and trapped some heat from the fire, as Toulac had intended, the ground beneath Zavahl seemed to leech what little heat was in his body, and he had nothing to protect him from the chill.

Shivering and miserable, Zavahl lay awake.

No wonder Toulac is so tough, if she's been doing this sort of thing all her life.

He wondered if he should go to join her, or if he should volunteer to stand watch for a while, since he seemed unable to get to sleep. Unfortunately, however, that would mean going even further away from the fire. Even as he was wrestling with his conscience, he saw a flicker of movement beyond the overhanging lip of the shelter. One by one, the Dobarchu were arriving, undulating over the rocks with a beautiful, fluid motion.

Zavahl stared at them with unashamed curiosity. The adults of the group were over three feet in length (or it should it perhaps be called height? he wondered, when they pulled themselves upright to stand on their hind legs). Of the three youngsters, two were only half that size, and still had the cute, rounded fuzziness of babyhood, while the other was a gawky adolescent, closer to the size of the adults. They settled in a ring around the fire, fluffing up their fur, basking happily in the warmth and, coincidentally, blocking out all the heat.

Zavahl hesitated. He wanted to ask them to move over a little, but did they understand the human spoken language? Besides, even the younger members of the group had powerful-looking jaws and pointed teeth, and their paws, so much like little human hands, had each digit tipped with a stubby but sharp claw. No matter what Toulac said, to the former Hierarch, born and brought up in a city, they still had the look of wild animals – and from all that he had heard, wild creatures were dangerous, unpredictable, and fierce.

'You're thinking like the old Zavahl.'

'I beg your pardon?' These interruptions from the Dragon in his mind still took Zavahl by surprise sometimes.

'All that wild animal nonsense is the sort of thinking that might come from a person who had never been to Gendival and seen the many races of intelligent and civilised beings who live and work there.' Aethon sounded slightly amused. 'You were thinking like someone who had never seen the firedrake Kazairl, and who didn't have a Dragon taking up residence in his mind.'

'I take your point on the Dragon business,' Zavahl replied, 'but remember that I can't communicate with Veldan's pet monster. He still looks like a ferocious wild animal to me. And as for Gendival, I might have been there, but I've never seen the place. I was blind-folded when they brought me in, so I don't really know what you're talking about. The only other strange creatures I've seen are the ones who brought us here, and I didn't find *them* particularly encouraging.'

'You're right. I had forgotten that,' Aethon said thoughtfully. 'Let me show you Gendival as it really is.'

Zavahl closed his eyes, and a succession of images appeared, each one like a brightly coloured daydream, as the Dragon began to show him the images of the Shadowleague settlement beside the lake, and its remarkable inhabitants. When eventually, blinking, he came back to the world of sea and stone and firelight, he didn't know how much time had passed, although the fire was beginning to burn low. While he had been transported by the dragon's visions, he hadn't noticed the cold, but now it struck back at him with redoubled force.

Sighing, Zavahl pushed himself up on one elbow. He was just about to duck out of the shelter and put some wood on the fire when, to his astonishment, one of the Dobarchu left their circle and went to the driftwood pile that he and Toulac had gathered earlier. Clasping a few pieces in his short arms, he shuffled back on his hind legs to the fire, placing his fuel carefully to build up a good blaze. Two of his fellows followed him, each with their own burden of driftwood, and between them, they made the fire up to a respectable size.

Something about their deliberate, practised movements wrought a change in Zavahl's perceptions that not even the visions of the Dragon had been entirely able to accomplish. The strange beings that Aethon had shown him had aroused his awe, curiosity, and sometimes even fear, but they had still not seemed real to him. Because he had never seen them for himself, they might have been a chimera that his mind had invented in a dream. But when he saw the Dobarchu engaged in their homely, and very human task, he stopped looking on them as animals, and started to see them as people: furry, oddly shaped folk, to be sure, but people none the less.

He looked at the little group of refugees, seeing them with new eyes. A mother was curled around her sleeping infant, holding it close to her and keeping it warm and safe. Another was using a stone to break open shellfish for the second little one. Two adult couples snuggled with their partners beside the fire. One of them whimpered in its sleep, and its mate reached out and gently stroked its soft, silvery brown fur, until the nightmare had passed. Zavahl was touched by the sight. If what Toulac had told him was true, the Dobarchu had experienced enough suffering to fuel a lifetime of bad dreams. He felt a great deal of sympathy with them. They had been reft of their homes and homelands just as he had, and they, too, had suffered in the transition.

And now we'll all have to build new homes and new lives in a strange place. I have a lot more in common with these odd-looking creatures than I do with most humans that I know.

It was a sobering thought.

Even Zavahl's fascination with the refugees, however, couldn't completely distract him from the biting cold. He shivered, and tried to tuck his chilled hands into his tunic – which, of course, only made him colder than ever. Suddenly, there was a stir of movement beside him, and he felt something soft and warm pressing against him. He looked down to see the other young Dobarchu, the slender adolescent who, it seemed, had succumbed to the insatiable curiosity of youth, and come to investigate him and his shelter. There was no doubt in Zavahl's mind that he was looking at a female. He could see a delicacy about her form, especially around her face and shoulders, a graceful fluidity of gesture and motion, and a melting look in her big, dark eyes, that all bespoke her femininity.

Zavahl was charmed. 'Hello,' he said with a smile. 'It's cold tonight, isn't it?' The little female tilted her head to one side in an obvious gesture of puzzlement, but the biggest male, the one who had been down on the beach with Toulac, looked up at the sound of the human voice, and nodded his head emphatically.

In his mind, Zavahl felt the Dragon stir. 'Mrainil is the only one that understands your language,' Aethon said. 'Only some of the Dobarchu have mindspeech, just as only certain humans do, and he's the sole member of this group who does. That's why he's a Loremaster. Though mindspeech comes into the consciousness as words, it deals in universal concepts that form a bridge between one language and another, which makes the understanding of different tongues a simple matter. That's why Mrainil can understand you, though his mouth isn't adapted to speak as a human does.'

Zavahl noticed the wistfulness in the Dragon's tone when he mentioned mind-to-mind communication. 'You must have had mindspeech, then, when you were in your own body,' he said.

'Dragons are different. As a race, we communicate entirely in mindspeech.'

'And now you can't communicate with others, because my mind lacks that ability?'

The Dragon hesitated for a moment. 'It's not your fault.'

'You must miss it.'

Aethon sighed. 'More than you could ever imagine.'

It occurred to Zavahl that there were more ways than one to be an exile.

Since the companion in his mind did not seem to want to speak any more, the former Hierarch turned his attention back to the big Dobarchu. 'I was just saying to this little lady that it's a cold night.'

Mrainil looked at him for a long, solemn moment, and he had the distinct impression that somehow, he was being assessed. Then without warning, the refugees broke into a flood of animated chittering, and every one of them leapt up from their recumbent positions beside the fire, and came rushing at Zavahl in an undulating brown wave.

Great Myrial! Maybe he didn't like me talking to the little one!

Unable to help himself, he flinched back from this sudden onslaught as the Dobarchu descended on him in a rush, pressing him down to the ground, and threatening to trample him. He yelled and flailed in panic, but he was completely overwhelmed. Then, as they pressed close to him, he realised what they were doing, and forced himself to relax. The furry creatures covered him like a warm, brown blanket, sharing their body heat with him, as they did with one another.

Mrainil looked down at him and chittered reprovingly, and he felt rebuked for his moment of panic. The adolescent female edged herself under one arm, and snuggled up to him with her head on his shoulder, watching him with her melting dark eyes. 'Thank you,' Zavahl said. 'I'm very grateful.'

A shadow at the mouth of the shelter blocked out the firelight. 'What's all the yelling about?' Toulac demanded.

'I'm sorry.' Zavahl, beginning to warm up nicely, squinted up at her silhouette, but made no attempt to move. This was the first time he'd felt vaguely comfortable all night. 'It was a misunderstanding. The Dobarchu all came rushing at me, and I got a bit of a shock,' he explained. 'I thought they were attacking me, but they only wanted to keep me warm.'

'My, what a lot you're learning today,' Toulac said drily. 'Try to keep the noise down, though. When the boat gets here, we'll be home and dry, but in the meantime, I don't want to go advertising our presence far and wide.'

'But this place is the back end of nowhere,' Zavahl protested.

'There can't be anybody around for miles.'

'Well, you're probably right,' Toulac admitted. 'But there's one thing been bothering me all day, and that's the amount of stuff we picked up from the beach that came from shipwrecks.'

'So?'

'So why would such a lot of ships get wrecked on this particular bit of coast?'

Zavahl shrugged. 'Well, all those reefs sticking out look nasty enough, and there may be freak currents, or something?'

'Freak currents, my eye. If there's a place like that, mariners normally know enough to keep well away, unless they happen to get blown onto the coast in a storm.' Toulac shook her head. 'No, I don't like this. I have a bad feeling that those ships didn't get wrecked all by themselves, and I won't have an easy moment until we're safely out of here.'

'Is it my turn to watch?' Zavahl had to drag the offer out of himself. He was so tired and so comfortable now that he really didn't want to move.

Toulac gave him a piercing look. 'Don't let me disturb you, sonny. I can manage a bit longer.' With that, she stumped off, back towards the water's edge, leaving him with an obscure but gnawing sense of guilt. Fortunately, however, he managed to master the uncomfortable feeling, and was soon drifting off to sleep in a warm haze of contentment. He didn't worry himself one bit about Toulac's dire prognostication that something was amiss. It was probably just another way of making herself appear more knowledgeable to an inexperienced adventurer like himself, he decided.

'You ought to listen to her,' Aethon warned. 'When it comes to these matters, she has far more experience than you do.'

But Zavahl didn't hear. He was already asleep.

Up on the clifftop, the wreckers were watching and listening. 'I wish the ship would come,' Shafol muttered. 'The old battleaxe is starting to get suspicious.'

Tuld shrugged. 'What if she is? That other idiot didn't seem too interested, and she can't prove nothing. She's not about to climb that cliff a second time today, not at her age, so she'll never find us up here, and she'll never see us light our bonfire when the ship comes. She might be waving a little torch down on the beach, but it's our beacon they'll be looking at. And you know how it works. No one lives along here, so the ships always come in to see if someone has lit a distress signal – and this lot actually have a reason, for once. Once we've lured them onto the rocks, it'll just be business as usual for us. The old girl won't be worrying about an attack from the land side. We'll just go down there and mop up.'

'What about those animals?' Shafol wanted to know. 'I've never seen anything like them before, and they're a fair old size. Look at them, all gathered round the fire like that, and sitting on top of that man. It's not natural, is that.'

'It makes no difference what they are,' Tuld replied. 'They're just animals of some sort, and they can't be very savage if they're sitting down there like a bunch of stupid lapdogs. They'll probably just run away when we get down there, but if they don't we'll deal with them when the time comes.'

'I wish that ship would get a move on,' Pelorm complained again. 'I'm freezing my backside off, up here.'

'I wish we didn't have to do this at all,' the fourth man said. 'Most of the folk we've wrecked might have drowned, but it's cold-blooded murder, just the same.'

'Shut your mouth, Feresh,' Shafol growled. 'What choice did we have? We were finished as fishermen when so many of the fish disappeared. We've got to feed our families somehow.'

Feresh shook his head. 'No good will come of this,' he warned. 'There'll come a day when we find we've pushed our luck once too often.'

'If that's the way you feel, why don't you just bugger off?' said Tuld. 'We don't need you anyway, and your whining is starting to get on my nerves.'

'All right.' Feresh got to his feet. 'I will. I'm taking my family away from here, and heading upriver. There must be somewhere we can work and eat.'

Tuld spat on the ground. 'Well, don't blame me when you're all starving to death in a ditch in the back of beyond.'

'At least we'll die honest,' Feresh said quietly, and walked away.

Tuld looked at the other two. 'Follow him and kill him,' he said quietly. 'I don't want him getting a fit of conscience and warning that lot on the beach.'

'Good idea,' said Shafol. He and Pelorm vanished into the darkness. A few minutes later there was the sound of a scuffle, and a muffled cry, quickly stifled.

Shafol and Pelorm came back, sheathing their knives. 'Bigger shares for us, then,' Pelorm said, settling back down among the bushes. 'Feresh always was a bloody fool, but I never thought he'd be getting a tender conscience at this stage.'

'I think his woman's been at him,' Shafol replied. 'You know how women are, and she never did like what we were doing.'

'She didn't do him any favours, then,' Tuld said, with a leering grin. 'Still, she may be a bit brainless, but what a looker! Now that she's a widow, I might have a go at her myself. She'll be needing a man about the place.'

As the night wore on, Toulac watched and waited with increasing anxiety, straining her eyes into the darkness to catch the first glimmer of the ship's lights on the horizon. Though she was weary and frozen right through, she had decided to keep vigil herself, rather than awaken Zavahl. She knew very well that he had not taken her uneasiness about the many shipwrecks seriously, he wasn't used to keeping watch, and she was afraid that he would let his attention wander at a critical time. Cold though she was, she had only been coming back to the fire when she lost all feeling in her hands and feet, or when the dimming glow told her that its wood needed to be replenished. Not that she was worried about the fire going out if Zavahl was left in charge – far from it – and the

Dobarchu wouldn't allow that to happen in any case. No, there wasn't any need to worry about spotting a light out at sea, then having to rekindle a signal fire from scratch. She did worry, however, about this business with the wreckers. She knew that she might be overreacting, and maybe Zavahl was right–

That'll be the day!

– about this being a difficult stretch of coast. But she didn't think so. There was something about this place, with its many shipwrecks, that caused her a good deal of disquiet, and she hadn't lived this long by ignoring her instincts and intuition, or by skipping optimistically through life, hoping that the worst would never happen.

Whoever is on watch tonight has got to stay alert – and that's just what Zavahl won't do. I'm better off dealing with this myself, and I'll sleep on the boat – when the damn thing finally gets here.

The time dragged by, and little by little, as her eyes grew heavy, Toulac felt her concentration slipping. Since there was no way she would admit that she didn't find staying up on watch all night as easy as she had done in her younger years, it only remained for her to berate herself for growing sloppy and careless, and this she did, at some length. It was a great relief to her when Mrainil left the fire and his sleeping people, and came down to the water's edge to keep her company. She had been trying, from time to time, to contact Veldan again but, without the stimulus of a crisis, she had been finding communication to be just too difficult over such a great distance. Mindspeech with the leader of the Dobarchu, apart from being interesting, distracting her from her worries, and keeping her awake, had the additional benefit of reassuring her that, with some hard work and a bit of expert training, her initial success could be repeated.

They talked for a while, perched out on the rocks, looking over the ocean. The previous time they had spoken, he had told her of his people and their exodus. This time, he wanted to know how *she* had left her own land, and come to be stranded here. As she spoke to him, she kept her eyes roving the horizon, but in the end, she was so engrossed in telling him of her adventures and misadventures that the faint, distant twinkle off the far headland came as a surprise.

Toulac gave an excited whoop. 'There it is!' She rushed back up the beach to get the torches, and thrust the ends of the first two brands into the fire. 'Zavahl, wake up!' she yelled. 'They're coming!' A vague, drowsy mutter came from within the shelter. Well, she didn't have time to wait around until he pulled himself together. As soon as the torches were well alight, she pelted back down the beach again, with the flames from the torches streaming out behind her, and a couple of spare, unlighted ones tucked under one arm, just for good measure. Mrainil, who had swum these waters, had shown her exactly where to stand and wave her signal, so that the ship had the best chance of making a clear approach. Forgetting her own injunctions about making too much noise, she jumped up and down, yelling and waving the torches over her head; knowing, even as she did so, that she was acting like a nine-year-old, but too excited to care.

Soon, it was easy to see that the lights were coming closer. Mrainil, however, in contrast to Toulac's exuberant behaviour, was sitting up on his hind legs, still as a statue, and staring out to sea. 'Does it look to you as though those lights are veering off to the side?' he asked.

Some of his anxiety communicated itself to Toulac, and she ceased her wild waving and simply stood as still as the Dobarchu, but keeping her torches held up high. 'I think you're right.'

Mrainil chittered anxiously. 'What do those idiots think they're doing? They're heading right for the reef!'

fourteen

On the Reef

Zavahl had been so deeply asleep that he found it remarkably difficult to pull himself back into wakefulness. When
Toulac's voice cut through his dreams, he had no idea, for
a moment, where he was, or why his bed was hard and lumpy, and
his coverlet so heavy and thick. Had somebody been calling him?
he wondered groggily. Well, never mind. He was sure it couldn't
have been all that important. He was just drifting back into his
dreams, when a blast of moist, fishy breath roused him more thoroughly than a whole bottle of smelling salts. He dragged his eyes
open to see a see a rounded, furry face with twinkling black eyes,
peering at him from a distance of a couple of inches. The Dobarchu
chittered interrogatively, tickled his face with coarse, bushy
whiskers, then nuzzled its broad, black, leathery nose into his ear.
Zavahl recognised his little friend, the young female, and finally his
hazy thoughts fell into place. In the distance, he could still hear
Toulac calling . . . Great Myrial! The boat must be here!

Dobarchu scattered out of his way as he heaved himself to his
hands and knees and scrabbled his way out of the shelter. As soon
as he left the hollow in the rocks and got out of the glare of firelight, he saw Toulac down on the reef, waving torches above her
head and yelling wildly.

Damn it! I should have a torch too.

Zavahl swerved back to the fire, scrambling as fast as he could
over the over the stony, rough terrain. He found a long, straightish
brand among the firewood, and held it in the glowing heat of the

174

flames until it was well alight. Then turning quickly, he ran back to help Toulac – at least, he ran at first, on the higher part of the beach where the rocks were dry and the footing was good. Further down towards the reef, in the tidal zone, they were coated with seaweed and slime, and here he was forced to slow his pace considerably, or risk a fall.

He was edging his way down towards the waterline when the men appeared, materialising out of the shadows to block his way. He looked from their feral, hard-eyed faces to the brutal knives that glinted in their hands, and felt a shock of stark, cold fear. They began to advance on him, stepping carefully on the slippery rocks, and Zavahl backed away, his heart in his mouth, swinging the torch, his only weapon, in front of him in wavering arcs. As they began to close in on him, he opened his mouth to yell for help from Toulac – and that was when he noticed, from the corner of his eye, that another man was creeping up behind her, armed with a sword this time, not a knife. Because she was making all the noise she had told *him* not to make, she didn't hear her attacker, and with all her attention fixed on the approaching ship, she was oblivious to his approach.

Zavahl yelled at the top of his voice – and at that moment, his own assailants rushed him. Trying to scramble away, he backed into a deep rock pool, and felt pain lance up his leg as his ankle turned beneath him on the slippery stones. He went down, floundering, and his torch flew from his hand and went out. Then they were on him. At the edge of his vision he saw the flash of a knife blade coming down, and knew it was all over.

Toulac was desperately trying to reach Veldan with mindspeech, but every time she tried it, her concentration kept slipping away. Suddenly, she heard Zavahl, yelling at the top of his voice, and an instant later, Veldan's voice resounded in her head. 'Toulac! Behind you!' She whirled round, and came face to face with a sword-wielding ruffian. In the next instant, the man had both the torches flung full into his face. He screamed and batted them away, beating at his frizzling hair and beard, and dropping his sword in the process. Toulac took the time his distraction had brought her to draw her own blade, and by the time he had picked up his weapon again, she was ready for him.

It was a clumsy fight, with both participants greatly hampered in their movements by the thick, green, slippery slime that coated the rocks underfoot. Toulac was furious with herself. How could she have let him sneak up on her like that? It was impossible to even attempt mindspeech with all her concentration on the fight, so how could she guide the ship in, now that she had thrown her torches away? And this miserable son of a bitch was stopping her from getting more.

'I will take care of the ship.' With a splash, Mrainil plunged into the water, and was gone, leaving Toulac to focus her attention on her opponent.

With his advantage of surprise gone, the wrecker suddenly appeared a lot less brave, but he was still grimly determined to stand his ground, and he was right between the veteran and Zavahl. They moved carefully on the slick, uneven surface; edging for position, and trading hacking, clumsy blows which were curtailed by the need to keep their footing.

Though Toulac needed to keep her concentration on her own adversary, she had, like all good fighters, worked hard to develop her peripheral vision. From the corner of her eye she saw Zavahl go down, and her heart sank. Surely he hadn't suffered so much, and come so far in so many ways, just to end up spitted like a hog by some petty brigand? Then the dreadful screaming started. Toulac cursed and lunged forward, feinting to one side then dodging in the other direction. When she felt her feet beginning to slip, she didn't try to stop herself, or regain her balance, but threw herself into the slide, let herself fall forward, and rolled to one side as her enemy's sword came crashing down on the rocks in the place where she had been. Now it was his turn to flounder, and fight to stay upright.

The veteran didn't waste time trying to get up. From her prone position, she brought her sword around in a mighty, two-handed swipe, aiming for the wrecker's knees. She felt the jar of the blade biting into flesh and bone, then he went down like a felled tree, the sword falling from his hand as he measured his length on the rocks. Now it was his turn to squeal like a butchered animal. With some difficulty, Toulac scrambled to her feet on rocks that now were slick with blood, as well as slime. A quick glance made sure that her opponent would not rise again, so there was no point in wasting her time finishing him off – in a while he'd be dead anyway. Instead, she turned back to Zavahl and his opponents, though she knew in her heart that she must be too late.

Myrial had chosen to take him after all – or so Zavahl thought. He certainly didn't expect what happened next. Unbalanced by the force of his thrust, the knifeman slipped on the same slimy rocks. He fell forward, on top of his victim, his aim awry, and Zavahl cried out in pain as the blade ripped through his tunic and glanced along his ribs. The other attacker, also committed to his thrust and taken by surprise, drove his knife straight into the back of his companion. The wretch struggled to rise from his sprawling position across Zavahl, screaming obscenities and flailing helplessly with his own knife hand, as the other strove to pull the blade out from between his shoulders. Somehow, Zavahl managed to wriggle out from underneath, and floundered away out of the pool, desperately trying to reach Toulac, who was still in the midst of a vicious battle with her own attacker.

The wrecker abandoned his attempts to reclaim his knife, and snatched up the blade of his companion, whose struggles were becoming weaker. The sight of his fallen friend seemed to enrage him even further, and with a roar, he scrambled in pursuit of his terrified victim. Zavahl knew how lucky he had been to survive the first attack. He couldn't expect to be so fortunate again. Weaponless as he was, and unskilled at fighting, his only option was to flee.

Toulac, having downed her own opponent, was struggling to her feet, but she would never get to him in time. Zavahl wasn't good at running. A lifetime spent in the confines of Tiarond's sacred Precincts had ill prepared him for the kind of life he was leading now, and he was tiring quickly. He could hear his would-be murderer panting and cursing, just behind him, and he knew the man was gaining. The wrecker closed in on him and grabbed him by his sleeve, spinning him around. Zavahl, despite his struggles, was pulled closer, as the other raised his blade to strike.

All at once, a host of shadowy shapes, running low to the ground and unnoticed until now against the dark backdrop, rose up around the attacker's legs, pushing him off balance and tripping him so that he fell full length. The Dobarchu had come to Zavahl's aid. They swarmed all over the wrecker, fouling his attempts to rise, and snapping at him with their strong, sharp teeth while, screaming curses, he struggled to rise. Zavahl hovered anxiously nearby, waiting for Toulac and her sword to come and deal with the problem. He had forgotten that the man still had his knife. Suddenly the blade flashed up, and came down again into the midst of the Dobarchu. A dreadful squeal was cut off sharply, and Zavahl knew that the weapon had found a victim.

Images flashed before his eyes: the couple snuggling together by the fire; the mother feeding the infant, the melting eyes of the young female who had taken such a fancy to him. With a howl of rage, he threw himself forward at the man and twisted the knife out of his hand. Holding the weapon in both hands, he rammed it down as hard as he could into the wrecker's chest, wrenched it out, and struck again, deeper this time. He felt the sickening grate of steel on bone and hot blood welled up between his fingers. The man was choking, gurgling, vainly clawing at the knife, and the hands that still held it. Then blood gushed from his mouth, and his body convulsed, as his eyes glazed over, focusing on the sky in a blank, unseeing gaze.

'Well, may I be dipped in dog's dung! Well done, Zavahl. I never knew you had it in you!' Suddenly he realised that Toulac was at his side, clapping him on the back. Finally, Zavahl remembered to let go of the knife. He felt an instant of wild elation that he had survived, and eradicated that murdering scum of a wrecker. Then the reality hit him. He doubled over, vomiting, turning his face away so that he would not have to look at the carnage he had wrought.

Then, as if from far away, he heard Toulac speak again. 'Myrial up a tree, the ship! What's happening to the ship?'

The ocean-going barge had made good time. The sea was relatively calm, and the moderate wind, for once, was in their favour. They slipped through the dark waters, with Arnond at the helm, and Meglyn manning the sheets. Rowen was down below, putting a meal together, with Elion trying to help, and getting underfoot in the cramped living quarters. Kaz was dozing up on deck, but Veldan and Ailie had been keeping watch in the bows all the way along the coast. They had tried taking turn about, but the one who was supposed to be resting had inevitably ended up leaning on the rail and peering anxiously out into the night in any case, so they had decided that they might as well have one another's company.

It was impossible to say who saw the beacon first. They both called out together as the twinkling light sprang up on the clifftop ahead. Their yells brought Meglyn forward, and Elion scrambling up through the hatchway from below. After a moment or two, Rowen hauled herself up behind him.

On deck, the firedrake raised a sleepy head, and blinked at the twinkling light. 'About time, too,' he grumbled. 'Say what you like about Amaurn, but it's a good thing he had Skreeva killed when he did, and stopped her minions taking Toulac and Zavahl any further. Otherwise we might be stuck on this miserable floating prison for a month.' Kaz hadn't taken to life on shipboard very well. During the course of the day he had informed Veldan, more times than she cared to remember, that the deck was too cramped for him to move around with any comfort, he always had to be concentrating on where he was putting his tail and, furthermore, he was pretty sure that firedrakes couldn't swim, so the presence of so much deep water all around him most definitely did *not* put him at his ease. And though they weren't afraid of Kaz himself, the presence on board of a creature who could breathe fire was bound to make Meglyn and the others a little uneasy.

At the helm, Arnond was frowning. 'They *would* fetch up here,' he said. 'This is the rockiest stretch on the entire coast. It's claimed a lot of lives.'

Now they could hear the hiss and boom of the waves breaking on the reef, and see the border of white surf along the shore. 'Will we be able to get in close enough, do you think?' Veldan asked anxiously. 'You certainly daren't take any risks with Rowen at the moment.'

'Or my ship,' Meglyn added.

'Or me – if anyone cares about that,' muttered Kaz, but only the two Loremasters heard him.

'Do those friends of yours know anything about seafaring?' Rowen asked. 'Would they light their beacon just anywhere along the cliff, or would they take the currents and rocks into account?'

'I doubt it,' said Veldan. 'Zavahl certainly wouldn't. I don't know for sure about Toulac, though. She certainly has lived a full and colourful life. She never mentioned spending any time at sea, but that means nothing. In our talks, we've hardly had time to touch the surface of all the things she's done.'

'All right,' said Arnond, 'we'd better be on the safe side, and presume neither of them knows what they're doing. This is what we'll do. Meglyn, shorten sail to a bare minimum. We'll have to edge our way in very slowly and carefully. Rowen, will you get the lead and take soundings?'

'Of course.' Rowen went off, hurrying as best she could.

'What's the lead?' Ailie whispered to Veldan.

The Loremaster shrugged. 'If it's anything technical, you'd better ask Elion. His partner was a good sailor.'

'The lead is used to test the depth of the water,' Elion explained. 'It's attached to the end of a rope which is marked off into fathoms, and someone stands in the bows and throws it out ahead of the ship. There's a hole in the bottom of the lead, too. If you fill it with soft tallow, then it comes up with a sample of the bottom sticking to it, so you can tell whether you're sailing over sand, or mud, or rock.' He grinned at Ailie. 'There. Now you know as much about it as I do.'

Cautiously they felt their way forward. Veldan, in a moment of inspiration, explained to Arnond about Kaz's remarkable, adaptable vision, and the firedrake was immediately sent into the bows to watch for rocks in their path, or telltale changes on the surface of the water that would indicate currents.

Suddenly, Ailie gave a yell, and pointed. 'Look, everybody! Down on the shore, below and to the right of that beacon. There seems to be a fire on the beach – see, among those big boulders up near the cliff. And somebody is down on the rocks, waving torches at us!'

Kaz raised his head from his contemplation of the water, but lowered it quickly when Arnond roared at him. 'Keep your eyes on where we're going, you! Never mind what's on the shore, *you* have more important things to think about.'

Veldan followed Ailie's pointing finger with her eyes. 'It's Toulac! And is that Zavahl behind her?'

'It certainly isn't,' Ailie said positively.

'She's being attacked,' Elion cried. 'Toulac, look out . . . Damn. We're too far away for her to hear us over the noise of the surf.'

Veldan tried mindspeech instead. There was no response from the veteran, but she swung round to face her assailant, so at least she must have heard. With her heart in her mouth, she saw Toulac throw her torches at the man, and draw her sword. At the same time, Ailie shrieked, 'Zavahl! Zavahl! No!'

Only then did the Loremaster see Zavahl, who was a little further along the rocks, being pursued by two men. Suddenly they all went down in a heap, and she thought she saw a flash as a knife blade rose and fell. So near and yet so far. They had arrived moments too late to help. She cursed, and heard a stifled sob from Ailie.

Then, all at once, she heard a strange voice in her mind. 'Loremasters! You're heading straight for the reef.'

Almost in the same instant, Kaz let off a bellow. 'Rocks ahead!'
'Arnond, we're going aground!' Elion yelled.

'Drop anchor, Meglyn!' Arnond shouted. 'Rowen, lower sail!'

The crash of surf was growing louder. There was a few moments of intense activity on deck, then the barge swung round in the current. Its anchor bit into the sea bed, dragged a little way, then held fast. Suddenly, they could all breathe again. The brief, relieved pause was ended with Ailie's cry. 'Zavahl! He's up! Get away from him, damn you. Leave him alone!'

Veldan swung round to see one of the men still lying in a huddle on the ground, and the other on his feet, in hot pursuit of Zavahl, and gaining fast. She looked across the stretch of water that still remained between the barge and the shore. 'Arnond . . .' she began to protest.

'I'm sorry, Veldan.' The captain's voice was firm. 'I won't risk taking her in any further. We'll lower the dinghy and row to shore, but it'll take a few minutes.'

As they watched, a wave of lithe, dark-furred creatures seemed to rise up out of the rocks and pull Zavahl's opponent down. Elion cried out in astonishment. 'Veldan! Aren't they Dobarchu?'

'That's what they look like. But what are they doing here?'

They all heard the shriek as one of the creatures died beneath the attacker's knife, and an answering cry of rage from Zavahl. To Veldan's astonishment, he threw himself at the knifeman, snatched away the blade and plunged it, twice, into the man's chest. Toulac was running towards him but apparently he didn't need her help.

'Looks like he's throwing up,' Kaz commented wryly. Once the barge was safely anchored he had been able to watch the end of the fight without incurring the captain's wrath.

Veldan and Elion exchanged a look of sympathy. 'Remember the first man you ever killed?' Elion said softly.

She made a face. 'I'll never forget it. It was awful.'

'The dinghy is ready,' Meglyn said. 'Which of you is coming with me? Veldan or Elion? If we're bringing your two friends back, there won't be room for anyone else.'

'I would suggest I go,' Elion said to Veldan. 'I've had a bit more practice with boats, and that old shoulder injury of yours might make rowing difficult.'

Reluctantly, Veldan agreed that he was right. Backwatering with her oars, Meglyn held the dinghy steady against the side of the barge, while Elion climbed down a rope ladder into the little rowing boat. On shore, Toulac and Zavahl had spotted them, and were standing together on the rocks, waving and yelling wildly.

'Loremaster Veldan?' The mindspeech had a slightly odd accent, and with a start, she remembered the mysterious voice that had warned her they were heading for the rocks. Clearly Kaz had heard it too. He turned his head and gave her a puzzled look. 'Yes? Who is it?' she asked.

'I am Mrainil, the last surviving Loremaster of the Dobarchu.' A sleek, round head popped up on the surface of the water.

'Thank you for your timely warning, Mrainil,' Veldan said. 'You probably saved all our lives. But what brings you here, so far into these northern waters?'

'Alas, I have bitter tidings.' The sorrow of the Dobarchu washed over her in a wave. 'My race has almost been annihilated, and I have brought the poor, last remnants of my people to Gendival, seeking sanctuary. I know this goes against Cergorn's prohibition, but I no longer care. He is our one last chance, and if he will not take us in, the Dobarchu are finished.'

'You don't need to worry about that,' Veldan assured him. 'Cergorn is no longer Archimandrite and, in this current crisis, all policies are changing. You'll have a home with us, and welcome. I'm sure of it.'

'You ease my mind, Veldan, and your news is the best I have heard in a long, dark age. But if Cergorn rules no longer, then who is Archimandrite now?'

Veldan took a deep breath. 'Amaurn, once known as the renegade.'

'Amaurn? I thought that he must be dead!' There was a pause, while Mrainil digested Veldan's startling news. 'When we have a moment, you must tell me how such an astounding thing could have come about. I was very young when he was accused of treason, and like most young folk, I sided with the rebel. Since then, my perceptions of the world have changed a good deal, and with them, my opinions of Amaurn, who must have been misguided in some matters, if not all. But if he will save my people, then perhaps the views of my youth were the right ones after all. There is much to be said for a compassionate heart, especially in these times.'

Compassionate heart? Veldan thought of the merciless Lord Blade and shuddered, but kept her own counsel.

People can change, and I truly believe that Amaurn is doing his best to leave Blade behind him. At least I hope so, for all our sakes. For now, though, I must – we all must – give him the benefit of the doubt.

In the meantime, a change of subject wouldn't hurt. 'How many of your people are with you?' she asked Mrainil.

'Eighteen – seventeen, now,' he added, with a touch of bitterness. 'Oh, my people were right to help your friend. But we can scarcely afford to lose any of our number. Our future hangs by a thread.'

'I regret your loss most keenly,' Veldan said. 'Your people were very brave to go to Zavahl's aid like that, when they could have simply taken to the water and saved themselves. At least I can bring you one piece of news that might help ease your grief a little. You aren't the last surviving Loremaster of the Dobarchu, Mrainil. Kyrre made it through to us, and though she was badly injured, she is recovering now, and will be very glad to see you.'

Mrainil gave a squeak of joy. 'Kyrre? She's alive? Oh, this is wonderful news! I can scarcely believe it.'

Veldan smiled. 'You and your people have suffered indeed, Mrainil, but we'll take good care of you now. We'll get you all aboard the boat, if you're agreeable, and we'll take you up the river to Gendival in style. And later, if you want to come back to the ocean, I'm sure we can find you somewhere to settle along the coast. It'll be much colder than you're used to, but maybe we can find some way around that.'

'The lake at Gendival will suit us very well at present,' Mrainil said. 'Fresh water is not ideal for us, but under the current circumstances, it'll do just fine.'

'And if you get sick of freshwater fish, we can get the Navigators to bring you shellfish upriver from the coast,' Veldan promised. 'If we put them on ice, they should keep fresh enough.'

'I hate to break up this meeting,' Kaz interrupted, 'but the dinghy has reached the shore. They'll be on their way back soon.'

'I must get my people organised,' said Mrainil, and streaked back through the waves, towards the shore.

Veldan hugged the firedrake, then went to join an excited Ailie at the rail, to welcome the wanderers.

With piteous cries, the Dobarchu had gathered round their comrade. As Zavahl approached, they made space for him, and let him kneel down beside the still form. He laid a hand on the soft, sleek fur. 'I'm sorry,' he said softly. 'I'm truly sorry.'

When he had been Hierarch, Gilarra had often accused him of being too uncaring, and too detached from the lives of the folk who depended on him to care for them. Now he knew how right she had been. In one short night, these alien Dobarchu had become closer to him than any of his own Callisiorans had ever been. He had found out what it meant to care – and it cut both ways.

Would a single one of my subjects have laid down their life for me as this little creature did tonight? I know very well that they wouldn't. But I was so cut off from them. Why should they care what happened to me?

But someone here cared about him. He looked down to see his new friend the young female gazing up at him. She pushed herself under his arm, and snuggled close. Zavahl hugged her. 'Thank Myrial it wasn't you, little one,' he said softly. 'You probably can't understand me, but I'm glad to see that you're safe.'

Just then, he felt a touch on his shoulder. 'Come on,' Toulac said gruffly. 'Look, they're bringing a boat in. We'll have you back to your lady friend in no time.'

Reluctantly, Zavahl let her pull him away from the body of the

Dobarchu. 'Shouldn't we bury him, or something?' he asked.

'His people are going to take care of him before we leave,' Toulac told him. 'Mrainil said they always bury their dead at sea.'

'As long as he has a proper resting place,' Zavahl said. 'I owe my life to him and his friends.'

'And we won't worry about the wreckers,' Toulac added. 'Let the carrion take care of itself. At least the crabs will have a feast tonight.'

Together they went down to meet the boat, which by now was close inshore. Zavahl saw that it was being rowed by a strange woman with dark, cropped hair and, to his relief, Elion. After everything that had happened, it was good to see another familiar face. It was difficult to clamber from the slippery rocks into the light, pitching craft, and Zavahl came very close to plunging headfirst into the sea, but the tall woman reached out an arm, grabbed a handful of his shirt, and yanked hard, so that somehow he found himself in a heap in the bottom of the boat, wondering rather dazedly how he had managed to get there. To his surprise his little friend, who had accompanied him down to the sea, leapt in after him, clearly determined not to let him out of her sight.

Elion was grinning at him. 'I hope Ailie isn't going to be jealous.'

Zavahl didn't know what to say. He wasn't used to being chaffed in this way – after all, who would dare tease the Hierarch of Callisiora? – but, though it was a little embarrassing, he liked the warm feeling of belonging that it gave him.

He and Toulac settled in the stern while Elion and the woman, who had been introduced as Meglyn, bent to the oars. Zavahl glanced back at the lonely beach where so much had happened. The Dobarchu were gone now, taking their comrade to his last resting place. Up on the beach near the cliff, a dim glow of firelight marked the position of the shelter on which he and Toulac had worked so hard and, glad though he was to be leaving, he felt a pang at having to leave it behind. It would always stand out in his memory as the first thing he had ever created with his own two hands.

A real bed would be welcome, though. He was shivering with exhaustion and delayed reaction to the attack, as well as from the cold. Sea water had got into the shallow cut along his ribs, and the wound burned and stung from the salt. It was an infinite relief to reach the rescue vessel. After hoisting his Dobarchu friend, who had obviously decided never to forsake him, onto the deck, he climbed awkwardly aboard himself, and his relief on reaching safety at last was so profound that he almost wept.

For the first time in his life, Zavahl found himself among friends. Ailie came rushing forward and hugged him. Caught up in the exuberance of the moment, he hugged Veldan too. After an instant of frozen astonishment, she hugged him back, with a smile that lit up her whole face. For the first time, he looked past her scar at what lay beyond, and was stunned by the extraordinary beauty that he saw.

Dear Myrial! And I called her a monster! No wonder she hated me.

Then he was hugging Ailie again, alight with pure happiness, and if anyone had come up to him in that moment and offered to spirit him back to his old life as Hierarch of Callisiora, with all its attendant pomp and wealth, he would have laughed in their face.

FIFTEEN

SOLID AIR

S call rode helplessly through the darkness, torn between anger and fear. He could feel the clutch of the Summoner's mind, overriding his wishes, trapping his own thoughts deep within him. It was forcing him to stay on the horse and keep riding through the storm, away from shelter and safety and familiar surroundings, away from the trader and Rochalla, away from all his hopes of making a new future for himself.

Inwardly, he raged at Dark.

How could he do this to me? I trusted him! What right has he to tear me away from Tormon and the others like this?

Beneath the anger, however, fear gnawed at him. If only he could see Dark's face, it might give him some clue as to his captor's state of mind, but even such glimpses as he could get were useless, for the Summoner's features were hidden and inscrutable beneath the expressionless mask of bone, and the boy could find no answers to his questions. Why had Dark run away like that, when he could have identified Grim's killer, and had Scall's evidence in support? It made no sense. Why had he involved Scall in his flight? Surely, if he wanted to escape, a reluctant captive could only be a hindrance.

What does he want with me? Where am I being taken? What's going to happen to me now? Will I ever see my friends again?

As well as being afraid for himself, he was also concerned for the safety of the others; especially Rochalla, who was unaware of the changes that had taken place in Presvel, who was now as dangerous and unpredictable as a wild beast. Presvel had lain in wait for him, and threatened him. Presvel had killed the old Summoner, Grim. Tormon had warned Scall to beware of the man and he had been right, but he could have no idea of the extent of the threat. Presvel had been finding it increasingly difficult to cope with life beyond the luxury and security of Tiarond's walls. It had been plain, even to Scall, that the balance of his mind had been deteriorating with every step that took him further from the city, and now it seemed he had lost his last, lingering hold on sanity. Rochalla was trapped with him in the Reiver stronghold, innocent of her peril – and he, Scall, was unable to warn her.

In that moment, he detested Dark with all his heart. His only goal now must be to bide his time – not that he had much choice, at present – and await his chance to escape. Surely the Summoner couldn't keep him under this unnatural control for ever. As soon as the opportunity presented itself, Scall knew he must be ready. He looked at the cloaked figure who rode ahead of him, dimly visible through the driving sleet.

You'd better watch out, Dark. I don't plan to be a prisoner for ever!

Only the faint hope that he might somehow get away kept him from sinking into utter despair.

Unfortunately, the Summoner's unyielding hold over him didn't keep away the night's bitter chill. Scall's ears, jaw, toes and fingers were aching with the cold. The wind seemed to blow straight though his wet clothing, and kept on going till it reached his very bones. He was more concerned, however, with the fact that his little mare was in distress. She was too finely bred for a climate such as this, and was without the shaggy coats that let the Reiver horses weather the wild moors. She lacked their sturdiness and stamina, too. The long journey from Tiarond had left her badly in need of a good rest, and now she was exhausted from fighting the cold and the storm. He could feel her trembling beneath him, and wondered how much longer she could keep going before she collapsed. Scall couldn't bear to think of her suffering as she was. If any harm came to her, he would find a way to make Dark pay if it took him the rest of his life.

All thoughts of escape, his friends, and even his beloved horse fled from Scall's mind as he and his captor drew close to the border of the only land he had ever known. Though naturally he had heard of the Curtain Walls, he had never had the opportunity to see them, and had only half-believed the stories. Now the vast, multicoloured sheets of light that stretched across the horizon and towered up into the sky struck awe into his heart. They shone brightly even through the drifting veils of sleet, and he shrank beneath such immensity, unnerved by the flickering, unnatural radiance that lit the landscape for miles around, and the snarling, buzzing sound that vibrated through his body and set his teeth on edge. There was a smell on the wind that reminded him of the air during a thunderstorm, and he could feel an uncomfortable prickling all over him, like insects crawling on his skin.

After a time, Dark slowed his pace, and seemed to hesitate, peering around as if looking for some landmark. Again, Scall wondered where he was being taken. A dreadful thought had begun to grow in him. Had the Summoner somehow been driven mad by grief over his master's death? Had some temporary insanity sent him out onto the moors in this dreadful storm? Scall had heard tales of such things happening, though he had no way of knowing whether there was any truth in them.

If he hasn't lost his mind, then I don't know what the idiot can be thinking of. There's absolutely nothing out here, and if we don't find shelter soon, we'll die for sure.

Finally, Dark appeared to have come to a decision. He turned aside from the route they had been taking, and followed the curve of the slope round the bottom of a steep hill. Suddenly, the unnerving glow of the Curtain Walls was straight ahead, and both the buzzing and the crawling discomfort on Scall's body were increasing. He saw that they were in a narrow vale, with steep grassy slopes and high ridges on either side. Several narrow streamlets, edged by occasional clumps of gorse and thorn, ran through the valley from springs that trickled here and there on the steep, grassy slopes, but he had little chance to notice such details. His mind quailed from the sight before him, refusing to believe that they could be heading directly for that glowing barrier. Had the Summoner decided to end his life by riding into the Curtain Walls? What would happen to someone who rode right into such sheets of fearful energy? Would he survive the experience? Scall very much doubted it. Dark, however, appeared to have other ideas. With his goal clearly in sight, he picked up the pace a little, dragging a reluctant captive on his equally reluctant horse, behind.

Suddenly, the shrieking in the air that Scall had assumed to be the wind, grew louder – loud enough to drown the buzz of the Curtain Walls – and he recognised the shrill, discordant voices which had haunted his blackest nightmares ever since he had left the city. The winged fiends from Tiarond were coming and here he was, penned in this bottleneck of a valley like a cornered rat.

Scall's mouth went dry. Panic caused his heart to thunder in his chest. Desperately he tried to move, to speak, to warn Dark of their peril, but the Summoner's hold was too complete. All he could do was sit helplessly in the saddle, and wait for his death to come plummeting from the skies. But Scall was not the only one who remembered. Without warning, the little chestnut took off at a gallop, running away from the threat, towards the Curtain Walls.

Dark was taken completely by surprise. During the entire journey, the mare had been dragging at her tether, and he had been braced against that pull. Now she darted ahead, jerking him the other way, and almost yanking him out of the saddle. To save himself, the Summoner let go of the rein, and the mare, unfettered now, moved even faster. Her panic was contagious, and set the other horses wheeling and plunging, so that Dark's concentration was bent on restraining the frightened beasts.

Scall felt the iron grip that had subdued his mind slacken abruptly, letting him regain the mastery of his body. Gradually he got his bolting mount back under control – an endeavour made much easier by her weariness, and the fact that she was almost as afraid of the barrier that lay before her as she was terrified by the horrors she had left behind. Scall had no disagreement with that. He was going nowhere near that barrier – not if *he* could help it! Pulling her head around, he turned her back the way he had come, and found Dark in pursuit some little way behind, unaware of the black airborne shape, half-obscured by the skeins of drifting sleet, that was gaining on him fast.

In that instant, Scall's resentment of the Summoner seemed insignificant. No matter that he had got them into this predicament, he was human, and not some vile and brutal monster. Besides, maybe he had some sort of mysterious power, or knew some way of defending them, of which Scall was unaware. 'Dark! Look out! Above you!' With all his might, he screamed the words into the storm.

Without waiting to see if Dark had heard, he cast desperately around for a weapon of some kind. One of the streamlets was nearly at Scall's feet, its shallow bed littered along the edges with smooth, water-worn stones of various sizes. Scall slid out of his saddle, remembering to put an arm through a loop of the reins, as Tormon had taught him, so that his horse would have no chance of running away. Stooping, he snatched up a missile. Back when he had been an apprentice in the Precincts, he had always been the best among his companions at throwing stones. He took aim in the direction of winged shape that was swooping low over Dark's head, and threw.

Dark had heard Scall cry out, but had been unable to make out the words over the discordant drone of the Curtain Walls, and the shrieking of the wind. He barely had time to wonder at the terror on the boy's face, when Scall started throwing rocks at him. Though the Summoner had been present during various discussions of the winged fiends, such peril that came from above was still an abstraction, outside his normal experience, and it was completely unnatural for him to look up in response to a threat. Besides, no one had expected the deadly creatures to have come so far from Tiarond so soon. Thinking that *he* was Scall's target, he crouched low on the neck of his mount, which impeded his vision even further.

All at once, something hit him with tremendous force, driving his breath from his body and knocking him from the saddle. He hit the ground hard, banging his head, and narrowly missed being trampled by the two panic-stricken horses. Dazed, he tried to roll over onto his hands and knees so that he could lever himself up to his feet, but he was prevented by a weight that pressed down on him, pinning him underneath. As the shock of the fall subsided and the flashes of scintillant coloured light cleared from his vision, he opened his eyes – and looked into the face of death itself.

The narrow, bony features of Dark's attacker were far more terrifying than his own skull mask had ever been, perhaps all the more so because they were a hideous travesty of the human face. The mouth was the wide maw of a predator and filled with cruel, pointed fangs. Its stench was foul, like rotting meat, and its pitiless eyes burned with an unearthly crimson light. All of this Dark saw in a single, frozen instant of horror which branded the image indelibly on his memory.

The fiend stooped over him like a hawk on its prey, and gave a drawn-out hiss. Its great, black wings stretched over him, blotting out the light. The long, sharp talons on one sinewy hand pierced straight through his clothes into his skin, while the other was upraised, razored claws extended, ready to tear him open. Dark cringed away, crying out in terror, convinced that his last moment had come, but the creature hesitated, its head cocked on one side. It was plainly puzzled by the Summoner's skull mask. Making a small, interrogative sound, it extended its talons still further, reaching out tentatively towards his face – then suddenly it gave a lurch, and toppled over to one side with a cry that was cut off abruptly as Scall appeared behind it, and hit it a second time with the rock he held in his hand.

The lad stood over him, weighing the bloodstained rock in his hand as if contemplating whether to hit the Summoner with it, too. Dark noticed that the last of the boyishness had left his face. 'You know what *that* was, I expect,' he said, in a voice that was dangerously calm. 'Now that you've got us into this mess, would you like to tell me what you plan to do next? Because if there's one of those creatures around, then there'll soon be more, and I don't think it'll take very long for them to find us.' Abruptly, his fragile calm shattered. '*This is all your fault!*' With a howl, Scall attacked the Summoner, who was still trying to rise, kicking him and pummelling him with his fists. 'Why?' he cried. 'Why did you do this, you stupid fool? Don't you realise that you've killed us both?'

Though the boy was too exhausted, and too numb and stiff with cold to do much damage with his blows, they stopped Dark from concentrating enough to get Scall's mind back under control. 'Stop! Scall, stop it!' he shouted, struggling to get to his feet and defend himself.

Suddenly Scall broke away and began to run towards his horse, which he had tethered to a thorn bush at the edge of a nearby thicket.

'Damn!' Finally, Dark managed to scramble to his feet. Without bothering to run after his escaping companion, he simply threw all his will in Scall's direction and, once again, took control of his body.

Scall fought back, but to no avail, as the Summoner overwhelmed him. The brief, brutal battle was fought in silence, but in the recesses of his mind, Dark could feel the boy's struggles, and hear him screaming. Each cry tore at his heart. He knew, however, that he had no choice. There was no way that the lad would go through the Curtain Walls voluntarily yet, judging from what he had said, more of those foul creatures might be on their way right now.

The two Reiver horses, still joined by their tether, had managed, in their panic, to entangle themselves in a thorn thicket a little way downstream. Keeping his will firmly on Scall, Dark hurried to reclaim the straying beasts, and finally managed to get himself and his captive safely mounted once more. This time he didn't let Scall ride, but used the length of rope from his pack to bind the boy across the saddle. He'd need all his concentration to find his way through the Curtain Walls, without wasting any on keeping his captive under control.

Dark was ready to leave when he happened to glance down at

the creature as it lay on the ground not far from his feet. It was unconscious, but still alive, for he could see the rapid rise and fall of its breathing. He forced himself to overcome his revulsion, and scrutinise it carefully – while still maintaining a safe distance. As he looked at it, a thought struck him and, in his mind, he heard his mentor's voice.

'*Whenever you believe you have an adversary, remember that you must seek beyond the obvious, for your true enemy is ignorance itself.*'

This was one of Grim's favourite lessons, and he had repeated it many times. Now, his pupil wondered whether the Shadowleague had ever been given the opportunity to study a live specimen of one of these fearsome predators. He doubted it. They wouldn't be too easy to capture alive. It had only been a fortunate chance that this one had happened to be alone, and that Scall had been there with his rock while it was preoccupied with Dark. Surely, then, any knowledge they could gain from this particular creature would prove invaluable in working out a way to destroy its brethren. Dark looked again at the wiry body, built for speed and strength, and at those evil fangs and claws, and knew an instant's doubt. Would the Shadowleague really be grateful for such a gift? Or would they punish him for bringing such a deadly threat into their midst? He had no way of knowing. All he had was the courage of his own convictions: in his very bones he *knew* that studying these fiends was the right thing to do.

'*In many cases, when you come to understand your foe, you find out that he isn't really your enemy at all.*'

Again, Grim's words came flashing into his mind. He looked down at the formidable natural weapons of this adversary, thought of its ability to strike from the skies, remembered the glare of those pitiless red eyes and doubted, in this instance, whether Grim could be right – but there was only one way to find out, and little time to waste.

It was a good thing that Grim had insisted they bring plenty of rope. As quickly as he could, he bound the dreadful fiend with hands that were clumsy with cold, and tied it across the back of Grim's horse. It took longer than he would have wanted, especially as he was continually nagged by the possibility that more of its brethren might come flying out of the storm. All the while, he was shrinking from the foul stench and the greasy, unclean touch of the pebbled, greyish skin, and terrified that the creature would awaken suddenly, before he had a chance to make it secure. The horse was even less impressed, and it took several precious moments and the full force of the Summoner's will before it calmed down, and reluctantly accepted its burden.

By this time, Dark was almost frantic. The shrieking in the wind was increasing once more, and with it, his sense of unease. At last everything was ready, and with a sigh of relief, he mounted his horse, and led his odd little cavalcade at a gallop towards the Curtain Walls.

As he drew near, the crawling sensation on his skin increased to the point of real discomfort, and that was another reason for Dark to hurry. He knew that the horses wouldn't stay close to such an unpleasant phenomenon for long. Closing his eyes, the better to remember Grim's last, whispered instructions to him, he reached out towards the barrier with his mind, trying to somehow pene-trate beyond it, to the arcane intelligence – if it could be called that – which lay at its core. It was much harder even than he had expected. Grim had warned him that this was no human mind with which he was trying to make contact, but something vast and alien. 'I can't explain it,' he had said, 'but when you find it, you'll know.'

Well, thanks, Grim. That's a lot of help.

Dark squeezed his eyes shut, and tried harder – then, all at once, he had it. He felt a peculiar sensation of merging as his mind locked with a *Something*. It was not a human consciousness, such as he had found in his encounters with Scall, or with the young boy whose Passing he had conducted, nor was it an intelligence such as that of Grim's mind when they communicated in their thoughts. This was more of an *Awareness*, and one so vast that it beggared all belief. For a giddy instant, Dark merged with an entire world – a world that, until now, he had never known existed. His mentor had told him that there were other realms beyond the Curtain Walls, and he had thought he understood the concept, but now he was overwhelmed by the immensity, the bewildering complexity, the beauty, the terror, and the sheer fascination of his first encounter with the world of Myrial.

The buzzing of the Curtain Walls changed in volume and pitch, and at the edge of his awareness, Dark realised that the barrier had parted, to let him pass. Taking a deep breath, he rode through, and as he did so, he felt the *Awareness* leave him with a wrenching snap. As the aperture began to close behind him, he slumped down on his horse's neck, utterly drained by his contact with the overmind of a whole world.

It was the shrieking cries that warned him. Dark jerked upright, his exhaustion dispelled by a jolt of white-hot fear. One, two, three black-winged shapes came hurtling through the diminishing gap. A fourth came just too late, and he heard its agonised screams as the barrier closed upon it. Ignoring the death of their companion, the other three came straight for Dark, their talons extended and their eyes glowing with a demonic light. There was nowhere to run, and no way to fight.

I'm finished!

Even as the thought went wailing through his mind, he remembered what Grim had done the day they'd been attacked by the father of the young Reiver boy. Concentrating all his will, he threw up a barrier of his own – a shield of force that enclosed himself, his prisoners, and the horses within a dome of solid air. As the fiends impacted with his transparent obstacle, Dark flinched, but somehow he kept his concentration, and his structure held firm. The creatures stopped dead in the air, as though they had collided with a stone wall, and fell back in a tangle of flailing wings and limbs, sliding off the curved surface of the dome.

Baffled, their eyes blazing with anger, the predators launched themselves at Dark once more – and once more fell back, thwarted, only a couple of feet away from their prey. In a frenzy, they redoubled their attacks, determined to batter their way through to the feast they could so clearly see. It was terrifying to be so close to them. The barrier did nothing to keep out their foul carrion stench, nor the piercing, discordant shrieks of their voices. He was sure that he could hear the faint scrabbling, scratching sound of their claws upon the shield he had created.

It was dreadful to be surrounded by such fiends, for they had placed themselves at intervals around the dome, and were attacking it from different angles, but in time, Dark came to realise that this was a good thing. If all three of them had concentrated their efforts on one place, he doubted that he would have had sufficient strength to keep them out – and besides, the horses, in trying to bolt away from the threat, would be putting pressure on the shield from within. As it was, they had been driven into a sweating, panic-stricken huddle in the centre of the dome, trying to keep as far away as possible from the threat outside.

Dark was proud of his barrier. Grim had taught him the technique after they were threatened by the grieving father of the Reiver boy, but this was the first time he'd actually had the chance – or the need – to put his lessons into practice. But there was no point in congratulating himself too soon. Effective the shield might be, and his only hope of survival, but unfortunately, it was also a trap. Dark had not yet perfected the technique of moving around while keeping his defence in place. Maybe if he only had himself to cover, he could manage it – at least, he was *fairly* sure he could – but he couldn't extend it far enough to keep it in position for long over three moving horses, which were so scared that they might they might bolt off over the horizon at any moment.

To make matters worse, the three winged fiends showed no signs of being discouraged by their failure to reach their prey. They could see quite clearly that there was food under the dome, and they would simply keep up their onslaught with mindless ferocity until Dark's strength and concentration gave out, and his defences could be penetrated.

Wonderful. So what do I do now, Grim?

The strain of keeping up such a large shield was immense, and Dark could already feel himself beginning to tire. Despite the cold, he could feel sweat beginning to form on his brow and beneath his clothes, and his breathing was growing faster. He was glad that he had remained on his horse. He was starting to tremble now, and he doubted very much that his shaking legs could have supported him, had he been standing on his feet. Beyond his frail barrier, could the predators sense that he was weakening? Was it only his imagination that made them seem to be redoubling the ferocity of their attacks? Grim had trusted him to get through the Curtain Walls and reach the Shadowleague. How could he fail his mentor? Surely he wasn't destined to end his life as scraps of meat in the belly of these foul creatures?

Help! Please! Somebody help me!

The cry in his mind had been a reflex, a simple voicing of despair; the actions of a man at his wits' end. No one was more surprised than Dark when he received a reply.

'Stand firm. I'm coming.' A moment later, a flaming shape came hurtling out of the darkness like a comet, trailing a long tail of sparks. It exploded into the midst of Dark's assailants, aiming straight for the eyes of one of the foul creatures. There was a blood-freezing scream, and the sharp stench of burning flesh came through the Summoner's shield. The fiend fell to the ground, clawing at its eyes, still emitting those ghastly shrieks, while its two companions scattered in opposite directions. One of them fled, taking a course at right angles to the Curtain Walls, and the fiery entity streaked round to follow. The other predator flew off parallel to the mysterious barrier, heading north at a tremendous speed.

What in the name of all creation was *that?*

Dark slumped in the saddle, running out of strength and desperate to let his shield go, but too suspicious of his alien, unknown bene-factor to let himself relax just yet. Now that the first crisis was over, he realised that the strange creature had addressed him in mind-speech, just as his mentor had been wont to do. The Summoner shook his head, trying to clear his mind. He knew he wasn't thinking clearly: his thoughts were a seething mix of confusion, exhaustion, and fear. Was the fiery being one of the Shadowleague, then? Grim had claimed that all sorts of weird and incredible creatures were part of that elite order, but Dark had only half-believed it. His master had been known to tease him before now.

Well, whatever it was, at least it got those foul demons off his back. He was just weighing up the possibilities of letting the shield go, and continuing on his way, when he caught sight of a distant flicker of light in the sky, too golden to be a star, and moving fast across the horizon. After a few moments, it was plain that the burning one – or another of its kind – was returning, and Dark steeled himself for the inevitable confrontation.

Closer and closer came the fiery shape, growing both in size and brightness as it approached. Finally it slowed and hovered just beyond his shield, and he was astonished to see that it was a beautiful bird, about the size and shape of an eagle, with a fiery crest and every feather on its body marked in shades of gold, and delineated in dazzling flame. From the beak and fierce eye of an raptor, to a streaming tail of fire and sparks at least a yard long, the effulgent being was a preternatural vision but, even more miraculously, Dark could actually *feel* the heat that the creature radiated penetrating his shield, and for the first time that night, he actually felt warm.

'Who in the name of wonder are *you?*' The voice, when it resounded through his mind, managed to sound both puzzled and sharp with annoyance. It was, however, definitely feminine. 'You aren't a member of the Shadowleague,' the glorious entity accused him. 'Who taught you how to penetrate the Curtain Walls? How do you know mindspeech? And what in the name of perdition were you playing at, to let those foul monsters through into Gendival? They both got away, you know. I couldn't catch the one I was chasing, and goodness only knows where the other is by now. Whoever you are, the Archimandrite isn't going to be very pleased with this night's work, let me tell you.' She – he supposed he should be calling it a she – paused to regard him beadily. 'Well? Did the Ak'Zahar steal away your tongue? And for pity's sake, why don't you drop that shield, before you collapse. What do you think I'm going to do? Eat you?'

With that savage, curving beak, she looked as though she *could* make a meal of him – *and* cook him first. With an effort, Dark pulled himself together. 'I . . . I'm sorry about letting the fiends through,' he answered in mindspeech. 'I couldn't help it – they just came out of nowhere when I opened the Curtain Walls. No one thought they would get here from Tiarond so fast.'

'You came from Tiarond?'

'No. From the lands of the Reivers, not that far from here. But my clan are sheltering a handful of refugees from the city, including this boy.' He gestured at Scall, who was still bound across the saddle of the chestnut mare, and twisting his head to gape at the fiery vision. 'My mentor, Grim, said that I must—'

'Wait! You're a friend of Grim?' Suddenly, much of the sharpness had vanished from the voice of the avain vision. 'Why didn't you say so before? Take off that ridiculous mask, so I can see your face. And while we're at it, will you *please* drop that shield, before you collapse?'

'Oh.' In his amazement at being addressed by such an exotic being, Dark had forgotten all about the shield. With relief he let it go, and felt it fall away from him as though he had finally stopped carrying a heavy burden on his back. Reluctantly, he removed his mask, feeling very vulnerable without it. For years now, the only people who had seen his naked face were Izobia and Grim. A shiver went through him as the cold night air struck his unprotected skin. Belatedly, he remembered his manners, and bowed his head to his bright companion. 'My name is Dark, and I was Grim's apprentice – until tonight.'

She nodded her fiery crest to him. 'I am Vaure, Phoenix and Listener, and . . . Wait! What do you mean, you *were* his apprentice?'

Once more, Dark felt the weight of his sorrow descend upon him. 'Grim is dead. He was murdered tonight by a companion of this lad, who had lost his reason, I think, in the attacks of the . . . What did you call them?'

'Ak'Zahar,' Vaure replied absently. 'Dark, this is grievous news! It is long since Grim was in Gendival, but I remember him when he was young, as you are now. He had another name then, but he was greatly respected and loved among the Shadowleague.'

'I loved him too.' Dark discovered that even a mental voice could still break on a sob, 'And I don't know what I'm going to do without him. With his last breath he charged me to come to you, and to bring this lad with me, and some strange artefacts that he found beneath the city, when he was escaping Tiarond.'

'And so you came as he asked you, and that is to your credit. But you bring more than this lad, I fear.' Suddenly Vaure's voice was censorious once more. 'How dare you bring with you one of the foul Ak'Zahar to endanger our land?'

Damn! I knew there would be trouble about this.

But Dark was still convinced that he was right. 'By a fluke I managed to capture the creature alive. Surely that can't happen very often, so I thought the Shadowleague might like the opportunity to study a living specimen. I thought we would need all the information about them we can muster, if we are ever to remove their threat.'

'*We?* Presumptuous indeed! But we will see what the Archimandrite Amaurn has to say about your temerity. He may have very different ideas about the future of one who has unleashed the Ak'Zahar on Gendival.'

For a moment, Dark almost capitulated, and suggested that they kill the creature here, and be done with it – but the promptings of his stubborn conscience would not permit it. He knew that he was right. These creatures should be studied.

I'm already in enough trouble for letting those fiends through the Curtain Walls. A little more won't make too much difference at this point.

But could he – dared he – argue the Archimandrite round to his point of view? Dark hoped so. Otherwise his sojourn with the Shadowleague was going to be brief indeed.

Sixteen

Beneath the Temple

There was no sense of time passing in the Elsewhere that was Thirishri's prison. Though the Magewoman Helverien had created her beautiful illusions of sky and ocean, they remained constant and unaltered, with none of the subtle changes in colour, shadow, and light that marked the passage of a normal day. This should have been wearying, but the Wind-Sprite could feel no sensations of tiredness and, though she did not eat in the normal way of other creatures, but absorbed energy from her surroundings, she now had no need to do even that. It was a good thing she had company, or eventually she would have lost her mind. She was seething with frustration at being trapped in this dreadful place, unable to even communicate with the outside, when the world was in such a state of crisis – or at least, it had been when she was first imprisoned. She had no way of knowing how much time had passed on the normal world while she had languished here. Was it mere moments? Hours? Days? Or would she be released some time in the future, and find that centuries had passed, and all her friends and everything she had known were all long gone? Would she end up like Helverien, doomed to be trapped here for millennia, while history passed her by, and the world altered beyond all recognition?

How could it be borne? How had Helverien stayed sane? Or had she?

'Thirishri?' The Mage was looking up at her, the faint lines of a frown between her brows. 'You're very quiet. Are you all right?'

As right as I can be, in this place, Shree replied grouchily. *I was just wondering how you had managed to stand it for so long.*

'I wonder that myself, sometimes. Somehow I managed never to lose hope that one day I would get out of here, and that helped. The other way was creating this landscape you see all around you from my memory, in all its multifarious detail. That must have taken me a few aeons, let me tell you. It wasn't as simple as it might appear. I can't imagine how the Creators managed to put together our whole world.'

Well, whatever they did, they don't seem to have built the place to last, the Wind-Sprite told her ruefully. *If we can't find a way to stop the collapse of the Curtain Walls soon, there won't be much of a world left for us, and goodness only knows what few species might be left alive at the end of it all.*

Helverien sighed. 'You don't know how deeply I've yearned to see the world again, and for how long. It would be hard indeed if we ever get out of here and there's nothing left. If only we could get out, we might be able to do something to save it. But as things stand, we're helpless.'

What do you mean, we might be able to do something? Shree asked sharply. *What in the name of wonder could we do?*

'Don't you know?' asked the Mage, in what Thirishri considered to be an irritatingly superior tone. 'Beneath the surface of Myrial there are several access points left behind by the Creators. They lead down to the artefacts and mechanisms which maintain the planet's systems. I know for certain that there's one beneath the Basilica in Tiarond. If we could only escape from here and find our way down there, maybe we could work out what was going wrong.'

Do you mean to say it's that easy? That the Ancients would just let anyone walk into these special places and start altering the balances that keep our world running as it should? I don't believe it! And supposing you did find what was amiss? Just how would you propose to put it right? We don't have the powers of the Creators.

Helverien shrugged. 'We would worry about that when we got there – if we could only get there. You're right about it not being as easy as it seems. As far as I know, the access is fairly open, but once you get down below, there are all sorts of lethal traps and obstacles, designed to put paid to any unauthorised trespassers.'

*And what do you propose to do about *them*?* Shree said tartly. The casual attitude, almost bordering on arrogance, of this Magewoman was beginning to get on her nerves. *Or do you think you're so special that the hazards simply don't apply to you, and that you can walk straight through a series of obstacles designed by the folk who were clever enough, and powerful enough, to create a world?*

'I wouldn't go that far,' Helverien said calmly, 'but I do stand a fairly good chance of finding my way. You forget that I'm a Recorder and an Archivist. I must be the only person still living who can read the script of the Creators. If only we could get out of here and find one of the control points, I would wager that they must have left some sort of instructions there to help us get in and put the problem right. If the world is in as bad a state as you say it is, it would be worth a try, surely.'

The Wind-Sprite was astounded. What utter temerity, to want to go and meddle with the devices of a race who were powerful enough to build a world! She thought of what Cergorn would say, if he were only here. This was exactly the kind of irresponsible interference that he had been trying to stamp out.

But in this case, would we really be right not to interfere? If matters continue to deteriorate as they are doing, surely there won't be any of us left to inhabit this world anyway. And wouldn't that be against the wishes of the Creators who had given us sanctuary here, in order to preserve our various races?

Cergorn is my Archimandrite, my partner, and my friend. I must respect his wishes.

'Even at the cost of the entire world?' For an instant, Shree did not register the fact that the final voice of her inner debate had not been her own. When the realisation hit her, she exploded into anger. *You were snooping in my mind. How dare you!*

Helverien shrugged, completely unmoved by the Wind-Sprite's outrage. 'Let's just say that I've had a lot of time in here to develop bad habits. That doesn't make me any less right, though. Whoever this Cergorn is, he's an idiot if he's just hiding his head and hoping that this situation will rectify itself. It won't. The Curtain Walls are only the start of it, you'll see. Once the systems start breaking down, one will impact on another which will impact on three more until, realm by realm, the world will become an uninhabitable wasteland full of corpses. If we don't start meddling, my friend, and pretty damn soon, there won't be a world left for us.'

For a moment, Thirishri felt paralysed by horror. *Are you absolutely sure of this?* she said at last.

'Why would I say so, if I wasn't sure of my facts? My people managed to gain access to a fair amount of information belonging to the Creators, before they caught on to what we were doing – thanks to me.' She sighed, a shadow of old pain passing across her face, then rubbed a hand across her eyes as if to wipe the memory away. 'Anyway, at one time, before I became a traitor, I came across an account of what had happened to another world of their creation, when the systems had started to break down. For some reason the usual checking and maintenance had been missed, and the place had been left to its own devices – very much like our own situation, it seems.' She shook her head. 'They discovered the mistake too late. By the time they came back to the place, there was very little left alive. We don't want that to happen here. If there are no longer any Creators to take care of our world, then we'll just have to do it ourselves.'

Somewhere deep in the earth, far below the Temple of Myrial, Aliana stopped, and slumped against a wall, letting herself slide down until she was sitting on the floor. With a sigh, she stretched out her aching legs. It seemed as if she'd walked for miles through endless, featureless dark tunnels. After the last few strenuous days, she was just about at the end of her strength. 'I don't know about you,' she said, 'but I need a rest.'

'About bloody time, too.' She heard Packrat sinking down beside her. 'I thought you were going to keep us walking till we dropped.'

'I was scared that we'd be caught,' Aliana admitted. 'I wanted to get as far as we could before we rested.'

'Well, I notice you didn't bother to ask how far *I* could go without a rest.'

'I don't remember asking *you* to come along at all.'

For once he was without a retort – they were both far too tired to start bickering – and Aliana celebrated her reprieve by getting out the food she had brought with her, while her fellow Ghost did the same. Briefly, she considered offering to pool their resources and share, but thought better of it. She wasn't sure she fancied anything that had been in Packrat's pocket. The air down here was very dry, and they both were desperately thirsty, but Aliana only had a little leather flask that she had filled the previous night in the brewhouse, and Packrat had none at all. They only dared ration themselves a couple of sparing sips each, and Aliana hoped that they could find a supply somewhere down here, or they were going to be in trouble.

After they had eaten, she blew out the candle to conserve it for when they were moving, and the two of them were swallowed by absolute darkness. Unfortunately, as soon as the light had gone, she couldn't seem to control her drooping eyelids any longer. 'Do you think it's safe to go to sleep without posting a guard?' she whispered.

Packrat grunted. 'I couldn't give a damn.'

That was about the last thing she remembered, before she fell asleep herself.

Aliana awakened abruptly, panic sweeping over her. How long had she slept? How much ground had Galveron gained on her? So far there had been no major division in the corridor they followed, though occasionally she had seen openings set high into the wall, large enough for a person to squeeze through, with short ladders leading up to them. The apertures were covered in fine grilles, and appeared to be vents of some sort. Perhaps they were used to keep the place clean, somehow. There was no dust on the floor, where she would have expected to find it, but she could see plenty of muck caught in the rusting grilles. More than once, she had considered climbing into one of these vents, to look inside for a hiding place for the Hierarch's ring, but the grilles looked to be set solidly in place, and she hadn't wanted to waste the time it would take to free them.

They were strange, these corridors. The walls, floor, and ceiling all seemed to be made of a dark metal with a bluish sheen; not reflective, but polished to a soft gleam. Oddly, it felt quite warm to the touch. The air, too, was fairly warm, and whispered gently past her face in the softest of breezes, carrying a faintly acrid tang that she could not quite identify. So far as her circle of candlelight had shown, there had been nothing of particular interest to see up to this point, but on the other hand, no danger had threatened either, so all in all, Aliana was not unhappy with her surroundings. There was only one problem: how was she going to find a hiding place for the ring if these underground passages continued to be so feature-less and empty?

Don't be silly. They must lead somewhere. We just haven't gone far enough, yet.

She lit the candle again, then, because it was very unwise to awaken a Grey Ghost suddenly, she took herself prudently out of reach of Packrat's knife before she gave a shout to rouse him. As she'd expected, he was on his feet, knife in hand, almost before his eyes were open. 'Come on,' she said. 'It's time we were moving again.'

Packrat glared at her, and muttered a curse. Aliana thought of reminding him that no one had forced him to come along, but on seeing his sour expression, she thought better of it. They might as well not start the day – if day it was – with an argument.

After another meagre sip of water each, they continued on their way, driven by Aliana's urgent need to keep on going. 'Galveron's not stupid,' she told her complaining companion. 'Once we're missed, it'll only be a matter of time before he works out where we've gone. They'll look everywhere else, and then they'll realise that we can't be anywhere but down here.'

'Right in her precious Holy of Holies, where no one but the

Hierarch is allowed to set foot,' Packrat said thoughtfully. 'That puts her in a bit of a fix, doesn't it? Will she break her own rules, do you think, and let Galveron come down here after us?'

'Well, she can't send anyone else, that's for sure. Galveron is the only one who knows about the ring. She won't risk her secret going any further.'

'What about Alestan and the rest of the Ghosts? They know. Maybe she'll get them to help. That brother of yours would be anxious to find you, especially once he knows that you're in trouble.'

'That brother of mine is locked up in a prison cell – if Gilarra hasn't thrown him, and the others, out of the Temple already.'

'Nah. Not yet, anyway. Your friends are the only bargaining counter she has.' Packrat's voice took on an accusing tone. 'You know, if it was anyone else, they'd get thrown out of the Grey Ghosts for this. You know damn well what Galveron said about stealing – and then you only go and run off with the most valuable thing in the whole accursed Temple. You've done it now, you stupid fool. We're all finished here. There'll be no more sanctuary in the Temple for *us*. Even if you could manage to talk your way around old Blue-Eyes, there would still be the Hierarch to deal with, and she won't forgive you if you live to be a million – which, seeing as she's going to throw us all out into the streets, isn't very likely.'

Packrat began to stamp along faster, as his voice grew angrier. 'I don't know what you were thinking of. After everything we went through to get to the safety of the Temple – after all *you* did, risking the winged fiends and crawling through all those corpses to bring the blasting powder across – why did you throw it all away? And how could you put the rest of us in such danger? I though we were supposed to be your friends.'

'It's Gilarra,' Aliana protested. 'It's not just the fact that she hates us, and we can't trust her, and she had Alestan arrested. She's no damn good at being Hierarch. She doesn't know how to inspire people, and make them feel they matter. And she's such a cow! Galveron would make a much better leader, but he's so upright and honourable and loyal, it would never cross his mind to take the ring for himself . . .'

'So you decided to take it for him.' Packrat threw wide his hands in a gesture of despair. 'For pity's sake, Aliana, I always thought you had some sense! When did you stop thinking like the leader of the grey Ghosts, and start acting like some woolly-headed simpering virgin without a sensible thought in her head?' He drove one fist into the other. 'I can't *believe* this. You fall for a handsome face and a pair of blue eyes, and the next thing we know, you've broken your word to the most powerful person in the city and betrayed your friends – your only *family* – and for what? Do you really think that Mister Honourable is going to say "Oh, what a good idea, Aliana, I never would have thought of that, I'll seize power at once"? You idiot!'

I don't believe this. Surely it can't be true. He actually sounds as though he's jealous!

Aliana stopped in her tracks, so abruptly that Packrat almost fell over her. 'You're wrong!' she yelled. 'Gilarra started this, the lying, conniving bitch, when she arrested my brother. I'll get her for that if it's the last thing I do. And I did *not* fall in love with Galveron! It's not like that. It's just so obvious that he *should* be the leader! I just thought that if I hid the ring, so that he couldn't hand it over straight away, then there would be a chance of persuading him, that's all. And Gilarra can't throw us out in the meantime, other-wise the ring would be lost to her for good – and surely Galveron wouldn't? Especially if we'd just handed him power?'

There was a long pause before Packrat spoke again. 'You do know, don't you, that when you eventually try to give the ring to Galveron, he'll only take it from you, and give it back to Gilarra.'

Aliana sighed, and sank down to the floor, feeling wretched and spent. 'I know. It's the part I hadn't quite worked out yet – how to cope with that bloody integrity of his.'

Packrat sat down beside her, and when he spoke again, it was in tones of someone picking their way across an unsound roof, knowing that one false step would collapse the whole structure.

'Aliana, if you're determined to get rid of Gilarra as Hierarch, the only way you could possibly do it would be to get rid of Gilarra herself.'

Shock sheeted like ice across Aliana's skin. 'You mean . . . Kill her?'

'Why not?' Packrat's tones were matter-of-fact. 'Do you reckon she would lose any sleep over killing us? You think about it. Ever since we set foot through the door of her accursed Temple, she's been desperate to kick us out again. What else is that but murdering us? She's just telling herself that if the winged fiends *did* happen to kill us, our blood wouldn't be on *her* hands. She's wrong about that. It would still make her a murderer – just a dirty, cowardly one. That wouldn't matter to us, though. Either way, we'd be just as dead.'

The notion of actually killing the Hierarch, however, was too extreme for Aliana to deal with all at once. She had begun this escapade when she was exhausted and angry, and her thinking had not been at its clearest. She was still sure that her plan to make Galveron leader had its merits – if only she could find a way to bring it off. But to actually murder Gilarra? If Packrat was right, it meant that what had started off as an apparently simple plan was getting way out of control, and the consequences, in the long term, would be staggering. 'Come on.' She scrambled hastily to her feet. 'We'd better get moving. Our first priority is to get this ring hidden.' Without waiting for him, she set off down the corridor, walking fast.

'It's no good trying to run away.' Packrat's voice followed her. 'You'll have to face this sooner or later.'

'Oh, shut up, Packrat.'

They travelled on for a while, though Aliana had little idea of exactly how much time had passed. It was easy to lose track down here in the darkness, and besides, her mind was still wrestling with Packrat's suggestion. Though she had twice killed someone in a fight since she first became a Grey Ghost, she had never murdered in cold blood. The knife in the back was the mainstay of a very different sort of thief from a Grey Ghost – which was one of the reasons the gang had survived so long undetected. Even when Lord Blade had been the Godsword Commander, Galveron had been directly responsible for the men who policed the city's streets, and he took a very dim view of murder.

Aliana sighed. Galveron again. Why did everything keep coming back to him? She wished she had never set eyes on him, or the damned Hierarch.

Maybe I should just take the ring back, apologise, and say that it was all a mistake, that I forgot about it and fell asleep somewhere. But how can I? No matter what Packrat was trying to imply, this isn't just about Galveron. When she had Alestan arrested, Gilarra proved that she couldn't be trusted. If I give her the ring, we'll have lost our only hold over her, and she'll be free to do what she likes with us.

As far as she could see, there was no other option other than to carry on with her original plan. Once she no longer had the ring, no one could take it from her, but with it hidden, she would have some room to negotiate. Right now, that seemed the only hope for herself, her friends, and her poor brother.

And what about Packrat's plan to murder Gilarra? Was it true that she would really have no choice?

Dear Myrial, I hope it doesn't come to that!

Aliana was finally distracted from her gloomy thoughts by a glimmer of light that came from somewhere ahead, round a bend in the passage. 'What's that?' She stopped and blew out the candle to get a clearer look at the faint gleam then, with Packrat moving cautiously at her side, she tiptoed closer. It was not a constant radiance, but seemed to wax and wane in pulses like a heartbeat made visible. With each pulse the colour changed, moving from red to orange to yellow to green to blue to violet.

'Myrial's backside,' Packrat muttered. 'That's enough to make your eyes water.'

'But why?' Aliana wondered. 'If they wanted to light it at all, why not just use ordinary light? It would be much more practical. What's the significance of all these colours?'

'Well, there's only one way to find out,' Packrat said. 'We can go round that corner and see what's there. On the other hand, we could do something sensible for the first time today, and go back.' In the dim, chameleon light, he met her eyes. 'Give it up, Aliana. We've precious little water, we'll soon run out of food, and there's nothing down here – or nothing that's ever likely to do us any good.' He put his hand on her arm. 'It was a good try, but it just didn't come off. We weren't to know what it was like down here. Look, let's go back, give that ratbag her stupid ring back, and break Alestan out of jail. Then we should all just get out of there altogether, and go back to the city. Surely we can find a place somewhere that's safe from those monsters? Maybe we could stay in one of those crypts you told us about, where you spent the night before. We might as well face it. No matter how hard we try – or *you* try, at any rate, because you're the one who's made all the sacrifices so far – we'll never fit in with that Temple crowd.'

His words were like a slap in the face for Aliana: all the more so because she knew in her heart that they were true. For lack of a better target – probably Gilarra – she kicked the wall and swore viciously. 'It's just not fair, Packrat! Why should we always be excluded, suspected, and looked down on? In the end, we're no different from those other folk!'

'Oh, but we are,' Packrat said quietly. 'Don't fool yourself, Aliana. We're thieves, we're dregs, we're scum. They don't want us because we live outside their rules, and there's no getting away from that.' He gave her another very direct look. 'I suppose it's harder for you to accept that. Once, you were inside their cosy little community, before your family fell on hard times. That's why you keep wanting to change things. It's not like that for me. I've always been an outcast. I don't know any different.'

In all the time that Packrat had been one of the Ghosts, she had never known him to be so candid and forthright, and Aliana didn't know how to reply to him. Luckily, he let her off the hook. 'Come on, then,' he said roughly. 'I'll make a deal with you. Let's go and look around the corner at these stupid lights, and if it turns out to be just more of the same, only with pretty colours, we'll go back. All right?'

'Maybe,' Aliana hedged. 'These lights must have *some* significance. Let's have a look before we decide.'

Heading towards the pulsing, changeful radiance, they crept cautiously around the corner of the passage. 'See,' Packrat said. 'It *is* the same.'

'No, it isn't.' Aliana pointed. 'Further down the passage, there's no more gleam from the walls and floor. Either it changes from this metal stuff to some very black material, or it just stops.'

Packrat squinted. 'I don't see any difference. 'Let's go back.'

Aliana gave him a hard look. 'You're only saying that because you don't want to go on. Well, I'm going to have a look. You can please yourself whether you come or not.' Without waiting to see whether he was following, she strode off down the corridor, unable to stop her feet from keeping time with those weird pulses of light that faded from one colour to another. Though she looked hard to find the source of the radiance, it seemed to come from nowhere and everywhere, emanating from the walls and floor as well as the ceiling. As she walked further down the passage, even the very air itself seemed to be vibrant with colour.

It's all very pretty, but why? I can't think of any practical reason for the light to change like that, but it makes me feel as though this place is alive, somehow.

When Aliana had gone on a little further, she had a much clearer view of the place up ahead, where everything changed. It looked as though the passageway ended abruptly in a blank, black wall, but when she drew close, she realised that it was nothing of the kind. The corridor just ended – that was all. Another step would send her plummeting, and as far as she could tell, there was nothing beyond the edges of the walls but a featureless black void. It looked as though Packrat had been right. This idea of hers had been doomed to failure from the start.

Without warning, Aliana's eyes began to swim with tears, but she was saved from a most uncharacteristic and embarrassing fit of weeping by the sound of Packrat's mocking voice from behind her. 'Told you so. *Now* can we go back?'

'I suppose so.'

'Hooray.' Sarcastically, Packrat clapped his hands. As he did so, light – bright, white light – came pouring down from somewhere in the featureless black spaces up above, to illuminate the void. Aliana gasped. Where before there had been only darkness, she could now see a shaft, about eight yards wide, and extending unguessable distances above and below. In the centre was another platform, about six feet across, which was simply the flat top of a square pillar which rose up from below. As far as Aliana could see, it was floored with a metal grid, with spaces about an inch wide. Through these holes she could see only a dark background, though from this distance, that wasn't surprising. On the other side of the shaft was a square opening that presumably must be the continuation of the corridor. It looked the same as the passage they had just traversed, except that, for some reason, the lighting had gone back to normal.

Packrat looked at the gap, measuring it with his eyes, then peered down into the shadowy depths below. 'Like I was saying, it's time to go back.'

'Now hold on a minute,' Aliana protested. 'We said if nothing had changed we would go back, but this is different. We can do this.'

'Yeah, right,' Packrat sneered. 'Take too big a run at this end, jump a bit too far, and you'll go straight over the far side of the platform, with nothing to stop you. And if you *do* manage to land on target, then you've got a precious short run up for the jump on the other side – or either side, for that matter, because it'll be just as impossible to jump back again. You'll have a choice of starving to death on the platform, or taking a plunge off the side to end it quick.'

Annoyed by his obstructiveness, Aliana rounded on him angrily. 'Will you stop being so bloody feeble, Packrat? In second-story work we do bigger jumps than that all the time.'

'But when you're burgling there's always something to hold on to,' Packrat countered, 'a ledge, or a shutter, or a drainpipe. But misjudge a jump here and you'll just keep right on going – all the way to the bottom.'

Ironically, had she been alone, Aliana might have thought twice about continuing. But Packrat's objections were having exactly the opposite effect to the one he wanted, making her all the more determined to succeed. Mostly, however, she was driven on by her acrimony towards the Hierarch. From their very first meeting, when the thief had risked her life to bring the desperately needed blasting powder from the Citadel to the Temple, and had been met with so little appreciation and gratitude from Gilarra, the two women had disliked one another, and the feeling had not improved with further acquaintance: on the contrary, relations between them seemed to deteriorate all the time. Had Gilarra not arrested Alestan, however, Aliana might have given up this mad scheme, in the face of the difficulties she was encountering. But no one, not even the Hierarch, was going to fabricate charges against her brother, and get away with it. As far as Aliana was concerned, the more difficult it was to recover the wretched ring, the better. 'I'm not giving up,' she said stubbornly.

Packrat let out a long sigh, and she could see how difficult it was for him to keep his irritation under control. 'You know, maybe there's another way to get at Gilarra,' he said. 'One that you haven't thought of. Why don't you just chuck the ring down there?' With a wave of his hand, he indicated the seemingly bottomless shaft in front of them. 'She'd never get it back then.'

Aliana shook her head. 'Packrat, I daren't. They all seem to feel that the wretched thing is significant, somehow. I can't imagine what sort of practical use it might have, but I just can't take the risk, in case it really is important. No, I'm going to jump. Listen, you wait here for me. There's no need for you to risk yourself. Hopefully, I won't need to go too far on the other side to find a hiding place for the ring, then I'll come straight back.' Without waiting for a reply, she went little way back down to the passage, turned and ran forward then, right on the brink of the shaft, she launched herself into the air.

Her feet hit the platform hard and, as Packrat had predicted so gloomily, her momentum was such that she had a difficult time stopping before she went skidding over the far edge. For a heart-stopping instant she teetered right on the very brink, flailing her arms for balance, then she managed to throw herself backwards, and landed hard on her backside, bereft of dignity but extremely relieved to be safe and sound. Scrambling to her feet, she turned back to Packrat, to tell him that there was nothing to it. The words froze on her lips, however, as saw him getting ready to jump.

'Packrat, no!' she yelled. The leap suddenly seemed to be a lot more risky when one of her friends was attempting it, and Packrat wasn't the most athletic person in the world. Pausing only to make a rude gesture at her, he broke into a run, and hurled himself across the gap.

There was no danger of him overshooting the platform, as Aliana had done, for he landed short of the centre, but at least he had made his leap safely. Aliana steadied him as he landed. 'Get off me.' He shrugged himself out of her grasp, his movements jerky with anger, and Aliana realised that his face was white with fear. Her heart went out to him. Irritating though he might be at times, he had overcome both his apprehension and better judgement to follow her, because he didn't want to leave her alone. She knew better than to mention that fact, however. 'Oh, so you've decided to come along after all,' she said. 'I thought you had more sense?'

He gave her a dirty look. 'I came because you aren't to be trusted on your own,' he snapped. '*You* haven't the sense of a baby sparrow. Come on – stop blethering, and let's hurry up and get off this damned thing. I don't like being perched up here with a drop on all four sides.'

Here in the centre of the shaft, the distance to the opening on the other side looked far greater than it had done from the edge of the corridor, though Aliana knew that the gap to be leapt over was the same size as the leap she had already made. Packrat had been right, however. The jump would be far more difficult to accomplish this time, because the small area of the platform left little room for a decent run up. For a moment she stood, breathing deeply, collecting herself and, incidentally, putting off the evil moment when she must commit herself. Then, all at once, she discovered that they had run out of time to hesitate.

A thin jet of flame, about as tall as herself, shot out of a hole near the centre of the grid. With a loud whooshing sound it leapt high, then sank down again and vanished, just as another came roaring up from another area of the grid, to be replaced by another and another, all springing up at random, so that there was no knowing where the next one would appear.

'Come on,' Packrat yelled. 'Shift your backside before we both get fried!'

Aliana gathered herself, sped towards the brink of the platform, and leapt. She wasn't quite ready, and it was a clumsy jump, with one foot slipping a little on take off. In the instant that she hurtled through the air, she was horribly aware of the gulf that yawned beneath her. Would she make it?

With a rush of relief, she felt her feet touch the solid floor of the corridor. She stumbled forward, falling to her knees, but with Packrat still on the other side, there was no time to register her own good fortune. Leaping up, she turned and saw him preparing to launch himself – and it was clear from his face that he was not confident. Even as he ran forward, another roaring jet of flame sprang up, almost beneath his feet, so that he was forced to swerve to one side. She was certain he must abort his leap, but even as the thought crossed her mind, she saw him reach the edge and recklessly throw himself out into space.

From the very first instant, it was clear that he wasn't going to make it. His face a distorted mask of horror, he slammed into the edge at chest level and, as he began to slide backwards, scrabbled in vain for a handhold on the smooth metal of the corridor floor. Aliana threw herself forward with a yell, landing on her belly, and with her arms outstretched as far as they would go, made a wild grab for his slipping hands. Holding on tightly, she tried to pull him to safety, but it was difficult to stop herself from sliding forward as Packrat was dragged down by his own weight. Then, just as she was thinking she had lost him, he managed somehow to wedge the toes of his boots against the wall, and keep himself from sliding any further. It was a slow and difficult business, but inch by inch, they managed between them to pull him out of the abyss, and get him safely back up into the corridor.

Aliana rolled over onto her back, wincing. Her arms felt as though they had been pulled out of their sockets. Packrat sprawled face down on the floor of the passageway, gasping and shuddering. Finally he raised his head and scowled at Aliana. 'Next time, you stupid bitch, maybe you'll listen to me.'

'Maybe next time, you'll listen to *me*, you pig-headed bastard,' Aliana snapped back. 'I told you to wait for me.' Then, ignoring his usual disreputable appearance, she grabbed him and hugged him hard, until his trembling stopped.

Poor Packrat. He didn't deserve to be dragged into this. I only hope that things will get easier from here – but I have a really bad feeling that this is only the beginning.

Seventeen

The One to Blame

Seriema was amazed at how quickly she had come to look on the Reiver stronghold as home. Right now, as she rode over the brow of the hill with Cetain and his warriors, she had never seen a more welcome sight than Arcan's valley: its little settlement of roughly built houses with their roofs of turf, the tower of the Summoners by the brooding waters of the tarn, and the fortress standing foursquare, sturdy, and secure on the hill above.

Today the bad weather had vanished away to the south, leaving a calm, bright day with nothing but a skimming of high, grey cloud to veil the sun. They had left the ruined tower at daybreak, and made much faster time on the return journey without the storm to fight, getting back to the Reiver settlement not long before noon. There had been no sign of the predators on the return journey, which indicated to Seriema that she had been right about them being nocturnal. Nevertheless, she hadn't dared to relax for an instant, all the way back, in case she should suddenly hear the horrendous screeches of the hunting fiends, and see the sky grow dark with wings once more.

Knowing that its stable was ahead, her tired little horse quickened its pace, and Seriema gladly let it have its head. She knew exactly how it felt. After the night she had just spent out on the moor, sheltering in the cellars of a ruin, and trying to hold off the marauding winged fiends, she too was looking forward to food, and rest, and the security of those thick and solid walls. She glanced across at Cetain, who rode beside her, keeping pace with her as

220

always. To her surprise, he wasn't looking happy to be home. Noting his frowning silence, he realised that he must be worried about telling his father that he had failed in his mission to warn the other clans of the impending threat.

Seriema reached across and touched his arm. 'You made the right decision,' she said quietly. 'Those vile creatures were abroad on the moors last night, so the chances are that they'll have found the other clans already. There's no point in throwing more lives away, when your warriors will be much more use – *and* stand a far better chance of surviving – here in their own home.'

'I only hope my father will see things as you do.' Cetain shook his head. 'The trouble is that anyone who has not experienced your demons for themselves will have difficulty understanding just how lethal they can be.' He hesitated. 'I have a confession to make, lass. When I first heard your account of what had happened in Tiarond, I didn't take it as seriously as I do now – though I did believe you,' he added hastily. 'All the same, I thought your descriptions of those creatures were the outpourings of a bunch of scared townsfolk who were so used to the soft life that anything would seem a threat.'

He gave a wry, self-mocking grin. 'I learned my lesson last night, and no mistake. When we came out this morning and found those few bloody remains of my poor warriors who didn't escape them, I realised just how much my people owe to you. Had it not been for your timely warning, the entire settlement could have been slaughtered last night. But will my father realise that?' Once more, his brows were knitted in a frown. 'He doesn't have the benefit of your unique experience, my Lady. What you see as prudence, he may well view as cowardice on my part. I have disobeyed his orders, and he is not a man who tolerates being crossed.'

That gave Seriema something else to be concerned about – but surely Cetain was worrying over nothing? Any reasonable man would surely see that he had done the only sensible thing?

I certainly hope so. I've scarcely had a single moment's peace since those winged fiends invaded, and I could sorely use a respite. And what about poor Cetain? There was nothing more he could have done last night

— in fact, he did very well to get so many of his warriors back here in one piece. Surely his father will have the sense to see that?

Neither Seriema nor Cetain, however, could have guessed what trouble awaited them within the stronghold. As they rode through the arched gateway into the courtyard they were astonished to see a number of warriors dismounting from their mud-spattered horses and leading them inside. Arcan was striding about, looking thunderous and hurrying his men along with the occasional barked command. He looked up as Cetain approached, with Seriema at his side. 'What in the name of perdition are *you* doing back here?' he demanded.

'My Chief, surely it would be better to discuss this matter inside,' Seriema tried to intervene.

Arcan, looking first surprised and then annoyed at her temerity, scowled at her. 'Hold your tongue, woman.' He turned his glare back onto his son. 'Well?'

'The winged fiends have spread out beyond Tiarond, just as Tormon and Grim predicted. They attacked us last night out on the moor, and I lost four of my men, unfortunately, before we could take shelter in the old tower.' A hush fell across the courtyard as the warriors heard Cetain's news. With a glance at the chieftain for permission, he continued: 'Father, the threat of these creatures is far worse than we could ever have imagined. We were besieged until daylight, when they dispersed, but there seemed little point in going on with our mission. If the fiends were at large last night, then it is likely that they would have found the unprotected settlements of the other clans. I decided not to risk any more of my men, just to deliver a warning that must have come too late.'

Arcan cursed. 'As if we hadn't problems enough!' he muttered. Addressing his warriors, he bellowed across the courtyard. 'Ho, you men! After you've eaten, you can be checking your gear, and our supplies of weapons. It seems that war has come upon us sooner than we expected.' Some of the men gave a ragged cheer at this talk of war, but others, having seen the haggard, haunted faces of

Cetain's weary comrades, looked a great deal less sure of themselves than they had done the previous day.

The clan chief turned to his eldest son, who had apparently been out with the riders. 'Lewic, you come back to my quarters with your brother. I might as well have both your reports together – though it looks as though neither of you have been much use at performing the tasks I gave you.'

Arcan led the way into the fortress, and his sons, having left their men with orders to rest, and get something to eat, followed the chieftain, with Seriema staying firmly at Cetain's side. As she left the courtyard, she heard a babble of voices breaking out behind her, and suspected that his newly returned men were being badgered by their comrades for the details of their narrow escape. She wondered where Tormon and Presvel and the others were. This news would come as a blow to them, as it must to anyone who had experienced the horrors of Tiarond.

As they followed the clan chief up to his chambers, Seriema noticed that there was something odd about the atmosphere in the fortress. Yesterday the place had been filled with bustle and talk, as people busied themselves with their allotted tasks. Despite the threat that hung over them, there had been a lot of good-natured gossip, laughter and chaffing. Today, however, the Reivers seemed subdued and quiet, going about their work in near silence, and with sombre faces. They seemed particularly keen to keep out of the way of their chieftain, and she wondered what on earth could have happened to bring about such a change. Nothing good, that was for certain.

Arcan looked none too pleased when Seriema accompanied his son into his chambers. 'Who invited you?' he demanded.

'I did.' Cetain put an arm around his companion's shoulders. 'The Lady Seriema knows more about these predators than either you or I, and her account of what happened last night should bear just as much weight as my own.'

'I don't care what she knows,' Arcan snapped. 'I wish to speak privately with my sons. You had better know what took place here last night, Cetain. Summoner Grim was murdered: stabbed by someone right here in our stronghold. We don't know what happened, but Dark, his assistant, has fled, and with him that lad who came with trader Tormon.'

'Scall?' Seriema exclaimed. 'But that's ridiculous. What could he possibly have to do with it?'

Arcan glared at her. 'Go and ask your friend Tormon. He knows as much about this business as any of us.' With that, he closed the door in Seriema's face.

Seriema was fuming. 'Of all the rude, obnoxious . . .' Though her first, angry impulse was to burst in on him and tell him what she thought of him, common sense prevailed. Presumably because of Scall's alleged involvement in the murder of the Summoner, she and her companions didn't seem to be too popular with the chieftain right now. This was the only refuge they had, especially considering that the winged fiends were at large in the vicinity, so it would be wise to practise a certain amount of discretion until Arcan's mood improved. Besides, there was a guard on his chambers as always; a husky young man as broad as a barn door. Seriema assessed him realistically, and rated her chances of getting past him as zero. Since the chief of the Reivers had so pointedly excluded her in the sentry's presence, she couldn't even bluff her way in. She glared at the offending door then, with a shrug, turned and went away. She had better find Tormon as soon as possible. It was time to put aside their ridiculous quarrel of yesterday. There were things she needed to find out, and she had information that would be equally important to him.

First of all, she looked in the little chamber that Tormon shared with his daughter. The merchant was not there, but Annas and Rochalla were sitting on the bed, playing cat's cradle with a long piece of blue yarn. A pair of thick, blunted knitting needles with something that looked like a coloured bird's nest between them, lay discarded on the bed, mute evidence that the blonde girl had been trying to teach the child to knit. Seriema smiled when she saw it. 'My attempts at knitting still look like that,' she said.

Rochalla looked surprised at being addressed in such a friendly fashion, but essayed a tentative smile. 'But knitting's easy,' she protested.

'To you, maybe,' Seriema snorted. 'I was all thumbs when it came to anything like that. My sewing's even worse.' She tried to keep the conversation on a light note because, despite her patience with Annas, Rochalla looked so tired, pale and worried. Clearly, the girl had been losing sleep over the missing Scall.

'Well, we all have our talents,' Rochalla was saying. 'I couldn't begin to imagine how to run a successful mercantile empire. I don't know how you did it.'

'Sometimes I wonder myself. And I'm not sure that I would have it in me to start again, even if the circumstances were right. I suspect knitting and sewing are going to prove a damn sight more useful in the months to come.' Seriema decided that it was definitely time to change the subject. 'Have you ladies seen Tormon anywhere?'

'He went to find Scall,' Annas piped up. 'Scall ran away, and he took his pretty horse. He didn't take Esmeralda, though.'

Rochalla stared at her. 'How did you know all that?' Her voice grew stern. 'Annas, were you listening at the door when I was talking to your dad outside?'

The little girl flushed and lowered her eyes. 'It was an accident. I couldn't help it. You didn't shut the door properly.'

'Well, next time, go and close the door instead of eavesdropping. It's not a very nice thing to do.'

Annas's lower lip began to protrude, but to Seriema's relief, they were saved from the approaching storm by the arrival of Tormon himself. He too looked very weary, and was spattered with mud and in need of a shave. 'What are you doing back?' he demanded of Seriema. Though he sounded surprised, she was relieved to see that all traces of yesterday's hostility and bad temper had left his face.

She looked significantly at the child. 'Is there somewhere we can talk?'

Rochalla took the hint, and rose immediately. 'Come along, Annas,' she said. 'Let's go and see if we can find some food for your dad and the Lady Seriema. They must both be starving.'

'All right.' Annas scrambled down from the bed, and grabbing Rochalla by the hand, led the way out. 'I'll get some for my dad, and you can get some for Lady Seriema.'

But before she left the room, Rochalla hesitated beside the trader. 'Tormon . . . ?'

He shook his head. 'I'm sorry, lass. The tracks went all the way up to the Curtain Walls, then stopped. There were some signs of a scuffle there, and horses milling around, but no trace of Scall.' He frowned. 'Oddly, there were no tracks leaving that valley, either. It was like they just vanished into thin air – but don't give up hope. We'll keep looking, I promise.'

The blonde girl nodded once and swallowed hard, biting her lip as she left the room. Tormon sighed. 'Poor little thing. And poor Scall, too.' He looked at Seriema. 'You didn't sound as if you were bringing good news, either.'

'We've got trouble,' she said, without preamble. 'It's not just Scall.' Seriema took a deep breath. 'Tormon, I have some bad news for you – for us all. The winged fiends have left Tiarond. They attacked us last night, on the moor, and killed four of Cetain's men. The rest of us were lucky to get away.'

The trader blanched, and sat down heavily on the end of the bed. 'Oh, dear Myrial, not that! What's to become of us all? And what happened to that poor lad, out there on the moors last night with those brutes roaming at large?'

After a moment, he got his feelings under control once more. 'So that was what all the commotion in the courtyard was about. I just got in myself – as you probably guessed, I went out with Lewic and his men this morning to see if we could track Scall and Dark, and I got a bit behind the others on the way back. Those little Reiver horses certainly take some getting used to after the Sefrians. When I got back, I hurried straight back up here to see Rochalla. I knew how worried she must be, and I didn't want to waste any time hanging round and gossiping with the warriors.'

'Speaking of warriors, Arcan didn't look too happy with us,'

Seriema said. 'I got the distinct impression that he'd rather we were anywhere else right now.'

Tormon nodded. 'You're right. For some reason, the chieftain is convinced that Scall was involved in poor Grim's murder.' He scowled. 'As if!'

Seriema sat down beside him. 'It's more likely that the lad chanced upon the real killer, and . . .' She didn't want to follow that thought any further. 'But that doesn't make a lot of sense, either,' she added hastily. 'If the murderer escaped, then why would he take Scall with him? It wouldn't make any sense to encumber himself like that.' She frowned. 'Arcan said that Grim's assistant was missing, too, didn't he?'

'Aye, you're right. But I've been coming here for years, and I know Dark as well as I know any of the Reivers. He's always struck me as a fine young man, and I would say that his integrity's beyond question. Every time I came here, I used to go down to the tower for a chat with Grim about what was happening in the world – he was a glutton for news – and Dark was always there too. In fact, I used to joke about them being inseparable. He loved the old man like a father, and whatever Arcan says, I *know* he would never have killed his master.'

'Then who did?' Seriema wondered. 'Why did they do it when Scall and Dark were there as witnesses, and what have they done with those two poor young men?' She sighed, and thumped the coverlet with her fist. 'Damn it, we're just going round in circles! None of this makes any kind of sense!'

'Well, until we find them, we'll never know,' Tormon said. 'And your news about the winged fiends makes that task a whole lot more difficult. As it was, I felt bad about leaving Annas this morning. I have a responsibility to her, now that her mother . . . isn't here. She must always come first, and I know I haven't any business putting myself at risk of being caught out on the moors by one of those accursed creatures – but I feel I should be helping Scall, too. He's a good lad, and he's come to mean a lot to me in a short time. How can I just abandon him?'

A lesson that Seriema had learned very early in life was never to run away from her responsibilities. There was a bond, now, between the escapees from Tiarond, and if she could help both Scall and Tormon, then she owed it to them to do her best. Besides, if Arcan was displeased with his visitors now, then it was important that the mystery be solved as soon as possible. The chieftain was a tough, irascible man, and who knew how long his gratitude would last?

Seriema remembered how unpleasant it had been out in the storm yesterday, and how terrified she had felt when the predators attacked. She had been so relieved to get back to the safety of the fortress's strong walls. How could she have guessed that that security would have been so short lived? She sighed. 'Let me talk to Cetain,' she said to Tormon. 'Maybe we can go out and look for Scall, then you can stay here with Annas, where you belong.'

For a moment, the trader said nothing – just looked at her as though he had never seen her before – but Seriema could see the relief written plainly on his face. At last he spoke. 'You know, back when you were Tiarond's foremost merchant, I never doubted your courage. You had to be brave, to make the kind of decisions you were making every day and, as a woman, to have reached the position that you held. But for some reason, you never had a reputation for generosity and kindness.' He smiled. 'All I can say is, maybe folk weren't looking deeply enough.'

Seriema was touched by his words. 'Or maybe they were right,' she said wryly. 'Perhaps I'm attaining kindness and wisdom at long last, instead of just mere cleverness. These recent events have changed us all. Now, Presvel, for instance . . .' She paused. 'Have you any idea where he is, by the way? I thought he spent every waking moment dogging Rochalla's footsteps these days.' It was surprising how little the change in her assistant's loyalties mattered to her now. 'He doesn't seem to have been hanging around her today, though.'

Tormon shrugged. 'Maybe she told him to get lost.'

'I very much doubt that. Rochalla is far too nice for her own good, sometimes. She would probably be afraid of hurting his feelings.'

'I wish she *had* told him to go away,' the trader said. 'No offence, Lady: I know he was your friend and your assistant, but the way he's been acting lately, I've sometimes wondered about his state of mind, and . . .'

With a gasp, Seriema seized the trader's arm. 'Tormon, has anyone seen Presvel since last night? Since Grim was murdered? Don't tell me that *he's* missing, too.'

Tormon stared at her, open-mouthed. 'You don't think . . . You don't think he did it?'

'What?' Seriema was shocked by the notion. 'No, surely not. Why, he's always been the least violent man I ever met. And Arcan said that Grim was stabbed – I'm quite sure that Presvel barely knows one end of a knife from the other. Besides, why should he want to kill the old Summoner? He doesn't even know him. Surely it must have been one of the Reivers with a grudge against Grim.'

'I suppose you're right,' the trader conceded. 'When you put it like that, it doesn't make a whole lot of sense. Still, I think we'd better keep an eye on Presvel, if we can find him in the first place . . .'

'Dad, Dad, we've brought you some good things to eat.' Annas burst in with such abruptness that Seriema jumped. Rochalla followed her, laden down with a heavy tray. 'Annas, you should knock,' she scolded.

'What for?' said Annas, unconcerned.

Rochalla stretched her arms and flexed her shoulders as Tormon took the tray out of her hands. 'Did you say you were looking for Presvel?' Rochalla asked. 'Sorry, I couldn't help but overhear. I've just seen him downstairs.' She frowned. 'Do you know, he insists he's all right, but I don't think he's very well. He looked absolutely dreadful.'

Seriema looked at Tormon. Though neither of them spoke, she was certain they were thinking the same thing.

Dear Myrial, no. It can't be possible. Presvel has always been a good man. He would never murder someone – would he?

*   *   *

Surely they must know I did it. They must be able to see it in my face, in my eyes, in my hand that held the knife . . .

There was no rest for Presvel and nowhere to hide. No fleeing from the dreadful thing he had done. No escaping the horror that lurked at the back of his every thought, bringing back time and time again the memory of Grim's face, contorted in shock and pain; the jarring of the knife as it entered the old Summoner's body, and the hot gush of blood that followed.

Yet despite the hideous clarity of those recollections, Presvel still had difficulty believing what had happened. He'd had vivid, very realistic nightmares before – everyone did, didn't they? If only the horrific scenario of Grim's death had been nothing more than that.

In his heart, he knew it was not.

Dear Myrial, I didn't mean to kill him! I would give anything if I could turn back time and undo the harm I did last night!

And what would happen now? He had lost the knife; had dropped it in the straw, when he fled in panic. He didn't dare go back to look for it – that would only draw suspicion to himself. Besides, what would be the point? They were sure to have searched the area. They were certain to have found it. Even now, Arcan must know that the killer had been one of the party that Tormon had brought from Tiarond.

How long will it be before they start questioning us all?

So far, Presvel had managed to lie low that morning, changing location from time to time, lest he be suspected of skulking around in a suspicious manner, yet always staying in places that were sparsely occupied, or where folk were too busy with their own tasks to pay him much heed. He had finally come up onto the flat roof of the tower, though he knew it would only be a matter of time before the cold drove him back down. While he'd been up there, he had seen Seriema return with Cetain and his warriors. His heart had leapt and, for a mad, wild instant, he had thought of running to her and confessing all. She would protect him, surely? She would know what to do.

Then doubt assailed him. His Lady had changed now. She had thrown herself in with these barbarian Reivers, seeming to fit into

Arcan's clan as though she had been born to it. He could no longer be sure that she would take his side, or support him in any way. Besides, a core of honesty within him made him ask himself why she should. Caught up, as he had been, in his obsession with Rochalla, he had paid Seriema no heed over this last day or two, and had neglected and ignored her at every turn. If she was angry with him now, she had every right to be.

For all that, if he should be compelled to unburden himself, there was no one, not even his precious Rochalla, that he would rather trust. For a moment, he considered doing exactly that. This was a dreadful secret to bear alone, and if Arcan had found the knife, then Presvel would be putting all his comrades at risk – for the entire group, including Rochalla, must find themselves under suspicion. But should he confess? Surely if he admitted his guilt to Seriema, she would – she *must* – tell the Reivers who had slain their Summoner.

I can't. I can't! They'll kill me for sure. It was an accident, I didn't mean to do it, and I'm desperately sorry, but they won't believe that – or at any rate, they won't care. All that will matter to them is punishing the murderer, and these wild barbarians won't have any mercy. Oh, why did this happen to me?

Presvel was seized by a wild and desperate rage: against the dreadful circumstances that had snatched away his safe, secure, and useful life in his beloved city, and driven him out to be a wanderer in this hostile, Myrial-forsaken wilderness; against that stupid Tormon, for bringing them to this uncivilised place, and landing them amongst these miserable savages; against Seriema, for throwing in her lot with the Reivers; against Scall, for causing this entire situation by following Rochalla around like a lovesick puppy, and for being in the wrong place at the wrong time.

He's to blame, damn him! They're all to blame! It's not my fault at all.

He was even angry with Rochalla herself, for encouraging the boy. It was her fault too! He should have known better than to try to rescue her out of the squalid life she had been leading. Oh, she looked so pretty, so young and so innocent, but underneath it all, she was still the same little slut she had always been.

Suddenly, an idea struck him. Maybe he could save his own skin, and at the same time pay them all out – or one of them at least – for getting him into this terrible situation. Surely, if he were quick and clever, it would be possible to fabricate enough evidence to lay the blame where it belonged – squarely at the feet of one, or more, of his companions.

On the freezing rooftop of the tower, Presvel smiled to himself. At last he had the answer. Only one thing remained to be decided. Which one of them would it be?

Eighteen

Vifang

All morning, while Amaurn had seemingly been busy with various other matters, he was, in truth, still preoccupied with Vaure's message concerning that unknown young man who had managed to penetrate the Curtain Walls and, in doing so, had unleashed a pair of Ak'Zahar on peaceful Gendival. Even worse, was the reason that the stranger had been forced to travel alone and meddle, unsupervised, with the faltering barrier. Unbelievably, Grim was dead.

Would it be too much to ask, to hear some good news for a change?

The death of his old friend had grieved Amaurn deeply. In all the time he had spent in Callisiora under the guise of the Godsword Commander Blade, he had been very much alone. Such isolation had been necessary in order to build his power base in Tiarond, and to preserve the secret of his identity, but it had not been easy. Sometimes he wondered if it had not been the self-imposed detachment from friendly human contact that had allowed him to be so cold-blooded and pitiless during those years. He had been forced to construct a carapace around himself that had prevented him from giving rein to his own feelings, and had forbidden him access to the emotions of others. This return to Gendival however, to the places of his past and the folk who were once his fellows, seemed to be hammering crack after crack in the iron shell with which he had enclosed himself, and his newly exposed sensibilities were very raw. To lose his oldest friend, the one who had supported him in secret for so long, and whom he had been so looking forward to seeing once again, was a bitter blow indeed. To be honest, Amaurn couldn't help but wish that the assistant had been the one who'd died, and that Grim had been on his way home right now.

All those times he begged me to let him come back to Gendival, and I kept putting him off. Oh, why didn't I let him return when he asked? If I had done so, he would still be alive now . . .

Also, they had not parted on the best of terms, with Grim suspecting his intentions towards the Tiarondian boy he was supposed to be bringing with him, and himself reacting with cold anger.

It's hard for old friends to part for ever on such a misunderstanding. I only wish I could have one more chance to talk to him, and put things right.

Much as his common sense told him that such notions were destructive, unproductive, and downright irrational, he had to fight to keep his thoughts from slipping into a chain of regrets and self-blame at every unguarded moment. He didn't have time for such luxuries. He had so much to do, and so many problems to consider, particularly since the Curtain Walls on the Callisiora side seemed to be in so unstable a state, that there was no opportunity to come to terms with his sorrow.

Amaurn had been working without rest since his return to Gendival – indeed, he had never left this chamber since entering it the previous morning. Though he had sent his fellow Loremasters off to sleep, he himself had spent all night poring over maps and charts and despatches from the other realms, trying to co-ordinate his resources and allocate his Shadowleague agents – who seemed such a small and inadequate army to combat the chaos into which the world was descending – so that they could go where they would do most good.

From time to time, as he worked, he had been reminded of the former Archimandrite. Cergorn's influence was everywhere in this fearful mess, making so many situations far worse by his neglect, and his refusal to utilise some of the Shadowleague's more esoteric knowledge to help the realms in crisis. If the centaur lived,

Amaurn thought grimly, he was going to find that more than a few changes had taken place while he had been recovering. So far, he seemed to be holding his own, kept alive, ironically, by the same advanced medical aid that he had refused so many others. On the whole, Amaurn was relieved that it was so. Though Cergorn's survival might cause him a lot of problems further down the road, his immediate death would cause a whole lot more in the present. At least his fight for life was keeping Syvilda, who would have proved a bitter enemy indeed, out of the new Archimandrite's hair.

Yet as time went on, he had at least begun to see why Cergorn had been so willing to hide behind the excuse of non-interference. The temptation to run away from so many problems was overwhelming. Only the discipline and determination he had learned in his years as Blade had kept Amaurn bent sternly to his tasks, plus the knowledge that, after all this time, he had finally attained the goal he had striven for at such a cost, both to others, and to himself. There was another reason, too: one that he dared not dwell upon too closely in this land of telepaths. The guilty knowledge, buried deep within his heart, that it had been he who had tampered with the Curtain Walls in the first place.

When the Loremasters who were assisting him had returned that morning, they had found him exactly where they had left him the previous night – weary, gritty-eyed, his face grey with pain from his cracked rib and injured arm, but determined to continue. Despite their urgings, even those of the formidable Maskulu, he had refused to go to and rest, so Bailen and Kyrre of the Dobarchu had brought him some food, some tea, and something to dull the pain – and stood over him until he had swallowed them all.

Though the breakfast had kept him going for a few hours more, however, Amaurn was beginning to flag. When he found himself reading the same passage for the fifth or sixth time, and still with no idea of its contents, he finally admitted defeat (according to his own estimation), or used his common sense (according to the views of his companions). Maskulu all but chased him out of the chamber, and Kyrre sent him on his way with stern instructions not to return until he was thoroughly rested. He emerged into the sunlight, blinking and rubbing his eyes, and took deep draughts of the cool autumn air. After all of the reports of horrors which had been his preoccupation for the last day and night, he felt a vague astonishment at the sight of the tranquil and beautiful valley. Its colours soft in the pale, hazy sunshine, it seemed as ethereal as a dream. But if even the Gendival Curtain Walls were failing, how long would this sanctuary remain?

Amaurn was walking away from the Meeting House when it dawned on him that he had neglected to organise a bed for himself. While he'd been all wrapped up in the woes of the world, such mundane details had never entered his mind. Until now, of course, when he needed to rest. To go and stay in Veldan's house was the first idea which occurred to him. He knew it well, for it had once belonged to her mother, though he gathered that it had been much altered since those days to accommodate the needs of the firedrake. As natural as it felt, however, to seek refuge in the former home of his lover, he realised that he would be imposing on Veldan, and she might not take such an intrusion kindly. He didn't want to put her at odds with him so soon after they had come to know one another. It wouldn't take much effort to have someone organise a place for him to stay, but somehow, he just didn't want to ask. Surely it would undermine his new-won authority, if the Archimandrite had to beg for a bed like some wandering mendicant! Besides, he was still a curiosity in Gendival, and it would be good to escape for a while, from all the many eyes that looked on him with curiosity, or with resentment.

It was ironic, having spent so many years yearning towards the Shadowleague, that Amaurn suddenly needed to get away from it for a time.

I must clear my head.

Ignoring the curious glances from passers-by, he walked down to the roofless arch which led out of the settlement. He took the way which led away from the village, along the farther side of the lake, where there were no Loremaster dwellings.

After a short distance the road forked. Here the valley was split into two separate arms by a long, steep spur which was outflung from Wisdom's Seat, the great hill which reared its bulk above Gendival. To the south of the spur was the deep and sinister vale which held the cold, grey waters of the Upper Lake; where dark, stunted evergreens clung to the steep escarpments on either shore, and buzzards cried in the lonely heights. To the north, the road left the lakes and climbed up steeply through a cutting, with the green Wisdom's Seat on the left hand, and barren, stony fells on the right – a relic from long ago, when they had been blasted by the cataclysmic power struggles between two rival factions of Loremasters. The ruined settlement, with its crumbling remnants of walls and buildings, was a little further on; a sorrowful, ghost-ridden monument to the last time there had been schism and conflict within the Shadowleague.

And it didn't teach me a thing.

Amaurn had no intentions of going as far as that bleak and haunted place. At this time, it struck too close a chord in his own heart. He took the steep northern road, but struck away from it after a short distance, making for Wisdom's Seat. Though there was no distinct path, he needed none, for his memories of the way were clear. The hill climbed very steeply in a series of small cliffs, crags and near-vertical slopes where ivy, gorse and bramble proliferated and hardy little trees – rowan, hazel, holly and birch – clung stubbornly, surviving, it seemed, against all odds.

According to local folklore, Wisdom's Seat was unclimbable, but in the great underground library of Gendival, the young Amaurn had discovered an ancient journal belonging to Iskander, the chief founder of the Shadowleague. Among a great deal of other fascinating information that might be very useful to an ambitious young man, it described the locations of two secret places near Gendival, to which Iskander would go if he needed to meditate, or make plans, or simply be alone. One was a cave, hidden away in the crags above the Upper Lake. Amaurn had tried it a time or two, but found it cold and cramped and miserable. The other refuge, however, lay close to the summit of the great hill which overlooked the home of the Shadowleague, so close that Amaurn often wondered why no one else seemed to bother to come up here.

All those generations of Loremasters, and not one of them, apparently, ever bothered to investigate why the hill was called Wisdom's Seat! Well, my methods may be suspect, but someone has to shake the Shadowleague out of its lazy complacency. We should be learning and progressing, and instead we stagnate in our little backwater of Gendival, doing nothing more useful than impeding the progress of other realms.

Though the ascent was far from easy, especially for someone with a cracked rib and only one hand at his disposal, there was a way to reach the hilltop – if you knew exactly where to go. Amaurn toiled steadily upwards, hacking clumsily at vegetation with his sword in his uninjured hand, and shoving his way through thickets of gorse and bramble. In the steeper parts, he carefully searched the craggy places for hand and footholds that would let him climb, and sheathed his sword to free his good hand and pull himself up by clinging to the branches of trees. Despite its toughness, he enjoyed the climb. After sitting indoors for so long, surrounded by reports of death and destruction, it felt good to escape into the clean fresh air, and good to use his muscles for a while, instead of his weary brain.

The precipitous rocks and the bark of trees felt rough and solid to his touch as he made his ascent. The crisp air was cool and tingling on his skin. He could smell the sharpness of autumn, like the taste of water from a mountain spring, mingling with other forest scents, each more invigorating than the last: the woody musk of damp earth and fallen leaves, the heady green smell of ferns and moss in damp and secret places, and the exotic, piquant spice of the gorse blooms which blazed on the hillside in patches of flaming gold.

A breeze whispered among the trees and the air was shrill with birdsong and, less melodiously, with a riot of noise from the flocks of squabbling thrushes which had come to gorge themselves on the vivid scarlet berries of the rowan trees. Nature's generous gifts were everywhere providing now, at the end of the growing season, against the frugal winter months ahead. Clusters of mushrooms poked their pale heads out of the woodland loam, and the tree trunks sprouted bizarre fungi, some good to eat, others deadly poison. Blackberries hung in heavy clusters, shining and dark, and the boughs of the hazels were laden down with nuts. Suddenly realising how long it had been since his hasty breakfast, Amaurn filled his pockets as he climbed.

Eventually, with his muscles aching and his skin torn by stinging scratches from briar and thorn, the new Archimandrite reached his goal. Not far below the precipitous summit of Wisdom's Seat was a little hanging meadow; a surprisingly smooth, green plateau thrusting out of the hill's craggy face. In the very centre grew a single, enormous oak tree, exquisite in shape and form, a perfect example of its kind. This was a magical place, high and isolated, with a compelling atmosphere of clarity and peace. The only sounds were the distant birdsong from the forest, the sighing of the breeze in the long, lush grass, and secrets whispered among the bronzing leaves of the oak.

Amaurn crossed the meadow, his footfalls soundless on the springy carpet of green. There was a sense of timeless serenity about the tree which was solace to his troubled thoughts. Approaching it with reverence, he laid a hand on its trunk, letting his own aura mingle with that of the ancient giant, and felt the tingling energy of its life-force pervade his body.

For a time he stood entranced then, with a sigh, he took his hand away. He found his old seat, remembered from long ago, where two roots formed a comfortable resting place, overlooking the lower lake and the Gendival settlement, far below. Amaurn took off his sword and laid the naked weapon close to his hand – a habit adopted in his time as Lord Blade and one which he wouldn't shake off easily – not that he would want to. He settled back, leaning comfortably against the trunk of the tree, and let the peace of the meadow wash over him and clear his mind, as it had done so long ago, for the founder of the Shadowleague himself.

I wonder how many other folk have discovered this magical place in the ages since then? Not many, I'll warrant. I could find no other record of it anywhere, but that's hardly surprising. Anyone who found it would naturally want to keep it for themselves, as I did. Aveole was the only person I ever told, and we both swore that it would remain our secret.

Amaurn ate the nuts, mushrooms and berries he had collected during his climb, then let himself relax, firmly putting all his problems behind him for a little while. Soon he felt his eyelids beginning to droop, and was content to let it happen. Here, in this peaceful, isolated sanctuary, he could be sure of remaining safe and undisturbed. Or so he thought.

Well, well! Fancy Amaurn knowing about this place.

The Takuru, of course, had always known. The shapeshifters, exiled as they were to the sidelines of the main Gendival community, knew every inch of the area that surrounded the settlement itself. Vifang, following the renegade upstart, had been surprised to see the human heading up here, but from an assassin's point of view, there couldn't have been a more suitable place. Amaurn, exhausted as he was, would be off his guard and easy prey. Amaurn would be all alone and far, far from help. Amaurn – and Vifang chuckled grimly – had even been kind enough to hide his own body. No searchers would come up here in the foreseeable future. It was unlikely that the fool's remains would ever be discovered. With a little help from Syvilda and her supporters in spreading the right rumours, the Shadowleague might even decide that the renegade, having sown the seeds of chaos for reasons of revenge, had vanished again, as he had done so long ago.

Imagine coming to an isolated place like this without bringing a bodyguard, or even telling anyone where he was going! A man with so many enemies must be insane to act so rashly.

It had been worth the wait for such auspicious circumstances. Events could not have worked out better.

The human had not the slightest idea that he had been followed. Concealment was child's play for a skilled shapeshifter, especially in the forest. As they had progressed up the hill, Vifang had melted from one form to another, becoming a bird, a tree-stump, a shadow on the grass. Now there was a new bush growing at the edge of the meadow – a holly, its glossy leaves dark and inconspicuous against the backdrop of the escarpment behind. From this vantage point, the Takur watched with avid attention, waiting until the Archimandrite relaxed and began to drowse. What form would it be best to adopt, for an attack? What would be the right shape, that would throw the prey off-guard? As soon as Amaurn's eyes were properly closed, the assassin sent a cautious tendril of thought towards the man's unguarded, sleeping mind and found the perfect shape. It was but a moment's work to make the change.

Amaurn was lost in a dream of the past. He was young again; innocent and idealistic, and free from guilt and doubt. He had brought Aveole up to the plateau, to show her this magical place, and they were sitting beneath the great tree in the warm summer sun. His arm was round her shoulders, and she leaned against him as they talked the idle inconsequentialities of lovers, and looked out at the valley far below.

Suddenly the dream seemed to shimmer and fade, and when Amaurn opened his eyes, the honeyed sunshine of a summer's day had changed to the silver-gilt of autumn. Aveole was no longer there. But what was this? He could see her, coming from the forest, walking through the soft grass of the meadow. He blinked and shook his head, dazed and disorientated, and not sure whether he was awake or still asleep. Then came the hard, black realisation that such happy times were a long way in the past, and his beloved Aveole was dead. The figure, however, kept on coming, and as she drew nearer, he saw the scar running down the side of her face. Veldan. Of course. He must be tired indeed to have let himself get so confused. She had returned from the coast much earlier than he'd expected.

He hailed her, but she did not answer, and suddenly he began to feel a sense of something wrong. How had she come here? How had she known where to find him? Why was she so silent, her expression so unchanging? She came closer still, almost within reach, and he suddenly saw what was wrong: what his instincts had been trying to tell him all along.

Her scar was on the wrong side of her face.

Wrong-handed, Amaurn snatched up his sword, and was on his feet, all in one swift movement. His arm was actually moving to deliver the deadly blow, when a single thought made him falter.

Are you sure?

If he was wrong, then Veldan would be dead. It was too late for him to pull the blow – his body was already committed to the swing – but that split-second's hesitation cost him.

Before his eyes Veldan vanished.

The sword, robbed of its target, clove through the air with nothing to stop it, pulling him off-balance. Even as he tried to recover himself, something tightened round his ankles, binding his legs so that he toppled, falling headlong into the grass, loosening his grip on the sword, and sending a stab of agony through his injured ribs. Amaurn looked down at his feet, and saw a huge, green serpent; its body, thicker than a swordsman's arm, was wrapped around his legs.

A shapeshifter! How Amaurn cursed his carelessness in coming up here all alone, without telling anyone where he was bound. He had sent away all the Loremasters who could fly to patrol the Curtain walls, and by the time any help could reach him on foot, it would already be too late. Nevertheless . . . Amaurn had learned a thing or two, lately, about not being too proud to ask for assistance. With all the force of his mind, he flashed an image of his location to Maskulu, along with a desperate plea for help.

The serpent had already thrown three or four coils around his legs, and was working its way up higher, constricting as it went. It opened its mouth and hissed, revealing long, curving fangs, and its menacing eyes – cold, flat, and black as obsidian – never left his face.

Constricting snakes tended not to be venomous, but he didn't want to take any chances. Barely daring to move, Amaurn groped in the long grass for his fallen sword and, with relief, felt the hilt slide into his hand. He rolled – the snake lunged at his face, but by that time the blade was already coming towards it, in a travesty of a decapitating blow. Again, the whistling steel struck nothing but thin air. The pressure around his legs vanished, and a hawk flew up out of the grass, went hurtling through the branches of the great oak, and vanished amid the leaves.

Swearing heartily, Amaurn clambered to his feet. Now what? Where was the damned creature? It could be anywhere: look like anything. In what form would it come at him next? He didn't have long to find out. From the edge of the forest came a low, rumbling growl – loud, full of menace and somehow, oddly familiar. There, emerging from the trees, came the very double of Veldan's firedrake friend, Kazairl.

Bloody wonderful!

Even as he thought it, he was already diving to one side. A great jet of flame came shooting from the killer's maw, missing him by inches, and burning a great, black swathe through the soft, green meadow. As Amaurn rolled over, and got back to his feet, his brain was working like lightning. There was no point in even trying to fight the Takur in this form. As a firedrake, the thing was faster, tougher, stronger and better armed – *and* it could incinerate him from a distance. Without another thought he took to his heels and ran, swerving back and forth to avoid the blasts of fire, and heading for the edge of the plateau where the hillside dropped away. The firedrake started after him but, impelled by a jolt of pure terror, he reached his goal in time. Without hesitation he leapt over the edge, and went sliding down the steep, wooded bank beyond.

Out of control, Amaurn went slithering down the slope, carried downwards by a shifting, rolling layer of leaf mould, loose soil and stones. He tried desperately to hang on to his sword, and to keep his feet from sliding out from underneath him, but he knew it was only a matter of time before he fell. Had it not been for the trees, he must surely have lost his balance, but he kept colliding with one sturdy trunk after another, doing no good whatsoever to his injured arm and ribs, but slowing his momentum enough to let him stay upright. Above him, he heard a roar of fury from the firedrake, then nothing. Its body was too large and ungainly to pass easily between all the trees, and he was pretty sure that it wouldn't want to flame him, and risk setting the woods on fire. A forest fire in damp autumn would warn the Loremasters that something was amiss up on the hill, and with Kazairl far away at present, the circumstances surrounding the Archimandrite's death would raise too many awkward questions. Besides, a shapeshifter had innumerable options. If the firedrake's shape proved unsuitable, it would simply try something else, and something else again, until it finally succeeded.

In what form will it come at me next?

Amaurn had managed to keep his footing for a goodly distance down the hill, and had even succeeded in avoiding the most precipitous parts of the slope, but such good fortune couldn't last. Scrambling to one side to miss a large rock that stood in his path, he managed to hurtle headlong into a low clump of bushes and briars, where he came to an abrupt – and thorny – halt.

Painfully, he disentangled himself, never once letting go of his sword. The tension of waiting for an attack to come out of the unknown was overwhelming.

Where is it?

From what direction will it come?

What will it look like?

Grimly, Amaurn set off again down the hill, skirting the thicket and making all the speed he dared. There was no point in waiting around for the damn thing to strike. Here, on the lower portion of the hill, the slope had grown more gentle and he could make a more controlled descent, though he certainly wasn't dawdling. By this time, he was certain that the Takur assassin must be toying with him. How far would it let him get, before it pounced?

Not far. In a thicket to his right, a shadow moved, just on the edge of his vision.

So there you are.

The temptation was either to go on the offensive and attack the creature, or at least put himself in a defensive position, with his back against a tree or a rock, and wait for it to come. Amaurn did neither – in dealing with a shapeshifter, both options would be a deadly mistake. So long as it didn't know he had spotted it, he would have one slender advantage: surprise. Gritting his teeth, he continued on his way as if nothing had happened.

Fast as lightning, it came at him out of the bushes. The Takur was using its own shape at last. This time, it took no recognisable form, but attacked as a dark, amorphous creature, almost as big as a man, but with a shadowy, shifting body that seemed to shimmer and melt from one guise to another, too fast for the eye to detect. A cluster of small eyes could be seen in the midst of the shape, glowing with a cold, white glitter. There seemed to be a number of flexible and elongated limbs and Amaurn saw, to his horror, that some were tipped with curved and savagely pointed claws, while others ended in knifelike blades which had the keen-edged gleam of sharpened steel.

All this he absorbed in a single, horrified instant – then the Takur was upon him. Amaurn, however, was ready for it, and as the long, black tentacles reached out towards him, he clove desperately at them with his sword, managing to lop off several which twitched and writhed upon the ground, their weapons useless. The creature hissed and snarled with pain, but already the severed ends of its limbs were elongating once more, and growing a new collection of blades and claws.

Again, Amaurn attacked the groping extremities and, though he had lost the advantage of surprise this time, he was gratified to see that the injuries and the effort of growing replacements seemed to be slowing the shapeshifter a little. He certainly hoped so. He, too, was tiring, he had begun this battle with injuries from a previous fight, and he was being forced to fight with the wrong hand, although in his years as Godsword Commander he had trained himself to be adept, at least, with both left and right.

Right-handed or left, however, Amaurn only had one arm, and one sword, against a host of deadly weapons wielded by many limbs. Desperately, he kept on hacking at the creature's flailing tentacles which came snaking in at him, now high, now low, now slicing at his guts, now gouging at his eyes, forcing greater and greater efforts from his tiring muscles to defend himself.

For a time it seemed as if the two combatants were stalemated – but something had to change, and soon. The Archimandrite, hurt and exhausted, knew with a deadly certainty that he was running out of time. The assassin also seemed to be in some distress, and both were slowing noticeably in their timing and reactions. But which would give way first?

Amaurn never saw it coming. He only knew he had been wounded when an icy shock in his side sent him reeling away as agony scored through him. He could feel blood soaking into his tunic, his vision swam, and giddiness overwhelmed him. The Takur followed up without mercy. It bore down on him, the bloodstained blade that had proved his undoing poised to strike again.

All those years, all those schemes and sacrifices, and it ends like this.

He had to admit there was a certain grim justice in it.

Then, without warning, the ground erupted underneath the assassin, sending it flying backwards, wailing, in a shower of soil and stones and fallen leaves. One of the trees tilted and fell with a crash that shook the hillside. Out of the ground came Maskulu, length upon monstrous length of him, with an armoured hide that could turn any Takuru blade, and formidable weapons of his own, in his multitudinous claws and razor-edged diamond mandibles. Amaurn had never seen a more beautiful sight in all his life, but his huge comrade was at a disadvantage amid the trees. As the shapeshifter fled he went to pursue it, but before he'd had time to turn his long, unwieldy body, his prey had vanished once again.

'Stay here,' Amaurn called as Maskulu seemed about to set off in pursuit. 'It's a Takur – you won't find it.'

'I can try.'

'No – don't go anywhere,' the Archimandrite gasped. 'Keep in my sight. That's the only way I can be sure you're you.'

'I never thought of that,' Maskulu rumbled. 'But how dare we leave such an assassin at large? He can come at you from anywhere, at any time. You could be dead before you even knew what had happened.'

'Tell me about it,' Amaurn grunted. Each small movement sent white hot agony lancing through his side. 'Come over here. I'll need you to help me get back.'

Coming closer, the Loremaster lowered his hideous head to make a closer examination of the wound. 'As far as I can tell, it mainly went through muscle. It doesn't look deep enough, hopefully, to have done any serious damage.'

'If I don't bleed to death, that is.'

'You'll never walk back,' his companion told him. 'Maybe, if you could manage to climb up, I could take you on my back – or maybe I should go and fetch some help to carry you back to the settlement.'

Amaurn looked at him. 'But who can you trust?' He grimaced, half in pain, half in anger at the clever way in which Syvilda had wrought his undoing. She had to be behind this – of that he was absolutely certain. Though her assassin had failed to take his life, its amorphous nature had cut him off from friend as well as foe.

Well, I'm damned if I'll let her get away with it!

He was growing light-headed now, and his limbs felt very cold. He realised that he was going into shock, but the last thing he could afford to do at this point was pass out. 'Come on,' he said to Maskulu. 'There's no time to lose. I'm going to climb up on that fallen tree, and get up onto your back from there. When we get back to the settlement, we'll work out the rest, but we have to get there while I'm still conscious.'

Maskulu rumbled in concern. 'Are you sure you'll be able to manage?'

Amaurn thought back to the night he had fallen down the cliff and had managed to claw his way back to safety only by refusing to consider any alternative. It was a comfort to know that he still had the iron-hard Lord Blade within him, to handle these emergencies. 'Oh, yes,' he said grimly. 'I'll manage.'

Nineteen

Traps and Conundrums

'They can't possibly have gone across *there*!' Galveron's face, in the pulsing, coloured light, was a picture of dismay. Alestan, standing on the brink where the passage ended so abruptly, looked again at the seemingly bottomless shaft in front of him, the small square platform in the centre that seemed to be topped with some sort of fine-meshed grid, and the long jump to the other side, where the corridor began again. In truth, he didn't like it any better than his companion, but he certainly wasn't going to admit that. 'Where else could they have gone?' he pointed out.

Galveron frowned. 'Those side vents . . .' he began.

'Galveron, we checked the grilles on every one of those vents,' the thief retorted. 'Judging from the muck on them, and the rust, not one of them had been opened in living memory. You've got to face it. Aliana and Packrat must have crossed this shaft, if they came down here – and we know they must have done. The food crumbs we found back there, the place where somebody relieved themselves – who else could it have been?'

Despite the ever-changing hues of his skin, the Godsword Commander looked very pale as he studied the awful drop down the shaft, but he set his jaw firmly. 'You're right,' he admitted. 'We're going to have to jump across.'

'You could always wait here,' Alestan suggested hopefully. 'I'm much more accustomed to the climbing and jumping side of things. I'll go on ahead and find the others, and bring them back here to you.'

Galveron gave him a withering look. 'You'll go on ahead and join with them, and leave me sitting here like an old maid at a wedding,' he retorted. 'Do you think I was born yesterday?'

'But we'd have to come back this way.'

'Yes – but only if you can't find another way out.'

The thief cursed under his breath. He kept forgetting how astute the Godsword Commander was.

'Anyway,' Galveron continued. 'What if you went on alone and came across another ladder?'

Alestan glared at him. 'Trust you to throw *that* in my face!' With his broken arm in splints and a sling, he had been unable to manage the ladder down from the podium platform and had been forced to wait while Galveron fetched a rope, then suffer the ignominy of being lowered down. But, much as he hated to admit it, the Commander had a point. 'Very well, then.' He gestured floridly with his free hand towards the shaft. 'After you.'

His companion hesitated. 'With that arm of yours, are you sure you're all right to do this?'

'I jump with my legs, not my arms.'

'But when you land, you use your arms to help keep your balance,' Galveron pointed out. 'You know, after I brought the rope all this way in my backpack, it's a real pity there's nothing here to which we can tie it. It would have been good to do this without worrying about falling all the way to the bottom. Still, if I go first, at least I can catch and steady you as you land.'

'If you haven't mucked it up and fallen down the bloody shaft,' Alestan said sourly, his pride stung by the implication that he might not be able to manage – and the knowledge, deep inside, that it might be true. 'Go on then,' he muttered. 'Get on with it.'

Galveron stood on the brink, taking in the length of the two jumps, the inadequacy of the bare platform in the centre – and the depth of the shaft. He swallowed hard, walked back a good distance down the corridor, turned, ran – and took a gigantic, flying leap that boasted a lot more force than grace. He came down hard on the central platform, and stumbled as he landed. Alestan heard the crack of his knee hitting the floor, and winced. 'Clumsy as a pig on ice,' he called, unable to resist such a good opportunity to needle the Godsword Commander.

Galveron's lips were moving silently as he got back to his feet, and by the look on his face, he wasn't saying his prayers. Limping slightly, he turned and glared at Alestan. 'At least I didn't break my arm.'

Now it was the thief's turn to scowl. Muttering dark things about Galveron's probable parentage, he stalked off down the passage until he was sure he had given himself a long enough run. He steadied his breathing, focussed on the jump ahead of him, sped lightly to the take-off point, and launched himself just at the right moment.

For someone who was used to making his way across Tiarond via the rooftops, the jump presented no problem. Alestan landed lightly, took a step or two forward to keep himself balanced, then turned to Galveron and bowed. 'Any time you need some lessons, Commander . . .'

'Next time I'll just leave you in prison,' Galveron grumbled – then he grinned, and clapped the thief on the shoulder. 'Good jump,' he said. Alestan was just opening his mouth to reply, when a rumbling, roaring sound came up from under his feet. Reflexively, he jumped aside, just as a jet of intense flame came up through the grid, right where he'd been standing, and, a split-second later, another shot up inches from the Godsword's face.

'Jump,' Alestan bellowed. 'Now!' Without waiting, he dashed to the edge of the platform and threw himself across the gap. The leap lacked both the power and grace of the first but it got him to safety, a few inches past the corridor's edge. As he landed, he turned, anxious about his companion. Galveron, with a desperate, do-or-die look on his face, was just jumping, but clearly he had been hampered by the short run-up.

He's never going to make it!

The thief looked on in horror, fully expecting to see the Godsword plunge to his death, but somehow, he managed to find that extra ounce of effort, coming to earth right on the brink where the passage began once more. Off-balance and teetering, he threw himself forward and Alestan winced as his knee, the same one as last time, cracked down hard against the floor. White-faced, he raised himself carefully, grimacing with pain, and looked at the thief. 'When I see your sister,' he said in pleasant, almost conversational tones, 'I'm going to wring her neck.'

Alestan looked back at the platform, where random flames were still shooting upwards at a tremendous rate. 'Join the queue.'

They stopped for a while to rest and eat, relieved that those irritating colours had gone, but still mystified as to why they had been there in the first place. 'I think they might have been some kind of alert, or alarm,' Galveron suggested. 'Maybe our passing through the coloured lights triggered the traps in some way – you know, like cocking a crossbow.'

The thief shrugged. 'It's as good an explanation as any – not that it's any use expecting anything in this place to make sense. I mean, who would think of constructing that shaft, and putting a platform in it with flames that shoot out? If you ask me, the builders of this place were seriously deranged.'

Galveron, who was busy tearing some strips off the hem of his shirt to strap up his knee, clearly had other concerns. 'I don't think it'll ever be the same again,' he said ruefully, rubbing gingerly at the offending limb. 'Let's hope there aren't any more leaps like that to contend with.'

'Look on the bright side,' said Alestan. 'Maybe there won't be.' He hesitated. 'On the other hand, how do we know that the next obstacle won't be a whole lot worse?'

For a time, however, it seemed that this strange place beneath the city had nothing more to throw at them. They walked on through those same, monotonous corridors for a hour or so, and Alestan was just beginning to think that the greatest danger down here would be perishing with boredom when Galveron stopped him with an out-thrust arm. 'Wait,' he said. 'What's that?'

For a stretch of several yards, the walls on either side were covered with tiles, about a foot square, that bore pictures of little stylised figures, all busy with a variety of activities. Alestan went closer to examine them. 'Myrial's teeth and toenails!' he gasped. 'Look – they're moving!'

The little figures on each tile seemed to go through a short sequence of actions which then started from the beginning once more, repeating themselves over and over. A man was being swallowed by a giant fish; the same man was leaving a house on a hill, and waving goodbye to a woman and children who were weeping; now he was returning to the house on the hill, leading a donkey laden with boxes of treasure; now he was deep underground, battling with a dragon; now he was confronting three hideous ogres; now he was on board a ship which was engaged in a desperate battle with another vessel bearing a pirate flag. There seemed to be no particular order to the tiles; all the activities of the little man seemed random and unconnected with one another.

Galveron, fascinated, couldn't seem to take his eyes off the amazing wall, and Alestan, too, had never seen anything like it. Reaching out a cautious finger, he touched one of the tiles, wondering if such interference would affect the movements of the figures in any way. All he could feel, however, was a smooth, cool surface, while the activities went on, unchanged, beneath his finger, like fish swimming beneath a layer of clear ice. After a time, however, he began to wonder what it was all for. The tiles with the moving pictures were astounding, and the antics of the little hero were quite diverting to watch, but what purpose did these things serve? And why place them all this way underground, in the middle of a corridor?

Alestan knotted his brows. These moving images had not been put down here for entertainment. They must serve some other purpose. Seeking answers, he looked further down the passage.

Just as the tiled stretch of the walls turned back to the smooth, blue metal, the floor of the corridor changed to another chequerboard of tiles, the same size as those on the wall, which were mainly white, but interspersed at random intervals with blue. The blue tiles seemed to be sunken, about the length of a fingertip below the level of the others and, though they were irregularly spaced, were each about a long stride apart from one another. This tiled stretch lasted for about thirty yards, then they could see that the floor changed back again to its original composition.

Galveron, still entranced by the images, was laughing heartily at one particular tile where the little man, in trying to shoot a bird in a tree for his supper, hit a hornets' nest instead, and was chased all the way through the woods by a swarm of angry insects. He turned away reluctantly when Alestan tugged at his arm. The thief rolled his eyes to the heavens.

Maybe that's their purpose. Perhaps they're meant to be some kind of diversion, to delay us here and put us off our guard. Then something awful, like those accursed flames, will happen.

But at present, nothing seemed to be happening that was any worse than Galveron's irritation at being interrupted. 'Well?' he snapped.

With great restraint, Alestan forbore to remind him why they had come down here. Instead, he indicated the tiled stretch of corridor up ahead. 'What do you make of that? I don't like the look of it, myself.'

Galveron frowned. 'You're right. It looks very suspicious.' He unslung his backpack, and took out one of the hard, doughy griddlecakes. 'Stay back,' he said softly, and with a flick of his wrist, he flipped the cake onto the white tiles.

From the walls on either side shot something that looked very like sizzling bolts of energy, which criss-crossed the corridor from floor to ceiling, as far as the tiled section continued. After a few moments, they died away, leaving the passage looking as innocuous as before.

'I thought as much.' Galveron started forward cautiously. 'It was bound to be another trap. It looks as though we have to keep to the blue tiles, to get safely across this part.'

'Wait.' Alestan pulled him back. 'That's too easy. The last obstacle looked simple, remember? And look what happened there.' From out of his pocket he pulled a half-eaten pastry of his own, and lobbed it, with impressive accuracy, onto one of the blue tiles. Galveron jumped back, cursing, as the bolts went searing across the passageway once more.

Alestan looked at him curiously. 'You know, before we came down here, I'm not sure that I ever heard you swear.'

The Godsword Commander glared at the offending stretch of corridor. 'In this place, I'm learning fast. What do we do now, then?'

'You have to learn to think like a thief,' Alestan said, with an evil grin. 'You would be amazed at the number of snares and locks and obstacles that people invent to protect their belongings from the likes of us. After a while, we learn how to deal with them – or starve.'

'Or end up being caught.' Galveron sounded disgruntled.

'Yes, that happens sometimes – but not nearly as often as you would like to think,' the thief retorted.

At that, Galveron settled himself down on the floor, leaned back against the wall and put his feet up on his backpack, and tucked his arms behind his head in a most irritating manner. 'Off you go, then. Wake me when you've found out how to get through.'

Alestan ground his teeth. Damn the Godsword! If only he actually *would* go to sleep, then he himself could find out how to get across this trapped area and head off in his own, where Galveron couldn't follow. By the time Galveron had managed to work out the solution for himself – if he ever did – the thief could be miles away, and hot on his sister's trail.

And if you think for one moment that this accursed Godsword was telling the truth about going to sleep, then you'll be able to cross this trapped stretch on a flying pig.

Pretending that he hadn't noticed Galveron watching him surreptitiously through half-closed eyes, Alestan turned to examine the puzzle. Not just the blue squares, nor yet the white – then what? He toyed with the idea that there might be some sort of sequence to crossing the tiles, but if there was, they wouldn't stand a chance of getting across. They didn't have enough pieces of griddlecake, or anything else, for that matter, to test out every damned tile, and couldn't throw accurately enough to the further stretches in any case. Muttering sourly, he began to pace back and forth across the corridor – and once again, he started to think about the pictures on the walls. All his instincts were screaming that this must be significant. But how?

Come on, Alestan – think! With every moment you waste here, Aliana is getting further away.

Galveron, in the meantime, had clearly decided that he had irritated Alestan enough, and stopped pretending to be asleep. Within moments, he was back at the wretched wall tiles, engrossed once again – which, of course, only had the effect of irritating the thief still more. Alestan continued to pace, glaring at the offending stretch of floor. There must be an answer here. There must be!

Then Galveron spoke, almost echoing his thought. 'I think I've got the solution.'

Alestan whirled to face him. 'What? *You?*'

'Not bad for a plodding Godsword, eh?' His grin was wide and malicious. 'Maybe we're one step ahead of you thieves a little more often than you seem to think.'

'That's supposing you're right, of course,' said Alestan. 'Go on, then, if you're so bloody clever. What's the answer?'

'Look.' Gently, Galveron pressed one of the wall tiles with its fingertips. There was a soft click and, to the thief's surprise, the tile came loose from the wall. 'You see?' the said Godsword said. 'You can take them out and move them around.'

'How absolutely fascinating. Perhaps, when you've stopped playing around with those ridiculous things, you can tell me how you propose to get across the floor.'

'But this is the way to get across.' Galveron's smug expression made Alestan's fists itch. 'Don't you see? These moving tiles make up a story. Right now, they're all mixed up, but if we can get them into the right order, we then put them into those recessed blue spaces on the floor. Unless I'm mistaken, they'll disarm the lightning bolts – either that, or we can then step safely on them, and get through that way.'

Alestan looked at him in disgust. 'A *story?* We have to make a story out of these damned things? Have you lost your mind?'

'Have you any better suggestions?'

'I wish to Myrial I had. This is ridiculous! What in the name of all creation could be at the end of this passage, to make whoever built these tunnels go to such elaborate lengths to protect it?' His voice grew thoughtful. 'It must be something pretty valuable.'

'Right at the minute, the Hierarch's ring and your wretched sister are down this passage,' Galveron reminded him grimly. 'As far as I'm concerned, anything else is incidental. Come on, help me get these tiles down. We'll lay them out on the floor, and see if we can put them in order.'

Alestan still only half-believed his companion's theory, but it wasn't as if he had anything better to do. As he took down the tiles, he was surprised to see that the images kept moving, with the little hero repeating a sequence of actions in an endless loop. But how? What made the pictures move like that? Curiously, he looked at the backs, but they were simply a plain, featureless white. By this time he was beginning to understand why Galveron had become so fascinated with the things.

How did they – whoever they were – manage to do this? It's incredible!

Galveron was holding up two tiles. 'I think these are the beginning and the end,' he said. 'See? Here the man is leaving his family and setting out on his adventures, and here he is coming back with all the treasures that he won.'

'Well, that's a start.' Alestan frowned. 'But what order does the rest of it take? I mean, does he get eaten by the fish before he fights the dragon, or what? And where do the hornets fit in?' He flung his arms up in the air. 'How do they expect us to do this? The bloody thing's impossible!'

'No it isn't.' Galveron was walking up and down the line of tiles that lay on the ground. 'Let me see . . . He must have been in the pirate battle before the ship got sunk and the fish ate him . . . And here he is, boarding the ship, so that goes before the others . . . And when he's walking into the woods – where the hornets are – he's still dripping, so I would guess that must be after he escaped from the fish, but before the dragon . . . Come on, Alestan. Help me out.'

Admitting defeat, Alestan joined him. Already, the line of tiles looked to have more of a sequence. 'Why couldn't the dragon be before the pirate ship?' he asked.

'Because he comes away from the dragon with a big sack of treasure.' Galveron pointed out the tile. 'And he doesn't have it on the ship.'

'Maybe the pirates took it off him?'

'Don't be ridiculous. He still has it when he comes home. Look, there it is on his donkey.'

Alestan gritted his teeth. 'I hate this bloody stupid thing.'

'I think it's fun, myself.' Galveron grinned at him.

'Aren't you forgetting that with every minute we waste on this nonsense, Aliana will be getting further ahead?'

'No she won't. Don't forget that she needed to work this out for herself, before she could go on, and that must have taken her a fair amount of time. In the end, it all evens out – at least, it will if we get on with this, and stop wasting time.'

'Hold on.' Alestan's heart sank. The Godsword's stupid idea might be annoying, but at least it had been *some* sort of solution. But . . . 'Galveron, I think we have a problem.'

Galveron looked up from his tiles. 'What now?'

'Well, Aliana is ahead of us, and if she *did* solve this puzzle as you've done, and she worked out the story, and put the tiles down in order . . .'

'Yes?'

'Then why aren't the tiles still down there on the floor? Why did we find them up there on the wall?'

Galveron's face reminded Alestan of the time, far back in his childhood, when he and Aliana had opened their birthday presents and found clothes instead of toys. Then the Godsword set his jaw. 'Damn it, no. I'm *sure* I'm right. I have no idea how the tiles got back on the wall, but I'm not going to worry about that now.'

'I would if I were you,' the thief replied. 'Because if you're right, then as far as I can see, the only way the wretched things could get back to where they were, is if someone came along and *put* them back – and if there's someone else wandering around down here, then we had better be prepared.'

'Good point. I'll be prepared, all right. If whoever invented these damned traps and conundrums is walking around down here, I'd be delighted to meet them,' Galveron said grimly, before turning back to his tiles once more.

With a shrug, Alestan joined him. If there was no alternative, he supposed he might as well get into the spirit of the thing. 'Look,' he said, after a moment. 'The donkey belongs to the ogres, and the hero runs away with it when he outwits them. And if he didn't have it on any of his other adventures, then this must be the last one before he gets home.'

'Well done!' Galveron clapped him on the shoulder, and for some reason, he felt ridiculously pleased with himself. Maybe the Godsword had been right after all, about this being fun. He pointed at the tiles again. 'That only leaves the part when the man gets captured by a witch, and, since his clothes have scorch marks all over them, and he has the sack of treasure but no donkey, she must come between the dragon and the ogres. That's it! We've done it.'

The two men grinned at one another. 'Come on,' Galveron said. 'Let's start getting them into place. This is the part where we find out whether I was right or wrong.'

Carefully, they stacked the tiles in the right order. At the edge of the trapped area, Galveron squatted down, wincing at having to bend his knee so far. 'Hand me the first one,' he said, reaching behind him. Alestan gave him the picture of the brave little man leaving his family and setting off on his adventures, and the Godsword reached forward and placed it in the nearest blue indentation. The tile slotted into place with a loud click. 'Now,' Galveron said. 'Give me another piece of that bread stuff, whatever you want to call it, and let's test this out.'

Alestan fished in his backpack and broke off another portion from their ration. 'Let's hope we don't have to do this too often, or we're going to starve down here.'

Galveron took it from him and looked at it critically. 'Best use for it, if you ask me. It's like chewing rocks.'

'I'll tell Telimon you said that. I'm sure he'd be interested in your opinion.'

'If you do, I'll make you eat the whole lot yourself,' the Godsword threatened. He took a few steps back. 'Right – stand clear.' He broke the hard, flat griddlecake in half, lobbing one bit onto the white tiles, as he had done before. Again, the captive lightning sizzled across the corridor and the smell of ozone filled the air. Galveron nodded to himself. 'So putting a tile in the right place doesn't disarm the trap,' he said, half to himself. 'I didn't think it would. Let's try it the other way. Aiming carefully, he tossed the other piece of his improvised missile onto the animated square.

Nothing happened, and a broad grin of relief spread across his face. 'I told you so. Come on, hand me the next tile.'

Cautiously, he stepped forward onto the tile he had just placed. In order to be able to reach the next blank space, he had to put both his feet on the tile, which left him very little space. 'This is no good,' he muttered. Returning to the safety of the normal corridor, he sat down and removed his boots, stuffing his rolled socks inside them and fastening them carefully to the outside of his backpack. 'You'll have to follow me with the pieces,' he said to Alestan. 'I suggest you take your shoes off too.'

'I'll be all right.' The thief showed him the light, flexible, soft-soled shoes that were so necessary in his trade. 'Are you ready now?' he prompted the Godsword. 'I really want to get on with this.'

'Come on, then.' Galveron got to his feet again, and squared his shoulders. 'Let's do it.'

Step by step, they picked their way along the trapped section of corridor, being very careful to put their feet only on the areas with pictures that Galveron had just laid down. With each step they took, Alestan handed out another of the tiles from the stock he carried, and the Godsword squatted – a difficult task, with his feet crammed together on one constricted spot – and placed the tile in the next blue indentation before straightening, very carefully, until he was upright again. Alestan admired his fortitude. Going up and down like that must be putting a great strain on his thigh muscles, and what it must be doing to his injured knee didn't bear thinking about. It was much easier for himself. All he had to worry about was not dropping the tiles, and he had nothing else to do but follow Galveron, which meant that he could stand with a foot on each of two squares – a luxury that was denied the Godsword while he was placing his tiles, as that stance, with one leg stretched back, made it impossible for him to reach far enough.

Their progress was slow and painstaking, and the thief was grinding his teeth with impatience long before they reached their goal. Eventually, however, they reached the end of the trapped area, and stepped onto the smooth, metallic floor of the passage with profound relief. Galveron stretched mightily, rubbing his thighs. 'Thank goodness that's over. I—'

'Look, Galveron! Quick!' Alestan had been looking back over the area they had just traversed, so he saw the change beginning to take place. One by one, the tiles bearing the pictures sank down a little below the level of the floor, then every one of them turned blue again, so the surface looked exactly as it had when the two men had first approached it. With a feeling of inevitability, the thief looked back at the wall on which they had first found the tiles, and saw the pictures appearing there once again, until everything looked as it had done before. 'Well, I'll be damned!' he said. 'Well, at least that's one mystery solved.'

'It's just as well,' said Galveron. 'I didn't really like the idea of a bunch of strangers wandering around here resetting these traps behind us.'

Alestan turned to his companion. 'Shall we go on now, or do you need to rest your knee a bit, first?'

'No, let's go on. Maybe I can work the stiffness out with a bit of exercise.' The Godsword shouldered his backpack and limped off determinedly down the passage. With a shrug, Alestan followed.

It wasn't so far between the tile puzzle and the next obstacle. Galveron groaned when he saw it. 'I don't believe this! Not again!'

Another shaft bisected the corridor. Swearing under his breath, Alestan walked to the edge and examined it – and felt his heart sink. 'The accursed thing's about twice as wide as the last one. And this time, there isn't even a pillar – or anything else, for that matter – in the middle. It's just a bloody great pit, and we'll never get across it!' Hurling his backpack savagely to the ground, he sat down on the floor, weary, disgusted, and defeated.

Galveron looked over the edge in his turn. 'At least there's a bottom that we can see this time, but it makes no difference. That shaft is deep enough to kill us ten times over.' He slumped down beside the thief, his expression thunderous. 'This is just all wrong,' he complained. 'There were ways around the other obstacles, but this time, they haven't given us a chance.'

'You know what?' Alestan said. 'You're absolutely right. This *is* all wrong – but not in the way you think. If it isn't passable, how come Aliana isn't here?'

The Godsword's face brightened. 'Good for Aliana! I might have known she would do it! Well, if she can get across, we can.'

Alestan looked at him quizzically. 'I thought you were mad at her?'

'I am,' Galveron protested quickly. 'What makes you think I'm not?'

Aliana's brother just chuckled. 'I believe you,' he said. 'Thousands wouldn't.'

The Commander of the Godswords glared at him. 'If you've finished being stupid, I suggest you help me find a way to get across this pit.'

Wondering if it was once again a question of standing on the right place, they made a minute search of the passage floor for some twenty yards back from the shaft. They searched the walls, running their fingers over the smooth metal and peering closely until their eyes ached. Hanging perilously over the drop, they searched the inner walls of the shaft itself, as far as they could reach and, with Alestan sitting on Galveron's shoulders, they even searched the ceiling.

They found absolutely nothing.

Eventually, Galveron shook his head. 'I don't know what else to do,' he admitted. 'I don't see how we can give up, but I've run out of ideas.' He scowled. 'A plague on Aliana! I trusted that damned sister of yours – I can't believe she would turn traitor. But, by Myrial, if the little wretch *had* to betray us all, I wish she had come anywhere but here.'

It was too much for Alestan. 'You leave my sister out of this,' he yelled. 'You can talk about betraying people – what about your promises to take care of us? You think you're so high and mighty, you and that damned bitch of a Hierarch, but for all your airs, you're no better than we are! You're . . .'

'QUIET!' Galveron's bellow was so unexpected that it startled Alestan into silence. 'Listen,' the Godsword said. 'Can you hear water?'

As one, the two men turned towards the shaft, and looked over. Just below the level on which they were standing, four round apertures had opened up, one in each of the walls. Water was gushing out of them at a tremendous rate, and they could see the shaft filling rapidly, even as they watched.

Suddenly, Galveron started to laugh. 'Well done, thief!'

'What the blazes are you talking about?' Alestan snapped. He was still fuming, and frankly, he couldn't see why that thick-headed Godsword was so pleased. 'So the pit's going to be full of water . . . So what? And what did it have to do with me?'

'You set it off – I think,' Galveron told him. 'I don't know if you could get away with just yelling anything, or whether the right word just happened to be somewhere in your tirade, but it must have been the shouting that triggered the water. We didn't do anything else. And no matter that it was an accident, you've solved the whole problem. All we have to do is wait until it fills up, then swim across.'

Alestan's jaw dropped open. If he hadn't been so angry with the Godsword, he would have worked it out sooner. 'I wonder who did the yelling when Aliana and Packrat found this out,' he said.

'I can guess,' Galveron said drily. 'You are twins, after all. It's only natural that you'll react to situations in similar ways.'

The pit was filling up fast. Soon the water would have reached the four inlets, and the two men would be able to swim across. Then another problem struck Alestan. 'What about this?' He held up his splinted arm. 'It's all very well for you, but . . .'

'Well,' said Galveron thoughtfully, 'you could always wait here while I—'

'*No!*'

The commander shrugged. 'Funny, you seemed to think it was a good idea earlier, back at the fire shaft, when the boot was on the other foot. I might point out, however, that if you had gone ahead and left me, you'd be looking pretty stupid about now – that is, supposing you had ever managed to work out how to use the story tiles.'

'All *right*,' the thief snapped. 'You've made your point.'

'Can you swim, anyway?' Galveron asked him curiously. 'I mean . . .'

'You mean, considering my background.' Alestan scowled at him. 'As a matter of fact I can, though I haven't done it for a very long time. We weren't born and bred in the Warrens, Aliana and I. Our father was a merchant who lost all his money, and killed himself when we were nine years old. Our mother was already dead, so we had to fend for ourselves after that.'

Galveron looked away. 'I'm sorry,' he said. 'I didn't know.'

'Why?' Alestan challenged him. 'Would it have made any difference to the way you treated us?'

'If you can swim, you can float.' The Godsword changed the subject abruptly. 'I'll tow you across. We'll manage all right.'

They stuffed their outer clothing into their backpacks, and tied their boots securely to the outsides. Then they fastened the rope to the packs, and tied the free end around Alestan's waist. The plan was to leave the heavy packs behind, then once they had reached the other side, they would pull them across. The trickiest part of the proceedings was getting the thief into the water, but Galveron got in first, and helped to support him as he slid over the side, then put a hand behind his head until he was floating confidently. The water wasn't too uncomfortable: on the cold side, but not icy. All too aware of the considerable depth beneath him, Alestan found find it very difficult indeed to relax, as he knew he must do, and trust the man who was towing him. In the end, he managed to distract himself by imagining what he would say to his wretch of a sister when he finally caught up with her.

The crossing didn't prove too difficult – especially when compared with the previous obstacles. When they reached the far side, Alestan clung to the edge with his good hand and trod water, while Galveron, after several attempts which involved a good deal of spluttering and cursing, managed to haul himself out. As soon as he was safe, he pulled Alestan to safety, then paused for a moment to catch his breath – he *had* been doing all the hard work in swimming them across – before pulling the backpacks over to their side.

The water had managed to seep into the packs to a certain extent, but they were Godsword-issue oiled canvas, and so their contents had stayed fairly dry, at any rate. Alestan thought of his sister, forced to go on her way dripping, with her soaked clothes sticking to her skin. Now that he came to think of it, he could see the odd little puddle and damp patch heading away down the corridor in front of them. A smile crept over his face.

That'll teach her to go acting like an idiot, and running off down here.

Galveron must have been thinking along similar lines. 'Poor Aliana,' he said. 'She can't be very comfortable now.'

Alestan raised his eyes to the heavens, but forbore to comment. 'At least Packrat will have had a good bath, for once,' was all he said.

'I forgot about him,' the Godsword said. 'You mean *he* can swim?'

'He grew up on the Middens, and you know how they flood every spring. The children who didn't learn to swim didn't survive.'

'Dear Myrial,' Galveron said softly. 'It seems that there's an awful lot I didn't know about your people, Alestan. I'm sorry. I think I've been jumping to a lot of conclusions, and misjudging you all a great deal. Stealing is still wrong, of course,' he added quickly, 'but what's really wrong is that youngsters like you and Packrat were forced into that kind of life in the first place. If we ever manage to rebuild this city, we're going to have to do better by our children.'

Alestan stared at him.

Amazing! We're not even sure how we're going to survive the next few days, and he's talking about rebuilding the city. Maybe Aliana was right. He would do a much better job of leading us than Gilarra.

Picking up their belongings, they went on their way once more; both of them silent now, and very thoughtful.

Twenty

The Newcomer

The closer Dark came to the Shadowleague headquarters, the more relieved he was that he had been provided with an escort. After his battle with the winged fiends – or the Ak'Zahar, as he was learning to call them – he had been taken to the wayshelter by the Phoenix, and told to wait, along with Scall and his winged captive, until someone could come to see him safely to the settlement. She was unable to do it herself she said, because she was needed to patrol the Curtain Walls, but she assured him that he wouldn't have too long to wait. Though the Summoner knew full well that the amazing bird was less bothered about his own convenience, and more concerned about preventing him from wandering at large through Gendival, he was more than content with this arrangement. Even though Grim had tried to warn him that he would be meeting with some very strange-looking individuals, the appearance of the large, exotic, golden avian, who could communicate in mindspeech and who left a fiery trail behind her as she flew, had shaken him to the core, and he had wondered what other shocks this day would have in store for him.

Still, at least he had half an idea what to expect. Poor Scall looked utterly terrified. Dark wanted desperately to untie him but, until his new custodian arrived, he didn't dare risk the boy running off. The Summoner hadn't exactly made an auspicious start here, by accidentally letting three winged fiends through the Curtain Walls and deliberately bringing a fourth one with him as a prisoner.

In the wayshelter, he had tried to apologise to the boy, and explain why he had brought him here, but Scall had refused to respond, save to glower at his captor with hatred in his eyes. Eventually, Dark had given up trying to explain, and was concentrating instead on making the poor lad a little more comfortable, when he heard someone calling him from outside – speaking aloud as well as using mindspeech and, to the Summoner's relief, sounding very human.

The escort turned out to be a young man of medium height, with long blond hair that fell past his shoulders, and a cheerful countenance. He was riding a lively, dark bay horse with three white socks and a white star on its forehead. Across his back was slung an unfamiliar, complicated-looking weapon, with what looked like the stock of a crossbow at one end, attached to an oddly shaped construction of metal and crystals, which in turn led to a long, shining tube made of some unidentified substance. Dark thought of Scall's arcane discoveries, and realised that he had brought the artefacts to the right place.

The young man introduced himself as Loremaster Kher. 'It'll be my pleasure to escort you back to Gendival,' he told the Summoner. 'To tell you the truth, patrolling the Curtain Walls was getting really boring. I'll be glad of an excuse to get back to headquarters for a while.'

When he slid down from his horse, Dark saw that he was limping very heavily. He removed a staff that was slotted through a loop on his saddle, and used it to help him walk as he went into the wayshelter. His eyes widened when he saw the winged fiend, bound and stinking in its corner. (It had been brought inside, very reluctantly, by the Summoner who was afraid that if he left it outside, its fellows might come back to rescue it – or prey on it.)

'So Vaure was telling me the truth!' Kher said. 'When she told me you had a live Ak'Zahar with you, I thought she was pulling my leg – what's left of it.'

Dark sighed ruefully. 'Since I had captured one alive, I thought it might be some use to the Shadowleague – maybe to help them pinpoint its weaknesses – but Vaure seemed to think it wouldn't be well received. I hope it's not going to get me into too much trouble.'

Kher frowned. 'To be honest, I don't know how it will be received,' he said. 'If Cergorn had still been Archimandrite, I hate to think how much trouble you would have been in. Now that the leadership has changed, though – well, it's anybody's guess. Amaurn is still very much an unknown quantity to most of the Loremasters; especially us younger folk. It's hard to say how he'll react, though I wouldn't be at all surprised if he was very interested in your idea.' He grinned at Dark. 'Let's hope so, eh? You look like the sort of fellow we could do with in the Shadowleague right now.'

Next the Loremaster turned his attention to Scall, who was lying on the bed. 'And who's this?'

Dark was opening his mouth to answer, but the boy beat him to it. 'I'm Scall, and I was staying with the Reivers – until this *bastard* kidnapped me.'

'I couldn't help it,' the Summoner protested. 'This lad found some very interesting artefacts beneath the city of Tiarond, and the new Archimandrite ordered us to bring him here, according to my mentor, Grim. He was once a Loremaster, and an old friend of Amaurn.' Again he felt the anguish overwhelm him at the mention of Grim's name. 'With his dying breath he told me to carry on and bring Scall here, and so I did.'

There was sympathy on Kher's face. 'I don't know a Loremaster here called Grim, but I'm sorry that you lost your friend, and you were right to carry out his wishes. But how came he to be killed?'

'He was murdered.' Dark's voice turned hard. 'By *his* companion.' He indicated Scall. 'The man was going for the boy with a knife, but Grim got in the way.'

'It wasn't my fault,' Scall yelled. 'I couldn't—'

'That's enough.' There was an unexpected snap of authority in Kher's voice as he looked from one to the other. 'Scall, you listen to me. You're on the other side of the Curtain Walls now, and your only hope of safety is to stay with us. Do you understand?'

Scall nodded.

'Good. Now, you can either make the journey tied across your saddle like a sack, or we can untie you and let you ride properly –

as long as you promise to come along quietly, and not give us any trouble. Which is it to be?'

Scall hesitated. 'I promise,' he said sulkily.

'That's a sensible lad,' said Kher. 'Now, I'm going to untie you, and you'll ride to the settlement with us. Once our leader has found out what he needs to know from you, I'm sure he'll send you back where you belong. All right?'

The boy's face lit up. 'He will?'

Kher, in the middle of undoing the ropes, patted him on the shoulder. 'I can't make any promises, but I don't see any reason why he shouldn't, especially if your information is of use to him. At least this way you stand a damn good chance of getting back through the Curtain Walls. But you'll never do it on your own. Without one of us to open them for you, you'll be stuck here for ever.'

Scall nodded. 'I understand.' He glared at Dark. 'Why couldn't you just have told me this, instead of tying me up and scaring me half to death? And after I saved your life, too, when that winged monstrosity attacked you.'

'I'm very sorry, Scall. But if you remember, there wasn't time for explanations when we left,' the Summoner pointed out. 'And besides, would you have come? Honestly?'

Scall flushed and lowered his eyes. 'I suppose not,' he mumbled.

'Let's get going,' Kher interrupted. 'It's quite a ride, and with those accursed Ak'Zahar on the loose, I want to get there before sundown.'

As a travelling companion, the young Loremaster proved to be good and cheerful company. He could certainly talk – as Dark soon discovered – but his light-hearted chatter helped take the Summoner's mind off Grim's death, and he certainly had some interesting tales to tell. Even Scall, who had started out by riding pointedly at a distance from the others, soon drew near, the sulky look vanishing from his face, to hear what his new companion had to say.

Kher explained that his leg had been injured while he was on a mission in another realm, and he had been sent home to recuperate.

'I'm all right on horseback,' he told Dark cheerfully, 'but I still walk with a dreadful limp. I was attacked by yehteh in the Cloud Mountains, and one of them managed to mangle my leg pretty thoroughly before my partner managed to drive them off.'

'What are – what did you say? Yehteh?' Dark asked curiously.

'Think of a sort of cross between an ape and a bear, and . . .'

'What's an ape? We don't have them where I come from.'

Kher sighed. 'Never mind. Yehteh are very big, very shaggy, and light grey or white in colour. They live up above the snowline, where food is so scarce that they prey on just about anything that moves. When they had plenty of space up there, they were quite content to stay put, but unfortunately, because of the Curtain Walls failing, the snowline is receding rapidly, and they're starting to come down off the mountain peaks and prey on the Angel hatcheries . . .'

'What are Angels?'

The Loremaster threw out his arms in surrender. 'I'm sorry – I keep forgetting that you only just got here, and you don't know anything. Because Vaure said you knew mindspeech, I was thinking of you as just another Loremaster. Still, I wouldn't worry about it too much. If you had arrived a couple of days ago, when Cergorn was still in charge, it might have been a very different story, but now that Amaurn is Archimandrite, all the policies have changed too. I know for a fact that he's absolutely desperate for able-bodied Loremasters just now, and there's a rumour that he's planning to rush the current trainees through the end of their tutelage, and get them out into the field. So that should leave plenty of room for new candidates like you. I expect Amaurn will welcome you with open arms.'

'I hope so,' the Summoner said fervently. 'Grim said he was going to ask Amaurn to take me, but now that he's gone . . .'

'You miss him very much, don't you?'

Dark swallowed hard. 'More than I could possibly tell you. He was all the family I had, after I was chosen to be a Summoner, and he was like a father to me.'

Kher frowned slightly. 'What exactly is a Summoner? The term is unfamiliar to me.'

271

Dark felt his face grow hot. 'This is going to seem awfully primitive to you,' he began, 'but it's like this . . .' But he needn't have worried. Kher responded to his tale with interest, not amusement, and as they rode on, deep in talk, the Summoner began to realise just what he had missed in spending so many years without a friend of his own age.

'This makes a nice change, I must say.' Toulac, who was standing with Veldan in the bows of the wherry, looked on appreciatively as the banks of the river slipped by. 'It's years since I was on a boat. I had forgotten how good it feels to float along, instead of having to walk or ride.'

They had made good time getting back, reaching the port of Neymis in time for breakfast at the inn where everyone, but particularly Toulac and Zavahl, ate like starving wolves, and the quayside fish market had been emptied of fish and shellfish for the hungry Dobarchu refugees, who were finding their first taste of shipboard life very strange indeed. Immediately after the companions had eaten, they said their thanks and farewells to Arnond and Rowen, and transferred to the wherry for the trip upriver. So far the journey had been uneventful, though both Veldan and Elion had come perilously close to falling overboard while learning to help Meglyn and Chalas pole the boat through the stretches where the current, now against them, was running at its swiftest. Now the difficult part was over, however; the river had broadened once more, and the high-peaked sail on its tall mast had taken over the work. Soon they would be back at the Shadowleague settlement.

'How long will it be before we get there?' the veteran asked Veldan.

'Not that long. An hour, maybe a little more, until we get to the trading post, then about the same to ride on to the settlement.'

Toulac glanced at her shrewdly. 'And are you planning to wait until we get all the way back before you tell me what's bothering you, or shall we get it over with now?'

Veldan flushed, making her scar stand out white against the rosy skin of her face. She opened her mouth, closed it again, and sighed. 'Is it really that obvious?'

'Well, let me put it this way – don't ever try playing cards for money.' Then she sobered. 'Seriously though, girlie, what's wrong? You and Elion have been mighty short on information about what's been happening back at the settlement since we were abducted. Is that leader of yours still giving you trouble?'

There was a pause, then: 'You're right.' Veldan spoke abruptly. Suddenly, she seemed to find the view of the passing riverbanks very absorbing. 'You've got to find out sooner or later – but I'll warn you now, you aren't going to like it.'

The veteran shrugged. 'There have been a lot of things in my life that I haven't liked. I'll survive. Go on, spit it out.'

Veldan turned to look at her. 'Do you really hate Lord Blade that much?'

'What's *he* got to do with this? Stop changing the subject, Veldan.'

'I'm not.' She looked down at her hands. 'Toulac, Lord Blade is a great deal more than you think he is. Before he came to Callisiora, he lived here, in Gendival, and he was a Loremaster, like me.'

'*What?*' Toulac couldn't believe her ears. 'That son of a bitch came from *here?*'

'That's right. He didn't like the way that Cergorn was running things—'

'I never thought I'd say this, but I agree with him there,' the veteran snorted.

Veldan ignored the interruption. 'And so he led a rebellion, which failed. Then the Archimandrite had him tried and sentenced to death but, with my mother's help, he managed to escape. All these years he was hiding in Tiarond, waiting for his chance to come back here, and . . .'

Toulac stared at her younger friend in horror. 'Myrial down a sewer! *Please* don't tell me that the bastard has!'

'I'm afraid so. He defeated Cergorn and became Archimandrite, and . . . And we helped him, Elion and Kaz and I,' she finished defiantly.

'*You did what?*' Anger flashed like fire through Toulac's veins.

'I helped him,' Veldan answered, sounding calmer now the truth was out. 'He was the one who rescued you, when Cergorn wouldn't have bothered. Cergorn didn't believe that Zavahl held the spirit of the Dragon Seer, so he didn't think that the two of you had any value. Amaurn – that's Blade's true name – wants to use the knowledge of the Shadowleague to help the folk who are suffering in these dreadful times. He told me that after Cergorn took away everything that ever mattered to him, he learned ruthlessness in Callisiora, so that he could finally return to Gendival and take back his life. He wants to atone for the way he acted when he was Lord Blade, and . . .'

'And you actually *believed* those lies? Where were your brains? Up your backside? He's a monster, you stupid girl – an unscrupulous, merciless cold-blooded murderer.'

'I know, damn it!' Veldan shouted, before continuing more calmly. 'I know that's what he was, and I also know that people don't change their entire character overnight, and that he might revert at any time. But I don't believe that he was always like that. He had many supporters in Gendival, and not all of them could have been stupid. He was my mother's friend, and she wouldn't have been so easily deceived. And I'm telling you here and now that at the moment, he's the best choice we have for Archimandrite. You don't know the inner workings of the Shadowleague, Toulac. Right now we're desperate for a strong leader: one who isn't afraid to take chances. It's the only hope for our world. You have no concept of the sheer scale and complexity of our whole world, and the potential for disaster if something isn't done to stop these systems from breaking down . . .'

'Maybe not, girlie,' Toulac snapped, 'but I know a damn bad lot when I see one. Still, as long as he lets me go my way, I wash my hands of it.'

'What, leave?' Veldan gasped. 'But Toulac . . .'

'There is no way that I'll be staying where that bastard is, and nothing you can say will convince me otherwise. He almost wrecked my life once, back in Callisiora all those years ago, when he got rid of the female Godswords. He won't be getting the chance to do it again. And while we're on the subject, you or Elion had better have a word with Zavahl. Blade very nearly burned him at the stake – or have you forgotten? You may say I know nothing of the inner workings of the Shadowleague, but you don't know much about the workings of Callisiora. Blade has been undermining the Hierarch for years. Have you thought how that poor sod is going to feel when he finds out that the man who wanted him dead is now running things back at the settlement?'

'Elion is talking to him now,' Veldan said coldly. 'If you're planning to leave anyway, what do you care?'

'He might want to come with me,' Toulac said.

'And leave Ailie behind? I very much doubt that. No, Toulac, I think you're on your own this time. I'm sure someone can be spared to escort you back through the Curtain Walls, and you can enjoy being stuck back in Callisiora again. You ought to give a thought, however, to the opportunities you'll be missing by letting your prejudices run away with you. Amaurn is more than happy to let you join the Shadowleague – which is more than Cergorn ever was.' And with that, Veldan turned and walked away.

Down in the cabin of the wherry, Zavahl felt himself turn cold at Elion's words. 'He can't be here . . .' he whispered. 'It can't be true!' Damn it, this just wasn't fair. He had been through so much these past few days – these past few *years* – and at last it had looked as though his life was taking a turn for the better. The demon in his mind who had frightened him so badly at first had proved to be no evil spirit, but a member of an ancient and knowledgeable race. Aethon was intelligent and pleasant company, and he was very considerate about not intruding himself upon the thoughts of his host.

The practical things Zavahl had learned from Toulac had given him hope that he might be of some use in this strange new land

and Cergorn, who had wanted him out of Gendival, had been removed from power. There was the inn, and Ailie, who was sitting on the bed beside him, holding his hand as if she never intended to let it go. Furthermore he suspected he had the beginnings of a tentative friendship with Elion. But now, just when things looked to be improving, and he'd dared to hope that he might make a new life here for himself, the Loremaster had told him this dreadful news, and all his hopes and plans had come crashing down in ruin.

Zavahl felt anger kindling within him. 'Curse him – he took everything away from me once, and even tried to rob me of my life. I won't let him do it again!'

Elion's face split in a grin. 'Good for you, Zavahl! Stand up to him! You'll have support from all of us, I promise. Amaurn will listen to me and Veldan – especially Veldan. His position isn't so secure yet that he can afford to go about alienating his supporters.'

'It won't do him any good to lose all the help he gets from the village folk, either,' Ailie put in fiercely. 'We do a lot for the Loremasters – in fact, most of them would be lost without us to take care of them – and we could do a great deal to make them very uncomfortable, if we were provoked.'

'And don't forget about me.' The voice of the Dragon echoed softly through Zavahl's mind. 'I remember how this Lord Blade acted when he captured you, and I, too, almost lost my life when he put you on that pyre. He will have none of the answers he seeks from me until I have assurances of his change of heart, and until he makes reparation to both of us for his former misdeeds.'

Zavahl was so moved by all their support that he almost wept. He thought back to the way he had been when he had left Callisiora: beaten, cowed, terrified and defeated. A lot had changed in a very short time, and though he wouldn't regain his confidence overnight, he knew that he had made a good start and set his feet on the road to a new, and more fulfilling life. With shame, he remembered his earliest reactions to Veldan and Toulac, those two remarkable women who had saved his life and given him this future. How he had feared and loathed them at first! How cruel he had been to

Veldan when first they had met. He owed them both his apologies and his thanks.

Suddenly Zavahl became aware of the silence around him, and the expectant faces of Ailie and Elion. 'Well?' the Loremaster asked him.

'I won't let my fear of Amaurn drive me out,' Zavahl said firmly. 'I'm going to face up to him, and stay. I've let myself be a slave to fear and hatred for too long. I've found out where I belong now, and feel as if I'm truly coming home.'

With a cry of delight, Ailie flung her arms around him. Elion grinned. 'I'm proud of you, my friend,' he said. 'And now *that's* settled, I'll leave you two alone.' On the way out, he paused in the doorway. 'Now that he has come home from Callisiora, I really believe that Amaurn is trying to set his feet on a different road, Zavahl. I don't think you'll have anything to fear from him this time.'

Perhaps – but will he have anything to fear from me?

The thought took Zavahl by surprise, but he kept it to himself. Only Aethon had heard it – and the Dragon kept his own counsel.

'Why does she have to be so stubborn?' Veldan fumed.

Elion shook his head. 'I don't know – but that's half the trouble. Toulac was right about one thing: we *can't* know what it was like to live under Blade's rule in Callisiora. He admitted himself, he's done numerous things of which he isn't proud. Perhaps we'd be less forgiving ourselves if we'd been there all the time, and knew that we and all our loved ones were really in his power.'

'But we weren't – I mean, they weren't,' Veldan argued. 'Not really. Blade was only the head of the Godswords. It was actually Zavahl who was in charge. It's all very well him playing the victim now and saying that Blade deceived him, subverted him, and almost had him killed, but he was supposed to be the ruler. Surely the ultimate responsibility had to rest with him.'

'Beware of making too many excuses for Amaurn, Boss,' the firedrake warned. 'You're right to say that Zavahl can't wriggle out of all his responsibilities, but he wasn't a strong ruler, it seems, and we all know who was *really* in charge. And if some of Toulac's grudges are personal, as she says they are, then it doesn't matter who was ruling the city, and who should have been. Personal is different.'

'That's true.' Veldan sighed. 'But she's my friend, and I hate to see her come so close to joining the Shadowleague, and then lose it all at the last moment. It would be awful if we had to wipe her memory and send her back to being what she was. Besides, I would really miss her – even if she is so pigheaded that I'd like to throttle her.'

'I would miss the old battleaxe too,' Kaz agreed.

'And me,' admitted Elion. 'Even if she does call me "sonny" all the time.'

'Well, it's no good sending Veldan back to talk to her,' the fire-drake pointed out. 'It didn't work the first time, and besides, they both need a little while to cool off with one another. We still have a bit of the journey left. You and I can work on her, Elion, as we go upriver, but we'll have to be really subtle . . .'

Elion burst out laughing. 'Subtle? *You?*'

Kaz glared at his fellow Loremaster, baring his great fangs and lashing his tail – and, incidentally, almost knocking down the mast. 'You have a problem with that?'

'Me? No, not at all,' Elion said hastily, holding up his hands and backing away while Veldan laughed in the background. 'I think it's a splendid idea. We'll be as subtle as we possibly can.'

The firedrake contented himself with one last, dirty look. 'Right,' he said. 'Subtle it is. Will you have the first go at the stubborn old ratbag? Or shall I?'

Feeling much better about the whole business, Veldan left them to it. She didn't think that even Toulac's pigheadedness could stand up for long to a determined assault from both of them. She wandered to the stern and talked to Meglyn for a time, but knew that really, she shouldn't be interfering with the captain's concentration while she was steering. Instead she leaned on the rail, and watched the ever-changing river, and the woods and meadows that were slipping by on either bank. Almost in a half-doze after the last few sleepless nights she was content to let her mind wander for a while, and make the most of her chance to relax.

Then Amaurn spoke to her, and woke her up in no uncertain terms. Briefly, he told her of the attempt on his life by the Takuru assassin, and warned her to be on her guard when she returned to the settlement. 'I don't want the shapeshifter doing away with any of you, and taking over your form,' he said. 'It's no good trying to alert Zavahl and Toulac to the danger – you'd never be able to explain it to them,' he added, 'but make sure that Elion and that firedrake friend of yours are told.'

'Shall I warn Ailie?' Veldan asked. 'She understands about the Takuru, and at least she could keep an eye on the other two.'

'No, don't do that. I absolutely don't want this to go any further at present. Maskulu took me to his dwelling, because it's safe and secluded. I don't want the rest of the Shadowleague to see that I've been hurt until Kyrre, who is on her way here now, has had time to patch me up. Then I'll stand a chance of making light of the situation. You three Loremasters come up to Maskulu's dwelling immediately you get home, and I'll talk to you then – but don't tell anyone else where you're going.'

'I won't. Oh, by the way, did you say that Kyrre was with you? Well, I have some good news that you might like to pass on. I think I forgot to mention it earlier. Before we found them, Toulac and Zavahl had met up with a small group of Dobarchu refugees. Mrainil, their Loremaster, has brought them to Gendival, seeking sanctuary; he thinks they may be the last of their race.'

'They'll be welcome, of course,' Amaurn replied. 'Our seas may be somewhat less hospitable than the warmer oceans they're used to, but we'll do whatever we can to help them settle down and adapt. Are you bringing them here?'

'Yes. I thought it best. They're on the boat with us right now. I know it'll be a blow to Kyrre that there are so few of her people left but, on the other hand, it'll be wonderful news for her that any have survived at all. Tell her that Mrainil will talk to her later, when we get closer to the settlement. He isn't getting his mindspeech very far at present, because he's still very tired. It was quite some journey that he made to bring his folk through so many dangers, not to mention all the Curtain Walls that lie between their islands and here.'

'They were all very brave,' Amaurn told her. 'You can reassure them that they're safe now. The Shadowleague will take good care of them.'

'Speaking of being brave, are you all right? Really?' Veldan could tell by the texture of his thoughts that he was hiding pain from her. She couldn't imagine why it should matter to her, but somehow, she didn't like to think of him being wounded and forced to hide out while he was hurt in Maskulu's uncomfortable tunnels.

'I'll survive,' he told her. 'But hurry back, Veldan. I need you here. You're one of the very few people in the world that I trust.'

And with that he was gone, leaving a very surprised Loremaster staring out at the river.

Twenty-One

The Path of Reflection

Helverien never would have thought that she'd get so tired of talking, so soon. She hardly knew whether to laugh or cry at such perversity within herself. Throughout all those lonely aeons, she had been filled with a desperate yearning for company – and now that she had it, all she wanted was a bit of peace and quiet, and a chance to be alone with her thoughts for a while. Not that this Wind-Sprite was not good company, she told herself hastily. Endlessly they had discussed the past, as she herself had seen it, and the present, as it was known to Shree, and each had found a great deal of interest in what the other had to say.

But the trouble is, we can't discuss the future. Until we get out of here, there can be no future for us, and because of the nature of this place, there's nothing for us to do but talk, and that's hard for both of us. It's in our natures to want to act, and to influence the course of events. This enforced inactivity and helplessness is galling in the extreme, and we're going to have to be very careful not to start taking our frustrations out on each other.

After a time, however, it became clear that the Wind-Sprite's feelings were similar to her own. The two of them fell silent, each lost in her own thoughts, contemplating the landscape that Helverien had recreated from her memory and imagination, with its groves of silvery-green trees, its eternally bright sky, and its sea of shimmering peacock blue.

Couldn't we try to make it night-time for a while? Shree said eventually. *I'm sure, if we put our heads together, we could come up with stars, and maybe a moon. It's a lovely place you've created here, but you have to admit, some sort of change might be in order.*

The Mage felt a flicker of annoyance. 'Some people are never satisfied! Do you think you could do any better? I'd like to see *you* create a landscape of this complexity.'

Maybe I should then, Thirishri retorted. *Perhaps I should take another area in all this nothingness, and make some mountains or something – just for a change.*

'Go on, then, Wind-Sprite,' Helverien challenged. 'Let's see how good you really are.' Suddenly, she was thoroughly enjoying this discussion, with its slight edge of contentiousness. The idea of a competition between the two of them certainly added a touch of interest to life.

All right then. I wi— Abruptly Shree stopped in midsentence. *Was it my imagination, or did you feel something just then?*

Helverien nodded, excitement running through her like wildfire. 'There was a change in the fabric of this place – almost as though a door had been opened somewhere.' She looked at the dancing sparkle and shimmer in the air that was the Wind-Sprite. 'I felt something very similar when you came here.'

There was a moment of silence, with neither of them daring to put their hopes into words. Then finally, Thirishri spoke. *Do you think someone is trying to release us?*

The Mage shook her head. 'I doubt it. Surely we would be aware of that? What I do think, however, is that someone – or something – else has been put in here with us.' She sighed. '*I* don't know. You get no visitors for a couple of millennia, then suddenly a whole bunch of them come along all at once.'

Galveron and Alestan had been walking long enough for all the residual dampness to dry out of their clothes, following their swim across the water trap. They had stopped to rest and eat, and then gone on their way again, stubborn – or hopeful – to the last. Surely sooner or later they must catch up with Aliana and her companion?

They couldn't keep on like this for ever. Now that they were becoming accustomed to dealing with the traps, they made fairly short work of the next one – a charming combination of some half-dozen whirling blades which thrust in and out of the wall at staggered intervals, just at neck-severing height, combined with clusters of long, lethal spikes which sprang up and down through small holes in the floor. Though it looked very nasty, they discovered that once the sequences of blades and spikes had been triggered, the intervals and patterns were the same each time. Though their timing had to be perfect, all they had to do was work out exactly when to run, when to pause, and when to duck. There was absolutely no room for error, and when they reached the other side of the lethal obstacle, they both felt as if their hair must have turned pure white – but it had done nothing of the sort, and both of them were safe.

With so many successes under their belt, the two of them were beginning to get quite cocky. Soon they were talking confidently of catching up with Aliana – though by unspoken consent, they avoided the subject of what they would do when they had found her. In the unchanging passages, it was easy to let their guard drop. Apart from the occasional traps – and there was usually some warning of those – the way they travelled continued much as it had done before, with occasional sharp corners, or stretches of varying length where the floor sloped up or down. They were completely unprepared, therefore, when they walked around a corner, and found that the passageway ended in a blank wall.

'What the . . .' Without thinking, Alestan walked forward to examine the obstacle. Galveron gave a warning cry, but it was too late. The floor at the end of the corridor, a section about five feet square, dropped down abruptly, taking Alestan with it.

Galveron threw himself down on his hands and knees at the edge of the hole. 'Alestan? Alestan!'

'I'm all right.' The voice of the thief came echoing back. After a moment, Galveron heard an odd, metallic whining, and heard and felt a whoosh of air. The section of floor came rising up majestically from the depths, with Alestan, white-faced but grinning, still on board. 'Jump on – quick!' he shouted. 'It takes us down to the next level.'

Galveron recognised the device as being kin to the one in the temple that led down to the first platform with the podium. Even as he ran onto the moving area, it began to sink once more. He found himself in a shaft with the same smooth, metallic walls – and a floor that was dropping rapidly, making him feel as if he had left his stomach behind. He was sure it was travelling much faster, and further, than the one up above. Suddenly, one of the walls vanished. The floor gave a sudden lurch, its downward motion stopped, and he sat down hard. Alestan, standing well-balanced, with legs apart, looked down at him and laughed. 'Come on, let's get off this thing – unless you'd rather spend all day riding up and down.'

Galveron would most definitely rather *not* spend a minute longer on this contraption than was absolutely necessary. Hurriedly, he got to his feet, and jumped off onto a nice stable floor, even as the mobile area began to rise again, vanishing out of sight beyond the ceiling of the small antechamber in which they now found themselves. It did not return.

Godsword Commander and thief shared a worried glance. 'It looks as if it only works when someone's standing on it,' Alestan said. 'For the rest of the time, it must wait up at the top of the shaft.'

Galveron frowned. 'That's all very well, but what happens if we want to go back? How are we supposed to get it back down here again?'

'Who knows?' Alestan's shrug was eloquent.

Having satisfied themselves that there was no obvious way to summon the moving floor – a task which took no time in the feature-less little room – they decided to worry about that problem later. After all, there might even be another way out, somewhere ahead of them – at least, so the ever-hopeful Alestan suggested. Galveron sighed, and kept his doubts to himself.

There were two doorways, set into opposite walls, leading out of the chamber. The opening on the right led onto another corridor, indistinguishable from the one they had followed all the way to this place. The passageway on the left, however, was entirely different. It was like the inside of a pipe or a tube, with its sides and floor curving round to form a perfect circle, apart from a narrow, flattened area of walkway at the bottom. The walls were soft, warm and springy to the touch, making Galveron think of flesh. In a peculiar way, they seemed horribly alive. The weird, changeful luminescence within the tube reminded him of the lighted area through which they had passed so many hours ago, just before they reached the first of the traps. It moved through a spectrum of soft, misty radiance, changing from purple to blue, to green, to yellow, to red, and each pulsing change was like the beating of a heart.

As one, the two men drew back from the outlandish route. They looked at one another. 'It seems to me,' Alestan said carefully, 'that this could be another trap, or even a series of them. We went through a stretch of these coloured lights, after all, before the last obstacles started.'

Galveron nodded. 'It stands to reason that the passage we should follow would be the same as the passage we just left . . . Don't you think?'

'Almost certainly.'

'And do you suppose that your sister would be thinking along similar lines?'

Alestan nodded. 'It's a fair bet that she would – we usually think alike.' He frowned. 'At least we always did, before the last couple of days. Now I don't know what she's thinking any more.'

'Never mind,' Galveron said. 'That's good enough for me. Let's go.'

With indecent haste, the two men left the disturbing tunnel, with its perplexing lighting and its uncanny resemblance to living flesh, and hastened down the familiar route of the other passage, which ran straight for some distance, before angling sharply to the left. But even this place was not without its surprises. As they rounded the corner, Alestan stopped with a sharp cry, and Galveron cleared his sword from its scabbard with a steely hiss. In the distance, coming towards them, were two figures – one tall, one shorter – who were definitely *not* Packrat and Aliana.

As he stopped, Galveron saw the distant figures stop too, and one of them drew a sword. The truth began to dawn on him at that point. He took a couple of steps forward, and burst out laughing. Beside him, the thief let out an exclamation of disgust. 'We *are* a couple of lummoxes! Getting spooked by our own reflections!'

Galveron felt similarly sheepish. 'I don't think we need to tell anyone about this when we get back, do you? I presume there's another wall across the end of this corridor – only this time, it's a mirror.'

'It could also be another trap of some sort,' Alestan pointed out. 'I don't know about you, but I learned my lesson last time, with the moving floor. Let's go and look at it – but carefully.'

They moved on with caution, keeping a sharp lookout for any places where there was a difference in the walls, floor, or ceiling; any change in colour, or texture, or even the soft sounds of their footfalls, that might warn them of a trap. But there was nothing. The corridor continued, unchanging, until they reached the mirrored wall itself.

The Godsword Commander looked at his own reflection. It was not a prepossessing sight. He was haggard, hollow-eyed and unshaven, the half-healed scars on his face didn't improve his appearance one whit, and his clothes were a mass of wrinkles after being stuffed into his backpack while he swam across the water shaft.

'Come on, Galveron,' Alestan urged. 'You didn't come down here to admire yourself. Is there a way through here, do you reckon? Or do we have to backtrack and go the other way?'

The very thought of the other, weird-looking tunnel was enough to stir Galveron into action. 'Let's find out,' he said, and began to push and prod at the wall, leaving fingerprints on the reflective surface.

Suddenly there was a shearing sound from behind them, and they spun round to see a see another wall, its surface mirrored like the first, slide down from the ceiling, cutting them off from the way they had come. Galveron experienced an attack of violent disorientation that sent his senses swimming – and then the world around him vanished, and everything went black.

So this is what it's like, being dead? I often wondered.

All things considered, Aliana felt unnaturally calm. She seemed to be floating in some dark and soundless limbo, and if her body still existed, she couldn't feel it any more. She had a feeling she ought to be panicking by now, but she was buffered by a sense of absolute unreality – due to shock, perhaps. She suspected that this delightful, dreamlike state wouldn't last too long, so she decided she had better make the most of it. If being dead was all like this, then she would have the rest of eternity to panic and go mad.

Had Packrat died too? Was he here with her? She tried to call out, but was unable to make a sound.

If he's dead, it's all my fault.

Anguish began to erode the edges of her blessed numbness. Just because she didn't dare go back to face Galveron and Gilarra until she had hidden the ring somewhere safe, she had kept them going, though Packrat had been vociferous in his pleas to turn back. She had led them further and further into the mountain via these featureless corridors, and persevered with the traps until she had solved them, one by one.

All except the last one, presumably.

What happened to us, anyway?

She had a confused memory of a corridor, and some sort of bright, silvery surface – then the next thing she could remember, she was here. Wherever *here* might be.

She wondered what had happened to her brother, and was wrenched by grief that she would never see him again. Was he still imprisoned? Had he been released? Would he find out where she had gone, and come in search of her? Would he fall into the same trap, and would she have his death on her conscience, too? Would

Galveron follow her down beneath the city in search of the Hierarch's ring? Would he take it from her body, and give it back to Gilarra? If so, she had killed Packrat – and herself – for nothing. Worse still, Galveron might also die. Aliana was crushed beneath the weight of her remorse. Before now, during her life as a Grey Ghost, she had always managed to escape the possible consequences of her impetuous behaviour. Too late, she realised that she had managed to get away with such rashness because she had been in surroundings that were familiar to her, and she knew the rules on a deep, instinctive level. In venturing beneath the Temple, she had entered a place where all the rules had changed, and her ignorance had led her to make a fatal mistake – and drag her friends down with her. For the first time, it came home to Aliana that her impulsive actions could have serious repercussions, not only for herself, but for others.

For a while, Aliana was lost in a pit of guilt and self-blame that was even darker than her surroundings, but eventually she was saved by the very circumstances which had given rise to all her pain in the first place. In the black nothingness with which she was surrounded, she found it increasingly difficult to focus on any coherent thoughts, let alone the ones which had been causing her such distress. Images seemed to flash through her mind at random, scattering and regrouping like shoals of bright fish. Some came from her imagination, and there were those that made no sense to her at all. Others came from her memories, and she even saw the face of her long-dead father, whose features had long been lost to her as time clouded the recollections of her childhood.

Then suddenly there was another image, clearer than the rest, that did not go away: a woman with dark hair, in which occasional strands of silver glinted. She was wearing robes of vivid blue, and her blue eyes were shrewd in her imperious face. She held out a hand to Aliana. 'Come,' she commanded. 'Follow me.'

Without knowing how she did it, Aliana drifted towards the woman, who turned and began to walk away, with the thief floating after her like a kite on a string. The darkness was split apart by dazzling light, and Aliana felt herself falling. There was a jolt that rattled every bone in her body, and she found herself on her hands and knees, on a stretch of pebbly strand at the edge of a lapis-blue ocean. Her father had taken her to the coast when she had been very small, so she had vague memories of the sea, but they were nothing near so wonderful as this. She could hear the seething of the waves as they rolled back and forth across the shingle at the water's edge, and she could hear birdsong, the chirring of insects, and the whisper of wind through a grove of trees. Sunlight was hot upon her skin, and she could smell salt air, flowers, sun-warmed herbage and sun-baked earth. After the deprivation of the terrible, dark void, it was as though all her senses were being overwhelmed.

Now that she was released from the dark limbo in which she had been imprisoned, Aliana found herself beginning to tremble violently. She bit her lip against an overwhelming urge to cry, but in spite of her best intentions, she found tears flooding down her face. Kneeling where she was in the sand, she cried out her relief.

'Well, isn't that just like a girl! There's nothing to bawl about, you silly cow.' The voice came from behind her.

'Packrat!' Aliana spun round and got to her feet in one undignified scramble, and threw her arms around her friend. 'I thought I had killed you,' she said softly. 'I thought we were dead.'

Packrat disengaged himself from her arms and glared at her. 'If we aren't, it's no thanks to you. The next time I say we go back, we go back – even if I have to knock you out and drag you every inch of the way.'

'Next time, I would appreciate it if you'll knock me out before I even set off,' Aliana told him ruefully.

'It'll be my pleasure.' Packrat gave her his gap-toothed grin. 'Now, if you've finished playing silly buggers, there's a woman up there who says she wants to talk to you.'

Aliana looked up, noticing for the first time what lay beyond the beach. A short flight of steps led up a steep bank to a terrace of white marble. Beyond was a house, constructed of the same materials and set in the midst of a beautiful garden. At the edge of the terrace, leaning on the railing, stood a tall, dark-haired woman clad in robes that were the same colour as the dazzling sea. Immediately, Aliana recognised the guide who had led her out of the darkness. Slightly above her, and to the right, there was a weird distortion in the air: an odd shimmer and sparkle that seemed to be there and not there, all at the same time. Trying to focus on it only made Aliana's head ache and her eyes water, and she looked away from it quickly. She turned her attention back to the strange woman, who beckoned, and called out to her. 'Come up and join me. We need to talk.'

There was no disobeying the note of command in her voice. Staying close together, Aliana and Packrat set off up the beach and climbed the stairs.

Though Helverien was burning with curiosity, she concealed it well. 'Welcome,' she said, as the two strangers reached the top of the marble steps. 'Make yourselves at home.' She gestured casually in the direction of the table, and two more chairs appeared, along with two extra cups. Their gasps of astonishment forced her to hide a smile. How gratifying!

They're only humans, the Wind-Sprite pointed out tartly, in mindspeech. *They're a lot more easy to impress than me.*

'They suit me just fine,' the Mage retorted. 'Do you know how many aeons have passed since I impressed anybody?' She turned back to the two newcomers, who were perching gingerly on the edges of the chairs as though afraid that they might vanish again. 'Now,' she said, with a pleasant smile. 'Introductions are in order, I think. Who are you, and how did you get here?' But before the girl could answer, she was distracted by a repetition of the feeling she had experienced earlier – an odd ripple in the landscape, and within herself, that indicated that the fabric of this Otherplace had been breached once more. In consternation, she looked up at the Wind-Sprite.

Yes, Thirishri said. *I felt it. *Someone else has come through.*

Helverien felt a pang of irritation – and concern. 'How in blazes are they all suddenly getting in?'

I don't know, Shree said thoughtfully. *But if people are getting in somehow, then maybe, just maybe, we can find a way out.*

There was no way out for the refugees in the Temple. They were trapped, all together in a limited space – and Kaita's worst nightmare had just become reality. It had started. And though the Healer had been expecting it since Tiarond's remaining population had been shut up in a single building with a pile of decaying corpses outside, the first cases that she identified still made her stop dead, with horror knotting her guts, a sickness in her stomach, and her heart pounding fast.

The disaster had begun through an act of charity and kindness. Cerella, the woman who had been rescued by Galveron and Aliana, had carried disease into the Temple. Already weakened from loss of blood, she had been racked by vomiting, diarrhoea, and fever, and had died within hours of the symptoms first manifesting itself. Kaita, already worried about infection and fearing the worst, directed her helpers to wrap the body carefully and take it through the passages behind the Temple, so that they could open the barred gate of the hidden entrance on the mountainside, and throw it off the ledge. It was far from being ideal, but it was the best alternative that she could think of. Burning would have been far better but, under the present circumstances, she simply didn't have the facilities.

She was directing the poor woman's disposal when Shelon came running up. 'Kaita! Cerella's child has started vomiting, too – and the woman who was nursing it along with her own babe says she doesn't feel very well. Her little one's whiny and fevered, too.'

That was when Kaita knew. The dead woman had been hiding in a house in the Precincts. There were bound to have been rats and flies there, which would have been feeding on the decaying corpses outside. They had carried the contagion to Cerella, and she had passed it on to her own babe, who had carried it to Irline, the wet-nurse, and she had passed it to her own child – not to mention her other children, who by now would have played with half the youngsters in the Temple, who would have gone back to their parents . . .

For an instant, Kaita felt faint. She groped for a chair and sat down, taking deep breaths until the dizziness passed. Her assistant was looking at her with concern. 'There's going to be an epidemic, isn't there?' he said quietly, looking around to make sure he could not be heard.

Quickly, Kaita pulled herself together. 'Yes,' she said. 'Get a couple of messengers who are discreet, and send them round to the other healers and the folk in charge of the day-to-day workings of this place. Get them here as quickly as possible for a meeting. And you go straight to Gilarra, Shelon. Get her here right now.'

As the young man rushed out, Kaita's mind started to race, trying to work out ways to keep the infection from spreading. One thought, however, kept intruding itself.

Oh, how I wish that Galveron were here.

Twenty-Two

A Different Perspective

S call noted with appreciation that the weather on this side of
the Curtain Walls was much better than it had been in
Callisiora for a good long while. High clouds scudded across
the sky, making shadow patterns on the exposed green fellsides far
beneath, and then parting altogether to create long spells of dazzling
sunlight. Though there was a bracing bite to the wind, the air lacked
the miserable, damp chill of his mountain home, and it was clear
that winter was not nearly so far advanced here. On such a day it
was impossible to feel too downhearted, and after his talk with Kher
in the wayshelter, when their guide had explained that his stay here
didn't have to be permanent, he had been greatly comforted.

There was another reason, too, for Scall's brightening mood. As
he rode with his two companions across the airy uplands and
through lush, green valleys, he realised that he was well on his way
to forgiving Dark. The Summoner had apologised so many times
that it was just too much of an effort to stay angry with him any
longer. He had liked Dark, right from the first time they had met;
even though, at that time, the man's appearance had been
concealed by the mysterious and frightening skull mask. Then, Scall
had only known that he was slightly more than medium height, he
wore his black robes with an easy grace, and his hair was long,
black, and curled down past his shoulders. At the time, it had been
much more important that – despite the intimidating appearance
of his mask – he had been kind to the nervous boy.

Now that he could see his companion's face, however, Scall liked him even better, though even without the mask he could still appear intimidating. His skin was very white – a result, Scall realised, of having kept his face covered up for so long. He had high cheek-bones, a high-bridged nose, and a firm chin. When he brought his black eyebrows together in a frown, he could truly look formidable, and the fine lines around his eyes hinted that he was somewhat older than he looked. Scall soon found out, however, that they were lines of laughter, and though Dark was too sad and worried to smile much at present, when he did smile, his eyes crinkled at the corners in a kindly way, and his face lit up with a boyish charm.

When he had been abducted, Scall had been deeply disappointed and aggrieved at what he had seen as Dark's treachery. Now, at least, he understood a little better. He could see how deeply the Summoner was grieving for Grim – how could he really blame the poor man for acting on his master's last request? And though he was still upset at having been torn away from Tormon and Rochalla, Kher had told him that, in all probability, he would be sent back to them as soon as possible. If the sunny-natured young man was any indication of the people Scall might find ahead of him, he wouldn't have anything much to worry about. Now that his terror had had time to fade, and he understood Dark's motives a little better, he could look on this extraordinary journey beyond the Curtain Walls as a tremendous adventure. Surely Rochalla would have to be impressed?

This is bound to put me ahead of stupid Presvel! That citified nerk is too scared to go outside the door!

Kher was beginning another of his traveller's tales, and Scall put his own reflections aside so that he could listen. For someone who looked so young, Kher seemed to have had an astonishing number of adventures, with creatures that sounded so bizarre that his young companion wondered whether he could be making them up. Nevertheless, Scall listened avidly, storing every detail in his memory. Already, he was thinking about telling them to Rochalla – with himself replacing Kher as the hero, of course! As he wondered how many of them he could manage to get away with, he looked at the two men who rode beside him, and sighed. Both of them had more than their share of good looks; Kher with his blond hair and his open, merry countenance, and Dark with his raven curls and his features that were so imposing. Scall thought sourly of his own gawky frame, his face that kept breaking out in spots, and his hair that would keep sticking up all over the place. The fact that he had inherited its coppery red colour from his aunt Agella didn't help, either. He sighed.

It's just not fair. How will I ever stand a chance with Rochalla?

Leading Grim's white horse, with the winged abomination strapped firmly across its back, they rode on through the afternoon and into the early evening. Though the sun had a distance to go, it had begun to dip now, and the light was turning a deeper gold. The three riders came down from the crown of the moors on a snaking track, descending into a valley beyond. Green fells swelled up on one side, and on the other, the valley bottom was concealed by a belt of trees. Looming above them, Scall could see the peaked roof of a tall, round tower.

The road rounded a sharp bend, almost doubling back on itself through some cultivated fields, then went through a village with a single street. The houses were built of clean grey stone, so different from the buildings of Tiarond, which over hundreds of years had been gradually stained and darkened by the smoke from countless chimneys. All were different in shape and size, but all were well-built and attractive, combining with the adjacent buildings to form a harmonious whole. The doors, the window frames and the shutters were painted in cheerful colours, and flowers growing in long, narrow boxes full of earth brightened the windowsills on every dwelling. Children playing in the village street stopped their games to look curiously at the riders and the adults, who had been moving briskly up and down the street on various errands, paused to stare and gape at the hideous winged predator. It wasn't lost on Scall that every one of them was desperate to ask Kher what was going on, but all of them maintained a respectful silence.

'Here we are,' Kher said, gesturing around him. 'Home at last.

Scall, you'll be staying here at the inn for a little while. They'll feed you and take good care of you, and you can rest. You didn't get any sleep last night, by all accounts. Dark, you're to come with me. The Archimandrite wants to see you right away.'

Scall swallowed hard, his newfound courage deserting him abruptly as he realised that the only two people he knew in this whole place were planning to go off together, and abandon him among a bunch of strangers.

Kher reached across and clapped him on the shoulder. 'Don't worry, laddie,' he said. 'They're good folk, Olsam and his daughter Ailie. They'll make you feel at home, and Ailie is the best cook in the whole valley. I'll come back for you as soon as I can – but I warn you, once you've had a taste of Ailie's cherry pie, you'll never want to leave.'

He grinned at Scall, who began to feel a little better – especially when he compared his own situation with that of Dark. The Summoner looked absolutely sick with nerves, twisting the mane of his long-suffering horse in restless fingers, and darting nervous glances here and there. His pallid face had taken on a slightly greenish cast and Scall felt sorry for him.

I don't know who this Archimandrite is, but I'm glad it's Dark he wants to see, and not me.

He tried not to think about who might want to talk to *him*, at some point.

At least they can't get mad at me. It's not my fault I'm here.

The inn was a large building at the end of the village street. Laboriously, Scall spelled out the words *The Griffin* on the signboard, and gaped at the fantastic creature, half-lion, half-eagle, that was depicted there. Kher dismounted stiffly and unhooked his staff from his saddle. 'Just hang on there for a moment, Dark, and keep an eye on that monstrosity of yours. I'll take Scall inside, and I'll come straight back. Then we can go on to the settlement.'

Dark tried to smile, but it came out more like a grimace. 'You take as long as you like. I'm in no hurry.'

Kher clouted him on the leg as he went past. 'Chin up, man. Amaurn won't eat you.'

'How the blazes do you know?' There was an edge to the Summoner's voice. 'You haven't even met him yet.'

Kher paused, looking up at him. 'Because he was your mentor's old friend,' he said quietly. 'For Grim's sake, he'll be kind to you, you mark my words.' He turned back to Scall. 'Are you ready?'

While the other two had been talking, Scall had dismounted, but he stayed where he was, clinging tightly to the reins of his chestnut mare. 'What about my horse?' he asked. 'Who's going to look after her? Is there a stable at the inn?'

'Leave her with Dark just now,' Kher said. 'She'll go down to the Shadowleague stables with our own beasts.'

Scall clutched the mare's bridle more tightly. 'I want to take care of her myself,' he said stubbornly. 'I don't want to leave her among a bunch of strangers. How do I know they'll look after her properly?'

Kher sighed. He had been all affability so far, but clearly, his patience had its limits. 'Look here, boy, I've coddled you so far, but now I've got to take Dark to see the Archimandrite and I don't have time for this. Now listen to me. She'll be safe with Harral. He takes good care of all his horses, and he'll be so careful with your mare that it'll be as if she was made of cobwebs and silk. Now give those reins to Dark, and *get inside*!' He grabbed the boy's arm and, before he knew what had happened, Scall had been hustled through the door, to stand in the long, whitewashed hallway. 'Olsam!' Kher bawled. 'Ailie! Where the blazes are you?'

'I'm coming, I'm coming.' The voice seemed to emanate from beneath their feet. After a moment, a door that was tucked underneath the staircase creaked open, and a little man with greying hair came hurrying out. 'Oh, it's you,' he said shortly. 'What can I do for you?'

'Is that any way to talk to your best customer?' The edge of reprimand in Kher's voice was so slight that Scall wondered if he had imagined it.

The innkeeper seemed unconcerned. 'If you don't like it, you can trek all the way down to the trading post and try Ruthar's evil brew,' he snapped.

Kher's eyebrows went up. 'What's got into you today? Did you drink too much of your own ale last night? You're certainly acting as if you've got a sore head.'

Olsam sighed. 'All right, all right. But I'm that busy I don't know where to turn. Ailie has been away since yesterday, jaunting off downriver in a boat, *if* you please, with Loremaster Veldan and her outlandish partner, and Loremaster Elion, too. And here's the inn in such a mess after those accursed Dierkan attacked the other night, coming in here and knocking down walls, and I don't know what-all else. And here I am left at home to do all the work, and I've only got one pair of hands . . .'

It looked like becoming a long tirade, but Kher interrupted swiftly. 'Well, just to crown the pleasures of your day, I've brought you a new customer. This is Scall, come all the way from Callisiora, beyond the Curtain Walls. He's here at the invitation of the new Archimandrite, so I'm sure you'll make him very welcome.'

Olsam shot him a sour look. 'I would make the lad welcome whoever had invited him, as well you know, Loremaster Kher.'

'That's fine, then,' Kher said quickly. 'You'll need to feed him pretty soon, by the way. We've been in too much of a hurry to eat, and he's hardly had anything since yesterday. We don't want him fading away.' Turning, he clasped Scall's hand. 'You get some rest, laddie. I'll come back later, when I know what's what. And don't worry about that little horse of yours. Harral will take good care if her, I promise.' He paused. 'Come to think of it, he has a beast in his stable that looks very like your mount. She's the darling of his heart and the apple of his eye, so I'm sure he'll look after your mare just as well. See you later.' He ducked out of the doorway, oblivious to the fact that Scall was staring after him in horror.

Elion? Elion came from this place? And Kher said that Harral, whoever he is, has a horse just like mine . . .

In Scall's mind, the pieces all fell into place. 'Kher, no! Wait!' He made a lunge toward the door, but Olsam caught his arm and hauled him back. 'Come on now, youngster,' he said sternly. 'Strangers aren't allowed to go wandering around the place by themselves –

those are the rules. You just stay right here, until Loremaster Kher comes back for you.' With that, he pushed Scall ahead of him, up the stairs, and onto a broad landing. Through an open door, the boy caught a glimpse of a mason repairing a sizeable hole in the back wall of the room, and a carpenter hammering together a new window frame to replace the splinters of the old. 'Sorry about all the banging,' Olsam said. He scowled. 'Blasted Dierkan. Breaking up my inn.'

Scall wanted to ask the him what a Dierkan was. It sounded pretty alarming if it could put a hole like that in a solid wall. Experience as an apprentice, however, had taught him that when adults had *that* expression on their faces, it was wise to keep his head down and his mouth shut. Olsam ushered him into a bright, clean room that overlooked the village street. 'There, now,' he said. 'You rest yourself, young fellow. I'll be back shortly with something for you to eat.'

By this time, Scall's other worries had crowded out the Dierkan again. Too numb with dismay to notice his surroundings, he sank down on the bed.

Firefly didn't belong to Elion at all! She belonged to this Harral, and she was the darling of his heart and the apple of his eye, and now he'll take her back, and I'll never see her again. I've lost her!

Throughout his abduction, the loss of Rochalla and Tormon, his fight with the winged monstrosity, and his journey beyond the Curtain Walls to this strange new place, Scall had remained brave. This, however, was one blow too many. He rolled over and punched his pillow until the feathers flew, and then he burst into tears.

'Does it still hurt?' It was hard for most people to imagine that a creature of Maskulu's size and appearance could actually sound so concerned. Amaurn, however, knew better. He had been bearing the brunt of his companion's overwhelming solicitude since the Senior Loremaster had brought him back from the hillside where he had been attacked. 'Of course it still hurts,' he snapped. He wished Maskulu could leave him alone for a while. He was desperate to rest, and collect his thoughts, and sleep. Unfortunately, it just wasn't possible. There was too much to be done – too much to attend to. It was vital that he play down his injury as much as possible, so that people didn't lose confidence in him. Cergorn's supporters would be quick to take advantage of any weakness. Certainly, no one must know he had almost been killed by an assassin. One attempt was bad enough – he didn't want anyone else getting the same idea.

Besides, if I fall asleep, that accursed Shapeshifter might creep up on me again.

Even though the fearsome Maskulu was guarding him, it was an uncomfortable thought.

'So what are you going to do about it?' Clearly, Maskulu had been picking up his thoughts. 'There must be something we can do to find the assassin! How can you function properly as Archimandrite, with this constant threat hanging over you?'

'I'm working on it,' Amaurn said. 'If I could, I'd clear every damned one of the Takuru out of Gendival. But the only way to be certain they wouldn't come sneaking back is to kill the lot of them, and even then, how could I be sure I'd managed to get them all?'

But there might be another way . . .

'Maskulu, I want you to mindspeak a message to the leader of the Takuru, and ask him – or her – to come here. And be polite. Then contact the archivists, and tell them to find me every scrap of information we have on the Takuru. Tell them to be quick.'

The Senior Loremaster stared at him. 'Amaurn, you must be delirious. You can't invite the Takuru leader *here*.'

Rather than take Amaurn back to the settlement when he was clearly wounded and vulnerable, Maskulu had carried him to his own underground dwelling, and put him in a chamber with only one exit that was easily guarded. He had made the Archimandrite as comfortable as he could, given the nature of the surroundings, then, in mindspeech, he had told Bailen, and Kyrre of the Dobarchu, who was adept in healing skills, what had happened, sworn them to silence, and summoned them to his lair.

Once more, Amaurn summoned Blade, and felt his face settle into those obdurate, granite lines. He gave Maskulu the cold stare that had intimidated everyone in Tiarond from the Hierarch on down. 'Firstly, I'm not delirious; secondly, yes, I want the Takuru leader here. Thirdly, I want that information as soon as possible, so why are you just standing there, wasting time?'

Grumbling, Maskulu turned away and began to send the messages, leaving the Archimandrite to concentrate on staying awake until the healer came. Luckily for Amaurn, the Takur's hurried blow had sliced rather than stabbed, but the gash in his side, though it did not seem too deep, had been bleeding freely. Though it hurt like perdition, he had managed to bind a pad of cloth torn from his shirt tightly over the wound and, though it was in an awkward place, kept pressing down on it with the heel of his hand. The bleeding seemed to have slowed right down now, but the injury would need expert medical attention, none the less.

When the two Loremasters arrived, Amaurn was pleased to see them, yet he remained wary until Maskulu, who knew them better, had asked them certain questions to which only they would know the answers. It was the only way that he could think of, at this point, to make sure that his friends *were* his friends, and not some Takuru assassin in disguise. This worked quite well for close confidants, such as Bailen and Kyrre, but the system was too clumsy, inaccurate, and open to abuse to be used with everyone. Amaurn knew he was going to have to think of something better, but right now he was finding it difficult enough to stay conscious, let alone focus his brain on such a difficult problem.

Kyrre and Bailen were laden down with bags and baskets. 'We told people that we were going on a picnic,' the blind young man said, with a smile. 'You'd be amazed at the number of folk who warned us that we'd get into trouble with the Archimandrite for sneaking off when the whole place has been stirred to a ferment by his new plans and instructions.' As he spoke, he was unpacking the baskets, identifying objects mainly by touch, but occasionally using

Kyrre's eyes for confirmation. 'You couldn't have a fire down here, so we – er – borrowed some of those heating crystals from the collection of advanced artefacts that we don't really understand. You know, the ones that Cergorn wouldn't let us use in case we accidentally broke them somehow in our ignorance, or wore them out.'

'Well, you have *my* heartfelt permission to use them,' said Amaurn, who was shivering violently; partly, no doubt, from blood loss and shock, and partly from the dank chill of Maskulu's underground home.

There were about two dozen of the precious crystals. Bailen took them from the basket one by one and carefully unwrapped them from their individual coverings of felt. They were irregularly shaped, the biggest about the size of two fists held together, the smallest about the size of a hen's egg. They glowed with a warm, red-golden light, and when they were rubbed against one another, they began to radiate heat which, in a short time, grew so intense that it could be used to boil water. Working by feel, he began to place them around the Archimandrite, so that the warmth was coming from all sides. The last four he saved, and grouped them together, a little out of the way, beside the wall. Borrowing Kyrre's sight for a few moments, he went to fill a metal pot at a trickle of water that dripped out of a crack in the wall on the far side of Maskulu's artificial cavern. He wedged the pot between the glowing crystals, and left it there for the water to boil. 'Some tea would be welcome right now,' he said. 'It might warm you up a bit. And I brought us plenty of food, too.'

Kyrre, in the meantime, had activated a number of glims, and the Archimandrite was grateful for the extra light. From a bag she extracted a tightly rolled quilt, and proceeded to open it out with her stubby little fingers. Though her lack of size gave her a certain amount of difficulty, she persevered, refusing to let Amaurn help her. 'It looks as if your wound has almost stopped bleeding,' she told him sternly, in mindspeech, 'so don't you dare exert yourself, and open it up again.' She spread out the large quilt on the floor, and made him lie on one side of it. 'We'll wrap the rest of it over you, once I've examined your wound,' she told him.

Amaurn began to feel the warmth from the crystals spreading over him, and with it came drowsiness. Finally, he gave up the struggle, and let himself relax. He was safe here – for the time being, at least. Guarded by Maskulu, and tended by this earnest young man and this healer of another race, he felt himself to be among friends – a sensation he had not experienced for many years.

Pain stabbed through his side as Kyrre opened his tattered shirt and unwrapped his clumsy bandages, and Amaurn caught his breath sharply. Holding a glim close to the wound, the Dobarchu examined it minutely. 'Still leaking blood,' she muttered, 'though you did well to stop the worst. You did the right thing to put pressure on it as you did. The blade didn't penetrate far enough to hit anything vital, though it did slice through some muscle, and that's going to take a while to heal, I'm afraid. Your movements will be constrained for some time to come.'

'They can't be.' Amaurn spoke through gritted teeth. 'I don't have time for that.'

'I'm afraid you'll have to make time,' the Dobarchu told him. 'It's not as if you have much choice. If we can get you down to the infirmary, we can use the healing lights on you, and we have certain medications which can speed things up. Nevertheless, those tissues won't knit up overnight, and the more you move about, the longer it'll take.'

As she spoke, she was rummaging in another basket, sorting through packets and powders. 'If you're doing what I think you're doing,' Amaurn told her, 'I don't want to be unconscious.'

'You'll be sorry,' Kyrre told him, 'but if you insist, I can give you something instead that will dull the pain a little.'

'Haven't you got anything to take it away completely?'

The Dobarchu made the chattering sound that passed for laughter in her kind. 'Yes,' she said. 'Unconsciousness.'

'Not an option,' Amaurn said firmly. 'Are you going to stitch it?'

Again, she laughed. 'You're not in Callisiora now, you know. We have something else from the technology of the ancients that will seal the tissue together – but before you ask, you'll still have to be very careful until the wound has time to heal. And yes, it will still hurt.'

He sighed. 'If that's what it takes. All right, Kyrre. Let's get this over with.'

Suddenly, Bailen interrupted them. 'I have a message from Kher, Archimandrite. He says he's here with that stranger, Dark, who found his way through the Curtain Walls – the stupid idiot who let those Ak'Zahar through at the same time.' His eyes widened. 'This man even captured one, and brought it with him! Of all the nerve!'

Amaurn looked across at Maskulu. 'I want to see this young man. He's the associate of one of my oldest friends. Tell Kher to bring him here.'

'Are you sure that's safe?' said the Senior Loremaster doubtfully. 'You've already summoned the leader of the accursed Takuru, and now you want a total stranger and one of the most deadly predators in the world.'

'I can't hide away from everyone for ever.' Amaurn shrugged – and winced. 'The Ak'Zahar has been immobilised, so that's all right. You can check out Kher, and if the newcomer attacks me, you have my permission to kill him. That goes for the leader of the Takuru, too.'

'And what if the leader sends the killer instead? You're putting a lot of trust in the belief that I'll be faster than a Takur assassin,' Maskulu grumbled.

Amaurn smiled. 'I'm sure you can handle it. This wouldn't be the first time I've trusted you with my life, and the way things are going, it probably won't be the last. Why don't you and Bailen go and bring him down here? Ask him about Grim's little messengers, if you want to check out his background. No accursed shapeshifter would know about them.'

'I wish *I* didn't,' Maskulu said with feeling. 'Ever since Grim sent them here, they've been nothing but a downright nuisance.'

Amaurn still couldn't talk about Grim without pain. He took a deep breath. 'Well, that'll be one advantage of having his assistant here. If this young man is genuine, you'll be able to turn the care of the imps over to him.'

'I'll go and fetch him at once. Bailen, will you come with me, and bring a torch?' Maskulu chuckled grimly. 'We don't want to scare him *too* much at first, do we? We'll leave it to our esteemed Archimandrite to do that.'

Amaurn waved him away. 'Get away with you, you idiot.' He turned back to Kyrre, the Dobarchu healer. 'In the meantime, I suppose you had better get busy. Much as I would like to, we can't put off dealing with this wound for ever.'

Twenty-Three

Homecoming

Outside the inn, Kher paused, clearly listening to some private message in mindspeech. 'The Archimandrite is on the opposite side of the valley right now, so we're going to skirt around the settlement and ride over there,' he told the Summoner. 'We'll have to take your captive Ak'Zahar with us, and I don't propose to carry him up that hill on my back.'

Dark had no objections to riding. He was feeling so nervous that his knees probably wouldn't hold him up if he tried to go on foot.

Oh, how I wish you were here, Grim! We had planned this day to be so very different. It was to be your joyous return to the place you had missed for so long. And will it ever become my place, now that you're not here? Without your support for me, will these people accept me? And what will I do, if they don't?

By this time, they had reached the end of the village and crossed a swift little river on a bridge of stone. On the other side was a crumbling, ancient wall, and a short flight of steps leading up to a gateway that had clearly been a tunnel once, though, judging by the moss and weathering on the stones, it had lost its roof a long time ago. 'That gateway leads to the settlement,' Kher said, 'but there's an easier route for horses if you follow the wall round to the left. Today, though, we're going another way, up round the far side of the lake.'

They left the inviting gateway and turned right, following a narrow road that ran along beside the river, passing an old mill. Gradually, the walls at the side of the road dwindled to a much lower, newer boundary that had clearly been constructed from the same fallen stones. On the other side of it was a narrow belt of trees and, through them, Dark could catch tantalising glimpses of mirror-bright water. 'That's the Lower Lake,' Kher told him. 'If you look back over your shoulder, you can just catch a glimpse of the settlement on the lakeside, and see the Tower of Tidings above the trees.'

Obediently, Dark looked and saw the high, round tower that he had glimpsed earlier, and a number of lower, stone-built buildings clustering around its foot. 'Why are we going away from the settlement?' he asked.

'I told you, we're supposed to meet Amaurn elsewhere.'

'Yes, but you really didn't tell me why.'

There was a pause while Kher wrestled with Scall's little mare, which he was leading along by its reins. For some reason, she seemed to want to head in the opposite direction to the one in which they were going. After a tussle, he got her following obediently again, and returned to what he was saying. 'The Archimandrite is meeting us at the home of Maskulu, one of the Senior Loremasters. Goodness knows why – it's underground, and it's cold, dark, damp, and damned uncomfortable. It's certainly not the sort of place I would choose to receive a newcomer.' He shrugged. 'Maybe he wants to keep you and your Ak'Zahar under wraps for a while, for some reason. Mind you, that's unlikely, too. We've already gone through the village with the critter, so the entire settlement will know about it by now.'

After a time, the trees ended, and there was nothing between them and the lake but a stretch of rough and marshy-looking ground, with clumps of tall reeds growing down near the water. The sounds of birdsong and the sigh of the breeze in the branches changed to the shriller whispering of wind through reed and sedge, the flap and splash and strident calls of ducks in the shallows, and the deep-throated rattle of frogs.

They were forced to cross another bridge, as the river took a sharp bend to the left and ran down to the lake. The wall ended here and, once they were on the other side of the bridge, they left the road and turned towards the calm expanse of water. They had reached the head of the lake now and took a curving route along its edge, picking their way with care across the soft ground. To his surprise, Dark saw that there was another lake just beyond the first, and he and the Loremaster were threading their way between them across a narrow neck of wetland and water meadow.

There wasn't another human soul in sight. Dark looked around this wild and lonely spot, and a shiver went through him that was not just cold and weariness. 'Are you sure the Archimandrite said he'd meet us in this forsaken place?'

Kher glanced back. 'Not exactly here. We've a little way to go, round the head of the lake, and then up the hillside.' He shrugged. 'Don't ask me why. I don't know Amaurn, he's only been here a couple of days, though I heard tell that he was a Loremaster in Gendival many years ago and had to run away after a dispute with Cergorn, who was Archimandrite here before him.'

Dark nodded. 'I know. Grim told me. Amaurn made an un-successful bid for the leadership back then, and Cergorn sentenced him to death. One of the other Loremasters, a woman I think, helped him to escape, and he's been hiding out in Callisiora all these years, waiting for a chance to come back. All that time, he had a lot of secret supporters, like my mentor, in the Shadow-league.'

The Loremaster's eyebrows went up. 'For an outsider, you're certainly well informed. I didn't . . .'

His words were cut off by a loud bellow. The waters of the Lower Lake erupted in a ferment of boiling foam, and huge waves sloshed across the marshy banks and swirled around the feet of the panicked horses. With a scream, Scall's mare broke her reins and ran, bolting back the way they had come and careering down the road towards the settlement – but the Summoner had no eyes for her. He bit back his own scream of terror as a ghastly head, with enormous jaws, weed-hung and dripping water, came rising out of the lake, climbing up and up towards the sky on a neck that seemed to go on for ever. An immense, gleaming, dark-green body broke through the surface of the water like an emerging island.

'Oh, damn,' Kher muttered. 'It's the Afanc.'

'Who has had the temerity to bring that abomination to our valley?' The mindspeech was so loud that it almost blew Dark's head apart. Only his desperate desire to prove himself worthy of becoming a Loremaster prevented him from letting his horse have its head, and bolting with it all the way back to Callisiora. Using all the power of his will, he somehow managed to keep control of his terror, his plunging mount, and Grim's horse with the Ak'Zahar tied to its back.

Kher was facing the monstrosity with a frown on his face that might have been irritation, worry, or a bit of both. He addressed it in mindspeech that Dark could also hear. 'Senior Loremaster Bastiar, you have no right to detain us. We are summoned to the Archimandrite, and we are already late.'

Dark was astounded. This – this *monster* was a Loremaster, too? Though Grim had said there were races other than human in the Shadowleague, he had never warned him about anything like this!

Kher's reply had obviously not pleased Bastiar. The creature's eyes glittered coldly, and it swung its head down towards the two men, enveloping both in a cloud of fetid breath. 'And did that renegade interloper ask you to introduce a deadly predator through the Curtain Walls? Answer me!'

'I must answer to the Archimandrite first and foremost, and he told me to bring this stranger and the Ak'Zahar to him at once. He did *not* say that I could stop and chat along the way,' Kher replied coolly. 'Word travels fast among the Shadowleague, and it is no secret that you are Amaurn's enemy. When he wishes to share his thoughts and plans with you, no doubt he will do so.'

'How dare you speak to a Senior Loremaster in that fashion!' Bastiar angled his huge head down to block the riders' way. 'You will go to the renegade when I have finished with you, and not a moment sooner, and I *will* have answers, Loremaster Kher.' He lowered his voice, and his eyes narrowed with a cunning gleam. 'If you are going to see the Archimandrite, what are you doing up here at the head of the lake? Where is Amaurn, that you do not seek him in the settlement?' The tremendous head swung around towards Dark. '*You* give me some answers, stranger!'

The Summoner almost stopped breathing. Then, from the corner of his eye, he saw Kher watching the exchange closely with an uneasy expression, and his thoughts began to race. If this monster was a Loremaster, and a senior one at that, it would hardly dare to hurt him physically, he suspected, but that did not mean that he and his companion weren't in a great deal of trouble. A lot would depend on his answer, and it would certainly be a test of both his loyalty to Grim's old friend, the new Archimandrite, and his suitability to be one of the Shadowleague.

'Well?' the monster rumbled. 'Where is Amaurn, and why has he summoned you?' The massive head swung down even closer. For a moment, Dark thought of feigning ignorance, and pretending he didn't understand mindspeech, but he realised that, if he really wanted to join the Shadowleague, such a deception might well backfire. Instead, he hid his fear as best he could, looked up at the terrifying Loremaster, and shrugged. 'Why ask me?' he said. 'Kher only just brought me here. What would I know about this place?'

Bastiar swung his head back to Kher. 'And just who is this outsider? Where did he come from, and why did you bring him here?'

The Loremaster was clearly taking a leaf out of Dark's book. 'Because the Archimandrite asked me to,' he said.

The Afanc rumbled ominously in its throat but, before it could speak again, something changed. The serpentine neck lengthened, and the great head shot up into a listening position. If the Loremaster was receiving some sort of message in mindspeech, Dark certainly couldn't hear anything, but something certainly had a profound effect. With a hiss of displeasure that almost split their eardrums, the monstrous Bastiar backed away from them, and sank back into the lake. 'We will meet again,' it promised them in ominous tones, and disappeared.

Gradually the horses became calmer, and the humans followed suit. Kher let out his breath in a long sigh, and Dark swallowed hard. 'What do you think happened? What made it go away like that?'

'While his attention was on you, I called on the Archimandrite for help,' Kher told him. 'He sounded a bit pressed, but he said he'd have a word with Bastiar.' His eyebrows went up. 'I'd have given a lot to hear what he said.'

'Just as long as he wasn't saying it to *me*,' Dark amended. 'I wouldn't want to get on the wrong side of a man who can scare a creature that size.'

'Me neither,' Kher agreed. 'Come on, let's get out of here before the Afanc changes his mind and comes back for us.'

Trying to stay as far away as possible from the shoreline, the two men skirted the head of the lake. Dark was not the only one who breathed a sigh of relief when they reached the other side of the valley, and began to climb up a rough track that crossed the rocky hillside at an angle. Though the steep slopes on this side of the vale were thickly wooded lower down, a twist of the track took them in the opposite direction, towards the other lake, and threaded its way around thickets of bramble and whin, and occasional clumps of holly and thorn. As they went on, the slope became more craggy, until they were climbing with a low cliff on their left. Kher dismounted, signalling to Dark to do the same, and then pushed hard on the rock in an area that looked indistinguishable from the rest. A slab of the cliff face pivoted, to reveal a narrow opening. 'This is where we go,' the Loremaster said. 'We'll have to—'

Suddenly he was interrupted by a voice that both young men heard within their minds. 'Thank you, Loremaster Kher, for bringing Dark here. Before you rest, will you please take the horses down to the stables? You, Dark, will wait there a moment with your – captive. Someone will come to fetch you.'

Kher looked at his companion, and shrugged helplessly. 'Sorry about that. It seems I've been dismissed. It's a pity – I really wanted to get a look at the mysterious new Archimandrite.' He helped Dark untie the captive Ak'Zahar from the saddle of Grim's white horse, and between them they lowered it to the ground. Though it had refused to eat or drink all the way here, and must surely be suffering the effects of such deprivation by now, it was still full of fight, straining at its bonds and snapping at the two men with its jagged fangs. Now that he was so close to his meeting with the Archimandrite, Dark was beginning to have doubts. 'Goodness only knows how they'll be able to restrain that thing in order to study it,' he said. 'I hope I've done the right thing in bringing it here.'

'Well, it's too late to worry about that now,' Kher said, dumping the last of the Summoner's packs on the ground. 'Besides, if they don't want it, they can always just stick a knife in it. What's the problem?' He clasped Dark's hand. 'Take care of yourself,' he said, 'and don't worry. Everything will be all right. The way you faced down the Afanc was magnificent, and if they don't take you as a Loremaster, they must be insane.' Waving away Dark's thanks for guiding him, he mounted and set off down the track, going back towards the settlement, and taking the two Reiver horses with him.

The Summoner felt very lonely, unwelcome and vulnerable, standing by himself on the exposed hillside, with all his worldly possessions in two small packs by his feet, and no one to keep him company but a deadly predator which by rights, he should not have brought with him at all. He looked into the tunnel mouth, and shivered. Why would the Archimandrite want to see him in such an inimical place? Why had he not been permitted to go to the settlement? This beginning did not bode well for his future here.

Then he heard the scrape and slither of movement in the lightless void beyond the portal. A strange, cool, greenish glow blossomed forth from the hand of a sturdy young man, with light brown hair tied back in a long, neat tail. To Dark's Summoner perceptions there seemed something odd about him; as he approached, it became clear that his eyes were glazed and sightless. Yet he still walked forward with confidence and, when he addressed Dark, he seemed to know exactly where to look. How could that be?

'You must be Dark,' the young man said. 'I'm Bailen. We've come to take you to Amaurn.' He stepped back, lifting the hand that carried the pale, glimmering light source. As the shadows fell back, a long, gleaming shape, bristled and armoured and with many clawed legs, emerged from the gloom. Its face was more hideous than all the monsters in the worst of Dark's childhood nightmares. It made the Afanc, that terrifying lake monster, look positively cute. The Summoner gasped, unable to prevent himself from taking a nervous step backwards. Bailen smiled. 'And this,' he said, 'is Senior Loremaster Maskulu.'

Getting hold of himself with difficulty, Dark stammered out a greeting in mindspeech. Privately, he hoped that Amaurn would be less terrifying. He'd had quite enough shocks for one day. Then, in his mind, he heard the gritty, clicking voice of Maskulu. 'Less terrifying than me? I wouldn't count on it, if I were you.'

Toulac hadn't realised how hard it would be to stay angry with Veldan. All the way back upriver she stayed aloof and alone in the bows, ignoring her shipmates with great determination – but the memory of their conversation kept going around in her head and, after a while, she began to wonder if she'd been entirely in the right.

Don't be stupid! Of course you were! You know what a monster Blade is – imagine what will happen to the world once he's managed to get his hands on the sort of power the Shadowleague have at their disposal.

But Veldan said he had changed.

What the bloody blazes does a girl like that know? She didn't have to live in Callisiora when Blade was in power behind the scenes. I thought I had escaped him by coming here – I won't live under his rule again. How long will it be, before he starts acting as he did when he took over the Godswords? He got rid of the female warriors then – how soon before he does the same with the female Loremasters? And Veldan will be no exception. That treacherous snake will turn on her, just as he turns on everyone.

Her thoughts went round and round in endless debate but, in the end, the answer always seemed to be the same. She should forget about the glorious future she had been planning, and just go. All along, it had seemed too good to be true. Of course there was always the other alternative: she could apologise to Veldan, and give Blade a chance before she decided to leave. But Toulac's pride wouldn't let her admit that she might have been too hasty in her judgement, and so many years' worth of experiencing human nature at its worst made her certain that she couldn't possibly be wrong.

Suddenly she heard a step behind her. Had Veldan come to admit that she was in the wrong? But a surreptitious glance over her shoulder showed her that the girl was amidships, talking to Kaz, and it was Elion who stood beside her in the bows. He hesitated before he spoke. 'Zavahl's going to stay here with us. I thought you might like to know.'

Toulac shrugged. 'He can do what he likes.' Her heart, however, had sunk at the news. If Zavahl, who had been so badly treated by Blade, was prepared to stay in Gendival and give the man another chance, didn't that make her own behaviour look both petty and cowardly?

I don't care.

Even in the privacy of her own mind, it had a hollow ring. Toulac sighed.

Why did this have to happen? Everything was going so well, then Blade had to show up and ruin everything. That man poisons whatever he touches.

There was another long pause before Elion spoke again. 'Please don't be so hasty, Toulac. Veldan's very upset to be losing you, you know. Are you sure you won't reconsider? For her sake?'

That was a low blow! Toulac gritted her teeth. 'Sonny, I would do a lot of things for Veldan, but this is asking too much. I wish it could be otherwise, but it can't.'

'You stubborn old baggage!' This time, the voice was in mind-speech, and it belonged to the firedrake.

'Leave me alone!' Toulac put her head in her hands, feeling as though she was being attacked from all sides. To her surprise, Elion intervened. 'Come on, Kaz. That's not very subtle, is it? Insults won't help this situation any more that they did when *we* used to hurl them at one another.' He turned back to Toulac. 'When we get back, why don't you go to the inn, have something to eat and a good long rest. You never know, this situation might look different when you've had a chance to sleep on it.' With that he left her, returning to the firedrake and Veldan.

The three Loremasters went into a huddle in the stern, and seemed to be having a very intense discussion about something.

Are they talking about me? Or am I just being a suspicious old woman?

Toulac felt more alone than ever. All the joy in her rescue and homecoming had been lost now. It didn't help that the closer she came to the Loremaster settlement, the more her doubts were growing. Was she stupid? Was she wrong? Was she throwing away her entire future because of prejudice, and a stubborn refusal to admit that she might have been mistaken?

When the wherry arrived at the trading post, its passengers and crew received the warmest of welcomes. A stocky man with silver hair and merry, twinkling eyes hailed them from the landing place and a younger, dark-haired man, who bore a distinct resemblance to Meglyn, came hurrying out of the building. Toulac's eyebrows went up as he extended a hand to help Veldan jump ashore, and caught her up in a hug. It seemed clear that he was fond of her.

She didn't tell me about him! Not that it's of any interest to me, of course.

Then the older man was doing the same for her, extending his hand to her with a courtly bow and laughing all over his face. Despite her black mood, Toulac found it impossible not to smile in return. The two men were introduced as Skeryn and Ruthar, and they were very keen to spend some time listening to the tales of the rescuers and the rescued, but Elion, Veldan and Kaz seemed to be in a tremendous hurry to get back. 'We'll do it another day, I promise,' Elion told them, 'but right now, we want to get home.'

'Amaurn will be anxious to speak to Zavahl, too,' Veldan said.

Toulac did not miss the grimace of annoyance that crossed Ailie's face – and the flicker of fear that crossed Zavahl's.

Maybe he'll want to come with me after all?

Then the veteran looked at Ailie, with her full, ripe figure and smiling face, and realised that, for a man who had lived his life so alone and unfulfilled, neither fear nor reason could contend with such a powerful inducement to stay.

He's beginning to find himself at last. Who am I to interfere? I remember how happy I was, when I thought I was going to be starting a new life.

'Well, nobody's making you go,' said a voice in her mind.

Toulac turned to glare at the firedrake. He knew very well that she wouldn't answer him aloud, and bring everyone into the debate, and unless she could manage to broadcast her replies in mind-speech, she would be helpless to respond.

She could ignore him, though. When Ruthar brought the horses around from the stables at the back of the trading post, she chose to ride one, instead of getting on the firedrake's back. Veldan made no comment, though Toulac caught the hurt expression on the girl's face, and again felt an uncomfortable twinge of guilt. She thought of Blade with increasing anger. It was all his fault – it must be. It was easier to blame him for this situation, than to blame herself.

As they rode off down the track by the river, the veteran found her enjoyment of being on horseback again marred by sad and wistful memories of her warhorse, Mazal. Though the dark brown gelding that she rode was an adequate beast, well cared for and well schooled, he seemed very dull and tame to ride in comparison to the grey stallion. Kaz, however, soon provided her with a distraction, by picking up their one-sided conversation right where he had left off.

'Why don't you wait, and talk to Amaurn, at least?' he said. 'Personally, I would trust the son of a bitch about as far as I could spit him, but I think the Boss is right. For the time being, at any rate, he's the best leader for the Shadowleague. Just talk to him, Toulac, for Veldan's sake. When will you get another chance to confront him with what he did in Callisiora? He says he had his reasons. Why don't you listen to them, before you judge? If you don't, you'll spend the rest of your life wondering whether or not you made a mistake – or even worse, they'll tamper with your memory when you leave Gendival, so that you won't remember me and Veldan, and you'll forget that you were even here.'

Toulac gasped. This was something she hadn't considered. How could she bear to have the memories of the last few days stripped away from her and return to being the bitter, unhappy, spent old woman who was eking out the last of her days in the sawmill?

The firedrake turned his head back to look at her. 'If it's just Blade that's the problem, you needn't be worrying about *him*.' His tongue lolled out in a firedrake grin. 'If he gives you any trouble, I'll fry the bastard.'

Toulac couldn't help but smile. 'Why, thank you, Kaz. I might just take you up on that.'

She hadn't noticed that she was using mindspeech until the firedrake's head came up sharply, and turned to her once more. 'Toulac, you did it again! I heard that! That settles it. You can't go now. You belong here, with the Shadowleague.' His eyes glittered. 'And if I hear any more nonsense about going away and leaving us, I'll fry *you*. I haven't eaten a human for a while.'

Toulac's eyes grew wide. 'You never!'

Kaz glanced back and grinned again. 'One of Blade's guards, at your sawmill,' he told her. 'So there.'

'Well, I wouldn't bother eating me,' Toulac retorted, trying her best not to be shocked – or at least, not to show it. 'I'd be far too tough and stringy.'

A wisp of smoke drifted out from between the firedrake's jaws. 'Not when you'd been *cooked*.'

At that point, Toulac suddenly realised that this entire conversation had been conducted in mindspeech. Kaz had – deliberately, she suspected – distracted her from the fact that she'd been answering him quite naturally.

I can do it! I could do it all the time! I only have problems sending my thoughts out when I try too hard, but I can work on that. And can I really leave now? Can I just go, and return to Callisiora, and turn my back on Veldan, and mindspeech, and all the adventures I would have with the Shadowleague? How can I let that accursed Blade take all of this away from me? Why should I?

But I told Veldan in no uncertain terms that I won't stay where Blade is. How can I back down now, without looking stupid and pathetic?

Toulac, still wavering, changed her mind back and forth several times before the end of the ride and Kaz, having made his point, left her alone to do so. He must have been talking to Veldan however, because every now and then, she was sure she saw the girl glancing back at her surreptitiously.

After a while they reached the lane that led off to the neat stables of the Shadowleague, with a number of horses, who made Toulac think sadly of Mazal, grazing peacefully in the fields round about. Ailie was plainly anxious to be getting back to the inn – preferably with Zavahl – and Veldan offered to save them time by taking their horses back to Harral. 'I'll take the others, too, if you like,' she said. 'On Kaz, I'll get back just as quickly as the rest of you.' Elion accepted her offer with alacrity, but said that he would stay with the fire-drake. Toulac wondered why he seemed so reluctant to go into the stables.

In the meantime, the veteran had decided that her own best course was to postpone her decision. When they dismounted, she went to Veldan. 'All right,' she said. 'I'll do what you want. I won't leave tonight, after all. I'll wait until tomorrow to decide what I want to do, once I've had a chance to talk to that miserable, flint-hearted son of a bitch. But I'm staying at the inn, mind you,' she added, determined to be independent to the last. She didn't want Veldan to spend the whole night persuading her to stay. 'Will that suit you, girlie?'

Veldan smiled. 'It'll suit me very well, Toulac, and I think it'll suit you, too, if you decide to stay. I told Cergorn, I told Amaurn, and I'm telling you – you were born to be here.'

'In that case, the fates left it a bit bloody late to bring me here,' the veteran grumbled, but she found it impossible to keep the grin from her face.

'In that case, you'd better stop wasting time, hadn't you?' Looking smug at having managed to get the last word for once, Veldan set off up the lane, almost being towed along by the horses, who scented their stable.

Toulac knew just how the animals felt, and probably with better cause. The previous couple of nights, and the day between, had tired her out. She couldn't wait to get back to the comfortable inn, and put her feet up at last. As the little group walked back up to the village, however, she began to wish she had stayed with Veldan after all. Elion had remained behind with Kaz and, with both him and Veldan gone, the closeness of the other two definitely made her feel superfluous. Clearly, they couldn't wait to be alone – and that was fine with her.

When they reached the inn, she left the two would-be lovers as quickly as possible. While they looked in the bar for Olsam, she searched out the kitchen, and took some bread, cheese, a jug of milk, and half a meat pie that happened to be lying round unattended. Clutching her booty, she went straight upstairs. Hearing voices, and the sounds of scraping and hammering from Zavahl's room, she peeped in on her way past, and saw the carpenters and masons at work on the damage that the flying drones had caused. She shuddered briefly at the memory of the horrible creatures – and then grinned evilly to herself.

Let's hope that Ailie's bedroom is nice and private and comfortable, because those two are going to need it. They'll have a bit of a problem frolicking around in here, right now.

Feeling a little smug, because Zavahl's chamber had been wrecked, while hers had been spared, she went straight on to her room, lured on by the siren call of her lovely, soft bed. It came as a nasty surprise, therefore, to find that there was already someone in it: a gangling adolescent boy who, by the look of his smeared face, had cried himself to sleep. Though she was sure she didn't know him, there was a vaguely familiar cast to his features that reminded her of someone she did know.

Toulac dumped her food down on the table, and planted her fists on her hips. 'Well, of all the nerve! And who the bloody blazes are *you*, might I ask?'

The boy opened his eyes, looked up at her, and blinked. 'I'm Scall,' he said. 'Who are you?'

Twenty-four

A Different Perspective

Dark had never known anything like Maskulu's underground lair. The black tunnels seemed all the more constricting after the open skies and far horizons of his moorland home, and he felt enclosed and trapped beneath the weight of earth and stone that surrounded him. With his heart beating fast, he walked beside the blind Loremaster, gingerly holding the luminous egg-shaped object which Bailen had given to him and which, apparently, was called a glim. At any other time the Summoner would have been fascinated by the glowing object, but today his thoughts were very firmly fixed elsewhere.

Bailen carried the extra pack that had belonged to Grim, while Maskulu brought the captive Ak'Zahar by the simple expedient of hooking a claw into the ropes with which it was bound, and dragging it along. If he hadn't witnessed, at first hand, the pitiless ferocity of the creature, Dark might almost have felt sorry for it as its narrow head banged repeatedly against the rough floor of the tunnel. As it was, however, he was far too worried about his own fate to spare much concern for something that had come so close to killing him.

They walked through the twisting, branching passageways for what felt like a long time, though the Summoner suspected that his discomfort at being beneath the ground, combined with his trepidation at his coming interview with the Archimandrite, were causing the moments to seem about five times as long as they normally did. It came as a relief when the frightful-looking Senior

Loremaster began to ask him, in great detail, about his capture of the Ak'Zahar. Telling the story of how he had come to be there, and explaining why he was accompanied by a predator that was anathema to the Shadowleague, helped him get his thoughts organised before he met Amaurn, and also helped to take his mind off the ordeal to come.

Dark had reached the point in his tale where they had arrived at the village and left Scall at the inn, but had not yet reached the part where he and Kher had met the Afanc of the lake, when Maskulu interrupted him. 'We have arrived. Keep your distance from the Archimandrite, and make no sudden moves towards him. Your life depends on this.' He squeezed through a roughly arched entrance, still dragging the Ak'Zahar behind him, and led the way into a chamber which, like the tunnels, had been hewn out of the solid rock. All at once Dark felt relieved that, no matter what the result might be, his ordeal would soon be over. He straightened his spine and followed Maskulu into the chamber, with Bailen bringing up the rear.

The appearance of the formidable Archimandrite was pretty much as he'd anticipated. Cropped grey hair, cold grey eyes, and a face that looked as though it had been carved from granite. What he had not expected, however, was to see this daunting figure lying prone on a quilt on the floor, being tended by a creature who looked like a very large, upright otter with paws like clever little hands, and a furry, round face.

Despite the muted lighting that came from the glims, Dark's eyes, accustomed to working in the dimly lit homes of the Reivers, were still very keen. He could see that Amaurn's clothes were bloody, and there was an open gash on his side. The otterlike creature, presumably another Loremaster, was doing something with a short, narrow tube that gave forth a slender beam of very bright light. Judging from his grey pallor, his clenched jaw, and the sheen of sweat on his face, the procedure seemed to be causing Amaurn a good deal of pain. Curious, the Summoner took a step closer, to be halted by a warning rattle from Maskulu.

Amaurn looked up. He ought to have seemed less intimidating when he was lying on his back, in pain, but Dark, looking at that face, wasn't fooled for a moment.

He should have been the one called Grim, and not my master.

Suddenly, Dark understood why his mentor had followed this man for so many years. If you tied him up in a sack, weighted it down with rock, and dropped him in the lake, he'd still be a force to be reckoned with.

The flint-grey eyes flashed. 'Thank you for that assessment,' Amaurn said drily. 'I trust that you won't feel tempted to try it out.'

Embarrassment and anger flooded Dark's face with heat as he realised that, in the stress of the moment, he had been forgetting to shield his private thoughts, and Amaurn had casually gone in and picked them from his mind. For a moment, he found himself wishing desperately for his mask of white bone, which could hide the expression – and the blushes – on his face. At some deep level, however, even the memory of the mask was enough to give him back the authority he had possessed as a Summoner. 'I may have been unguarded,' he said sharply, 'but what gave you the right to pry?'

His brown eyes, hot with anger, met the Archimandrite's cool, grey gaze. Neither man would look away, and the duel of wills might have continued interminably, if some action of the furry little Loremaster who was tending Amaurn had not caused him to flinch in pain, breaking the deadlock.

When their eyes met again, his expression was a little less hard and cold. 'I was intruding on your privacy because I thought it necessary,' he said to Dark. 'As you can see, we are not meeting under the best of circumstances. What I'm about to tell you is not yet common knowledge among the Shadowleague, so I'll require you to keep your mouth shut, and your thoughts under *control*, young man. Earlier today, I was attacked by an assassin, and barely got away with my life. Unfortunately, the killer also escaped. He is one of the Takuru – a shapeshifter who can take any form he pleases – even that of my oldest friend's valued companion and assistant.

So you can see why I must be very careful until my attacker is caught. That is why Kyrre is treating my wounds here in Maskulu's home, instead of the settlement. We don't word of my vulnerability getting around the Shadowleague, in case it gives similar ideas to anyone else.' He gave a grimace that might have been more pain, or might have been a wry attempt at a smile. 'So I don't apologise for prying into your thoughts. I know now that you are who you say you are, and not some impostor.'

His expression and voice became more gentle. 'I am so very sorry about poor Grim. He was one of my best and oldest friends. He had looked forward for such a long time to returning to Gendival, and now he never will.' Amaurn looked away for a moment, before turning back to Dark with a smile that was genuine, if strained. 'But his assistant is doubly welcome. I know he thought very highly of you and your abilities, Dark, and if you wish to stay here, I can use every loyal follower I can get . . .'

Another spasm crossed his face. 'Will you put that bloody thing down, Kyrre!' he barked. 'How in perdition am I supposed to have a conversation while you're searing my flesh off with that damned contraption?'

'Suit yourself, my Lord Archimandrite.' The mindspeech of the Dobarchu healer had a distinctly feminine tone. 'But you know that the longer I put off using the sealer, the more difficult the wound will be to repair – especially if you keep moving about, and trying to sit up as you are doing. I did warn you that there would be a good deal of pain, but you wouldn't let me put you to sleep.'

Dark wrestled with his own diffidence for a moment, wondering if he dared speak. But he had to prove himself worthy of becoming a Loremaster and if, at the same time, he could help his mentor's oldest friend, then he owed that much to Grim. He cleared his throat and spoke. 'Sir, maybe I can help you with that wound.'

'*You* can help?' Amaurn, clearly still in a good deal of pain, glared at him in some irritation. 'I'm sure that Grim must have explained to you the history and background of the Shadowleague?'

'Yes, he did, but . . .'

'In that case, you must be aware that what we have here is medical equipment from a race whose knowledge and power was far superior to our own. Now what – no offence intended – can a wet-behind-the-ears shaman from a race of backward barbarians do to rival such a device as this?'

Dark gritted his teeth. 'Well, I can certainly put a stop to the pain without knocking you unconscious. Grim has been working for years on ways to extend the powers of mindspeech further, so that we can use our minds to affect the physiology of ourselves, and others. We couldn't do much for the Reivers – shamans we may be, but the backward barbarians aren't ready for what they would see as witchcraft. According to Grim, Cergorn's restrictions forbade what we were doing, so we had no idea how far we could take our methods. But if you'd rather rely on the half-understood relics of a race long gone to dust, then be my guest. It's your pain. You keep it, if you're so attached to it.'

Amaurn's mouth opened, then closed again. Clearly he hadn't expected such a temeritous response from this newcomer. He rallied well, however. 'What, exactly, would you want to do with these new techniques of yours? And how do you know they'll work?'

Dark smiled. 'Now I can pick the thoughts from *your* head, Archimandrite. You're thinking that if Grim invented these methods, they must be all right – but though you're certain *he* could help you, you're not at all sure that I won't muck things up, and damage you in some way.' He shrugged. 'I'm afraid I can't help you, there. In the end, only you can decide whether you trust me, or not.'

The Archimandrite's eyes grew hard. 'Are you trying to say that I'm afraid?'

'I'm saying that I understand your doubts,' Dark replied. 'After your experience today with the assassin, you have every right to be cautious. I've come out of nowhere making some outrageous claims, you haven't known me an hour, but I'm asking you to trust me.' He smiled wryly. 'If I were in your shoes, I doubt that *I* would trust me.'

'But you're willing to stand by your claims, none the less?'

Dark nodded. 'I can take the pain away while your healer is using her device, and it's possible that I can help you fight off infection and speed up the healing process to a certain extent. I may not be as experienced as Grim but, as his friend, you must know that he wasn't the sort of man who'd keep secrets for secrecy's sake. He taught me everything he knew about this sort of healing – at least, he taught me the theory,' he added truthfully. 'Don't forget that he didn't have much chance to put his theories into practice, either.'

There was a moment's silence before Amaurn spoke again. 'I appreciate your honesty, and I think that your apprenticeship with Grim left more of a mark on you than you realise. I can see a lot of him in you,' he said. 'Very well, Dark, you've convinced me. Let's give it a try.'

'Amaurn, no! This is purest folly.'

'Archimandrite, there is no justification for taking this sort of risk.'

Both Maskulu and Kyrre had spoken at once, but Amaurn waved away their protests. 'Let him try,' he said, and turned back to Dark. 'Deal with the pain first,' he said. 'If that works, then you're at liberty to try anything else you feel appropriate.'

Dark swallowed hard, aware of the responsibility that the Archimandrite was placing on him. Then, unbidden, the face of the young boy whose life he had helped to end came into his mind, and with it, understanding and acceptance. Though he'd had no chance to save the child, the lessons he had learned that day, and the experience he had gained, would help him now. In his mind, he heard Grim's voice:

'I have every faith in you.'

And he knew that he had every faith in himself. 'Right,' he said, stepping forward. 'Let's get started.'

The Summoner approached Amaurn cautiously, aware of the watchful Maskulu's disapproving glare. He knelt down, and was about to place his hand gently on the Archimandrite's head, when he noticed the healer Kyrre standing beside him, waiting to continue her own work. Dark could feel her interest, her doubts, and her hope. 'Do you mind if I attune my thoughts to yours?' she asked him. 'I won't intrude, but I would like to see just what you're doing. New methods of healing are important to us all.'

'You're very welcome to observe,' Dark told her. 'I'm interested in your device, too. Maybe we'll have a chance to discuss them both later. It would be good to talk with a more experienced healer.'

'I would like that,' Kyrre said – and he knew that he was on his way to making a new friend.

Gently, Dark laid his fingers on the Archimandrite's forehead, and probed with his thoughts into Amaurn's brain – at least, that was what he planned to do. Instead, he came up against a blank grey wall; firm and obdurate, and as impenetrable as granite.

Damn!

Helping the Reivers with this method was one thing, but working on telepaths who were trained in mind control was clearly going to carry a whole new set of complications.

But maybe there'll be benefits, too. It will be helpful if the patient can actually be taught to assist the healer.

But that was a thought for later. 'Sir,' he said patiently, 'you're shielding. You're going to have to let me in, or I won't be able to do anything at all.'

Amaurn glared at him. 'What do you mean? I *am* letting you in.'

'No, I'm afraid you aren't.'

'Oh.' Amaurn looked slightly abashed. 'Old habits die hard, I'm afraid. Try again, Dark, and I'll do my best to be more accommodating.'

Once more, the Summoner touched Amaurn's forehead, and let his thoughts sink into the other's mind. This time, though the wall was still there, there was a narrow chink in it through which he could pass. Clearly, the Archimandrite wasn't a man who believed in taking chances. Just as he had done with the dying Reiver child, Dark located the centres that registered pain, and blocked the impulses between the nerves in Amaurn's side, and the receptors in his brain. He nodded to Kyrre, and spoke aloud in stilted tones, because he was keeping all his concentration focussed on Amaurn's mind. 'You can carry on now, and seal the wound properly. He won't feel a thing.'

I hope.

Dark was just as interested in Kyrre's sealer as she had been in his mental techniques. He watched with fascination as the searing beam from the narrow tube fused the layers of injured muscle, and finally the flesh itself, leaving a dark brown scar behind. Amaurn lay quietly and let them get on with their ministrations. His eyes were wary, but it was clear that he was in no discomfort.

'What in perdition are you doing?'

The voice was feminine, but Dark, fighting to keep his concentration, was too preoccupied to look up and see who had spoken. He saw Amaurn's face light up however, in a way that made him look like an entirely different human being. 'Veldan!' the Archimandrite said. 'I'm glad you're back. And Kazairl and Elion, too.'

Someone knelt down beside him, but Dark still did not dare take his eyes off Amaurn. The girl was saying something more, and he felt his concentration beginning to slip. 'Will you all *please* shut up?' he said through clenched teeth. 'Just for a few more minutes?'

No one said anything further, but he was so closely linked to Amaurn's mind that he was aware, at the edge of his attention, that a tightly shielded conversation was taking place in mindspeech between the Archimandrite and the girl. He could feel her eyes on him, and knew that Amaurn must be telling her all about him. Dark would have given a lot to know what they were saying, but told himself to mind his own concerns. He wished that Kyrre would hurry up and finish. While she was actually working on the wound, and giving Amaurn so much pain, it wasn't easy to maintain his block on the nerve centres, and all this concentration was giving him a headache. Besides, he was very curious about Blade's new visitor, or visitors.

At last it was done and he only needed to leave a mild block in place to dull any residual pain from the healing. He exited with relief from Amaurn's mind, and stretched his kinked spine. As he straightened, he met a pair of huge, grey eyes in an exquisite face. He didn't realise that he was staring, until she slapped him. It was so fast he didn't even see it coming, and it almost knocked his head off his shoulders. It was only then that he gave any thought to the scar down the side of her face, and realised that she must have thought he was staring at *that*.

This wasn't going to be easy to get out of. If he denied looking at her disfigurement, it would only prove that he had been looking at it. And the longer he delayed, the worse trouble he'd be in. Dark's mind raced. 'I'm sorry I was staring,' he said. 'It was very rude of me. But has no one ever told you that you have the most amazing eyes?'

The amazing eyes narrowed suspiciously – but what could she say? If she accused him of staring at her scar, then *she* would be drawing attention to it. Suddenly, on a very private strand of thought, he heard a snicker. 'Heh, heh. That's confounded her. Nice one, stranger. I could get to like you.' The Summoner looked past the girl to see a large, dragonlike creature standing with a bearded, dark-haired man – and it definitely wasn't the human who had spoken.

In the meantime, the girl seemed to have gathered her wits. 'In that case, I owe you an apology,' she said stiffly. He could tell from her tone that she didn't believe him, but she was trying to put the best face she could on the entire matter.

The Summoner had been peripherally aware that, during the entire exchange, Amaurn had been looking very closely from one to the other. Now, at last, he spoke. 'Well done, Dark. That was very impressive. I didn't feel a thing. As I said before, you are truly Grim's successor. He would be very proud of you, and you certainly belong in the Shadowleague.' He turned to the girl. 'Veldan, would you do me a favour? Dark is very new to us. Would you show him around, and generally explain things to him?'

'Why me?' the girl said bluntly. 'Wouldn't Elion be a better choice?'

'No, I don't think so,' the Archimandrite said mildly. 'What do you think, Dark? Would you like Veldan to introduce you to the settlement of Gendival?'

'I would like it very much,' the Summoner said.

Amaurn smiled to himself. He had seen the way Dark was looking at the girl, and he had a strong feeling that her scar had genuinely been the last thing on his mind.

'This should be an eye-opener for Veldan. She's so convinced that everyone is looking at that damned scar of hers that she's losing out on the best parts of her life.' The words had come, in *very* private mindspeech, from Kazairl.

The Archimandrite exchanged a conspiratorial look with the firedrake. 'My thoughts exactly,' he said. 'I don't want to see her hiding behind her work as a Loremaster – she deserves more than that. Dark will be good for her.'

The firedrake's tongue lolled out in a firedrake grin. 'You know,' he said, 'for an evil despot, you're not half bad, sometimes.'

Trying not to smirk, Amaurn turned back to Dark. 'That's settled, then,' he said. 'Veldan will take care of you. Now, I had better introduce you properly. Dark, this is Loremaster Veldan, and her companions, Loremasters Elion and Kazairl. Kazairl is the one with the teeth and the tail. He's a firedrake, and Veldan's partner.' He gestured to the Summoner. 'And this is Dark, who was a Reiver Summoner and the assistant of a very old friend of mine. He's a new, and very welcome addition to the Shadowleague. And speaking of new additions, how are the Dobarchu refugees faring, Veldan?'

The Loremaster tore her attention away from Dark. 'We sent them off to the infirmary for the time being. We were thinking about settling them in one of the buildings down near the lake shore.'

'They send their thanks to you,' Kyrre put in. 'I've just been talking to Mrainil. I will go down and see them as soon as I've finished here.'

At that moment, Maskulu interrupted. 'The shapeshifter leader approaches. Shall I go and bring her down here?'

'Please, Maskulu, if you would.' Amaurn turned to Dark and Veldan. 'Would you two help me up? I can't face the Takuru leader lying down like this.'

Veldan looked at Kyrre. 'It's not what I'd advise,' the Dobarchu said, 'but you can depend on it that he'll get up anyway, so you might as well assist him. I don't want to put any more strain on that wound than we can help.'

Helped by Dark and Veldan, Amaurn struggled to his feet, swearing under his breath as pain stabbed through his side. 'I thought you were supposed to be blocking this,' he complained to the Summoner.

Dark looked unrepentant. 'If I do, you won't remember to take care of yourself and rest. If you start moving around too much, you'll undo all of Kyrre's good work.'

The Archimandrite glared at him, and Veldan stifled a chuckle. Kaz, in the meantime, had moved up with the others, and now took up station at Amaurn's side, as an additional – and very menacing – bodyguard. Elion, too, closed the distance between them. Though he leant against the cavern wall in the attitude of a casual observer, his hand hovered close to the hilt of his sword. Amaurn was grateful for their support. Only now was he beginning to realise how lonely those bitter years in Callisiora had been.

At that moment the Takuru leader entered, with the Senior Loremaster, bristling with disapproval, looming threateningly at her side. She had taken the guise of a silver-haired woman, robed in white, and tall and regal in bearing. Halfway across the floor, she was halted by a warning rumble from Maskulu. Stopping immediately, she inclined her head to Amaurn. 'I am Kalevala, leader of the Takuru.' She spoke pleasantly, but her eyes were wary. 'I am pleased to greet the new Archimandrite. How may my people be of service?'

Amaurn gave her a long, level look. 'The question is, how can the new Archimandrite be of service to your people?'

Even though she was wearing a different form from her own, she could not hide her astonishment. 'What do you mean?'

'Before we talk about that,' Amaurn said, 'please feel free to take your true form. I'm sure you would feel much more at ease.'

Again, he had caught her off balance. 'But . . . Are you sure?' she floundered. 'I had thought to set you at your ease by taking this semblance. Frankly, many other races find our true forms repulsive.'

'That sort of prejudice is exactly what I'm trying to change,' Amaurn said. 'Please change shape, Kalevala. We are all friends here.'

'Very well.' The Takur leader blurred and twisted as she morphed into her shadowy, ever-changing, many-limbed form, with the cold, white glittering eyes somewhere in the centre. Beside him, Amaurn heard the sharp hiss of Dark's intaken breath but, to give the young man credit, not a trace of shock or revulsion showed on his face.

He'll do very well.

'Now that we're comfortable,' Amaurn said to Kalevala, 'I wish to discuss the position of the Takuru within the Shadowleague.'

'We *have* no position in the Shadowleague,' the shapeshifter hissed. 'We are outcasts, pariahs, tolerated only because we are occasionally useful.'

The Archimandrite nodded. 'Ah, yes,' he said smoothly. 'Cergorn kept you as his spies, did he not? He graciously let you live in the most inhospitable area around the two lakes, and he would never allow you to become Loremasters. And with such token gestures he bought your loyalty, telling you that you could expect no better. Well, I intend to change all that – with your approval, of course. You certainly deserve a better life here than you've been having under Cergorn's rule. And I'm going to see that you get it.'

For an instant, there was stunned silence in the chamber. Amaurn could see that Maskulu was about to launch into a furious protest, and gestured urgently for the Senior Loremaster to be quiet. Kaz was growling deep in his throat, Veldan was staring at him wide-eyed, and Elion's mouth was hanging open.

'If the reaction of your colleagues is anything to go by, you may experience more than a little opposition to your plan.' There was an edge of bitterness in the Takur's voice.

Amaurn shrugged, trying not to wince as pain stabbed once again through his side. 'They'll come round to the idea, when I've explained a few things to them.' Suddenly, there was steel in his eyes, and in his voice. 'I'll see to that. But really, all this fuss about shapeshifters is most unnecessary, and the Shadowleague ought to know better. I believe that there's a simple solution to the problem. Apart from your somewhat – unconventional – appearance, most people fear and suspect the Takuru because you can conceal yourselves in their very midst. Meanwhile you, for the most part, conceal yourselves because you know you are unwelcome and reviled. And while you are living apart, as you do, people will always distrust you. Your people originally come from the Forest of Rakha, do you not?'

'I – well, yes.' Kalevala was obviously confused this sudden change of tack.

Amaurn shook his head. 'Then you must feel desperately uncomfortable and exposed up on that bleak, rocky stretch of hillside above the Upper Lake that Cergorn was generous enough to allot you.'

'You are quite correct. My people are miserable there.'

'If you are forest dwellers, would I be right in assuming that you are mainly arboreal by nature?'

The Takur's amorphous, shifting forms blurred even faster. 'Clearly you have been doing some research, Archimandrite. I am assuming that you already know the answer to that question. What is your point?'

'I am inviting the Takuru to come and make their homes with the rest of us, Kalevala. As far as I know, you are the only truly arboreal species within the Shadowleague, and the slopes above the settlement are covered in oak woods. You wouldn't need to compete with the rest of us for space to build your homes. All the treetops will be yours.' He paused. 'Furthermore, I would like you to submit any candidates from among you who wish to train as Loremasters, and take their proper place among us.'

The Takur leader sank to the ground, clearly overcome. In the dark, shifting mass of her body, the clustered eyes were glowing. She soon recovered herself, however. 'Your offer is generous beyond belief, Amaurn. But what is it that you want from us in return?'

'I want the Takuru to use their true shapes within the settlement and the surrounding area,' he said. 'People suspect you just now because they don't know where you might be lurking, in disguise. I want to remove that fear by removing your disguises – and the need for them. You say that people are revolted by you, but there are many other creatures in the Shadowleague who are also terrifying in appearance. Maskulu is an excellent case in point. And what of the Afanc? And the Alvai? People don't bother about them because they're so familiar, and if they saw you around all the time, people would soon get used to the way you look.'

'Is that all?' Kalevala asked suspiciously.

'Not quite. I'm sure you're very well aware that Syvilda sent a Takur assassin against me.'

'Yes,' she admitted. 'Though I'm sure *you* are well aware that I did not sanction Vifang's actions.'

'Indeed. And that's why we're having this conversation now. I want to make one exception to the Takuru taking on other shapes within the settlement. By sending that assassin against me, Syvilda has sealed the fate of herself and Cergorn. As soon as he is sufficiently recovered to travel, they both will have their memories wiped of any vestige of the Shadowleague, and they will be sent back to the islands of their people. In the meantime, I want some of your people to shadow them constantly, without them knowing, to make sure that they don't plot anything else against me.'

'You'll exile them?' Kalevala sounded surprised. 'Is that all? I thought for sure that you'd execute Syvilda, at least, when you found out.'

Amaurn shook his head. 'Cergorn was the one who was keen on executions – as I have reason to remember all too well. I would rather not emulate his mistakes, but I'm not exactly acting out of the goodness of my heart. If I execute the former Archimandrite and his lifemate, then I'll permanently destroy any chance I might have of winning over their supporters. A seeming act of generosity, however, might just make some people think twice. And if I wipe Cergorn and Syvilda's minds, at least I won't have to be looking over my shoulder every minute.'

The Takur's eyes glittered. 'So you want us to act as your spies? As we did for Cergorn? Despite all your fine talk, you only want to use us as he did!'

'I don't intend to make a habit of it. This is a special case, however. And if you or your people feel any conflict of loyalties about this, you should be aware that you'll be saving the lives of Cergorn and Syvilda by preventing them from making any further moves against me. Because if they try anything else, I *will* execute them.'

The shapeshifter leader considered – but only for a moment. 'Very well,' she said. 'On behalf of my people, I accept your terms, and . . .'

'Just a moment,' Amaurn said. 'There's just one more small condition. I want the head of the assassin who attacked me today.'

Kalevala sighed. 'I thought as much. You do realise that if you do this, particularly if you spare the life of Syvilda, who commissioned the assassination in the first place, you will make further enemies among the Takuru? My people will be outraged at such injustice, and I'm sure you don't want to be worrying about any shapeshifters with grudges at this point.'

Amaurn scowled. 'He damn nearly killed me. Are you saying I should just *overlook* that?'

'I did not say so,' Kalevala replied. 'As a mark of gratitude for your generosity today, *I* will take care of your assassin. Vifang will never trouble you again, Amaurn. You have my word on it.'

'Thank you, Kalevala. I appreciate your help in this matter more than I can say.' The Archimandrite inclined his head to her in a gesture of respect. 'I hope that you'll let me have the night to rest my injuries before I break this happy news to the rest of the Shadowleague? I won't deny that getting them to accept these changes is going to take some fast talking on my part. I'll call a meeting in the morning, if you will wait until then to tell your people what we're planning.'

'That seems reasonable.' For the first time, there was humour in the shapeshifter's tones. 'I suspect that I will have an easier time of it than you, Archimandrite. I wish you luck.'

Amaurn smiled thinly. 'I'll deal with any objectors, don't worry. Between us, we'll make this work, and I look forward to all sorts of benefits for both sides, once the Takuru have been integrated fully into the Shadowleague.'

'Indeed. And with such a good beginning from a new leader, I think we can all look to the future with renewed confidence.'

When Kalevala had gone, Veldan let out her breath in a long sigh. '*Well!*' she said. 'Now there's something you don't see every day. After your reign, Amaurn, the Shadowleague will never be the same again.'

'It was certainly an inspired method of getting rid of your assassin,' Maskulu said doubtfully, 'but how are you going to convince the Shadowleague that it's a good idea to have the Takuru living among them?'

'Oh, I'll just point out to them the basic fairness of my plan and its long-term advantages to the Shadowleague as a whole,' Amaurn said airily. 'And if that fails, I'll remind them in no uncertain terms that I'm not asking them if this new arrangement should exist. I'm telling them that it *will*.'

Twenty-five

Horse Sense

Toulac regarded the interloper balefully. 'I'm the person whose bed you're sleeping in.'

'But I'm not – I mean *it's* not,' the boy protested.

'*What?*'

'It's not your bed. It's mine.' The boy sat looking at her warily. 'That man – the innkeeper – put me in this room and told me I had to stay here.' His voice took on a note of complaint. 'He said he would bring me something to eat, but he never did. And I'm *starving.*'

By now, Toulac had recognised the accent. 'You're from Tiarond, aren't you?' The boy nodded, looking so utterly wretched that Toulac felt sorry for him. 'What did you say your name was, again?' she asked.

'Scall.'

'And what in the name of all that's holy are you doing *here?*'

'It wasn't my fault!' he blurted. 'I didn't want to come here. He made me!'

'Who made you?'

'The Summoner . . . Dark. He put me on my horse and did something to me so I couldn't move. It was horrible!'

Toulac interrupted quickly, heading off what looked ominously like tears. He was an adolescent boy – if he wept in front of her now, he'd be so embarrassed that she wouldn't get another word out of him. 'Whoa, back up there. Summoners belong with the Reivers. I thought you came from Tiarond.'

'I did.'

'Then how did you escape?'

'It's a long story,' Scall said. 'It started when my aunt asked me to take the trader's horses up to Mistress Toulac at the sawmill . . .'

'Now just hold on a minute, sonny. *I'm* Toulac from the sawmill.'

His eyes grew wide. 'You are? But how did you get here?'

'I am – and I'm also the one who is asking the questions right now. You'll get your turn later, if you're lucky. Why is it that I never saw a sign of you, or any horses? And who the bloody blazes is your aunt?'

'Smithmaster Agella. I'm – at least I was – her apprentice.'

Toulac smacked a hand against her forehead. 'Agella! That's it! I *knew* I recognised your face.' All at once, she realised that Scall's story really *was* going to be a long one. With a last, regretful look at her comfortable bed, she crossed the room, and built up the fire with an armful of logs, then patted one of the chairs beside the table. 'Come on. You said you were hungry, didn't you?'

Scall didn't need telling twice. He bounded out of bed and fell on the food like a starving wolf. Toulac pulled out a chair of her own, then grabbed her share of the meat pie before he could scoff the lot. 'All right,' she said. 'Let's have your story. Start at the beginning, and don't leave anything out.'

Scall's tale held a number of surprises for Toulac, one of them being that Scall had met Elion. An amazing number of things had been happening on the mountain, during her last couple of days in Callisiora, but the events that had happened to Scall since he left Tiarond with his companions were equally astonishing.

Worst of all was the news that the winged marauders had left Tiarond and were spreading through the country. Almost as bad, however, were the tidings of Grim's death. In her younger days, Toulac had made a good living as a mercenary fighting for various factions of Reivers against the others, and she had known Grim when he, too, had been young and vigorous – *very* vigorous, as she recalled. It had been years since she had seen him but his loss hit her hard, none the less. Another of her old friends had gone on and left her, and the world was a poorer place for his passing. It was strange, she reflected, how such news had a way of changing one's perspective. The loss of an old friend had suddenly brought home to her the value of her new ones.

And I can't leave them. How could I?

She realised that her mind had wandered from Scall's tale somewhere in the midst of his kidnapping, but now a rising note of protest and outrage brought her attention back to him. He was talking about his arrival in the Gendival settlement, and the loss of his beloved horse, that had been a gift from Elion.

And they wouldn't know that here, of course – or maybe the beast wasn't really Elion's to give away.

Toulac the horsewoman could understand Scall's misery. He had lost his home, his family, and his companions. Losing his little chestnut mare might not have seemed so very dreadful in comparison to all the other terrible things that had happened to him in recent days, but clearly she had been a tremendous comfort to him, and now she had been taken away.

Poor little bugger. It's just not fair. And I'm not going to stand by and let it happen!

'Listen,' she told Scall. 'I've a friend who has a lot of influence with the man who's running this place. I can't make any promises, you understand, but I'll have a word with her when I see her in the morning, and get her to talk to the Archimandrite.' She smiled at him. 'I reckon there's a good chance of us getting your little Firefly back for you.'

If only there was someone who could get Mazal back for me.

The boy's face lit up at her words. 'Really? You mean it? This is wonderful – I can't believe it. Thank goodness you were here.'

Toulac noted that he was far too excited about his chestnut mare to give any further thought to how or why *she* had come to be here. If she could do something about getting his precious horse back for him, that was all that mattered. Inevitably, her thoughts slipped back to Mazal. She could understand what Scall was going through. When she looked up again, she noted with dismay that his face had fallen once more. 'Now what?'

'How do I know they're looking after her properly? What if she's unhappy? What if she's scared?'

'Scall, that's hardly likely,' the veteran pointed out. 'If she came from here originally, then she'll be in her own stable, among familiar people. She'll be quite happy tonight.'

'But what if she misses me? I always visit her in the evening. Tormon says that routine is very important to a horse.'

Oh, blast Tormon to perdition!

Toulac sighed. 'Scall, if I take you to see your mare, and you assure yourself that she's all right, will you shut up?'

'Oh, Mistress Toulac, if you take me to see her, I'll do anything you say.'

'In that case, never, *ever* call me Mistress Toulac again, do you understand? Just plain Toulac will do. Now let's get going – and Scall, you've got to keep quiet. Olsam will be short-handed tonight, and Ailie is very preoccupied at present. If we can sneak out of here, then hopefully we might get back before anyone even notices we've gone.'

Toulac lurked on the landing, peering through the bannisters until the coast was clear. Then she beckoned to Scall to follow her, and they slipped out of the inn door with no one any the wiser. Dusk had fallen, and the villagers had all gone home for their evening meal. No one noticed the two fugitives as they crept along the deserted street. Once they were safely beyond the village, they hurried down the shadowy track by the river. Toulac was glad she had come this way earlier, and discovered the whereabouts of the stables. She was even more glad that the path was now illuminated by nets filled with glims, that were suspended from the boughs of trees.

When they reached the stables, the veteran pulled them down to lurk behind a hedge while she surveyed the place. Lamps still burned in the buildings, and folk were still moving to and fro as they settled the horses for the night. 'We'll have to wait for a while until everything's quiet,' Toulac whispered.

Time passed. Gradually, the stars came out overhead, and the lights in the stables began to go off, one by one. The evening held the chill of autumn, and the grass was soaked with dew. Toulac could feel Scall shivering beside her – in fact, sometimes, she could almost hear his teeth chattering – but he never once complained. Briefly, she toyed with the idea of letting him have her disreputable, fleece-lined coat, but common sense made her harden her heart. He was a damn sight younger than she was, he didn't get rheumatism, and if anybody should catch a chill from this escapade, it would be better all round if it were him, because he had more resilience to fight off illness.

Suddenly, a hideous shriek ripped through the darkness, as though someone were being tortured beyond all endurance. Scall jumped violently, and clung to Toulac, panting and shivering in terror. 'What . . . What . . . ?' His voice was a strangled squeak.

'It's all right,' she whispered. 'It's only a barn owl – a big, white bird.'

'Was something killing it?'

She was glad that the darkness hid her smile. She had forgotten that Scall was a city boy, born and bred. 'No, they always sound like that. Gives you quite a turn, coming out of the darkness, doesn't it? Don't get a shock if you see one – they fly absolutely silently, and they have huge, dark eyes that make them look like ghosts.'

'I'm glad you warned me,' Scall whispered. 'I hope Firefly is pleased to see me, after all this.'

'She will be – don't worry.'

Finally all was quiet, and Toulac judged that it was safe to go ahead. In the darkness, she poked Scall. 'You remember our backup plan, if everything goes wrong? Don't forget what I told you about being ready to run at a moment's notice. If anyone comes, I'll distract them, because I can get away with being out here, but you can't. Go straight back to the inn, and *don't* let anyone see you going inside. If they've found out that we were missing, and there's any trouble, get Ailie, and explain the whole thing to her. She'll take care of you until I get back. All right?'

'All right.' Scall sounded tense and excited.

'Come on, then. And for pity's sake, be quiet.'

They moved silently around the perimeter of the field, with Toulac keeping low, and Scall copying her clumsily. As she went on, it occurred to the veteran that she could probably have done this whole thing legitimately by contacting Veldan and Elion in mind-speech, explaining the situation, and getting her to arrange permission for the boy to visit his horse. So why hadn't she?

Partly because she didn't want to get into another conversation with the Loremasters tonight about whether she should stay or go, and partly because she was determined to show them – and Blade – that she was independent, and they couldn't tell her what to do. The main reason, however, if she were being honest with herself, was because sneaking around after nightfall was so much fun.

You daft old besom. Will you never grow up?

Not if I can help it!

When they reached the stable block and crept through the gate into the yard, a solitary light was burning in the tackroom. A lone figure could be seen through the window, sitting at a table writing something, against a backdrop of a wall covered in pegs for saddles, bridles, and other bits of paraphernalia. Toulac approved of the way this place was run. There should always be someone around at night, in case one of the horses was taken ill, or there was some other emergency. Of course, it didn't make things any easier for people who were trying to sneak in, but she could cope with that. She was pleasantly surprised that there were no dogs around, but she knew that some horses didn't like them. Mazal, for instance, couldn't stand to have them anywhere near him, and had disposed of one or two in his time, when they came within reach of his hooves. He had been bitten by a large dog when he was a foal, and had apparently been taking his revenge ever since.

Scall gave her a dig with his elbow and she realised, with some chagrin, that she had been letting her mind wander. Beckoning to him to follow, she slid around the yard, hugging the walls, until they reached the main door of the stables. Opening it only as far as she needed, she pushed the boy through, and hurried after him into the warm, horse-scented gloom. Only a little light came filtering through the windows, disguising the colours of the horses but, as they crept down the row of generous loose-boxes, Scall had no trouble recognising his mare. She nickered happily as he went to her, and Toulac caught her breath in alarm. 'Shush!' she said softly. 'Keep her quiet, Scall.'

The results were not what she had expected. As she spoke, absolute pandemonium broke out in the box at the far end of the row. There came a series of splintering crashes as a horse tried to kick its way through the door, and a loud, joyous whinnying that Toulac would have recognised anywhere. It couldn't be possible, but . . . Her heart leapt. 'Mazal,' she cried. 'Oh, Mazal!' Then she was in the box, tears running down her face, her arms round the stallion's neck as he nuzzled into her shoulder.

The stable door slammed open to reveal a stocky, square-jawed man carrying a pitchfork in one hand, and a lantern in the other. The sound of running feet in the yard outside revealed that he was not alone. 'What the bloody blazes . . . ?' he gasped. 'What are you doing with that horse?'

'What are you doing with my horse?'

Both of them spoke together. 'So he's *yours*,' the stableman said. 'I can see that he is. You're the first person who's been able to get anywhere near him since he was brought in. I had to lock the dogs away, and he bit two of the grooms, and kicked another one into the middle of next month. You don't know how glad I am to see you. I had planned to run him with some of the mares, but it seemed as if he was going to be impossible to handle. You'll be glad to see him safe, I reckon, a glorious beast like that. Er . . .' He hesitated. 'Would you mind if I did run him with my mares? I bet his foals would be something to see, and it would be nice for you if his line was to go on.'

'Of course I don't mind,' Toulac said. 'I'm sure the arrangement would suit everybody – especially Mazal. As long as I can have my pick of the foals, of course.'

The stableman chuckled ruefully. 'I thought you might say that.

Still, it's only fair.' From one horseman to another, they exchanged a conspiratorial smile, and the man held out his hand. 'I'm Harral. These are my stables.'

'I'm Toulac. It's good to meet you.'

A noise from the doorway made them both turn, and Toulac found herself the focus of a number of curious stares from the grooms who were gathered there. 'It's all right,' Harral said. 'Nothing to worry about. You can go back to bed.' She noticed that they all obeyed him without question.

Harral smiled at her. 'Now, where were we? Toulac, did you say your name was? Ah, yes. Now I remember. That was the name I was told. But who are you?' Harral asked her. 'You're not one of the Loremasters, and I don't recall seeing you in the village.'

'I only just got here,' Toulac admitted. 'I came from Callisiora with Loremaster Veldan. She said I had some talents that the Shadowleague could use.'

'Did she, now?' The man's bushy eyebrows went up. 'That would be just like Loremaster Veldan, all right. It's a good thing for you there's been a change of Archimandrite, though, or my guess is that you'd both have been in trouble. Cergorn didn't approve of bringing strangers here. You might be all right with Amaurn, though. He's a lot more easy-going.'

Toulac's eyes opened wide. 'He *is*? Are you sure we're thinking about the same Amaurn? The one who just came from Callisiora?'

'That's him, all right. You don't sound as if you like him much.'

'I've never had much cause to.'

'Really?' The bushy eyebrows lifted once more. 'I'm surprised at that, considering he brought your horse back for you, and all.'

The veteran gasped. 'He did *what*?'

'Didn't you know?'

'He brought Mazal here?' She couldn't seem to take it in.

'Rode it all the way himself – and I must say that *he* never had any problems.' He smiled. 'Now that fellow's a horseman, if ever I saw one. To the very bone.'

Rage flooded through Toulac. 'He *stole* Mazal? I don't believe this!

That son-of-a-bitch has stolen my horse! Of all the bloody nerve! I *told* Veldan he was an unscrupulous, treacherous snake.'

'No, no. Hold on a minute!' Harral had to shout to be heard. 'Didn't you hear me tell you? He brought it back for you.'

Toulac's tirade stopped abruptly. 'For *me*? Don't be daft! As if that nasty bugger would do anything for anyone but himself.'

Harral put a hand on her shoulder, keeping a wary eye on Mazal as he did so. 'Now, just calm down there, and listen to me. I reckon you've got the wrong idea about our new Archimandrite. He struck me as a real gentleman. He brought the horse to me himself, and told me to keep it for you. He gave me your name, and described you, and everything. Said your warhorse was a superb animal, and you'd be glad to have him back. He said to tell you thanks for the loan, and if you bred any foals from him, could he have one?' He chuckled. 'With everybody wanting foals the way they do, I reckon that stallion of yours is going to be a busy lad. Still, I dare say he won't object. *I* wouldn't, if I were in his shoes.'

'Blade – I mean Amaurn – brought Mazal all the way back here for *me*?' Toulac was undergoing some difficult readjustments to her thinking.

The stableman shrugged. 'That's what he said. Are you feeling all right?'

'Yes, I'm fine.' With an effort, Toulac gathered her wits about her. As she realised that Mazal had truly come back to her, a huge, daft grin spread across her face. 'I can't believe this,' she said. 'I thought I would never see him again.'

'I know exactly how you feel.' Harral was smiling too. 'You're not the only one who got a precious horse back today – only mine was a mare. It was pretty much the same thing, though. Some gormless Loremaster had gone and lost her, and I had despaired of ever seeing her again.'

Over his shoulder, Toulac saw Scall standing with his arms around Firefly's neck. His expression was stricken, but his eyes were beseeching her to help.

'Oh,' she said. 'The little chestnut mare.'

'How did you know about her?' the stableman asked in surprise. 'And hey, who's that boy there with her? You, lad! What do you think you're doing with my horse?'

'Harral,' Toulac said, 'I can explain. But I need to have a private word with you. Urgently.' Putting an arm through his, she steered him out of the stable towards the tackroom. As she passed Scall, she gave him a ferocious glare. '*Stay there!*' she hissed. She only hoped he would obey her. If he tried to run off with the mare now – and she could understand why he would be tempted – they both would be in trouble, and there would be no salvaging the situation.

All the way across the yard, Harral was trying to hang back. 'But what about that boy?' he demanded.

Toulac hurried him into the lamplit tackroom. 'Scall won't hurt your precious mare,' she told him. 'In fact, who do you think has been taking such excellent care of her while she's been away?'

'What? That young lad?'

'Yes. And that's what I need to talk to you about.' She sat down at the table. 'You wouldn't happen to have a drink handy, would you?'

'I don't hold with drinking around my horses,' Harral said sternly, 'but there's tea on the stove, if you'd like some.'

'That'll do just fine.' She yawned mightily. 'It would be better, in fact. I'm desperate for a good night's sleep. These last couple of days have been beyond belief.'

Harral grinned as he put the thick, black tea down in front of her, and sat down with his own cup. 'Sounds like foaling time,' he said. 'This should perk you up a bit. Now, tell me about this young lad, and what he has to do with my mare.'

Toulac told him the story as she had heard it from the boy. 'So you see,' she summed up, 'Elion actually *gave* the animal to Scall, and told him he could keep it. The poor lad thinks it's his now, and if he hadn't been brought here against his will, then you would probably never have known what had become of it. He's already lost his home, and probably his family in the fall of Tiarond. Please don't take the his precious horse away from him as well.'

Harral shook his head. 'That's all very well, Toulac, and I'm not saying I don't sympathise with the lad, but the mare wasn't Elion's to give away. She's one of the best I ever bred, and she's the joy of my heart. I saw you with your warhorse – you *know* what I mean. I couldn't believe my eyes when she came pelting back into my yard, all on her own, after that idiot Kher had gone and let her get scared by the Afanc. It was like a miracle.' He sighed. 'What can I do? I'm sorry for the boy, but Kher told me what was going on in Callisiora just now. There's no way I'm letting him, or anyone else, take her back there to be eaten by those accursed Ak'Zahar. She's staying here, where she's safe.'

'Well, I can understand that,' Toulac admitted. 'But it'll break Scall's heart to lose her.' She thought for a moment. 'Look, isn't there some way the two of you could compromise? I mean, what do you want out of this whole affair? You want the mare safe with you, and you want her bloodline – her foals. Why don't you let Scall stay here with her? He has a way with horses, and you must admit, he looked after her beautifully under some very difficult conditions. Surely you could find him work in your yard? Let him keep the mare on condition that she stays in Gendival, and work something out between you over her foals. You'd be getting a damn good worker, and let's face it, there's no future for the lad back in Callisiora. Don't you think he deserves a chance?'

Harral thought for a moment. 'It might work,' he said. 'I'm loath to let anybody else call her his own, but you're right – it would be hard on the boy to lose her after that imbecile Elion actually gave her to him.'

Toulac smiled. 'Thank you, Harral. You're a good man. You deserve all the foals that Mazal can get for you.'

He grinned back at her. 'Why do you think I've been so accommodating over this? I've got to stay on the right side of you, haven't I?'

'Come on,' said Toulac. 'Let's go and break the news to Scall. I can't wait to see his face.'

They were so pleased with their neat little plan, that neither of them was prepared for the boy's reaction. When they told him of Harral's generous offer, his face became a mask of horror. 'Stay here?' he gasped. 'But I *can't!*'

Toulac suddenly remembered why she'd never had any children. 'Myrial in a cesspit! Why the bloody blue blazes not?' she snapped. 'What's the matter with you, you stupid boy? You can't possibly want to go back to Callisiora.'

Why not? That's exactly what you *were planning.*

Toulac told her inner voice to shut up, and took a different tack with Scall. 'Come on,' she wheedled. 'This would be a fine, safe place for you to grow up. You'd have your mare, and you could build yourself a decent future here.'

Scall put his arms around the mare's neck, his face twisted in anguish. 'But what about my friends?' he said. 'What about Tormon and Rochalla? I can't just abandon them – especially now that the winged fiends have reached the Reiver lands.'

'Son,' Harral said gently, 'your loyalty does you great credit, but maybe you shouldn't be so hasty. After all, what difference could you make? *You* can't fight the Ak'Zahar . . .'

'I fought the one that Kher and the Summoner brought in,' the boy replied with great spirit. 'If it weren't for me, Dark would be dead now.'

'Well, that's as maybe,' Harral said. 'But you can't fight them all, and what it comes down to is a choice. If you want to stay here, there's a place for you, and welcome. If you choose to go back to Callisiora, you're welcome to do that too, as long as the Archimandrite says you can. But if you *do* go back, you'll go without the mare. I'm not letting her go away from here again, and that's final. And if you want my opinion, you'd be insane to go back to a land that's overrun with some of the most vicious creatures known to the Shadowleague. I'm sorry, lad, but you'll have to decide. There's a future for you here. There's none in Callisiora. I'm sure your friends – if they really *are* your friends – would tell you the same thing.'

'But . . .' Scall fell silent. Toulac felt sorry for him. She could understand what he was going through, since she was in a similar situation herself. She patted him on the shoulder. 'You think about it, sonny. Don't rush into anything – it's a big decision. But think very carefully. You'll never get a chance like this again.'

And neither will I.

Twenty-Six

An Unexpected Question

The quarters of the chieftain's son were a lot more luxurious than the rooms allotted to Seriema and her companions, and she frankly admitted to herself that she was enjoying the pampering. Cetain, trying to make amends for his father's earlier unpleasant behaviour, had invited her to dine with him and, guilty as she had felt about abandoning Tormon and Rochalla when they were so worried about Scall, she had decided that there was nothing additional she could contribute, and that the two who had been closest to the boy were better off keeping one another company. She would be better off with Cetain, she decided – and, if she needed to salve her conscience, she could always talk to the chieftain's son about riding out with another search party in the morning.

Seriema soon decided that she'd made the right decision. Cetain had been most welcoming. He had given her mulled wine to drink, which was especially good after her long, cold ride earlier that day. Furthermore, she knew that she could look forward to a far better supper than the scraps that Rochalla had been able to scrounge from the Reiver kitchens. Soon the two of them were seated in deep, comfortable chairs on either side of a roaring blaze, talking, thinking, and soaking up the warmth, and Seriema would never have believed that she could feel so at home and so comfortable in the company of a man – especially one she had known for such a short time.

There was a definite masculine ambience about the chamber, which was cosy but uncluttered. A table beneath the window was covered in a neat and businesslike array of leather-bound books, parchment scrolls, and paper written over in a dashing, sprawling hand. 'What are you studying?' Seriema asked, secretly impressed by the universal signs of scholarship. Warrior he might be, but clearly this was no thick-skulled barbarian.

'I'm trying to find out a little more about the history of this land of ours, and the part the Reivers have played in it,' Cetain told her. 'It was Grim who got me into it – he taught me to read, and write, and study, and a whole lot more besides.'

When he spoke of the Summoner, his expression became still and preoccupied, and Seriema, recognising pain when she saw it, reached out and touched his arm. 'It must have been a dreadful shock for you, to come back to the news that he'd been killed.'

'It was. I still can barely take it in. He was one of the best, and kindest men I've ever known – though I had to make him a solemn promise not to spread *that* around. I was lucky that he spotted the one child from Arcan's brood with an inquiring mind, and took me under his wing – though my parents were never very keen on the whole business. Until Grim took Dark as an apprentice, I think my father worried that he might select me. He would never admit it, but his relationship with the Summoners still has that edge of super-stition, the same as everyone else. I know most folk were afraid of Grim, but that stemmed from ignorance, mostly, and tradition. You know, mothers warning their children that if they were bad the Summoner would come and get them.' He smiled wryly. 'Of course, my mother never had to do that. The threat of telling our father was always enough to scare us into obedience.'

'Yet clearly Arcan liked Grim,' Seriema said. 'Though he was trying to conceal it, he was very upset about his death.'

'I'm sorry about the way my father acted towards you,' Cetain said. 'I think it comes of the clans all being so tightly knit, each one against all the rest. When something bad happens, his instinct is to close ranks against outsiders.'

She sighed. 'I know. I got the distinct feeling we weren't welcome here any more.'

'As far as I'm concerned, *you* are.' Cetain smiled at her, and gave her a very direct look.

Seriema, though far from displeased, wasn't used to having a man regard her in that way.

He can't be serious! What could he possibly see in an old maid like me?

Awkward and embarrassed, she scrambled to her feet. 'I just remembered. There's something I have to tell Tormon . . .'

'Not so fast, lass.' Cetain leapt up and put his arms around her. 'Whatever it is, you can tell him later.' Then, giving her no chance to escape him, he kissed her.

Seriema froze in his arms. 'Why did you do that?' she said suspiciously. 'There are lots of younger, prettier girls in the fortress. Why choose me?'

Cetain showed no sign of letting her go. 'Because I want to kiss you every time I see you, but I can never seem to get you alone. Because the girls in this fortress are fine lasses, to be sure, but none of them can hold a candle to you. Because I want to capture your strong, proud spirit for myself. Because I want to wed you, if you'll have me.' He took a deep breath. 'I want you to be quite certain that, though I'm moving very quickly here, and I've probably taken you by surprise, I'm absolutely serious.' He leant down and kissed her again, then gave her a wicked smile. 'And because I've been longing to get you into my bed ever since I first set eyes on you.'

'*What?*' It was hardly the most graceful of responses, but Seriema was reeling with shock. She absolutely couldn't believe what she had heard.

'That's not exactly the reaction I was hoping for.' Cetain spoke in injured tones. 'Which word are you having the most trouble with? Bed, or wed? Or is it both? Is the merchant queen of Tiarond too grand for the younger son of a brigand chieftain?'

'What?' She couldn't seem to get beyond that word. 'I'm not, I mean, I don't, I . . . Oh, blast you, Cetain! Stop playing games with me! You've had your little joke at the expense of a plain old maid, and it's gone far enough.' Her vision shimmered with tears. Cursing herself for a fool, she tore herself out of his grasp, dragged a sleeve across her face, and made a dash towards the door.

Somehow, he got there before her, and captured her in his arms again. 'Whoa! Just hold on there, you daft woman.' He held her tightly, so that she had no choice but to look at him. 'Now, I don't know whether it's true about you being a maid – though I plan to find out before very much longer . . .' Again, there was that white flash of a grin. 'But don't you *ever* let me hear you describing yourself as plain and old again. Do you hear me?'

'Well, I'm older than you,' Seriema muttered.

'Not by much, you're not, you idiot.' Leaning down, he kissed her forehead. 'You know what I think, lass? Those years of shouldering all your responsibilities as the head of a mercantile empire have made you *feel* old, long before your time. You did a truly remarkable job, and all the more so because you had to manage all alone, with no one to help you, or take care of you when you were tired, or sad, or at your wits' end. I think you must have been very much alone for most of your life – but all that's over now. If you stay with me, I'll make damn sure that you're never lonely again.'

Seriema shook her head. 'But *why?*'

'Aaagh!' Letting go of her, Cetain waved his arms in frustration. 'Because I *love* you, you irritating woman! I fell in love with you the very first day I saw you. There – I've said it. What more do you want? Do I have to spell it out for you? Do I have to write it on the wall in blood?'

'But . . .'

'Oh, I've had enough of this.' Before she knew what was happening, he had swept her up in his arms, carried her across the room, and dumped her unceremoniously on the bed. 'Right,' he said. 'You won't believe me when I tell you, so I'm going to *show* you. And what's more, I'm going to keep on showing you until you do believe me – supposing we have to stay here for a month.'

It didn't take a month. Sometime during the next couple of hours, Seriema's scepticism melted away in the face of Cetain's determination. He didn't push her or force her – but he wouldn't let her get off the bed either. He lay beside her, holding her, talking to her, and kissing her, until she began to relax, and respond to him. Though Seriema felt awkward, uncomfortable, and shy, he was patient and gentle. Eventually she came to trust him, and said goodbye to the old maid of Tiarond for ever.

Seriema awakened to find the grey light of early morning glinting through the cracks in the shutters. When she realised where she was, her eyes flew open in a mingling of amazement, delight, and dismay. How on earth could she have behaved in such a wanton fashion? And why hadn't she thought of it years ago?

Because the right man never came along, that's why.

But what if he wasn't the right man? What if he hadn't really meant what he'd said last night? She rolled over, to find an empty bed.

Damn him! I knew it!

She wanted to cry, but beneath it all was the empty satisfaction of having been right, after all. Everything was back to normal. The only person she could really trust was herself. Then, just at that moment, the door swung inward, shouldered open by a half-dressed Cetain, who sidled in bearing a perilously tilting tray. He looked across at her and smiled. 'I thought you might be hungry,' he said. 'I seem to have worked up a tremendous appetite, myself.'

Though Seriema felt herself going very red, she couldn't help herself from bursting out into an enormous grin. She felt ridiculously happy to see him. Not even the inevitable porridge, oatcakes and cheese could put a damper on her spirits, and she didn't crave her morning cup of tea as much as she normally did. It seemed, however, that she was not to get her breakfast yet. Cetain put the tray down on the table, and came and lay down beside her on the bed, putting a possessive arm across her body and easing himself up on one elbow so he could look down into her eyes. 'Well?' he asked her. 'Have you slept on it? And what's the answer?'

She blinked at him. 'Slept on what?'

He sighed. 'My question, of course. The one from last night, that you so conveniently dodged. Have you made up you mind yet? Will you be my lifemate?'

Seriema gasped. 'You mean, you meant it?'

He smacked his palm against his forehead. 'May the gods of heath and tarn preserve us! Of *course* I meant it!'

'You did?'

He drew back and glared at her. 'You're really pushing your luck, lass.'

'Yes,' Seriema whispered, hardly able to get the word out around the lump in her throat. 'I would love to be your lifemate. So get out of that, if you can.'

Cetain let out an enormous whoop, and crushed her in a hug that made her ribs creak. 'I never want to get out of it for as long as I live.' He kissed her soundly. 'Truly, I thought you would never say yes.'

Seriema laughed, and used a corner of the blanket to wipe tears of happiness from her eyes. 'I can't believe it,' she said. 'When Tiarond fell, I thought I'd lost everything. I didn't realise then, what a fortune was waiting for me, just around the corner.'

'There, now, lass – you'll have me blushing in a moment. Do you want some breakfast?'

'I'm absolutely starving,' she admitted. 'Even cold porridge is starting to look pretty good, right now.'

Cetain tucked the blanket around her shoulders. 'I'll put some more wood on the fire, before you freeze.'

They didn't linger over breakfast – it wasn't the most delicious meal in the world, and the room really was too cold for sitting around in a state of undress. When they had finished, Cetain took her hand. 'Well, lass? Shall we go and break the good news to my mother and father?'

'Let's hope I won't come as a terrible disappointment to them,' Seriema said doubtfully. Suddenly, she felt terribly nervous.

'You won't.' Cetain looked sheepish. 'I, er . . . I already took the liberty of mentioning my plans to my family. When I was talking to my father yesterday, I had already made up my mind to ask you and I was thinking about it so much that it – it just came out. So they knew, you see, what I was going to do.'

Seriema gaped at him. 'You already *told* them? What if I'd said no?'

'Well, in that case, I would need all the sympathy I could get.'

'And they didn't *mind*?'

He shrugged. 'Well, there was a bit of grumbling at first about our Reiver girls not being good enough – you know the sort of thing. So I reminded them that if I hadn't fixed on one of our own lasses by now, it wasn't likely that I would, so my only option would be to look to another clan. You'd be astonished at how fast they changed their minds at that point. My father said that, as far as he was concerned, you had already proved yourself to be one of us when you rode out with me and my men, and my mother decided that you still were the heir to a great fortune, if Tiarond should somehow be resurrected, and that would all be to the benefit of the clan.'

'Huh,' Seriema snorted. 'I hope she's not holding her breath. But as long as they're both happy, they can think what they like.'

Cetain smiled, and let out a sigh of relief. 'I'm glad you don't mind,' he said. 'Shall we go and tell them now?'

'Wait,' Seriema protested. 'At least let me wash, first.'

'Of course.' He kissed her again. 'Who would have believed that you'd really be a maid? Well it's said that the men of Tiarond have too much between their ears, and naught between their legs! Though personally, I'd have said that they had naught between their ears either, to have let you pass them by. I really am most uncommonly pleased with myself, to have come by such a treasure.'

Such was Seriema's awkwardness with men, that she still was unsure whether he wasn't having some dreadful joke at her expense. Nor was she used to discussing such intimate matters. Her face flaming, she fled behind the curtain to the area where he kept ewer and basin. Looking at herself in the polished silver mirror propped on a shelf, she still couldn't believe that he could have chosen her. Her face was the same, plain, old-maid's face – or was it? She had to admit that the last few days had wrought some changes. All the riding in the fresh air had given her sallow cheeks some colour, and her recent antics had brought brightness to her eyes and a glow to her entire demeanour that had never been there before. For once, because she didn't have a headache from poring over reports, inventories and balance-sheets, her thick, dark brows weren't all screwed up together, and her new habit of wearing her hair loose and unconfined had softened her heavy jaw, and was a better frame for the strong bone structure of her face. Happiness had somehow softened and relaxed her, and though she would never look pretty, she had certainly been transformed.

Amazing. Everything's still there, just as it ever was – but somehow, it all looks totally different.

She began to wash herself, with much brisk splashing, in cold water. After a moment, a hand appeared around the edge of the curtain, holding a gently steaming kettle. 'We wouldn't want anything to freeze, now, would we?' said a cajoling voice. In spite of her blushes, Seriema burst out laughing.

She had just finished dressing when there was a knock on the door. She recognised him as Lewic, Cetain's older brother – so far, the only one that she had met. One of them, the next youngest to Cetain, had been killed the previous year when another clan had raided their cattle. Two of them, she knew, were not yet out of childhood, and the others were at various stages of adolescence, the oldest of the three being about the same age as Scall. Seriema hoped she'd get them sorted out eventually.

Lewic, bearded and more burly than his brother, but with the same dark red hair, smiled at her. 'Well?' he demanded of his brother. 'Did she say yes?'

Cetain put his arm around her shoulders. 'She certainly did.'

The bearded warrior let out a loud whoop, and hugged his brother, then Seriema. 'Well done, lass, and welcome to the family.' He winked at her. 'And I owe you my thanks. The stakes were running high last night. I've just won myself a damn good sword from Attan, because you said yes.'

Cetain, who had desperately been trying to hush his brother, groaned, and buried his face in his hands. Seriema turned on him in a flash of anger. 'Did you tell the whole bloody *fortress* about this?'

He backed away from her. 'Seriema, I didn't. I swear!' He glared at his older brother. 'I can guess who did, though.'

Lewic only grinned, but she was too happy that morning to stay angry at him. 'I just hope it *was* a damn good sword,' she said sweetly, 'since you're no doubt planning to give it to Cetain as a wedding present.'

Cetain roared with laughter at his brother's chagrin, and Lewic shook his head. 'The Reivers have always been known as a parcel of rogues,' he said. 'I can see that you'll fit in just fine.'

'So what brings you here so early in the day?' Cetain asked. 'Were you really so desperate to collect on your wager?'

Lewic sobered. 'I wish that *was* all,' he said. 'I finally persuaded our father that Seriema would be on our side and he, with his usual thoughtfulness and sensitivity, demanded that I bring the knife to her straight away, to see if she could identify it.'

'What, *now?*' Cetain scowled. 'Lewic, you can't be serious!'

His brother shrugged. 'It wasn't my idea. I'm sorry, both of you, for spoiling what should be such a happy time.'

'It's all right,' Seriema said quickly. 'Grim's murder was a dreadful thing, and I'm willing to help if I can. But why is Arcan so sure that the murder had something to do with us?'

'Not you,' Cetain corrected her quickly. 'You weren't even there at the time. You were out on the moor with me.'

Seriema waved that distinction aside. 'Well, my friends, then.'

'Did Tormon not tell you about the knife?' Lewic asked in some surprise.

'Knife? No, he didn't mention one, but Rochalla and Annas came back and interrupted us before we'd finished talking. What knife?'

'It was found by Grim's body, covered in blood. It's not a Reiver knife, Seriema. I'm sorry, but it came from Tiarond.' Lewic put a hand into the deep pocket of his jerkin. 'I have it here.' He pulled out a cloth-wrapped bundle, handling it with some distaste, and handed it to her. With a similar feeling of revulsion, she took it from him and unwrapped it carefully.

At the sight of the weapon, a chill went through Seriema. The haft and blade were encrusted in dried blood, but she would have recognised it anywhere. She had seen it in its owner's hands on several occasions, during the journey from Tiarond. The gruesome find trembled in her hands, and she looked at Cetain with eyes that were wide with dismay. 'This belongs to Presvel,' she said softly.

Quickly, Cetain took the knife from her, wrapping it in its cloth again, for which Seriema was extremely grateful. She was glad to get the horrible thing out of her sight. Lewic poured her a cup of wine from the flagon on the table, and she took a grateful swallow. 'You're absolutely sure?' he asked.

She nodded. 'He picked it up when we left Tiarond. It's a Godsword knife. I have one, too. We armed ourselves from the Godsword guardhouse just before we left the plateau.'

'But doesn't that mean that you all have one?' Cetain asked with a frown. 'And aren't the Godsword weapons standard issue?'

Seriema shook her head. 'Tormon didn't take one at all. He already had a knife of his own. The rest of us did, but Presvel was a bit smug, because he had found an officer's knife, while the rest of us had ordinary ones. It had silver banding round the handle – just like the one you have there. I happened to be with him when he found it, and he offered it to me – that's how I know about it. I don't think anyone else was around just then.' She sighed, and took another sip of wine. 'He seemed so pleased with it, I told him to keep it for himself.'

'It's just as well that you did,' Lewic said softly. 'At least we can identify the murderer now.'

'But how *could* it be Presvel?' Seriema cried. 'He's just a clerk, for Myrial's sake! I was just saying to Tormon last night that he hardly knows one end of a knife from the other. In all his life he's never done anything more violent than swat a fly! How did he come to this?'

Cetain shook his head. 'Who can say?'

Seriema got up and began to pace. 'If only I had spoken to him sooner. Maybe there would have been some way to head this off. I noticed – we all did – that he'd started to behave a bit strangely since we were forced to leave the city. He's been spending a lot of time alone, and he has some kind of infatuation with Rochalla, though I don't think she reciprocates . . .' She stopped, and frowned. 'In fact, I think they must have known one another before all this happened, because it was Presvel who brought her into my house to take care of Annas, when we thought she was an orphan.'

She began to walk back and forth again. 'You know, Grim's murder might well have been a dreadful accident. Because of Presvel's obsession, I think he had grudges against both the other men in our party . . .'

'Scall?' Lewic's eyebrows went up. 'You call that youngster a man?'

'He's old enough,' Seriema said wryly, 'and I happen to know that he and Rochalla have been seeing a bit of each other since we got here.'

'Ah. That might explain a lot.'

'It may have been that he was trying to kill Tormon or Scall, but somehow Grim got in the way,' she suggested.

'But there can still be no excuse for him, lass,' Cetain said quietly. 'Even if what you suggest is true, and it may well be, the intent to kill was still there. Whatever the true circumstances were, surrounding Grim's murder, they still point to Presvel being a very desperate and dangerous man.'

Seriema stopped pacing, and bit her lip. 'There's no help for it, is there? We're going to have to go to Arcan with this information.' She paused, then spoke again in a very small voice. 'What will they do with him?'

Cetain put his arms around her, and held her close. 'They'll hang him. I'm sorry, lass.'

The news was very hard to take. For years now, Presvel had been her assistant, her shadow, her confidant, and, frankly, the nearest thing she'd had to a friend. Now it seemed the efficient, unassuming clerk had lost his sanity and turned into a murderer. Presvel would die a horrible death, strangling at the end of a rope – and it would be her evidence which would put that rope around his neck.

For a few minutes Seriema let herself be comforted by her life-mate-to-be, then firmly, she pulled herself together. Slipping out of Cetain's embrace, she walked to the fireplace, wiping away her tears as she went, and took another draught of her wine. When she turned back again, her eyes were dry and her breathing steady. 'Come on, then. There's no point in putting this off. Let's go and tell your father now.'

Presvel had it all worked out. In his plan to shift the blame for Grim's murder to one of his companions he had, after some thought, decided to implicate both Tormon and Rochalla. It was only fair. After she had betrayed him by running after Scall and the trader, she deserved whatever was coming to her. Besides, he'd discovered that she had taken Annas off to bed at more or less the same time as Scall had left the great hall, so chances were that she and Tormon had been together at the time of Grim's death. If both of them did not appear to be guilty, then one could exonerate the other.

And what had she been doing with Tormon, when they were together? Had she been allowing the older man to put his hands on her, as she had with the boy? The slut deserved to bear the blame for this whole mess. Had it not been for her, none of it would have happened.

The first thing that Presvel had done was to steal himself another weapon – a Reiver knife, this time. Though the feel of it in his hand filled him with revulsion, he knew that it was best to be prepared. Secondly, he stole the Godsword knife that Rochalla had taken from the guardhouse. She had never really wanted it in the first place, and had never used it. He had taken it from the small bundle of oddments that were all her belongings and, with luck, she wouldn't even notice it had gone.

He had also managed to steal a jerkin and a shawl, respectively, from the selection of clothes that Tormon and Rochalla had managed to put together thanks to the charity of the Reivers. A chicken, killed the previous night while it roosted, had provided the blood with which he had daubed the clothing and the knife so convincingly, though he still couldn't believe how much harder it was to deliberately kill the fowl, than it had been to kill the old man by accident.

Now it was time for the next step of his plan. This morning he would take the weapon and the bloodstained garments to Seriema, say that he had found them hidden in Tormon's room, and let her do the rest. Presvel wrapped the gory bundle in an old sack, and went in search of her.

At first he couldn't believe it when he discovered that the Lady was with the chieftain's son, and as for the gossip that was running through the fortress like wildfire – well, that was just impossible. On reflection, however, he decided that in the unlikely event that the rumours were true, then things might well work out for the best. This business of Cetain asking Seriema to be his lifemate had distracted everyone from the murder, and while the focus of their attention was elsewhere, his story might be accepted much more easily. If he sought out Seriema right now, while she was with the chieftain's son, then whether she had said yes or no, they would both have their minds on other things, and Arcan would hear his version of events all the quicker. Moreover, a barbarian like that would surely be more inclined to take the objects at face value, and not ask the awkward questions that might have occurred to the astute Seriema.

Presvel paused outside Cetain's door, his hand frozen in the act of knocking, as he heard the murmur of voices from within. His curiosity getting the better of him, he lowered his hand, he put his ear to the door instead.

When Presvel heard what they were saying, however, he almost stopped breathing, and his guts twisted in fear. Lewic, the chieftain's oldest son, was there too. And he had the knife! That accursed Reiver brigand was showing Seriema the knife.

Will she recognise it? Oh please, Myrial, don't let her identify it as mine! And if she does, please don't let her say anything!

For a moment, he dared to hope. Maybe it would be all right. Surely, after he had served her so well and so faithfully for so many years, she wouldn't betray him out of hand, without giving him a chance to explain himself first. Then the floor seemed to fall away from under him as he heard her identify the weapon as his.

Dropping his gory bundle, Presvel fled. There'd be no chance now for him to shift the blame. The time for subterfuge was past. When he reached the bottom of the staircase, however, and the more populated areas of the fortress, he had the sense to force himself to slow down, and walk along as if everything was normal. It wasn't easy. Though he knew it made no sense, he felt that every eye was on him.

There hadn't been enough time yet for Seriema and Cetain to go to Arcan with their information. He expected that they would want to talk things through a little, first. Despite the damning evidence of the knife, he hoped that Seriema would find it difficult to accept that he could do such a thing.

I still find it very hard to believe, myself.

It wouldn't take them very long, though, to make up their minds. Soon they would go to the chieftain. He would have a brief respite while they talked to Arcan – and then the hunt would be up. The hand of everyone in this place would be raised against him. Presvel's mind raced as he tried desperately to think of a way to save himself. Even if he fled the stronghold now, Arcan's men would pursue him in order to exact their vengeance. They knew these moors far better than he did, and they were far more accomplished horsemen. They would catch him easily and, he suspected, they wouldn't even bother to bring him back to explain that it had all been a terrible accident. They would slaughter him then and there, and leave his body for the buzzards.

You need a hostage.

The calm inner voice of his intellect cut through the brute panic of the hunted animal. Presvel stopped in his tracks. Of course! Why hadn't he thought of it sooner? If he had a hostage with him, how would they dare approach him? Shreds of a plan began to come together in his mind. He might even make it back to the city, and hide in those tunnels that Scall had found. Surely he would be safe from the winged fiends down there?

All that remained was the choice of his victim, but it took little thought to decide who he should take with him. Tormon's child, of course. She was small, and weaker than him, so that he could capture her without much effort, and she could easily be cowed. Besides, it would be a perfect way to get back at that insufferable itinerant peddler, and show him that city-bred Presvel was a force to be reckoned with after all.

He knew that he would have to make his preparations quickly. Turning, he went down a different corridor, to the kitchens. During the previous day, he had been too nervous to eat, so he was owed a substantial amount in the way of rations. He chose oatcakes, cheese, and cold meat, and wrapped them in a discarded apron when no one was looking. Then, moving quickly now, he headed for the stables. Once there, he saddled both the animal he had ridden from Tiarond, and one of the Reiver horses. He had a vague idea in the back of his mind, from something he had read, no doubt, that he would make much quicker time if he had a spare mount, so that he could change when one of them got tired. He hid his supplies in a pile of hay nearby, unaware that the man he'd killed had done the very same thing, and hurried back upstairs.

A quick check assured him that Tormon was in the great hall, eating an early breakfast. That would mean that the brat would probably still be in bed by now. It was a real stroke of luck that her father wasn't with her. Would Rochalla be minding her? If that was the case, there might just be a change of plan . . .

It had taken an age to get Annas off to sleep the previous night. Rochalla had been well on the way through her supply of stories before she realised that the child was playing her up because she wanted to be downstairs with her father, and listen to the storyteller in the great hall. A brief battle of wills had followed, but the blonde girl's firmness had eventually prevailed.

This morning, however, it was a different story, and Annas simply had not wanted to wake up. Rochalla had offered to watch the child so that Tormon could have breakfast, then go and see to the horses. Now that Scall had gone, he was really missing the boy's help, and needed to take extra time to do the additional work.

Having managed to rouse her at last, Rochalla was helping the child to dress, to the accompaniment of the usual string of questions. It was hard to be patient, and answer cheerfully. She felt very tired this morning. Annas was a demanding bundle of energy, and took a lot of looking after. Part of the trouble, of course, was that she had still not adjusted to her mother's death. The sudden disappearance of Scall, another member of her small, immediate circle, hadn't helped either. The poor little thing was very insecure, needing constant attention and reassurance – and stopping at nothing to make sure she got them. Hopefully, she would settle down with time. She deserved to be happy. She was a lovely child, with such a droll way of looking at the world that Rochalla often found it hard to hide her laughter. She didn't feel like laughing today, however – not when she was worried sick about Scall. Until Annas had awakened there had been nothing to distract her, and nothing to do but think, and fret, and worry about the gawky, gangling boy who had somehow, before she was aware of it, stumbled awkwardly into her heart.

Poor Scall. Where are you now? Are you all right? Are you hurt? Are you . . .

The thought of him being dead was too horrible to contemplate. Yet Seriema had said that there were winged demons about on the moor, and Tormon had been unable to track the boy beyond the valley of the Curtain Walls.

But he didn't find any – remains – either.

Rochalla clung to that thought, and hoped. She was tempted to pray, but remembered all the prayers she had wasted on her brothers and sisters when they were ill. After she had buried the last one, little Derla, she had railed against Myrial, and vowed that she would never pray again, and she had seen or heard nothing since that would persuade her to change her mind. Indeed, if Myrial existed, then He had let Anna's mother and Tormon's beloved lifemate be murdered, too – and in front of the child's eyes, at that. And what about all the hundreds of dead in Tiarond, actually slaughtered during a religious ceremony? How could Myrial have permitted such a thing? If He existed at all, Rochalla had no time for such a cruel deity.

As she brushed Annas's hair, she heard the sound of footsteps approaching along the stone-flagged passage. Rochalla wondered if Tormon could be coming back already. She hoped so. Then she could get off to her own room for some well-earned sleep – if she *could* sleep, when Scall was lost somewhere, out on the bleak moors. As the door opened, she turned towards it – and the welcoming smile dropped from her face.

Presvel. Oh no – not now! I just can't cope with him these days.

She got to her feet. 'What brings you here . . .' The words died on her lips as he shouldered his way past her. He made a grab for Annas, and suddenly he had one hand across her mouth, and a knife at her throat. Rochalla made an involuntary movement forward, and froze as the blade twitched against the child's neck.

'Don't move – either of you,' Presvel said in a calm, almost conversational voice. 'I know how much this brat means to you, Rochalla, and want to reassure you that I mean her no harm – unless, that is, you do something stupid like calling out, or trying to run away. Now, we're going to take a little walk down to the stables. You'll stay in front of me, in my sight the whole time. If you make one wrong move, or say one wrong word, Tormon will be short of a daughter as well as a lifemate. When we reach the stables we're going for a little ride. I'm taking you back to Tiarond.'

Rochalla gasped. The city? Presvel had been acting very strangely these last few days, but he must truly have lost his mind to propose such a thing! A chill ran through her. Such desperate behaviour could only mean that he was the Summoner's murderer – and a man who had killed once could kill again. 'Presvel,' she said carefully, 'I would love to go back to Tiarond with you. But what about the winged fiends?'

'We'll take our chances,' Presvel said shortly. 'Now, move!'

Twenty-Seven

Revelations

The members of what Amaurn was coming to regard as his own little band of conspirators spent the night at Veldan's house. The only exceptions were Kyrre, who had gone to spend some time with her own people; Maskulu who, with the best will in the world, wouldn't fit inside; and Bailen, who wanted to visit his friend and fellow Listener Dessil, who was still recovering from being stung by a Dierkan on the night the dreadful creatures had raided the inn.

The sleeping arrangements didn't quite turn out as planned. Originally, Veldan had only offered Amaurn a bed at her house. Maskulu's dark, dank dwelling was a sanctuary in times of trouble, but it was no place for a wounded man to recuperate. However, until word came back from Kalevala that the Takuru assassin had been neutralised, it was best if the Archimandrite had a powerful body-guard, and Kaz could fulfil that role. Furthermore, Amaurn had been missing from the settlement for hours now. It was important that he be seen by the Shadowleague, and make his presence felt. Veldan's house was a much more central place from which to run things – though she had warned him not to get too comfortable. 'Decide whether you want to build a new place, or convert one of the existing ones,' she'd told him, 'but whatever you decide, get the artisans from the village working on it as a matter of priority. The Archimandrite needs his own dwelling. It's the hub of his power. And besides, Kaz and I want you out from under our feet as soon as possible. I'm not having the entire Shadowleague trooping in and out of my home all day while you run your administration from my best armchair.'

So it had been decided that Amaurn would go home with Veldan, and Elion would take Dark to stay with him for the night, as Ailie already had Zavahl, Toulac, and Scall at the inn, with one room out of commission as a result of the Dierkan attack. In the end, however, it hadn't happened that way. Elion and the Summoner called in at Veldan's house on the way back home, and that was as far as they got.

On the way from Maskulu's dwelling to that of Veldan and Kaz, the firedrake had taken Amaurn to the outskirts of the settlement on his back, then the Archimandrite had walked the rest of the way with the surreptitious support of Elion and Veldan, who walked on either side of him, ostensibly deep in conversation but, in reality, ready to put out a helping hand if he should falter or stumble.

In a community of telepaths, it was difficult to keep all emotions under control. Wherever he went, Amaurn caught spreading ripples of feelings – some disappointed and some relieved to see him again. He hadn't even been missing for a whole day, but clearly it hadn't taken long for the rumours to start flying. Luckily, Maskulu had come along too, bringing with him Dark's bound Ak'Zahar captive. Having given some thought to the young man's notion of having a live foe to study, Amaurn had been very impressed. Grim's apprentice was exactly the sort of new blood, intelligent and unafraid of new ideas, that was needed in the Shadowleague. And of course, the appearance of such a dangerous predator in their midst, and Amaurn's instructions that a safe, and extremely secure, housing was to be designed and built for it at once, was enough to set tongues wagging with a vengeance, distracting everyone from the Archimandrite's mysterious disappearance.

After her attempt on his life, Amaurn had contemplated having his unavoidable confrontation with Syvilda that night but, at the urging of Elion and Veldan, he had decided to put it off until the following morning. Word of his return would soon be reaching her, and she would know that Vifang had failed. Furthermore, if the Takuru leader had been true to her word, Cergorn's lifemate would never hear from her assassin again, and she would never get another – not a shapeshifter, at any rate. In addition, Kalevala's spies were already in position around her. She would not be able to make a move without Amaurn knowing of it immediately. He wondered how she would react when she discovered that her plots had come to naught, and allowed himself a cold, mirthless smile of triumph.

The Takuru are mine, now.

Amaurn's triumph only lasted as far as Veldan's house. When he crossed the threshold his mind was flooded with memories of Aveole and, even after all this time, he was almost felled by the wrenching pain of her loss. He staggered, and Veldan and Elion closed in on either side to support him. 'Come on,' Veldan said. 'That walk has taken a lot out of you. You had better lie down for a while.'

He turned, his footsteps unerringly taking him towards the door that led to the staircase, and Veldan looked at him with her eyebrows raised. 'I see you've been here before.'

'I – I used to come and visit your mother here.' Somehow, Amaurn could not bring himself to meet her eyes. To his relief, she didn't comment, but led the way upstairs, and opened another door off the landing. 'There you are.' She gave him a penetrating look, but her tones were very neutral. 'You should be comfortable here. It used to be my mother's room. I don't use it for myself, because I had another one built on the ground floor when I had the house remodelled, so that Kaz and I could sleep together. I keep this upper storey for guests now, otherwise it doesn't get used at all.'

Veldan pushed open a familiar door, and within minutes Amaurn found himself in Aveole's bed. Just then Elion came upstairs with a glass of water, and the two Loremasters closed the curtains and made sure that he was comfortable before they left him, promising to be back with some tea and some hot food in a while, once they had got themselves organised.

They might as well have strapped him to a rack.

How well he knew this room! Some of the happiest times of his life had been spent here. And because Veldan didn't use it for herself, she had never bothered to change the colours or the furnishings. Aveole's presence was everywhere; so powerful that he was almost convinced he'd find her lying beside him, if he only turned his head. But she would never come here again, except maybe as a restless spirit. All those years ago she had died, and he had not been with her. He had thought he'd been protecting her by not telling her his whereabouts when he had fled Cergorn's death sentence. Following his brush with the assassin, however, when Maskulu had taken him to his dwelling and they had been waiting for Kyrre and Bailen to arrive, the senior Loremaster had finally been persuaded to tell him what happened to Aveole once he had gone. Apparently her child had been conceived during their last, desperate meeting in the tower, the night she had helped him to escape. As the days passed into a month, then two, then three, without him getting word to her, however, she had finally begun to lose hope. Apparently she had left the settlement before her pregnancy had begun to show, so that Cergorn couldn't know for certain that her child had been fathered by Amaurn the renegade. For some time she vanished without trace, and no one knew where she had been when she was found, dying of a fever, on the borders of Gendival, all alone save for a small child and a firedrake egg.

Amaurn, however, knew exactly where Aveole had been. To have got the egg, she must have made the near-impossible journey, alone and pregnant, to the hidden lands of his people. She must have assumed that he'd gone back there. The thought of her fruitless journey tore his heart.

Forgive me, Aveole! I always meant to get word to you when my position was secure, but I never thought it would take so long! I was too caught up in my own loss, my own bitterness, my own plans for revenge, to realise the anguish you must have been feeling, and the desperate courage it must have taken to go through your pregnancy, homeless and alone. If only I had sent for you – but I was afraid that through you, Cergorn would track me down. I loved you so much. How could I have been so thoughtless and selfish and cruel? If it weren't for me, you might still be alive today.

While he was in Callisiora, Amaurn had always managed to block out any thoughts of his beloved's death, because he couldn't bear to believe that he would never see her again. Here, in her house, in her room, he accepted the truth at last, and the part he had inadvertently played in her death. Burying his face in his hands, he wept scalding tears of anguish and remorse, mourning for the love that he had lost, and all the barren, wasted years that they might have spent together, in joy, if only Aveole had lived.

When Elion went downstairs, Veldan hung back, and ducked into the other, smaller bedroom. She didn't want to talk to Elion and Dark, or even her beloved Kaz, just yet. She had too much on her mind, and she needed a brief time alone, to think. Her suspicions about her relationship to the new Archimandrite, which had been growing for a while, were getting stronger.

Amaurn seemed to like and trust her more, somehow, or in a different way, than he trusted her companions. If she wasn't mistaken, he seemed to rely on her more. Yet the first time they had met, on the mountain above Tiarond, she had seen the naked shock, almost akin to fear, on his face.

Just as if he had seen a ghost.

And was she imagining things, or had she discerned an odd guardedness about Maskulu's behaviour when he saw them together: a feeling somewhere between speculation, interest, and a sort of wry humour?

In addition, why did she feel so oddly drawn to Amaurn? Why was it that every time they met, she seemed to be drawn into defending and supporting him, even though she knew perfectly well what he had been like as Lord Blade?

Why wasn't she uneasy around him? Most people seemed to be nervous of him, for one reason or another.

He had said he was a good friend of her mother.

He knew the way to Aveole's bedroom.

And through the wall now, she could hear the sound of weeping: deep, racking sobs that bespoke the misery and abandonment of a wretched, tormented heart that was overcome by a grief beyond all bearing.

Veldan found that she was trembling; torn between hope and fear and doubt. Did she really want a man like Amaurn, with his shadowy past and reputation for ruthlessness, to be her father? And if he was, did she really want to know? She was well aware that the most sensible course of action would be to march next door immediately, and demand some answers of Amaurn, but somehow, she couldn't seem to find the nerve.

This particular room looked out upon the wooded hillside which climbed steeply behind the house. Veldan went to the window, her eyes seeking the nearby forest clearing where her mother had been buried. She rested her forehead against the cool glass, and sighed. 'I wish you'd told me,' she said softly. 'Couldn't you have left me something – a letter, a message, a clue? I wish I could have known you, Mother. I wish you were here right now, to tell me the truth.'

'You don't need her, sweetie. I think you already know the truth.' Even though Kaz couldn't get upstairs, he was still hovering close to her in his thoughts. She was glad that he was there. It was such a comfort to know that, even in these uncertain times, they would always have each other, and that would never change as long as they both lived.

Veldan straightened, and took a deep breath. 'I had better go and talk to him, hadn't I?'

'It would be best, Boss,' Kaz agreed. In his thoughts, she felt his evil firedrake grin. 'And if you don't like the answers he gives you, just lure him back downstairs, and I'll incinerate him for you.'

Veldan smiled ruefully. 'I just might take you up on that. It would certainly make my life a damn sight simpler.'

'You know,' Kaz said softly, 'it isn't easy being alone in the world. Both of us grew up severed from our roots, having no other family save one another. I know that if I had the chance, I would want to know who my people were.' He paused. 'Even if they *were* a bunch of bastards.'

'Thanks for that last contribution,' said Veldan drily. 'All the same, you're right.' And before she could dredge up any more doubts, she squared her shoulders, went back to the room next door, and stood in the doorway. She could only think of one way to do this. 'Are you my father?' she demanded.

Amaurn took his hands away from his face, and her heart twisted at the desolation she saw in his eyes. Then he seemed to focus on her, and his expression softened a little. 'I believe so.' He paused, and took a deep breath. 'Do you want me to be?'

Now it was Veldan's turn to hesitate – but only for a moment. She went into the room, and sat down on the bed. 'I believe I do.'

'When did *you* start to suspect that he might be her father?'

Elion had no need to ask who the firedrake was talking about. 'That first night he came to Gendival – or at least the following morning,' he answered.

'Me too.'

'You know Veldan best, Kaz. Do you think she started to suspect at the same time?'

'Well, if she did, she never let me in on the secret.' Kaz paused, looking thoughtful. 'All the same I expect she did, somewhere deep down. She just wasn't ready to admit it to herself at that point.'

The best part of an hour had passed, and Veldan still hadn't come downstairs. Elion and Kaz had lit the fires on the ground floor, by the simple expedient of the human throwing an armful of logs into each fireplace, and the firedrake igniting them with a huff of his breath. Elion had made tea for himself and Dark, but he was loath to take any upstairs and interrupt whatever was going on between Veldan and Amaurn. Now he was pacing back and forth in front of the hearth, and sighing a great deal. 'I wish I could find out what's happening up there,' he said. 'This suspense is wearing me out.'

'They're talking, of course,' the firedrake said. 'Though if they keep on doing it much longer, I think I might start getting jealous.'

'Yes, but what are they talking about?' The Loremaster kicked the hearth in frustration.

'Veldan's mother, actually.' Kaz had far less scruples about eavesdropping and, because he knew his partner so well, was able to achieve it, on a superficial level, at least, without her noticing – or so he thought. Elion sometimes wondered if Veldan let him think he was getting away with it because she knew how much fun he got out of it.

Dark, who had been dozing on the couch by the fire, woke up with a start and looked around wildly. For a moment, it seemed that he had forgotten where he was. Elion felt a pang of guilt. 'Are you all right?' he asked the stranger.

The young man struggled to dredge up a smile. 'Yes, of course. Never better.'

'He's very good at putting a brave face on things, isn't he?' Kaz remarked clinically.

'He shouldn't have to,' Elion said. He sat down beside the newcomer. 'I'm sorry we haven't done more to make you feel at home, Dark. We've been neglecting you, I'm afraid. Our manners are usually better than this, but it's been a very unusual day.'

'At least, *my* manners are usually better than this,' Kaz snickered. 'Elion's don't bear talking about.'

'You!' The Loremaster's voice rose in indignant protest. 'You haven't got any, you overgrown lizard!'

Dark laughed.

'Elion, why don't you go over to the inn, and get us all something to eat?' the firedrake suggested. 'There's practically nothing in the house, because we've been away so much lately. If I don't get something soon, I'll be forced to eat our visitor, here.'

'But . . .' Elion looked upwards, as though he were trying to see through the ceiling.

'Don't worry,' the firedrake said drily. 'If there are any developments, you'll be the first to know.'

Before Veldan finally put in an appearance, Elion had time to go all the way to the inn and wait while Olsam, bemoaning Ailie's preoccupation with Zarahl, packed up some food. When he got back she was just taking leave of Kyrre, who had come to place some portable versions of the coloured healing beams around Amaurn. Even from a distance, he could feel the happiness of the Dobarchu healer. 'Excuse me for hurrying away,' she was saying to Veldan. 'I must get back to Mrainil, and the rest of my people.' And with that she hurried off into the night.

'I've got some food.' Elion held up two heavily laden baskets and a sack which contained half a fat lamb for Kaz. Veldan took the sack, staggering slightly under the weight, and they went inside. 'Thank goodness for that,' she said. 'I'm so hungry that I could eat the Afanc, and have Maskulu for dessert.'

'That would be worth seeing.' As they began to lay out the food – just bread, cheese and cold meat, but plenty of it – on the kitchen table, Elion waited for her to say something about what had happened between herself and Amaurn. He didn't really want to ask her out loud, so he cleared his throat and caught her eye, hoping to put all his questions into his expression. Veldan met his gaze with a cool, impassive stare. 'What?' Her tone dared him to stick his nose into her business. 'Nothing,' Elion said quickly, and looked away. He knew then that no one, not even Kaz, would ever find out what had really taken place in that upstairs room.

Veldan, her emotions wrung dry, was almost too weary to eat, but too hungry not to. She didn't want to dwell on Amaurn any more that night – her whole world had changed very suddenly, and she wanted to give her impressions and emotions time to settle down and be assimilated before she saw him again. It was no good talking to Elion, however. He was too curious, and kept darting quizzical looks at her until she wanted to hit him. Instead, she turned her attention to the newcomer. 'I'm sorry everything has been in such an upheaval today,' she said. 'You must be wishing you hadn't come.'

Dark smiled his charming smile. 'I won't deny that it's been nerve-racking – especially the monsters. When I was coming round the head of the lake with Kher, and that behemoth came rearing up out of the water, I nearly turned tail and ran all the way back to Callisiora. And my nerves were still in shreds from that, when I was introduced to that terrifying underground creature.' He shook his head. 'To believe that they were both Senior Loremasters of the Shadowleague required a lot of readjustments in my thinking. After those two, your own big partner looks almost cute.'

'You'd better not let Kaz hear you saying that,' Veldan chuckled. 'I warn you, he'll devote his entire life to reducing you to a quivering wreck – just to teach you a lesson.' She yawned. 'I don't know about you people, but I could sleep for a week.' Suddenly, for some reason, she found she didn't want them to go. After the shocks of the day, their company was more than welcome – and if Amaurn wanted anything in the night, there would be someone else to go. 'Are you two staying here tonight?' she offered.

'Thanks, Veldan,' Elion said. 'It's so late now, I haven't got the energy to walk home. As long as it's not too much trouble.'

'I'd be glad to have you. Elion, will you take the couch, and Dark can have the other spare bedroom?'

Elion nodded. 'No problem.' He turned to the Summoner. 'We didn't get you off to the easiest of starts in Gendival, Dark, so I think we owe you a comfy bed, at least.'

They said their goodnights, and Veldan showed Dark to his upstairs room, helping him carry the two packs he had brought all the way from his former home. When they reached his door she handed him the lamp. 'There are some glims in the bedroom, if you want to use them,' she said. 'Just twist the two halves in opposite directions, and they'll start to glow.' She paused, feeling a sudden twinge of concern as she looked into his face. He looked hollow-eyed and exhausted, as did they all, but there was a pallor about his face that worried her.

'Are you feeling all right?' she asked him. 'You look awfully pale.'

'I'm fine,' the young man said. 'It's – well, this is going to sound really silly, but it's because, for the last few years, I've had to wear a mask day in and day out.'

Veldan frowned. 'You did?' She wondered why. There was nothing wrong with *his* face. On the contrary, it was a very pleasant face indeed. 'What on earth for?'

He grinned sheepishly. 'Where I come from, folk are far more simple and superstitious than they are here in Gendival. The mask was the mark of the Summoners, and it was supposed to frighten people into a sense of awe and obedience. It used to work, too, I might add. You see, it was made out of a real human skull.'

'Ugh!' Veldan shuddered. 'Better you than me. But I do know how awful it is to wear a mask all the time. I did it myself, for a while.'

'You? But why?'

Veldan felt herself colouring. 'Why do you think?' she snapped.

He frowned. 'What? Your scar? But it doesn't make any difference.'

'Well, it makes a bloody big difference to me!' Veldan didn't know whether to be glad of his casual attitude, to hit him for being so obtuse, or to run away somewhere and hide her embarrassment.

Now it was Dark's turn to colour. 'I'm sorry,' he said. 'I didn't put that very well. I realise that it must have had an impact on your life, and I didn't mean to dismiss it. But you see, to me it's just part of you. I haven't seen your face any look different – and I like it just the way it is.'

As if they both realised that this conversation had gone too far, too fast, they both looked away from one another. Muttering a hasty goodnight, Veldan fled downstairs, as Dark dived into his bedroom.

By the time she reached her own downstairs chamber, where Kaz was curled up in his nest by the fire, Veldan was already telling herself off for being silly. 'This has been the weirdest night of my life,' she said to Kaz, as she shed her clothes in a trail from the door to the fireside.

The firedrake opened one eye. 'Never mind, sweetie. I'll take care of you.'

Needing to be comforted, Veldan pulled the blankets off her bed, and brought them over to Kaz's nest, where she curled up with the firedrake. 'Thank goodness I've got you,' she murmured. 'Between unexpected compliments from strange young men, and long-lost fathers turning up out of the woodwork, a girl needs someone she can depend on.'

Twenty-Eight

Beginning with Breakfast

Toulac had stayed up very late the previous night, talking with Harral down at the stables, but mainly just being with Mazal. She had sent Scall back earlier, with a message for Ailie to the effect that his absence had been her fault, and when she had eventually dragged herself back to the inn, she had been so sleepy that she'd barely noticed the scolding the innkeeper had given her, or the fact that she had hauled the poor woman out of bed to open the door for her. All she cared about was that Ailie had found another room for Scall, and she had her bed to herself again. The last few days and nights had finally caught up with her, and she barely had time to take her boots off before she was under the covers and lost in the deepest of sleeps.

The following morning, she slept late – and would have slept a damn sight later, had she not been awakened by a frantic hammering on her door. She rolled over and opened a bleary eye. 'Bugger off, whoever you are.'

The banging started up again. 'Toulac, Toulac! You've got to help me.' It was Scall again. The veteran groaned, and hauled herself out of bed, muttering curses. She marched over to the door, and flung it open. 'What the bloody blazes is it *now?*'

The boy looked nervous, shifting from foot to foot as he stood in the doorway and wringing his hands. 'Please, Toulac,' he blurted, 'will you come with me? The head man wants to see me – the Arch . . . The Archi . . . Well, the same as the Hierarch, anyway, and—'

'And you're scared,' Toulac said flatly, not sufficiently awake yet to be tactful.

Scall flushed crimson. 'I am *not!*' he yelled. 'Oh, who needs you anyway? You're nothing but a stupid old woman.'

Wonderful. An adolescent tantrum before breakfast. Just what I need to start my day.

She gave him a cold, level stare that made him step back a couple of paces. 'That's as may be, sonny, but I'm not the one who's frightened of the Archimandrite. Now do you want me to come with you or not? Because otherwise, I'm going back to bed.'

'All right,' Scall mumbled.

'All right what?'

'Yes, I would like you to come with me . . . please. Not that I'm scared, or anything,' he added defiantly.

'Of course you aren't.' With difficulty, Toulac resisted the urge to pat him on the head. 'Just let me wash my face and pull myself together, and I'll be right with you.' She yawned mightily. 'Do you know if there's any tea around here, this morning?'

A pained expression flitted across Scall's face, and she knew he was wondering how, with the Archimandrite in the offing, she could think of such mundane things as tea. 'There wasn't any downstairs,' he told her, 'but the meeting is being held in someone's house, and there are quite a few people coming, so Ailie's coming along too, to make breakfast for everybody. Then they're going to look at the stuff I found.'

Breakfast! Suddenly, the day was improving. 'Just wait there a moment,' Toulac said, and ducked back into her room for the quickest wash of her life. It was only then that she noticed the note that had been pushed under her door. Judging from the print of her boot-sole on it, it must have been there since the previous night, she realised. Obviously, she had been so tired that she had never noticed. It was from the Archimandrite, and invited her to that morning's meeting too. Toulac beamed. Notwithstanding her opinion of Lord Blade, it was always nice to be wanted.

As she had suspected, the meeting was being held in Veldan's house, and Ailie was going to take them there. Toulac and Scall were hanging around by the inn door, waiting, when the innkeeper came hurrying out, with Zavahl right behind her. At the sight of the former Hierarch of Callisiora, Scall turned pale. He dug Toulac with his elbow. 'What's *he* doing here?' he demanded, in a whisper loud enough to be heard all the way down to the Navigators' trading post.

Zavahl looked round at the boy, and smiled. 'I live here now,' he said. 'If you remember, they were going to burn me at the stake back in Callisiora, so I decided to find a friendlier place. I like it much better here.'

Toulac smiled to herself as Scall went crimson at being addressed by such an august personage.

They followed Ailie along the path that led around behind the village, and crossed the river over a small footbridge, instead of the stone bridge on the road that would have taken them right through the settlement. As they went along, Toulac caught up with Zavahl. 'Did you sleep well?' she asked slyly.

He shook his head. 'As a matter of fact, I didn't – but not only for the reasons you're thinking of.' His eyes looked haunted. 'Ailie tells me that I'll be meeting Blade this morning, and I'm not looking forward to it one bit.'

'You and me both,' Toulac said. 'Veldan kept trying to tell me that everything was different here, and he was trying to change and be a better man, and all sorts of other complete hogwash.' She waved her arm dismissively. 'I'll believe it when I see it – maybe.'

Ailie looked back over her shoulder. 'But Scall was telling me this morning that Amaurn rescued your horse for you, and you were wild with delight. Doesn't that make you feel a little more charitable?'

Toulac shrugged. 'I bet he wouldn't have done it if he hadn't needed a mount to bring him here.'

'On the other hand, he's the Archimandrite, and he can do what he wants,' Ailie argued. 'Scall said you have a truly magnificent warhorse, which must be very valuable, and Zavahl was telling me that Amaurn loves horses with a passion. What was to stop him keeping the animal for himself?'

'Scall and Zavahl would be better off minding their own affairs,' growled Toulac, 'and I can't be doing with this ridiculous "Amaurn" business. To me he's Blade, and always will be.' With that, she dropped back to stamp along in the rear.

This was the first time that the veteran had seen Veldan's house in its forest clearing. Elion answered the door, and greeted Scall kindly. 'Why, fancy seeing you here! Have you still got the little mare I gave you?'

'I did have,' the boy said bitterly, 'until I came here and that Harral took her off me.'

'Ah.' Hurriedly, the Loremaster changed the subject. 'Don't stand there on the doorstep, everyone. Come inside.'

They all followed him into the main room – and came face to face with Kaz, who was curled up by the fire. Toulac had never thought to prepare Scall for his first sight of the firedrake and, clearly, neither had anyone else. He made a choking sound, and as his knees began to buckle, she grabbed his upper arm in a vicelike grip. 'Steady,' she hissed. 'It's all right. He's Veldan's friend and partner, and he lives here.' She couldn't resist the opportunity to brag. 'I rode here on his back, all the way from Tiarond.'

Scall, looking sceptical, was opening his mouth to reply, when two figures came slowly down the stairs. Veldan came first, followed by Blade. On her other side, Toulac felt Zavahl stiffen. She didn't blame him. At the sight of the former Godsword Commander, she could feel her own hackles rising, though she had to admit that he looked far less cold and intimidating now that he was out of his severe black Godsword tunic, and wearing a soft green shirt. One arm was bandaged and in a sling, and Toulac was the veteran of enough wounds of her own to see that he had been hurt elsewhere, for he walked stiffly, with his arm clasped close to his side, and she could see him catch his breath at every step.

Serves him right.

There was no time to take in any more. Just as Blade reached the bottom step, there was a sudden movement at Toulac's side. Zavahl sprang forward, and hit him square in the face, hard enough to knock him off balance, so that he fell on his back on the lower stairs.

'Zavahl!' Veldan pushed her way between the two men. 'You can't do that – he's wounded!'

The former Hierarch looked down at the sprawled figure. 'That's nothing to what he'll be if he ever interferes with me or mine again,' he snarled. 'Leave me alone in future, Blade – I warn you. Or on my very life, I'll make you sorry.'

Veldan and a dark-haired young man that Toulac didn't recognise, helped Blade to his feet. Rubbing his jaw, the Archimandrite glared at the former Hierarch – then threw back his head and laughed. 'Well,' he said. 'I see that leaving Tiarond hasn't done *you* any harm.'

Zavahl's mouth fell open.

The former Godsword Commander held out his hand. 'Zavahl,' he said, 'I treated you very badly back in Tiarond. I was in a position of trust, I abused that trust, and you have my most profound apologies. I used you mercilessly to further my own plans, and thanks to me, you lost your place in the world, and very nearly your life. But when I look at you now, I've never seen you look better, or happier – and that being the case, I very much hope that you'll come to forgive me in time. If there's anything I can do for you, to make up for the way I treated you, you only have to say the word. I wish you a long and prosperous life here in Gendival, and I promise you that you won't have anything to fear from me again.'

Toulac stared at the new Archimandrite in astonishment.

Well, may I be dipped in dogs' dung! I wonder if Blade has a twin brother? Because I'd bet my life that this can't be the man I know.

The gracious apology seemed to have taken the wind out of Zavahl's sails, too. He looked at Blade doubtfully and Toulac could see, from the changing expressions on his face, that distrust was at war with hope. 'Why?' he asked, in an unsteady voice.

Blade smiled wryly. 'Firstly, because I feel I owe it to you. Secondly, because you now share your body with the consciousness of the Dragon Seer Aethon, and between you you can help me, the Shadowleague, and the entire world. Ironically, you're more important as the host of Aethon than you ever were as the Hierarch of Callisiora, and you're in a position to do a lot more good.'

'It's all right, Zavahl,' Veldan put in softly. 'You can trust him this time. He'll keep his word.' She fixed Blade with a steely stare that was so like his own, it sent a shiver down Toulac's spine. 'Won't you?'

'My daughter, I will.' When Blade looked at Veldan, his expression underwent such a fundamental change, softening from sternness into tenderness, that Toulac couldn't believe her eyes.

His daughter? *Myrial up a pole! What in perdition is going on?*

She saw similar shock on the faces of Ailie and Zavahl, and even Scall was looking in puzzlement from Blade to Veldan, and back again. On the other hand, it was clear that Elion, the dark-haired stranger, and the smirking firedrake were already in the know.

Zavahl was the first to pull himself together. 'Very well, Blade. I accept your offer, and your word. After all,' he added wryly, 'you're where you always wanted to be, now: on the top of the heap. I don't have what you want any more, neither rank nor power, so I expect I should be quite safe.'

Blade smiled thinly. 'You show a good grasp of the situation, Zavahl. You've learned a lot, since last we met.' With the air of a man who was anxious to change the subject, he turned to the veteran. 'And you, Toulac? Will you not stay? It would mean a tremendous amount to Veldan.'

'Answer me one question,' Toulac said. 'Why did you throw all the female warriors out of the Godswords, all those years ago?'

A shadow of old sorrow crossed Blade's face. 'Because they reminded me so painfully of the love that I had lost – Veldan's mother. She was a Loremaster here, too.' He put his arm around his daughter's shoulders. 'Grief and guilt and loss can make us selfish, sometimes. They can change and harden us beyond all recognition. I know that "sorry" is a very small word to say for ruining someone's life, but if you'll join us here as a Loremaster, at least I can try, in some small way, to make it up to you.'

As he spoke, an odd thought came to Toulac.

Did he really ruin my life? All the places I saw, all the adventures I had, all the friends I made as a mercenary – I would have missed all that if I had become a Godsword, and stayed in Tiarond.

She looked from Veldan to . . .

Drat it! I suppose I'll have to get used to calling him Amaurn, now.

'All right, sonny. Count me in.'

With a whoop of joy, Veldan ran across to hug her, and the Archimandrite looked round at them all. 'Now,' he said. 'If there's nobody *else* I need apologise to, I suggest we have some breakfast.'

Breakfast was a good opportunity for the introductions, and some filling in of the backgrounds of those who were strangers to one another. After they had crammed themselves around Veldan's large kitchen table, and eaten every scrap of Ailie's excellent food, they returned to the other room, and found various places to sit. Amaurn addressed them all. 'I wanted you people to be the first to look at the artefacts Scall discovered, for the simple reason that they were found beneath Tiarond, and I have a feeling that will prove to be significant. The people in this room have all been in Callisiora recently – and some of us, for considerably longer than we wanted to be,' he added wryly. 'Before I make the discovery of these arte-facts more public among the Shadowleague, I wanted to hear our interpretation of Scall's finds, the relevance of the place in which he found them, and our present crisis in general.'

'What about me?' the innkeeper asked. 'I've never been to Callisiora in my life.'

Amaurn smiled at her. 'You are here, Ailie, because of your asso-ciation with Zavahl, your common sense, the fact that you make superb breakfasts – but more particularly, because you run the inn, which is always a great repository of *unofficial* information among off-duty Loremasters. You also have regular links with the Navigators, who tend to pick up news and gossip, and a lot of local knowledge in their travels. If you find any links between anything you see or hear today, and anything you've heard elsewhere, be it fact or rumour, then it may be of great use to us.' He looked around his associates. 'Now, Dark, if you please, would you show us the items that Scall found?'

Dark went upstairs to fetch Scall's strange artefacts, and while they waited for him to return, Amaurn asked the lad to tell everyone how he had come to discover them. With much blushing and stammering, Scall told his tale, and everyone listened with avid interest – though when they heard of Tormon's involvement, Amaurn and Zavahl exchanged uneasy glances. Between them, they had almost killed the trader, and had slain his lifemate, and Amaurn knew that if they ever met him again, they could expect no quarter – nor would they deserve any.

At least, for once, I don't have to bear the blame for this one. It was Zavahl's idea to get rid of the folk who found Aethon's body, so he could claim the discovery for himself.

He felt a stab of bitterness.

I know who'll get the blame, though. I seem to be required to apologise and atone for everything – mostly, to be fair, with good reason – but they all seem to have forgotten that the Hierarch of Callisiora wasn't always a paragon of goodness, either.

By this time, Scall had finished his tale and Dark had returned, carrying a small cloth bag. Amaurn could scarcely contain his excitement. He hoped desperately that there might be some clue here to the restoration of the failing Curtain Walls. Kneeling on the hearthrug, the Summoner pulled out the two objects – a small, silver sphere, and a thin disc about a foot across – and handed the sphere to Amaurn, who examined it closely.

'Cradle it in the palm of your hand,' Dark instructed.

Cupping the silvery object in his palm, Amaurn held his hand out – and everyone gasped. There, hovering in the air above the artefact, was a large, solid-looking image, with brown and green land, blue oceans, and a flickering fretwork of blue-white lines that could only be the Curtain Walls.

This reminds me of that gigantic circular object in the Holy of Holies in the Temple of Myrial, in which the Hierarch could see what was taking place in other parts of Callisiora – or at least, he could until I came along, and stole his ring.

'Open your hand, and close it again,' Dark urged. 'Think of a place you want to see. Grim thought it seemed to work by some sort of connection to mindspeech, though if Scall can make it function, there's obviously no need to have any marked abilities in that direction.'

Amaurn did as he was bidden – and suddenly, there was an image of Tiarond on its mountain. He opened and closed his hand again, and there was Gendival, and the settlement beside the lakes. And again . . . He caught his breath. There, on the opposite side of the globe, was a blank, grey, curving dome, bounded by the ocean on one side, and mountains on the other. His own land, the realm of the dispossessed Magefolk, covered and hidden by the mysterious force-field of the Creators.

'What in the name of perdition is *that*?' Veldan demanded.

Amaurn turned to the firedrake. 'That's your home, Kazairl – the home of your people. Yours and mine.'

'But why can't we see it?' Elion wanted to know.

'Because the Creators of Myrial thought the Magefolk – my people – were getting far too powerful, and were a risk to their own plans. They locked us away from the rest of the world, long aeons ago. What you see there is a force field a thousand times more impenetrable than the Curtain Walls. It blocks mindspeech, and other very powerful abilities of the mind that once we had.'

'And the firedrakes live there too?' Kaz interrupted.

'Indeed they do. Your people are trapped with mine.'

'But how did *you* get out?' Toulac demanded.

'Underground. I discovered a cave system that went deeper than the barrier.' With an effort, he shook away the memories. 'Anyway, this is getting us nowhere.' He put down the small, silver sphere, and after a moment, the image faded and vanished. 'This will be very useful to the Shadowleague, in allowing us to see what's happening along the Curtain Walls, and what's taking place in other lands, but offhand, I can't think of a way in which it will solve our current problems. Let's have a look at this other item, instead.'

He took out the flat, thin disc, with the mirrorlike surface and the narrow band of gold about its rim – and with an oath, he almost dropped it again, as the surface turned deep black and lines of writing, formed in characters of bright green light, began to appear at the bottom and move slowly up the page – for a page it clearly was, even if it was like nothing that Amaurn had ever seen before.

The writing was formed from strange runes that he didn't recognise. He wondered how old they were, and a shiver went through him. Was this the language of the Creators themselves? He handed the device to the former Hierarch. 'Zavahl, may we talk to the Seer, please? And Aethon, is there anything like this in your memories?'

There was a slight, indefinable change to Zavahl's expression. 'This is very old indeed.' There was an odd, new resonance to his voice. 'It appears to be a list of some sort, but there's a lot that I cannot understand. Maintenance – what can that mean? Overmind? Ah, here's something . . . Tunnel Plan . . .' He put his finger on the place to point it out – and the moving writing instantly vanished, to be replaced by a series of drawings and maps, all delineated in that same glowing, green light. Zavahl's voice shook with the Dragon Seer's excitement. 'Amaurn, Veldan, see . . . It's the mountain – Mount Chaikar! This picture is meant to represent Tiarond!'

They all gathered around, getting in one another's way, as more of the pictures began to slowly emerge, one by one, from the bottom of the page. Zavahl choked at the sight of a stylised bridge and platform over a great drop, and a massive circle suspended in midair above. 'That's the Holy of Holies in the Temple, where none but the Hierarch may tread!' he gasped, in his own voice.

Amaurn looked away from him, feeling guilty.

That's what you think.

Below that, there was the image of the Hierarch's ring. Amaurn shuddered. He knew that this was significant – it was obviously leading somewhere – and now that he had seen the ring, he was pretty sure that there was a connection with the Curtain Walls.

Zavahl spoke again, with Aethon's resonant voice, and confirmed his suspicions. 'Amaurn, there is a memory of my people that concerns a concealed locus of entry – or maybe even more than one – which gives access to the intelligence that maintains this world. I think you have one right here, beneath the Temple. Maybe it is accessed from the place that the Hierarchs call the Eye of Myrial, or maybe we can get in through the tunnels Scall found. To find our answers, it looks as though we must go back to Tiarond, notwithstanding the presence of the Ak'Zahar. Also, we may need to obtain the ring from Gilarra – if she survived.'

Amaurn buried his face in his hands, and groaned. 'So the ring holds the key?'

'I suspect so.'

'Then we're in big trouble.' He looked up at Aethon/Zavahl. 'When Toulac, Kaz and Veldan rescued you, the ring slipped off Gilarra's finger when the platform collapsed. I saw it happen, but I was trapped under a piece of timber, and I couldn't reach it in time. The Ak'Zahar took it. They have it now. It could be anywhere.'

There was a long moment of silence. Amaurn glanced at Veldan, who was sitting beside him, and saw that she had gone very white at the mention of the Ak'Zahar. Belatedly, he remembered Elion mentioning that she had been badly wounded during her last encounter with the deadly winged predators. Clearly, the scars went deeper than the one on her face, and his heart went out to her.

Finally Toulac spoke up, breaking the silence. 'So it looks as though we're going back to Tiarond – whatever might happen when we get there.'

'But why should we? Surely there's no point, if we don't have the ring, and we don't even know what we're doing,' Elion argued. Belatedly, Amaurn remembered that the Loremaster had lost his own partner in the same skirmish that had wounded his daughter. No wonder he was reluctant.

'Well, we won't get anywhere sitting on our backsides in Gendival, that's for sure,' the veteran retorted.

'Toulac is right,' said Aethon, through Zavahl. 'We may not know exactly how we can fix this disaster, but the heart of the secret lies somewhere under Tiarond, and the device that Scall found can show us maps of the tunnels. Maybe, when we get down there, we'll be able to find out what to do. Perhaps I may see something that will awaken some memories from the past of my people . . .'

'And perhaps we'll all get killed for nothing,' snorted Kaz.

Though returning to Tiarond was the very last thing he wanted to do, Amaurn knew that he, at least, would have to go back.

This is all my fault. I can't start a new life here, and build a future for my daughter, and for the world, until I put right the mess I made. And I won't send others into danger to pay the price that should rightfully be mine.

'You're absolutely right, Toulac,' he said. 'We'll have to go back – and there's no time to lose. Each day we delay, the chances of finding the Hierarch's ring grow less and less, and what's worse, the rate of deterioration of the Curtain Walls seems to be increasing. The longer we hesitate, the more races will go the way of the Dobarchu.' He looked around at everyone, trying hard not to let his gaze linger on Veldan. 'However, not all of us need to make the journey; indeed, not everyone should.'

'Well, *you* shouldn't, for a start.' The blunt words had come from his daughter.

'What makes you think I was planning to?' he asked her, stalling for time.

She gave him an old-fashioned look. 'By your expression, your voice, the words you were using . . . Need I go on?'

'No, you're quite right.' A firm hand was obviously needed here. 'I was planning to go – and what's more, I fully intend to.'

'Despite the fact that you were wounded only yesterday,' Veldan said flatly. 'And you're the Archimandrite now, if you hadn't forgotten. There's no way that the leader of the Shadowleague should be risking himself on missions. That's not how it works, and you know it.'

He glared at her. 'In an emergency – and I'm sure you wouldn't deny that this *is* an emergency – there can be exceptions. My local knowledge will be needed in Tiarond. I must go back.'

'How can you even *think* about leaving here just now?' Veldan exploded. 'You've only just taken over as Archimandrite, and you haven't really had time to consolidate your hold on this place. Cergorn's supporters will be conspiring against you before you get as far as the Curtain Walls.'

'Cergorn won't be here.' Suddenly, there was absolute silence in the room, and all eyes were turned his way. 'Oh, for goodness' sake,' he said testily, 'I'm only talking about exile, not execution. I'm sending him back to his home island, and Syvilda with him. I've been talking to his healers this morning, and they say that he can be moved, with care. The three of them – Quave, Myssil, and Shimir – have all volunteered to accompany him on the voyage, so he ought to be all right.'

'With all respect,' Elion said, 'isn't it a mistake to leave an enemy roaming loose like that? What if he returns, just like you did, sometime in the future, when you're not expecting him? Or what if his followers bring him back?'

Amaurn shook his head. 'That won't happen. I'm going to have a full, permanent memory wipe done on both Cergorn and Syvilda and a new, false set of memories put in their place. They won't even know that Gendival and the Shadowleague exist. And it won't be any use for their followers to track them down and try to remind them, because those memories will have been permanently destroyed.'

'But . . . To be robbed of his memories like that, and sent away,' Ailie said hesitantly. 'Surely that's a cruel fate.'

When Amaurn looked at her, his eyes were cold as steel. 'It's a damn sight better fate than the one he had planned for me.'

'And his followers?' Veldan asked. 'Will you explain your reasoning to them, or will you tell them after the event?'

'That's a very tempting suggestion,' Amaurn said, 'but regretfully, I'll have to tell them. That way, they'll know exactly what happened, and it should put a stop to any rumours that I spirited Cergorn away and put an end to him. Besides, if I confront them and face them down, it'll also have the effect of letting them know who is the leader around here. If I do it behind their backs, they might start getting the idea that I'm afraid of them.'

'When are you going to do it?' Elion asked.

'Today. I've already made arrangements with the Navigators, and a ship will be ready to take him downriver. I want to get him away as quickly as possible after I've made the announcement, before his followers can start thinking up ways to interfere.' He shrugged. 'I plan to tell everyone at the same time as I let them know they'll be having the Takuru as their neighbours . . .'

'*What?*' cried Ailie, in horror.

Amaurn smiled wryly at her. 'That's about the reaction I'm expecting. I'm hoping that one outrage will cancel out the other.'

Elion shook his head. 'Maybe you're right to be leaving for Callisiora. I have a feeling that you aren't exactly going to be popular round here.'

'I know. However, if I succeed in repairing the Curtain Walls, then maybe they'll come round to my way of thinking, and see that I was right after all. But we seem to have strayed from the original point of this discussion. Who shall we take back to Callisiora with us, and who will be staying behind?'

Zavahl looked sick. 'I'm going to have to go, aren't I?' he said in a low voice. 'Without me, you won't have Aethon, and you need his memories.'

Amaurn nodded. 'I'm very sorry, Zavahl. I know that you're starting to make a life here, and returning to Tiarond is the last thing you want to do. But we do need Aethon's memories. Your own knowledge as Hierarch probably wouldn't come amiss, either.'

Ailie looked at the pair of them in horror. '*No!*' she cried. 'Zavahl, you can't! You're not one of the Shadowleague. They can't ask this of you!'

He looked at her helplessly. 'Ailie, I have to. There are more folk than just us to consider. You've got to understand – it's more than just carrying Aethon along. As a Hierarch, I failed my people. If I can do something to help them now, then I can't neglect that duty.' He tried to smile at her. 'After all, it'll be my last. Once we've put the world to rights, and I get back here, I don't plan to go more than a hundred yards away from the inn for the rest of my life.'

Ailie's mouth set itself in a stubborn line. 'Then I'm coming with you.'

'No,' Amaurn said firmly. 'You aren't. This isn't a jaunt down the river, Ailie. We'll be facing some of the deadliest creatures in the annals of the Shadowleague. You aren't trained to defend yourself, and we'll be hard enough pressed as it is. Having to look after you will weaken us in general.'

'You'll have to look after Zavahl,' the innkeeper retorted angrily.

'We can't do without Zavahl.' The Archimandrite was implacable. 'We can justify having to defend him. You would just be dead weight in our party – in more ways than one, probably. Don't try to cross me in this, Ailie, and don't get any wild ideas about following us. Without my permission, no one will take you through the Curtain Walls. I've done enough to wreck Zavahl's life – I'm going to make damn sure that you, at least, are going to be safe at home, waiting for him to come back.'

'Damn you!' Ailie snapped. She turned to Zavahl. 'Are you going to let him get away with this?'

Zavahl sighed. 'I'm sorry, but I think he's right. I'll miss you very much, but if you don't come, then at least I'll only have one of us to worry about.'

'If you want *me*,' Toulac volunteered, breaking the tension, 'I'll be more than willing to come along.'

'You'd be more than welcome,' Amaurn said.

'I think you can be sure that if you go to Tiarond, the rest of us are coming, too,' added Veldan.

He gave her a very direct look. 'You don't have to, you know. I think that you and Kaz and Elion have seen enough of the Ak'Zahar to last you a lifetime, and all three of you suffered in various ways from your last encounter. You've done your share, and more. I wouldn't have you put yourselves through all that again.'

Veldan shook her head. 'If you're going, I'm going.'

'And if *she's* going, I'm going, too,' Kaz added. 'Although you can bet your life that I'm going to do my best to talk her out of it.'

'And I would like to go,' Dark said. 'If you think I would be any use.'

Elion looked at the floor, and said nothing. Had he decided not to go, or was he still making his mind up?

'Maybe we should discuss who will be going later, when we've all had time to think things through,' Amaurn interjected. 'There is one other person I would like to take with me, however.' He looked at Scall. 'Scall, you found the tunnels in the first place. I won't try to coerce or even persuade you to go – I promised a good friend that I wouldn't. But if you could find it in your heart to volunteer, you would be of tremendous use to us, and I promise we'd do our very best to keep you safe. Then, when we're done, we can bring you back with us, and you can live here, if that's what you want, or we'll take you back to join your friends in Callisiora. It's up to you.'

Scall's eyes grew wide. 'You want me to go back there? There's no way . . .' Then something seemed to occur to him. 'I don't want to come and live here, if it's all the same to you. I would rather go back to my friends. But there is one thing I want, and if you give it to me, to keep, I'll come with you and show you everything I can.'

Amaurn leaned forward. 'Whatever you want, Scall. Just name it.'

'Well,' the boy said, 'Elion gave me this horse, but that Harral says she belongs to him . . .'

Beside him, Toulac burst out laughing. 'I might have guessed!'

Twenty-Nine

Hunters and Prey

Seriema and Cetain were with Arcan, showing him the knife, when a Reiver warrior came bursting in after the most perfunctory of knocks. 'My Chief! The Tiarondian, Presvel, has lost his mind! He kidnapped trader Tormon's child at knifepoint, and has ridden off with her, and that blonde girl who was looking after her.'

Arcan leapt to his feet, scowling. 'He stole a child? And was allowed to escape the fortress? Who permitted that? Why was I not sent for immediately?'

The warrior took a step back. 'I'm sorry, my Chief, but it all happened so quickly, and there was so much confusion. He made his move when most people were at breakfast, so the corridors were nearly empty. He got most of the way down to the beast quarters before he was even seen, and by the time someone had run and fetched the guards, he was mounted and ready to leave. He had two horses already saddled, so this was no sudden fit of madness. He must have planned it, and prepared well in advance. When he threatened to cut the little girl's throat, the gates were opened for him at once. What else could we have done, my Chief? Tormon begged us to let him go. The poor man has already lost his wife, and he didn't dare take the risk of his little daughter being killed, too.'

'Where is Tormon now?' Arcan asked.

'Saddling up,' the messenger replied. 'The ground is wet enough for tracking. Presvel said he would kill his hostages if anyone pursued him, so the trader plans to follow at a safe distance until nightfall, keeping out of sight, and then await his chance to take the little one back.'

'If the winged demons don't get him first,' the chieftain said. 'I'll go down and speak to him at once, and see what help we can offer. He cannot take on this madman alone – especially not now that we know Presvel is Grim's murderer. That makes it our business, too.' He looked down at the knife in his hand, and cursed. To Seriema's surprise, he inclined his head to her. 'My apologies,' he said brusquely. 'If I had not shut you out yesterday, you would have identified this weapon much sooner, and we would have arrested the miscreant before he could foment this new mischief.' Beckoning them to follow, he swept from the room.

As they hurried down the stairs, Seriema clutched at Cetain's arm. 'I must go with poor Tormon,' she said. 'I can't let him face this alone. In a way, I was the one who brought Presvel here, so I feel a responsibility.'

'Then I'll come too,' Cetain replied firmly, 'and I'll bring some of my best men. A few archers would be welcome, too, with those winged fiends around.'

Seriema felt a glow of gratitude towards him for his unquestioning support.

I'm so lucky to have met Cetain. After all those lonely years, who would have thought it possible that I would find such a man?

When she saw Tormon, her heart went out to him. Anger and fear seemed to emanate from him in waves, and she could not bear the torment in his eyes. As Arcan's little group came down the stairs into the beast quarters, the trader was just mounting his great, black stallion. 'Tormon, wait!' the chieftain called out. 'Let me send some of my men with you. You can't do this alone – not with the winged demons at large.'

'I don't have time to wait.' The trader set his face and rode his horse towards the great doors. The two warriors who were guarding them and blocking his way exchanged nervous glances.

Seriema ran forward. 'Tormon, let us help. You've got to stay out of Presvel's sight until nightfall in any case. It won't take long to get the men mounted up – and they know this terrain far better than we do. They can help us stay hidden while we're chasing him. And Annas needs protection from the predators, as well as Presvel. If they strike after dark, you'll be glad of all the help you can get.'

Tormon reined in his plunging horse. 'We?'

'Of course.' Seriema, already heading for the fleet little Reiver horse that Cetain had given her, threw the words over her shoulder. 'You didn't think for one minute that I'd let you face this alone? Cetain's coming too, with some of his men.'

The trader hesitated, common sense warring with his desperate need to find and rescue his daughter. Then he nodded. 'Hurry, then,' he said.

It didn't take long before they were riding away from the fortress. Though Tormon had offered her the use of his Sefrian gelding again, Seriema had decided that, since she was about to join the Reiver community for good, it would be better to ride one of their horses. In any case, she was already becoming attached to the smaller, faster animal. It also put her at the right height to talk to Cetain, and since the trader seemed to have no desire for conversation, that would probably work out for the best.

They set off across the moors in raw, wintry weather. Spits of sleet, and sometimes even a brief flurry of wet snow, fell half-heartedly from an iron-grey sky. The wind was light but, in the moorland hollows, the heather, bracken and whin were white with frost. Cetain's little band – eight warriors in all, three of whom had a reputation as skilled archers – rode steadily, guided by the clear trail that Presvel's horses had left behind. Accustomed as they were to years of raiding and battle, the Reivers didn't follow the track of footprints directly, but instead moved in their general direction, following the secret folds and hollows in the land. Cetain, who was leading them, knew how important it was to stay well back, out of sight. If Presvel should catch even a glimpse of them, it could spell the end for Annas. Nevertheless, Seriema could see how difficult it was for the trader to keep his distance, when every fibre of his being was straining to go to his little girl's rescue. She closed the distance between them. 'We'll do it,' she said quietly. 'If it's humanly possible, we'll get her back.'

He gave her a look that was filled with pain. 'It's hard to have faith, Seriema, after everything that's happened. I lost Kanella, then I became fond of Scall and he vanished. Now it's my daughter.' He lifted his face to the skies. 'What have I done? I never hurt anybody in my life. What have I done to deserve this?'

To that, there could be no answer.

They rode in silence for a little while, then he turned to her again. 'He killed Grim, didn't he?'

'I'm afraid he did. I recognised his knife as soon as I saw it.' Seriema shook her head. 'I don't understand what can have happened to him, Tormon. He always seemed to be the most sensible, level-headed person in the world, but since the fall of the city, he's changed beyond all recognition.'

The trader nodded. 'I got the feeling that he was bothering Rochalla, though she never said anything about it. I know she was fond of Annas, but I think that she volunteered to look after her so much because it let her keep her distance from Presvel.'

Seriema sighed. 'Well, why didn't the silly girl say something to one of us? Maybe if we'd had more warning . . .' Then she shook her head. 'No, I'm not being fair to her. We all noticed that Presvel's behaviour was becoming increasingly strange, but we had our own concerns, and we were too busy finding our own feet after our everyday worlds had collapsed all around us. But there must have been some sort of relationship between them at one point, I'm sure of that. He introduced her into my household to take care of Annas with some trumped-up story about her being a distant relative, or the daughter of a friend, or something like that, but I wasn't convinced, right from the start. But she seemed a kind, decent girl, and good with the child, so I let it lie. I meant to look into her background in more detail after the Great Sacrifice, but . . .'

'Well, whatever happened between them before, she doesn't want him now,' said Tormon bluntly. 'I was beginning to get the feeling that she was a bit sweet on Scall, in fact.'

Seriema looked at him, wide-eyed. 'Tormon, if he murdered the old Summoner, you don't think he killed Scall, too?'

'I don't know,' said Tormon. 'The fact that Dark is also missing gives me some hope. Maybe they thought they would be blamed, and ran away – though it wouldn't be like Scall not to leave some kind of note, or message.' He shrugged. 'Hopefully, we'll be able to get the truth out of Presvel – before I kill him.'

She felt sick to hear him talk so bluntly about killing a man who had been her friend and confederate for so many years. Cetain, who noticed everything, rode up between them, and put out a hand to touch her arm. Tormon, seeing the gesture, looked down at them with a frown. 'You two seem thick as thieves, all of a sudden. Is there something going on between you that I don't know about?'

'Yes,' Cetain said. 'I asked Seriema to be my lifemate, and she said yes.'

Tormon stared at them for a long moment, his face betraying no emotion. 'Congratulations,' he said bleakly then, spurring his horse, he left them and rode on ahead.

Seriema watched him go, and shook her head. With his own life smashed to splinters, it was too much to expect, at this time, that he could find it in himself to appreciate the happiness of others.

Poor Tormon. No one can ever bring back his lifemate, but somehow we must find a way to get his daughter back safely. If we fail, it will be the end for him.

Rochalla had, perhaps, been a little more afraid when the winged monstrosities had invaded Tiarond, but it was a close-run thing. Somehow, one of the most frightening aspects of the situation was the fact that the person who had been her protector then, was now the very one who threatened her life.

Everything had happened so quickly when Presvel had abducted Tormon's daughter at knifepoint that Rochalla had been stunned into obedience, unable to think of a way to save herself or the child.

Now, as the distance grew between herself and safety, her mind was starting to work once more – but what was the point? It was already too late. If she couldn't do anything to save herself and Annas back in the fortress, where there were people around to help her, what hope did she have now, when she was all alone with a helpless child and a madman in this bleak and isolated place? For there was no doubt in Rochalla's mind that she was dealing with a madman now. The only possible way she could hope to get herself and Annas safely through this nightmare was to convince Presvel that she was on his side – no matter what it took to do so.

I've got to save Annas, no matter what becomes of me. Poor Tormon has lost so much already – he couldn't bear it if anything happened to his little girl.

Already, Rochalla was worried about the child. Annas had no coat or cloak and the day was bitterly cold. Already, her skin had a chilled, pinched look. Much more alarming, however, was the way she had lapsed into that same, numb stillness and silence that had followed the death of her mother. Presvel had put her in front of him on the saddle and she sat there like a rag doll, her eyes glazed, taking no notice of her surroundings. It was as though she had shut herself off once again, just as she had done before.

It was hard for Rochalla to keep her hatred of Presvel from showing in her face.

How could he do this? How dare he? The poor little thing was just beginning to regain her confidence. Goodness only knows how badly this will affect her.

If we survive.

Did Presvel know that the winged fiends had come out onto the moors? Did he care? If they should manage to get all the way back to Tiarond undiscovered by the creatures, what would happen then? Did Presvel really believe he could survive in a place that was swarming with such deadly predators? Did he have a plan at all? Or was he simply running?

As they rode on, Presvel decided to pick up speed so, for some time, Rochalla was too busy trying to cope with her horse to worry about anything else. Though Presvel was no great horseman, at least he could manage, but she had never ridden on her own before. It was a lot different from riding double and being a mere passenger, as she had done when they had escaped from Tiarond. Not knowing how to hold the reins, or how to sit properly and balance herself in the saddle, she slithered and bounced around all over the place, perpetually on the brink of disaster, and staying on only by clinging for dear life to the front of the saddle. Her horse, sensing, as all animals will, who was the boss, eventually tired of following his stablemate and stopped abruptly, putting his head down to graze. Rochalla shot over his neck and landed face down in a scratchy clump of heather.

With an oath, Presvel turned his own mount and came back to her, wrestling with his reins and keeping Annas in place with one hand, while leaning over to catch the girl's straying mount by the bridle with the other. Rochalla, winded, scratched, muddy and bruised, burst into tears, but he looked down on her with no trace of pity. 'Get up,' he said coldly.

'I can't,' she sobbed. 'You know I can't ride this bloody thing!'

Suddenly, he had the point of his knife at Annas's throat once more. 'Learn.'

Cold hatred dried her tears. Glaring at him, she managed, somehow, to haul herself up onto the back of her fidgeting mount. Leaning across, he hit her, an open-handed blow across her face. 'And take that look off your face.'

Rochalla dropped her eyes, resisting the urge to press a hand to her flaming face. 'I'm sorry, Presvel,' she said meekly. It wasn't difficult to pretend to be cowed. It had been one thing to think he might hurt her, but quite another to have him do it. It had brought home to her, in a way that nothing else had, just how much danger she and Annas were in. Better to let him think he had intimidated her – otherwise, she knew she could expect further punishment.

Presvel tied her reins to a ring on his saddle, and led her along. They rode in silence for some time before Rochalla gathered her courage, and spoke. 'Presvel, I'm trying to understand. Why did you kill the Summoner? You did kill him, didn't you? But surely it must have been a mistake? An accident?'

Presvel gave a short laugh. 'Oh, it was a mistake, all right. It was your good friend Scall that I was after, when the old fool intervened.'

Horror washed over her in a dizzying wave. 'You were trying to kill *Scall?*'

He gave her a black look. 'Oh, you don't have to worry about your little friend,' he sneered. 'At least, not on *my* account. I was only trying to frighten him, and warn him off you – at *that* point, at least. No, it seems to have been Dark who dragged him off to who-knows-where.' He grinned nastily. 'What with one thing and another, I doubt that they survived the night out here, but that's hardly *my* fault. And now that the competition's out of the way, you'll go back to being mine, and only mine.' He squeezed Annas cruelly, so that the child whimpered. 'We could make a nice little family, don't you think?'

Rochalla fought to keep her voice level. 'Of course we could. But Presvel, how are we going to survive in Tiarond? Is there nowhere else we could go?'

'We're going home,' Presvel said firmly. 'I don't believe that the winged demons will be there any more. I don't believe that there were all that many in the first place. Seriema panicked, and so did that ignorant oaf Tormon. There was no real need to leave, and put ourselves through all this. You saw for yourself that there were still Godsword troops around, because we passed that patrol. They'll have taken care of the problem by now and everything will be as it was, except that *I* will take over the reins of Seriema's empire – not to mention her mansion.'

He smiled at Rochalla, his earlier violence apparently forgotten. 'Everyone should have a home. Seriema doesn't want her house any more – she's going to wed that dolt of a barbarian, the chieftain's son, and spend the rest of her life running around like a savage on the moors. So I decided that we might as well have it, instead. After a whole lifetime of pandering to her Ladyship's every whim and fancy, I think I've earned it, don't you? And why shouldn't you be a great lady? You may be a lying, treacherous little slut, but I'm sure we can cure you of that.'

A chill went through Rochalla. More than ever now, she knew that she and Annas must escape from this madman but, while he continued to hold Annas at knifepoint, she had no idea how she could get the two of them away.

Tormon and the Reivers must be following us by now, I'm sure of it, but they won't dare come anywhere near us until after nightfall, when the winged fiends will be on the loose. Dear Myrial, I don't know how we'll ever manage to get out of this.

In the Otherplace of Helverien's long exile, the Mage gathered that it was time for recriminations among the new and unexpected visitors. As soon as the second pair arrived, caught by the same trap into which the first couple had fallen, there had been a very noisy shouting match, with much yelling and waving of arms, between the woman from the first pair, and one of the men who arrived subsequently. They were so preoccupied with their dispute that they had ignored Helverien completely, and she had stepped back into the background, not very pleased, but listening with one eyebrow raised to all the commotion. 'They may let slip more information in the course of their quarrelling than they would tell us voluntarily,' she commented to Thirishri.

Truly. Shree, quite literally invisible to the human eye, was also watching and listening closely, hovering above the humans. *They certainly come from my time,* she said. *Though I don't know the others, I recognise one of them as a Godsword – a Temple warrior from Tiarond. I wonder what he's doing here? He would be the one who could tell us exactly what had been going on in the city, but I doubt that we'll get much sense out of him until these four idiotic humans have finally settled their differences.*

Helverien nodded agreement. From the hot words that passed between them she gathered that the quarrellers were brother and sister, that she had stolen something and run away, and that he had followed her. Though the field of human emotions had been closed to her for a very long time, she soon realised that beneath all the shouting and shoving, they loved each other very deeply and, as she had expected, the argument ended in a tearful embrace, and peace was restored.

In the meantime, she noticed, the girl's companion was staying well out of reach of the tall, blue-eyed Godsword with the air of command about him. When Shree turned her attention to him, the skinny, unkempt little man was protesting his innocence. 'But it wasn't my fault. I saw her sneaking around the Temple and I saw her nick the food, but I didn't know what else she had stolen until later. I followed her because I could see that she was getting into some kind of trouble, and I wanted to help. All along I've been trying to persuade her to go back, but she wouldn't.'

Helverien, rather piqued that the quartet were far too preoccupied with their own affairs to take any notice of her, decided that it was time to intervene. Drawing herself up into a dignified pose, she stepped forward, so that all four humans fell silent and turned to look at her. 'I am Helverien,' she said. 'This place has been my dwelling and my prison for long ages uncounted. Before you say another word, I want to know who you are, how you came to this place, and what you are doing here.' She gestured them towards the table on the terrace, and created chairs for the two newcomers. Judging from their reactions, the materialisation of furniture out of thin air impressed them quite as much as it had done with the first two. Shree, watching, invisible from above, sighed. Helverien ignored her, focusing all her attention on the four new arrivals. 'Well?'

It took some time to sort their stories out. Even with Shree, their contemporary, helping her with occasional pertinent comments, it took a while for Helverien to get all the facts straight – and to be honest, she found it difficult to care about the politics and petty machinations within the ranks of the Tiarondian survivors that had sent Aliana down into the tunnels beneath the Temple. Out of the entire tale, only one thing was of any importance whatsoever. 'Can I see the ring?' she asked.

Reluctantly, with a wary glance at her tall companion, the girl pulled it out of her pocket, unwrapped it, and laid it on the table, where the large red stone glowed like an ember. Helverien gasped. 'I knew it! Do you know what this is? It's a key. A key that can be used to repair the Curtain Walls. With this ring, and my knowledge, we stand a chance of putting things right.' Then she sighed. 'If we could get out of here, that is.'

Galveron had turned very pale. 'So, are you saying that without this ring, no one in our world outside this place has a chance of putting things right?'

The Mage shook her head. 'There may be other ways, but the ring is the only one I know. But it's doubtful that your people could have made use of it in any case . . .'

But Galveron was no longer listening. He was looking at the girl, his expression a daunting mixture of anger and contempt. 'There,' he said. 'Do you see what you've done? The lives of all those people will be on your conscience. I hope you're proud of yourself.'

With a cry of distress, Aliana leapt up from the table and ran off. Packrat got up to go after her, but Alestan restrained him with a hand on his arm. 'Leave her. Give her a few minutes to get it out of her system. I'll go after her in a little while.' He turned to Galveron, his eyes hard. 'Sooner or later, you'll pay for that.'

The Godsword shrugged. 'Really? Well, sooner or later we'll all pay for what *she* did.'

'Oh, come, Galveron,' Helverien intervened. 'You were far too hard on the child. She was only thinking of you.' She looked down at the crimson jewel that glittered on the table. 'She couldn't have been expected to understand the significance of the ring. According to you, not even your Hierarch knows that.'

'But she ought to know the difference between right and wrong,' Galveron replied implacably. 'She was perfectly well aware that she was doing wrong when she stole that ring – but she went ahead and did it anyway.'

The Mage shook her head. 'Maybe,' she said, 'but in truth, this entire business has come down to a gamble. If someone should come looking for you all, and happen to free us, then Aliana will have done the only possible thing that could have saved the world, by bringing the ring to the one person who knew how to use it. If she hadn't stolen it, and had just given it to your Hierarch – well, you would all have been doomed in any case.'

'How do you know?' said Galveron indignantly. 'We might have learned how to use it.'

'And pigs might fly.' Helverien gave him a long, level look. 'For my part, I think it almost impossible that you would have done any such thing. Whatever that poor, misguided girl's motives were for stealing that ring, it was wrong and cruel of you to put the deaths of a whole world on her conscience. You owe her an apology.'

Galveron spluttered. '*I* owe *her* an apology?'

'You heard me. Just think for a moment, Galveron, why she did what she did. She never thought for one moment of keeping the ring for herself. She took it for you – because she believes in you, and she's sure you'd make a damn sight better leader for her people than the current Hierarch.' Helverien smiled. 'You have to admit, there aren't many women who would have the gumption to try to steal a whole realm as a gift for the man they love.'

'What?'

'That's bloody ridiculous!'

'There's no *way* Aliana would fall for an accursed Godsword!'

The objections came from all three men simultaneously, and with such force that Helverien was almost rocked back on her seat. 'Well, well,' she said to the watching Wind-Sprite, in mindspeech. 'We may be trapped here, but this situation looks like providing us with some entertainment.'

Who cares about yet another example of human folly? How can you be so flippant, when the future of the world is at stake?

The Magewoman shrugged. 'If I could alter the fate of the world I would, Thirishri, as well you should know. But since currently I'm not in a position to influence a damn thing, I might as well work with the material I have right here.'

Muttering, Shree left the terrace, venting her frustration in a violent blast of wind that threw dust and leaves up into the air, almost flattened the olive trees, and sent a huge wave thundering up the beach. Before it could reach the humans, however, Helverien waved her hand, and the wall of water suddenly collapsed, spreading out across the beach before draining harmlessly back into the sea.

'What in the name of perdition was *that?*' Alestan demanded. Packrat was trying out some of his more colourful curses – but Galveron sat silent and grave, so deep in thought that the phenomenon had passed him by almost unnoticed. Suddenly, he got to his feet. 'I'm going to find Aliana.'

Alestan also rose, to block his path. 'Leave her alone. You've done enough damage.'

Galveron's eyes flashed, but when he spoke his voice was almost conciliatory. 'You don't understand. I'm taking Helverien's advice. Aliana was wrong to steal the ring, and nothing can change that, but I was equally wrong, to treat her as I did. I don't want to hurt her, Alestan. She – she means a lot to me. I'm going to apologise to her, and maybe then the two of us can talk this whole business through.'

'Don't let him,' Packrat said. 'Make the stinking bastard leave her alone.' But Alestan stepped back. 'All right,' he said. 'For once, I actually believe you, Godsword.'

Briefly, Galveron clasped the Grey Ghost's hand. 'Thank you, Alestan. I appreciate that,' he said. 'And don't worry. I'll be careful. I know that the last couple of days must have been very hard on her, since she stole the ring.' With that, he strode off in the direction in which the thief had vanished.

Alestan shook his head. 'I hope this situation isn't going the way I think it is,' he said. 'If I end up with a blasted Godsword for a brother-in-law, I'll never live it down.'

Packrat gasped. 'But you wouldn't let her . . .'

'How the blazes could I stop her? She's her own woman, you ought to know that by now. That's how we all ended up here in the first place. Just so long as she's happy, and he takes care of her, I can stand it, I suppose.'

Helverien watched them all with a faint, indulgent smile on her face. It was nice to have people around her again.

Aliana sat beneath a tree with her arms wrapped around her knees, and stared at the ocean. She wasn't weeping, and she didn't even feel any anger – not yet, at any rate. Within her was nothing but a void: a numb emptiness where all her feelings ought to be. She didn't even want to *think* about Galveron's words, let alone take them in. Packrat had been right. Her whole impetuous scheme had ended in disaster, but just for a little while longer, she could pretend that it had not. By keeping her mind in this precarious state of blankness, she could pretend that the dreadful scene between herself and the Godsword Commander had never taken place.

When Alestan and Galveron had appeared, Aliana had felt weak with relief at the sight of them, safe and apparently unhurt. Unfortunately, the pleasure didn't seem to be mutual. She had never seen her brother so angry with her. It was much easier to think of Alestan's stormy anger than Galveron's cold contempt. She and her brother could never stay vexed with each other for long. They were all the family each other had, and they shared the close, mysterious bond of twins. Their quarrels tended to be noisy, tumultuous, and of short duration, but once they had managed to get whatever-it-was out of their systems, forgiveness was as natural to them as breathing.

I wish he was here with me right now. It would be such a comfort . . .

But that thought was taking her in a direction in which she did not want to go, and she cut it off abruptly, returning to her contemplation of the vivid blue sea.

She never heard him coming. One minute, it seemed, she was alone and the next, Galveron was sitting beside her. She stiffened, not knowing exactly what to expect, but bracing herself for whatever was to come.

'Aliana, I've come to say I'm sorry.'

'What did you say?' This was without a doubt the last thing she'd expected.

'Don't push it,' he growled. 'One apology is all you get.'

She kept on looking out to sea, rather than look into his face just yet. It made things easier, somehow. 'I'm sorry too, Galveron. It was a stupid idea.'

Galveron picked up a pebble, and threw it towards the water. 'You know, all the way through those accursed tunnels, I've been rehearsing, at great length, all the things I wanted to say to you. In the end, though, it all comes down to a single word. *"Why?"'*

Aliana took her courage in both hands, and gave him a very direct look. 'Why did I take the ring? Because you wouldn't take it for yourself,' she said quietly. 'You're so damn loyal to Gilarra, but everyone except you can see that she can't cope as Hierarch. She concentrates on the wrong things, she can't seem to get herself, or anyone else, organised, she has no idea how to encourage people and make them feel that they are important – just the opposite, in fact. She almost seems to feel it's beneath her to say "thank you". If it hadn't been for you, she would never have lasted beyond that first night, and neither would the rest of those poor refugees. I wanted you to see that *you* should take charge – at least for as long as the emergency lasts. The situation in the Temple needs a military mind, not a religious one. If I had just said to you that you ought to step in and take over, you wouldn't have listened – either that or you'd have scoffed at me, or told me to mind my own business. I wanted to make you see how serious I was about this, so my idea was to go down into the tunnels and hide the ring – to use it as a sort of hostage, until Gilarra consented to step down, and you agreed to lead us all. It wouldn't just have been me, you know. Apart from the priesthood, maybe, you'd have had the entire Temple behind you.'

The Godsword Commander shook his head. 'But what about the penalties for stealing, you little idiot?'

'You could hardly do anything to me if I was the only person who knew the whereabouts of the ring.'

He sighed. 'To you, maybe. But what if I, or Gilarra, had elected to torture your friends until you gave it back?'

That came as a blow. Aliana's mouth fell open. 'You – you wouldn't have, would you?'

'You have no idea what I would have done,' Galveron said sternly, 'and furthermore, you had no idea what *you* were doing, either. It was the most hare-brained, impractical, ill-conceived idea I've ever heard, and it was doomed to failure from the start.'

Aliana felt very small. She hung her head. 'I know that now,' she admitted. 'I didn't really have time to think it through properly. I knew I wouldn't have the ring for long before Gilarra demanded it, and it was just a stroke of luck that I had it at all. It just seemed like fate, somehow . . .' She swallowed hard. 'But then once I got into the tunnels, there was nowhere to hide the wretched thing, and so I kept on going because I didn't dare go back, and by that time Packrat had become embroiled in the whole business too, and it all just got so out of hand . . .' She heard the tremor in her voice and swallowed again. She was *damned* if she was going to cry in front of him!

He put an arm around her shoulders. 'Well, it's done now, and Helverien says that if someone finds us in time, you did the only thing possible to save Callisiora.'

'But what if they don't find us?' Aliana said miserably. 'Or what if someone comes after us and falls into the same trap, as you and Alestan did?'

Galveron sighed. 'I don't know. But don't worry. We'll find a way to make it right somehow.'

Thirty

Fitting In

Slightly away from the Gendival settlement, around the
northern edge of the lake, on the opposite side from the tree-
clad slopes where the Loremasters dwelt and a few hundred
yards past the village and the mill, there stood an abandoned house.
About ten years previously, the place had been built by the miller's
eldest son whose increasing family – his wife was one of those
cheerful, fecund women who seemed to drop another offspring
every year – had forced him to move out of the mill and into a larger
home of his own. His choice of site had proved unfortunate,
however. It was a pretty spot, on the edge of the water but, two
winters after the family had moved in, a freak storm had caused the
lake to rise and break its banks and the floodwaters had come
pouring around the house.

Everything had happened so quickly and unexpectedly that two
of the family's small children had been drowned while they were
trying to make their escape, and after that no one had wanted to
live there any more. Though such a storm happened only once in
a blue moon, people now knew that particular location to be flood-
prone, especially since such a large section of the banks had been
washed away. The villagers thought the place was unlucky and
haunted, and it was on the wrong side of the lake, and too distant
from the other Loremaster dwellings and the settlement in general,
to be of interest to the Shadowleague.

Now, however, the abandoned house had come into its own once
more, as the new home and prison of the captive Ak'Zahar. The

412

main living area of the building was being caged off – walls, floors, and ceiling – with a sturdy, specially reinforced mesh which would withstand even the strength of the winged predator. A team of Shadowleague volunteers whose scientific curiosity had overcome their apprehension and revulsion, were moving into the remainder of the dwelling to study the creature, turning the kitchen into a makeshift laboratory and the bedrooms into study and meeting rooms. The third bedchamber had retained its original function, and would hold beds for off-duty researchers to rest from their day and night vigil.

As dusk fell around Gendival, lighting had been put into position around the house, inside and out, and the research team, plus a number of labourers and artisans from the village, were continuing to work into the night to get the place ready for its new occupant. The sound of hammering, sawing, and the tumult of voices trying to be heard above the background noise could be heard from within, and flashes of brilliant light could be glimpsed through the windows as the cage was welded into place.

Veldan leaned on the low garden wall and watched all the activity from a safe distance. She had put in an exhausting day with Amaurn, doing nothing, it seemed, but argue and fight with Cergorn's supporters – not to mention other members of both Shadowleague and village. They hadn't wanted the Takuru shapeshifters living in their midst, they didn't want to keep the captive Ak'Zahar alive to study, and many of them hadn't wanted Cergorn's memories to be wiped. Due to nothing more in the end than Amaurn's sheer strength of will, they had ended up getting all three, but it had taken an awful lot of wrangling and debate before they had given in. Veldan felt battered and drained from all the violent arguments and strong feelings flying around the settlement, which were even more wearing than usual, because the protagonists were all adept in mindspeech. She had come out here to escape all that, and the last thing she wanted now was someone volunteering her for a job.

'Too damn right.' Kaz, as always, was at her side. 'Honestly, Boss,

I could hit you sometimes. Somebody ought to knock some sense into you. In a couple of hours we'll be leaving for Callisiora again. This was our last chance for a while to have supper in front of a nice, roaring fire, and instead of making the most of the opportunity, we're standing out here on a cold, damp evening looking at the ugly face of that accursed monstrosity.' He twitched his tail in irritation.

'Oh, shut up, Kaz.' Veldan made a rude gesture at him. 'You know very well why I came out here.' Her eyes went to the Ak'Zahar, which was in a temporary cage on the other side of the garden wall, while its new enclosure was being constructed. It was crouched in a corner, watching her with a flat, unblinking stare that promised her no mercy, should she stray within its reach. The Loremaster shuddered. All that day, the planned return to Tiarond with Amaurn had been preying on her mind. There had been no doubt that she would go, but the thought of having to face those winged predators once more was filling her with terror. She had brought herself out here to the captive Ak'Zahar, in the hope that spending time in the presence of her old enemy would somehow inure her to the fear of its fellows, but it didn't seem to be working. On a night like this, the raw cold stiffened the scars on her arm and shoulder and set them aching, reminding her all too clearly of her last encounter with the Ak'Zahar. Unconsciously her hand went to the side of her face and, once more, she became aware of the difference in the texture of her skin, and the eerie numbness that existed in the new-grown tissue.

Will it happen again?

Will it be worse this time?

Will I die in slow agony, as Melnyth did, torn into a thousand pieces by talon and tooth?

The firedrake growled, low in his throat. 'No, no, and no!' he snapped. 'This time, I'll be with you, and I'm not going to let *anything* happen.'

Veldan put an arm around his curving neck, and decided that there was no point in trying to hide her doubts from her partner.

'But you heard what Scall said. There'll be tunnels again. What if it's the same as last time and you can't be with me?'

'Ah,' the firedrake said smugly, 'I knew you'd be worried about that, so I talked to Amaurn. He's agreed to take blasting equipment and a couple of those plasma beam weapons, like the one that Kher is so good with, so that we can enlarge any openings that aren't built for beautiful and intelligent and *proper* sized beings such as myself.'

He leered at her, and Veldan burst out laughing, feeling relief sweep over her at the thought of having her partner at her side. 'Oh, Kaz – I do love you.'

Suddenly the firedrake's head snapped round, as he peered into the shadows. 'Who's there?'

Dark stepped out, looking a little discomfited. 'Sorry, I didn't mean to interrupt. Amaurn sent me to find you, Veldan. He says we should all be getting some rest, since we'll be riding through the night.' It had been decided that the journey would begin at such an uncivilised hour so that they could reach the Curtain Walls at daybreak, and be travelling through the predator-ridden lands of Callisiora in the daylight.

The Loremaster laughed. 'Amaurn says *we* should be getting some rest? Coming from him, that's rich, the way he's been charging around all day with that wound, keeping going on drugs and your painkilling skills.'

'I know,' Dark agreed. He came up beside her, and took up a similar position, leaning comfortably against the wall. 'I had to refuse him in the end, just so that he would slow down a bit, and act sensibly – or at least, that was the idea. I know that Kyrre knit those tissues with her sealer, but the repair needs time to strengthen. Only his body's natural healing processes can complete the job. He's crazy to push himself as he's doing, and this trip to Tiarond in his condition is nothing short of ridiculous.'

'I think so, too,' Veldan agreed, 'but he doesn't seem to feel he has a choice.' She shrugged. 'I feel a bit like that myself, I suppose. Once you've tangled with the Ak'Zahar, things become personal.'

'You did?' Dark looked surprised.

'I certainly did.' Lightly, Veldan touched her disfigured face. 'It was the Ak'Zahar who gave me this.' Somehow, possibly because the subject had already been broached with Dark, she could talk quite comfortably about her scars. 'We were in Ghariad, their own lands, a good way to the north of here beyond the Curtain Walls. Cergorn was Archimandrite then and he had sent us to gather information; Kaz and me, and Elion with his partner Melnyth.' She swallowed hard, against memories that still were painful. 'In a way, I got off lightly that day. When they discovered us, they tore poor Melnyth to pieces, and the rest of us were lucky to escape with our lives. We thought Elion would never get over it.'

'And yet the three of you are prepared to go up against them again,' Dark said wonderingly. 'That takes a rare and special kind of courage.'

In the darkness, Veldan felt herself blushing. 'What about you?' she asked, to cover her embarrassment. 'You must be the only person ever to have captured one of the Ak'Zahar. That's a pretty impressive feat.'

The Summoner laughed. 'Don't tell anyone, or I'll never live it down, but I'm afraid the laurels have to go to Scall for that one. The creature was attacking me – in fact, it had me on the ground – when he bashed it with a rock.' For a moment, his face grew sombre. 'I thought it was the end for me, to tell you the honest truth.'

'And yet you're willing to pit yourself against them, too,' Veldan said.

Dark nodded. 'It's for all the folk I left behind, in Arcan's clan,' he said. 'I may have left them without a Summoner, but that doesn't mean I've stopped feeling responsible for them. Grim would expect no less of me.'

'Grim was Amaurn's old friend?'

'That's right. He was my friend too, and my teacher and mentor, besides. He was like a father to me.' His voice thickened with unshed tears, and unthinkingly, Veldan tucked an arm through his. 'It's hard when you lose someone you love,' she said.

Abruptly, he changed the subject. 'Have you tried mindspeech on our captive here?'

'No.' Veldan shuddered. 'To be honest, I'm not even sure how intelligent they are. Thank providence, they don't seem to have much idea of working or hunting cooperatively, or we would be in bigger trouble than we are, but on the other hand, they do strike me as being brighter than the average animal. Why do you ask, anyway? Have *you* tried mindspeech with this creature?'

The Summoner nodded. 'I walked over here earlier today. I thought that if we could somehow work out a way to communicate with the Ak'Zahar, it might solve a lot of our problems. It would have given Amaurn a lot more ammunition for the argument that we should keep it here, besides.'

'And what happened?'

'Nothing. All I got was a blank, like a wall. But I couldn't decide whether it actually lacked the ability to use mindspeech, or whether it was shielding itself from me, because we're its enemies.'

'I wonder . . .' An idea began to form in Veldan's mind. 'If we can get one of the Takuru to join the research team, and it takes on the form of the Ak'Zahar, it might get our captive specimen to be more trusting, and to communicate.'

Dark's face lit up. 'That's a brilliant idea!'

Veldan grinned back at him. 'It was pretty inspired, if I say so myself. Also, it might help to justify Amaurn's promise that they could come and live here in the settlement.'

'I know I'm only new here,' Dark said, 'but I can't quite understand the antipathy people have towards the Takuru. There are so many weird and wonderful beings in the Shadowleague; so why such prejudice against one particular race? I thought there was going to be a riot today when Amaurn announced that they were coming to live with everyone else. They almost seemed to object to the Takuru even more than they did to the Ak'Zahar, and that's ridiculous.'

'The Takuru have a bad reputation in the Shadowleague,' Veldan told him. 'People are unnerved by a creature who could be right in their midst without them knowing, and though most of them seem to be decent enough, there have been various shapeshifters in the past who were more than willing to cause mischief by spreading gossip, and passing on secrets that they'd overheard.'

Dark nodded. 'And so the problem escalates. The Takuru make mischief because they aren't accepted, and they aren't accepted because they make mischief.'

'Exactly. And Cergorn's habit of using them as spies didn't help, either. That's why there's a fair-sized community of them living here – on the outskirts, of course. The Archimandrite found them far too useful to allow them to go home, yet he wouldn't bring them right into the settlement, either. I think he felt he would retain power over them by throwing them the occasional crumb of acceptance, while leaving them hungry for more. It's very sad, really.'

'Well, let's hope it will change now,' the Summoner said. 'I thought Kalevala spoke very well today. Her solemn oath that the Takuru would stick to their true forms within Gendival did a lot to set people's minds at rest.'

'That's true,' Veldan agreed. 'And because Cergorn used the Takuru himself, even his supporters couldn't really find a lot to object to, in the end.'

Dark turned to look at her. 'Tell me to mind my own business if you want to, but I thought it was hard for you when Cergorn left today.'

'You're right.' Now Veldan was the one who felt close to tears. The parting from Cergorn and Syvilda that afternoon had been diffi-cult for her. She had known them all her life – in a sense, they had practically brought her up. Though her relations with them had soured lately, they were still an important part of her life, and she was conscious of how much she owed them. The worst part of all had been the lack of any recognition on their blank faces as Cergorn was carried on board the waiting Navigator vessel, with Syvilda following. Though Veldan knew that the mind-wipe would have been painless, and she was also aware that they had a whole life-time's fabricated memories waiting to be triggered once the ship had departed from Gendival, it seemed that part of her past was being erased, as well as theirs. Though they would survive, and hopefully would live out a happy life, to her it would be as though they had died. She knew that she would never see them again.

She sighed. 'I think the hardest part of losing them was knowing that we had parted on such bad terms. Cergorn was far from pleased with me and Elion when we returned from Callisiora, but maybe we could have patched that up in time. Once Amaurn came on the scene, though, and I sided with him against them . . .' She shook her head. 'There's such a lot of old hatred there. Even if there had been some way for Cergorn and Syvilda to have stayed in Gendival, they never would have forgiven me for choosing Amaurn, just as he never forgave them for his own trial and exile and, indirectly, for my mother's death.'

Suddenly, Veldan didn't want to talk about it any more, and it was her turn to cast around for a change of subject. 'If you don't mind me asking, is Dark your real name?'

He shrugged. 'It is now. Grim gave it to me when he took me as his apprentice, and even though I've left the Reivers for the Shadowleague and I'm not really a Summoner any longer, I want to keep it for his sake.'

Suddenly, they were interrupted as the Ak'Zahar made a leap to the front of its cage. Hissing and snarling, it reached out a bony arm between the bars and flailed at Dark with its claws extended. With an oath, Veldan jumped back, and then grinned sheepishly at her companion. 'Old habits die hard. Even with that monstrosity behind bars, I don't think I'll ever really get used to having it around.'

'You and most other folk,' Dark said ruefully. 'Amaurn had to push very hard to get the Shadowleague to accept it, and the villagers were almost worse.'

'Amaurn's good at pushing, though. It took some fast talking, but they came round to the idea in the end.'

'Only because he didn't leave them with a lot of choice,' Dark retorted. 'Nobody but that handful of researchers actually wanted it.'

'Maybe you're being a bit too pessimistic,' Veldan argued. 'It's only natural that people are going to feel uneasy about living so close to one of the Ak'Zahar. I do myself, even though I know it's locked up quite safely. But I also believe in your argument that knowledge is the most powerful weapon. When Amaurn put that to them, I think most folk accepted it, albeit reluctantly.'

'I'm glad that *he* put it to them, and I didn't have to,' Dark said. 'They would have made mincemeat of me – especially that Afanc. He scares the pants off me. We didn't get off to a good start when he came rearing up out of the lake and threatening me and Kher, when I first arrived, and I got the impression that our second meeting today wasn't much better. His objections against the Ak'Zahar were violent, to say the least, and I just *know* that he was blaming me for bringing it here.'

'Bastiar's objections were more against Amaurn being leader than you and your Ak'Zahar,' Veldan told him. 'He's one of Cergorn's most loyal supporters.' She shivered. 'I've never seen him so angry as he was when Amaurn announced Cergorn's exile, even though he must have known, in his heart, that it was a kinder and more charitable act than executing him.'

'Is it always like this when the Archimandrite changes?' Dark asked. 'It seems a little extreme.'

'No.' Veldan shook her head. 'As far as I'm aware, the progression from one leader to the next is usually quite smooth. But you've joined the Shadowleague in tumultuous times, my friend. Partly, I think, it's due to the breakdown of the Curtain Walls, and all the associated problems. Suddenly, the isolationist position of the Shadowleague was hampering our attempts to help the victims of the resulting wars and climate shifts and, more importantly, it was interfering with our ability to put the situation right. If that wasn't bad enough, we had Cergorn and Amaurn, whose positions and opinions were so polarised that they *had* to be natural enemies and, of course, we still have their followers entrenched in their opposing camps.'

She picked a piece of lichen off the wall, and sighed. 'It was so tedious today, having to go through all those tired old arguments about tradition versus innovation yet again. The fact is, no one will know if the new ways are any good until they've been tried, and no one would ever try them before now, because once the knowledge is out there, and available, it can never be taken back again. I know it's a risk, but I don't think we can keep suppressing this stuff for ever. Take those lamps over there.' She waved a hand in the direction of the brightly lit house. 'They're powered by crystals which are found in the deserts of the Dragonfolk, and there's certainly a tradition that the dragons used them on their home world. But were we allowed to use them here? Of course not. Cergorn and his predecessors wanted to keep even the Shadowleague to a low level of technology, so that we wouldn't get dependent on it, and go around hankering after it to solve problems while we were out in the world. Amaurn actually had those lamps hauled out of the museum and told the researchers to use them, but a lot of people aren't too happy with the idea. It's the same with his notion of using blasting powder against the Ak'Zahar, while they roost.' She was talking about a suggestion that Amaurn had made, towards the end of that morning's meeting. 'It's the only way I can think of to deal with them, and it's certainly the safest – apart from the poor soul who has to go in and set the charges, of course. But to hear the Afanc talk, you'd think the world was coming to an end. I'd like to think that, with Cergorn gone, we should see an end to the dissension, but it won't happen. His followers are still here, they're still very resentful, and while the former Archimandrite is alive, they'll keep looking for a way to bring him back.'

'Do you think they'll ever manage it?' Dark asked. He shifted position uneasily. 'Judging from the Afanc's behaviour, I wouldn't give much for the prospects of Amaurn or his supporters if they succeed.'

'I don't think they'll be able to bring back Cergorn as leader,' Veldan said. 'Not after a full mind-wipe. But there would certainly be nothing to stop them aligning themselves behind another candidate.' As she spoke, she thought of the lost Wind-Sprite, Cergorn's former partner.

I wonder what happened to Shree? Because if she ever returns, Amaurn will really have to watch his back.

A silence fell between them, and they stood for a while, turning their backs on the brightly lit house to watch the stars glittering in the darkness above, and the wind ruffling the surface of the lake.

'I hate to interrupt, but Amaurn wants to know where you two are. He says he's finished working out his plans for the blasting powder with Kher, and we're nearly ready to go.' The firedrake snickered. 'Naturally, I didn't tell him where to find you – but I think you and your new friend had better hurry right along, sweetie, before he comes looking for you.'

Only when she heard Kaz speak, did Veldan remember that he had been there, and wonder when he had actually left. 'Where are you?' she wanted to know.

'I've been enjoying that supper in front of the fire that you won't get now. I didn't think you needed me around.' He paused, and she could sense that he was grinning. 'I like Dark. I think he shows a lot of promise – especially for a Callisioran.'

Veldan was glad that the darkness hid her blush. 'I'm happy you like him, Kaz. So do I.'

She turned to the Summoner. 'We'd better be getting back. Kaz said that Amaurn is ready to go.'

Dark's eyes widened in surprise. 'What – so soon? The time has just flown by.' Even as Veldan turned to go, he hesitated. 'Veldan – do you really think I'll fit in here?'

She stepped back towards him, and took his hand. 'I think you're going to fit in just fine.'

Thirty-One

The Way Back

Annas was afraid of Presvel, but it was more than that: she hated him, too. He had handled her roughly, he had hurt her with a knife, he had hit poor Rochalla – and worst of all, he had taken her away from her Dad. He was a Bad Man, just like the Bad Men who had killed her Mama. Some instinct of survival made the little girl stay very still, slouching in the saddle, and pretending to be asleep. If she didn't do anything or say anything, she reasoned, maybe he would forget that she was there, and not hurt her.

Beneath her eyelashes she caught the occasional sidelong glimpse of Rochalla. Because she had been brought up with horses, and riding them before she could walk, she could tell that the blonde girl didn't have a clue. Rochalla was sitting all wrong, and sliding around in the saddle because she wasn't holding on properly with her legs. She looked uncomfortable and scared. Annas wanted to help her and tell her what she was doing wrong, but if she spoke up, it might make Presvel angry, which was the last thing she wanted. All too well, she remembered what the other Bad Men had done to her Mama. What if this one did the same thing to Rochalla – or even to herself?

The rain was beginning to turn into big, wet snowflakes, and Annas didn't have a coat or a cloak to keep her warm. She was cold, and tired, and hungry, and scared, and getting wetter by the minute, and she wished that Dad was here. He wouldn't let Presvel hurt her. Where was he? Why wasn't he here? Why had he let the Bad Man get her? Surely he must be coming. Oddly, the other person who would have been comforting to have around was lady Seriema. She might be a bit grumpy, but she wasn't so bad, really, and she wouldn't put up with any nonsense from Presvel. She could tell him what to do – Annas had seen her do it before.

My Dad will be coming. He must be coming. All I have to do is look after Rochalla till he gets here, and not let the Bad Man get me. Then everything will be all right.

Of course, if she could get away, somehow, then that would be even better. It didn't seem very likely that she could manage it, but Annas was determined to be on the watch. If a chance did come along for her to run away, she had better not waste it.

Presvel was actually beginning to hope that he might get away with this. It was getting dark now and, so far, there was no sign of any pursuit. Though he had more sense than to believe that Tormon and the Reivers weren't after him, if he could keep them at a sufficient distance he might actually have a chance to get up into Scall's tunnels before they realised what his intentions were. Then, safe and sound from any threat of the winged demons, he was sure that he might lose his pursuers altogether.

Though the valleys were falling into shadow, there was still a little daylight left in the evening sky. Ahead of him he could see the looming mountains, with the peak of Mount Chaikar standing up tall and proud above the others, a landmark and a beacon to guide his way. Now that it was beginning to get dark, and he was coming closer and closer to the city, he began to worry about the winged predators. Once or twice he thought he heard a harsh cry in the distance, but with Presvel's innocence of anything to do with nature, it might just as well have been a night bird, or some hunting animal. The wind was getting up now too, and as it whistled across the open spaces of the bleak foothills, it distorted and masked all other sounds.

As the mountain drew closer, and the hills around its skirts became more steep and rugged, the half-hearted snowfall began to thicken, though the soft wet flakes didn't lie, but sank into the muddy ground and vanished. Now that the clouds were coming down it was growing increasingly difficult to see without carrying lights of some kind, which the fugitive dared not do. Besides, the two horses were exhausted; stumbling and staggering along the slippery trail. When the little group of refugees had left the city, going the other way, Tormon had rested their mounts frequently, making everyone dismount and lead them for a time, but Presvel hadn't been interested in walking – especially when he knew he was being pursued. Now, even though he was no horseman, it was beginning to come home to him that if he didn't stop soon, he would lose the horses altogether. The prospect of finishing his journey on foot, combined with the threat of the winged demons, brought him to his senses. For some time now, as they had drawn nearer to Tiarond, they had been passing the odd farmstead, not to mention isolated cottages belonging to labourers and shepherds. Much as it made him uneasy to stop when he knew that Tormon and the Reivers must be on his trail, and much as he begrudged losing the time, he knew he would have to find somewhere to shelter for the night. His only comfort was that his pursuers would be in the same position.

For some time he had been following a track which seemed to be leading him in the right direction, and finally it had joined a clear, if primitive, road. As it wound across the side of a hill, Presvel saw a narrow track leading up to his left, and a cluster of buildings nestling into a hollow in the hillside above. Clearly, they had been abandoned – there were no lights in the windows, and no smoke could be seen from the chimneys – and he decided that they would be as good a place as any to stop for the night.

It was difficult to persuade the horses to drag their way up the steep hillside, especially with the riders still aboard, but there was no way that Presvel was going to *walk* all the way up there. When they finally reached the cluster of buildings he found a stable, and they dismounted and led the drooping beasts inside. Rochalla was limping stiffly, grimacing with pain but, nevertheless, he made her take the saddles and bridles from the horses and give them a perfunctory rub down with a wisp of musty straw while he stood nearby, still holding Tormon's child at knifepoint. Leaving the weary animals to roam loose within the stable, to find any bits of fodder they might scrounge, Presvel made sure that they were securely fastened in. Then, tucking the child under one arm, he made Rochalla walk in front of him to the house, carrying the saddlebags from his horse.

The farmhouse was dirty and squalid, and smelled of mould and damp, but at least it was a shelter from the predators that stalked the night. When he put Annas down, the child ran to Rochalla, who knelt and put her arms around her. 'Are you all right?' she asked softly.

'Mostly,' Annas said. 'But I'm cold and I'm hungry.'

'Here,' Presvel said, pulling the cloth-wrapped package out of his saddlebag. 'I brought us some food.'

'What about a fire?' Rochalla asked. 'We're frozen.'

'No fire,' he said flatly. Though it would have made sense for Tormon and the Reivers to have found their own shelter by now, the trader's concern for his daughter might have overridden all considerations of safety, in which case Presvel was not about to take the risk of betraying his whereabouts. Smoke from a chimney might attract the winged fiends too, and that was the last thing he wanted. Rochalla looked as though she wanted to protest, but she compressed her lips and said nothing. The memory of the earlier blow must still be clear in her mind. Presvel smiled to himself. Evidently, he had been too indulgent with her in the past. He should have taken a firmer hand with her long ago.

After he had fed them, he made Rochalla put the little girl to bed in one of the upstairs rooms and, once Annas was settled, locked the door behind her. Then, ignoring the blonde girl's protests, he took her arm and hustled her back downstairs. He'd had no chance to get her alone since they had left Tiarond – but that was about to change. He had a lot of lost time to make up, but on the other hand they had the whole night in front of them. Presvel looked hungrily at Rochalla who was his at last. The last few days had been bad ones, but maybe things were looking up.

It was a long night. Cetain's Reiver band spent the hours of darkness in another abandoned farm, but this time, the house was an empty, burnt-out shell, and they were forced to camp out, horses, warriors and all, in the large, sturdy barn. Looking around at the walls of solid stone, Seriema was reminded of the night when they had been attacked by the predators on the moor, and forced to take shelter in the cellar of the old, ruined tower. She reflected that she was lucky to be living in a region where stone was cheaper and more plentiful than wood as a building material. That one fact might make all the difference to the survival of human beings in these mountains.

There was nowhere safe for a fire in the barn, which was going to mean a chilly night, but the straw and dried bracken in the upper loft could make a cosy bed, and they found a small but precious supply of hay squirrelled away in a corner, to feed the horses.

As always, each rider carried rations with him, so supper was not a problem. After watches were set, the men began to settle down for the night, making themselves at home in their new surroundings. Word of Cetain and Seriema's intentions to wed had spread through the troop and so they had to endure some good-natured chaffing on the subject of sleeping arrangements, but she didn't care. Drowsy after the long ride, she wanted nothing more than to snuggle down with Cetain, and fall asleep in the warmth of his arms. Unfortunately, however, she was too concerned about Tormon to do anything of the kind.

When Cetain had insisted on finding shelter for the night, the trader had argued long and vehemently against the decision, and had only changed his mind in the end when Seriema had pointed out that they ran the risk of losing Presvel's trail in the dark – or even worse, they stood a chance of running into him, and frightening him into harming his hostages. Finally, Tormon had acquiesced, though with ill grace, but now he had taken himself apart from the others and was standing near his horse, looking as if he intended to stay there all night.

Seriema, sitting on a pile of bracken up in the hayloft, looked down helplessly at the trader. 'I feel as if I should go to him,' she told Cetain, 'but I just don't know what to say. He already lost his poor lifemate in the most horrific circumstances and now his little girl is very much at risk, and frankly, her prospects don't look good. Any words of comfort I could try to offer him would be so empty right now. He would know it, and so would I.'

'I'll go and talk to him, shall I?' Cetain got to his feet, brushed straw and bracken fronds from his clothing, and scrambled down the ladder, leaving Seriema looking after him in astonishment. He approached Tormon, and seemed to be admiring the big black Sefrian stallion, and to her surprise, the trader was soon talking to him. The conversation went on for a while, and though Seriema, eaten up with curiosity, strained her ears, she was too far away to hear what they were saying. After a time, Cetain clapped Tormon on the shoulder and set off back up the ladder, and in a few minutes the trader followed him and settled down in the bracken.

Wide-eyed, Seriema looked at the Reiver. 'What in the name of all creation did you say to him?' she whispered, as he settled back down beside her.

Cetain looked a little uncomfortable. 'Just man stuff,' he said.

'*Man stuff?*' Seriema's eyebrows almost went up to her hairline.

He sighed, 'Oh, all right – if you really want to know. I said I understood why he was in a hurry to get his hands on Presvel. I told him that if it were you, or our child, who had been taken hostage, I would feel just the same.' He spread out his hands. 'Lass, it's no good trying to tell a man in Tormon's position that every-thing will be all right. He knows damn well that there's a good chance it won't.'

'So what did you tell him?' Seriema was still a little baffled by all this.

The Reiver sighed. 'I promised him that whatever happens tomorrow, I'll help him hunt down Presvel and kill him, like the dangerous animal he's become.'

'Oh.' It was as though someone had kicked Seriema in the stomach. For a moment, she felt physically sick.

Cetain was looking at her with concern, searching her face carefully with his eyes. 'I'm sorry,' he said. 'But you understand, don't you, why it has to be this way? I know he was your friend and companion for so many years, but we aren't hunting the old Presvel, the one you knew. This one has already murdered one man, and now he has a young girl and a child at his mercy. It we let him go, next time it could be you, or me, or our child if we ever have one, or someone else's.'

Seriema took a deep breath. 'If he ever goes after you, I'll kill him myself,' she said fiercely – then she shook her head. 'Just listen to me, would you? As if I'd have the faintest clue how to kill a man!' She nestled into the curve of his arm. 'I know you're right, Cetain. In my heart, I've known all along that we weren't going to bring Presvel back alive. But it took a while for the reality to sink in, I suppose.' Her eyes filled with tears. 'And I can't help but mourn for the man I used to know,' she finished, in a small, muffled voice.

Cetain held her tightly. 'I shouldn't have brought you, really,' he said. 'But I was selfish. I needed you to be part of this. I don't want to involve you in Presvel's death, but you were a part of his life. For the sake of our future, lass, I don't want you wondering if I took part in the needless slaughter of your oldest friend. Such a doubt would fester between us, and ruin what we have together. This way it's hard for you, but at least you'll be there, you'll know what happened and why, and you won't spend the rest of your life wondering.'

Seriema wiped her eyes with the back of her hand. 'I understand,' she said, 'and you're right, even though it isn't easy to be a part of it all.'

'Aye, life can be very cruel, sometimes.' He kissed her gently. 'But it does have its compensations, too. Let's try and get some sleep now, shall we? Hopefully, by this time tomorrow, it'll all be over.'

As Seriema snuggled down into the bracken beside Cetain, the last thing she saw before she closed her eyes, was the lonely figure of Tormon, sitting alone with his arms wrapped around his knees, staring vacantly into space. And in that moment, she knew without a single doubt that they were doing the right thing.

As the bleak dawn broke across the hills, Rochalla cleaned herself as best she could in cold water in the farmhouse kitchen, wishing that she could wash away the memory of Presvel's foul touch upon her skin. The previous night had been one of the most difficult of her life, but it would have been far worse had she not spent those hard years as a whore, to keep her family alive. During that time she had learned to distance herself from what was happening to her body, no matter how distasteful it might be.

When Derla died, I swore that I would never again lie with a man I didn't love, for as long as I lived. I broke that oath when I put myself under Presvel's protection because I was alone and scared, but little did I know then that I would have to play the whore for him to save my own life, and that of another little girl.

Presvel had been outside, checking that their horses had made it safely through the night. He knew he didn't have to worry about her running away – not with poor little Annas locked in the room upstairs and the key in his pocket. She heard his step outside and rearranged her clothing hastily. He had been insatiable through the night, and she didn't want to give him any glimpses of flesh that might set him off again.

As he came in, he was whistling. 'All ready to go?' he said. She couldn't believe how well she had deceived him. He was so desperate to believe that she still wanted him, that he had never paused to consider how she might feel about a man who had done murder, and who had now captured herself and a little child at knifepoint.

He won't ever trust me completely – even Presvel has more sense than that. Besides, this violent jealousy of his would never allow it even under the most ideal circumstances. But the more I can get him to relax around me, and the more happy and wanted I can make him feel, the better my chances will be to get him to drop his guard and give me a chance to get Annas away from him.

Putting on a bright smile, she turned to her captor. 'Just let me give Annas something to eat, and get her ready, then we can be on our way. I'm looking forward to seeing Tiarond again.'

'Oh – of course. Here, you'll need this to get into her room.'

As she took the key, Rochalla realised that Presvel had been too wrapped up in his own concerns to consider Tormon's child. As she went upstairs, she knew she would do whatever it took to protect the little girl. To save Annas, she was willing to debase her own body and her own emotions, and to lie until she was black in the face. She only hoped that her subterfuge would eventually bear fruit. At the moment, she could see no way out.

All I can do is hold on, and try to keep us safe, and hope that help is on its way. Otherwise we don't stand a chance. Sooner or later the winged fiends will get us – or Presvel will kill us himself.

On the other side of the Curtain Walls, a crowd of people were encamped around the Gendival wayshelter. Amaurn's little force from the Shadowleague settlement had ridden hard all night, arriving at the refuge not long before dawn. Now they were taking a couple of hours' rest, as much for the horses as for themselves, before venturing back into Callisiora. Though the trail over the Snaketail was bad at this time of year, they had seen in Scall's world-viewing artefact that it was not blocked by snow as yet, and so they had decided to risk the quicker route that would get them there by about noon, rather than circle further south-west into the lands of the Reivers, and take the long way round, climbing up to the plateau by the steep cliff road.

The morning had dawned cold, grey, and damp, as though Callisiora's miserable weather was reaching out through the Curtain Walls to touch them, and they had built campfires for comfort and cheer on such a gloomy day, as well as for cooking and heat. People gathered round them, weary after the long night's ride, and checked equipment or sat talking quietly, content to make the most of the break in their journey.

They were a fair-sized group, Toulac thought, as she walked among them. Blade – Amaurn, she corrected herself – had come in person, leaving the nightmarish Maskulu in charge of the Shadowleague in his absence. At present he was inside the wayshelter itself while Dark, the other new recruit to the Shadowleague, checked his wounds. Veldan, still faintly disapproving of the Archimandrite's having included himself, was with him and, of course, where she went, Kaz was never very far away. Though he wouldn't fit inside the small stone building he was sitting just outside, only separated from his partner by a wall.

Elion was sitting by one of the campfires, talking to the strange Zavahl/Aethon partnership, and Scall was at the same fire, but keeping his distance. Though Elion was an old friend, the boy was still too overawed by the presence of the former Hierarch of Callisiora to be able to relax around the two men.

Around a fire of their own was a group of eight Loremasters who were strangers to the veteran. Although she had been introduced to them before they set out, there had been too many names for her to fix them all in her mind. The only one she could remember was the leader of the group: a cheerful young man with shoulder-length blond hair and a peculiar-looking contraption slung across his back that was clearly a weapon of some sort. His name was Kher, and he would be leading his little group – a hand-picked band of archers, fighters and explosives experts – who would have the unenviable task of going into the heart of the city and blowing up the tunnel that led into the Sacred Precincts.

The information that Elion, Kaz and Veldan had brought back from their disastrous foray into the lands of the Ak'Zahar indicated that the predators always roosted together, and the larger the group, the better they seemed to like it. Reports from Elion, Scall and Amaurn, who had been the last to leave the city, suggested that the fiends appeared to be settling in the Precincts tunnel, so it had been decided that one single explosion could solve the greater part of the Ak'Zahar problem at a stroke, for if the Curtain Walls could be repaired, no more could come down from the north to replace them. The operation could be carried out through the day, while the creatures were all roosting, and the charges must somehow be laid without alarming them. To that end, Amaurn had brought with him a secret weapon, the nature of which he refused to divulge, even to Veldan, much to her irritation.

The veteran paced up and down on the crisp turf, easing the stiffness of riding out of her legs before she sat down and had some breakfast. She had been mounted on a strange horse, which always took a bit of getting used to. Having just had Mazal restored to her, against all the odds, she had decided not to risk taking him back to Callisiora again. If, perish the thought, anything should happen to her, then Harral would take care of him – only too well!

Toulac smiled to herself. Judging from the number of mares that the head of the stables wanted him to cover, the stallion was going to be having a fine old time in her absence. One of the candidates was Firefly, the little chestnut, who luckily had come into season a day or two before she arrived in Gendival. Though Amaurn had given her back to Scall, overriding Harral's furious protests, the boy had been persuaded – albeit very reluctantly – to leave her behind in safety while he made this journey back to Tiarond. Even more reluctantly, he had been made to promise her first foal to Harral, so that her bloodline could be continued in Gendival. Scall himself was still adamant that he was going back to the Reivers to be with his friends when all this business was over. The veteran was surprised to see such steadfast loyalty in one so young, even if it *was* at the expense of common sense.

As for herself, Toulac was beginning to wonder if she shouldn't have stayed behind in Gendival, with the fortunate horses. She shivered, feeling glad of her thick sheepskin coat, and looking forward to a cup of tea when the water boiled. A drop of something stronger wouldn't go amiss, either. These bleak, early morning hours were a breeding ground for doubts.

I'm an idiot to be going back. What do they need me for? I could have stayed in Gendival, in comfort, with my nice, soft bed at the inn, and Ailie's cooking, and Mazal to keep me company . . .

Who am I trying to fool? I would never have had an easy moment. Back at the sawmill, before Kaz turned up on my doorstep with Veldan and all this started, I was despondent and desperate because all of my old friends were dead and I had no one but Mazal. Well, now I have a whole crowd of new friends. And Ailie and Harral might be back at the settlement, but most of them are here: Elion, Zavahl, Kaz and even young Scall – and most particularly, Veldan. A whole new part of my life is beginning and I'm not going to start by deserting my new friends. Besides, they're going to need to have somebody there with common sense.

Nevertheless, she didn't feel easy in her mind about this venture. There were too many imponderables. Her own rule of thumb, proven again and again over the years, was that every unknown element in a plan would increase the risks tenfold – and this so-called plan of Amaurn's was positively bristling with unknowns. Basically, they were going to go marching in, armed with very little information, and just hope for the best. But what other options did they have?

Ah, well. Even more reason for me to go along and look after them all.

Amaurn was in the wayshelter itself, letting Dark examine the wound in his side and listening to Veldan as she voiced much the same doubts with which he himself was wrestling. 'The one thing we'll never do is get the ring back – how can we? Either it's on one of hundreds of Ak'Zahar or they've stashed it somewhere in the city, and in that case we wouldn't have a clue where to start looking.'

'I couldn't agree with you more,' the Archimandrite replied. 'And if our plan to blow up the tunnel into the Precincts succeeds, the ring is likely to be buried under tons of rubble – if it's there at all. We had better hope it isn't the only option, that's all. Maybe Aethon will be able to dredge up some alternative course of action from his memories once we get there.' He spread his hands apart. 'We have to try, Veldan, The only alternative is to watch the world as we know it slowly being destroyed.'

She sighed. 'I know. And I'm sure we'll come up with something. One way or another, we'll have to. At least if we can get rid of the accursed Ak'Zahar, that'll be something.' She paused, her face expectant. 'Go on, tell me. You can't keep it a secret for ever. How are you going to get the charges into the tunnel, without the predators finding out?'

She really was hard to resist, Amaurn thought. And besides, now that they were under way, he didn't mind his daughter knowing – nor Dark, he added to himself. He felt compelled to take the young man under his wing for Grim's sake but, apart from that, the Summoner clearly had the potential to become a first-rate Loremaster. Until there was time and leisure for Dark to be properly trained, however, he wanted to keep him under his eye. Besides, right now he needed the pain-blocking techniques which Grim had pioneered and taught to his apprentice. His injuries – his arm, his ribs, and particularly the wound in his side – were healing well, thanks to Kyrre's prompt and expert treatment, but they would still take some time. He knew he ought to be resting, to save himself a lot of discomfort and give himself the best chance of a rapid recovery, but that was out of the question and, in the meantime, there was the pain. He wanted to avoid taking any painkilling medications in case they slowed his reactions or clouded his thinking at some critical moment, so Dark's nerve blocks, though they had to be renewed every two or three hours, were the perfect solution.

'Amaurn?' Veldan sounded impatient. He gathered his thoughts with a start, and realised that he was a lot more tired than he had expected to be. His daughter was looking at him with a frown. 'I *knew* you shouldn't have come.' Her tone was accusing. 'You should have stayed at home and rested.'

'Never mind that.' At least he had something to distract her. 'All right, I give in. I'll show you my secret weapon.' He raised his voice a little. 'Will you show yourself?'

A bench in the corner began to flicker, then shimmered, and changed into an amorphous black outline. Veldan gasped. 'A shapeshifter!'

'That was my idea,' Amaurn said, a little smugly. 'I asked Kalevala if she could spare one of her best people to come with us and take the form of an Ak'Zahar, to put the charges into the tunnel. She said she would send someone to meet us here. I didn't want anyone to know about this before we were safely away, in case there might be objections.' He turned to the Takur. 'Thank you for joining us. You are very welcome.'

'I thank you for your welcome.' To his surprise, the voice was feminine. 'I am honoured to join you – but before we proceed any further, there is something that you must know; something that my honour compels me to divulge to you. Then you may not be so pleased.'

Amaurn smiled. 'I doubt that.'

The Takuru flexed its many limbs in what was clearly a shrug. 'So be it. Then you should know that my name is Vifang.'

'*What?*' Amaurn scrambled to his feet, but Veldan was faster, leaping in front of Amaurn with drawn sword.

That shapeshifter assassin did not move. 'I did warn you,' she said wryly.

Amaurn felt anger burn within him. 'Kalevala promised she would kill you herself,' he snarled. 'Is this all the word of the Takuru is worth?'

'No. Kalevala did not *say* she would kill me. She merely promised to take care of the problem. And she did. She came straight to me and told me that you had not demanded my death after all, though you would have been well within your rights. Since you preserved my life, the honour of the Takuru demanded that I should place it in your service. You need never fear me again, Amaurn. You needed a shapeshifter, and now you have one.'

The Archimandrite was astounded. 'Now just hold on,' he protested. 'What about your loyalty to Cergorn?'

Again, Vifang shrugged. 'Cergorn used me – used all of us – for many years. Always he held out promises to us, as did Syvilda when she engaged me to kill you, but the good things were always going to come tomorrow, next month, when we had completed what he asked of us, or whenever. We kept on with him because we wanted to be useful, wanted to be part of the Shadowleague, and we hoped that eventually we would be accepted. But it never happened. Cergorn never kept his word, but kept putting us off. But you . . . Within a day of your agreement with Kalevala, my people were claiming sites for their new homes.' She folded her limbs and bowed. 'You have earned my respect, Archimandrite, and the respect of my people. I place myself at your disposal to complete this mission and afterwards, if I survive, I swear that you will never again lack for a bodyguard.' A ripple of wry humour seemed to emanate from the Takuru. 'No one else will ever get the chance to sneak up on you, Amaurn. You have my word on that.'

Amaurn was lost for words, but Veldan was not. Close association with Toulac had been increasing her vocabulary. She looked at the shapeshifter, and a grin appeared on her face. 'Well, may I be dipped in dog's dung!'

Thirty-Two

Sacrifice

Far beyond the city and the Temple, Amaurn's group of Loremasters and their companions had left the moorland's slopes and swales, and had climbed the steep track that zigzagged up the south-eastern slopes of Mount Chaikar, to the high gap where the Snaketail pass curved round the shoulder of the mountain. At the head of the pass, they paused to catch their breath and let their horses rest where generations of travellers had rested before them. It was an inhospitable spot in winter; cold and bleak and exposed, with flurries of soft, wet snow swirling around and soaking into their cloaks and hair, and the coats of the horses. The upper slopes of the mountain loomed menacingly above, still carrying their burden of conifers, loose rock and waterlogged earth which could come avalanching down without warning, as once it had done before. The wind whined and whistled between the craggy walls of the deep cutting into which the road plunged as it left the hilltop, and a shallow river still ran down the constricted trail, draining from the slopes above.

The pass marked a turning point in the journey of the travellers. Behind them lay the moors, and the Curtain Walls, and their own land of Gendival. Before them, they could look down the other side of the pass to the river valley, and the craggy slopes where a landslide had almost caused the deaths of Kaz and Veldan and had transformed Zavahl's life beyond all recognition. Beyond the landslide they would pass Toulac's old home, and then descend to the city on its plateau.

People were mostly silent, lost in their own private thoughts and

438

concerns, but Veldan knew that everyone was uneasy for a whole number of reasons. To the Loremasters, the chief source of anxiety must be the state of the Curtain Walls. When they had reached the barrier, they had been dismayed to discover that the veils of energy were flashing in and out of existence, in place one minute and gone the next. The once-clear colours had changed to dirty, muddy hues, and the sound had become a screeching, crackling dissonance that made their ears ache and set their teeth on edge. Worse, however, were the moments of dead silence when the barrier failed completely. Every one of them had been thinking of similar failures throughout the world, and the chaos that must ensue as a result. It came home to them, then, how little time they had left in which to act.

And in addition to our ignorance and our desperation, we have the Ak'Zahar to deal with.

She only hoped that Amaurn and Toulac were right in their theory that the winged predators would not nest in the lower cliff tunnel because of the frequent flooding. She dreaded the notion of having to fight them again – but they were not her only source of evil memories. Veldan viewed the steep, dark cutting of the pass without enthusiasm, remembering the mountain shaking free its covering of mud and trees and hurling the whole mass down onto the trail to bury herself, and Kaz, and Aethon. 'This all seems very unnerving,' she commented to the firedrake. 'It's almost as if time is running in reverse. It's an unsettling feeling, to find ourselves going back to the place where everything started.'

Kaz shrugged a shoulder, almost unseating her. 'Time can run as it likes, as far as I'm concerned,' he said, 'just so long as we don't have that accursed landslide again.'

'I'll second that,' said Veldan, with feeling. The route was seemingly unchanged from the last time she had seen it, but she couldn't believe she had been there only a few days before. So much had happened in the meantime, it seemed like years. She only hoped that this journey would prove less eventful than the last – though, frankly, she doubted it.

We may escape the landslide this time, but we'll still have the Ak'Zahar to contend with, not to mention whatever may await us underneath the Temple.

The others, who were similarly silent, stood nearby and she wondered what they must be thinking at this time. For a whole number of differing reasons, every one of them must be harbouring mixed feelings.

Elion was remembering the last time he had taken this road in this direction, and Thirishri's warning that snow would soon block the pass for the rest of the winter. In a normal year she would have been right. Once those early, heavy falls blocked the pass, that route was buried for months at a time but, thank providence, the current freak weather patterns had proved her wrong this time.

Though in a way I wish the snow had fallen thick and deep and blocked all the routes to Tiarond. I don't want to go back there!

But there was no choice. Apart from Veldan and the firedrake, he was the only one who had any familiarity with the Ak'Zahar and their habits. And if the other two were going, how could he refuse? He had paid an appalling price for his knowledge – if he backed out now, he would be cheapening all the sorrow and suffering of his loss, and rendering Melnyth's death pointless – and he wasn't about to do that. His only true regret was that, because he felt he ought to stick with Kaz and Veldan, he would be going down beneath the Temple with Amaurn and the others, when what he really wanted to do was join Kher's group and blast into oblivion those thrice-accursed killers of the woman he had loved.

'So why don't you?' It was the voice of the firedrake. 'If you want to avenge Melnyth, I would understand, and so would Veldan. In your position, either one of us would feel the same.'

Elion felt a flash of anger that the firedrake had dared to snoop into his most private thoughts. 'Blast it, you overgrown lizard, are you eavesdropping again? Will nothing break you of that unconscionable habit?' Then the import of Kaz's words came home to him. 'You – you wouldn't? But are you sure?'

'Well, despite being an immoral, despicable snoop, *I* certainly wouldn't mind.' As usual, the firedrake sounded completely unrepentant. 'As for Veldan – why don't you ask her yourself?'

But the Loremaster was already smiling at him. Clearly, she had started to pick up some very unsavoury habits from her partner. 'Elion, you do what you have to. It seems only right and fitting that we three survivors of Ghariad should have our vengeance at last.' Sliding down from the firedrake's back, she put her arms around Elion and hugged him hard. 'And when you do blast those flying sons of bitches to smithereens, you'll be doing it for me and Kaz, as well as for poor Melnyth.' Grasping his shoulders, she held him away from her, and looked into his eyes. 'Just you take care of yourself, that's all. Do you hear? We wasted too long in pointless enmity as it is, and I don't want to lose you just when we've put all that nonsense behind us. You have a lot of friends in Gendival who care about you, including myself and my partner here. If you end up as a predator's dinner, we're going to be *very* cross with you.'

She was saying far more to him than her words conveyed, and Elion knew exactly what she meant. She was telling him not to take risks so that he would follow Melnyth into death – and to his surprise, he found that he no longer wanted to. The last few days had seemingly wrought changes in everyone and, in his case, he had rediscovered that life was precious after all and still held meaning and purpose – and perhaps, at some future time, even joy – despite the loss of the partner he had loved so deeply.

'Don't worry,' he told her. 'I'm over that now, with some help from you and Toulac, and one or two others. Though I'll never stop loving Melnyth, it's time to let her rest.'

And, enjoying the look of surprise on her face, he kissed her soundly. He looked at Kaz, and grinned. 'I'm not going to kiss you, you ugly great brute,' he said. 'But thanks, anyway.'

Kaz leered at him. 'You'd better not try,' he warned. 'I've already thrown up on the old Archimandrite – I don't want to repeat the experience with the new one.'

'I wouldn't worry.' Veldan glanced across at Amaurn, a slight frown on her face. 'He looks as though he has far worse things to worry about than one of your furballs.'

Amaurn was far too wrapped up in his own thoughts to notice Veldan's glance, or register her concern. Confronted once more by this land of his long exile, he felt a disquieting coldness settle over him.

I thought I had escaped this wretched place. Why must I return so soon?

Just as the old Amaurn had returned to him in Gendival, beyond the Curtain Walls, was heartless Lord Blade awaiting him here in the city, ready to take control of his life once more?

That's pure nonsense! Blade and Amaurn are not two different people. They're both part of me.

But maybe that was the problem. As he remembered those long years of loneliness, of bitterness, of ruthlessness and hungry ambition, Amaurn felt uneasy. His existence here had not been a life to be proud of and many of his deeds, which had seemed logical and necessary to the driven Godsword Commander, appeared expedient and reprehensible to the Archimandrite of the Shadowleague.

A shiver ran through him and he had to keep repressing the urge to look over his shoulder. The spectre of his old life had come back to haunt him, and try as he would, he was unable to shake off the superstitious notion that, in some way, he would be made to pay for his past misdeeds. He looked across at his daughter, who stood talking to Elion and Kaz.

If I must make restitution, then so be it. But please don't let the price be Veldan.

Further down the mountain, below Tiarond's plateau, Presvel and his captives had been toiling their way up the vertiginous cliff road. They had been forced to make the final part of the ascent on foot, because their exhausted horses had proved unequal to the climb, and had simply lain down and refused to go any further. Presvel would have been a good deal more angry with the stupid beasts had his spirits not been lifted by the night he had spent with Rochalla, but he was aware that everyone needed to be under cover and hidden from any potential pursuers as soon as possible.

The climb was gruelling. He had made Rochalla and Tormon's brat ascend the path in front of him, and so they could go no faster than the child's best pace. Everyone was too breathless to speak, though it made little difference, for Annas had not uttered a word since they had set out that morning and Rochalla had said very little, pleading cold and weariness as a reason for her prolonged silences. After the night they had spent, he was a little injured by her lack of warmth, but he assured himself that everything would be all right once they had a little more time together. It was a real shame, he reflected, that the damned child had to be there, distracting Rochalla and getting in the way, but for now he decided that he still might need a hostage. He could always get rid of the little wretch later, when it was safe to do so, and then his golden-haired beauty would be free to devote all her time to him.

Because one or the other of Presvel's captives kept needing to stop and rest on the way up, it seemed to take an age before they reached the black mouth of the tunnel. This time it was Rochalla who faltered. 'Please,' she gasped, 'my legs won't carry me any further. Just let me sit down for a moment or two and catch my breath back before we go inside.'

Presvel sighed. He was getting tired of their whining, but if he gave the girls one last rest now, before they tackled the tunnel itself, that should take them all the way to the entrance of Scall's tunnel. Besides, though he was loath to admit it, his own city breeding and sedentary life were beginning to tell on him. If he gave in now, he would not only be magnanimous, and please Rochalla, but he could give his own legs a much-needed rest. 'All right,' he said. 'Not for long, though. We don't have all day to be sitting about.'

With sighs of relief, Rochalla and Annas simply flopped down right where they were, ignoring the coldness of the stone and the wetness of the path. Presvel, loath to display a similar weakness, remained standing, leaning back against the cliff face for support, and looking down and out across the bleak landscape far below. Suddenly he straightened, with a lurid oath. Far below, where the trail wound between the hills like unravelled thread, he could see a cluster of tiny, moving specks. There were more than he had expected. Clearly, the Reivers were determined to capture the man who had killed their Summoner.

Ignoring his complaining muscles, Presvel strode across to Annas and Rochalla and yanked them roughly to their feet. 'Come on,' he snapped. 'There's no more time to waste. Get into that tunnel now!'

Just before he dragged her inside, Rochalla also caught a glimpse of the distant riders, far below. Her heart leapt, and for the first time since Presvel had abducted her, she knew true hope. She wished she could tell Annas that her father was coming at last, but she decided that it was too soon to raise the child's hopes.

Only when the darkness had swallowed them utterly did Presvel kindle the lamp he had taken from the abandoned farmhouse, sending the blackness springing away from them and making their shadows dance and waver on the slimy wet walls. Rochalla remembered the terror of the flood, and shuddered. Tormon, Scall and Seriema had been caught down here, and barely escaped, and Tormon had explained to her afterwards that the flash floods depended, not on the weather she could see, but conditions high up in the mountains – and there was no knowing, from one moment to the next, what might be happening high among the peaks. At any moment, without warning, another deluge could come pouring down here, and she and Annas would both be drowned. All at once, her fear overcame her weariness, and she was even more anxious than her captor to get this journey over. With a sigh, she hoisted Annas up into her weary arms, finding the strength from some reserve she had not known she possessed. 'Come on,' she said to a startled Presvel. 'Let's hurry.'

It took them some time to find the opening to Scall's mysterious corridors. The hand-hewn ceiling was very rough and the lamplight threw deceptive shadows across the stone, concealing the aperture so well that at first they walked right past it and went on, unsuspecting, up the tunnel, until they were startled by a glimmer of daylight at the far end. Rochalla, her back aching, her arms almost breaking, and her legs feeling limp and strengthless, felt like bursting into tears. Regardless of Annas's small ears, she gave vent to her feelings in a few choice phrases that she had learned while walking the streets of Tiarond. A dumbfounded Presvel clearly realised that she was at the end of her tether and finally condescended to take the heavy child from her as they turned and, resignedly, began to walk back down. And every single moment, Rochalla was expecting to hear the roar of the flood behind her, and feel herself being swept from her feet by the inexorable torrent.

This time they kept a more careful eye out, not only for the opening itself, but for the cross-strut to which Scall had clung when the floodwaters lifted him to the tunnel roof. Approaching from the uphill direction, they were looking at the roof from a slightly different angle. This time they saw the strut easily, and the circular shape of the aperture above. 'Finally,' Presvel said, putting Annas down and straightening with a sigh of relief.

Rochalla, her nerves so tightly strung by this point that they were stretched almost to breaking point, was equally grateful to find the escape route from this horrible, horrible place. Then she came to her senses, and thought of Tormon and the Reivers, following behind. How would they know which way she and Annas had gone? For all they knew, Presvel might be planning to head back to the city. And what if they missed the aperture completely, as she and her companions had done? They might even forget about it, and simply continue on up to Tiarond!

Presvel stooped and picked up Annas once more. 'Look,' he said to the little girl, 'I'm going to lift you up there, and you climb into the tunnel above, all right? Once you're there, wait for us, and *don't move*. If I climb up there and find you've gone, I'll kill Rochalla, and it'll all be your fault – do you understand?'

In the lamplight, Rochalla saw the little girl's face turn dead white and she knew that Annas was thinking of her mother, murdered before her eyes by soldiers, in the Godsword Citadel. In that moment, she was rocked back on her heels by the violence of her hatred for Presvel.

You cruel bastard, to bring that back to her! By Myrial, I hope that Tormon and the Reivers carve your guts out!

Then her common sense reasserted itself. First of all, their friends would have to find them. When Presvel turned away to boost Annas up into the tunnel, she stooped and tore a long strip from the already tattered hem of her skirt. Rolling it up quickly, she hid the wad of cloth in her hand, as her abductor turned back to her. 'Now,' he said, 'I'll climb up there, and pull you up after me.'

Rochalla gritted her teeth. He knew full well that she wouldn't try to run away while Annas was in his power. It took him several tries to leap high enough to grasp the metal strut, and he dangled there, his legs kicking, his face contorted with the effort. 'Don't just stand there,' he grunted. 'Give me a hand.'

Wishing that she had a weapon while he was in such a vulnerable position, Rochalla took hold of his feet and boosted him up until he sat precariously astride the rusting bar. Reaching up, she let him grasp her wrists and pull her after him, until they had both gained the perch. Then, balancing with difficulty, Presvel got hold of the rim of the aperture and hoisted himself up. Rochalla had only a moment in which to act. Quickly, she tied the strip of fabric to the strut, its end fluttering down like a banner in the draught that whistled constantly down the passage. She placed it near the wall, so that Presvel would be unlikely to see it from the opening, and by the time that he had turned around and reached down to her, her hands were empty, and she could confront him with guileless eyes that hid her secret thoughts.

Hurry, Tormon. Hurry up and find us – before it's too late.

Within Myrial's Temple Gilarra was sure that it was already too late to save her people. Existence for the refugees had become a living nightmare. Despite all the heroic efforts of Kaita, Shelon and their helpers, the sickness was spreading rapidly, making conditions in the building intolerable even for those who had not yet succumbed. Godsword soldiers, pressed into grim service, went back and forth through the route to the upper caves and the mountainside exit, carrying the bodies of the dead. There was little they could do to dispose of them safely; they couldn't bury or burn even one, let alone so many. All they could do was hurl them off the ledge into the valley far below. Presumably the winged predators and other scavengers would eventually clean up the grisly remains, but it was a terrible thing for the survivors to consign their loved ones to such a miserable, undignified end, and it only served to exacerbate the grief for those who had already suffered so much.

Gilarra just didn't know what to do any more. Galveron had not returned, and she had been worried sick about him. What had happened to the precious Hierarch's ring that he'd been sent to find – and, more importantly, what had become of the Godsword Commander himself? Had he perished? Along with everyone else in the Basilica, she was feeling the lack of his authoritative air, his organisational skill, his sound common sense, and his easy way of getting along with people.

The Hierarch was lost without him. She was at her wits' end, trying to comfort people who had already been reft of family and friends when the winged demons attacked, and who now had suffered further devastation through this dreadful affliction. The Temple was a scarcely endurable place, with its stench and filth from the sick, and the wailing and tears of the bereaved. Those who were still healthy were shocked, and grieving, and exhausted, while those who had already contracted the sickness suffered and, for the most part, died. There was a handful of survivors: generally, it seemed, those who were stronger and better nourished when they contracted the sickness stood a greater chance of struggling through, though they emerged as pitiful and wasted shadows.

In order to slow the spread of the disease, Kaita and her assistant Shelon were trying to enforce stringent rules of cleanliness and hygiene, but their precautions were impossible to implement within the confines of the Basilica. Kaita had wanted to boil all the drinking water, but there had not been enough fuel. Already, any wooden furniture or other combustible items were being devoured by the fires down in the makeshift kitchens, and the refugees were running out of options. Nor was there any soap, or any spare fat with which to make some. Everyone was imprisoned together in a confined space, with nowhere to go but outside, but the winged demons still infested the city and, no matter how desperate the circumstances became, no one was ready to risk being torn apart by the teeth and claws of the terrifying predators – at least, not yet. In the meantime, all the exhausted healers could do was to try to separate the healthy from the sick and those who cared for them, and hope for a miracle.

It was difficult to see how the spirits of the refugees could get any lower. The survivors of Tiarond, still devastated by the massacre that had sent them to the shelter of the Temple, were now reeling from this second vicious blow, that made their haven almost as dangerous as the city outside. Gilarra was certain that many folk were no longer making any effort to fight the disease. With their lives made intolerable by so many losses and tribulations, they had simply decided to stop fighting, and die. Telimon had been quick to follow his twin, and Agella's niece, Felyss, who had lost her lifemate and all of her family save her aunt, would also have perished, save that she had recently begun a friendship with Gelina, the former thief, who was nursing her with such dedication and determination that she seemed to be pulling through. There was very little good news of that sort, however. Stablemaster Fergist had not been so fortunate, and Agella was fighting her sorrow by dedicating all her time and energy to helping the healers, in whatever way they required.

The Hierarch was becoming desperate. It had only taken a couple of days for sickness to sweep through the Temple and people were dying with incredible speed, often within hours of showing the first symptoms. Kaita said it was because they were losing their bodily fluids so rapidly, but Gilarra was sure that the explanation went beyond the logical and the mundane. It seemed to her that Myrial's curse on his people had not been lifted with the end of Zavahl's reign, but had continued into her own. First the winged demons, and now this. Where was the justice in it all?

In searching for someone at whose door she could lay the blame, it was easy for her to settle on Aliana. If only the accursed thief hadn't made off with the ring, it would all have been different!

But would it, really?

Gilarra was beginning to wonder. It truly seemed as though the deity had turned his back on Callisiora, and was determined to make an end of the land and all its inhabitants. The strongest proof that Myrial had abandoned them had come with the deaths of both the infants who had been destined as the new Hierarch and Suffragan. Such a thing had never happened before in the entire history of the Temple. Was this a sign? She couldn't see how it could possibly be anything else. Whatever might happen to the Callisiorans, and whether or not there would be any survivors, it seemed that the Hierarchs had failed their god, and their reign had been brought to an end.

There was little Gilarra had been able do but move among the sick, trying her best to comfort the dying and those who cared for them. As she did so, she had an increasingly clear sense that the people were losing faith in Myrial – and in his earthly representative. Suddenly her own future seemed a good deal less secure. Again and again, the failure and fate of the previous Hierarch came into her mind.

Was this what Zavahl felt? This same frustration? This helplessness? This fear?

Over and over, she tried to block the chilling realisation that she was treading the same path as her predecessor. One that had led to the Hierarch's sacrifice.

Until recently, Gilarra had managed, with some difficulty, to keep such grim thoughts at bay, but now that was no longer possible. An hour ago she had walked up through the passages and caves behind the Temple, following the bodies of her lifemate and her small son. Though she had tried her hardest to keep her little family away from the sources of infection, it had not been possible in the overcrowded building. Once they had succumbed to the sickness, neither Gilarra's earthly powers nor her most fervent prayers had been enough to hold them to the world.

Hierarch or not, Gilarra had still wept and cried out, just like the poorest of the Tiarondians, when the bodies of her loved ones – one so pathetically small – were hurled over the edge of the cliff, to vanish from sight. As she returned from the high mountain ledge she had been beside herself. Too absorbed in her grief and too blinded by tears to see where she was going, she had needed to be helped by a sympathetic Godsword soldier who had lost children of his own. Clearly worried that the sight of so distraught a Hierarch might further demoralise the desperate refugees, an overworked and overtired Kaita had left her to rest on the stone ledge in the tunnel behind the sickroom, where she and Galveron had been wont to hold their private conversations. Shelon had arrived a little later with a cup of warm, bitter liquid, and said that it would help to calm her nerves. Longing for any respite from the pain which beset her, Gilarra swallowed it quickly, then the healer took the cup and left her alone once more.

Kaita's potion filled her with a dreamy lassitude that blunted the edge of her grief a little, and allowed her to think once more. That the medication might also blunt the edges of her intellect, she never considered. Looking back over the last few days, it seemed to her that she had failed in everything, both as a Hierarch, and as a life-mate and mother. No one was around to tell her that she'd been trying to cope with a disaster unparalleled in the history of Tiarond. No one reminded her that she had only been Hierarch for a few short days, and that mistakes were inevitable at first, and could be rectified with experience. No one was there to share her worries, or comfort her in her grief. Too late, she had discovered what Zavahl had always known: that the Hierarch of Callisiora was more isolated and more lonely that the meanest thief who lurked in the city's alleyways, or the lowliest peasant who tilled the land.

She who had decried Zavahl's leadership had made a far worse mess of everything than he had when her turn had finally come. She was useless as a leader of her people and she had no more influence with Myrial than her predecessor. Too late, she realised that her obsession with the Hierarch's ring had blinded her to her own shortcomings.

It was time to face the brutal truth. She was an utter failure as a leader, and there was nothing she could do about it.

Or was there?

There is one thing. That coward Zavahl never completed the Great Sacrifice. Were I to undergo it in his place, then maybe Myrial would listen to our prayers once more.

No one was there to dissuade her. As she passed through Kaita's busy sickroom, and into the Temple beyond, no one even noticed her in all the bustle. She felt detached from all the activity around her, from the lives and the fears and the tribulations of her people, as though she had died already and had drifted back to the Basilica as a restless ghost.

There was no question in Gilarra's mind about a way to carry out her plan, or the location in which she should perform the Sacrifice. Only one place was appropriate. If people noticed her slipping behind the silver filigree screen that concealed the entrance to the Holy of Holies, no one remarked on it. She was Hierarch, wasn't she? It was only natural that she would go there.

On the high platform before the darkened Eye, the lonely Hierarch paused. Before she jumped, she began to compose a final, heartfelt prayer to Myrial, begging him to accept her Sacrifice, and beseeching his aid for her beleaguered people.

Kaita had no idea that Gilarra was missing until Shelon brought her the news. According to his anxious report to the healer, he had been seeing the soldiers off through the tunnels with another grisly burden of corpses when he had noticed that the stone bench was empty. In the normal course of events, he would have thought little of it. Myrial only knew, there was enough for the Hierarch to be doing in the Temple right now. On the other hand, however, it was unlikely that she would be very fit to do anything practical for some hours, after the strong dose of sedative he had given her. Shelon had begun to feel the first twinges of alarm. He'd considered Gilarra's grief, her exhaustion, her increasing desperation, and all the other myriad pressures of her position as Hierarch – then he had come to find Kaita, as fast as he could run.

The healer's first reaction was irritation. Didn't she have enough to do, without scouring the Temple for a missing Hierarch? How dare the blasted woman heap more work and worry on her? Then all at once, she remembered that Gilarra had just lost her lifemate and her child. She remembered how she had grieved when Evelinden had been killed, and felt ashamed. 'Can you manage here for a little while?' she asked her assistant. 'I'm going to find Agella, and we'll have a quick look around.'

Shelon hesitated. 'Do you – do you think we ought to ask the Godswords to look for her?' he asked.

Kaita sighed. 'For morale's sake, I was hoping not to involve anyone else in this – but yes, you're right. Corvin is a level-headed fellow, and he seems to have taken charge in the Commander's absence. I'll ask him to organise a few of his most discreet men to mount a search.'

A concerned Corvin told Kaita that he would divide his men, sending some up through the storage caves and along the mountain ledge, and others down into the extensive lower caverns, to search there. Agella was also more than willing to assist, though the healer regretted having to ask her. The sturdy Smithmaster was thinner now, and looked much more frail and fragile, with her gaunt face and dark-shadowed eyes. Since Fergist's death the previous day, she had kept herself determinedly brisk and busy, but Kaita knew that she was bleeding inside.

Nevertheless, if Gilarra had possessed that kind of indomitable courage, we wouldn't have to waste our valuable time searching for her now.

Trying not to attract too much attention to themselves, the two women searched through the remaining refugees – a task made much more difficult by the fact that everyone wanted to talk to the healer. There was no sign of the missing Hierarch, but only when they reached the filigree screen, did Kaita realise that there was one place they hadn't looked. 'Come on.' She took hold of the Smith-master's arm. 'Let's go and see if she's in there.'

'We can't go in there!' Agella pulled her back. 'That's the Holy of Holies! We're forbidden! Only the Hierarch can go past that screen.'

'Oh, balls to that!' Kaita snapped. 'To my knowledge, there are at least four people down there right now who aren't the Hierarch, including Commander Galveron.'

Agella gasped. 'It's a good thing *that* isn't common knowledge,' she said in a low voice. 'People are bound to connect the violation of the Sanctum with this pestilence. You know how they are.'

'Yes, I do. Stupid,' Kaita replied, but in her heart, she knew that the smith was right. 'It doesn't make any difference, though,' she added firmly. 'If Gilarra is in there, we have to find her. She isn't thinking too clearly right now, and I don't know what she'll do. If you don't want to come, I don't mind going alone.'

Agella shrugged. 'If you're determined to go in there, then I'm coming with you. Come on – let's get it over with.'

Kaita nodded but, when faced with the actuality of entering the holy place, she couldn't help but think of the Godsword Commander, who had travelled this way before her, and had never returned.

I'm not the one who should be doing this, and neither is poor Agella. She has enough problems of her own, right now. Oh, Galveron – where in perdition are you? You've vanished just when we need you most.

Though both women were sensible, practical, down-to-earth and not in the least bit superstitious, they had to admit to a shiver of awe as they passed behind the silver filigree screen. When they entered the black room, and the floor dropped so suddenly, the two women clutched at one another and Agella swore. Having acted on the spur of the moment, neither had thought to bring a light with them, and when the sudden motion stopped, and the door sprang open, Kaita was glad to see the glimmer of a small lamp, away in the darkness. Her relief, however, was short-lived. As she and Agella walked out onto the open platform, she saw the narrow bridge without a railing, that spanned the dark abyss. At the far end, perched precariously on the edge of another small platform, was the Hierarch. It was clear from her attitude that the woman was working up sufficient courage to jump.

Kaita's mind raced. Her impulse was to call out loudly, but the last thing she wanted to do was startle Gilarra into jumping, so instead she walked to the edge of her own small platform, and spoke softly. 'If you really want to jump, Gilarra, that's your choice, but you might want to think about it for a little longer, first. It's not exactly a reversible decision.'

Gilarra whirled, and the two watching women gasped as her feet strayed perilously near the edge. 'Don't try to talk me out of this,' she warned. 'I know what I have to do.'

'I wouldn't dream of it.' Kaita spoke calmly, but she was gripping Agella's hand tightly in her anxiety. 'I'd be grateful if you'd tell me why, though. After all, we'll have to go up there and tell the refugees why their Hierarch is no longer with them.'

Gilarra gave a bitter laugh. 'As if they'd miss me! It's Galveron they really want – do you think I don't know that?'

'They want and need Galveron, yes, but as Godsword Commander, not Hierarch,' the healer told her. 'They are two very different roles, after all.' She took a deep breath. 'Don't leave your people like this, Gilarra. What will it do to folk who are already so demoralised? Some have lost their faith in Myrial, it's true . . .'

'Like you, you mean!'

Kaita didn't see any point in lying to her. 'Yes, like me. But a lot of them still believe, and in many cases that faith is the only thing that keeps them going. Your death might take their last hope away from them. Would you really want that?'

'You're wrong,' Gilarra said. 'My death will give them hope.

Zavahl was meant to undergo the Great Sacrifice, to intercede in person for his people at the feet of Myrial. Since he failed, I must act in his place.' She looked across at the healer with honest appeal in her eyes. 'Don't you see, Kaita? I'm a failure, as much as Zavahl ever was. This final act is the one remaining thing that I can do for my people. Forgive me, please.'

'Gilarra, no!' cried Kaita. Terrified as she was of the slender bridge, she ran forward, but it was already too late. Before she had time to reach the edge of her own platform, Gilarra lifted her arms, as if in supplication to her god, and launched herself into space.

Then there was silence. The platform across the abyss was empty, as if no one had ever stood there.

Kaita backed away from the edge of the chasm, and let her shaky knees fold under her. Agella was still standing, staring at the place where the Hierarch had last stood, and cursing softly. The healer's thoughts were a jumble. Had Gilarra been selfish, weak and deluded? Or had her final act been one of heroism and self-sacrifice?

Don't be stupid! The silly bitch has left us in a worse mess than ever.

But if she really believed that, why were there tears in her eyes? In the end, Gilarra had given her people the greatest gift in her power – her very life.

Once again, Kaita looked at the empty platform. Would there be any point in the Hierarch's sacrifice? Only time would tell.

Thirty-Three

The Tunnels

It had not been an easy night for Seriema and her companions, and daybreak had found them on edge and unrested. The trouble had started during the hours of darkness when they had been awakened by a scratching and scrabbling on the sturdy double doors of the barn, a slither and crash of loose slates falling from the roof, and a cacophony of strident screeching. Seriema awoke from uneasy dreams with a startled cry and saw Cetain already on his feet, reaching for his sword, while all around him his warriors had also roused, and were garbing themselves to fight. 'That's done it,' he said grimly. 'They've found us.'

Down below the horses were panicking, and Tormon was in their midst, trying to calm them. Luckily, there were no windows to worry about; the place was vented by the odd gap where a stone had been knocked out of the wall, high up near the roof, and not even the cadaverous demons could get through such narrow spaces. Cetain deployed his warriors to guard the building's vulnerable points: swordsmen to defend the doors, and archers up in the hayloft, ready to shoot any winged fiend that managed to break through the thick slabs that protected the roof. He ordered several of his men to go down and help the trader keep the beasts from harming themselves, or one another. In the face of danger, a horse's impulse was to run away but here, with nowhere for them to go, they stood a chance of doing themselves serious injury in their frantic attempts to flee the threat. Seriema could sympathise with the poor beasts. Unlike a horse, she possessed the intellect to realise that the sturdy building should keep her safe, but even so, she found her heart beating faster as dark and dreadful images slipped, unbidden, into her thoughts. She soon discovered that keeping busy was the best way to deal with an unruly imagination, so she had spent the night giving assistance to Tormon, who had his hands full with the horses.

Fortunately, the Reiver band had only to wait until dawn. The roof and doors of the barn were sturdy enough to hold out until then. Once daylight came, all sounds of the predators had ceased. After an interval that had Tormon fuming with impatience once again, they had emerged from their shelter to find that the skies were empty and the danger had passed.

They had pressed on swiftly then, aware that their later start must have put them further behind their quarry. What must the trader be feeling at this moment? Not only was this delay costing him vital time that might mean the difference between life and death for his little girl but, since these vile, voracious creatures were abroad in this area, he must be terrified that they had also found Annas.

On impulse, Seriema pressed forward to ride alongside him. 'Just because the fiends discovered us, it doesn't mean they'll find the others,' she said softly. 'We don't know whether the creatures are attracted by our scent, or our body heat, or the sounds of our voices, or maybe even something else but whatever it is, Cetain thinks that they were lured here to us because of our numbers . . .'

'Which means nothing.' Tormon cut her off, his voice harsh. 'Presvel is a madman, remember? We don't even know for sure whether he had the sense to take shelter for the night. And even if he did, what's to stop the predators finding Annas and Rochalla as easily as they found us?'

Sorry for him though she was, Seriema gave him a hard look. 'Absolutely nothing at all,' she said crisply. 'But that's no reason to despair yet, Tormon. Annas might be dead already. We don't know. But on the other hand, she might be perfectly all right. If you keep dwelling on the bad things all the time, you'll cloud your thinking with fear and anger, and then won't be any use at all: not to us, not to Annas, and not even to yourself. I can only imagine how difficult this much be for you, but please don't give up hope. In a day or two we might all be riding back to Arcan's fortress with Annas and Rochalla among us, safe and well.' With that she left him, but as she rejoined Cetain, the sound of her own inner voice was mocking her.

If we manage to rescue Annas and Rochalla, and get back to Arcan's fortress in safety, it'll be nothing short of a miracle.

At last they reached the great cliff, which seemed even higher than Seriema remembered. She wasn't looking forward to such a stiff climb! A number of the men had never been to Tiarond and more than one of the seasoned warriors blanched at the sight of the road that came snaking down from the plateau, high above. While Cetain was giving short shrift to his men's complaints about having to go on foot, and lead their horses all the way up *there*, Seriema joined Tormon, who was already scanning the escarpment with anxious eyes. He acknowledged her approach with an unsmiling nod. 'Are they going to take all day?'

Seriema shook her head. 'Only a moment or two. They might as well get their complaining over with now, because they won't have any breath to spare for grumbling once we start to climb.'

'Well, they can please themselves. I'm not waiting for them any longer.' Tugging at Rutska's bridle, he set off up the road at a pace a little faster than was wise, his shoulders squared and his chin jutting with determination. Watching him go, Seriema sighed. She couldn't blame him for not waiting. While they were riding down the valley, they had spotted the tiny figures, high up on the cliff road, and ever since then the trader had been a man possessed. Catching Cetain's eye, she pointed to Tormon and mouthed the words 'hurry up'. The Reiver nodded. Cutting short the complaints with a single barked command, he set off up the cliff, leading his own horse, with Seriema following. One by one, in single file, the other warriors fell into position behind.

At least she was fitter than she had been when she first left Tiarond. Then, she would probably never have managed such a steep climb. Now it was possible, at least, though far from pleasant.

Soon her legs were aching and she was gasping for breath. Judging from all the wheezing and panting from the warriors behind her, she wasn't the only one having a hard time with the gruelling ascent. Somehow, that made her feel a little better.

By the time they finally reached the tunnel, however, Seriema was no longer thinking about the climb. She had other things to worry about. All too well she remembered the flash flood that had almost killed Tormon, herself, and Scall. While they were waiting for the last of the warriors to catch up, she scanned the skies anxiously. Apart from the flurries of damp, sleety snow, there was little in the way of precipitation – as far as she could see. Unfortunately, she knew as well as Rochalla had done that the weather on the plateau counted for little, and it was the weather in the mountains, unknown and unseen, that would rule their fate.

Owing to the fact that she had reminded Cetain about the tunnel before they left, the Reivers had come prepared with torches. However, neither the light, nor the presence of a group of sturdy warriors, could make Seriema any easier in her mind. Tormon, caring only for the fate of his little girl, had other things than floods to think about and though she had tried to warn them, the Reivers could have no idea how quickly such a deluge could strike, and the terrifying power with which it did so. All the worrying was left to her and, she reflected wryly, she seemed to be doing enough for all of them.

Keeping up a steady pace, they went on through the tunnel. The air smelled of damp stone and the acrid smoke from their torches, while the flames streamed out behind them in the strong draught. The hollow hoofbeats of their horses, multiplied a thousandfold by the echoes, sounded deafeningly loud to Seriema, who was forced to abandon all ideas of straining her ears for the distant roar of rushing water, though her nerves remained as tense as before so that Tormon's voice, calling out loudly from somewhere ahead of her, made her jump. 'Look! There's something flapping there! By Myrial, it looks like part of Rochalla's dress!'

Cetain and Seriema crowded close to the trader, who was holding his torch up high. It was clear that the long, ragged strip of fabric had not become caught, but had been deliberately tied to the metal cross-strut near the curving roof of the tunnel. Above it, clearly visible from this angle, was the circular aperture that led to the mysterious passages within the mountain, that had been discovered by Scall during the flood.

'So he took them up there, instead of returning to the city.' Seriema frowned. 'What in Myrial's name does he hope to achieve by doing that?'

'He probably wants somewhere to hide, until we get tired of looking for him and go away,' Certain suggested.

'He'll have a bloody long wait, then,' Tormon growled.

Seriema tried to put herself into the head of the cautious, systematic assistant she had known for all those years. 'I suppose he doesn't want to contend with us *and* the predators, all at once,' she suggested. 'Perhaps he's even hoping that there's another way into the city, through these tunnels.'

The trader shrugged. 'Well, standing around here won't give us any answers. Let's get after him!'

At first, Cetain was intending to leave the horses in the tunnel to await the return of the Reivers, but that suggestion brought such a horrified response from both Tormon and Seriema that he agreed to spare four of his men to lead all the beasts back to the bottom and await the others there. 'I wish you folk had told me all this sooner,' he grumbled. 'It would have saved us a lot of trouble and the poor beasts a lot of needless effort if we had just left them there in the first place.'

'But I didn't imagine for a moment that Presvel would go up there,' Seriema objected. 'I was sure he would head straight back to Tiarond, in which case we would need the horses when we got to the top, to ride across the plateau. After all, they're on foot now. With the horses we might even have caught them in the open, before they reached the city.'

Cetain nodded. 'It's a good point that you make. Indeed we might have done.' He sighed. 'I only wish he *had* gone on across the plateau. It would have made our task so much easier.'

Seriema, who knew very well that their task was to kill her former assistant, shuddered, but said nothing.

By the time the horses had been organised, Tormon had already managed to haul himself up onto the cross-strut on which he was standing with his head and shoulders inside the aperture in the ceiling. Cetain called out to him from the tunnel below. 'We're coming now, Tormon. Don't be getting too far ahead of us.' Without replying, the trader pulled himself up and vanished into the hole, where Seriema caught a glimpse of the rungs of a ladder. Cetain caught her eye, and shook his head. 'We'd best be hurrying.' He sent Willan – the scar-faced veteran she remembered from the night they had sheltered in the ruined tower on the moors – up onto the cross-strut first, then held out his hands to Seriema. 'Right, lass. Up you go. I'll give you a boost.'

She extinguished her torch by knocking it against the wall, and thrust the stub into her belt. With Cetain lifting, and the older man pulling, she managed to scramble her way up somehow, very conscious of her flailing legs, and thanking providence that she'd had the sense to wear pants, like the rest of the Reivers.

I have quite enough on my plate at present, without a bunch of ribald warriors looking up my skirts!

Once on the strut she balanced there precariously, feeling both unhappy and uncomfortable, and dreading the next part, where she would have to stand upright. But the wretched Willan wasn't going to give her a chance to put off the evil moment. Clearly enjoying the spectacle of her maladroit efforts, he gave her a gap-toothed grin. 'Come on, my Lady. Up you go.'

Seriema suppressed the urge to give him a good, hard shove. 'You'd better make damn sure I don't fall,' she said sweetly, 'or Cetain will have your balls for breakfast.'

At that point, Willan stopped grinning like a loon. Balancing carefully, he reached up at full stretch into the opening above and caught hold of the bottom rung of the ladder, hanging on to it as he raised himself unsteadily to his feet. Clinging to the rung one-handed, he used the other to help Seriema into the same position and then helped support her weight as she pulled herself up into the opening. Finally, after what seemed like an arm-breaking, shoulder-wrenching, leg-flailing eternity, her feet found the bottom rung of the ladder, and she began to climb in earnest – to the sound of cheers, catcalls, and ironic applause from the Reivers assembled below.

When she reached the place where the tube opened out into the tunnel above, she recoiled in surprise as she almost bumped noses with Tormon, who was kneeling by the rim of the hole. 'You might have come and helped me, instead of sitting up here gawking,' she snapped. 'I just made a total fool of myself.'

Tormon brushed her protests aside. 'What are they doing down there? Why the bloody blazes don't they get a move on?'

Though she sympathised with his urgency, Seriema, personally, was glad of a few moments' respite. She climbed out unaided, sat down beside him on the soft, rather spongy floor of the tunnel, and leant gratefully against the curving wall, massaging her sorely abused arms and shoulders. 'They won't be long now,' she said. 'Cetain is sending them up one by one because he's afraid of putting too much weight on the cross-strut, all at once. But they'll be much quicker than I was, you'll see.'

As if to prove her point, the first of Cetain's warriors had pushed his head and shoulders out of the hole almost before she had finished speaking. Seriema and Tormon retreated a little way down the passage to be out from underfoot, and waited for the rest to arrive. Seriema sat down again, making the most of the rare chance to rest. There was no point in trying to talk to Tormon, who waited impatiently, his attention focused on the tunnel ahead. Instead, she took the opportunity to look around a little. Though Scall had tried to describe it when he had spoken of his adventures, this place was like nowhere she had ever seen. While she had been climbing up here she had been too preoccupied to notice when the light had changed to this uncanny, misty radiance, as faint as moonlight and changing colour in a never-ending cycle of varying hues. A warm, dry breeze, coming from somewhere ahead, blew steadily through the passage, carrying the oddest medley of scents, part acrid and part spicy, that made her want to sneeze. Tentatively, she poked one of the walls, curious about the odd texture. The warm surface yielded slightly under the pressure of her finger, then sprang back when she removed her hand, leaving no trace of her touch.

While Seriema was still investigating the strange substance, Cetain emerged from the access tunnel behind the last of his warriors. He exchanged a quick glance with Tormon, who had been pacing up and down a short stretch of the corridor, then beckoned to his men, who had been sitting around, taking a well-earned rest after their gruelling ascent of the cliff road. 'Come on, you laggards! Get off your backsides and let's be moving on!'

There was none of the groaning and grousing that usually would have accompanied such an order, and Seriema knew it was out of deference to Tormon's feelings. She turned to Willan, who stood beside her. 'They're good men, your Reivers.' He gave her a startled look, then his face creased in a gap-toothed smile. 'Aye, lass, they are. A bit rough-and-ready, maybe, but none the worse for that. And a lot of them have wee ones of their own. They can understand what the trader is going through.'

By this time Cetain had joined them, and as soon as he came up, Tormon was away again, striding quickly along the passage. Seriema knew that only the strangeness of this unknown place was stopping him from breaking into a headlong run, and was glad that he was showing *that* much caution, at least. The corridor curved gently ahead of them so that it was impossible to see very far – and who knew what might await them around the next bend?

Then they reached the massive chamber that Scall had described, and even Tormon was stopped in his tracks. Seriema gasped at the sheer scale of the place, which would have accommodated a hundred of Myrial's Temples with room to spare. Cetain was gripping her arm tightly and she could understand why he must be feeling overawed. This place affected her in the same way, and at least she'd had Scall's descriptions to forewarn her – although, until that moment, she had never quite believed him.

For the little group of humans who stood in the cavern entrance, dwarfed by the immensity around them, it was impossible to comprehend such an alien place. Just by being what it was, it threw the mind into confusion. Seriema gazed in perplexity at the strange formations, part organic, and part geometric, that were ranged across the floor of the chamber. Strange lights ran across the surface of the structures: some twinkling, some flashing on and off in patterns which almost – almost – conveyed some meaning to her mind, and others glowing softly like opal. Above her there were more lights, pulsing along what looked like vast spiderwebs, or leaping across the dizzying spaces in narrow, vibrantly coloured beams.

Again, the walls seemed to be formed from that odd, yielding substance. Bands, blotches, and starbursts of softly glowing light seemed to move and glide beneath its surface, changing colour and melting into one another in a medley of amorphous shapes. The air felt dry and prickly on the skin and the pungent scent was stronger here, with overtones of the smell that always accompanied thunderstorms. The sounds, though not particularly loud, were utterly alien: strange humming and droning in many different tones and pitches, sharp bursts of crackling and, beneath it all, a rhythmic, throbbing pulse that seemed to penetrate right through to their very bones.

Tormon was the first to recover from the bewildering assault upon the senses. 'Come on,' he shouted. 'What are we standing here for? Let's all split up, and search.'

Cetain, with the air of a sleeper waking suddenly from a dream, moved to forestall him. 'Let's do nothing of the kind,' he said firmly. 'This is not a good place, Tormon, and just look at the size of it, man! If we get split up, we'll never find each other again.' He paused in thought for a moment. 'We must divide into two groups – no more. I'll command one and Willan will take charge of the other. We'll go in opposite directions from this entrance, and stick to the walls. *Is that clearly understood?* Unless you get a definite sighting of Presvel and his captives, no one is to go wandering off into the centre of the chamber, and if *that* happens – though I doubt it will – you must leave the others some sort of sign to show the way you've gone. Otherwise, we must all keep going until we meet again – and by that time, we'll have an idea of the ways out of here; their position and, hopefully, whether anyone has passed that way lately. Rochalla seems to have her wits about her. She left us one clue to show where they had gone. Maybe she can manage others. If we get right around, and there's no other way out, or no sign of them having left the chamber, then, and only then, will we worry about how best to search the middle.' He looked around his men. 'Now, is everybody quite clear about what we're going to do?'

For a moment the trader looked truculent, but Seriema went up to him and spoke softly in his ear. 'Tormon, this is really the best way. We've got to be systematic, or we'll never find them in a place this size.'

He bit his lip, and sighed. 'All right. We'll do it your way. But let's stop wasting time!'

Quickly, they split into two parties. Tormon, Seriema and Cetain formed up with three of the Reivers and went to their left, while Willan took the other five warriors and went right. Before the two groups parted, Seriema pulled the torch stub from her belt. Though prudence had made her hang on to it, it really wasn't long enough to be much use. Carefully, she laid it in the entrance of the passageway. 'There,' she said. 'No matter what happens now, at least we'll be able to find our way back out of here.'

Cetain gave her a smile that was warm with pride. 'Well done, lass. You might not be so good at climbing, but when it comes to wits, you beat us all.'

It was a long walk all the way around the vast chamber, and the knowledge that Presvel had probably taken a much straighter route, thereby saving himself a lot of time and effort, added extra irritation. On the other hand, however, theirs was the safer and more sensible way. Who could say that Presvel and his captives weren't wandering around the cavern somewhere at this very moment, lost and unable to find a way out?

For her part, Seriema hoped that she and her companions would find an exit soon. All the shifting, flashing lights, coupled with the incessant sizzling and buzzing noises in the background, were making her head ache. Not only was she physically weary after her long ride and hard climb that day, but her brain was beginning to feel fogged by all her fruitless attempts to make sense of what was taking place all around her, and she was finding it difficult to concentrate. Then something happened to jolt her out of her trance. Finnall, one of Cetain's men, had wandered a little way apart from the rest. He was notorious in the Reiver band for having more curiosity than brains, and the warriors could tell a whole host of amusing tales at his expense. This time, however, it was no laughing matter.

Out of the corner of her eye, Seriema saw him wander over to a tall column covered in scintillating lights that looked for all the world like jewels. As he reached out to see if he could pick one off the surface, she let out a yell of warning, but it was too late. With a loud snapping sound, a filament of searing light lanced out from the structure and attached itself to Finnall's hand. In an eyeblink it had run up his arm, branching and multiplying as it went, until his entire body was covered in a blinding network of blue-white brilliance. Writhing and screaming, the Reiver fell to the floor, while his comrades clustered round him at a respectful distance, desperate to help him, but not daring to go any closer. Then the scream was cut off abruptly, as Finnall burst into a ball of silvery flame. When the fire died away, absolutely no trace of him remained.

There was nothing to do but go on, and as yet, everyone was too shocked to say anything about the terrible fate of their comrade. Seriema noticed, however, that the men stuck together in a tight bunch now, and avoided not only the structures in the chamber, but the walls as well. It wasn't necessary for Cetain to warn them to be careful. The dangers of this alien place had been brought home to them in the most horrific way, and no one was taking any chances. For herself, Seriema held tightly to the hand of a visibly distressed Cetain. She had waited too many years to find him, and she had no intention of losing him. If anything happened to him now, it was damn well going to happen to her, too!

Weary and sick at heart, they finally reached what was apparently the only exit to the chamber, and it was a subdued band of Reivers who met with their companions, who had arrived there a little while before. The others listened with horror to the tale of Finnall's fate, but there was little time for dwelling on what had happened. Every one of them was seized by an urgency to get away from this dreadful place as soon as possible. And now they could make some progress, for they had another clue. Balled up in the doorway was another rag of cloth from Rochalla's dress. The trail led onwards, out of the chamber and into the unknown regions ahead.

Seriema looked at Cetain, wondering what they would meet with next, and whether anyone else would be lost. From the look on his face, she suspected that their thoughts were very much alike.

Thirty-four

Unexpected Friendship

After they had rested at the head of the pass, Amaurn's little force continued down the trail, riding in pairs where the way was wide enough and single file where the rocks closed in. In the general scrimmage of departure, Elion had found himself riding alongside Vifang. To make people feel more comfortable, the shapeshifter had taken on human appearance, and was riding Toulac's horse. The veteran – thanks to a plot hatched between herself and Elion – had joined Veldan on Kaz, so that she could help to take the minds of the Loremaster partners off the landslide that had almost killed them on this very road.

As they rode down the trail, Elion couldn't help glancing across at Vifang. The form she had taken was distinctly feminine – which, he supposed, was hardly surprising. More unsettling, however, was the fact that the flame-red hair she had chosen was almost identical in colour to that of his dead partner, Melnyth. The face was not the same, being much more delicate and regular of feature, and this woman appeared to be younger, and neither so tall nor so lean. Nonetheless, the slight, superficial resemblance was sufficient to stir up a welter of memories in Elion, both good and bad. The most vivid, however, was his partner's horrendous death.

Was this some evil omen? Unthinkingly, he recoiled from Vifang, and saw her face take on a bitter expression: half anger, half regret. 'Do I repel you so badly, even in this form?' she challenged him.

Hastily, Elion shook his head. 'No, of course you don't repel me! It's not that at all. It's just . . . You remind me . . . I can't . . .' He

468

gave up, and took another approach. 'Why did you choose that colour for your hair?'

Vifang shrugged. 'I don't know. It's strange, but the image of it has been popping in and out of my mind all day, as though it were being projected from somewhere. I even increased my mental shielding, but the impression is so strong, it just keeps breaking through.'

Suddenly, Elion understood. He wouldn't be the only one who had Melnyth on his mind today. Veldan and Kaz would be thinking about her too, reflecting on that last encounter with the Ak'Zahar, and how badly it had failed. With all three Loremasters remembering her it was little wonder that, between them, they had created images strong enough to pierce Vifang's shield. Not for one moment did he think she'd been snooping deliberately. In order to take on the shapes of other beings the way they did, the Takuru must be extraordinarily receptive to form and detail. Due to the strength of the emotions that must be emanating from the three surviving Loremasters on this day of all days, she had unwittingly copied Melnyth's most distinctive feature – that banner of flaming hair. Elion found himself wondering just how Vifang's personality meshed with the other forms she created. How closely did the emotions shown on this human's face correspond with what was passing in the Takur's mind? If she took on a human form, did her mental processes become more human? But in that case, what would happen when she took the form of a tree, or a chair? Some time, if they both survived today, he would love to ask her . . .

He came back from his thoughts to find the shapeshifter staring at him. 'So what's the problem with this hair, anyway?' she demanded. 'I swear, against all the weird prejudices of you damn Loremasters, we Takuru just can't win.'

Suddenly, Elion saw himself jeopardising Amaurn's entire plan to integrate the Takuru with the rest of the Shadowleague. 'No, it's not a prejudice at all,' he told her hastily. 'It's just that you reminded me . . .' And with that, he went on to explain to her about his former partner, her violent death, and his theory that he and his colleagues had been projecting her image unconsciously.

To his surprise, he found it easier than it had previously been to speak of those dreadful times. By the time he had finished, the glint of anger had faded from Vifang's eyes. 'Oh. Now I see – and I understand what it must mean to you, to be going back to fight the Ak'Zahar today. I'm sorry, Elion, to have brought back such memories. I can change the colour – what shall it be? Black? Blue? Purple? Green?' As she spoke, her hair took on each colour in turn, with some startling results.

Elion burst out laughing. 'I'd stick to the red, if I were you. Besides,' he added softly, 'I always loved that colour. It's nice to see it again.'

Vifang shot a shrewd glance in his direction. 'I really don't think that would be a good idea,' she told him gently. 'I'll try the purple, if it's all the same to you – at least for today.'

As they went on down the trail, they continued to talk, and Elion learned more about the sad exile of the Takuru: always on the outskirts, always excluded, suspected, reviled. He felt angry that Cergorn had lured them into this unhappy existence with false hopes and promises, and ashamed of himself and his own people for being so prejudiced. 'But why did you keep on believing him?' he asked. 'Surely, in time, you must have seen that Cergorn was leading you on.'

The Takur shrugged. 'Of course we did, and it made us very bitter. That was when a few of my people actually started to make the sort of mischief that had been wrongly attributed to us before. But what alternative did we have, other than to keep hoping that sooner or later, the Archimandrite would keep his word? The Takuru have never been a prolific race. Even at the best of times, there were no more than a handful of us, and we were hunted down and killed wherever we were found. It was an easy matter for wrongdoers of any species to say that their crimes had been committed by shapeshifters, and if they could get anyone to bear false witness for them, they were generally believed. Just when it seemed that our race must be doomed, Cergorn offered us sanctuary and hope. Even if the Curtain Walls had not failed, I doubt that we would have survived much longer in our own lands. In spite of the way he used us, we still owe him a good deal, Elion. Had it not been for Cergorn, flawed and manipulative as he was, the Takuru would have been extinct by now.'

It was somewhere around noon when Amaurn's group of Loremasters came down the trail and onto the plateau. Elion looked ahead to the city of Tiarond, oddly surprised to find it so unchanged. But the invaders had not used fire, he reminded himself, nor had they attacked with siege weapons to subdue the city. All they had needed were teeth and talons, numbers, speed and strength. Not to mention the ability to strike without warning, from the skies.

All too soon, the time came for the two groups to split up. Amaurn, along with Veldan, Kaz, Toulac, Dark, the Zavahl/Aethon pairing and a reluctant Scall, would carry on across the plateau to the cliff road, and down into the passages that the lad had found. Elion, Vifang, Kher and two other Loremasters would head into the city to deal with the Ak'Zahar.

They didn't linger over the parting. They were all too aware that the group who were going into Tiarond would need all the remaining hours of daylight to complete their task – and if, in the meantime, the clouds should come down really low, even that margin of safety would vanish. There was only time for a quick hug from Veldan, a slap on the back from Toulac, and some last words of advice and warning from Amaurn, before Elion found himself riding away from most of his friends and heading towards the city, to face once again the fiends who had killed his partner.

Kher and Elion had talked it over on the journey and decided that the best plan would be to leave the horses near the city gate. Their hooves made too much noise on the cobbled streets, preventing any attempts at a silent approach to the Precincts' tunnel, and if the Ak'Zahar should be disturbed, and rush to the attack, being mounted would not convey any advantage to the Loremasters. On the contrary, the only way to survive would be to run and hide in the nearby merchants' houses, going to ground like hunted animals. Though the houses in this lower area were cramped and mean, the Loremasters chose one near the gates and led their mounts inside, leaving them safely tethered in the two downstairs rooms. Elion remembered Veldan telling him how Toulac used to bring her horse into her kitchen, and felt a prickle running down his spine. He mocked himself for being unduly superstitious but nevertheless it seemed to him, as it had done to Veldan, that circumstances were coming full circle, back to a peculiar echo of the events that had started this entire business.

Having made the horses secure they went back out into the street, where Vifang changed back into her own amorphous form, which would be much more efficient for either hiding or fighting, and vanished into the shadows. To Elion's surprise, it didn't bother him in the least. Somehow, that human figure sporting the flamboyant banner of red then purple hair, had made him view the shapeshifter in a whole new light, and since he had come to know her better, he had realised that she wasn't alien and frightening after all. What was more, he had discovered that he liked her very much, and was glad to have her at his side throughout this dangerous mission.

Since the presence of the Takur had made Kher's little group superfluous, Amaurn had sent all but two of them back to Gendival. Loremasters were in such short supply during this crisis that it seemed insane to risk any more of them than was absolutely necessary. If Vifang failed, then an extra handful of fighters was going to make little difference. Elion suspected that Amaurn had only brought them in the first place to mollify the more conservative members of the Shadowleague, who couldn't seem to see that on a mission like this, only abilities mattered, not numbers. Kher's two remaining assistants were Loremaster partners. Though well-versed in fighting skills, Alsive and Elysa were also skilled artisans and historians who had made a special study of the explosives and weapons that had come from the distant past. They were an oddly mismatched couple – while Alsive was short and dark, tending to be on the chubby side and explosive of temperament, blonde Elysa was willowy and languid, and a deadly fighter, if aroused.

As the little group crept through the streets, Elion was glad to have the two extra fighters. The deserted city was an eerie place. He shivered as they went on through the empty streets that were slippery and wet with sleet, and wished he had one of the plasma beam weapons, like the esoteric device that Kher carried, slung by its strap from his shoulder. It was one of the only two in existence and, like most of the young Loremasters under Cergorn's reign, Elion had sneaked it out of the museum of forbidden artefacts from time to time, and taken it off to some deserted spot for a bit of target practice.

I'm just as good a shot as he is and he needs one arm to hold his stick. Why should he have it?

But Kher had been given the weapon by Amaurn, because he'd been patrolling the failing Curtain Walls on the Gendival border. He wasn't about to let go of it now, no matter how much Elion coaxed or cajoled, so there wasn't any point in trying. There wasn't any point in wishing for its counterpart either, because Amaurn's group had taken it down into the tunnels with them.

Sternly, Elion told himself to stop wishing for things he couldn't have, and pay attention to his surroundings instead. The city was not as he had expected. Since everyone had been in the Precincts when the predators had attacked, there were no decaying or dismembered bodies lying about, and he was profoundly grateful for their absence. The place looked as though the entire populace had simply packed its bags and decamped elsewhere, and the Loremaster could almost let himself believe that they had fled – until a swirl of air brought a breeze down from the upper levels of the city, laden with the sickly pungency of decaying flesh.

Despite the emptiness and air of abandonment, Elion could not shake the sensation of being watched by unseen, hostile eyes. Time and again, he turned his head quickly, thinking he had seen a face or a shadowy figure at a window, only to be confronted by a curtain moving in a draught, a dead plant in a pot on the windowsill – or nothing at all. He only thanked providence that it was daylight. Even now, the menace and threat of the predators was ever present.

Every unexpected noise made the Loremasters startle and freeze, and they were surprised at the number of sounds there could be in such a deserted place: the whispering of the wind, the harsh cries of carrion birds, the slither and crash of a dislodged tile, and the creak of shifting timbers in the damp, deserted houses. Scrabbling and scratching sounds coming from the interiors of the deserted buildings showed that the rats, at any rate, were thriving.

As the Loremasters moved cautiously onward, heading uphill towards the Sacred Precincts, Elion could see that, in the absence of their inhabitants, the buildings of Tiarond were already beginning to decay. Missing roof tiles, broken window panes, a creaking shutter that had come adrift and was swinging perilously by one hinge: all of these foreshadowed the city's ultimate fate if the Shadowleague failed to take it back from the Ak'Zahar.

The clouds were thickening by the time Elion and his companions reached the merchants' houses on the edge of the Esplanade. Ahead of them, across the empty square, was the dark mouth of the tunnel that sheltered and concealed the colony of predators. Elion shivered and wiped clammy palms on his shirt. They were in there. He could smell them – that same foul, carrion stench that had filled the labyrinthine caverns in Ghariad the day that Melnyth lost her life. At the thought of his lost partner, hatred flared within him, turning the fear into anger.

Just stay put in there for a little while longer, you ugly, murdering bastards! This is the day when Melnyth's death will finally be avenged!

They took shelter in the garden of Lady Seriema's mansion, concealing themselves from view in a cluster of laurels while they organised themselves for the task ahead. Kher unslung his weapon and hung it carefully on the broken stump of a thick bough, while he sorted through the packs for the explosives. The sleet was coming down harder now and Elion glanced up uneasily at the lowering skies.

If this lot turns to proper snow, we could be in all sorts of trouble. Both the pass and the cliff road get blocked very easily, and I don't fancy spending the winter in Tiarond.

He turned to Kher. 'We'd better hurry, before it gets any darker.'

At that moment there was a stir of movement among the shrubs, and one of the bushes lost its glossy leaves and melted into the nebulous, many-limbed form of Vifang. 'Ah, er . . . There you are,' Kher said. Clearly, he was not quite comfortable yet in the presence of the Takur. 'Are you still prepared to go into the tunnel for us?'

'I've already been inside,' the shapeshifter told him. 'At least, a little way.'

'*What?*' Elion was horrified. 'You went in there without even letting us know? Well, of all the crazy, irresponsible . . .'

'Calm down, Elion.' Kher gave him a quizzical look. 'What's your problem?' He turned back to the shapeshifter. 'How far did you go, and what did you see?'

'As I said, I only went in a little way,' Vifang told him. 'I didn't want to risk disturbing them yet. I took the form of a bat, so I could get an idea of their numbers in the darkness.'

'And?'

'There are so many of them, all clustered together, that it's difficult to tell. I'd say there were a couple of hundred, anyway. At least that many.'

Kher's normally merry face looked closed and grim. 'That's good. Hopefully, we'll get the whole accursed lot of them with a single blast.'

'Are you ready then?' Vifang asked. 'The day is wearing on. As soon as you're ready for me to go I'll change shape, but I won't do it until the last moment, because as one of the Ak'Zahar, the daylight will hurt my eyes.'

'How can you be so calm about this?' Elion demanded.

'You forget,' the Takur said, 'I have been the foremost assassin amongst my people for some time before this. One way and another, I've had to teach myself not to let my nerves get the better of me.'

The Loremaster shook his head. 'How quickly can you teach me not to let *my* nerves get the better of me?'

'Not *that* quickly!'

'I was afraid you'd say that.' He thought for a moment. It was a concern to him that she planned to become an Ak'Zahar. He had seen them attack one another mercilessly before now, for no reason that would make any sense to a human. 'Wouldn't it be safer for you to keep the form of a bat when you sneak in next time?' he suggested.

'Indeed it would,' Vifang told him, 'but how would I carry the charges?'

'Oh.' Elion felt foolish. 'I hadn't thought of that.'

Vifang smiled her own, inner equivalent of a smile. She liked this human, who seemed to have accepted her so well. There was no way she could tell him just how nervous she really was, or how perilous her task would be. He would only worry all the more. Then she revised that thought. Elion already knew how dangerous the Ak'Zahar could be. They had killed his partner. And he was already worried.

'We have the charges ready now.' Kher broke into her thoughts. He handed her a sack and the shapeshifter opened it and looked inside. 'Those small, flat black discs are the charges,' he told her. 'There are eight of them. Just place them firmly against the walls or ceiling and they should stick there. If it's at all possible, try to distribute them as widely as you can throughout the tunnel. If we can, we want to kill all of those damned monstrosities in a single blast and it will be best if we can blow up the tunnel all along its length.'

From his pocket he took another device, about the size of his palm and rectangular in shape. 'Once you're safely out, this will detonate them.' He showed her the raised white square that gleamed against the black, metallic background. 'Just press this – and boom!' He paused. 'At least, I hope so. We took these devices from the collection of materials that we weren't allowed to use before Amaurn took over. Goodness knows how long they've been locked up in there, or whether they'll work at all.'

'But didn't you test them?' Elion asked him.

'We couldn't. We need all that we have, and we couldn't spare any charges to test. Once we've blown them up, we can hardly use them again.'

The Takur felt a stirring of unease. 'But what if I go in there, risk my life to plant your charges, and then they won't detonate? What then?'

Kher plunged his hand into the sack and came out with another small package. 'We use this – just ordinary blasting powder. There's not enough here to blow up the whole tunnel, but when this explodes, the blast should be enough to detonate the other charges.'

'Blasting powder?' the shapeshifter protested. 'Have you lost your mind? They'll smell that stuff at once. And how am I going to persuade the Ak'Zahar that I'm one of them if I have to go into that tunnel dragging a fuse?'

Kher thought for a moment. 'Well, I'll tell you what. Just take the charges in at first, and come straight out again. Then, if they *do* fail to blow, you can go back in with the blasting powder.'

'So now I get to go in there twice? Thank you *so* much!'

'Well, it's only as a last resort,' Kher said hastily. 'I'm sure there'll be no need – really. The charges should detonate all right.'

'If you're so sure they'll detonate, Kher, why don't *you* wager your life on it?' Elion snapped.

Vifang moved quickly to head off an incipient fight between the Loremasters. 'Well, there's no point in standing around here.' She fixed the image of the hideous Ak'Zahar in her mind, and felt the familiar cool, melting sensation that told her that her form was changing. Then her body settled into the new pattern, and one of the hideous winged predators squatted where the Takur had stood a moment before.

Before she had left Gendival, Vifang had made a close and detailed study of the captive Ak'Zahar. On encountering a member of any new species – or, for that matter, any inanimate object that they wanted to copy – the Takuru had the ability to shift their consciousness into the other's form while the subject, in the case of living creatures, remained completely unaware of the intrusion. In that way, they could make an imprint in their minds – a template of the way the new structure functioned and fitted together, so that it could be replicated by their own shapeshifting form. A difference in size created no difficulty. The amorphous bodies of the Takuru existed partly in the normal world, and partly in the Otherplace – that strange, alternative, adjacent dimension which, according to Amaurn, the Magefolk had also been able to access through the use of certain artefacts. Existing simultaneously in both dimensions, the shapeshifters could move part of their mass at will from one to the other, using as much as they needed to form the shape that they were using in the mundane world, and leaving the extra in the Otherplace.

Now that she had taken on the semblance of the predators, Vifang discovered that not only could she could mimic their smell, their appearance, and the way they sounded, but she also suffered the same problems as they did where daylight was concerned. Even the subdued light of a clouded afternoon dazzled her, lancing into her eyes like blades of steel. She put down the sack and covered her face with bony hands, almost drawing blood with her elongated, razor-sharp talons. Her one imperative was to get out of that dreadful light. 'I'm going now,' she said quickly. 'I won't try to communicate with you once I'm inside, in case those creatures can pick up mind-speech, but rest assured that I'll be as quick as I possibly can.'

Elion, who had been staring at her new form with a kind of fasci-nated revulsion, visibly pulled himself together. 'Well, you take care of yourself,' he told her. 'After this, I reckon that Amaurn owes you any favour that you care to ask of him – and I'll make sure he knows that, too.'

The shapeshifter laughed. 'I'd appreciate that, Elion. All being well, I'll see you soon. Stand back,' she warned, and extending her leathery wings, she took off with her taloned hands hugging the sack close to her body – one lone figure on her way to challenge the menace of the Ak'Zahar.

Thirty-Five

The Mirror Wall

'Come on, Scall. Keep up!' Though Dark's voice wasn't angry or unkind, there was a sharp note in it that the youth had never heard before. Since Amaurn's companions had said farewell to Kher's group, and gone their own way, tempers certainly seemed to be fraying. Had it not been for the fact that they were all adults, members of the mysterious, powerful Shadowleague and experienced in both fighting and the solving of problems, Scall would have sworn that they were nervous – if not downright scared. But that was hardly likely, was it? If anyone was going to be scared on this expedition, surely it was going to be him.

Not for one moment had Scall imagined that he'd be back here again, especially so soon after his escape from this grim place. Everything had served to remind him of his earlier flight from Tiarond. Everyone – Amaurn, Veldan, Kaz, Dark, Zavahl, Toulac, and the lad himself – had picked their way across the muddy, flood-ravaged plateau until they reached the guardhouse at the edge, where they had left their horses before taking the cliff road down to the waterfall. There was only one difference – to Scall, the most important in the world. This time, Tormon and Rochalla were not with him.

They'll still be at the Reiver stronghold, I expect – unless Tormon went looking for me. But no – how could he? He wouldn't leave little Annas. That wouldn't be fair. I wonder what they're doing now? And did Presvel get caught – or is he still chasing after Rochalla?

A shiver went through him at the thought.

'Scall, come *on*.' This time, though he was yelling to be heard over the roar of the waterfall, the Summoner really did sound annoyed and Scall realised that while he'd been woolgathering, he was holding up the line of people waiting in turn to pass behind the immense waterfall and enter the cliff road tunnel. Amaurn, Zavahl and Toulac were already inside. Dark, Veldan and Kazairl were waiting behind him, because the firedrake had insisted on going last in case his weight should crumble the edges of the water-worn road.

'Sorry.' Scall felt himself going red. Even after all his adventures it seemed that he was still as much of a daydreamer as he had been when he was Agella's useless apprentice. Quickly, he ducked beneath the sleek arc of water, letting the misty spray cool his burning face, and glad of the darkness beyond to hide his blushes.

In the tunnel, the others were waiting impatiently. 'What kept you, boy?' Amaurn barked. 'Sorry,' Scall mumbled again.

Toulac took his arm and steered him away from the irate Archimandrite. 'Try to keep your mind on business, sonny,' she said softly. 'Just think – the quicker we can get this over, the sooner you can get back to that little chestnut mare of yours. Not to mention that girl you left behind with the Reivers.'

Scall, however, was not to be consoled. 'It's just not fair. I didn't want to come back here in the first place, but they made me.'

The veteran shrugged. 'Welcome to the adult world, sonny. Life isn't fair. You've just got to get on with it.'

Scall fumed. This was just the sort of irritating thing that old people were always saying. It sounded good, but what use was it? Luckily for him, he was too much in awe of the veteran to answer back.

By this time, the last of the companions had entered the tunnel. Everybody lit the glims they carried, and headed on down the wet road, their footsteps echoing from the curving walls of the passage through the cliff. Scall hurried as fast as he dared, keeping his eyes on the ceiling despite the risk of tripping over the bumps and ruts in the uneven road. Reluctant though he was to re-enter the strange passages he had found, he couldn't get there soon enough. Firstly, the thought of the flood that had almost killed him last time made him desperate to get out of the tunnel, and secondly, Toulac had been right about one thing. The quicker they got this over with, the better – and then he could go back to Tormon and Rochalla, and get on with his interrupted life.

If I survive, that is.

To his great relief, the downward journey didn't seem to take nearly so long as it had when the place had been strange to him, and he'd been all alone. When he saw the circular opening in the ceiling he called out to the others. 'Look! There it is.'

They all hurried towards it, and clustered underneath. Amaurn frowned. 'It's going to be interesting, trying to get Kaz up there.' He unslung the peculiar weapon, a twin of the one that Kher carried, from his shoulder. 'It looks as though we'll have to bring down part of the ceiling, and use the rubble to make a ramp of sorts.'

Toulac, in the meantime, had been scouting around the area in which they were standing. 'Hey, look at this,' she called. 'Someone's been here before us.' There, at the edge of the road, was a pile of horse droppings.

Amaurn bent to examine them. 'What in the name of perdition . . . ?'

'Whoever they were, I don't think they went any further than this.' Toulac frowned. 'We didn't see any more dung, or any other signs of horses further up the passage or the cliff road, and the ground was pretty muddy in places.'

Then Dark made the second discovery. 'Look up there!' Tied to the metal cross strut was a strip of fluttering material. Lifting the glim above his head, he examined the cloth more closely. 'Why, this is Reiver patterning. What can *they* be doing here?'

Rudely, Scall shoved his way past the Summoner. That cloth looked so familiar . . . 'That looks like Rochalla's dress!'

Dark put a hand on his shoulder. 'Steady, lad. That's a pretty common weave among my people. More girls than one have dresses with that pattern – it could belong to anybody.'

Scall remained silent, but he was certain that the Summoner was wrong. What in the name of Myrial would some other Reiver girl be doing here? For some unknown reason, Rochalla had returned, just as he had. But who was with her? Tormon and Seriema? Or was it Presvel?

Amaurn called them all to order. 'Standing around here is getting us nowhere. Let's get moving, shall we? Everybody stay well back.' Once they had all retreated to a safe distance, he lifted the weapon, aimed carefully at a spot on the ceiling near the rim of the circular hole, and fired. There was a brilliant flash of light, a reverberating crash, and a section of the ceiling came down in a cloud of dust that set them all coughing and choking. As the haze began to clear, Scall could see that a chunk of the roof had come down, exposing a length of the strange, circular corridor above. As they had hoped, the rubble had formed a large pile underneath that could be scrambled up with care.

'Myrial in a ballgown!' Toulac said. 'You haven't gone and blocked the whole tunnel?'

Amaurn squinted through the dust. 'I don't think so. If some of those rocks were moved, there would be a space to squeeze through. Probably.'

'Who cares?' Veldan said impatiently. 'We don't need to get down there anyway. The way back up isn't blocked, and as long as we can still get out, that's all that matters. Let's get on with this.'

Scall couldn't have agreed more.

Ramp or no ramp, Kaz still had a certain amount of difficulty scrambling up into the tunnel above and, before he could squeeze into the passageway, Amaurn was forced to lower the settings on the plasma weapon, and fire short bursts at the walls to enlarge the space. The results were unexpected. All the layer of spongy material, which turned out to be four or five feet thick, seemed to shrivel and shrink away, leaving a tube of polished stone that went like a wormhole through the interior of the plateau.

'What in the name of Myrial *was* that stuff?' Zavahl wondered aloud. 'Aethon says he can't find anything in his memories that mentions it.'

'We can worry about that later,' Veldan replied. 'At least there's room enough for Kaz now, and that's what counts.'

When the spongy substance had gone, the soft, changeful, coloured lights also vanished and once again the glims were needed as they crept along in single file, walking with difficulty on the curving bottom of the tube. To Scall's annoyance, Amaurn wouldn't let him take the lead. Instead he was forced to trail along behind the Archimandrite and Zavahl, even though *he* had been the one who'd discovered this place, and he was the only one who'd been here before. Not, to be perfectly honest, that he particularly wanted to be the first to encounter any dangers but, on the other hand, it just went to show what they really thought of him: that he was just a boy, and didn't count for much. Fuming, Scall stomped along, muttering under his breath. Tormon had never treated him like that. And this lot had sung a different tune back in Gendival, when they had wanted to see the strange devices he'd discovered in this very place.

Suddenly Toulac, who was walking behind him, tapped him on the shoulder. 'Never mind,' she said in a low voice. 'None of this lot ever had the nerve to tackle one of the winged fiends, armed with just his bare hands and a rock.' After that, Scall felt much more cheerful. When the tunnel opened out into the gigantic cavern, and Amaurn stopped, and gestured for him to lead the way, his pride was restored completely.

In truth, Scall had forgotten how bewildering and dauntingly strange the massive chamber seemed at first, with its bizarre, moving patterns of light, its weird sounds and its unnatural structures, all different shapes and sizes, that seemed to be growing out of the floor. As they came out of the tubular tunnel, all the adults stopped and stood gaping at their alien surroundings. He noted with some satisfaction that they all looked as awestruck as he had been on his first visit. If truth be told, he was just as dumbfounded the second time around, but he concealed it as best he could, cultivating a studied, casual air. 'Come on. The place where I found that weird stuff is over this way,' he said, and set off bravely in what he hoped was the right direction.

'Damn it, we've lost him!' Seriema planted her fists on her hips. 'Honestly, I can understand why Tormon is so anxious, but we've asked him time and again not to get too far ahead – and now look what's happened!'

They had reached a place where the tunnel widened and three passages intersected: the one they had come in by, and two others. The trader, who had been getting increasingly far ahead of them as time went on, was nowhere to be seen. Gesturing to his men to keep silent, Cetain went and shouted down each tunnel in turn. 'Tormon! Hi, Tormon! Come back!' There was no answer and the Reiver turned to Seriema with a shrug. 'Well, he's really done it this time. And didn't even have the gumption to leave us some kind of sign to show us where he'd gone. Why, even that young lassie had more sense.'

'Aye – and if *she* left a sign to show which way they'd gone, that gormless muttonheaded trader has gone and moved it,' Willan said disgustedly.

'So what do we do now?' Seriema asked in a worried voice.

Cetain shrugged. 'I'd toss a coin, if I had one. The two ways look the same to me, with nought to choose between them.'

'We might as well take the nearest one then, I suppose,' Seriema said doubtfully. 'If there's no sign of him further on, we can always come back.' She sighed. 'We've walked so far already, I could do without this extra fuss and bother.'

When they had left the vast chamber above, the tunnel had proved to be the same as the one by which they'd entered. The tubular walls were still covered with the soft, spongy substance and the light, once again, had reverted to the soft, changeful rainbow hues. Sometimes the passage ran straight, and sometimes it curved gently. Occasionally, just to vary the monotony, there was a sharply angled bend, and sometimes the floor sloped downwards with a steep gradient, letting them know that they were going further down beneath the plateau. But that was all. There had been no cross-roads, and no rooms leading off the endless passage, so there had been nothing to hold up the hurrying Tormon. Even when the rest of them had been tiring he had gone forging ahead – until they had discovered, too late, that he had left them well and truly behind, and they could no longer find him.

Seriema sighed. 'Well, we'd better try not to let him get too far ahead of us. Has anyone got something to mark the tunnel we came in by?'

Willan took a clean square of linen that formerly had been used to wrap some oatcakes, and skewered it with a dagger to the soft, yielding material of the passage wall. It hung there like a flag, marking the way home.

That is, if we ever get the chance to come back this way.

Trying to set aside such gloomy thoughts, Seriema squared her shoulders, and set off down the new passageway – however, she was fighting a losing battle to keep up her spirits. 'None of this make any *sense*,' she complained.

Cetain, surprisingly, disagreed. 'It may, though,' he said. 'Among the Reivers, when a chieftain dies, we bury him beneath the moor, and raise a great barrow over him. His prized possessions go with him to his tomb – whatever might contribute to his wealth or comfort in the worlds beyond.' He looked at Seriema and grinned. 'Of course, because the Reivers aren't wealthy people, there are certain folk among them who think it's a waste to bury so many valuables under the ground where it will be lost for ever. Inevitably, there are those who are brave, or foolish, enough to break into the tombs in search of forbidden riches. But to protect the chieftain's spirit from unseemly disturbances, we build the barrows with a maze of false passages inside and a lot of them contain pitfalls and traps. A would-be thief, breaking into the resting place of a Reiver chieftain, very seldom seems to find his way out again – not that it seems to stop them trying, however.'

His grin grew sly, and he winked at her. 'Mind you, 'tis said by some that the chieftains, before they die, will often pass on a plan of the barrow to their sons or daughters. That way, honour is satisfied, yet the wealth is not lost to the clan. Bit by bit, the items are recovered and find their way back into use, and no one ever remarks on their return.'

Seriema looked him with a frown. 'So?'

'Ah, the point of my tale is this, lassie. This place with all its tunnels made me think of the barrows, but on a much grander scale, of course. I don't think all these endless passageways are here for any particular reason – other than to hide something.'

'You know, I believe you're right. I hadn't thought of that, but it's the only thing that makes sense.' Seriema looked with increasing respect at the young man she had promised to wed. How lucky she was! Cetain was a Reiver warrior who could ride and fight with great skill. He commanded great respect in the rough, wild world in which he lived – but in addition, he had a brain, and he used it. 'I wonder who built this place – and I wonder what it is they're trying to protect,' she mused.

Cetain looked grave. 'I'm not sure if I want to know,' he said.

They had been walking for quite a while without any sign of Tormon when they were confronted with another choice of route. To their surprise the tunnel, which had remained round in cross-section like the others, with walls of the ubiquitous, yielding substance, opened out into a small chamber that looked almost normal by comparison, with walls of smooth, dark metal that were straight and squared-off in the usual way. Seriema gave a sigh of relief and looked around appreciatively. 'Thank Myrial for that! Maybe now we're finally getting somewhere. I never want to see another of those blasted tubes, ever again.'

'I'll drink to that,' said Cetain with feeling. All around him, his men had brightened perceptibly to find themselves between solid, comparatively normal looking walls, and in plain, white light that stayed the same unchanging colour.

This time they had no difficulty choosing a route. Leading off from one side of the room was a sort of doorless antechamber and, when they walked cautiously inside, they discovered that not only were there no other doors leading off it, but it didn't even have any ceiling. Instead, a squared-off shaft went on upwards for some indeterminate distance, its end lost in the shadows, high above. Back in the main chamber, the only other exit, apart from the one they had come in by, was a long corridor that led off from the opposite side. Again, it was built on conventional lines with straight, right-angled walls and ceiling, and clad in the same dark metal as the walls of the room itself.

Willan took the lead for a while with a couple of his best warriors accompanying him. Relieved to be heading into an area which seemed a little less alien, Seriema strode forward with Cetain at her side, and the remainder of the men following after. After walking for a while they came to a place where the tunnel angled to the left. As she rounded the corner, Seriema froze in shock. There, coming towards them, were a group of warriors. Willan cursed, and as his men reached for their weapons, they saw the others do the same. It was only after another half-dozen steps or so had brought the figures close enough to recognise that they understood what they were seeing.

'Well, I'll be damned,' the grizzled veteran muttered. 'It's a mirror!'

Abruptly, Cetain halted, stopping the rest of them in their tracks with a barked order. 'Aye,' he said softly. 'And a bloody sight more perfect a mirror than was ever found in Arcan's fortress. But what would such a thing be doing all the way down here? Who would make a blank wall into a perfect mirror?' He half-turned and looked at Seriema. 'Well, lass, not for nothing was I telling you all about the barrows, before. Call me a suspicious fool if I turn out to be wrong – but to me, this has the smell of a trap.' He grinned at the older man. 'Willan, are you still as deadly with a knife as you used to be?'

'Why, of course I am!' said the veteran indignantly. 'I can put out the eye of a fly at twenty paces.'

Cetain's grin grew even more wolfish. 'Ah, you don't have to go that far,' he said. 'All I want you to do is hit that mirror up ahead.'

From nowhere a sleek, balanced little throwing knife appeared in Willan's hand and, with a smooth cast, he launched it towards the reflective wall. With a loud splintering sound, the mirror shattered into countless fragments. There was a flash of eye-searing light and their ears popped from the change of pressure as a strong wind went whistling past them, heading towards the shattered mirror and whatever lay beyond. Then the light vanished, leaving dazzling purple after-images in front of Seriema's eyes. The wind died away and the pressure in her ears equalised as she swallowed hard.

Seriema scraped tangled hair away from her face and blinked tears from her smarting eyes. She didn't know what she had expected to see beyond the mirror. Not a plain wall, or an ordinary room, that was for sure. What she had *not* expected, however, was to see the Godsword, Galveron, come hurtling out of what looked like a dark and swirling void with four other figures trailing after him. All five of them ended up in a tangled heap on the floor of the passage while behind them . . . Seriema blinked. Behind them, the wall was a perfect mirror once again, unmarked and flawless as before.

'Well!' The voice belonged to Willan. 'You surely don't see *that* sort of thing every day!'

It was a wonderful feeling to be free again. No matter how convincing Helverien's illusion had been, it was an incredible relief to be back to the normal, solid world. Galveron strode forward to meet Seriema and her companions. 'By Myrial, but it's good to see you, my Lady! It must be you we have to thank for our rescue.'

Seriema was still looking dumbfounded. 'Lieutenant Galveron! I'm glad to see that you survived the attack on the city. But what in the world are you doing down here?'

He shook his head. 'Oh, my Lady, that's a long, long story. These days, I'm no longer Lieutenant. Lord Blade seems to have been lost during the attack of those hideous winged monsters, and Hierarch Gilarra made me Commander in his place.'

'Gilarra? She's still alive, then?'

Galveron nodded. 'There are a few hundred survivors from Tiarond. We took refuge in the Temple and, from the Holy of Holies there, we found our way down here. In brief, my Lady, Gilarra sent me in search of the Hierarch's ring.'

Seriema's eyebrows went up. 'What? Down here?'

'Don't ask,' he told her wryly. 'In any case, we found it, my companions and I, but we were caught in that trap from which you've just released us and we were beginning to think we'd never see the outside world again. But what brings you down here, Lady Seriema? However did you find your way to this place?'

'We are also searching – but for companions, not a ring,' Seriema told him. 'Again, it's a lengthy tale, but the short of it is that Presvel – you remember my assistant? – has lost his mind following the fall of the city, and has kidnapped trader Tormon's child, and another girl. We came down here with Tormon, to help him get his daughter back, but he went too far ahead of us, and we lost him. We were searching for him when we found *you*.' She turned to her tall companion with the dark red hair and the piercing eyes. 'I think some introductions are in order. Commander Galveron of the Godswords, this is Cetain, son of the Reiver chieftain Arcan – and soon to be my lifemate.'

Galveron felt his jaw drop. One of those unregenerate rogues the Reivers? And she was betrothed to him? How in the name of Myrial had that come to be?

Cetain laughed, and held out a hand. 'I can guess your thoughts, Godsword, and as you said before – it's a long story. But we'd be glad to tell it to you when we've more time. At present, though, I suggest we'd best put away any old enmities. We humans must band together against a far more menacing foe.'

In spite of himself, Galveron was impressed. There was something about this young man that he liked. 'By Myrial, but you're right,' he said. 'And in the interest of our new cooperation, I would suggest that we help you find Tormon and his little girl, as a matter of priority.' He frowned. 'That poor man. Is there no end to his ill-fortune? Still, we'll do whatever we can to help him – then we can think about some way of getting out of here.' He grinned at Seriema. 'But before we do, there's someone I want you to meet.' With an arm around her shoulders, he drew Aliana forward. 'Lady Seriema, this is Aliana, joint leader of the city's finest thieves – and soon to be *my* lifemate – that is, if she'll have me?' He looked down at Aliana, suddenly worried. He had a feeling that she might not appreciate being put on the spot like this. To his surprise, however, the thief looked up at him with a beaming smile. 'Just try and stop me,' she said.

Shree was paying little attention to all this trivial human chatter. The Wind-Sprite couldn't quite believe her good fortune – she had given up hope of ever escaping from the timeless Otherplace in which the renegade Amaurn had trapped her. The final, incredible detail that put the seal on her joy was the face of Lady Seriema, who stood with a bunch of rough-looking men down this strange, metal-walled corridor.

I can't believe it! Not only did I actually manage to get out of there, but I've been released back into my own time!

Heleverien flicked a sideways glance at the Wind-Sprite, where she hovered near the ceiling. 'It's more than coincidence, if you ask me. I've had a long time to reflect on the way life seems to work, and what we tend to dismiss as providence or serendipity are usually part of a much larger pattern, acted out on a scale of history that's too large for us to comprehend.'

Privately, Shree thought that sounded like claptrap. The only reason she could possibly see for being released so soon was that she would return within Amaurn's lifetime, and bring the renegade to justice at last. In the midst of dwelling on this happy prospect, she suddenly realised that the humans below her were already deep in conversation, and she had better stay aware of their intentions.

It was as she had suspected, having heard Galveron and Aliana's stories of their recent adventures. They had emerged in a continuation of the place in which they had found themselves when they ventured under Myrial's Temple. Though she was barely concerned about their plans to rescue the trader's child, she decided that she had better remain with them for the present and investigate this strange place further. Clearly, it was some construct of the Ancients and, as such, it concerned the Shadowleague closely. Perhaps, between them, she and Helverien might be able to make some sense of it all.

It occurred to Shree that she ought to be trying to reach Cergorn. Judging by what she had gleaned from Galveron and Aliana in the Otherplace, and was now hearing from the Godsword Commander and Lady Seriema, she had been missing for a few days at least. She needed the kind of detailed information that she could only get from the Shadowleague, and she needed to let her partner know that she was all right. It probably wouldn't be easy to reach Gendival from here – she was a long way away, and who knew how far underground. Solid rock seemed to have a somewhat inhibiting effect on mindspeech. But if she tried her hardest, there should be Listeners on duty who could pick up and boost her thoughts, and it was desperately important that she reach the Archimandrite. He had to know as soon as possible that the renegade Amaurn was still a threat.

While the humans were talking, Shree took her chance to send her message. Focusing her thoughts down to the narrowest, most private beam, she reached out beyond this tomb of stone, beyond the Tiarondian plateau, beyond the land of Callisiora, and through the Curtain Walls to Gendival.

Immediately, she could sense that there was something wrong – something more than could be explained by a few short days' absence. The team of Listeners on duty were new to her, and very young. Thirishri, concentrating even harder on reaching them, saw a hazy image beginning to form in her mind's eye of the trio in the

Tower of Tidings. There was a human girl, fresh-faced, young and pretty, with golden highlights glinting in her light brown hair. Two others were next to her: a young man with stubble making a darker shadow on a shaven head, and a girl with pointed features, her braided hair a shade or two darker than that of her companion.

Shree was puzzled to find that the trio were all human. Single-species groupings were traditionally rare among the Listeners, for the obvious reason that the abilities and talents of the different races could augment and boost one another. This trio, though able enough, were also very young: final-year students, she suspected, who had been promoted before their training was complete. Again, she felt a frisson of unease. Cergorn would never have allowed such a thing!

The leader and focus of the group was the girl with the lighter hair, who identified herself as Devera. Shree didn't give her time for anything further. *This is Senior Loremaster Thirishri. I need to get a message to Archimandrite Cergorn as soon as possible.*

On the other end of the link, she could feel the girl's confusion. 'But – I'm sorry, Senior Loremaster, but that isn't possible.'

Shree wasn't feeling very strong on patience. *What do you mean, it isn't possible? Just get him, girl!*

'But . . . Senior Loremaster, didn't you know? Cergorn is no longer Archimandrite. He's no longer in Gendival at all.'

What did you say? Thirishri was stunned, but she was not a Senior Loremaster for nothing. Within a moment, she had recovered herself, and resolved to find out what had been going on in her absence. It took a while to bully the whole story out of the girl who had, by this time, come to realise that she had slipped up badly in blurting out the news as she had. However, by the time the Listener's explanations had stumbled to a close, she had heard all she needed – and far more than she had wished to hear. Almost absently, she broke her contact with Gendival, her other feelings overwhelmed by her grief. Truly, it was as though her partner had been killed. After such an intensive mind-wipe, there was no hope that Cergorn could be restored as he had been. The Archimandrite was no more.

Her partner in the Shadowleague had gone for ever. Then black rage gripped her, as icy and infinite as the very depths of the ocean.

I'll find you, Amaurn! You can't be far away! Finally, it's time for the execution you've avoided for so long!

After all, it shouldn't be difficult. Her heart had leapt when the Listener had told her that her foe was right here, somewhere in these very tunnels. How convenient! It would spare her from wasting needless time in hunting the monster down.

Below her, the humans were preparing to move off and Helverien, who had been talking as animatedly as the rest of the pathetic fools, looked up to the corner where the Wind-Sprite hovered. 'What about you, Shree? Are you coming with us?'

Thirishri decided that she might as well – at least for now. Because of the nature of these tunnels, it might well be that Amaurn's party would fetch up in the same place as these other missing humans. If not, she could always split away from the others and begin a search of her own for the traitors who had brought down her partner, for as well as the renegade, there were also the back-stabbing turncoats who had supported him – mainly Veldan and her cronies. As she drifted down the corridor above Helverien and the humans, the Wind-Sprite's thoughts were grim and bleak. It was time to settle a few scores.

Thirty-Six

The Colony

It was a good thing that Vifang only had a very short distance to glide, because her squinted eyes were watering so hard that she couldn't see a thing, and her maiden flight wobbled and veered wildly from side to side. She managed to get herself levelled out just in time to avoid missing the tunnel entrance, and was rather proud of herself as she made a neat swoop into the dark opening. Then all such trivial thoughts vanished as she made her cautious way into the lair of the Ak'Zahar.

It was just as well that her long, successful career as an assassin had taught her to submerge her fear in absolute concentration. On her earlier reconnaissance she had observed the ways in which the Ak'Zahar moved and rested and reacted to one another. Now she would find out just how much she had learned. The predators were clustered thickly in the central part of the tunnel, where the light from the entrance and exit could not reach them. In the darkness, the night-eyes of the Ak'Zahar began to function properly, giving Vifang clear but colourless images in varying shades of greenish-grey. For the first time, she could see that their groupings were not random, but had a certain informal structure, with the smallest and weakest on the edges of the cluster, nearest the light, the cold winds, and any creature that would be insane enough to threaten the voracious monstrosities.

Like me.

There were no young to be seen, and briefly, the Takur wondered how they were born and raised. She decided that the interior of an

Ak'Zahar nursery, whatever form it might take, was the last thing that she wanted to see – apart, of course, from the interior of an Ak'Zahar belly.

Before she came too close to the group, Vifang flew to the wall of the tunnel and attached herself firmly with hands and feet to the rough stone, just as she had seen the other Ak'Zahar doing. In the process, she discovered the secondary reason for the long, curved talons. They allowed her to cling tightly to the tunnel wall and even the ceiling, supporting the negligible weight of her emaciated, hollow-boned body with no difficulty or discomfort at all.

Copying the odd, sideways scuttle of the Ak'Zahar, she moved cautiously along the wall towards the colony. There was a muted hissing, and the rustle of dry skin and leathery wings as all heads turned as one to view the newcomer, the knowledge of her approach passing through the group in an expanding ripple. Dozens of eyes, seen with her new vision as spots of bright, white light, were fixed on her with a flat, unblinking stare. A shudder ran through Vifang. She felt chilled and physically sick, but she knew it was essential that she find some way to control her mounting fear. If they scented it on her, they would exploit her weakness and tear her to pieces.

For a moment she paused in her approach, and thought of Amaurn and the hope he had held out to her people. She thought of the joy and triumph she had felt when she had finally been permitted to join a group of Loremasters, and the warm and totally unaccustomed sense of belonging it had given her. She thought of Elion; the way she was beginning to enjoy his companionship, and the way in which he had accepted her. Most of all, she thought of the future, where all sorts of adventures, possibilities and opportunities lay open to her – if only she could survive the next hour or two.

The Takur's reflections steadied her and boosted her courage, allowing her to regain the cool, calm nerve with which she had always faced her assignments. Taking a deep breath, she began to move forward with great caution. In order to plant the charges as Kher had asked, she was going to have to go right through the centre of the group of predators and out of the other side – and she had a feeling that the Ak'Zahar weren't going to approve of that at all.

At least the stench of the creatures didn't seem so overpowering when she smelled the same way herself. Vifang laid her first charge at the edge of the throng, sticking it to the ceiling of the tunnel, and then began her perilous journey towards the centre. As she had expected, the puny specimens on the outskirts of the group didn't give her any trouble. On adopting this new shape, she had taken the precaution of making herself larger and more sinewy than most of the Ak'Zahar. In her studies of the captive specimen she'd learned as much of their body language as she could in a short time, and at this moment, her body said 'Don't mess with me'. The lower-ranking predators moved aside without protest to let her pass, and she shouldered her way through them as if she didn't have a fear in the world, laying her charges at intervals as she went. As she penetrated further into the cluster, she was aware of their ranks closing behind her, cutting off any hope of a quick escape.

As she went on, the crowds of creatures grew more dense, their bodies so tightly packed together that she was forced to have increasing amounts of physical contact with them. It took all the willpower she possessed not to cringe away from the foul touch of their leathery skin. Within inches of her own flesh were innumerable sets of fangs and talons, ready to tear her to shreds if she made the slightest wrong move. And always, those eerie, glowing eyes were watching her; following her every move with their savage, pitiless gaze.

Nevertheless, Vifang had progressed much further than she had expected before the real trouble began. In the very centre of the mob, there were a handful of predators, about a dozen or so, who were every bit as large and sinewy as she was – and a damn sight meaner looking. Pushing their lesser fellows aside to make more space, they hissed menacingly at her, baring their fangs and beating their leathery wings.

Well, I certainly won't be going through the middle of this lot!

With her escape blocked behind her, the shapeshifter realised that it would be a bad mistake to try to fight the predators, or to provoke them in any way. Carefully, she backed off a little – far enough to nullify any suggestion of aggression on her part, but not so far that she appeared to be intimidated. As she did so, she glanced around the tunnel for an alternative route.

For the first time Vifang noticed that, while the walls and ceiling seemed to be the favoured roosting-places, the floor remained comparatively unoccupied. By this time, she had occupied this body long enough to begin to see the world from a predator's point of view, and suspected that they avoided the floor for the same reasons as she had done. For one thing, it was covered in a thick and stinking layer of guano. For another, any Ak'Zahar who tried to roost down there was just too vulnerable to his fellows who were perched above.

But I'm not going to roost.

Opening her wings a little, the shapeshifter loosed her hold on the wall and glided down, swallowing hard as her feet sunk into the malodorous muck.

I damn well hope Amaurn appreciates this!

Moving as quickly as she dared, she left the next two charges in the central part of the tunnel, sticking them to the lower part of the wall, one on either side of the passage. Then she continued on her way.

It was nerve-racking in the extreme to be down there on the floor, with the mass of the Ak'Zahar clustered above her. She heard the scratchings and rustlings as they moved, and from the corner of her eye, she could see their glowing eyes following her every move. Her skin crawled under the impact of so many eyes, and chills were running down her spine. If any of them decided to drop on her, then the others would be sure to join in the attack and she would be finished. Keeping her nerve, so that she could make her way steadily onward to the end of the tunnel, placing her charges as she went, was the bravest, and the most difficult thing she had ever done. To plant the last two devices she returned to the roof, and as she shouldered the weaker predators roughly aside, striking out at them with her talons, there was real venom behind her actions.

By the time she had laid the last charge in position, her eyes had begun to hurt again, pierced by the gleam of faint light that came from the opening ahead. Vifang could stand it no longer. She changed herself into a hawk and shot out into the clean, free air. From behind her there came a chorus of hisses and harsh shrieks. Her transformation seemed to have stirred the Ak'Zahar thoroughly. But the sky was still light outside, and none of them dared leave the tunnel – not yet.

Wheeling over the Sacred Precincts, she kept her eyes carefully averted from the piles of carrion below, reluctant, after her recent experiences among the predators, to think of the appalling fate to which the populace of Tiarond had come. Soaring high, she flew over the massive barrier of rock through which she had just passed, and swooped down to the Esplanade, where she landed in the garden of the merchant's house and changed back into her own shape, contriving to lose the last of the filth and the stench from her body as she did so.

The Takur was deeply moved by the welcome her companions accorded her. Never before had she felt such a sense of belonging. As she accepted their congratulations and praise, she began to feel that her dreadful experiences in the tunnel had been worthwhile. Elion stood close to her as Kher prepared to detonate the charges. 'What were you *doing* in there?' he demanded. 'You seemed to take *ages*! I was worried sick.'

Vifang shuddered. 'You don't want to know. Trust me, Elion, you really don't.'

Kher interrupted them. 'Is everybody ready?' he asked. 'Stay down, behind the wall of the house. This is going to be a big explosion.' As they all crouched down, he pressed the white button on his detonator.

There was a long pause.

Nothing happened.

'Shit! Damn, blast and balls!' Kher stood up, and hurled the device into the bushes.

Vifang had turned cold all over. 'I don't know what *you're* swearing about,' she said quietly. 'I'm the one who'll have to go back in there.'

Elion blanched. 'No!' he protested. 'You can't.'

Kher laid a hand on his arm. 'She has to go back, Elion. We all knew it might come to this.'

'You don't understand what she'll be going through in there.' Elion turned away from his fellow Loremaster, shaking off the restraining arm. 'It's just not fair.' Vifang knew that his thoughts were echoing her own. He knew as well as she did what the outcome of a second trip into the tunnel was likely to be.

I pushed my luck getting through there once. I'll never manage it again.

She thought of Amaurn, and they way he had welcomed her into the Shadowleague, even though she had once done her best to kill him. She thought of her people, already beginning to settle into their new homes. She thought of Elion and his fellow Loremasters, and being accepted amongst their ranks. To be part of the Shadowleague carried certain responsibilities. She had no choice.

The former Takur assassin turned back to Kher. 'All right,' she said. 'Let's get on with this. I'll change back into one of the Ak'Zahar, and you can give me the blasting powder and the fuse. I'll need about the same time as I took before. If I'm not out by then, I won't be coming. Light the fuse, and make sure you finish those creatures off – for me.'

Kher nodded. 'Don't forget, you won't have to go all the way in this time. Plant the blasting powder by the first of the charges, and get out of there as fast as you can. Once the first is triggered, it should set the others off.'

'You'd better hope so,' the shapeshifter told him grimly, 'because there's nothing in this world that could induce me to go in there a third time.'

For the first time since she had joined them, Kher reached out and touched her. 'Take care,' he said softly. 'I salute your courage.'

Once again, Vifang made the change into the Ak'Zahar. 'See you later, Elion,' she said, but the Loremaster would not acknowledge her, or turn and look at her. She reached tentatively towards his mind – and saw the vivid image of the red-haired woman, and heard the sound of her screams as the winged horde descended on her and tore her to shreds.

Vifang got out of there as fast as she could, and slammed her shields up for good measure.

That'll teach me to intrude.

Badly shaken, she set off for the second time towards the tunnel mouth – and this time, as she approached, she could feel that they were ready for her.

There was a stir of movement as Vifang entered the tunnel, clutching the package of blasting powder with its fuse attached and trailing out behind it. As soon as she approached the darker areas, where the predators clustered, she found herself the focus of an untold number of eyes. This time, there were more than the weaker members of the group at the edge of the crowd. The larger, dominant specimens had pushed their way forward, and were regarding her with a threat apparent in every line and angle of their stance. She knew then that they didn't intend her to leave that place alive. And there on the floor, right beneath the largest and most threatening of her foes, was the place where she would have to leave the blasting powder.

Carefully, Vifang selected the spot where she would put her package – a small protrusion in the tunnel wall that was just about underneath the spot where she had left the first charge. Since most of the guano was concentrated nearer the centre of the tunnel, the floor here was still fairly clear, so she hoped that the fuse would stay dry enough for long enough to do the job. Slowly, so as not to provoke the Ak'Zahar into a sudden attack, she inched her way forward, until she had almost reached the spot she wanted. They were right above her now, watching, waiting. She didn't dare go any further. Stealthily she stretched out her arm as far as it would reach – but it wasn't quite far enough. There was only one thing for it. Making a slight alteration to the image in her mind, she changed her shape, just a little, just enough to make her arm long enough to reach the ledge.

Harsh cries of challenge sounded overhead, and leathery wings unfurled. Vifang dropped the package with its trailing fuse neatly on the ledge, and turned to fight or flee – but it was too late. There was no time for her to change shape. They were on top of her, clawing and rending at her flesh with their teeth. As the pain ripped through her body, she sent one last, desperate message in mind-speech. 'I'm caught. Light the fuse now. Elion, goodbye!'

Among Amaurn's group of adventurers, Aethon had his own pre-occupations. As everyone followed Scall across the cavern floor, he was the only one of them who was not completely baffled by the esoteric surroundings. Because Dragons communicated with a language of music and light, he could read a certain amount of meaning into the displays of coruscating, coloured radiance all around him. Some faint echo of memory told him that the lights carried massive amounts of information, coded in some ancient language of which he could almost make out the odd word here and there. It didn't help that Zavahl's human eyes could only register a limited spectrum. Aethon suspected that there was a great deal more going on around him than he was able to perceive.

The Dragon tried hard to glean any snippet of information that he could, but he found it hard to concentrate. For the past few days, since the kidnapping by the Dierkan and the subsequent rescue and return of himself and Zavahl to Gendival, he had been fairly quiet; remaining, for the most part, in the background of his host's mind and not communicating much. He had found himself faced with an agonising dilemma: if he returned to his people, and passed on the memories to a successor then he, or at least the consciousness and personality that was all that remained of Aethon the Dragon Seer, would cease to exist at that point. And he didn't want to die. Even riding as a passenger in someone else's body was preferable – and he had to admit that, now that he and Zavahl were coming to terms with their peculiar arrangement, he was quite enjoying this entirely new perspective on life.

On the other hand, if he did remain where he was, he would die in any case when his human host perished. The memories would die with him, and the most valuable resource that the Dragonfolk possessed would be lost for ever. How could he do that to his people? As Seer, he had a responsibility to pass the memories on at whatever cost to himself.

At that moment, Scall led the little group to the centre of the chamber, and all thoughts of the future fled. Aethon's awe matched that of Zavahl as they stood and stared at the circular, sunken area of floor, about twenty feet across, that looked like the inside of a large silver bowl. Spaced at equidistant intervals around the edge were six great columns of light, about as thick as a human body, that soared upwards, converging slightly until they vanished and, presumably, met at some distant point up in the shadows, far overhead. Each beam was a pure, clear hue: red, yellow, green, blue, violet or dazzling white, and the colours moved in order from one column to the next, travelling endlessly round the circle so that the spire of light above the silver bowl seemed to be turning gently in place. In the centre of the sunken area was a large iridescent sphere, for all the world like a gigantic soap bubble, with streaks and swirls of rainbow colours in constant motion around its translucent walls. Scall pointed to it. 'That's it,' he said. 'Inside that bubble is where I found those weird contraptions.'

'You went inside it?' the Archimandrite asked. 'How did you manage that?'

'I just walked right though it. It seemed to vanish, and I thought I had burst it, but when I left the bowl and looked back, it was still there.' Scall frowned. 'I think you can only see it from the outside, if that makes any sense. When you're inside it, it's invisible.'

Amaurn's eyes were bright with curiosity. Clearly, he couldn't wait to investigate. 'Come on,' he said, and slithered down into the bowl, beckoning to the rest to follow him.

To Aethon, there was something vaguely familiar about all this, but if the details did exist in the memories of the Dragonfolk, they came from the very distant past and were difficult to detect. Amaurn didn't hesitate but pushed straight through the wall of the bubble, with the others following after him a little more circumspectly. Aethon, coming last with Zavahl, noticed that as each of them passed through the wall of the sphere, it seemed to grow in size to encompass them all, even the firedrake. Once he himself had joined his companions on the inside, however, he could see nothing of the walls at all.

In the very centre of the bowl was a slender, waist-high plinth of the same silvery material. 'This is where I found those things,' Scall said.

Aethon felt a stir of interest. 'Zavahl, will you go up close and look at the plinth?' he asked. As he had expected, there was a narrow slot in the top of the waist-high column. He concentrated as hard as he could, trying to summon the fleeting, phantom memory in detail, but it remained hazy and indistinct. 'Something goes in that slot,' he said to his host. 'I think – I think it's the device that looks like some sort of mirror.'

Zavahl passed on the message, and Dark knelt at once to remove the artefact from his pack. He took out the thin, silvery disc with the rim of figured gold around its edge, and gave it to Zavahl. Aethon used his companion's hands to position it correctly, pushing its edge into the slot. About an inch or so of the device fitted into the narrow aperture and it rested there, standing upright on its edge. There was a sharp click, and a series of stylised diagrams began to move slowly across the dark face of the disc, outlined against the black background in shining green light.

Veldan bent close. 'These must be rooms,' she said. 'See? Here's where we are now, with all those weird things growing up out of the floor, and this silvery dip in the middle, with the columns of light all around.'

'And – great Myrial!' Zavahl said excitedly. 'There's the Holy of Holies in the Temple, with the high platform, and the Eye beyond.' Then he frowned. 'And there it is again – but it's different. See? There's another high platform, but there's no bridge. There's a metal walkway going across the room, instead. And there's another huge Eye, much bigger than the one that I know – but look, it seems to be set against a wall instead of suspended in mid-air.' He reached out to point, and accidentally brushed the screen with his finger.

The diagram of the unknown room grew brighter for a moment then vanished, and three short lines of symbols appeared. Again, they almost seemed to convey a meaning to Aethon that, frustratingly, lay just beyond his reach. Then Scall called out, drawing his attention away from the artefact. 'The bubble has come back!'

It was true. The view of the massive chamber was screened by the translucent, iridescent walls of the shimmering sphere that enclosed them all as they stood in the centre of the bowl. Scall made as if to run, but Toulac grabbed a handful of his tunic and held him fast. 'Just wait a moment, sonny. Let's check that it's still safe to go through there.' She pulled a leather gauntlet from the deep pocket of her sheepskin coat, and threw it at the wall of the sphere. There was a blinding flash in the place where it hit, and a crackle of energy. The glove dropped to the floor – not burnt as such, but smoking gently. The firedrake looked at it with startled eyes and hastily tucked his tail underneath his body, out of harm's way.

Before anyone could speak, there was a single, resonant chime, like the deep sound of a bell, and everything seemed to move in an odd, sideways wrench that sent them clutching at one another to keep their feet. Then the walls of the enclosing bubble seemed to melt away and Aethon realised that the silver, bowl-shaped concavity in which they stood was no longer where it had formerly been but, apparently, had moved to a new location. The great cavern had vanished, and they now stood in the corner of another vast chamber of polished black stone.

Scall immediately recognised the place from the diagram that remained on the screen of the mirrorlike device that was still slotted into place on the plinth. There, on the far wall, was the thing that Zavahl had referred to as the Eye – a massive circle, outlined in low red light, its centre like a black hole into nothingness. Scall tore his eyes from it with a shudder and noticed a platform on the floor near the front of the chamber, formed from what looked like gleaming white marble and standing a few inches proud of the black stone with which it was surrounded. It glowed with its own inner radiance, and apart from the red circle of the eye, and the six tall columns of light that still glowed in their changing colours on the periphery of the silver depression in the floor, it was the only source of illumination in the room.

Suddenly, his attention was torn away from the ground by Toulac's voice. 'Myrial in a thunderstorm! Look up there!'

High above was a long metal walkway which stretched across the vast room from wall to wall, just about at the level of the centre of the Eye, looking perilously slender and fragile from that distance. In the centre a short extension stuck out at right angles, with a circular platform on the end of it. A spiral of metal steps led up to the walkway from the ground at each side, and at either end of it there seemed to be an open archway in the wall, leading out of the chamber. Three figures were on the lofty perch, and Toulac's yell had stopped them in their tracks about halfway across.

Scall stared in disbelief. There, up on the gantry, was a man dragging a little girl roughly along by the arm, and grasping a knife in the other hand – and beside them, stumbling with weariness, a slender girl with pale blonde hair. Though the walkway was far above the light, in the shadowy upper vaults, Scall recognised them instantly. 'Myrial save us!' he gasped. 'It's Presvel, and Tormon's little girl. And there's Rochalla!'

Then his eyes caught a stir of movement to his right, and the golden flicker of a torch appeared in the exit at the end of the walkway. There stood Tormon in the archway, frozen with horror. Presvel swept Annas up in his left arm, and put the knife to her throat. 'Get away from me, Tormon,' he yelled. 'Don't come any closer, or she's dead!'

At the sound of the trader's name, Amaurn felt a chill go through him. Since he had taken over the role of Archimandrite, it seemed that all of his past mistakes were coming back to haunt him. Here in this room was the child he had orphaned when, acting on Zavahl's instructions, he had ordered his men to kill Tormon's wife. And there was the trader himself, forced to carry on alone.

Just as I was, when I lost my Aveole.

All at once, Amaurn understood how much pain he had inflicted on the other man, and felt a surge of self-revulsion.

How could I have done that? What possessed me, all those years, that I could have let myself become such a monster?

Suddenly he remembered what Veldan had said to him the day he had wrested the Archimandrite's authority from Cergorn:

'There's no undoing those dreadful deeds, and you'll pay for them all eventually, in one way or another. So you should. But if you really seek redemption . . . Everyone should have at least one chance to atone for their past.'

He looked at Zavahl and saw the same guilt mirrored in the other's eyes, then he looked back up at the gantry. The man that he now recognised as Presvel, formerly the assistant to the Lady Seriema, had been alerted by the sound of Toulac's voice, and was looking down at them, as well as along the walkway at Tormon; turning his head from side to side like a beast at bay, afraid to take his eyes off either threat. His knife, still held against the child's throat, flashed in the torchlight as the hand that held it shook. 'Stay away from me – all of you!' he shrieked.

'Dark?' Amaurn said softly. 'Didn't you tell me that Presvel was the one who murdered Grim?'

'He did,' Dark replied, his voice harsh with anger. 'Seriema and Presvel were with Tormon and Scall, here, when they all took refuge with the Reivers. Presvel was threatening Scall with that knife, and Grim got in the way.'

Two birds with one stone. Perfect. Not only do I have a chance to make some sort of atonement to Tormon, but at the same time I can avenge my old friend.

Amaurn looked at Zavahl with Blade's chilling smile. Understanding passed between them. 'You distract him,' he told the former Hierarch. 'I'll take care of the rest.'

'Wait – I can help distract him, too,' Dark said. From his pack he produced the Summoner's skull mask, and put it on. 'From that distance, he won't be able to tell whether it's me – or the spirit of Grim, come back to haunt him.' He looked at Amaurn. 'Just make damn sure you kill that bastard, will you?'

'Don't worry, Dark. I loved Grim too.' With that, Amaurn unslung the weapon from his shoulder and melted into the shadows, keeping one eye and ear open for the little scene that was unfolding behind him.

Zavahl spoke. 'Stay back in the shadows, Scall. You and Dark should try not to attract his notice – at least at first.' With that, he strode out into the centre of the floor, standing on the glowing slab so that he was clearly illuminated. 'Presvel?' he called. 'Do you believe in ghosts?'

Presvel started, but recovered quickly. 'There's no such thing as ghosts,' he said, but his voice lacked conviction.

'You're gambling a lot on being right,' Zavahl replied. 'Otherwise, you wouldn't be looking to add another to your list of innocent victims.'

Amaurn, creeping around the walls of the room, heard the little girl cry out, and looked up quickly in alarm, but it seemed that Presvel was just clutching her too tightly.

Good. He's rattled.

He reached the bottom of the spiral staircase on the opposite side of the room from Tormon's entranceway. Presvel's attention was on the arch along the walkway to his left, and the folk on the ground below him. It was doubtful that he'd have much chance to worry about his right-hand side. The Archimandrite began to climb, moving slowly and stealthily as, right on cue, Dark stepped forward. He had pulled up the hood of his black cloak, and was wearing the spectral mask of bone. 'Did you really think you could kill a Summoner and escape so easily? No grave can hold my kind.'

As he spoke, a shiver went down Amaurn's spine. Somehow, Dark had changed his voice to sound exactly like his mentor. Presvel stared in horror at the apparition, as Grim's voice spoke again, with a ring of irresistible authority. 'It's time to pay your reckoning, Presvel. You can't escape. Put the child down, and come to me.'

For a moment, it looked as if the ruse might actually succeed. Presvel hesitated, and the hand that held the knife wavered and dropped to his side. On the ground, Dark took a step forward. 'Let her go, Presvel,' he repeated in Grim's voice. 'Put her down. Don't add to what you owe.'

Amaurn had reached the top of the staircase. He lifted the weapon to his shoulder, but with Presvel still clutching the child, he couldn't get a clear line of fire. Then it happened. Apparently, Tormon's patience snapped. With a roar, he came charging out of the arch and along the gantry. 'No!' Presvel howled. 'Not another step!' Lifting the child high he dangled her over the railing, holding her in position with one hand clutching tightly to the loose material at the back of her tunic. In his other hand, the knife was once more against her throat.

Tormon, his face white, skidded to a halt. At the same instant, Zavahl shouted up to Amaurn. 'Fire!'

There was no time for hesitation. The madman was holding the little girl away from him. Zavahl was already running forward. Amaurn had a clear shot at last. Lifting up the weapon, he fired.

Thirty-Seven

Act of Vengeance

Elion's memories had been haunting him ever since Vifang had first ventured into the lair of the Ak'Zahar. When she was attacked, and he heard her cry out in farewell, his past rose up to overwhelm him completely. For an instant his surroundings vanished, submerged in the vision of Melnyth being swarmed by hordes of voracious predators while he was powerless to help her. He was assailed by the same panic, the same helplessness, the same wrenching sense of loss. Events had come full circle. History was repeating itself . . .

It damn well won't. Not if I can prevent it!

Without warning, he snatched Kher's arcane weapon down from the branch on which it hung. The other Loremasters were taken completely by surprise, and by the time they had gathered their wits and realised what was happening, he was already halfway across the Esplanade, running faster than he had ever run in his life. Last time, Veldan had stopped him. This time, no one was going to get the chance. 'Hold on, Vifang! I'm coming,' he called to the Takur in mindspeech he didn't have enough breath to shout aloud.

'No! Get back!'

Elion could sense that she was too beset to answer him further. For an instant, he touched her mind, and caught a fleeting glimpse of talons and teeth and wings; panic and pain and a multitude of gleaming eyes. No way would he go back. Better to die fighting to save a companion than go through that guilt and torment once again. He gained the tunnel mouth, and the darkness swallowed him.

For a moment Kher and his Loremasters were frozen in shock and confusion, then Alsive and Elysa collected themselves, and set off after Elion. 'No, stay here! That's an order!' Kher roared. 'It's too late.'

Though they were clearly astonished that he had stopped them, at least they had the sense to realise that he was right. Reluctantly, they returned to him, looking back over their shoulders at Elion vanishing into the black maw of the tunnel. As they turned back, Elysa wiped tears from her eyes, and Alsive began to protest, but Kher forestalled them both. 'I was afraid of this,' he said. 'Elion has been unstable ever since Melnyth's death. There's nothing we can do – and I'm not letting anyone else get killed because of him.'

He squatted down beside the fuse, ready to light it. 'I'll give them a moment or two – that's all I can do. Then I'm setting off the charges.' Privately, he was upbraiding himself for being sentimental, taking risks and jeopardising the mission. He knew he should detonate the explosives straight away. Elion and Vifang were as good as dead already, but if they had disturbed the Ak'Zahar sufficiently to make them leave the tunnel, then all would be lost. Nevertheless, he was determined to give his companions that one last chance.

Under his breath, Kher counted to two hundred. Then, with shaking hands, he reached out and lit the fuse.

Down beneath the plateau, Tormon, frozen in horror, could only watch as the drama unfolded on the walkway. Everything seemed to happen tremendously slowly, as Amaurn fired the plasma weapon, and Presvel's head exploded in a burst of flame. The knife went flying, in an arc of glittering silver. Screaming, Annas dropped from his hands and plummeted towards the ground. Down below, both Zavahl and Dark darted forward, but Zavahl got there first –

right underneath the falling child. Just in time, he grabbed her out of the air, staggering beneath her weight and collapsing on the ground with her on top of him. There was a moment's silence, then a loud wail from Annas proved that she was very much in one piece.

It was as if a spell had been broken. With a cry, Tormon rushed to the nearest spiral staircase and all but flung himself down it. He ran across the floor of the chamber and knelt down, snatching his little girl up into his arms. 'Annas! Oh, Annas!'

Zavahl rolled over and got to his knees, clearly winded, gasping and clutching himself around the ribs. Other folk were clustering around, but neither father nor daughter paid them any heed. She clung to him, sobbing. 'You're safe now,' he kept saying to her. 'I've got you, I've got you, you're quite safe.' He couldn't believe how close she had come to dying. How close he had come to killing her. If it hadn't been for . . .

Tormon looked up at Zavahl, who had caught his child, and saved her life. He looked beyond him at Lord Blade, who had slain Annas's abductor as he'd been about to cut her throat. Blade had reached the bottom of the spiral staircase, and was walking across the vast chamber, a wary, inscrutable expression on his face. At the sight of the two men, the trader felt all the old hatreds came boiling back. He thought of Kanella, helpless and terrified in the brooding Godsword Citadel, dying in agony on the Hierarch's orders, at the hands of Blade's soldiers.

Then he looked down at Annas. She was trembling, her face was smudged and tearstained – but she was very much alive, thanks to these same two individuals. The trader felt his hands begin to shake. He was so dazed and torn apart by the conflicts within him that he felt dizzy, and physically sick.

They had killed his lifemate.

They had saved his daughter.

He tore his eyes away, from Amaurn, from Zavahl, from Annas, seeking a brief moment of respite from the confusion. And there on the ground, within reach of Tormon's hand, was the knife that Presvel had dropped from high above in the moment of his death.

There, within striking distance of the knife, if he were to snatch it up and use it, was Kanella's killer. He looked at the glittering blade, and imagined it sinking into Zavahl's flesh.

At least that would be one less of them to plague the world.

Almost of its own volition, one hand freed itself from Annas, and snatched up the weapon.

Out of nowhere, a hand came down and gripped his shoulder. 'Don't be daft, sonny,' a gruff old voice said softly. 'Killing Zavahl won't bring Kanella back. Nothing you can do will alter the past. It's the future you've got to think about now – for you and for that little girl.' Tormon looked up into the shrewd blue eyes of Toulac, who had once owned the sawmill on the Snaketail Pass, the last stopping-place, in happier times, for his gaudy wagon before he and his family settled down in Tiarond for the winter. Dazedly, he wondered how she had come to be here. 'Anyway, these two aren't the same men who ordered your lifemate to be killed,' she said, puzzling him still more. 'The men who did that are dead now. The two you see before you may look the same, but they're not – they've learned compassion, and contrition, and common sense. That doesn't justify what they did, and I don't expect you'll ever forgive them – in your position, I certainly wouldn't – but please, Tormon, let the killing stop now. They may have slain your lifemate, but they saved your daughter. At least there's a sort of balance in that.'

There was truth in her words, and a man as fundamentally honest and decent as Tormon couldn't fail to see that. For a moment he found himself wavering, still torn between gratitude and hatred. Then Lord Blade, with a look of regret and compassion that the trader would never have thought to find in a man with such a repu-tation as a cold-blooded killer, opened his mouth to speak. In that instant Tormon knew.

If Blade utters one word – if he dares to try to apologise, or make excuses, or he attempts to justify his actions in any way, then I'll use this knife in my hand and everything will end in a nightmare of blood, hatred and revenge that will not only reach into my existence, but will blight the future of my daughter, too.

Still holding Annas, he got to his feet. 'Shut up!' he snarled. 'Don't you dare try to speak to me – either of you!' Glaring, he looked from Blade to Zavahl and back again. 'Whatever Toulac may say, you *are* the same monsters who killed an innocent and helpless woman. Much as you try to bury your deeds in the past, they'll stay with you for the rest of your lives. There's no way that either of you will ever begin to comprehend what you've taken from me and Annas, and I want you to understand that I'll hold you in contempt and loathing to the end of my days . . .' He took a deep breath. 'But you saved the life of my little girl, and as Mistress Toulac says, there is a kind of balance there. So I'll leave it to fate to mete out the punishment you deserve. Just as long as I never see your miserable faces again after today, I'll leave it at that, and get on with trying to live my life alone.'

'You don't have to be alone, Tormon.' Scall stood there, with his arm around Rochalla. 'We'll be coming with you, if that's all right with you. I know it won't be the same as the family you lost, but we all seem to fit together, somehow, and at least you won't have to be alone any more.'

Tormon stared at the youth – no, the young man – in astonishment. When had Scall found time to grow up like this? Where had he been, following his disappearance? What had he been doing to bring about this new confidence and maturity? And the trader was delighted by their offer to join him. He was fond of both of them, and Annas loved Rochalla. Suddenly, he felt as if a weight had been lifted from his shoulders. Even Annas had stopped crying, and was scrutinising Scall and Rochalla with great curiosity. 'Are you two going to be lifemates now?' she demanded.

Scall turned crimson, and it was left to Rochalla to speak. 'Yes,' she said firmly. 'Yes, we are.'

'And you're going to stay with me and my Dad?'

'That's the idea.'

'Good,' said Annas firmly. 'It's a very good idea. Can we go home now?'

'Yes, let's find the others and get out of here.' Tormon turned back to Toulac, studiously refusing to look at Amaurn and Zavahl. 'We can find our own way out, the same way we got in, and we'll be taking Scall with us.' He turned without another word, and began to walk back towards the staircase. Before he got there however, he heard Seriema calling his name. Looking up, he saw her emerging from the arch at the end of the walkway. To his surprise, there were a number of extra people with her, including the Godsword, Galveron.

Now how in Myrial's name did he get down here?

But before he could open his mouth to hail them, there came a loud roaring sound, and a wind came out of nowhere, strong enough to snatch the breath from him and blow him off his feet. Pressed flat to the floor, trying his best to shield Annas, he turned to see the scar-faced girl he'd noticed in the background running forward in front of Blade, a look of terror on her face. The sound of her scream was loud enough to be heard even above the deafening howl of the gale:

'Thirishri! *No!*'

As Elion ran into the tunnel, the noise was deafening. Screeches and shrieks echoed and re-echoed, the volume almost painful in this constricted space. The further behind he left the entrance, the darker it became, and he suddenly realised that he wasn't going to be able to see a thing. Also, if Vifang had kept the form of the Ak'Zahar, how could he help her? He wouldn't dare kill any of them, in case it might be her. He kept on going however, and found, to his relief, that only the very centre of the tunnel was pitch black. On the edge of the colony, where all the commotion was taking place, there was the faintest glimmer of light – just enough to let him see the predators swooping and striking at something on the ground, where a whole mass of them were clustered. Good. Now he knew where the shapeshifter must be.

'Vifang, hold on. I'm here!'

'Elion! Get away!' Even in mindspeech, the voice was faint and stifled, and filled with pain.

'No chance.' The Loremaster raised the plasma weapon, and fired a short burst towards the ceiling. A blue-white bolt of energy leapt forth, sizzling, and several of the winged monstrosities turned into balls of flame, and plunged to the ground. The reek of burning flesh joined the stench of the guano, and oily black smoke began to fill the tunnel.

Elion's triumph was tinged with bitterness.

If Cergorn had let us take this into the Ak'Zahar labyrinths of Ghariad, Melnyth needn't have lost her life.

The rest of the Ak'Zahar had fallen back in a terrified, shrieking mob, blinded by the brilliance of the searing beam. Only one was left – a small, huddled heap on the bloodstained ground.

Firing one more burst with the weapon for good measure, Elion crouched down by the body of the predator. 'Vifang? Is that you?'

'Yes.' The mental voice was very faint.

Suddenly, he heard the faintest rustle, and caught a sight of furtive movement from the corner of his eye. Glancing upwards, he turned cold. The Ak'Zahar were stalking him again, making the most of his preoccupation with the Takur to creep up on him across the roof. Swearing, Elion leapt to his feet and moved away from Vifang to get a clearer shot. As the predators came swarming towards him, he lifted the weapon to his shoulder, and fired – and nothing happened. Frantically, he pressed the lever again and again, but the ancient artefact had chosen the worst possible moment to malfunction. Panic seized the Loremaster. He ran, trying to buy himself time, frantically hammering and wrenching at the weapon as he went, but to no avail. He had only managed a few strides before the predators caught him. Claws ripped at his clothing, and long fangs snapped at exposed flesh, making him cry out in pain as he was borne to the ground by the winged horrors.

All this time, Elion had wondered what Melnyth had really gone through the day she died. Now he was experiencing for himself the stench, the terror, the pain as claws sank into his flesh. He could not fight them off – there were too many. All he could do was curl into a ball, to try to protect his vital organs for as long as possible, and pray for a miracle.

Then all at once there was a deafening bellow, and a jet of flame went searing over his head. Again, the stench of burning flesh filled the tunnel as a number of the predators fell writhing to the ground. Shrieking in pain and fear, the remainder fled.

Elion opened his eyes to see the dim form of a firedrake. 'Kaz?' he said muzzily.

'No, me. Get up, quick.' The voice belonged to Vifang.

Somehow he found himself on the firedrake's back, still clutching the accursed faulty weapon, and they were hurtling towards the tunnel mouth, and safety. Then, to his horror he saw a spot of light in the darkness, racing towards him along the floor, and showering sparks as it went. Kher had lit the fuse!

They had scant seconds to reach safety before the charges ignited.

With no thought for her own injuries, the firedrake hurled herself at the spot of daylight up ahead, leaping forward with every muscle straining. Daylight burst forth all around Elion as they cleared the tunnel mouth, brilliantly bright after the darkness. He was almost unseated as the shapeshifter wrenched her body around, out of direct line of the tunnel mouth, and leapt to one side, staying close to the cliff. He clutched the wounded Takur tightly, determined not to let her go.

We're going to make it! We're going to . . .

There was a deafening boom from behind him, and both man and shapeshifter were knocked off their feet by a blast of scorching air. They hit the cobbles hard as, behind them, smoke and flame billowed out of the tunnel mouth, and the earth shook with the force of the blast. A huge crack snaked right up the face of the cliff and Elion could hear the rumbling, grinding roar as the tunnel collapsed. Then everything went quiet, except for the ringing in his ears, and the uneven sound of Kher's feet, limping across the Esplanade towards him, with the other two Loremasters racing ahead.

Far below the city, Thirishri erupted into the underground chamber of the Eye with a howl of rage. *Amaurn! Renegade! Usurper! You dared to destroy my partner – and now it is your turn to face destruction!*

A blast of wind caught and buffeted them. When Tormon lost his balance and fell, so did Rochalla and Scall. Zavahl, who had been climbing to his feet, went down again hard. Veldan reacted quicker than Amaurn, who clearly was still caught up in regretful thoughts of the trader. 'Thirishri! *No!*' There was no time to think – she ran forward, acting on pure impulse, putting herself between her father and the threat, but another blast of wind caught her, knocking her off her feet and sending her sliding back along the floor to collide with Amaurn, who went down too.

Die Amaurn! The Wind-Sprite roared. Far above, Veldan saw the telltale shimmer in the air. Shree was right above them, about to crush them with another deadly hammer-blow of wind.

Then there was another roar, loud enough to drown the howling of the wind, and Kaz was there, standing over his fallen partner. 'You leave my Veldan alone, you overgrown fart!' Stretching his neck, he sent a long jet of flame scorching upwards, but it was dispersed and blown away by another powerful blast from the Wind-Sprite. Then it happened. Thirishri turned her anger on this new defender of her prey. Kaz was picked up bodily, despite his great weight and size and hurled through the air, right across the chamber, to smash against the further wall.

In her mind, Veldan heard the sharp, dry sound of snapping bones, and was overwhelmed by the explosion of her partner's pain as his agony raced like fire along her own nerves. All at once there was silence and the buffeting wind fell still, as though even the Wind-Sprite was overwhelmed by the mindless violence of her act. Then Veldan was on her feet and running. She heard the pounding of boots on stone as someone followed, but her anguish was too deep to spare a thought for whoever might be coming after her. Everything had happened so quickly – how could it have happened so quickly? Within the space of a few heartbeats, her life had been shattered into pieces.

The firedrake lay beside the wall; a twisted, distorted mass of abraded flesh and broken bone. A creature of his weight, hitting a solid object with such tremendous force, was certain to have suffered irreparable damage. Veldan threw herself down beside him, tears streaming down her face. 'Kaz – oh, Kaz!'

'Don't worry, sweetie – a couple of days rest and I'll be fine.' His mindspeech was faint and fading. The shared pain in Veldan's mind had almost gone now: was Kaz managing to shield it from her or was he, too, unable to feel it because he was dying?

Then Dark was kneeling at Veldan's side, touching the firedrake's body with gentle hands. Shaking his head, he looked up at the Loremaster. 'I'm sorry,' he said, 'there's all sorts of damage. I don't know if there's anything that can be done – maybe there's another of those healing beam devices down here that they had in Gendival. I can hold him to this world a little longer, to give us time to think, but . . .' Now there were tears on his face too. 'Oh, Veldan, I wish I could do more!'

Across the chamber, Toulac, sick at heart, had scrambled to her feet. She was heading straight to Kaz and Veldan, when a movement in her peripheral vision stopped her dead. Abruptly, she turned and ran towards the place where Amaurn and Thirishri were confronting one another. The veteran had heard a good deal about Cergorn's former partner but, somehow, she had never imagined that a creature of the element of air could be capable of such power and violence. Clearly, she would have to be stopped before she hurt anyone else – though Myrial only knew how.

At any moment, the storm was going to break again. The earlier fit of berserk rage, engendered by the loss of her partner, had left the Wind-Sprite. The dreadful thing she had done seemed to have shocked her back to an icy calmness. She seemed, for the moment, to have exhausted all her violence in her attack on Kaz, and now, it was to be hoped, remorse was setting in – but Toulac could see the faint distortion in the air as she hovered lower than before, closer to Amaurn, and could feel the dreadful tension in the air as they faced one another. The Archimandrite, white and shaking with rage, lifted the plasma weapon to his shoulder. In a flash of prescience, Toulac saw that, if either of these two killed the other, the resulting schism between the supporters of the old and the new would rip the Shadowleague apart beyond all repairing. Though she was afire with the urge for her own revenge, for her love of Kaz and for the anguish of her friend Veldan, she knew that it couldn't be allowed to happen.

Taking a deep breath, she stepped between Amaurn and Thirishri. 'Well,' she said, both aloud and in mindspeech, in a voice that shook with grief and anger. 'There's your revenge, Wind-Sprite. But why Kaz? Why? He was the only one of his kind at large in the world: he was unique. And Veldan wasn't the one who mind-wiped Cergorn, but you've just blighted her life beyond all repairing. Just as you and Cergorn wrecked Amaurn's life so long ago, when he was condemned to death and forced to live in exile, and his Aveole died. Just as Amaurn blighted Cergorn's life by deposing him, and yours, by robbing you of your partner.' Her voice grew stronger, more forceful, more urgent. She only had this one chance to stop them – she would have to make the most of it. 'Don't you think it ought to stop, Thirishri? Amaurn? Don't you think it's time? Or will you destroy the Shadowleague by taking this senseless feud any further?'

For a moment, nothing happened. It was as though neither of them had heard a word she'd said, and Toulac started to get really worried. 'Look,' she pleaded with them. 'Just postpone your damned hostilities, at least. You're supposed to be down here to find out what's wrong with the Curtain Walls – at least that was the idea, Thirishri. Myrial knows what *you're* doing down here, but it doesn't matter right now, and I suppose we'll make sense of it all eventually – if we live that long. But first of all, you ought to be concentrating on your task as agents of the Shadowleague, which is putting the world to rights. That should be enough of a problem, without complicating things any further by trying to slaughter one another. Once this is all over, you can have a talk – a long talk. Try to understand each other for once. *Then* you can kill each other, if that's still what you really want.'

Again, nothing happened at first – then slowly, the Wind-Sprite backed away. *I agree,* she said. *And I – I deeply regret what happened to Kazairl.*

Amaurn lowered the weapon. 'Fine, we'll have a truce for now,' he snarled, 'but I'll never forgive you for killing Kaz and breaking my daughter's heart. This isn't over yet, Wind-Sprite.'

Oh, wonderful!

The problem was, that Toulac sympathised with him completely. But she was wise enough to see that this was not the time to allow personal feelings to get in the way of doing what was right. She went to Amaurn, put both hands on his shoulders, and looked into his eyes. 'What about Tormon's lifemate?' she said softly, and saw him flinch. 'The two situations aren't that different, you know.' And then, leaving him to work it out, she went to comfort Veldan.

Thirty-Eight

Within the Eye

All this time, Helverien had been watching from her vantage point on the walkway, letting matters settle down before she intervened. She had been astounded to see a firedrake, and shocked and sickened by his fate. She was appalled that Thirishri had done such a thing – and disgusted with herself for not noticing the Wind-Sprite's distress and anger sooner, and finding out the cause.

There must have been something I could have done to forestall this tragedy!

But at least there was something she could do now. She turned to Seriema and the other humans, who were gathered in the archway and looking down in puzzlement at the events below. She didn't blame them for being confused. They didn't possess mind-speech and, not being able to see the Wind-Sprite, they had no idea that she existed. As far as they were concerned, the firedrake – a creature that, in itself, was alien enough to give them pause – had been flung through the air by some unseen force and Toulac, who definitely had been addressing her words to two people, had only been talking to one.

And that one . . . Looking down at him, Helverien felt her pulse quicken with excitement. He wasn't . . . He couldn't be . . . She knew very well that he was. Even after all this time, like called to like, and she could still recognise one of her own race. This man they called Amaurn was a Mage, as she was. But why was he here? How had he escaped? The discovery was enough to galvanise Helverien into

521

action. 'Stay here,' she barked at her human companions. 'It's too dangerous for you ordinary humans to be wandering around down there – yes, even you, Galveron and Cetain. I'll go down and find out what's happening.'

Before they could question her or raise any protest, she was gone, speeding down the spiral staircase as fast as her legs could carry her. Halfway down the metal steps she stopped, and came speeding back again. 'Give me that ring,' she ordered. Aliana, unusually for her, seemed surprised into obedience, and promptly handed over the Hierarch's ring with its glowing red stone. Jamming it on her finger with scant regard for ceremony, Helverien set off down the staircase once more.

When she reached the floor of the chamber, the Mage was piqued to discover that everyone seemed so wrapped up in the fate of the firedrake that no one took any notice of her. Even Shree seemed too upset to speak.

She singled out a man with brown hair and an ascetic, serious face, who was standing a little apart from the others. 'Hey, you! What's happening here?'

There was surprise in his eyes, followed by a flash of anger. 'I don't know who in perdition you are, Lady, but you ought to show a little respect. One of our friends is dying.'

Helverien took a deep breath. Damn it, had all those aeons spent alone made her forget how to deal with people entirely? 'I'm sorry,' she said. 'My name is Helverien, and I was simply wondering if I could do anything to help.'

He shook his head. 'Thank you for the offer, but there's noth . . .' Suddenly he tilted his head slightly, as though were listening. Then his eyes widened. 'Did you say Helverien? *The* Helverien?' Then he seemed to collect himself. 'No, no – of course it couldn't be. That was so very long ago, you couldn't be—'

'Oh, it's me all right,' the Magewoman said grimly. 'I mean, I'm her. I've been imprisoned out of time down here for so long . . . But how did you know? How could you possibly have recognised me? And who are you, anyway?'

His name was Zavahl – but he was more than just a man. Briefly, he told her his story, and it seemed to be just as incredible as her own. How could it be possible that he shared his body with the mind and spirit of one of the Dragonfolk? And a Seer, at that? It was the Dragon, of course, who had recognised her from his memories. Then all at once, she realised what his presence signified. 'Aethon?' she addressed him directly. 'This might be the miracle we're looking for. Between us, with my knowledge and your memories, we might just be able to find a way to fix the malfunction in the Curtain Walls.'

Aethon was filled with excitement. At the sight of this woman's face, the memories, first experienced by some long-gone predecessor, had come rushing back. Helverien of the Magefolk, the one who had betrayed her own kind to stop them from getting out of control and overrunning the world. Her people had paid an appalling price for her actions and so had she, but to the Dragonfolk, she was a hero nonetheless. How she should have come to him now, out of the mists of ancient history, he had no idea, but this was not the time for such questions. They didn't have much time to spare. Just maybe, if they could find a way to put right the malfunctioning systems that controlled this world, they could also find a way to help the firedrake. If Kaz could cling to life for long enough to let them try.

The main problem, of course, was that Zavahl had no mind-speech, so everything would have to be passed through the human, and spoken out loud. But they could manage that, though it was cumbersome, and Zavahl, who had been keeping in close contact with Aethon during these new developments, was more than willing. 'Kaz saved my life when I was going to be sacrificed and at the time, I didn't even have the decency to thank him. Of course I'll do anything in my power to help save him. Just tell me what you want, and I'll do it.'

Aethon decided that this wasn't a good moment to remind him that the main priority was the restoration of the Curtain Walls, and saving the firedrake was a forlorn hope at best. Instead, he directed Zavahl back to the silvery area with the coloured pillars of light that somehow had transported them to this chamber. 'Quickly! We must fetch that disc-shaped device that Scall found. We'll need it – I don't know why, but we will.'

Helverien, in the meantime, was already climbing the spiral stairs that led back up to the walkway, though she had chosen the staircase on the other side this time so as not to pass the humans that waited for her up above. This was not the time to be bothering with their trivial concerns and answering their endless questions. She only hoped they would have the sense to stay out of it. When she had nearly reached the top, she was aware of Zavahl, pounding up behind her, his footfalls making the delicate, twisting metal structure vibrate and ring like a bell. By the time she had reached the centre of the walkway he had caught up with her, clutching a disc-shaped artefact in his hand. 'Here,' he said. 'You'll need this.' She looked at him questioningly, and he shrugged. 'Aethon says the memories tell him so. He doesn't know exactly how it'll work, but it's certainly a way to communicate with the Eye – or whatever lies behind it.'

'Thank you.' Helverien felt relief wash over her. She had known where she had to go, but she hadn't been too sure of what to do when she got there. Maybe, between them, she and the dragon would be able to work it out. 'Come on.' Beckoning to him to follow, she led the way out to the long, slender gantry that sprang out at right angles from the centre of the walkway, extending in the direction of the great Eye. At the end of it was a platform with another waist-high plinth of silvery metal – except that this one was broader, about three feet in width, with a slightly angled top, the depth of which was the same as usual – about a foot from the top edge to bottom. Zavahl ran his hands over the sloping surface. 'Look,' he said, indicating a shallow, circular depression on the far left. 'This looks as though it would fit Scall's mysterious disc. But what are all these symbols next to it?' There were maybe a couple of dozen of them, arranged in a neat rows and columns, and slightly raised against the background. Each of them glowed with a faint red light against the silver surface.

Helverien took a closer look. 'They're runes,' she said. 'The same runes the Ancients used.'

'Can you read them?' Though the words were uttered in Zavahl's voice, she was somehow aware that it was Aethon who was speaking now, through his intermediary. She shrugged. 'I was the Archivist and Recorder for my people. Of course I can read them.'

Zavahl – or was it Aethon? – shot her a reproving look before continuing to examine the top of the plinth. On the right of the runes was a smaller depression, not made to take a discshaped item this time, but deeper, and its bottom curved to fit a different object entirely. Zavahl's voice shook with excitement – and this time, he was definitely speaking for himself. 'This looks similar to the one beneath the Temple. It's a place to put the Hierarch's ring.' His face fell. 'If only we had the ring, of course.'

Helverien couldn't resist. 'What, this ring?' she said casually. Slipping it from her finger, she dropped it into his shaking hand.

He stared at it, open-mouthed, in total shock and disbelief. 'Where in Myrial's name did you get this?' he shouted at her.

'Never mind. It's a long story. Do you know how to use it?'

'Of course I do,' Zavahl snapped. He placed the ring in its proper position in the plinth, and the huge red stone clicked into place within its aperture. Immediately, the chamber darkened. A low, thrumming vibration, so deep that Helverien could feel it in her very bones, breathed a single organ note into the air. The dark, smoky red of the Eye's periphery began to brighten to copper, to gold, to glowing flame, to searing, incandescent white.

Zavahl was muttering, half to himself. 'It's just like before, except then the centre of the Eye stayed dark and dead . . . Oh, Myrial, don't let it be dead this time.'

For a moment, it seemed as if his prayer was about to be answered. The formless void in the centre of the Eye began to pulse with the rhythm of a heartbeat, and with each pulse a faint, blue spark of light within it brightened. Zavahl was holding his breath, and Helverien realised that she was doing the same. The spark grew in brightness until the entire centre of the Eye was suffused with a vivid, blue-violet light.

Zavahl's fingers were clenched tightly round the edge of the plinth, the knuckles showing bone-white through his skin. 'Now, speak to us,' he was murmuring. 'Please, please speak to us!'

But it seemed that the Eye could go so far, and no further. A discordant sound began to grind at the edges of that profound and lovely note, setting the Magewoman's teeth on edge, and the blue interior of the Eye was marred by ugly bursts of nothingness, like bolts and streaks of black lightning running across its surface. The blinding white periphery of the Eye was splintered into rainbow sparks.

'It's breaking up!' Zavahl cried. 'Stop it! Don't let it slip away again!' Then he grew unnaturally calm, as the Dragon spoke. 'Helverien, use the disc! If the normal channels of communication aren't functioning, you still can use the disc.'

Damn! She had forgotten. Quickly, Helverien took the artefact and positioned it in its own depression in the top of the plinth. Immediately, the colours of the Eye stabilised once more, as the small dark screen lit up in its centre with the same blue-violet of the centre of the Eye, and the outer ring, formerly gold, blazed with incandescent light. Helverien squinted at it with watering eyes.

Well, not even the Ancients were free of their conceits. This might look very impressive, and I'm sure it's very symbolic and all; but as Packrat might say, it's going to be a bugger to read.

Be that as it may, there were words forming on the screen even as she looked, in letters that stood out white against the glowing blue background. Though they were in the runic symbols of the Ancients, she could read the words quite clearly:

SYSTEM MALFUNCTION

Helverien cast her eyes to the heavens. 'Well, tell me something I *don't* know!'

Experimentally, she touched the glowing runes upon the plinth, and as her fingers brushed each one, the corresponding symbol appeared on the screen:

IDENTIFY

Once again, words materialised on the screen – and she caught her breath in horror.

COMPLETE SYSTEM FAILURE. BURNOUT IN CORE CEREBRAL PROCESSOR. RUNNING ON EMERGENCY SYSTEMS AND PERIPH-ERALS ONLY.

Helverien clung to the edge of the plinth to stop her knees from buckling. Emergency systems and peripherals – whatever they might be – wouldn't be able to run an entire world for long. The enigmatic screen had just pronounced a death-sentence on Myrial and all its inhabitants.

In desperation, not knowing what else to do, the Mage abandoned all attempts at the stilted phrasing of the Ancients. Her fingers flew across the symbols on the plinth and new words, a plea straight from her heart, appeared on the screen:

HOW DO I FIX IT?

No one was more surprised than she to get a reply. Her eyes widened as, step by detailed step, it told her.

All this time, Amaurn's chief concern had been for his grieving daughter, who sat huddled beside the firedrake with Dark, as the two of them strove with all their might to hold him to the world by the pure force of their wills. It was increasingly clear that they were failing. According to the Summoner, there were serious internal injuries as well as broken bones, and bit by bit Kaz was slipping away. Finally, the Archimandrite got to his feet, unable to bear the sight of Veldan's anguish any longer. His eyes fell on the plasma weapon, discarded on the ground, and despite Toulac's warnings, he wondered longingly whether it would be possible to blast the accursed Wind-Sprite into oblivion.

Why didn't she take me? At least there would have been some logic,

*some twisted and ironic sense of justice in that. After all, it's my fault
that the Curtain Walls are failing in the first place. I got us into this
mess. Why should Kaz be her victim, instead of me?*

It would almost be better if I used that damn weapon on myself!

Reluctantly he tore his eyes away from the weapon – and that
was the first time he noticed what was going on above him, on the
walkway. Zavahl was up there, out on the platform, with . . . 'Shree,
who in perdition is that woman you came with?'

Her name is Helverien. The Wind-Sprite sounded very subdued.
*She is one of the ancient Magefolk. I met her when you trapped
me within your accursed device. She too had been imprisoned, and
had been there for thousands of years.*

Amaurn reeled as though she had hit him. Helverien? *Helverien?*
He knew the story, of course. Her name was still reviled among the
Magefolk as though she had only betrayed them yesterday. But
really, were her crimes any worse than his own? She had only put
her own people at risk, not the entire world. And, on the other hand,
if she knew what she was doing . . . He damn well hoped that she
did. She had activated the Eye, and providence only knew what she
was doing now. Amaurn started to run, heading for the spiral stairs.

When he reached them, he was out of breath from his rapid
ascent. 'What the blazes is going on here? What are you doing?' he
gasped. Slowly, Zavahl turned to face him, his eyes dark with shock
in a face as white as chalk. 'Helverien got the Eye to tell us how the
world can be restored,' he said, in an oddly toneless voice. Clearly
Aethon was speaking through him. 'Think of this world as a being;
an artificial version of a living being, crafted with infinite skill. It's
the same as a body, it has a heart, in other words a power source
to run its systems, and methods of exchanging energy, and of
healing itself. It also had a brain, but somehow, that has been
destroyed. It's burned out – dead. And that's why our world is dying
too.'

'But you said that it can be restored?' Amaurn demanded
urgently.

'Oh, yes.' Zavahl – or Aethon – sighed. 'All it will take is for one of us to sacrifice ourselves, and merge with Myrial, so that its body becomes that person's body, and their minds become the great Mind that runs and maintains all the systems, and the climate, and the Curtain Walls. Whoever volunteers will cease to be what they were. Time will cease to be what it was. Whole generations will pass in an eyeblink to the eternal Mind. It will be omnipotent, but changed for ever – and isolated and lonely beyond all imagining.' He hesitated, then Zavahl was back behind his eyes. 'It isn't fair to ask Helverien to do this. She's been imprisoned for aeons as it is. She's suffered enough – if suffering this will be. The thing is, we just don't know what it will be like.' He hesitated, and the Archimandrite could see him gathering his courage. 'Look, Amaurn,' he said. 'I'll do it. I was supposed to have been Sacrificed anyway – at least this is better than being burned alive. I am – I *was* the Hierarch. It's my responsibility. I've talked to Aethon, and he agrees. At least that way, the memories of the Dragonfolk won't be lost for good.'

Amaurn felt sick. For a moment, he was tempted just to let Zavahl get on with it, and sacrifice himself – but he couldn't.

I was the one who caused this disaster in the first place, by exchanging the Hierarch's ring for a facsimile. It's not Zavahl's responsibility – it's mine. I'm the one who has to go.

But what about Veldan? I've only just found her – I've hardly got to know her! And how can I leave her now, when this terrible thing has happened to Kaz?

It's her world I'll be saving too. She'll understand. And she has other friends who'll help her get through her loss. Elion will understand what she's going through, and Toulac will always be there. And if I'm not much mistaken, young Dark will be the greatest solace of all to her – far more than I would ever be.

He turned to Zavahl, while he still had the courage, before he could change his mind again. 'No, Zavahl. You go back to Ailie, and have a happy life. You don't have to sacrifice yourself again. I'm the one who should go.' He took a deep breath. 'Say goodbye to Veldan for me, will you? Ask her to forgive me.' Then he turned to Helverien. 'Right,' he said. 'Let's not waste any more time. How do I do this?'

She gave him a look that was filled with compassion. 'Farewell, Amaurn. I salute your courage. I'm sorry I never got the chance to know you – I should have liked to talk with one of my own people again. I'll show you how to extend the gantry now, and then Zavahl and I will leave. The gantry will elongate, taking the platform – and you with it – into the centre of the Eye. The platform will then return to its old position, but you . . . You will be incorporated into Myrial.'

Amaurn sighed. 'Well, I suppose there are worse fates than immortality. After all, I've been living on borrowed time after Cergorn sentenced me to death all those years ago. Goodbye, Helverien, goodbye, Zavahl and Aethon. I'll try my best to do a good job, I promise. And be sure to tell Dark and Toulac to take care of Veldan – not that they'll need any telling.' All at once, he realised that he was stalling. 'Now, Helverien, show me how to . . .'

Wait! The voice came from Thirishri. *You don't have to go, Amaurn. I will. Let's face it,* she added wryly, *I will not be troubled by the loss of a body, as you would. And I realise now that Cergorn is lost to me for ever.* She sighed, as only a Wind-Sprite could. *Besides, I could never go back to Gendival and face Veldan again, after what I did. I must go, Amaurn. I must volunteer to be the new Mind of Myrial. Perhaps, by saving a world, I can atone for what I did today.*

And with that, she left them. Before they could object or argue, Shree had departed, with only a shimmering disturbance in the air to show that she was streaking like a comet towards the Eye. She plunged into the centre – and was gone, leaving no trace of her passing.

For a long moment, nothing happened. Then once again, the resonant note began: growing, swelling, soaring to a triumphant climax. The menacing black lightning vanished from the centre of the Eye, and it cleared to the soft, calm blue of a twilight sky. In the glorious, celestial music, the sound of the Wind-Sprite's voice could be heard. *Ahhh – now I see. I see it all: the entire world of Myrial in its infinitely complex wonder.* She laughed. *I'm so glad I did this instead of you, Amaurn. You still exist in your fragile form of flesh, but I . . . I am a whole world.*

'And can you fix the Curtain Walls?' the Archimandrite demanded waspishly. He was glad he wouldn't have to talk to her on a regular basis. All this showing off was starting to grate on him already.

I am learning how to repair them as we speak, and it will be done by the time you are back above ground.

Ah well, with that sort of efficiency, I suppose she has a right to a certain amount of conceit.

He supposed he ought to be relieved and excited that the problem was solved and the world was saved, but right now, all he could think of was his grieving daughter and the dying firedrake.

I had better get back to Veldan and poor Kaz . . .

But Amaurn was disturbed from his thoughts by Thirishri's voice. *Amaurn! I may have the answer! The firedrake might have a chance after all!*

Kher was panting as he stumbled to a halt beside Elion and Vifang. 'By my life, but I'm glad to see you two! I didn't think you stood a chance! Are you all right?'

Am I?

For a moment, Elion wasn't sure. Thick dust hung in the air, mingling with the smoke from the explosion, and he had started to wheeze and cough. His skin tingled and smarted from the heat of the explosion, but as far as he could tell, he had escaped any serious burns. The surge of desperate energy that had supported him through the last few moments was dying away and, now that he was aware of them, his wounds had started to hurt like perdition. He glared at Kher. 'Don't be bloody stupid! Do we *look* all right?' Then all at once he was struck by the realisation that, against all the odds, he and Vifang had survived. Relief and amazement washed over him and he started to laugh helplessly, the tears running down his cheeks and cutting tracks through all the dirt and blood.

'You're all right,' Kher said disgustedly, 'which, after those antics, is more than you deserve.' He sent Alsive back to the garden to fetch his pack, which contained the small kit of basic medications that the Loremasters carried at all times.

Elysa, in the meantime, had been investigating the tunnel. 'It looks like it's collapsed completely,' she called. 'I can't get any further than a few feet in, and even that part is very unstable. I can't imagine that any of our winged friends could have survived that.'

Elion realised that somehow, he was still clutching the ancient weapon. With a grimace of disgust, he thrust it back at Kher. 'Here. Take it and welcome. The bloody thing went dead on me right at the most crucial moment.'

Kher's face fell. 'You broke it? This thing has existed for hundreds of centuries, and you *broke* it? What's Amaurn going to say?'

'Well, he can say what he likes but there's nothing I can do about it. It only existed for hundreds of centuries because no one was trying to use it. Either way, it's not much good, is it? If Cergorn is right, and we keep the thing locked up in a museum, it's useless to us. If we do use it, it malfunctions. Maybe there's a lesson in that. Maybe there's a third way, between Cergorn's views and those of Amaurn. Maybe we'd be better off developing our own new methods, and let the Ancients go hang.'

All the time he had been speaking to Kher, Elion had been watching the Takur. Somewhere in all the confusion, Vifang had changed back into her normal form, and he could see that she was beginning to heal herself. Already, she seemed better, though the rents of her injuries still could be seen here and there, in the indeterminate darkness of her body. Though Kher was still fussing around Elion, trying to clean his wounds, the Loremaster ignored him. It was as though he and the shapeshifter were all alone. 'I thought I was too late,' he told her. 'I thought you were dead.'

'It takes a lot to kill one of my race,' Vifang told him, 'but if you hadn't come for me, either the Ak'Zahar or the explosion would have finished me for sure. You lured them off me long enough for me to change form into something more . . . suitable.'

'Why a firedrake?' Elion asked curiously. 'For a moment, I thought Kaz and Veldan had come for me.'

'I thought the flames might come in useful,' the Takur said wryly. 'Besides, that was one of the forms I used when I was trying to kill Amaurn. I already had the image fixed in my mind, it was easy to make the change. Then I could come to *your* aid.' Within the nebulous, many-limbed form, the bright eyes glittered. 'Why?' she asked softly. 'Why did you take such a risk for one of the reviled Takuru?'

Why did I?

As Elion looked at this weird, disquieting being, who had engendered such strong liking and respect in so brief a space of time, a jumble of thoughts and feelings whirled through his mind – and suddenly, he knew the answer. 'Because I didn't want to lose another partner,' he said firmly.

There was a long moment of silence before Vifang answered. 'But . . . But I'm barely a member of the Shadowleague. I can't be your partner.'

Elion smiled at her, and held out his hand. 'You can if you want to be.'

Thirty-Nine

Returning

Far underground, Dark's strength was failing. Veldan could see the strain and effort clearly on his face, as he tried to hold her dying partner to the world. It was no use. Though her heart was breaking, and she didn't know how she could face the future without Kaz, she knew that it was pointless to put them all through any further suffering. Blinded by tears, she reached out and touched the Summoner on the arm. 'Let him go, Dark. Help him to sleep.'

Dark darted a glance at her in which she saw concern and compassion mingled – and something more. 'Are you sure?' he said. 'Veldan, are you certain? I can hold on a little longer . . .'

'No.' Veldan's voice broke on a sob. 'He doesn't even know we're here any more, and he's dying by slow inches. Help him to go, Dark. Set him free.'

'I . . .' But whatever the Summoner had meant to say, he never got the chance to finish. Suddenly Amaurn erupted into their midst and, seizing Veldan's hands, pulled her up from the floor. 'Veldan, there's no time to explain. Just trust me, that's all. Just trust me.' He looked up at the Eye, high above them on the chamber wall. 'All right, Shree,' he called aloud. 'Go!'

Before Veldan's eyes, the twisted body of the firedrake rose up from the floor, supported on what seemed to be a column of shimmering air. 'Amaurn!' she shrieked. 'What's happening?'

He gripped her hands tightly. 'It's all right, Veldan. Hope and pray that it will be all right. Shree has amalgamated with the Eye, and

534

become the consciousness of Myrial. She thinks she knows a way to heal Kaz . . .'

It was too much for Veldan to take in. 'But Shree nearly killed him already. Stop her, Amaurn – it has to be a trick. Don't let her take him!'

'Hush.' He put his arms around her and held her tightly. 'You're overwrought, my love, and understandably so, but you don't realise what's been happening. This is your partner's only chance.'

This time, his words got through to her, and she understood what he was saying – though not how such a miracle could come to be. Even as she watched, the firedrake had reached the centre of the Eye, and vanished into its depths.

Veldan was aware that Amaurn had let her go, but had still kept one arm around her shoulders. She was aware that Dark was holding her other hand. She was aware of Toulac beside her, stalwart and strong as ever, though the veteran was looking up at the Eye with a worried frown on her face.

Time passed. And more time. Veldan remembered their childhood, when she and Kaz had grown up together. The little lizardlike baby who had hatched out of the strange-looking egg had grown up into such a magnificent creature, large and clever and strong. All through the years, he had been Veldan's protector, her comforter, her friend, and she had been his. They had taken care of one another through the good times and the bad. She thought of the gleam of mischief in his opalescent eyes, his wicked tongue, and that irritating snicker that usually meant that he intended to have the last word.

How can I live without him? It would be like losing half of me! Now I know how Elion felt. At last, I know.

And all this time, the Eye had continued unchanged, without any indication that anything was happening within its depths. After a time, Veldan began to doubt that anything would. The group of people above, on the walkway, were beginning to get restless, and she could hear a low murmur of puzzled voices coming from that direction. Her nerves were so tight-strung that she wanted to kill them, just to shut them up.

How dare they stand there muttering, while Kaz's life, and mine, hang in the balance?

Veldan thought she couldn't stand to wait a moment longer. She must move, scream, weep . . . And then she saw it. A long, dark shape drifting deep within from the enigmatic blue. A few moments more and Kaz emerged from the centre of the Eye, but there was no spark of consciousness to greet her worried calls. And while she couldn't see it properly from down here, his silhouette still looked oddly misshapen. Veldan's heart sank, and bitterness overwhelmed her.

Shree failed, damn it! For a brief time she let me hope – and then she failed.

It was just too cruel. Veldan didn't know how she could bear it. She closed her eyes to shut away the dreadful sight, and let the darkness of despair surround her. Then she felt Dark's hand squeezing hers, very tightly. 'Veldan,' he said urgently, 'don't look like that! Open your eyes. He's alive. Kaz is alive. He isn't conscious, but he's alive! I can feel the life within him.'

Then, and only then, did Veldan dare look. He was closer now – she could see him breathing, beginning to stir. And as the firedrake was lowered to the ground, her spirits soared. But that peculiar shape . . . Her eyes widened as he settled to the floor. 'Dark – look! Amaurn and Toulac – look at him!' She ran to Kaz and as she knelt down beside him, he opened his eyes. 'Hello, sweetie.' The voice was faint, but already growing stronger. 'I just had the strangest dream. I dreamed that Myrial gave me . . .' Suddenly his head shot up, and snapped around on his long neck to look behind him. '*Wings?*' In his excitement, his voice rose to a bellow. 'VELDAN! I HAVE WINGS!'

The Loremaster hugged him, and the tears streaming down her face now were tears of joy. 'I'm happy for you, Kaz. You always wanted them, and you deserve them. But most of all, I'm happy just to have you back.'

The firedrake gave her an injured look. 'Have me *back?* Bat crap! I wasn't going anywhere, Boss. You don't get rid of me that easily.'

Veldan looked up at the Eye. 'Thank you, Shree,' she called.

'Thank you for giving him back to me. And thank you for the wings. He's always wanted them.'

The chamber reverberated to the sound of the Wind-Sprite's laugh. *I'm glad I could do it, Veldan. And I'm glad my modifications meet with your approval. To restore Kazairl, I had to access the original template of the firedrakes that Myrial had stored in its memory when they first came to this world. No one was more surprised than me to discover that they had wings! If Kaz is anything to go by, they must have lost them somewhere through the aeons since then and now – but no matter, they seemed like a good idea to me, and I thought he might like to have them back.*

By this time, all of Veldan's other companions were clustering around Kaz, telling him how glad they were to see him, asking him how he felt, congratulating him on his beautiful new wings, and telling him how brave he'd been, and how worried *they* had been. Veldan could see that Kaz was basking in all the attention, standing in the middle of the floor and spreading his elegant, gleaming wings in all their new magnificence. His expression was looking more smug by the minute. 'Oh dear,' she murmured to Dark. 'He used to be conceited enough before this happened – now he'll be impossible.'

The Summoner put an arm around her once more. Between them, it seemed to have become the most natural gesture in the world. 'Don't worry – we can cope with him.'

Though it sounded like a statement, Veldan heard the lilt of a question in his voice. She looked into his brown eyes and smiled. 'We most certainly can.'

Kaz nudged Veldan with his nose. 'Hey!' he said peevishly. '*I'm* supposed to be the one who's the centre of attention here.' He looked at Dark with a leer. 'You can damn well wait your turn till later.'

At this point – luckily – Shree interrupted them. Her voice had changed; had become more resonant, somehow, and more impersonal. *And now, I think you all should go back home. I have a very great deal to do here, and a lot to learn. Already, I feel my old self fading, and becoming part of this world. If you want me, however, you know where to find me – although I think you should block off all access to this place. We don't want *more* folk wandering down here accidentally. If anybody needs to communicate,* she continued, *they can reach me through the Holy of Holies, below the Temple in Tiarond. The Hierarch's ring will activate the Eye there, just as it always did – though I think perhaps you'll find that the position of Hierarch has just become obsolete. But I'm sure that Galveron and Aliana can work something out. He'll make a perfect leader for Callisiora, and so will she. I shall watch their progress with interest.*

'That may be your opinion,' said a deep masculine voice, 'but Hierarch Gilarra might have something to say in the matter. Indeed, now that Zavahl has returned, the situation has become even more complex.'

Veldan looked up in surprise. She had forgotten all about the other intruders, who were still clustered on the edge of the walkway, standing very close to one another for support. She noticed that Tormon and his companions had joined them, and that Scall had his arm around a slight, blonde girl. The man who had spoken, presumably Galveron, had come out to the platform and was addressing the Eye directly. At his side, looking very determined, was a slim young woman with a mop of tawny curls.

Once again, Shree's voice was heard. It was difficult to tell whether it came from all around them, or directly from the centre of the Eye. *You need not worry about Gilarra – or Zavahl, if I'm not mistaken. When you get back to the Temple, you'll find that the situation has resolved itself. Now, if you are ready,* she added with heavy sarcasm, *I will transport you back to the first great cavern. You'll get out easily from there, without spending any more time blundering around my corridors, and triggering the traps.*

There seemed little point in lingering, and everyone seemed as anxious to leave as Thirishri was to see them go. The others came down from the walkway, and they all crammed into the silver depression in the floor, ringed by its coloured pillars. Once again, it expanded to accommodate them all. As the chamber vanished from sight, Veldan expected to hear Shree call out in farewell, but there was only silence. Already, it seemed the former Wind-Sprite had turned away from her connections with her companions, immersing herself in the persona of an entire world.

Once they had gained the mysterious chamber – still as enigmatic as ever – with the peculiar structures and coloured, moving lights, it took them no time to pass through the tubular corridor, and scramble down the pile of rubble into the cliff road tunnel. Veldan leant against Kaz in their habitual position of closeness and comfort. 'Thank Providence we're out of there! I never want to see that place again to the end of my days!'

'Me neither, Boss – me neither.' Caught off his guard, the fire-drake sounded very subdued, and his partner knew that his brush with death had affected him far more deeply than he would admit.

Veldan put her arms around his long neck, and hugged him. 'Come on, you,' she said. 'Let's go home.'

FORTY

AFTERWARDS

By the time Toulac took the chestnut mare back to an impatient Scall, the worst of winter had passed, and spring was coming round again. As she rode Mazal and led the little mare, who was now pregnant with the stallion's foal, up the valley that led to the Reiver fortress, there was a hail from the hillside above, and Seriema and Cetain came riding down towards her.

Toulac had to smile when she saw the former head of the Merchants' Guild. Seriema, as usual, was wearing the clothing of a Reiver warrior, and she looked radiant, tanned and healthy. Her shirtsleeves were rolled up and her dark hair was blowing out behind her in the wind. Though she lived with the Reivers all the time now, and had given up her great mansion on the Esplanade without a backward look, she had not abandoned her business ventures completely. Instead she had taken on a partner: Aliana's brother, Alestan. Already, after only a few months, the other merchants trembled in their boots to see him coming.

In the meantime, Seriema and Cetain had spent a busy winter rallying and aiding what remained of the other clans. Because they had been unable to get through with their warning, the Ak'Zahar had been able to wreak utter havoc among the unsuspecting Reivers, leaving so few survivors that the old, destructive clan system had been obliterated for good.

It had taken some considerable time for Arcan's archers to hunt down and destroy the last of the winged fiends that had spread out to the moors, and a number of lives had been lost before they had succeeded. Sadly, the chieftain himself had been numbered among the slain, and now Lewic, Cetain's older brother, was the leader. Luckily, he had been more amenable to Cetain's suggestions for amalgamating the clans than his father would have been, with the result that everyone was mingling now and sharing what they had. Some of Lewic's folk had gone to join the refugees in the fortress of the adjacent clan, and some of the strangers had come here. Everyone had been so shocked by the extent of the slaughter that there had been surprisingly little fighting, apart from the odd broken head, and Lewic, Cetain and Seriema were hoping it would stay that way. In the new spirit of friendship that seemed to be abroad, they had also made agreements with Galveron, Lord of Tiarond, to trade meat and wool for other goods from the city. It seemed that the raiding days of the Reivers had gone for good – and Toulac, for one, wasn't sorry.

'Toulac,' Seriema called as she drew near, 'it's good to see you. And you brought Scall's horse with you – thank Providence for that! He's been growing quite impossible to live with lately because he didn't think you'd get her back to him before they left.'

'Left?' the veteran asked. 'Is Tormon going back on the road, then?'

'Isn't he just!' Seriema laughed. 'He and Scall have been busy all winter long, building and fitting out their new wagon – with the help of Rochalla, of course, not to mention Annas, who's been keeping them right and telling them how it should be done.'

Toulac laughed. 'That child will go far!'

Seriema nodded. 'Rochalla has made a tremendous difference to her. It's not the same, of course, as having her own mother – but Rochalla does a marvellous job, and Annas loves her to distraction.'

'Are your other visitors here yet?'

'Yes,' Cetain said. 'You're the last, Toulac. That's why Scall was in such a state.'

'How is Blade – I mean, Amaurn? And how is Zavahl?' Seriema asked. 'You won't be wanting to talk about Gendival in front of the others, so I'll get my questions in now.'

'You wouldn't recognise Amaurn as that cold, driven monster that we both knew,' Toulac told her. 'Now that he's home, and Archimandrite, as he always wanted to be – and especially because he's been united with his daughter – he's mellowed considerably. Though if any of the other Senior Loremasters are unwise enough to try to cross him, we still see the odd flash of the old Lord Blade. And as for Zavahl – well, he's deliriously happy with Ailie, and suffice it to say, he's a damn sight better at being an innkeeper than he ever was as Hierarch!'

By this time, they were nearing the stronghold, and with a wild yell, Scall came running out through the gates to meet them. 'Toulac! You brought her! You brought Firefly back at last!' He ran up to the mare, hugging and patting her, and despite all the pampering she'd had in the Shadowleague stables, she looked very pleased to see him.

Toulac made a face at her. 'Ungrateful little wretch!' Then she left them to their reunion, and went inside with Seriema and Cetain. In the courtyard, a dazzling sight met her eyes: a brand new wagon, somewhat larger than the one the trader had previously owned, and twice as gaudy. A smell of fresh paint hung in the air, and the sound of hammering came from inside. When they went round the back, Tormon's head popped out of the door. 'Toulac! You're a sight for sore eyes! Have you brought Scall's mare back, then?'

'Can't anybody talk about *anything* but that bloody horse?' Toulac grumbled, but she was grinning as she spoke.

Later, when Scall could be prised from the side of his beloved Firefly, they all gathered over supper and a glass of wine in Cetain's chambers. Rochalla, who had joined them with little Annas, looked absolutely blooming. Clearly, life as Scall's lifemate was suiting her, and the veteran suspected that Annas might have a little playmate before too long.

There were a number of other visitors. As well as bringing the horse, Toulac had also come to collect Quave, the Shadowleague Healer who had been spending the winter in Tiarond with Healer Kaita, teaching her some new surgical and diagnostic techniques, and helping her eradicate the last of the sickness that had accounted for so many of the refugees. Amaurn was – very cautiously – releasing certain knowledge into the world via the Loremasters, though he had decided to restrict this to information that would help the various races of Myrial put their shattered lives back together. He had decided to hold back, however, on materials such as the blasting powder, which could so easily be turned into weapons.

Kaita had travelled with Quave as far as the Reiver fortress because Shelon, who had turned into a very able second-in-command, had taken a firm stance about making her take the occasional rest. Her eyes sparkling with amusement, she told Toulac about her new assistants: Felyss and Gelina – and, to everyone's surprise, Packrat. These days, clean and tidy and with his hair neatly trimmed, he was almost unrecognisable as the scruffy thief who had first appeared among the refugees in the Temple. But he had always been willing to help the healers then, and had remained interested ever since. Shelon, who was training the new recruits, actually thought he showed some promise – and if Kaita noticed the way his eyes kept lingering on Felyss, *she* wasn't going to say anything. They would have to work that out themselves.

Agella had come with Kaita, to bid farewell to her nephew before he took to the road with Tormon for the summer. The Smith and the Healer, who had worked together so well and ably during the crisis in Tiarond, were now the firmest of friends, and both of them were important and respected members of the Working Council of Tiarond, which had been set up by Galveron and Aliana to help them rebuild their ravaged city and the lands beyond.

The two of them, former Godsword Commander and former thief, now the rulers of Callisiora, had also ridden out with Kaita and Agella – probably on Aliana's insistence, Toulac suspected. Galveron, as conscientious as ever, would have worked every single hour of the day, and burned himself out within a month, had his new lifemate permitted it. She, however, had sufficient influence to put a stop to any such notions, and made sure that he put some time aside to relax – and to spend with her. Ostensibly, they had come to confer with Cetain and Seriema, who had become good friends with them during the winter – though Cetain had been heard to remark, on more than one occasion, that he could no longer call himself a Reiver now that he was making friends with the city folk instead of robbing them whenever the opportunity arose.

They were all delighted to see one another again, and spent a very convivial evening talking about that fateful day that had brought them all together beneath Myrial's Temple, and catching up on all the news. There was no doubt that a bond had been forged between all the people who'd been present on that momentous day, no matter what their reasons had been for venturing into the tunnels. Kaita and Agella, who had been in the Temple above but had met the adventurers in the aftermath, had also become included in that bond. As Toulac pointed out, their coming together seemed to have been more than mere coincidence: certainly they were now the ones who had taken up the responsibility for the future welfare of the Callisiorans.

Kaita poured the last drops of wine from the bottle into her glass. 'You know, Toulac, I've often wondered about this business of coincidence,' she said. 'I'll never forget that very morning, when Gilarra sacrificed herself to buy us a miracle. I never was religious in the first place, and we all realise now that Myrial doesn't exist as a deity in the way that the Callisiorans believed he did – but I can't help wondering: was it really a coincidence that we were saved within hours of the Hierarch's sacrifice? Did Gilarra waste her life to obtain something that would have happened anyway? Or somewhere, on some unknown level, were her prayers answered, and was her sacrifice redeemed?'

Her words were followed by a long moment of silence. The veteran picked up the empty bottle, squinted at it, and put it down again. 'That,' she said, 'is the kind of drunken talk that tells me it's definitely time we went to bed.'

It was quite late the following morning when Toulac mounted Mazal and set off home, with a remarkably uncommunicative Quave riding alongside her. Her head was still throbbing faintly though Kaita, bless her, had produced a concoction of her own devising that seemed to be making her feel better by the moment – so much so that she found herself whistling as she rode along. It had been nice to catch up on all the news, but she couldn't wait to get back to her friends in the Shadowleague, and these days, Gendival was a very pleasant place to be.

It was astonishing, after all the initial ill-feeling and conflict, how the Shadowleague at large had settled down and accepted Amaurn as their leader. The prompt restoration of the Curtain Walls had silenced the doubters very effectively, and since then everyone had been marvelling at how wise and careful a leader Amaurn the rene-gade had turned out to be. Veldan and Toulac, however, and one or two others, were pretty sure that he was lulling them into a false sense of security, and would sooner or later be setting them all by the ears once more – but whatever he was up to, only time would tell. He and Helverien had become great friends, though not in any romantic sense. He remained as faithful as ever to the memory of his lost Aveole, while *she* was busy cutting a swathe through all the young bucks among the Shadowleague – with a few notable excep-tions. Helverien, when not otherwise occupied in making up for lost time, was working closely with the historians and artisans in an attempt to restore as much as possible of the lost knowledge of the Ancients. She was often helped by Zavahl/Aethon, who could make pertinent contributions from the memories of the Dragonfolk – that is, when they could spare the time from running the inn with Ailie. In the meantime, Shree was trying to find a way to give the Seer's memories back to the Dragonfolk without destroying Aethon in the process, and everyone was hopeful that she would, eventually, succeed.

Elion and his new partner were very happy together, and though their pairing had caused a certain amount of consternation among the more conservative Loremasters, the Archimandrite had been firmly in favour, and so that was that. For Elion, there was never a dull moment. One day his partner might be a firedrake like Kaz, another time she might appear as the purple-haired woman, or a centaur, or a phoenix, or anything else he could possibly imagine. Mostly, however, when they were at home, she tended to stay in her own enigmatic Takur shape; an arrangement which seemed to suit them both. At present, they were away on assignment in the land of Nemeris, making sure that the peninsula and the archipelago were safe for the return of the Dobarchu refugees. Since the Curtain Walls had been restored, the climates of the various realms had been stabilising so rapidly that Toulac suspected that Thirishri had been working very hard to get everything back to normal as fast as possible. The winter just past had been very difficult, and the Loremasters had all been kept busy rendering what aid they could in all the realms. If things stayed stable during the summer, however, then hopefully the survivors of the catastrophe would have a good long season to recover themselves and their lands, and would be in much better condition to face the following winter.

All in all, the veteran reflected, things were going pretty well. She wondered how it would have been if Cergorn had remained in charge, and shuddered. The Curtain Walls would have failed completely by now, and the ensuing havoc didn't bear thinking about. No, she wished the former Archimandrite well in his new life, but she was extremely glad that he was gone.

Toulac and Quave made good time across the moors, and passed through the newly restored Curtain Walls around about noon. The shimmering sheets of pure, iridescent colour sang with a clear, humming note, and were barely recognisable from the clouded, muddy, discordant formations they had been before. In the golden light of afternoon, they reached the wayshelter – and found that Veldan, Kazairl, and Dark had come out to meet them.

'I'll leave you here,' Quave said. 'I'm anxious to get back to the settlement, and no doubt you four will want to catch up on all the news.' Skirting the foot of the hill on a horse that was distinctly wary of Kaz, he galloped off.

The veteran waved to her friends, glad to see them once again – even though it had only been a couple of days since she had seen them last. With Amaurn's blessing, the four of them had evolved a slightly different and unconventional partnership than the usual pairing of the Loremasters: Toulac and Dark had become, officially, partners, but in fact they shared a four-way partnership with Veldan and Kaz. Amaurn had been so delighted with an arrangement that made all four participants – and particularly his beloved daughter – so happy that he had undertaken to assign them all together in future so that they would not have to be apart. Though they all knew that there had been certain mutterings of complaint among the Shadowleague about favouritism, no one had ever dared to make any complaints aloud – not with Kaz's reactions to take into account, and certainly not where Amaurn could hear. As both Toulac and Kazairl had been expecting, Veldan and Dark had formed a partnership of their own, in which they were blissfully happy, though their love encompassed the veteran and the firedrake to such an extent that no one ever felt neglected or left out. Toulac smiled to herself.

To think, when winter began, how alone and embittered and bereft I was, with nothing to look forward to but death. Nowadays, my life is so wonderful, I feel that I could live for ever!

Suddenly, she was forced to pay attention to business, as Mazal shied skittishly. Kaz was charging down the hill towards them, with Dark and Veldan on his back. 'Stop that, you daft bugger,' she scolded the horse. 'You've known Kaz far too long for that kind of nonsense.'

Kaz came skidding to a halt in front of her, his claws leaving great gouges in the turf. He extended his magnificent wings for balance, and Toulac caught her breath. Growing out from his shoulders, where they seemed to have formed a new and complex pair of joints, they were ribbed like the wings of a bat, and covered with a skin that looked delicate, but was extremely tough, though soft and satiny to the touch. Like his scales, they were tinted in a medley of softly glowing metallic hues that looked at their very best in the sunshine.

The two Loremasters slid to the ground, and Toulac also

dismounted as Veldan came running across to hug her. 'About time you showed up,' the firedrake said. 'What kept you? I told you we should have gone with you. I could have taken you much faster than that walking breakfast.'

Toulac chuckled. It hadn't taken long for Kazairl to rediscover all his old ebullience after his brush with death. 'Our friends might have been all right, Kaz, but I don't think that most of Arcan's folk are ready for you.'

'Stupid humans!' the firedrake snorted. 'Since Veldan made me give up eating them, I can't think what use they are at all – except for the ones who become Loremasters, that is.'

'What about Zavahl?' Veldan reminded him.

'Yes, he's all right,' Kaz said condescendingly, 'but of course he has a Dragon inside him, and that makes all the difference. Ailie's worth having, too. Now *there's* a human with her priorities right.'

'Just because she always feeds you,' Dark said. 'How is everyone in Callisiora, Toulac?'

'All thriving. Cetain sends his best to you and, of course, he asked if you were sure you wouldn't consider going back and being a Summoner for them again.'

Dark sighed. 'I knew he would. That was one reason I didn't want to go with you.' He looked at Veldan. 'And, of course, I don't have to go very far to look for the other reason.'

Kaz rolled his eyes. 'Thank goodness you're back,' he said to Toulac. 'Now I can have a decent conversation without having to throw up every five minutes.'

The veteran grinned at him. 'You old fraud! You don't fool me for a minute. I know how happy you are that these two got together.'

'Shhh – don't tell *them* that!' The firedrake snickered, then turned to his partner. 'Come on, Veldan. If you two have finished drooling over each other, can we show her now?'

'Show me what?' said Toulac, though she could easily guess. The firedrake's wings were magnificent, but she had yet to see him take to the air. However, since both he and Veldan had been blithely unconcerned about him being earthbound, she suspected that they had been working on the situation. The two of them had been disappearing periodically all winter, telling no one where they had gone, and both Dark and Toulac had suspected that they were sneaking off to practise. Dark, grinning proudly but looking a trifle apprehensive, had obviously been let in on the secret already.

'Ah, Toulac,' Kaz snorted. 'You guessed!'

'We wanted to wait until all four of us were together to show you,' Veldan added.

The veteran suppressed a momentary twinge of disquiet. But of course they knew what they were doing. They had been practising all winter! She took Dark's arm. 'Come on then,' she said. 'Let's see you fly!'

Veldan, beaming all over her face, swung up onto the firedrake's back, and they headed up towards the brow of the hill. 'Is that it? We've seen you *walk* before,' Toulac heckled, and the Loremaster half-turned to make a rude gesture. 'Just you wait!'

At the top of the hill, the firedrake crouched and spread those glorious wings. Then suddenly he sprang upwards, caught the wind, and took flight with verve and grace, beating hard until he had gained sufficient height, then opening the great sails wide to swoop and glide.

Far above the watchers, Veldan let out a whoop of joyous abandon, echoed by a bellow of triumph from Kazairl. 'How about *that*?' he called down to Toulac. 'Let's see that walking picnic of yours match this!'

'Don't you listen to him,' Toulac said stoutly, stroking Mazal's arched neck. 'I wouldn't be without you for the world – even if Veldan *won't* let you in her kitchen.' Nevertheless, she couldn't take her eyes off the airborne pair above her.

What must it be like to fly like that?

The veteran watched in wonder as the firedrake soared above her; wheeling, dipping and gliding with joyous abandon. Linking to Veldan's mind, she felt the exhilarating rush of cold wind against her face and saw the moors wheel by below, and her own self and Dark, looking incredibly small and far away. It was glorious! She could see for *miles* – in fact she was certain that she could see, so faint and far away that it looked like a twig stuck in the ground, the Tower of Tidings in the Loremaster settlement.

Reluctantly, Toulac came back to herself and turned to Dark, her eyes glowing. 'Myrial in a handcart! Aren't they a wonderful sight?' She paused thoughtfully. 'I can't wait until they take *me* up there!'

DATE DUE

MAR 3 1 2003	
MAR 3 1 2003	
JUN 1 7 2003	
JUL 0 7 2003	
AUG 1 1 2003	
MAR 2 2 2004	
JUN 0 9 2005	
MAR 2 7 2006	
APR 1 0 2006	
aug 16/07	
JUN 2 0 2008	
Nov 4/09	
Midland	
JUL 30 2011	